The Fabric of Strife

SELANDU TALES BOOK 2

By J. A. Komorita

The Fabric of Strife

SELANDU TALES BOOK 2

Edited by George Verongos
Cover by George Verongos
Cover concept by J. A. Komorita
Quilts by J. A. Komorita

PAPER BACK
ISBN: 979-8-9911618-2-4

Website: jakomorita.com

ACKNOWLEDGMENTS

To my editor, George Verongos, for your knowledge, hard work,
and patience, and your EQ.

To George, and to Christy Lock, for keeping me sane during my ups
and downs in this process.

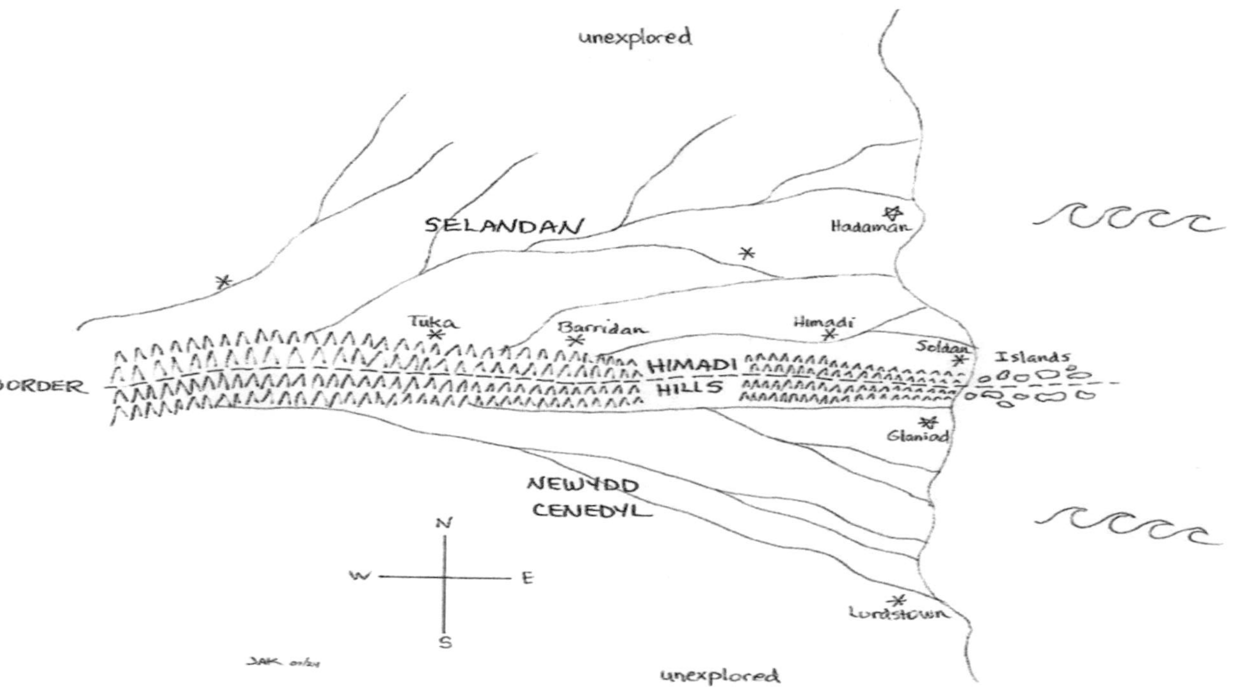

unexplored
SELANDAN
Hadaman
Tuka
Barridan
Himadi
Soldan
Islands
BORDER
HIMADI
HILLS
Glaniad
NEWYDD
CENEDYL
N
W
E
S
Lordstown
unexplored
JAK 01/21

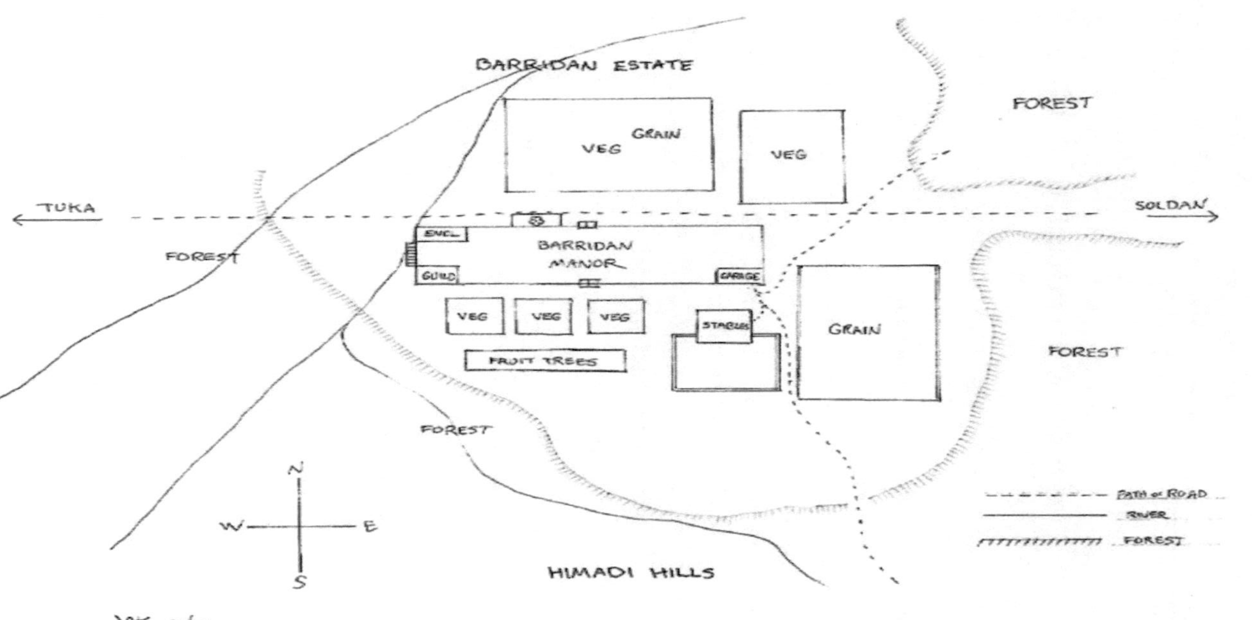
BARRIDAN ESTATE
FOREST
TUKA
SOLDAN
FOREST
VEG
GRAIN
VEG
ENCL
BARRIDAN MANOR
GUARD
GARAGE
GRAIN
VEG
VEG
VEG
STABLES
FRUIT TREES
FOREST
FOREST
N
W
E
S
HIMADI HILLS
Path or Road
River
Forest
JAK 07/24

VOCABULARY

Bolded names and words are the more important or most often use ones.

Cara MacLennan	crafter, the lone human visitor in Barridan	CARE-uh
Rodani	Security Fifth; Cara's guardian and lover	row-DON-ee
a'selaso	honorific form of addressing a high priestess	ah-sell-AH-so
a'taso	honorific form of addressing a taso directly	ah-TAH-so
a'temaso	honorific form of addressing the head of guild guardians	ah-tem-AH-so
Andrew Lieu	Ambassador Second; pronounced Andreh' by Selandu	Lee-ooh
Arimeso Osanin	taso of Barridan	Air-ih-MAY-so oh-SAH-nin
Baldar	physician; Master Healer	BALL-dar, as in "dart"
Chendal	head of the Guild of Guardians; the temaso	CHEN-dahl
Deneban	Security Twelfth (m)	DEN-eh-bun
Deremic	Cara's second servant; has some training in protection	Deh-REM-ick
Garidemu	potter; hates humans	gare-ih-DEY-moo; rhymes with "dare"
Hadaman	capital city; north and somewhat east of Barridan	HAH-dah-mahn
Himadi House	manor under construction on the Himadi Plateau where	same

	Selandu and humans are to live and work together	
Imal	Security Third (m)	IH-mul
kia	little one	KEE-uh
Kimasa	head of the Enclave of priestesses; the selaso	kih-MAH-sah
Kusik	the keso, Security First; Arimeso's husband	KOO-sick
Lanata	Security Fourth (f)	lah-NAH-tah
Larisi	Serano's lover; new acolyte of the Enclave	lah-REE-zee
Litelon	a mid-adolescent stablehand, who has a crush on Cara	lih-TELL-on
Menachem Mboto	Ambassador First; pronounced Mena'hem by Selandu	men-AH-(flegm) mm-BOH-toh as in "boat"
Misheiki	Security Seventh (m)	mish-AY-kee as in the letter "a"
Naremit	Security Eleventh (m)	nah-REHM-it
Newydd Cenedyl	land south of the hills; human lands (means "new nation")	Welsh; NEY-width KAN-a-dill
onana	familiar form of mother; mama	oh-NAH-nah
Pavanec	Security Eighth (m)	PA-van-ek, as in "pal"
poridi	a nasty, clawed, 100-150 lb. canine/feline animal; fast and always dangerous	pour-EE-dee

reiti	ambassador	ray-EE-tee
risheigi	homosexual person; also: mirrored	rish-A-gee
selaso	head of the Enclave; high priestess	seh-LAH-so
Serano	Security Sixth; Rodani's guild partner	seh-RON-oh
tem'u	informal name for guild partner; close companionship	TEM-oo, as in "temp"
temaso	head of the guild of guardians (only three people in guild council are higher)	teh-MAH-so
temichi	Selandu name for guardian	teh-MEE-chee
temichin	plural of temichi	teh-MEE-chin
Timan	the biso, Security Second; Kusik's guild partner	TEE-mun
Toranel	Security Ninth (f)	TOR-an-el, as in "tore"
Vanu	Security Tenth (m)	VA-new, as in "van"

CONTENTS

Welcome to the fallout.
Welcome to resistance.
The tension is here
The tension is here
Between who you are and who you could be
Between how it is and how it should be.
—Switchfoot

ONE

Security First Kusik, tasked with keeping the peace and safety of the Barridan estate and all who resided within, paced back and forth in a fury of frustration.

Arimeso, ruler of Barridan—and of Kusik—sat at her desk, watching her chosen mate fume.

"You are really going to allow this?" Kusik asked her, exasperation in his voice and every line of his face. "This…perversion? This blatant disobedience?"

"How many times do you need to ask?" she countered. "How many times do you need to hear my answer?"

"Until something makes sense to me, Arimeso," he shot back, stopping in front of her desk. "He broke one of the guild's oldest rules. Put in place for very good reasons, reasons you blatantly ignore."

"I am not the only one blatantly ignoring reasons, Kusik." She leaned back and took a fresh grip on her own temper. "If we never reach into the unknown, we never make progress."

"What kind of progress," he shouted, leaning toward her, "does guild rule-breaking create? Or does it just destroy?"

"There is more at stake here than just rules."

"Yes! Consequences!"

The death of one of her artisans remained in Arimeso's thoughts, but that tragedy was not directly caused by Rodani's rule-breaking. It was caused, ultimately, by fate…or the goddess. "Consequences," she said with a sigh, "can be positive as well as negative." She refocused on him, her mouth pursed and pupils narrowed. "So, as you can only see one side of this new issue, you continue to concentrate on the negatives. I will watch for the positives."

Kusik bowed, abrupt and perfunctory. He left the office grumbling.

TWO

Cara MacLennan shut off her sewing machine as her lover walked out of her bedroom.

Violet-eyed, alien—he didn't knock—just strolled into her workroom with the air of assumption that he had a right to go where he would. He was very tall, this alien. Sturdy but graceful, square of face and long in the limb. He was clad in black, the Guild of Guardians' color. Grey skin gleamed in contrast to the black, and the weapons belt around his waist gave testament to his deadly skills, and the pride with which he carried himself.

Cara smiled at him and received nothing much in return but a barely perceptible curve to his mobile mouth.

It was enough.

"The physician did not release you," he said. It was an oblique question, typical of the Selandu reserve.

Cara glanced at her puffy sleeve. It hid the bandage around her arm, courtesy of another silver and grey man who had tried to kill her. "He didn't."

Four days later, the gunshot wound was still healing, but at least one more trip to the physician's clinic was mandatory. She waved to his seat at the side of the worktable that held her quilting supplies, hoping he would sit next to her.

"What's the talk?" she asked.

Rodani folded himself into the chair with a dancer's grace. "Nothing I may tell."

Cara swiveled around to face him. "Nothing?" She thrust her hand upward and out as she glanced past the bedroom door. "I nearly lose my life at the hands of a bedamned Riverchild, and I'm forbidden to know why?"

"Be at ease, kia. His danger is past, and we have won this skirmish."

"I didn't know we were at war."

"Your naïveté is presenting its nose beyond the sticker bushes. Besides," he continued, "It makes your successful escape more noteworthy. The eyes of both our species are on the path you walk."

"All the more likely I'll make mistakes."

Rodani toyed with one of the pencils on the table. "I will not let you, kia."

He meant well, but for Cara, it wasn't easy handing her autonomy over to an alien. She was a human artisan living on an estate full of alien artisans, and she was used to ordering her own life. Fiercely independent, Cara bristled at the safety precautions Rodani insisted on. It was their main area of contention, and she was determined to win what she could, despite the dangers inherent in her situation. A life lived in perfect safety was no life for her. She was there on the northern continent to prove a point: that humans and Selandu could live side by side for long periods of time, long enough to join forces to make it back off-world. That is, if the unknown beings who had knocked both species out of hyperspace would let them.

Cara curled her legs underneath her. "Are you sure I can't tell Iraimin?"

"I am certain."

Short, sharp, and not unexpected. Cara rested her arm over the chair. "Why?"

"The more people who know what we've done, the more potential problems."

"Are you ashamed of me, Rodani?"

Rodani's vertical pupils widened, then narrowed past the point of normal. "I refrain from shameful acts, kia."

"Then why am I forbidden to tell her?"

"I have said." He reached out and pulled a paper toward him, idle fingers sweeping over the designs sketched on it. "Potential problems."

Cara sighed. "Do you distrust her? I don't believe she'd harm us."

"I cannot know, and cannot take the chance."

"She's my only female companion. I need to share my happiness."

Rodani tilted his head to the side, casting her a glance from the corner of his eye. "Share it with me."

Cara smiled, a wide stretch of mouth that ended at each ear. "That's different."

"We are in need of privacy, kia."

"Then tell that to her," she said, and huffed a breath of frustration. "Threaten her with guild retributions if she talks to anyone else. Just let me tell her."

"No." He drew a finger across the back of her hand, taking a bit of the sting from his refusal. "And you are still having dream fears."

Cara squeezed her eyes shut against the sudden influx of images. A booming pistol that deafened her. Bullets whizzing past. A frantic run down hall and stairs. Spurting blood. Brains that clung to her clothing and hands.

She pulled her knees up and wrapped her arms around them.

Rodani rolled his chair over and drew Cara into his arms. She uncurled, relaxing into his warmth. A few months ago, she'd have laughed if someone said she'd fall in love with an alien, let alone bed one. Such things didn't happen. It was unheard of. The two species were far apart in culture and codes of honor. Physiology was little known, and two ears, eyes, arms, and legs did not ensure compatibility in other areas.

Cara unfolded herself from Rodani's embrace. He released her as she turned to face him, to straddle his legs, and rest her weight on his thighs. His cheek and jaw showed fading mottled patches.

"Your bruises are healing," she said. It hurt that he had suffered because of her. She brushed the bruises with her fingertips, silently wishing mayhem on Kusik.

"I am well," he said. His pupils pulsed as Cara reached upward to touch the tip of his ear with a delicate finger. Soft. Tiny hairs, nearly invisible, stood tall and straight to catch the wind's direction, and the sound of prey...or predator.

"Kia," he whispered, and pulled her hand away from such a sensitive area.

"There's time before dinner," she said, waggling her trapped fingers a hand's breadth from his nose.

"Baldar has not given you leave to resume normal duties."

She fought playfully against his grip. "That doesn't matter." With her good arm, she wrestled him in a mismatched fight that brought forth a spate of laughter from her.

Rodani allowed himself a smile and wrapped his arms around her. Cara leaned forward for a kiss, which was rudely prevented as he stood and set her on her feet. "I will wait."

Damn.

Cara's stomach rumbled. "If we must."

Rodani followed her toward the door, then put a hand on her shoulder and moved ahead.

Security measures didn't change with a change in their relationship. Enemies in the household precluded Cara from poking her nose outside her rooms before her guardian had a chance to sight the corridor. Cara trailed Rodani out into the hall, and shut the door behind her, leaving it for him to lock. In the relative privacy of their out-of-the-way corner of the manor house, she took the opportunity of a teasing touch.

Rodani swept her hand away. "Cara, you do understand the necessity of restraint in the gathering?"

"I'll try."

"Do. Please."

They walked down the stone hall together, his bootsteps falling in rhythmic dissonance with the patter of her indoor slippers. She hadn't recovered from her attack, that was obvious. The wound on her upper arm still pained her. Reminded her. At every turn, she expected danger. At every corner she flinched, waiting for an armed man to reach out and grab her, or blow a hole through her chest. Patiently, Rodani held his stride to hers.

Stairs led to the first-floor main hall. Cara's senses began to spin as she walked them. She resisted an overwhelming urge to dash down the wide steps two at a time, as she had done days ago with her would-be killer on her heels. At the bottom of the stairs, Cara took a wide berth around the spot where she'd fallen onto the stone floor, waiting for a bullet to end her life. Rodani glanced at her temporary diversion in path without comment.

The huge gathering room was crowded as usual, Brownian motion in silver and grey. She pulled ahead of Rodani as they wended their way through the tables to the bar at the back. An unusual number of people turned to watch their passage, courtesy of Shurad. His attack, and his subsequent death by Rodani's handgun, had reverberated throughout the household, causing speculations on why and how, and whether there would be repercussions between Selandu and human authorities.

As they neared the bar, an apprentice caught some signal and poured two drinks for Rodani, much to the dismay of patiently waiting patrons. Rank had its privileges, especially when it concerned the taso's lone alien guest. Drinks in hand, Cara and Rodani joined the food line, loading their trays from tables laden with enough food to fill the approximately two hundred Selandu stomachs in residence.

By the time they returned to their customary table, Serano had taken his seat. There was a drink in his hand and another at his left, waiting. He was Rodani's guild partner, and was paying attentions, as it was called, to an acolyte of the goddess. Serano raked Cara up and down with his eyes as she settled into place at his right.

"Problem?" she asked.

"That is not mine to decide."

Cara turned to Rodani. His gaze flickered from Serano to her, then away into the distance.

Let it pass, he seemed to say.

A grin spread over Cara's face as she dug into dinner. Neither did Serano like this new affinity Rodani had enjoined. She'd give a couple of fingers to know what conversations had transpired between the two since that night. Rodani was the senior in their partnership and, more than once in Cara's hearing, had put Serano in his place on her account.

Good thing someone stood up to him. Cara put her fork down and chuckled over her plate, then reached for her drink.

Something tapped on her foot.

"Sobriety, Cara," Rodani whispered. Cara rubbed his leg with her slippered foot as her mirth gave in to frustration.

Serano leaned toward her. "Is that the best you can do?" His vertical pupils were slit in anger, one clenched fist rested near his plate. "Rodani, I thought you were to discuss this with her."

"I did."

"Then take her back to her rooms."

Rodani put his elbows on the table and clasped his hands before his chin. "Do not give me orders, tem'u."

Serano leaned back and scrutinized Cara. Her smile faded in the face of his ire; her blue eyes darted like a kumiri being hunted.

"You will get yourself killed, and Rodani with you if you cannot restrain yourself, human."

She knew Serano despised her. And when he called her by her species name, he was riding the precipitous edge of his temper. Cara took a deep breath. "Then I can't show any pleasure in my change in circumstances."

"Show what you wish in private. Contain yourself in public."

Cara slid her arms around the rim of her plate and interlaced her fingers. Her shoulders sagged. The corners of her mouth drooped.

Serano leaned closer, his voice deepened. "Must you show every emotion you feel, like a child of two?"

Rodani laid his palm flat on the table. "Serano."

"At least I have a spectrum of emotions, a'tem," Cara said, voice rising. "All I see of you is lust and anger."

Serano's eyes blazed. He raised his fist.

"No." Rodani put his hand in the air between Cara and his partner. "Arimeso forbids. Follow orders." Fellow diners turned their heads to look.

Serano composed his face and took a sip of his drink. "You remind me, ki'ono, of a child who clings to his mother's skirts. He steps out to taunt the other children, then hides when they come after him, knowing his mother will protect him."

She wanted to shout, "I'm not a little girl," wanted to make a scene. But there was Rodani at her right hand, still sporting discolorations on his face. She bit off a piece of meat and chewed over her plate as another body came into view.

Larisi, the acolyte, set her tray down and pulled out her chair. Her eyes roamed the table, settling last of all upon Serano.

"You do realize," he continued, "that everyone else in the room will interpret your attitude as pleasure in Shurad's death?"

Cara swallowed the mouthful. It went down like a lump of cold oats.

"Is that the image you wish to project to us?" His eyes were mere slits, deadly in their intensity.

"No."

"You do not think." His was an old complaint.

"You do not feel." And hers, a new rejoinder.

"You cannot conceive of what I feel, Cara, or how many worries I face."

"Fewer than I."

"And you are adept at ignoring them."

Cara clenched her fists over her plate and gritted her teeth. Rodani slapped his hand on the table, right between them. Dishes rattled. Flatware clanked. Heads turned.

"Cease."

"A'Cara," Larisi began.

Cara looked up into her face. The midnight pupils were gentle ovals, and her face bespoke a serenity that was a far cry from Serano's barely checked temper, or Rodani's face that seemed forever full of secrets. Cara envied the woman.

"The Enclave extends its sympathies," the acolyte said. "We regret that Shurad's misplaced honor put you in such danger."

"Thank you, a'Larisi."

"Would that it had never occurred."

"Yes."

The mood at the table grew suddenly somber.

"Goddess heal you both," Larisi said.

"Is that not a little late for him?" Cara asked.

"No."

Cara glanced over at Rodani, then back to Larisi. She had no idea of an Enclave acolyte's reaction to someone frankly disbelieving in the goddess. She kept quiet.

The meal finished without further rancor, and without Iraimin making an appearance. Cara wondered at her friend's no-show and toyed with the idea of asking Rodani to stop by the painter's rooms on the way back. But she decided Iraimin knew where she could be found and would find her when she was ready.

Rodani dropped her off in her rooms.

"Forgive my tempers, please," she asked.

"Forgiven," he said without pause. "Try harder next time."

He left with nothing more than a nuzzle at the nape of her neck and a parting "Safe night." He locked the door behind him, leaving Cara standing in the middle of her workroom feeling bereft. Not even a tease about when would she be healed. Not a touch in any newly appropriate places. Not a wink, which he had learned from her some weeks ago, nor a smile. He showed his non-humanity clearly at such times; responses acculturated not in Newydd Cenedyl, but in Selandan. Responses that didn't quite mesh with her expectations, responses she could never interpret with any surety.

Cara sighed against the frustration and tension the evening had induced and curled up in front of the fire in her study. Serano, especially, had been on edge tonight, frightening in his intensity. And she could discuss it with no one except the man who had already bid her goodnight.

And what of the future Himadi House? Twenty or more humans and an equal number of Selandu, rubbing shoulders in one location? Tempers, turf wars, all the myriad differences that put Cara and her guardians at odds, multiplied a thousand-fold. Would it work?

The logs crackled and popped in the flames. The fire warmed the study, which was small enough to feel cozy in, large enough to dance in when she wanted. The tiny dinner table took up space along one wall. A couch, a bookcase, a couple of chairs, a window covered in shutters—forever locked unless Rodani or Serano was in the room, and her 'corder.

Warmth at her front, cold at her back, Cara pulled the quilt off the couch and flopped it over her body. She was beginning to think a switch of rooms was desirable. The cold weather creeping southward would get worse before it got better, and she was already going to bed shivering.

And she couldn't count on Rodani keeping her warm every night.

There was so much she was ignorant of, so little she had learned. How often did Selandu make love? What were Rodani's expectations of her? What were the courtesies in requesting, offering, or declining amorous activities? The Cultural Studies Center didn't teach it. Didn't know it, as far as she could tell. If either of the male ambassadors had brought back such knowledge from their stays in the Selandu capital of Hadaman, neither had owned up to it.

Of course, Cara wouldn't either when she went home.

Went home. It hurt to think of it.

One passionate night with her guardian and she was hooked? Surely not.

Damn.

The door to the hallway rattled. Cara clutched the quilt to her chin in an unexpectedly strong reaction. Had Rodani changed his mind? Come back to sit beside her, lay beside her, warm and hard in all the right places? Her blood thumped in response as the door opened and shut, and boots crossed the workroom. First, they went toward the bedroom, then turned and made their way toward the study. Cara lifted her chin, ready to welcome her lover with a smile.

Serano strode into the room, stopped and stared at her, pupils too narrow in the low light. Half an inch taller than Rodani, grey-eyed, more slender in face and build, he was traditional to the core of his heart, and a womanizer to the core of his body.

Slowly, as if not to startle him, Cara stood up. Despite Arimeso's injunction against violence to her body, she didn't trust Serano to hold his temper.

"Sit down," he said. His face held the same tension she'd seen in the gathering. Meant to have his say about something, obviously. It didn't take a genius to figure what about.

Cara pulled the quilt away and motioned him onto the couch. He regarded her a moment longer, as if the unexpected courtesy and quiet in such a voluble person was suspect. He sat.

"I'll ask Deremic for tea," she said, and walked toward the workroom.

"No."

Cara turned in the doorway. The denial didn't bother her. She now stood where she wanted to be, next to an open door, with room to run.

"Sit down."

"I've been sitting all evening, a'tem. It would please me to stand." Formality, formality. She hoped it would put him in a less irritable state of mind. She slipped sideways, next to the fireplace and her back to the wall. It was an uncomfortable reminder of five nights ago, when she and Rodani had faced each other with their desires.

Come back, she wished to him in the cool air. "Is there a problem?"

Serano stared at her coldly from his place on the couch, like an arrogant craft master ready to upbraid a lackluster apprentice. "If you are wise, there will not be."

Good. Typical. Had he cleared this discussion with Rodani before traipsing over here to confront her?

No chance. Rodani would accept such talks as his own obligation, not foist it onto his junior partner.

"A'tem," she said, "I'll be as wise as I know to be. But Rodani made his choice in this matter, just as I did. And if you have concerns, he will understand them better, and do a—"

Not wise to say what she was going to say, that Rodani could explain things better than she ever could. *Wise as I know how to be* had better start now. Cara made the tossing gesture with her hand. "I'm listening."

"Are you?"

"Yes, Serano. I am."

Serano's face closed down. He froze into killer mode, still as a fox in a taxidermist's shop. Eyes just as sharp and steady. She'd seen Rodani do it twice, and it frightened the curl out of her hair.

Serano spoke, low-voiced and clear. "If you get him killed, I will kill you."

Chills crawled down her body, then were crowded out by tendrils of fear. "Serano," she managed to say. "I...if he dies because of me, I wouldn't wish to live."

"Then we are agreed?"

"No!"

Serano remained motionless, still projecting a deadly glare. "Your idiotic requests and errors in judgment have put his life in jeopardy more than once already."

She swallowed a painful lump in her throat. "He's free to say no. And has."

"He has given you more leeway than he should."

"That's his decision," she retorted. "And I have given him leeway with me."

His pupils widened, then narrowed. "Will you again?"

"That's between Rodani and me."

"It is a poor choice you two have made. And a dangerous one."

Cara waved her hand in the air, taking the edge of the quilt with it. "You're having this discussion with the wrong person."

"Do you wish to die?"

Her hand stopped, then clenched into a fist. "Vague threats may frighten me, a'tem, but not for long."

"They should."

Serano remained frozen a moment longer, then relaxed into the corner of the couch. But his narrowed eyes spoke a different truth. "Tell him you have changed your mind. Tell him you will no longer welcome his attentions."

No, she nearly blurted. And kept it between her teeth by the barest margin. *Calm. Calm and distance, fem.* "Put yourself in my place, Serano. Alone in my country, you find yourself with the only woman who has breached your barriers. You welcome her attentions, bask in her acceptance of your differences, then are told you must refrain—even though you walk your days at her side."

Serano was still. Still and watchful.

"What would be your answer?"

"Go home."

"To face what?" She shifted her position against the wall. "More than personal failure, that's certain. Who else is better suited to prove Himadi House can succeed than me? Rodani and me, Serano. A grand experiment that succeeded beyond anyone's expectations." She gripped the quilt tightly again and stood her ground, eyes narrowed in limited imitation.

"You are a child playing with guns."

"Would Rodani bed a child?"

"You misinterpret me, human. I—"

"No. I do not."

He didn't like the interruption, that was clear.

"I am an adult," she said hurriedly, to forestall any censure. Keep his mind on interpreting her accent, which had thickened in the heat of her emotions. "I choose what I wish to choose, face the dangers I consent to face. Find pleasures where I dare to find them, Serano. You are the guardian of my body, not my conscience. Or," she leaned forward, "Rodani's."

"You walk a narrow path with your eyes closed."

"Not closed," she spat. "Wide open as I can get them. I'm unused to the dangers, but Rodani guides my feet."

Serano slipped his hands into the deep pockets of his black jacket. He fingered something rhythmically as he stared at her. "You are no more amenable to reason now as in the beginning, Cara. I had hoped to prevent pain for both of you."

He rose, provoking in Cara a slow slide toward the doorway. "I can see," he continued, "that I have failed. May you both be a comfort to each other's woes."

Serano walked toward her, toward the doorway. Her heart beat with a heavy thump. Breath caught in her throat as he stopped at her side. "Remember my promise."

His words ricocheted painfully inside her head as he walked to the hall door and left. Selandu promises were not easily given and rarely rescinded. Would he kill her and risk breaking the fragile peace between their species, along with the chance to go back to space, all for his guild partner? Why?

The fire crackled and spat at her, contemptuous of her folly. What would it be: a knife in the dark or poison in her tea? A fatal encounter with a certain flower? *Greatest apologies, Ambassador Menachem, but she crossed over into Sela's arms before the antidote could be administered.*

Dark.

The room was firelight dim, the shutters closed and locked. The winter sun had set long before. Flickering shadows played over the sofa and created ethereal inkblots on the far wall, hypnotic in their trembling frailty.

Cara slid down into a crouch at the base of the wall. What the hell was she doing? She had walked many of her life's paths, gaze firmly ahead, determined not to see the perilous cliffs on either side. Had she finally found one too narrow for her feet? Maybe she was as naïve as Rodani said, as stubborn as Serano thought.

But she was here. Had been here longer than any of the ambassadors had been allowed in Hadaman at one stretch. It was worth something, this success, this crossing of barriers no one ever thought to cross.

It had to be.

She stood and flung the quilt over the back of the sofa, then padded into the bedroom.

Had to be.

She pulled out the clip that held the bun of her hair in place and let it unwind. It fell to her waist in wide brown rivulets, tresses that had caught and held Rodani's fascination.

Had to be.

She stared into the mirror at dark blue eyes, at round pupils that seemed so strange after months of vertical black in grey.

Or gorgeous violet.

She stripped off her clothes and crawled under the quilts on her bed, trapped a folded pillow under her arm, and closed her eyes.

***

Heavy; a dragging weight.

Something clung to her legs. Then it was water, and she waded through it in desperation, muscles bunched under the strain. The smell of rotting fish invaded her nostrils, the sound of waves crashed against her ears. Something followed behind her, gaining on her. A deadly miasma enveloped her and filled her lungs with the breath of terror. Moonlight showed her nothing but shadows on the water. Her breathing came in heaving gasps. The water rose to her thighs, draining her strength with its every ebb and flow.

Her unseen enemy neared. In the distance, the thump of a fist hit flesh.

Rodani!

Turn back. Protect him! But her own enemy breathed at the back of her neck, closing in.

Thump.

Helpless to fight the water or the enemy that clutched at her, helpless to save Rodani, she started to scream. Something grabbed her around the throat and threw her into the waves. She fought with waning strength as water closed over her head.

A hand tightened around her neck. Her lungs felt ready to burst.

Cara's eyes shot open as she struggled in the quilts wrapped around her. Desperately, she kicked them off. Shivering in the cold air, she reached for the bedside lantern and turned it up. The shadows fled into corners and under furniture, cowering in the light.

Footsteps whispered in the narrow servant's corridor. Cara grabbed for the quilt and flung it over her body as Deremic tapped on the door frame and stepped just inside.

"A'Cara?" he asked, soft behind the mask of propriety that hadn't left his face in the five days he'd been her servant.

"I'm well, I'm well."

Hamman's brother, replacement for young Falita who had unknowingly let Shurad into their suite, Deremic wasn't someone Cara could confide in. Not yet.

"Shall I call Rodani?"

"Unnecessary, Deremic." She took another deep breath. "Thank you."

Deremic remained in her doorway just long enough to incline his head at the lie-that-was-courtesy, then left.

Alone.

The shadows gibbered at her from their hiding places, and terror hunkered down in the dark of her workroom, watching. Waiting for the right moment to conquer her suppression and explode into memories.

She shivered, wishing she'd asked for Rodani. He was just across the hall. But he needed his rest, too. Only he and his goddess knew what nightmares crawled through his sleeping mind. He wasn't telling.

Cara rolled over and worked her way down under the covers. The bedside light radiated warmth and security.

THREE

Naremit, security eleventh, paced down the guild-only hallway. His still-new boots smacked against the stone floor and his fists dug curved nails into his palms. He opened the door to the range. "Goddess bless," he muttered into the empty room. "Finally."

Anger stole the finesse from his muscles. He fumbled with his gun, the magazine clattering onto the floor as if to reproach him for his ire. He refilled it from the storage closet and planted himself in front of the targets.

"Temi damn her." He raised his arms. "Damn her to an early grave." In rapid succession, he fired into the human-shaped target. One mag. Two. Three. Holes erupted in the target's head, chest, gut, pelvis. There was no tight pattern to the holes, but a sufficient number of them would do an adequate job.

Damn the taso, too, forbidding Shurad a proper Enclave burial. No one would even tell him where his cousin's body now lay. Garidemu, potter and close companion—and also a cousin, had been agitating him for days. Why couldn't Shurad have been decently burned, as the Riverfolk's traditions required? Treason, Arimeso had said. Treason!

Naremit shoved another handful of ammo into the magazine and fired into a neighboring target.

Treason was bringing an alien onto the manor's grounds and assigning a guardian to protect her. Treason was forcing every person on the estate to acknowledge her existence, and that of her dishonorable species. Treason was profiting from alien goods, ugly things they were, and displaying them for a whole gathering of the weak-minded to fawn over.

What's more, the keso agreed with him. Temi damn the man. Couldn't he convince the taso this was a bad idea? Said he'd been trying. How hard was it to convince a female of anything, anyway? Kusik had had months to accomplish the task, and here the human was, still in residence, still making her boring, haphazard blankets, of all things, and being watched and coddled by one of the worst guardians ever to win guild knives!

And his cousin was dead, killed by that same guardian.

Naremit shoved the gun into his belt and spun on his heel. He walked out, slamming the door behind him. Most of the guardians were already in the guild meeting room when he got there. Behind him, Kusik was talking to Serano.

"Success?" the keso asked Rodani's partner.

"No," was the answer.

"Try harder."

Lanata and Imal had returned from their meeting with Shurad's parents. Naremit glanced around. Everyone was here now, except...of course.

"Serano, where is Rodani?" Timan asked, as he took his place at the far end of the table. Kusik tossed papers and a pencil on the tabletop at his end.

"Unknown. He should be here in moments."

"He should be here now," Naremit said. He yanked a chair out and sat in his place at Timan's right hand.

Serano eyed him from mid-way down the other side of the table. "New knives still hanging heavy on your belt, I see."

"I am not the one with the perpetually broken timepiece, a'tem."

"And you have no—"

"Cease," Timan ordered.

As the last of the guild sat down, Rodani walked in. He took his seat across from Serano, facing the doorway.

"Last in, first to report." Kusik picked up his pencil. And glanced down at the paper. "How is the pet human?"

Naremit mentally tapped his forehead with his fist: *Good shot.*

Rodani leaned forward, his eyes narrowing. "Her arm is healing from Shurad's attempt to kill her. But she is having dream fears." He interlaced his fingers. "She has woken up every night since the shooting with difficulty regaining her sleep. She feels sadness for what has happened and evinces sympathy for Shurad's family."

Naremit uttered a hiss, barely audible above the rustling of clothing in the cold room. But Rodani turned to him with a piercing glare. He ignored it.

"She is crafting?"

"Yes."

Kusik turned to Guild Fourth Toranel. "Plans for this year's meet?"

"Advancing," the woman said. "There is a good supply of ammo, but the maze walls need shoring up, and the plan for the tracking event needs finalized." She passed a sheaf of papers down the row to the keso.

"Pavanec," he said, "you and Misheiki keep your eye out for likely guild candidates. Not only in the manor, but in the outlying cottages and the village."

"And please," Lanata added, raising an eyebrow. "Do not overlook any female candidates."

Goddess above, Naremit thought. *If women were supposed to be in the guild, Sela would fight alongside Temi.* It was obvious to him that females were not as strong as the males. There was not one thing they did better than men. He felt a momentary pang of sympathy for Shurad's parents, wanting to build their own society away from the fools who worshipped inclusivity. Women in the guild? Heresy, like men in the Enclave. He stared at Rodani. And crafters in the guild. Utter bilge. And aliens? Oh, for just a few missiles from shipboard. He would take care of the whole problem with a few clicks of a button.

Naremit came out of his reverie to hear his cousin's name.

"Shurad's parents were inconsolable, a'Keso." Lanata rubbed her fingertips against her thumb rhythmically. "It would not be a surprise to me if they knock on our doors or demand a hearing in Tendiman."

Her partner, Imal, took up the tale. "We believe what triggered Shurad's actions was his parents' failure to petition for redress from the Council of Three."

"How many attempts had they made, Imal?"

"Last week was their third."

Naremit leaned forward and laid his fists on the table in front of Timan. "And now they will be given another three attempts."

Every guild head turned his way—which was, of course, what he was looking for. "As long as those aliens share our world, we will never be safe. And yet the Hadaman Three natter about treaties and guidelines and waste the precious power of the earthmover to build a house in Himadi. The High Guild reviews their acceptance and training guidelines for the fiftieth time since we landed, and the Enclave chants and burns incense!"

"A'Keso," Rodani said, turning away from the diatribe, "I wish to be excused."

Naremit shot to his feet, burning with rage at the loss of his cousin and the muted attitude of his guild counterparts. "And you saunter back to watch over an alien child instead of helping secure this world!"

"Naremit, cease," Kusik said.

"Who gave you those bruises, a'tem?" he said. "Did you get down on your knees while she played childhood games?"

Rodani stood up slowly. Naremit growled at him across the intervening heads but was yanked back in his chair by Timan.

"Sit," Kusik told Rodani, then glared down at the end of the table. "We have heard your complaints every week since you arrived, a'tem. They grow tiresome."

"If they are—"

Now Kusik stood, and every guardian at the table froze. "You will obey me, as I obey the taso." Carefully, he placed his fists on the table and leaned. "The human's presence in the taso's house is the taso's decision. Is there any question about this?"

Only Naremit's heavy breathing came through the silence that filled the meeting room.

"Disperse."

The guild moved out in a discordant clatter of boots. Timan approached Kusik quietly. "Naremit is missing a few lessons, tem'u," he said.

"I cannot blame him for his pique," Kusik replied.

"But for his disruptions and discourtesies?"

Kusik waved his papers as if to shoo away an annoying bug.

Timan crossed his arms. "You know well that it is not wise to allow him to build obstructions between us. He is fomenting rebellion."

"He is hardly more than a youth."

"Which is a good time to set him on a path more befitting a guardian."

"I leave that to your best judgment, Timan. And in its place, I require your opinion."

"My duty, as always," he said, inclining his head.

"What do you suggest should be done about Rodani's shameful disregard of the rule?"

Timan hesitated. "What does Arimeso say?"

Kusik's expression fell into mask, his eyes hard. "It is your opinion I wish to hear. I am already aware of hers."

"You put me in a discordant position, tem'u."

"And you refuse to answer because I will disapprove of it," Kusik said. "Then you need not tell me what it is." He shuffled his papers with a restless energy, crumpling the rough edges.

"Kusik, I do not approve of guild rule-breaking any more than you. But I see this as extenuating circumstances."

Kusik ceased his unquiet fidgeting. His pupils narrowed. "And it does not offend you?"

"To which offense do you refer?" Timan asked him. "Rules, visceral reactions to aliens, insubordination? Or your original disfavor of the boy he once was?"

Kusik stuffed the papers in his satchel with a furious thrust of his arm. "You ever insist on making me analyze my judgments, tem'u."

Timan bowed. "My duty to us all, a'Keso."

Kusik made his way back to the quarters he shared with the taso, musing on the stubbornness of guardians. It wasn't enough that he had shown his displeasure with Rodani by gifting him with a few bruises. It wasn't enough that the man's own partner fought a dominance battle with him that very eve, after the shooting. Kusik ached to punish both guardian and human. But he was a keso. And his taso had a mind all her own.

"Difficult meeting?" Arimeso said, looking up from the book in her hands.

"One of the graduates is testing his new saddle."

"On the subject of?"

"The human."

Arimeso laid down the book in her hands and interlaced her fingers over top of it. "Another Riverchild?"

"Not that I am aware." Kusik tossed his satchel on a spare chair in the corner. "But the strength of his convictions concerns me."

"Make him understand, esuva."

"I find it difficult to disagree with him."

"Disagreeing is not the issue."

"A'Taso, this affinity of Rodani's, and the rule-breaking that brought it on, will not stop here."

"No one outside of the principals knows."

"They will. Someone will make a mistake. Likely it will be the human." Kusik poured a drink from the decanter at his desk. "This is the beginning, Arimeso. Heed me." He took a long swallow. "Heed me well."

***

Rodani stood on the other side of Cara's worktable, looking exotic and far too serious for her comfort. "Arimeso calls a meeting."

Cara shoved her cutting ruler aside. The fabric underneath bunched and lost its perfect alignment. Just the mention of the taso's name was enough to sour her stomach. The woman wasn't evil, just unpredictable. One never knew what was going on behind those grey eyes and calm demeanor. She held each life on the estate in the palm of her narrow, six-fingered hand.

"About what?" she asked.

Rodani shifted his shoulders, then pulled his hands behind him—into the small of his back—a stance of formality she least expected.

"Rodani?" Thoughts crowded her mind, one shoving another aside as her adrenaline rose. She was in trouble. Rodani was in trouble because of her. Kusik was mad at him. Arimeso was angry.

Cara's lunch solidified in her stomach. "Rodani," she prompted him cautiously.

He blinked. The broad shoulders sagged a fraction, and he shifted his empty stare to the worktable.

"Ambassador Mena'hem wishes to speak with you."

"What?"

Rodani looked at her quizzically.

"I mean, why?"

"We shall hear."

"Now?"

"Sai."

She changed into something more appropriate, a long skirt and tunic, and jacket against the winter chill.

Arimeso's quarters were centered in the middle of the first floor, well insulated against outside dangers both natural and sentient. Rodani ushered Cara into the taso's office.

The room wasn't large, but it was as ostentatious as anything Cara had seen north of the hills. A new tapestry of muted blues and greens covered the floor under the chairs in front of Arimeso's roanwood desk. Portraits adorned the walls. *Iraimin's?* she wondered.

"Sit," Arimeso said. Kusik sat at her right, looking as unpleasant as ever.

Cara took the chair on the right, Rodani the left, closer to Kusik.

"A'Cara, Ambassador Mena'hem called for you."

The ball in her stomach threatened an inappropriate getaway. A call from the Cultural Studies Center could only mean trouble. Dae? Her father had been fighting heart problems for years now. Had he finally lost? It hurt to think she'd missed his deathbed. There were things she still wanted to say.

Arimeso motioned to Kusik. He pressed a button on the desk.

"A'Reiti," she said.

"A'Taso," Menachem answered across the miles, across the hills. Home. Strange, how strange a human voice sounded now—nasal, weak.

"Cara is present, a'Reiti. You may speak."

"Thank you, a'Taso."

Cara waited out the slight hesitation that stretched into infinity. Ambassador that he was, still Menachem wasn't known for mincing words when it came to his fellow humans.

"Cara, we heard of your troubles."

Troubles. Ahh. He knew a taso was listening. Cara waited to see where he would go with his introduction.

"Are you well?" he continued.

"I'm healing."

"We regret the unfortunate circumstances."

Huh. Which unfortunate circumstances? Me being the only human with the requisite skills to come here? My success? Getting shot? Or Shurad's death? Surely, you don't know about Rodani.

"As do I," she said, at her diplomatic best.

"Cara, we wish for you to come home."

Thanks to Serano's threat, twice in twenty-five hours she was shocked into speechlessness. Her mind raced; her heart thumping close behind. Leave Rodani? Leave her work, her art? *No.*

A different freedom beckoned as well. Freedom to do what she wished, walk where she would, see whom she desired. But it was Rodani she desired. Few heartstrings still attached her to her home.

"Why?"

Menachem took his turn at silence. Arimeso, Kusik, even Rodani was still; an assassin watching, waiting. Waiting for her answer.

"It would bode ill for both races if you were killed, Cara," Menachem said, breaking the silence.

"As well if I ran away. I'll stay."

"Think long and hard."

Cara took a deep breath. "I've already done that, a'Reiti."

She could hear her pulse in her ears. Rodani hadn't moved a muscle.

The speaker crackled. "You have only to request a return, and it will be granted."

Cara glanced at Arimeso. Blank-faced, the taso regarded her across a chasm of status and responsibility that Cara could only imagine.

"Thank you, a'Reiti," she said. "Your concern is appreciated."

"As will be," Ambassador Menachem replied. "I thank you, a'Taso, for your time and effort."

"A'Reiti."

Given a wave of Arimeso's fingers, Kusik broke the circuit. He lifted his head and gave Cara a look like the one Serano had gifted her with last night. She dared a glance in Rodani's direction. Serano he could handle. He had the seniority. But Kusik?

Rodani was staring at the desk in front of Arimeso's folded hands. Cara molded her face into an expression of innocent waiting and relaxed back into the chair.

"I told the ambassador you would stay," Arimeso said.

Cara's eyes widened. She tilted her head. "I commend you for your insight, a'Taso."

"Is there aught that you need from me?"

"No, a'Taso. Of all that is possible to have, I have what I need."

Arimeso waved a dismissal. Cara and Rodani rose, bowed, and left.

"You didn't know?" Cara asked him as they reentered her rooms. She headed toward her worktable, and the quilt-to-be that lay in pieces on top of it.

"I did not." In the middle of her workroom, Rodani hesitated, eyes downcast. "I thought you might leave."

Cara padded back to him and placed a gentle hand on his waist, tucking it safely in between his weapons. "Why?"

He put his hands on her shoulders. "Safety, familiarity, freedom. All those things you find lacking here."

"And if I had said yes?"

His pupils grew wide, and he looked away as if uncertain of the advisability of answering such a question. "I would have regretted it, kia."

Cara smiled. "You are sweet."

"I taste sweet?" Now the pupils narrowed; he was thinking.

She laughed, then tugged on his jacket. "Let me find out. I've forgotten." Rodani lifted her up with an easy pull, slipped an arm under her rear, and returned her smile before Cara closed in on a kiss.

Not sweet, no. Just that hint of spice that always clung to his skin, the spice that now threaded its way into her brain to act on her hormones. Cara wrapped her arms around his neck and clung to him; harbor in a storm. If they had made her leave....

"Hamman will wonder if we were gnawing on each other's teeth, kia," Rodani said into her curls.

"Then someone will have to teach her how to kiss, too."

"We may start a new trend in intimacies."

Cara pulled back from him and smiled into his eyes. "Terrible thought." Then another occurred to her. "Are there any more wires in these rooms?"

Rodani set her down on her feet. "No. Deremic still searches for them. I have talked with the stablemaster. Do you wish to visit the colt?"

Cara halted her saunter toward the worktable and turned to face him. "Now?"

"If you wish."

Cara hurried toward her bedroom door. "When have I ever not?" she asked over her shoulder. This time, she left the door open, a measure of Rodani's new status. She slipped out of her dress clothes and into something more worthy of the stables, taking the opportunity to glance at him from the corner of her eye.

Pocket 'com in hand, he was watching her. She grabbed her coat from the many-armed pole next to her armoire. "Ready," she said, presenting herself in front of him.

They headed down the hall, past the door to the rooms Rodani and Serano shared.

"You don't need a coat?" she asked.

"It is not so cold as that, kia. Not yet."

It wasn't fair that cold and heat affected the Selandu so little. It made her feel puny, her species fragile. Normally content with her small size and creative capabilities, she'd seen her self-image change since her arrival at Barridan.

***

The garage was half-empty of its usual half-dozen vehicles. Stone walls did little to stave off the cold that whistled in through the open doors. Cara headed automatically for the dark carriage, which was, she surmised, fraught with any number of hidden guild weapons. Asking Rodani any questions on the subject was futile.

"Have you heard from Litelon, Rodani?"

"No. I have no wish to."

"Did you find out what happened?"

He unlocked her door and opened it, leaning in to look around before motioning her in. When he leaned back, Cara climbed in and took her normal spot in the middle seat. Rodani walked around the front and got in.

"Did you find out what happened?"

"Remember your seatbelt."

"Rodani..."

He pulled out of the garage and drove down the lane, eastward, to the stables. Cara leaned back in the seat and brooded.

It was her life that was at stake, her blood that was spilled, her screams that still echoed in the nooks and crannies of her brain. She had a right to know. But she and Rodani had already met on opposite sides of that ravine before. There was no bridge across unless he built one.

"This may be your last time to play with the colt, kia."

She leaned forward and put her arms on the seats ahead of her. "Why?"

"He has grown."

She waited for him to continue his explanation, something that made sense. "And?"

He glanced at her from the rearview mirror. "Their cantankerousness increases with the increase in size."

"Is he dangerous now?"

"Not when I am there." He pulled into the gravel drive and parked.

The stables were rather quiet for once, and noticeably neat. A man Cara didn't know stood at the small gate with the colt, Ichi, reined in hand and waiting.

When they neared, the man opened the gate and let the colt loose in the pen. He scampered around the wooden railing, snorting and snuffling among the dry rushes. Rodani followed Cara into the pen and latched the gate behind him.

Cara started walking toward Ichi, Rodani at her heels. The colt eyed her suspiciously, then trotted over and greeted her in the manner of his kind—a cold nose in a sensitive spot. Cara held herself still to keep from spooking him. He was taller than before, almost chest height, and had to bend his neck to sniff her. Cara rubbed the fuzzy round ears and tickled his wiry whiskers. He prodded her hands, looking for treats.

"I have none, little one. You must ask your master," Cara told him. He licked her palms and rooted at the soles of her shoes.

"A few more months and you could ride him, kia," Rodani said.

"I didn't realize they grew so fast."

She rubbed the colt down his back and ruffled the fur. Unlike the whiskers, it was soft, downy like the ears. She bent down to sniff it and received an earwash of saliva in return. Laughing, she rubbed it with her hand. It smelled like Ichi's breath—a little sour, with a tang of rushes.

"Are you hungry?" Cara asked. She grabbed a handful of rushes and held them out. He eyed them with disinterest and took off toward the water trough.

"Ah, I should have brought a rag for the dribbles."

Rodani stepped around to her side. "I will not leave you in here with it while I fetch one."

Cara eyed him top to bottom and smiled. "Will you loan me your shirt again?"

His eyes grew wide, as if she'd slapped him. "Not for a slobbering benatac."

"Then I'll think of a better reason." She patted him on the arm, grabbed a fistful of rushes, and walked up to the colt. They played face-tag, Cara trying to wipe his muzzle with rushes, he trying to nibble. She spotted a rope wrapped around the fence, walked over, and pulled it off.

"Here, Ichi. Do you play tug of war?"

He investigated the wiggling rope for a moment, then trotted off.

Cara turned to Rodani. "What catches the interest of an herbivore?"

"Grass."

She muttered and took off after the colt. They played catch me, catch you for a while, back and forth across the length and breadth of the pen, past a watchful Rodani. Cara had to stop far sooner than Ichi did. She halted near the gate and squatted, panting. Rodani came over and knelt in front of her.

"You are well?"

"Yes," she said. "Out of breath." She slid her hand onto his thigh, letting it rest ever so casually, as if maybe it belonged there.

"Kia," he warned softly.

She swiped her hand down toward his knee before reluctantly removing it.

Ichi sidled up to them and snuffled Rodani's neck. "Away with you." He pushed at the long snout.

The colt squealed and bared sharp incisors. Quick as Rodani was, he wasn't fast enough. Ichi attacked, knocking Rodani onto his back, biting at his arm. Rodani kicked at him, ineffective because of their size difference.

Cara shouted and yanked on his ears. He snapped at her and turned back. In that moment of freedom, Rodani walloped the colt upside the head with his fist.

The colt staggered. Rodani rolled to his feet as Ichi barked an insult and charged. Rodani bent forward and aimed his shoulder at the little beast. They met with a heavy thump. Ichi went sprawling, Rodani on top and trying to protect his face from clawed and flailing feet.

"Stablemaster!" Cara yelled. She ran over to the pair, trying to grab something on the animal, anything that would help Rodani. He laid one arm over the colt's forelegs and grabbed for his throat, squeezing at the lower jaw. Then he pushed Ichi's head against the stone and held it there with white-knuckled force.

"Grab the rope," he said, harsh with effort. "Wrap his hind legs."

As running feet approached from the east, Cara scrabbled in the rushes for the rope and ran back. But she didn't have enough strength to hold one furiously thrashing leg against its owner's will, let alone two.

"I can't."

She laid her body across Ichi's lower half as he twisted and turned under Rodani's greater weight. The gate banged open, and a handful of people ran in, enough for each leg and the head. They wrapped Ichi's legs together, bound his jaws, and carted him off.

Cara stood up and stared after them. "What happened?"

Rodani brushed the rushes and benatac fur from his clothes and tugged at his shirt. "I offended him, obviously. You see now how they have earned their reputation."

"Yes." She crossed her arms and shivered in reaction, frightened to see Rodani attacked but glad it wasn't her. She didn't have his reflexes or strength. "Are any more mares carrying? I need a new playmate."

"You have a new playmate."

Cara spun slowly on her heel. The lilt in his deep voice matched the light in his eyes.

"But you won't play with me."

"Your arm has not healed."

"I just used it in your defense. Twice." She flexed her upper arm against a renewed ache.

"And it is greatly appreciated." Rodani took a last swipe at his pants and motioned Cara toward the swinging gate. "Home."

Rodani drove, as usual.

"I suggest we shower," he said at her door. "Leave your clothes for Deremic to have cleaned."

Before she could reply, he shut the door and was on his way. Good thing he hadn't given her time. She'd almost invited him into the shower with her. It was on the tip of her tongue when he turned away, but interpreting slowed her speech.

It was probably for the best.

Cara stripped and left her clothes in a heap, knowing Hamman would come in at the sound of water running. Forever at hand, she would be waiting outside the door when Cara was done, towel in hand.

Cara let warm water hit the stone bench that served as a resting spot for tired bodies, or washing of dirty feet. In this weather, it would be icy if not warmed first. Her arm ached with the cold and injury, but she sat and washed everything twice while being cautious of the wound. Even if intimacies were still a few hopeful days away, she didn't want to offend Rodani's meticulous sense of smell with the afterodor of benatac.

She wrung her hair, opened the door, and put a bare foot out.

There was the outstretched towel, waiting. And behind it, wet-haired, bare-chested, and barefoot, stood Rodani.

He looked hesitant, unsure. But a smile crept across his face, a smile that mirrored Cara's.

"And where is Hamman?" she asked.

Rodani let the towel sag between his hands. "Busy with other chores."

"So, she asked you to take her place?" *Heh. As if.*

"I offered."

"Your courtesies have ulterior motives." She swung the door open far enough that it tapped the wall. "And I'm freezing."

He stretched the towel out and wrapped it around her as she walked into it. Her arms were folded against her chest; she could do nothing but lean against him. He smelled faintly of soap and spice, and his hairless chest was hard and warm beneath her cheek, the muscles producing an alien pattern of shadows across the grey expanse. Beneath it, Cara heard an odd lup-a-dup, strong and steady.

She rubbed her nose on his skin. "You changed your mind."

His grip loosened.

"Should I leave?"

It took extra effort to look him in the eye from this position, but it was worth the crick in her neck. "You do, and I will chase you across the hall, naked."

Rodani's eyes pulsed, and a grin spread across his face. "I am tempted to test you."

Cara nibbled down his chest toward the belt line. "What would you be testing? My lack of decency, or your willpower?"

"I have none," he said. "Hence my presence."

She gave a little dog-shake and pulled her arms free from the towel. It drooped across one breast. Rodani bent his knees, put an arm under her rear, and lifted her up. The towel fell to her waist, prompting him to take advantage of her gifts.

Cara wrapped her arms around his head and kissed his hair. "If you don't get me under the quilts, Rodani, I'll turn into ice."

He spun around and walked into the bedroom with her. "I prepared for you."

In the corner stood a small contraption on legs, black and square. It glowed a dull red.

"A stove?"

Rodani released his grip on her. She plopped onto the bed with a squeak of surprise. "A portable heater." He pulled off his weapons belt and laid it on the bedside table, then stripped off what clothes he had on and climbed in as she moved over to make room.

"You're quite thoughtful," she said.

"It is better to think while I am still able." Rodani scooted next to her and flipped an edge of the quilt over her legs.

"How can I tell when you're not?"

He leaned over her, nose-to-nose, arm on her other side. "The more often my pupils pulse," he said softly, "the less I am thinking."

He nuzzled her face, moving down to her neck. Ripples of pleasure ran down Cara's spine. Her skin warmed where Rodani's breath passed over it, only to chill again in the slowly warming air.

"You promised to teach me the way of your pleasures, kia."

"I haven't forgotten," she said.

Cara cupped his face in her hands and kissed him. He kissed her back, a quick study—the first time he hadn't known what a kiss was. Cara pushed him onto his back to work her way down one side of his long body and up the other, then brought her lips to his organ.

"No," he whispered, cupping her chin to prevent the oral touch. "Hands." He entwined his fingers in the curls of her hair, adding suggestions and revealing responses to her hands' efforts. Then she worked her kisses back up to his face.

With a few words, Rodani gently pushed her knees apart. Cara swallowed her modesty and taught him the beginnings of what he wished to learn. His attention to detail embarrassed her, but she preferred it to a dogged assumption that an alien would know what she needed. Gently, he probed and tested, scented and rubbed, watched her expressions and listened to her wordless sounds.

The lesson whetted other appetites, appetites they shared despite their differences. Rodani moved upward, rubbing his lips over her abdomen and around her breasts. Cara put her hands under his arms and coaxed him forward. He hovered over her, and on a gust of breath, joined her. She shuddered with the exquisite stretch and tension, then curled her legs over him, locking him into her body.

Slowly, he began as she asked, riding inward until he could no more, then withdrawing in infinite patience. His scent filled Cara's brain; his skin hot on hers. Their slow-motion movement begat a passion that burned with the intensity of the summer sun. The walls faded out. The world narrowed to the bed, and the heat, and the consummate push and pull.

When Rodani lifted his hips, she rode him from below, squeezing him rhythmically. He gasped and froze, pupils pulsing spasmodically as he watched her. He hovered an eternity of seconds, then a soft growl escaped his throat. He slipped an arm underneath her shoulders and began to thrust with a force that took her by surprise. She moved into his rhythm with ease as waves of pleasure cascaded over her.

As they fought to meld into one, Rodani growled and shouted, shivering in spasms Cara felt inside and out. He spent his voice and seed with shudders that repeated in decreasing intervals and strength. Cara held him in a fierce grip, her own body tight with unreleased tension. Rodani eased his arm from underneath her and whispered into the curls on her head, then pulled himself from her body and lay at her side.

Cara lifted her hand and caressed his face. "Will you do as you did before?"

Rodani placed his palm on her breast and ran it downward. A reply seemed unnecessary.

She guided him to that forever mischievous sweet spot, and his slender fingers began to work their magic. Warmth radiated outward. Rodani's gentle gaze faded into dark as Cara closed her eyes against the insistent itch that begged to be scratched. It faded frustratingly, then returned with a vengeance that broke through the last of her reserve and left her eager cries to fill the room. She rested her hand on Rodani's and turned toward him, clasping their paired hands between her thighs. Sated, they lay together in pleasant repose.

After a few minutes, Rodani opened the sliding door in the headboard with his free hand. From where there had been nothing the first time, he pulled out an oval of thick, soft cloth and placed it on Cara's hip. Releasing his hand, she reached for the cloth and picked it up.

"What's this?"

He took the cloth and brought it down to where his hand had rested, tucking it carefully into place. "It saves the servants changing the sheets every time."

"What's done with it afterwards?"

"It is thrown in with the day's laundry."

She smiled. "A useful item. Soft." Then the smile faded. "But they'll see it."

He regarded her steadily. "Yes."

"They'll know."

"They know already."

"But they'll know...more."

His expression didn't waver. Noise wasn't something she wished to contemplate. The walls were thick, but not particularly soundproofed. "Do they stay near?"

"They observe courtesies."

Maybe it was enough. Maybe she didn't need to care if Rodani didn't. She reached down and pulled the quilt over them both and snuggled down next to him. He wrapped an arm over her shoulders and rested his chin on the top of her head.

Strange, strange and so unexpected that she'd found such comfort in this cold land. A silver and grey alien male held her, touched her, listened to her as so few human men had. Why him? Not because he was her guardian. Not because he'd saved her life.

There was something more. He had reached down into her soul and begun the healing of a gaping wound, a wound she'd suffered under for a lifetime. A hole she'd thought unfillable. What power did Rodani hold over her? What in hell compelled her to trust this often aloof, deadly man? It made so little sense. She had no love of violence, no love of weapons, stealth, spying, or any other skill she imagined he knew.

"Kia," he said, "Do you know the word 'erinai'?"

"No."

Rodani rubbed her back with his hand, up and down, up and down. She'd taught him how to comfort her, and he hadn't forgotten. Hadn't dismissed the necessity of it either, like a lot of human men she knew. Maybe that was one of—

"An erinai is a name one bestows on an intimate."

Cara waited for him to continue his explanation, but only the hand remained in motion. Up and down her spine, up and down over her shoulder blades, upon occasion running afoul of her hair. Was he anxious about something? Or worried he would offend her? Maybe he expected her to take the next step.

"Like 'kia'?" she asked.

"Yes."

The silence welled up between them, a comfortable wait, but filled with unspoken expectations.

Ah. Obvious, like most things once seen. "You wish me to name you?" she asked.

His gaze roamed the room, as if in search of something to alight upon. "If it would please you."

"Would it please you?"

Rodani's grey face paled nearly to white. He didn't embarrass easily. Cara felt a mote of triumph and ran her hand up his bare chest to the neck. "How is such naming done?"

"One chooses an attribute—physical, psychological—and uses it to form a name."

There had to be something more to this. Something besides just a pet name. What was he looking for?

She slipped her fingers into the locks of silky hair that had fallen over his shoulder. "Rodani, what if I choose something that displeases you?"

"If you choose something that pleases you," he said, cupping her fingers in his hand, "then it will not displease me." His eyes bore into hers, looking, maybe, for something. Something she knew not what.

"Do I have some time to think of one?" she asked.

"Yes."

She smiled and kissed him, then rolled off the bed and padded into the bathroom, white cloth still tucked strategically in place. Cold again, she made quick work of her washup and came back to stand at the bed. Rodani lay on the sheets—her sheets, head resting on one of her pillows, his muscled body stretched out in languorous repose.

She pulled the quilt from the bed and wrapped herself in it, then looked at the bedside table. She ran her fingers lightly over his gun belt. Snaps and buttons, bumps and lumps made themselves known to her sensitive fingertips.

A six-fingered hand shot out from the side and grabbed her wrist. She jerked and pulled, but Rodani's vice-like grip kept her from moving. His pupils were slits.

She took a step back. "I'm sorry," she whispered, wide-eyed.

He slid off the bed, hand still firmly wrapped around her wrist.

"Rodani..."

He stood up, naked and remote, and pulled her hand away from his weapons.

"Never, Cara." His voice ran deep, the words clearly enunciated. "Never touch a weapons belt." He stared down at her. "What it contains could kill you."

"I'm sorry, okay?" Her voice broke at his unexpected reaction, at the strength in his grip. She'd forgotten. Forgotten how strong he was, how much and how often he contained himself around her. It was an ugly reminder of her vulnerability.

"You would be sorrier if you chose to ignore the warning."

Cara stepped back from him, their hands hovering in the air between them like a mismatched arm-wrestling contest.

"Is that a threat?" she asked.

Rodani released her. His arms fell to his sides, pupils relaxing into a more normal width. "No, kia. It was not my intent to end our ride in acrimony."

Cara closed her eyes, then reopened them. He still stood, naked before her, grey skinned, four-toed and six-fingered, silver hair streaming over his shoulders and down his chest to the waist. The recent evidence of his passion was tucked out of sight behind the pelvic orifice, protected until desire again brought it forth.

Alien, guardian, dangerous, and still very much an unknown. From passion to fright was the work of moments, and it unnerved her. A switch in his focus, but the same piercing intensity. *Stupid, Cara.*

"Kia," he said into her silence.

"Yes?"

"You are well?"

After a deep breath, she said, "Yes." She was, really, all things considered. As long as she didn't push one temichin boundary too many.

"I have seen this before."

"What before?"

"This expression," Rodani said, looking her over. "This stance, the quilt held tightly around you."

Expression? She fingered the fabric in her hand. Stance?

"Teach me what it means," he continued, "what you are thinking, so I will know."

Cara rubbed the sole of one cold foot on the stone floor. "Um, unsure."

"Unsure?"

"Of what to do, what to say." That much was the truth. She didn't know whether to approach him after his anger or walk away. "I just offended you, and I don't wish to do it again."

Rodani stepped up and pulled her into an embrace, quilt and all, then rubbed the curls on top of her head with his hand. "Will this suffice?"

His warmth bled through the fabric, and onto her skin. Times like these were made for purring. Cara wished she could. "Yes." She unwrapped the quilt and wrapped it around him, covering them both. "That was quite a turn of the tide for me."

"And only for you?" His tone rose with a lilt of humor. "You touch my body, then touch my weapons, both with an innocent curiosity."

"And only one is forbidden?"

"Only one." He released her. "I had hoped to craft this afternoon. I would sit with you, if I am still welcome."

Cara smiled. "Of course you are."

They dressed and then sat on adjacent sides of her worktable. Rodani opened his toolbox and retrieved a sanding brush and a hair clip. The silver clip reflected the afternoon light with a dull shine. Curves decorated it, left from the rectangular metal after the background was sawed away. Rodani flipped the clip in his hand and began to sand its curves.

Cara watched him bend his head and arc his hand toward the light.

"Aisu."

Rodani stopped, hand in the air, and regarded her quizzically. "Aisu?" he replied. "Su enmi erinai?"

"Sai," she agreed. "Aisu."

Night eyes.

Rodani pursed his lips, then the corners of his mouth curved upward.

***

Across the hall, Serano closed the door of their quarters behind him and headed downstairs. Another interruption, another meeting, this time alone. It was rest-day. He had better things to do, more pleasurable things, than a face-to-face with the keso.

Serano knocked on the security office door.

The intercom crackled. "Who?"

"Serano."

"Enter."

Kusik sat behind his carved do'e desk, itself a sinuously curved masterpiece that enfolded Kusik in its wooden embrace. Carvings meandered over the front facing, symbols from times long past, times before space flight.

"A'Keso," Serano said.

"Your talk with the human?"

No preamble, no courtesies. Kusik eschewed such things. Many years had ridden by since Serano first heard that tone of voice directed at him. Some things eased with time. Others did not.

"A failure, a'Keso."

"So I surmise, by their current activities."

Serano flinched inwardly at the revelation. Kusik had more than one method of garnering information. "A'Keso," Serano ventured, "my skills are such—"

"When I partnered you to him, I did not know I would need a spy, not a tracker." Kusik leaned back in his chair and eyed Serano darkly. Then his pupils expanded. "Or a poisoner," he said slowly.

Serano's intake of air was nearly audible. "A'Keso."

"Persuade her against this path of action she is riding."

"A'Keso, I have found it impossible to reason with her alien mind."

"Kenimandil reasons with the ambassadors."

"Sela did not give me a politician's skill, a'Keso."

"You manage with women quite well."

"A'Keso..." the hesitation in Serano's voice mimicked the hesitation in his thoughts. "A'Keso, I use no political skills on women."

"Do not play ignorance games with me, Serano."

He stiffened and raised his chin, just shy of being aggressive. "I am not, a'Keso. Cara is different. Nearly incomprehensible. Neither political nor amorous skills will work on her."

"Tell that to your partner."

Caught, Serano blinked and took a breath.

"If he can pierce her barriers, so can you," Kusik continued.

Trap closed; jaws clinked shut. "A'Keso..."

"Turn her against him, or him against her—I care not which. Take his place in her bed, if that will help. Then make her wish to go home."

"A'..." Serano shut his mouth.
"Dismissed."

***

Litelon kicked the pail of wash water with all his adolescent strength. It went flying across the stone floor of the stable, bumping and clattering, spilling water in a spiral fall. One of the slats splintered against the trough and broke. His shoulders bunched under his ragged shirt as he threw the mop after it. It spun through the air, walloping a saddle on the far wall. Saddle and mop fell into the rushes on the stone floor. The storm that had flooded Litelon an hour ago still washed through his body in hot waves.

That damnable guardian! He could not have. Could not!

Litelon shuddered. His fists clenched to the point of pain, his arms rigid at his sides.

She was adashi. She was forbidden. Everyone knew it. How could he have done such a thing? How many times now had Rodani forbidden him to see her? Talk to her? Always spouting safety. Precautions. Enemies.

Litelon spun around and pounded his fist on the stable wall. It wasn't his fault that bedamned Shurad had murder on his mind. Wasn't his fault that Cara had almost been killed.

How could Sela have allowed this...this forbidden alliance? He was the one who wanted her, deserved her. He, Litelon. Who else had braved the dangers he tended every day? Who else could tame a wild beast, quickly, competently?

And Rodani hadn't even given him a chance. No chance at all to win Cara's attentions before they were captured. Captured by that evil-eyed guardian who should never have approached her. There was no other explanation for her touch on him, the touch that burned into Litelon's mind as he stood behind the wooden slats in the stall, watching her.

Who else knew? The taso? The taso knew everything. Couldn't she stop it? Maybe she didn't wish to. She was curious. Why else bring an alien here? Should I tell her?

Litelon shied away from facing the taso. But—

There was someone else in the house. Someone else who had the power to ask, to investigate, to intervene.

He ran back to the half-stall that served as his living quarters and rummaged through the battered chest in search of something reputable to wear.

FOUR

Cara's newest quilt was coming along nicely. As opposed to the on-and-off pattern of work she was forced into at home, this every day crafting was showing results. Her accuracy in cutting and sewing the myriad pieces had improved noticeably over the months.

Arimeso's customers seemed to be taking notice as well. In fifteen weeks, she'd made eight wall hangings, all of which had sold. It was a record she couldn't expect to continue. But it was, Rodani had told her, a record few other crafters held. It seemed the outré was intriguing, even among Selandu. And less troublesome for the average Selandu to have human art objects nearer than the creators themselves.

Face-to-face, the fabric pieces went together, then under the presser foot. Feed dogs drew each duo across the faceplate and off the other side, leaving the way open for the next.

A rapid knock on the door surprised her, interrupting her train of stitch. She stared at the door suspiciously.

It couldn't be Rodani. She'd told him days ago that he didn't have to knock anymore. He was as welcome in her rooms as he was in her arms. Litelon's knock was softer. Iraimin always came in through the servants' rooms.

"Who's there?"

"Kusik."

Good gods of the wide deep. The security first! Kusik of the heavy hand. She didn't want to let him in. She forced her mouth to form the words, to allow a hated one entrance to her room. "Please enter." *And where the hell is Rodani?*

As the door opened, she stood up from her machine in deference to his presence in the room. "A'Keso," she said with as much composure as she could muster on short notice.

He gave no return greeting.

"Jacket."

He stood still in her doorway, tall, slender but solid looking. His pupils seemed to glow even in the daytime. Night-black clothing and stone demeanor spoke to a power that was not to be trifled with.

"May I ask my destination?" Cara asked formally as she headed for the bedroom.

A moment of silence, then, "the Enclave."

She stopped and turned to face Kusik, eyes wide. "Why?"

He let her question hang in the air just long enough to feed her fears.

"Move."

Cara swallowed heavily. She knew a command when she heard one. "Hamman?" There was no answer. "Hamman? Deremic?"

Cara peered timidly into the dim hallway that joined her bedroom with the servants' quarters. The air was still, the quiet chilling; her hands clenched the door frame.

"Hamman?"

Cara leaned into the doorway, then pushed backwards and grabbed her embroidered jacket. She kept her eyes on the floor as she neared the keso. Kusik opened the door for her, with a glare to his eyes.

"Where is Rodani?" she asked politely.

Kusik took her arm in a painful grip and propelled her out of the room ahead of him, causing her to nearly trip over her own feet. As he locked the door behind them, Cara's heart began to race in her chest. Her ratcheting pulse pounded in her ears.

"Is he well?" she tried again, against her better judgment.

"Silence."

Kusik's temper, the absence of Rodani and her servants, and the prospect of facing the Enclave of the priestesses made her feel nauseated. The priestesses? Not even Rodani mentioned them but in passing. They mediated. They interpreted the goddess's will and laws. And in their zealous application of Sela's law, they could sometimes command the guardians.

The guardians. Kusik's deadly men and women. Cara didn't know what was ahead of her, or where Rodani was, or in what shape. He had to be involved somehow if he wasn't here. Or dead.

The thought made her dizzy. Her breath caught in her throat. *No. They wouldn't.* Nor could he have been sent on assignment. He'd told her more than once she was his sole duty while she resided in Barridan. *Had someone shot at him?* Few knew what had occurred between the two of them.

That must be it. The priestesses took exception to their new affinity, and they were putting a stop to it.

Maybe they couldn't demand such a thing. Or if they did, maybe Rodani wouldn't listen.

Right. Between Arimeso, Kusik, and the priestesses, Cara wondered how much say he had in his own private life.

In much too short a time, Kusik led her to the northwest corner of the manor house, where the Enclave held court in more privacy than anyone else but the taso. Inside was a small antechamber with a young woman sitting behind a bare desk. Kusik yanked Cara forward, under the gaze of the coolly reserved acolyte, who only bowed her head at him. Cara needed no introduction. The woman led her down a hall to doors that faced each other in tandem. She opened the last one on the left with a key she'd retrieved from her pocket.

Cara stepped through the doorway. The room was bare of anything but a chair and a high window.

With bars.

Vertical bars. Cara stopped and stared open-mouthed at the sight. The door shut behind her. She turned back and grabbed the door handle. It was locked. She banged on the door and cursed the empty room, pacing its narrow width.

No Rodani. No answers. No knowledge.

An illicit love affair.

A locked cell.

Priestesses with a mandate to enforce their goddess's whims.

Cara's fingers began to tingle, and her knees felt weak. Winter sun shone through the barred window, casting striped shadows on the bare floor. A cold breeze came with it. Wisps of clouds floated high in the sky, flying in the freedom she dearly needed.

A Selandu-sized chair sat in the middle of the floor. Cara stared at it.

And back at the window.

And at the chair.

She put her weight against it and tipped the chair on one leg, then swung it around onto a second leg. Little by little, she walked the chair until it rested against the wall underneath the window. She climbed on top of the chair back and gripped the bars as high up as she could reach. With a massive pull, she got her feet on the windowsill. She tested the space between the bars with her head. Twists and turns got her through the gap.

With a last look down, she dropped onto the dry winter grass, ignoring the aching arm that Kusik had gripped.

With her back against the stone, the manor's west wall ran distant to her left, windowless for the first few hundred feet south to the water wheel. To her right was a short bit of wall, also windowless, then a corner. She sidled up to the corner and peered around. Far along the north wall was a trio of Selandu, conferring at the garden. Cara could only hope they didn't notice her.

She had to try to find Rodani. Had to see him. Had to know. Along the wall were two windows, then another stretch of unrelieved stone. She tiptoed to the first window. It was barred, and the room was empty. Frustrated, she yanked on the bars. But they remained solidly in place.

Where was he? Arimeso's quarters? She'd never find him there, not without being caught. She went on to the next one, which was lower and unbarred. Slowly, slowly, she approached the window. A flash of Enclave gold passed by. She ducked back and held her breath. *Was Rodani in there? Were they questioning him?*

Cara knelt and crawled under the window, then leaned against the stone. Mutters were all that came to her ears. Female voices only, no beloved baritone. The cold wind threaded its way through the gaps in her jacket and blouse, bleeding through the loose weave of her pants. Hands and knees in the grass, Cara trembled in agitation.

Where was he? What did they do with him? What was going on? She couldn't peek through every window, and she was bound to be missed. Well, they wouldn't take her if she could help it.

Full of fear, Cara crawled backwards until she was away from the window, ran around the corner, and headed south across the grassy field between wall and woods. The jacket pinched and pulled as she moved in the rhythm of running. Her shoes crunched the dry grass, and her lungs protested the cold air. At the edge of the woods, she looked around and up into the trees.

A glance behind her told her no one was trailing her yet. But now that the first hurdle was behind her, a second one loomed ahead. She had nowhere to go, and no way to get there except on foot.

What can I do? Where will I end up? Oh gods, Rodani, please be okay.

***

Kimasa, high priestess of the Enclave, turned her head when the acolyte returned. But when her eyes widened, Kusik spun around to see what caused her alarm.

The acolyte, Adonsa, alone in the doorway, bowed low to Kimasa. "A'Selaso, please forgive me," she whispered. "The human is not in the waiting room."

"Where is she?" Kusik spat.

"I...I do not know, a'Keso," Adonsa said, bowing even lower.

Kimasa shifted in her chair. "You left the door unlocked?"

Adonsa's pupils widened as she raised her eyes to her priestess. "No, a'Selaso. I would never! The," she swallowed visibly. "The chair is under the window."

Kusik shot out of the room as if a poridi were on his tail, and flung open the cell door. He gazed at the empty room, the chair, the bars, then yanked his 'com from his pocket. "Two, One. Two, One."

He waited, agitated, fist clenched around the 'com. *Temi fry that woman. How dare she?*

His 'com sputtered. "A'Keso?"

"Timan," he growled. "Find Serano, gather the two new trackers, and meet me outside the Enclave."

***

At the edge of the woods, Cara jumped for the nearest tree and swung up onto the branch. As fast as possible, she climbed from tree to tree, heading east, sometimes directly and sometimes with a jump and swing. *You can do this,* she thought, repeating the mantra. Panic stole the breath she needed to curtail her fear. It was a perilous method, but hopefully trackless.

Except when she misjudged the distance. She picked herself up off the ground and climbed again. Tree after tree after tree, and the wind bit at any exposed skin. Quickly, she began to lose strength. With another jump, Cara heard running water. She traveled east for a few more trees before she spied a clear stream that fed and watered the woods. In her haste and exertions, she tripped over one root, and caught a hanging branch with her temple, near the eye.

This might do, she thought, ignoring the sting. She swung down to the stream's edge and removed her shoes and socks, stuffing them in her pockets. Then she waded into the stream.

It was icy, of course. Splashing and shivering, Cara stumbled through the water. Rocks bruised her soles and turned her ankles. The water numbed her feet. She hadn't even gone as far as she thought she might before being forced to climb another tree. Quickly, she dried her chilled feet on her pant legs and slipped the socks and shoes back on.

Cara climbed to another branch and across to the next tree. Then to the next.

Voices? Was that someone behind her? No! She clutched at the tree trunk and listened for only seconds. The panic she'd been swallowing flooded her system. *Aisu, I love you!*

At the next tree, she made a jump for the branch, grabbing with her hands.

***

Rodani sat quietly in a carved wooden chair and stared at the blank wall in front of him. The high priestess had asked him some pointed questions, but he'd answered them truthfully, as honor demanded. He wondered who else was sitting in other rooms and what they'd said, but it was Cara he was the least sure of. He'd tried his best to make himself understood to her, and not take her gift for granted. But he knew better than anyone outside of the Hadaman government house what pitfalls there were in interspecies communication. Using his guild training, he willed away hunger and distress.

The sound of bootsteps clattered outside the room. A door slammed, then silence resumed.

A few minutes passed before his door handle rattled, and the acolyte that had been at the front stepped in.

"A'Rodani," she said quickly. Her eyes were downcast as befitting one new to the ways of the goddess and Her secrets. But Rodani caught a glimpse of her pupils. His heartbeat resisted his training, thumping in his chest as he rose from the chair. *Judgment already?* She motioned, and Rodani followed the acolyte down the same hallway he had earlier, and into the same dim room. Incense filled his nose, blocking out other scents that might have added to his meager store of information.

The selaso looked at him, still seated with her second and third on either side. Rodani faced her, feet apart, chin high, back straight, and hands clasped in the small of his back. He felt naked without his weapons, but Kusik had relieved him of his tools of trade when he had been escorted down from his room.

"A'Selaso," he said respectfully.

The high priestess looked Rodani up and down in silence, pregnant with power and dignity. Smoke curled up from the burner to her left. Heavy curtains draped across the back wall and around to each side, giving the room an even heavier, closed-in feel. The stylized sun and moon icon hung behind her.

Rodani willed his breathing to normal and concentrated on the design in the curtains, wondering for a moment if Cara had noticed it. Right or wrong, yes or no, he wished this judgment over with. It had to go with him and Cara.

Had to.

"A'Rodani," the high priestess said.

Rodani refocused. Kimasa's grey eyes stared into his. "A'Selaso."

"Why would Cara escape?"

Rodani's breath caught in his throat. Guild training jumped into high gear. "Escape?" he repeated.

Kimasa folded her hands on the table in front of her. "From the waiting room. Through the bars on the window."

Rodani's mind raced. *Ran? She ran? Where? Why?* She didn't fear him. He'd staked too much on that fact to challenge it. It was almost the first thing he'd asked before their joining. He could read fear on her face and body. He hadn't caused it since she first walked into his arms—except when she'd touched his weapons belt.

Then why run? It didn't make— Slow down. Track. Move in behind your quarry's eyes.

Likely, she had also been escorted by Kusik. He knew she feared the first. Next, she would've been full of questions, and she wouldn't have known of the Enclave's rules of silence. As well, she knew of

Kusik's temperament. Further, she would've been locked in, and he assumed she would interpret that as being held prisoner. And he had been nowhere she could find.

"Fear, a'Selaso," he said resolutely.

"Of you?"

"No, a'Selaso. Of you. Of this situation."

Kimasa's displeasure radiated. "Why?"

The three priestesses listened closely as Rodani gave them their first detailed glimpse into an alien mind and heart. Ignorance bred fear. Fear bred rash decisions, decisions based on alien honor and overwhelming emotions. Emotional decisions brought incoherent actions.

"Has she been found?" Rodani asked at the end of his explanation.

Kimasa bent her head and looked at him under lowered brows. "Not at this time. As soon as she was discovered gone and the orders for search given, you were brought back in."

"A'Selaso, I should join the search. She will come to me."

Quiet descended.

"You are so sure?" she asked.

"I will stake my reputation and my place in the taso's guard on it, a'Selaso."

Kimasa raised a finger.

The acolyte led Rodani back to the holding room and locked the door behind him.

***

Serano studied the ground outside the barred window, and the area surrounding it. Deneban, newly graduated, stood by him. Security Second Timan and Naremit waited behind. "Naremit," he said, pointing east along the front wall. "Ask the gardeners if they saw anyone."

As Naremit ran off, Serano turned to Deneban. "Run to the garage and see if she went back to her rooms. Or Rodani's," he added, as Deneban hastened south.

Beside Timan, Serano scoured the ground for tracks. He thought he saw a hint of footprints, but halted the search when Naremit ran up.

"A'tem," the young man said, breathing heavily. "One of them said they saw someone crawling along the base of the wall. He said he thought it was the human, because she seemed short when she ran off."

"What direction?" Timan demanded. "Did they see?"

"He said he ran to this corner to see what was occurring. He saw her running for the trees as if a monster were after her," Naremit said, pointing into the distance.

"Denaban," Serano 'commed. "Cancel your search. She went south." He strode over the grasses toward the south woods. Deneban caught up to them and walked at Serano's side. Half-sized footprints showed clearly in the fallen leaves.

Serano was confident he could find Cara and bring her back to the Enclave. Inside the wood's edge, he stared intently at the immediate surroundings, then turned to Deneban.

"Your thoughts?"

Young Deneban looked eager. "She has no woods skills?"

"That I am aware of."

"Left, right, or back, we would have noticed. She has no wings. And since the tracks disappear, there is only one alternative." He reached for the nearest tree branch and bent it down into their line of sight. Pointing to the newly ruffled bark, he said, "And here is my evidence." The lighter brown of newer growth showed fresh beneath the old. "And," Deneban continued, "the prints are deeper here, indicating more pressure was applied during her jump."

"Your suggested course of action?"

"Follow the path of the closest trees, watching for markings."

The pair studied the trees and the layout of the lowest branches, wending their way into the woods. At each new tree, they looked for evidence of the human's passage: broken twigs, ruffled bark, freshly torn leaves. They found more footprints further past the stream, then continued, Serano in the lead.

Again, they checked tree branches, ground disturbances, and anything else that caught the well-trained eye.

"That one," Serano said, aiming a finger up a trunk.

Deneban shimmied up. "Yes, here." He climbed back down. Beyond the adjacent tree, he rejoined Serano, who was staring at the ground.

She'd fallen, again. The mass of wet under-leaves that her body's landing had uncovered told the tale.

As did the tree she'd fallen from.

Serano turned to Deneban. Deneban looked at the ground, then at the branch she'd tried to grab. Then his eyes opened wide. His head jerked around to stare at the tree trunk in alarm. "A camabarin tree."

"And that is her blood on the bark," Serano added. "She is in a great deal of pain."

Wasting no more time, Serano followed the now obvious footprints that led away from the tree, whose bark mimicked a guardian's knife. Deneban scurried to catch up, Timan and Naremit behind.

"She did not recognize it?" Deneban asked, breathing deeply.

"She may not even know they exist," Serano said.

Deneban closed his eyes for a moment. "Goddess."

They sped up, following the trail east. Serano was certain she was within shouting distance. If she would listen to reason, this chase could end in moments. But so far, only his deep and gifted partner could talk reason into her. Luckily, the trail was clear. Perturbations in the leafy floor showed where Cara had tripped and fallen, then gotten up to run again. Serano stopped.

"Cara!"

His bellow passed through the trees and out into the distant hush.

"Cara!"

The whispering leaves were all he heard.

He took off again, faster. Knowledge that Kusik was back in the manor house waiting, put extra urgency into his stride in this last lap. He followed the trail, moving from one side of it to the other in an effort to avoid both trees and obliteration of her tracks. His gaze flicked from his feet to the path ahead, and back.

Again, he stopped.

"Cara!"

His guild allies settled in to follow behind him. Leaves rustled overhead. The damp odor of decay wafted around in the crisp wind.

A lone tic'idi broke the silence. Serano ran past great tree trunks, breathing heavily in this race he could hardly lose. In his element, he picked up the pace, following Cara's track impressed into the leaves. Minutes went by.

A movement that was not forest-borne caught his attention. With a burst of speed, he gained a few more yards. A brown head bobbed and wove through the trees ahead of him. He heard labored breathing that was not his own.

"Cara, stop!"

She had to have heard him. Serano spread his arms. Timan, Deneban, and Naremit fanned out in response to the guild gesture. With their quarry in sight, all renewed their efforts. The gap narrowed quickly. She was no match for a long-legged Selandu guardian in the prime of life. Serano reached around her and lifted her off her feet. As she twisted and turned, he made a grab for her legs with his other arm.

"Goddess above, Cara! Stop!"

She collapsed in his grip, gasping. The others closed in. Serano set her on her feet, which prompted a spew of Cene'l words. Leaves and small twigs clung to her hair, most of which had come unraveled from the bun. Streaks of dirt mixed with a smear of blood that stretched from her forehead to her cheek. Her jacket was decorated with the same woodland flourishes he saw in her hair. Her chest heaved with the effort to catch her breath. Her hands...

He grasped a wrist gently and turned her hand palm up.

A hiss of pain escaped through her teeth. She wrenched her hand away from him. Deep gouges ran down the lengths of her fingers and into the meat of her palms. A fresh upwelling of blood dribbled down her wrist and onto the cuff of her blouse.

"Come," he urged her. They'd wasted enough time on her fruitless attempt at escape.

"Where is Rodani?" she asked, avoiding his renewed grip on her arm.

"The selaso is waiting, Cara."

A coughing fit erupted with a strength that bent her double. "Where is Rodani?!"

Serano stared at the sorry sight in front of him. "He is—"

"No," came a voice from the side.

Timan was in command here. No one had forgotten it. Serano closed his mouth.

Cara looked from Serano to Timan. "Is he alive? Hurt? Prisoner?"

Serano blanked his face and looked away. Orders were orders, and punishments were swift.

Cara spat out another word and ran, east again. Serano mouthed an obscenity particular to guardians and took off after her, Timan close behind. Within seconds, they grabbed her. Timan wrenched her hands behind her, whipped out his cuffs, and slapped them on her. She gasped. Her lungs erupted in another deep cough.

"This is some form of game," Timan said, turning her to face him. "And we tire of it." He took her arm in a fierce grip and pulled.

She screamed.

They began the long walk back. Cara struggled beside Timan, unable to contain her voice. Serano and Deneban followed behind them. Naremit brought up the rear. One-handed, Timan retrieved his 'com from an inner pocket and flipped it on, calling to Kusik. With his response, Timan related their success and Cara's wounds.

Serano followed silently. Rodani would be livid if he knew. All guardians had a protective streak running through them. It came with the territory. But he had watched Rodani's personal investment in Cara's protection grow from a dutiful stream into a thundering waterfall over the past month. Serano had no illusions about his unconventional partner's strengths and weaknesses. He wondered, not without cause, what would happen if the high priestess decided against them. Cara's blood-striped hands wavered in front of him.

She stumbled in weariness and went down on one knee. Serano nearly tripped over her before Timan pulled her, sobbing, back to her feet. He seemed to be oblivious to the pain he was aggravating. They marched onward. Over the stream, to the edge of the woods, to the south side of the mansion-sized house. With more stable footing and a clear view, Timan hurried Cara along at a pace that left her breathless and stumbling. He pulled out his 'com and radioed their near position.

Over the south lawn they marched, through the double doors, down the passage to another set of doors Cara had stepped through less than an hour ago. The acolyte was still at her desk. And Kusik waited at the inner door, arms crossed, face cold and still. Cara's injuries and renewed fears crowded her mind as she passed by him.

Kusik said no word, just replaced Timan at her side, dismissed the sterling retrievers, and led her through the doorway. This time there was no walk past a dozen shut doors. The pair turned right and then left again, straight into a dim, smoky room that made Cara cough. Kusik led her to a place before a table where she faced three priestesses, her hands still locked behind her.

The three women regarded her in silence. Cara shifted her feet, twisted her cramped shoulders, and tried not to move her hands. The incense made her eyes water and her nose run. Her fears fed on the silence and strangeness of her surroundings, and of the yellow-robed priestesses. Her hair fell in wisps and strands around her scratched and stinging face. Her jacket hung awry. Leaves clung to the bottom of her pant legs, and the knees were stained. Clods of dirt adhered to her shoes. Her healing bullet wound, aggravated by Timan and the method of her flight, was a constant ache. But nothing overpowered the agony in her hands.

"A'Cara," the middle priestess said. "I am Kimasa."

She jumped at the sudden break of silence. Another wave of pain rolled upward. Her palms burned. "A'Selaso," she replied as steadily as she could.

Above her high collar, Kimasa's face was as stony as Kusik's had been. "I am required by our laws to interview you. But you ran. Why?"

Short and to the point. There was no good answer, Cara realized belatedly. Either she admitted to fear, or to arrogance, or to outright stupidity.

Take your pick, fem. And remember the formalities.

"Fear, a'Selaso," she said.

"Of what?"

"A'Selaso, I was nearly killed less than two weeks ago. I was afraid of what I might be facing here when my guardian was missing and the keso took his place, refusing to answer my questions."

"You fear the Enclave?"

Gods. What to answer? She needed Rodani's guidance to navigate this minefield. And he had disappeared. "I fear any unknown who wields great power, a'Selaso. Especially in the company of disturbing events."

"What disturbing events?"

"The disappearance of my guardians and servants. The refusal of answers to my questions. Locked doors to empty rooms. Other, less important things."

Kimasa blinked. "You were heard inquiring upon the status of your guardian."

Another question that was not a question. Yes. She certainly had. Cara refocused on the floor in front of her.

"It disturbed you that he could not be found?"

"Rodani is my safety, a'Selaso," she replied, bewildered at the question. "It disturbed me to feel myself in danger when I don't know where he is."

"How are your day-to-day dealings with Rodani?" Kimasa asked.

Closer, Cara thought in grim humor. "Pleasant."

"Does his presence disturb you?"

"No." *Ask me if yours does. Or Kusik's.*

Kimasa laid her palms flat on the table. "What is your impression of him?"

It was hard to think with a dull throbbing in your arm and fire in your hands. Cara closed her eyes, losing then regaining her balance. Her legs trembled with fatigue.

"He's quiet," she said, herself quiet in the intimidation that Kimasa and Kusik wove between them. "Honorable. Strong. Dutiful to his taso and his guild." *Brush it on thick while you're at it, hmm?*

"Some find it difficult to be so closely guarded," Kimasa continued. "Do you?"

"In the beginning, I did, a'Selaso," Cara said. Her feet and ankles complained about their hurried journey over roots, humps, lumps, and rocks. Her injured arm hadn't shut up yet. "But I've come to understand the importance of his duty. He guards my safety. And within my rooms, I can do as I wish, when I wish."

"Always?"

Quick. She was quick on the uptake, not one to underestimate. "Unless I'm destructive or foolish with my safety, a'Selaso. And that's rare."

"Does he spend much time with you?"

"We socialize. Play cards. Craft. Listen to music. Practice with gun and knife."

"As often as in the beginning?"

"More," she admitted slowly.

"Why?"

Gods. She had to know. This, a'Timan, was game playing. The selaso was getting at something. And she wasn't about to play her hand prematurely. Neither was Cara.

"We're not such strangers now as before."

"He is no longer strange to you?"

Tired, bewildered, Cara stared at the women in front of her. *Strange?* Strange, is a trio of witches who prodded her for intimate revelations they were probably already aware of. Ready to burn her at the stake for her offensive sexual liaison? Why else would she be brought here, in front of these women? And where was Rodani? Was he alive? Was he hurting, as she was? Had he been beaten again for his choice of lovers? All she wanted was a bed to lie in and the cessation of pain. Funny how fear can focus your mind on the real priorities. Safety. Stability. Shelter. Sustenance.

Love.

Comfort.

Get me out of here. And Rodani.

Alive and well, thank you.

Suddenly, the room swam back into focus. Kusik was a few steps closer. Every reflective eye was on her.

"Forgive me, a'Selaso," she stumbled over the Selandu words in weariness. "Please repeat the question."

Kimasa folded her hands in her lap. Her cohorts had not moved a muscle that Cara had seen. "Rodani is no longer strange to you?" she repeated.

"There will always be some strangeness, a'Selaso. We're two different species, after all."

"How and when did this lessening of strangeness occur?"

"Gradually. Over time. A greater understanding of each other."

Kimasa sat forward again, leaning her arms on the table. "What is your affinity for Rodani?" Cara blinked through the incense haze. Was she asking if they were lovers? In front of Kusik? Dammit, she knew the answer! "I wish him to remain as my guardian."

"Have you joined with him?"

She'd learned that word the hard way. The memory still burned. "I don't understand, a'Selaso."

Kimasa clasped her fingers near her chest. "Are you joining Rodani in sexual intimacies?"

Damn.

"Among my people, a'Selaso, that question is highly offensive."

The reflective eyes didn't waver. Kusik moved closer. "You are in Selandan," Kimasa reminded her unnecessarily.

Cara stared at the floor. "Yes."

A leaf from her shoe dropped to the floor and blended with the intricately woven tapestry. Cara, too, wanted to drop. Wanted surcease. Wanted to blend in and disappear.

"Are you engaging in sex with Rodani?"

She lifted her chin and composed her face as best she could, looking away from both Kimasa and Kusik in a Selandu rejection. Kusik stepped to her side. She flinched, her pulse rising. But she kept silent.

Until he slapped her bound and bloody palms with his hand. Cara cried out, twisting away from him and losing her balance. She went to her knees, the whole of her hands and arms a wash of agony.

"You will answer the selaso immediately and truthfully." Kusik nearly growled with suppressed outrage.

Cara shivered in anger and pain, biting down on all the insults she longed to hurl. Lurching to her feet, her hands on fire, she stared across at the curtains, over the heads of the seated priestesses.

"Yes," she whispered.

"Why?"

There had been no surprised silence. The witch had known. But the question dumbfounded her. "Why?"

"Why."

"For—" Cara stopped, breathing heavily and drawing a blank. Started again, hesitantly. "For the pleasure of the body and mind. For contentment and comfort. For easing of desires. For the pleasure of pleasing someone else."

Kimasa stared. "What caused this situation to develop?"

Deep dark demons! Cara wanted to shriek, to fall into a dead faint on the tapestry, and to hell with the blood that got on it. Would the questions never stop? She began to know how Rodani felt when she was in one of her pestering, questioning moods. *What caused me to want Rodani in my bed? I'm a woman. With a handsome alien man at my side every day. Nature happens. Leave it, witch.*

"Sharing of interests," she managed. Oh, if her hands would just stop hurting. "Finding common abilities and needs."

"Who approached whom?"

Cara's temper, already frayed, stretched to the breaking point. But Kusik's presence and her burning hands stopped her. "He approached me."

"How?"

She swallowed a deep breath of incense-filled air. "There were two somewhat humorous confrontations between us, and other situations where one might see evidence of unspoken sexual feelings. One evening Rodani sat down and told me of his desire."

"And you responded how?"

Cara closed her eyes, reopening them again when the dizziness returned. "I admitted my own."

"And he chose to explore those desires?"

"We both did."

"A mutual decision?"

"Yes, a'Selaso."

Kimasa sat back in her chair. "Truth is critical to this inquiry, a'Cara."

It was the first time Cara remembered the priestess using her name. "I do not lie, a'Selaso. It's against my honor."

Surprise spread over Kimasa's face, quickly hidden. "And it is part of your code of honor that the physical and emotional joining of two species is acceptable?"

Now we get down to it. Cards on the table. Place your bets.

"Yes, a'Selaso." She swayed on her feet, her hands a roaring fire at her back.

"Would your life be in danger if you said no to his advances?"

"No. Too much honor in him."

"Would you make the same decision again, knowing what you now know?"

Cara didn't hesitate. "Yes." She took a deep breath, fighting the pains. "Yes."

She saw Kimasa wave her fingers in their direction. Kusik took her arm and drew her out of the room.

Another wave of panic went through her. *Where now? Back to the cell? To the taso, maybe.* He was steering her toward the center of the manor. Or to public censure. It was a different route than she was used to. More crowded. More stares.

She noticed the stares. Knew why, too, as dirty as she was. Humiliation. Too many faces. Too many steps. Her legs wouldn't work. Kusik tightened his grip on her arm as a goad to her flagging strength. Stairs were a nightmare. So were the faces of the people she passed.

A door appeared in her vision. A jingle of keys. A room she recognized. Home. She stumbled in, barely noticing the click of the door behind her.

Kusik spun her around and slapped her to the floor. She hit, hard.

"You were unconscionably offensive to the selaso, human!" he shouted down at her. "And you ran!"

Injury to insult to injury. It was too much. When he deigned to uncuff her, she drew up in a fetal position, sobbing and mumbling in Cene'l. The world went away. All that remained was pain. Her body shook with crying that wouldn't stop. Kusik's booted feet scraped the stone near her head. Had he kicked her, she would not have cared.

Dimly, Cara realized she had something yet to do. Hands. She had to take care of her hands; they were the lifeline to her art. She put an elbow on the floor and levered herself to her knees. The pain made her head swim, almost toppling her. She managed to get one foot underneath her, but her strength was gone. Rising up was out of the question.

On knees and elbows, she crawled to the shelves holding her fabric, using it as a prop to stand. Halfway up she felt a hand on her arm, a welcome steadying anchor. It was Hamman, whispery sweet Hamman, who had braved the keso's displeasure to help another of Sela's children. As Kusik walked out, they made their way to the facilities. Cara collapsed on the lid of the toilet as Hamman filled the basin. She lowered her hands into the water, whimpering.

"Who did this?" Hamman asked.

But Cara was beyond words. Her hands were a burning fire from fingertips to wrists. Her head threatened to explode. She ached where she'd hit the floor. Her bullet wound throbbed. And still there was no Rodani.

Hamman swished the water around in the basin and adjusted the faucet, bringing the water to a comfortably warm temperature. "What happened, a'Cara?"

Another pair of boots impinged upon her awareness. She was attracting a crowd. Must have been Kusik's walk through the center hallways. She ignored the newcomer as she ignored Kusik's far-hovering presence. Only pain and loss filled her mind as she wiggled her fingers in the water.

"Kia?"

She froze, no belief in what her ears had heard. She looked up from her black cloud to see Rodani in the doorway. Cara pulled her hands from the basin, ran, and wrapped her arms around him, heedless of dripping blood.

He pulled her arms back around from his hips and looked at her hands. "What in Temi's name did you do, Cara?"

Her speech broke with sobs, her mind barely capable of interpreting. "Ran. Jump tree. Grab. Knives."

Rodani blinked and drew back his head. "Make some sense, kia. Please," he pleaded as blood dripped onto the stone floor.

She pulled her hands out of his grasp and mimed her words. "I jumped to a tree." She reached up. "It cut me. Like a knife."

His pupils expanded into saucerous orbs. "A camabarin tree." He turned to Hamman. "Did you call Baldar?"

"I assumed Kusik had, a'Rodani," Hamman admitted softly. "Cara could not tell me, and I had no chance yet to inquire."

Rodani strode into the empty workroom, then pulled out his 'com. "A'Keso, did you call Baldar?" he asked.

His superior responded coldly. "No."

"Her hands were torn by camabarin bark!"

"That is not my concern."

The call cut off.

Rodani stared at his 'com with an expression of absolute disbelief, then began to fume. He immediately rang the physician, then made two more calls before returning to the facility. Cara was back on the toilet lid, hands over the water, trying to pick a piece of bark out from under skin. Her hands would not hold still for the task.

"Aisu," Cara whispered. "Where were you?" She sniffled and hiccupped. "I thought they'd killed you."

"In a room near you." He took her hand by the wrist and bent down to peer at it. The long red gashes were ragged and swollen.

"No one would tell me where you were. Tell me anything!" Her voice rose in belated panic, where the worst was past, and lesser worries could be brought out and hashed over.

"It is not allowed."

"Why?" she asked, in a disbelieving tone.

"When facing the priestesses in an inquiry," Rodani said, "no communication is permissible. It prevents intimidation or collusion that hides the truth."

Cara stared at the same hand Rodani held. It wasn't hers; it was someone else's. It looked angry. As was she. "What did they want?"

Now Rodani looked at her. "They were ascertaining whether our affinity was through choice or coercion."

"Coercion!" she shouted up at him. Pink water splashed Hamman's skirt. "There was no coercion! Did you tell them that?"

He regarded her calmly. "The more important question is, did you tell them that?"

Cara tried to think back. Most of the inquiry had been in a fog of incense and pain. She barely remembered the questions. Or her answers. "I must have," she said slowly. "But not directly."

"Yes." His face was thoughtful. "You must have. Or I would not have been allowed to return to you."

It all started to fit together. Someone *had* questioned their new affinity. Had gone to the Enclave with concerns. And the high priestess had felt obliged to investigate.

"Is that their duty? To interfere?" she asked.

Rodani placed her hand back in the water. "In this case, yes. The goddess forbids anyone to misuse another. Especially through strength or status."

Cara's eyes widened. Both hands came up out of the water. "Isn't that what Kusik just did to me? To punish me?"

Neither Selandu would look at her. Another piece of the puzzle fitted into place. A security first should uphold the highest standards of goddess, consort, and taso. "I know he's one of them. Isn't he?" she demanded.

Rodani returned her searching gaze.

"One of those who doesn't want me here?"

Rodani reached over her head and took a small cloth from a container, passing it to Hamman. "She cannot wash her own face," he told the servant. "Brush the woods from her hair, as well."

"Forgive me, a'sel'ai," Hamman replied. Her expression showed a level of distress as deep as Rodani's.

"Aisu, answer me, please," Cara pleaded. "Does he want me dead?"

Hamman wet the cloth with warm water and began to wring it out.

"The taso forbids," he said.

Gods! More than her hands began to burn while Hamman plied the cloth across her face. "And he refused to call Baldar, hoping I would die?" she asked during a lull. Hamman rinsed the cloth and reapplied it to stubborn areas.

"Hoping you would be sent home, possibly," he admitted.

"Damn him!"

"He is guild, kia. That is Temi's duty."

It took her a moment to hear the humor—a light touch, trying to defuse her righteous anger. Hamman put the cloth back in its ceramic holder and took a brush from the drawer. She unpinned Cara's ragged bun and pulled the brush through in long, slow strokes.

"It should be washed," she noted quietly.

"Physician first."

The next few minutes went by with only the crackle of the brush through hair and the gentle splashing of water to be heard. A knock on the door announced Baldar's arrival. Rodani left to answer it. The tall physician trailed Rodani into the facility. He handed his bag to Hamman without preamble or permission, and pulled Cara's hands out of the water. Letting one go, he pulled the other closer and studied the scarlet slashes. Prodding caused an involuntary jerk and hiss.

Baldar spared her a single glance before retrieving a tiny pair of scissors from his bag. "Open the workroom shutters, Rodani," he said. He walked her into the workroom, pulled her sewing chair closer to the window and sat down, positioning her in front of him. With a surgeon's precision, he cut away the ripped and dead skin still attached to the wounds. Cara closed her eyes against the sight and breathed deeply, trying to keep quiet.

Baldar finished one hand, then the other. It was a quick job; he wasn't wasting time. When the task was completed, he took her back to the facility's sink and laid one forearm on the edge of it. From his bag, he took out a large brown bottle with a stopper.

"Hand cup," he told her, working the stopper loose.

Confused, Cara looked to Rodani for interpretation.

"Make a cup of your hand," he told her, demonstrating.

She imitated him.

"Hold her fingers together," Baldar told the guardian. He held her wrist with one hand and poured a clear liquid into her palm from the bottle.

Fire burned into her skin, doubling the pain she already felt. She screamed and tried to jerk her hand away. But Baldar's implacable grip on her wrist and Rodani's on her fingers prevented the movement, and the pooled liquid from spilling.

She swore in Cene'l and kicked the cabinet under the sink, adding another extremity to the list of hurts.

Baldar took a small sponge and soaked up some of the liquid, then spread it over the deep gouges on her palm. The burning followed. Her body shook convulsively with the effort to control her reaction. Mewling, she leaned back and turned her head away. But reality stayed put. She twisted her shoulders, stamped, and swore.

Methodically, Baldar poured more and repeated the sponge applications up and down her fingers and back across her palm. The burning redistributed itself after each of the sponge's passages.

"What is that, a'Baldar?" she asked, shivering.

He wiped the last of the liquid on the larger of her wounds. "Astringent."

"Why?"

He studied his handiwork. "It will draw up the tree's toxin that entered your hands through the cuts."

What? "Toxin?"

"Toxin," he echoed, reaching for the bottle again.

"Will it kill me?"

"Not when treated," he told her. "It is localized. It disseminates into the tissues slowly and does not travel far. Untreated, the skin and muscles would rot and die. Treated, your hands will simply be useless for a time."

Cara stared at Baldar in abject dismay. Useless? What would she do? And how? "How long?"

"If you were Selandu, I could predict with some accuracy, a'Cara. A month at least, possibly two, considering the amount of time that elapsed between the accident and the treatment."

Baldar's words exposed another layer of Kusik's cruelty. She stared up at Rodani. "All the time I was being questioned by the priestesses, poison was going into my hands?"

No reply.

"And while he paraded me down the central hallways in handcuffs?" she continued, her anger reasserting itself over the pain.

Rodani's eyes widened at her admission. His face went to mask, as did Hamman's, silent in the doorway. Even Baldar looked at her before tilting the bottle.

"Hand cup," he said, holding out his hand for her other one.

It didn't get any better.

Cara shivered and grimaced, not quite able to keep silent. She bent her head and rested it in the crook of her arm while fire burned down from fingertip to wrist. Only Baldar's grip kept her in her seat; that and the knowledge she was representing her whole species.

Not that she cared much at that point.

Ages later, he stood back, the deed done.

Cara glanced at her hands, expecting to see crisped, blackened flesh. But what met her eyes was a grotesque array of irregular stripes ranging from bright pink through livid red to almost purple. The wounds were puckering from the concentrated astringent, and her hands were swelling. They were absolutely untouchable.

"Those rings must come off," Baldar said as he replaced the bottle of liquid fire into his bag.

Cara tried to touch one ring with the fingers of the other hand. Uh-uh. She held her hands up to let some blood drain down. That worked sometimes.

No. Then Baldar tried. Cara gasped and bit her lip against the tugging around her wounds. No luck. Rodani even gave it a try, with a tenderness she hoped Baldar didn't see. But when faced with the same results, he gave up.

"Cut them off," Baldar told him.

Cara hugged her arms to her waist and cried at this final little loss, as Rodani went to get his wire cutters. One ring had come from her mother upon her becoming a woman, the other, years later, from Ambassador Second Andrew.

Rodani returned. With a little pressure at the side of each ring finger and a quick snap, the rings parted company with her flesh. Gently, he pulled them off and slipped them into an inner pocket of his jacket. "I will repair them," he said matter-of-factly.

"You can," she whispered. A glimmer of hope worked its way into her voice. Metal crafter that he was, his words eased just a little of her misery.

Sober faced, Rodani winked—a human reassurance he'd learned from her.

Cara turned to Baldar. "My hands will be well in a month or so?" she asked.

"Likely they will be useable," the physician replied. "When they will be pain free is unknown, as well as whether there will be permanent damage or not."

Another shock went through her, another layer peeled away from Kusik's honor. "Permanent?" she yelled. She was a crafter! She had to have hands. Cara leaned up against the wall behind the toilet and tried to will away a sudden nausea. Kusik had purposely tried to cripple her. And what's worse, he might have succeeded.

"When will we know?" she asked.

Baldar stuffed his hands into his pockets. "A half-month or so, depending on the severity. I will give you exercises to begin tomorrow. Your progress or lack thereof will tell the tale."

"What will improve the chance?"

"The exercises," he said bluntly. "Start using your hands as soon as possible, even through great pain. The more the muscles are worked, the sooner the toxin breaks down, and the less accumulation of damage."

She stared down at her devastated hands and tried to imagine using them. They burned and pulsed. She crossed her forearms on the sink edge and dropped her head onto them.

From his bag, Baldar brought out a pair of grey six-fingered gloves, and laid one on the back of Cara's hand for measurement.

"A'Baldar," Rodani said, placing his hand over Cara's as the physician removed the glove. "I would ask you to wait a short while."

"They need to be covered."

"Yes, but I have requested an audience with the taso, and I need her hands uncovered," Rodani nodded to Cara, "until we are finished. I will bring her by your office on the way back."

"Be sure you do," was the reply.

"Will you side with me on this, Master Healer?" Rodani asked.

The tall guardian and the taller physician regarded each other across the narrow space.

"I have no wish to be caught in the middle of a guild feud, a'tem," Baldar said. "I will testify to the facts at my disposal."

"That will suffice."

Baldar packed the gloves and left, with thanks from both Rodani and Hamman. Cara stared at her hands like a spectator at the scene of a disaster. Her lungs hiccupped. Neither throbbing nor burning had stopped, and didn't look to for a while. And now, Rodani was going to haul her down to face not only the taso, but Kusik again. She wasn't up to such a confrontation, which was what she was certain it would be. Otherwise, why now?

"Aisu," Cara began. Rodani pulled her up from her lidded perch and carefully led her into the bedroom.

"Hamman, clean clothes," he ordered.

She scurried to comply.

"What do I expect?" Cara continued. From inside the armoire came a click and clink and the rustle of fabric.

"You may expect," Rodani said as he unbuttoned her blouse, "another inquiry. Hopefully a short one."

"Will Kusik be there?"

Hamman turned around with clean clothes in her arms and stopped at the sight of Rodani's sartorial intimacies. She composed her face and walked over to them.

"Almost certainly," Rodani said. He finished with the buttons, then walked around her and pulled the blouse downward from the cuffs. Hamman slid the clean one on in reverse as Rodani worked on the pants. Socks, shoes, hair; cooperation sped the process.

All too soon, Rodani pulled her toward the door.

FIVE

Rodani and Cara headed down to face the taso, and the security first who had dishonored his duty. Cara held her hands waist high and palms up. The knowledge that she was absolutely defenseless in the event of a trip or fall made her steps slower, her motions unsure. Rodani hovered without seeming to hover; it was improper for a guardian to be overly solicitous—despite their illegal affinity.

They wound their way downstairs and through the corridors leading to Arimeso's quarters. Rodani announced their presence through the speaker. Timan opened the door. Cara's stomach dropped at the sight of those who had treated her pain and injuries so callously. Arimeso was seated, of course. But Kusik was standing to her right. A security first on his feet in a meeting was not an auspicious omen.

Rodani took up position to Cara's left as they approached the taso's desk. They took the formal stance.

"A'Taso," Rodani said, Cara repeating a moment after him.

"A'sel'ai," Arimeso said. Her eyes fixed upon the taller of the two. "What is the nature of the problem, Rodani?"

Rodani took a deep breath, and a firm hold of his emotions.

"There are two issues here, a'Taso," he began. "The first is Cara's injuries. She was extremely frightened at being called to an inquiry by the Enclave."

"Why?" Arimeso asked, before Rodani had a chance to continue.

"A'Taso, humans can be quite rational thinkers when their emotions are low, though their core assumptions are often very different. But given a situation where emotions rise, their ability to think through it is impaired. And their assumptions lead them to actions that may make no sense to us, though they do to the humans in question.

"I have repeatedly reminded Cara of necessary caution. When a'Kusik came for her today, frightened her, and refused to answer her questions, she became fearful. When no one would tell her of my whereabouts and health, her fear grew. By the time she was locked into a waiting room, her fears had overridden her ability to think logically." Rodani took a deep breath. Beside him, Cara trembled in pain and reaction.

"A'Taso, when a human lacks information, she lacks what is needed to make good decisions. Given my warnings, these events were interpreted to mean we both were in dire trouble. She thought her life, as well as mine, might truly be in danger. She is not a guardian, a'Taso. She had no skills to seek me out, even assuming I was alive. In her mind, she could only rescue herself. Self-rescue, given her lack of armament and skills, meant running. She ran.

"It was not dishonor, a'Taso, but a desperate attempt to save her life. She fought her trackers as she fought me months ago: to the end of her strength, human honor.

"This," Rodani grasped Cara's wrist and brought her left hand around to the front, "is the result of her lack of information, and her fear.

"This," Rodani repeated for emphasis, as Cara hissed in pain, "was preventable."

Arimeso took a hard look at Cara's hands. Her pupils expanded.

"In all respect, a'Taso," Rodani continued, "I submit to you that the rules for dealing with humans should be modified due to their differing nature and needs. Cara, and any other human who joins or follows her, should be given at least enough information that she can make more rational judgments. Lack of information coupled with high emotions is a recipe for disaster."

Demons and devils, Cara thought. *My whole species damned by him, all with the best of intentions.*

"What minimum information would have prevented your inappropriate actions, a'Cara?" Arimeso asked.

Cara stared at the floor, trying to think, trying to translate. "Knowledge that Rodani was unharmed, and that our lives were not in immediate danger, a'Taso."

"That would be sufficient?"

"Sufficient to prevent my escape attempt, a'Taso, not my fear."

"Do you agree with Rodani's assessment and his proposal, a'Cara?"

Damned if she did, and damned if she didn't.

"Yes, a'Taso," she answered with a grimace and clenching of her eyes, "much as it pains me to look my species' weaknesses in the face."

"The goddess has a mother's hand, a'Cara. Sometimes gentle, sometimes harsh."

Cara closed her eyes in resignation. This wasn't the place to debate theology. "A'Taso."

Arimeso turned back to Rodani. "I will consider your suggestion."

"A'Taso." Rodani bowed his head in acceptance.

"And the second issue?"

Cara tensed involuntarily. She'd bet her sewing machine that Kusik did, too.

"A'Taso," Rodani began again. "When Serano was tracking Cara in the woods, he learned what had happened to her, and saw the damage to her hands when he caught her. He will testify that a'Timan radioed her capture and her condition to Kusik.

"It took approximately ten minutes to catch her, and another fifteen to return. The toxin had already begun to work. When she was turned over to Kusik, he took her directly into the priestess's audience chamber. She was questioned for approximately ten minutes. The toxin was still working. When they were finished, he led her handcuffed and bedraggled through the main corridors on the way up to her room. He—"

Cara brought both burning palms up in front of her. "He also slapped my hands viciously when I wished to refrain from answering what was an inappropriate question."

Arimeso's gaze returned to Cara and the mutilation of her hands. "Viciously?"

"Viciously, a'Taso," Cara repeated, gaze firmly on the taso, and not the black clad man to the side. "I screamed and almost fainted in front of the selaso."

"He brought her up to her room," Rodani continued, "and let her try to cleanse her own wounds—"

"After knocking me to the floor, still handcuffed and almost incoherent with pain," Cara interrupted.

"—and refused to call the physician to attend her. That was another five to ten minutes. A'Hamman will testify to these events.

"Had I not been released so soon, it would have been even longer before she was seen. Hamman did not know Kusik had not called Baldar, and she would not have questioned the physician's absence for a while.

"A'Taso, what should have occurred was that Cara be brought to the physician immediately upon her return, instead of delaying it for almost three quarters of an hour. Camabarin toxin is insidious, as you know. The delay may cost Cara some use of her hands. Permanent damage," he added. "Baldar will testify as to the state of her injuries and the possible results of the delay."

The room fell silent. Cara's heart thumped in her chest, and in her swollen, burning fingers. Arimeso stared off into the distance. Timan stood behind them. Kusik... Well, Cara couldn't bring herself to look at him.

"A'Taso," Rodani said. "Is a'Cara still a guest in this house?"

Her pupils narrowed. "Yes."

"Then I submit to you, a'Taso, that she has been deliberately mistreated."

Cara shut her eyes and swallowed hard. Had Rodani stepped over some line? Kusik had not said a word, but she could feel the threats hanging in the air. Only Arimeso kept the lid on an incipient explosion.

She turned to her keso. "Is there falsehood in what has been related here?"

"Exaggeration, a'Taso," Kusik replied stonily, breaking his silence for the first time. He affected supreme arrogance, secure in his position at his taso's side. "The delay was not as long as has been estimated, and my discipline of a'Cara's impropriety was quite within acceptable bounds. She was rude from the moment I entered her room until the moment I reentered it with her."

Arimeso turned her chair so that she could easily see all three people.

"It is true you took her directly to the selaso, not the physician?"

"Yes, a'Taso."

"Why?"

"The selaso was waiting, a'Taso. She had priority."

"Did you ask her for a short postponement?"

"No, a'Taso."

"Did you slap Cara's hands during the inquiry?"

"Yes, a'Taso."

"Could not a more appropriate place be found?"

"Her attitude was quite improper, a'Taso. I thought a discipline to her hands would attract her attention to correcting her behavior."

Cara stiffened. Rodani gripped her, his fingers tightened painfully on her arm. Her own swollen fingers tightened in response, exacerbating her pain.

"You walked her through the central halls handcuffed, before she had a chance to cleanse and change?"

"Yes, a'Taso."

"Why?"

"It was the shortest route to her rooms, a'Taso."

Kusik was showing himself to be a master at obfuscation of motives. Cara could have spit in his face.

"And in her rooms, you knocked her to the floor, still handcuffed?"

"Yes, a'Taso."

"Why?"

"For her accumulation of offenses during the inquiry, a'Taso, and for the dishonor of running away."

"It could not have been postponed?"

"Punishments are most effective when delivered promptly, a'Taso."

Cara fumed silently. She could almost see the reasoning, harsh as it was, behind Kusik's actions. But her heart cried out for vengeance, or at least justice. Would Rodani's view seem nothing more than hormones run amok? She held her breath and tried to ignore her swelling hands and her misery.

"A'Kusik," the taso said formally. "Your adherence to standards of propriety is commendable. But your discipline was unnecessarily harsh, considering her wounds. You will apologize to a'Cara for that discourtesy; and in the future, you will deal with her more circumspectly."

The silence lasted only a moment. The taso's security first, the second-highest ranking person in the entire house, who made sure her every order was carried out, turned to Cara and pulled his hands behind him.

"A'Cara, forgive me. I meant only to teach you propriety, and keep you within its bounds."

Cara glanced in his direction but dare not meet his gaze. Vindication warred with disappointment. She was torn between the base desire to see him in like pain and the adherence to her own standards, where dealing pain for pain was dishonorable.

She felt a squeeze on her arm.

This wasn't what she wanted, but it made life safer for both her and Rodani. She couldn't face Kusik and say the words. They stuck in her throat. She turned her face away from him. "I accept," she managed to say. Slowly she turned back to face Arimeso, acutely aware of the heavy silence. The pressure on her arm eased, then fell away.

Arimeso regarded her with pupils minimized to the narrowest slits. No one moved.

"What is your meaning, a'Cara?" she asked.

"Meaning, a'Taso?" she replied, tense at the unexpected question. Wasn't it over?

"You turned aside."

Cara froze, her mind gone blank in sudden panic. There was meaning to her gesture? Then it came to her. Of course.

"Contradiction, a'Taso."

"Contradiction?"

"My words meant acceptance," Cara told her. "My body spoke my emotions."

"And your body said rejection."

She hung her head. Killed them both, she had. Damn her humanity. Damn her truthfulness. "Forgive me, please, a'Taso. I have no wish to worsen the situation."

"What will alleviate the contradiction?"

Deeper and deeper. It was going to swallow them both. Rodani had brought her here to get an apology from his superior, and she was fouling it up. "A'Taso...I...I fear to tread this path without guidance. There is too much at stake."

"If it would not offend, a'Taso," Rodani said from her side, "I would make a suggestion."

Please, aisu, get me out of this one. Please.

Arimeso motioned with her fingers.

"Possibly I can see her dilemma, a'Taso. An apology is quite acceptable if there is no permanent damage. But she is in great pain and is extremely disturbed that there might be such. My suggestion is to make an end here, subject to an inquiry if Baldar agrees there are signs of permanency."

Cara held her breath as Arimeso considered the proposal.

"Is that acceptable to you, a'Cara?" she asked.

"Yes, a'Taso," Cara replied quickly. She wanted out of here and back in her own little corner, and Rodani had led her to the path she needed.

"Then in two weeks, we will reconvene with Baldar in attendance."

"A'Taso." This time, Cara beat Rodani to the appellative. She ached to crawl under the covers and drown her pain in alcohol.

Arimeso waved a dismissal. The pair bowed and exited.

Outside the doors, Cara heaved an audible sigh of relief. She raised her still throbbing hands to an angled position, the better to keep the swelling down. "Forgive me, aisu, for almost starting your feud."

He turned, back to the wall and eyes sweeping the hallway. "There is consolation in knowing you recognized the danger."

"Thank you for offering an honorable way out."

"My duty, kia."

"You mean your duty to get me out of all the tight corners I walk us into?"

He smiled at her.

Gods above and below. She'd thought for a while she'd never see it again. She longed to crawl into his arms and let him take her pain away. She had to get a drink. Several drinks. One more prod to her patience, one more confrontation, and she'd run screaming out her second-story window.

A few more turns and an unfamiliar corner brought them to Baldar's medical suite. Inside the doors was a small waiting room. On a wall was a shrine of the goddess. Below it, a table rested on the six legs that represented the six directions. Seven candles of different colors sat on the table, their flames glowing steadily. A small bowl of incense sat in front of them. The stylized sun and moon oversaw the candles. Three long benches took up the remaining space, facing the shrine.

Seated in the second row were a man and his son; in the first, a young woman. As Rodani guided Cara to the inner door, the woman arose from her seat and approached the shrine. Taking a pinch of incense between her fingers, she dribbled it over the third candle—a red one.

Trying to reorient her thoughts on something less painful, Cara watched the woman's ritual as Rodani spoke to someone inside the inner room.

He didn't like the answer he got; that was evident on his face as he turned around. Surprisingly, he walked over to the shrine and repeated the woman's ritual, trickling powder over a different candle—the grey one—before retreating to the hindmost row of benches. He motioned to Cara to sit. She slid back carefully against the seat, cradling her hands, then rested them palm-up on her thighs. No other position was remotely possible.

"What do the candles signify, Rodani?" she asked.

"Areas of life where one may solicit Sela's good will. Grey is for health. We please Her with a gift of incense in hopes She will grant the wish."

"Then I should do it as well?"

"That was for you."

Cara swallowed the lump that rose in her throat, mightily resisting the effort to curl against his arm. Distraction. She needed a distraction from the pain, the throbbing and fire.

"The woman. She used the red one. What's it for?"

"Fertility. Likely she is carrying a child or attempting to conceive."

"Red for blood?"

"Yes."

Cara hunkered down in her seat, shifting her hands toward her, elbow resting on Rodani's hip. He gave it a glance.

"The black one?"

"Request for death."

That caught her off guard. Was there much incense circling the candleholder? She wished she could get up and investigate, but any movement was a pain. "For medical reasons, or guild ones?"

"Either. Temi is represented in the shrine as well."

"The moon?"

"Yes."

A shiver ran through Cara, whether at the idea of the black candle, or at the attempt to hold herself to stillness. Hissing pain escaped through her clenched teeth. She curled into it. Rodani glanced at her again, then tensed and got up and went back to the door, stepping just inside it. One hand remained on the doorframe. Cara could still see the back half of his long body, but for once she could draw no pleasurable response from the view. She squeezed her eyes shut and tried to go away.

"Security fifth you may be, a'tem," a strident voice rose from inside the room, "but the goddess recognizes no status. You may have a seat in the antechamber."

"No," Rodani's deep voice came back to her. "You may tell a'Baldar that we were here, and when it pleases him, he may send you up to Cara's rooms for her needs." The soles of his boots grated against the stone as he reached inside the room, then spun and trod back to Cara. "Come. I have made you wait long enough." In one hand, he held a bag.

He drew her out of the seat, guiding her around the corner until she gained her balance.

The long corridors she could manage in her weakened state, but this additional trip up the stairs almost proved her master. The second floor seemed to be an impossible distance away. Each step jogged her arms painfully, and there was no prospect of using the hand railing. Her attempts to put one foot before the other came in increasingly delayed intervals. Leg muscles strained and complained against the punishment they'd already taken. A ripple of weakness started in her thighs and threatened to wash her backward down the stairs.

"Help me, aisu," she whispered, leaning against the dark wooden rail that protected walkers from a crippling fall.

Immediately, Rodani bent down, wrapping one arm behind her back, the other behind her knees. A jolt to her hands was unavoidable when he picked her up, as was her outcry. He strode up the last of the steps with a smooth gait, reaching her doorway in a minimum of time.

With some awkwardness, he unlocked the door and opened it, kicking it shut behind him as they entered.

"Hamman!" he shouted.

Rodani never shouted. Not since their fight. But Cara could little afford the energy to think of anything but her hurts.

Hamman scurried at his commanding tone, pressing herself against the wall as Rodani twisted to bring Cara into the bedroom. He laid her on the bed and opened the bag to reveal a cup and umbrella on a pole. Quickly, Rodani set it up on the headboard behind her head and filled the cup with a dark powder. With the candle striker, he lit it. Smoke began to billow up and fill the umbrella. He moved the umbrella over her face.

"Breathe this, kia."

Hamman and Rodani tucked pillows around and under her arms in an effort to prop up her hands. It didn't last. They kept sliding off when she relaxed her muscles. Rodani stood solid and imposing at the bedside, arms crossed, and chin tucked down in thought.

"Stay with her."

Hamman bowed in obedience as Rodani exited the rooms at the same speed with which he had entered. She took the opportunity to slip what clothing she could off of Cara's unresisting body and tuck a quilt around her before settling into the cozy chair to wait out Rodani's absence. Cara's dark hair framed her pale face. The tension in her face gradually relaxed as the smoky medication began to take effect. Hamman began to relax as well.

She'd been quite as shocked as Rodani at the damage to Cara's competent hands, and the anger that had overcome Rodani at Kusik's perfidy had reddened her sight as well. But she kept her peace, knowing few could successfully face the keso and bring his dishonorable actions to the notice of the taso. Rodani was likely one of those few. Only partly by dint of his guild skills and his position in the taso's guard, he was incredibly tenacious and most willing to face censure when honor was at stake. Hamman had had more than one set-to with him in his years at Barridan. But this time she would be a firm ally.

Nearly a half-hour went by before Rodani's reappearance. On his shoulder rested a large wooden structure, hastily cobbled together. Functional but obviously not up to his usual standards, the H-shaped contraption slipped over Cara's hips and provided a variably slanting shelf. The upwardly extending sides kept her arms from slipping off. Servant and guardian padded the shelf with a many-times-folded quilt and placed her arms on it. She dozed, her swollen hands twitching slightly.

"Thank you, Hamman," he said, turning to the servant. "I will call if you are needed again."

She left, and Rodani settled into the chair she'd recently vacated. He stared morosely at the rhythmic rise and fall of Cara's chest as she breathed. Purposefully, he banked his anger in the way the guild had taught. But the residual was a ball in his midsection that didn't go away. It would take little to bring it to the fore. He wanted to kill. And knew he would, in turn, be killed if he did. It was a temptation to be relinquished.

But who had told Kimasa? Not Kusik, he decided. There were easier ways to cause trouble between him and Cara. Cause trouble. That was a key. Who wished them trouble? Forget the servants. Hamman knew too much and was bothered too little. Deremic would keep to himself. They knew quite well there had been no coercion. The look on Cara's face when she was with him was enough to tell that truth.

Serano?

Rodani closed his eyes and rested his head against the back of the chair. Would he? Possibly, if he thought he would not be caught. But then, Serano was straightforward in his dealings, not one to go to someone else to solve his problems.

Larisi? Did she even know? That was one question to get answered. Where were her priorities? Should he approach her directly? Or let Serano take that duty?

Iraimin? Surely not. Granted she was risheigi, but Rodani thought it unlikely she was the culprit. Whether the painter desired Cara or not, he couldn't see her wanting to cause Cara such devastation.

Had word been passed through the security ranks? He thought not. Guardians were a tight-lipped bunch. But then they *were* a tight-lipped bunch, and some might have their own reasons for silence on the subject.

Marica? The head of housekeeping was not someone with whom Rodani rode many paths. Possible. She was on the traditional side. Didn't think much of him, he knew. But Hamman was traditional, too. Rodani wished he'd seen her expression that first night he and Cara had closed her bedroom doors. He smiled at the memory. But the smile faded as Cara stirred and moaned in her sleep. He got up to check her hands.

Hot. They were hot and sweating. Where were those gloves? Where was the physician-assistant? Cara's forehead was hot as well. Did it mean fever, as it did in his own people? He slipped back into the servants' quarters to call Baldar.

In minutes, there was a knock on the door. Rodani opened it to the physician.

"Why did you not stop by, a'tem?" Baldar asked.

"We did," Rodani replied sourly. "Cibala did not tell you?"

Baldar turned in his walk toward the bedroom. "She did not," he said, eyeing Rodani as if looking for any hints of prevarication. Rodani kept an honorable silence, and Baldar turned back toward the bedroom...and his patient.

"She is hot," Rodani told him before he had even set his bag down. "Her hands are outrageous. Is there nothing more to do?"

Baldar palpitated the swollen fingers and probed the palms. "Not until evening. I will treat them again. How long will she sleep?"

"Unknown."

Baldar returned to his bag and retrieved three small balls. Squishy ones, Rodani noticed, like the ones babies played with. They varied in size and color.

"She should exercise her hands with these as often as she can manage," he said, passing them to the guardian. "Make it your duty to be sure she does. Her craft and her place here depend on it."

If the second instruction didn't implant that duty firmly in Rodani's mind, the explanation surely did. He pocketed the toys.

"How often will she be breathing the smoke?"

"As often as she needs it." Baldar continued, slipping the gloves on her. "Massage her hands while she is sedated. It will cause her no pain and hasten the healing."

"What kind of massage?"

Baldar demonstrated, then watched as Rodani imitated the pressing, pushing motion of his fingers. "No," Baldar corrected. "Work toward the palms, not the fingertips. That will push the toxin away from her extremities and toward better circulation." Rodani adjusted the direction, and Baldar stepped away, satisfied for the nonce. He snapped his bag shut with an emphatic click and headed for the door.

"How went your meeting with the taso?" he inquired belatedly.

"Adequately," Rodani said. "We reconvene in two weeks. Your attendance will be requested."

Baldar cocked an eyebrow at the news, then bowed and left.

Rodani resumed his massage. Time passed quietly. Cara remained motionless, which thankfully meant that the powder worked well on humans. He rested for a while in the chair, a cooling cup of tea his only accompaniment, his head full of an analysis based on too little information. There were no answers to be found in the Enclave. They were as close-lipped as the guild. A data gathering mission of his own would be censured and stopped; supplicants to the Enclave were protected from retribution.

Rodani had just resumed another round of massage when a pair of boots trod on his composure.

"How is she?" Serano paused in the doorway and raked his partner up and down with his eyes. His pupils narrowed.

"If I find out who started this..." Rodani began.

His threat hung in the air. Serano ducked under it as it slowly dissipated and came round to Cara's other side. He picked up a swollen hand and prodded it, then placed it back on its resting shelf.

"Would Larisi have told Kimasa?" Rodani asked.

Serano leaned against the headboard. "She does not know, though she has asked of the friction between us."

Rodani glanced to the side and concentrated on Cara's hand.

"Other thoughts?" Serano asked.

Rodani glowered and tapped his ear, as if someone might be listening. "I expressed my displeasure at this outcome to the taso," he said.

"You are radiating."

Rodani threw his partner a dark look. "What else but anger do you expect of me?"

Serano pursed his lips. "Nothing but what I predicted when I caught her." He perched himself on the edge of the bed near Cara's motionless shoulder, facing Rodani. "She slipped out through the bars. Ran into the forest."

Rodani's fingers pressed against Cara's, moving downward toward the palms with measured length and timing. "And if you simply followed her footprints, why was she attempting to embrace a camabarin tree?" One finger finished, on to the next.

"She was jumping from tree to tree, grasping for a limb."

The rhythmic motion stopped. Rodani closed his eyes against the painful image. If only… "Goddess, heal her. That explains the depth of the wounds." He resumed his digital work with the concentration of a surgeon.

"What are you doing?"

"Easing the toxins out of her fingers."

"That is painful, yes?"

"Yes." He moved his fingers into the palm, working downward to the wrist.

"How often for the massage?"

"Ten minutes a hand, twice an hour while she is asleep."

"It will keep you busy."

"Better that than riding circles through a labyrinth of prickly popi." He glanced at the timepiece on the headboard. "Trade sides." Carefully, Rodani placed Cara's swollen hand back in its resting spot.

"What do you seek?" Serano asked as he passed around the foot of the bed.

"Restitution," Rodani replied. "Likely the taso will call you to an audience."

"She has."

"Yes?" he prompted, taking Cara's other hand in his.

"I apprised her of my knowledge, including the fact that the only words out of Cara's mouth were queries upon your whereabouts and health."

Cara remained oblivious to Rodani's succoring. Her chest rose and fell beneath the quilts with comforting regularity.

"You have captured her spirit," Serano told him, settling into the cozy chair.

Rodani's eyes rested again on the face of his bedmate. "Wild ride."

"You were never one to dare the boring."

Rodani pegged him with a glance. "Look where the ride has taken me." His fingers worked their way down into Cara's palm.

"Into the stables with bit and bridle, led by a sprite as pale as the moon."

"Do not lock the door yet. We are walking in parallel, not chosen."

"In parallel?" Serano asked, confused.

"As benatacs do, shoulder to shoulder. As companions, not life-mates."

"Be cautious of the ground ahead," Serano advised.

"The path would be easier were we left alone to walk it."

"You ask the impossible."

Rodani worked his way down the next finger, carefully applying pressure as Baldar had shown. No results had become apparent as yet. The swelling was extensive and heading down into her wrists. He held his temper in check with the merest thread. "Why impossible?"

Serano crossed his leg over the other knee. "You are attempting a cross-species affinity, and it carries overtones of sacrilege."

"If Sela truly exists, She is the mother of Cara as well as me," Rodani replied.

"As usual, you state your assumptions as fact."

"As logical extrapolation of doctrine."

"Doctrine varies with the ears that hear it."

"Then it is not doctrine. It is interpretation."

Serano tossed the conversation with a wave of his fingers. "I must relearn the futility of discussing theology with you."

"Why?" Rodani countered. "Discussion is all it is worth."

"And what of Kimasa's help?"

Rodani suspended his massage to shut his eyes against another kind of pain. "What of it?"

"She helped you."

"The operative word being *she*, not goddess."

"You do not believe?"

Rodani sighed heavily against the tension in his chest and the memories of a lifetime. "I never claimed that. Serano, if you had the life I have had, you would question as well."

"My—"

On the bed, Cara startled, coming out of a drug-induced haze with an anguished cry of pain. Serano sat up in alarm; Rodani gently replaced the hand he'd been rhythmically rubbing.

"Cara?"

Her medicated gaze flickered between the men in front of her. "Aisu?" she whispered.

"Are you better?"

"No," was her slowly considered opinion. "Can we start the day over?"

"One might wish," he said gently.

"What time is it?"

"Not quite dinnertime." He laid his hand on hers, featherlight. "Are you hungry?"

"No." She looked away, into the space beyond her walls. "Maybe."

Serano leaned forward and rested his forearms on his knees. "Why did you run, Cara?"

She closed her eyes. "Fear."

"To where were you going to run?"

"Toward the Himadi Hills."

Serano pursed his lips. "What good would that do? You would never get there."

Cara's temper flared. She pulled her hands off the resting board. "Then I would die trying! If all you can do is offend me, Serano, you can leave! Why didn't you tell me Rodani was unharmed?"

"It is forbidden," came a voice from the servants' corridor. A trickle of recognition slipped through Cara's memory banks as her guardians stood at attention. A flutter of gold became visible inside Cara's peripheral vision. The fluttering turned into a robe as Kimasa strode into the room. Her face was a reminder Cara didn't want. She closed her eyes in a desperate attempt to flee the painful situation.

Kimasa glanced at the two men and folded her arms under the voluminous sleeves, then looked down at Cara. "Why did you run from me, child?" she said quietly.

A handful of answers came to mind, but only one escaped Cara's lips. "I am not a child."

A curt reply was unexpected. Kimasa regarded her distantly, studying the swollen hands. "You need not have run."

"You need not have had us hauled down for a frightening inquiry, but talked to us together, here," Cara responded heatedly.

"Cara." The tone in Rodani's voice was unmistakable. Kimasa turned to him.

"Is this discourtesy a purposeful offense?"

"Unlikely, a'Selaso," he replied. "I think it pain that overwhelms learned manners."

"A'Cara," she continued, "I did not know you were wounded when I questioned you."

Finally, she opened her eyes to the high priestess. Pride, hauteur, power, Kimasa wore those things like she wore the golden robe of her calling. Her face held a remote expression, as if mundane earthly matters were of minor concern compared to her responsibilities to the supernatural. She was neither comfortable nor comforting, this emissary. Cara wished she'd leave.

"The laws prevented me from talking with you and Rodani jointly," she continued.

"Laws can be bent in fairness for those unfamiliar with them," Cara replied, closing her eyes against another confrontation she was in no shape to face.

"Not in honor."

"Sometimes it is a higher honor to bend them than to adhere to them."

"Cara."

Cara's throat began to tighten. The throbbing in her hands increased as the effects of the smoke wore off. The tone in Rodani's voice hurt. It wasn't what she needed to hear. Hot tears leaked out from under her eyelashes and began the long trail down her cheeks.

"Aisu," she whispered. "This is not...a good time for philosophy. Please. Beg my forgiveness of the selaso and let us be alone."

It was shock. Pain. Physical, emotional. The vestiges of pride that had held her on her feet in the Enclave's meeting room washed from her body through the tears that were beginning to soak her pillowcase. Rodani said nothing, but there was a rustle of clothing and a tap of boot heels. The side of her bed compressed with weight and a kerchief brushed her face. She cried harder. Humiliation replaced pride. Pain overpowered anger. Hard won knowledge replaced the ignorance that had caused such a disastrous decision in the first place. And she wanted to hide from it all. If they'd just leave her alone, leave her to be miserable in private, she might just pull herself together long enough to regain her sense of reason.

Go away!

Her sobs became louder, tears flowed faster. Her body shook with release. A warm hand momentarily cupped her wet cheek; the mattress rose with the lifting of a body.

"A'Selaso," Rodani said respectfully. "I have seen her in this state before. It is fruitless to discuss anything with her until she regains control over her emotions. May I bring her to you when she is calm?"

"Such a bizarre seizure, Rodani. This is dangerous?" Kimasa asked.

"Not to my knowledge, a'Selaso."

"When will she regain her sensibility?"

"It varies. A few minutes to half an hour."

Kimasa considered. "I will wait." She swept around the end of the bed. Serano stepped back from her in deference to her status. She took the overstuffed chair. "I have had no time to study the creature since she arrived."

Cara's sobs grew louder. Rodani pulled his hands behind his back. "I beg you, a'Selaso, do not refer to her as such."

His tone was respectful, but there was a firmness behind it that spoke of courage, and of affection.

"Explain this affinity to me, Rodani."

Rodani slid a hip onto the bed. "Is that necessary, Kimasa?" he asked softly, his eyes riveted on hers. Unspoken messages exchanged between them.

She hesitated. "Perhaps not." Kimasa studied Cara's tears with the same dispassionate curiosity that Baldar had that first time. "What is the purpose for this?"

Rodani sighed. "Release of emotion."

"Emotion is to be contained."

"She has explained to me that some humans' emotions are too strong to be contained and must be released. She is one of those humans."

"A poor survival mechanism," Kimasa judged.

"Why would the goddess design them as such?" Rodani asked.

"I do not second guess Her, Rodani. Why do you?"

"I am not satisfied with answers that are no answers."

"The Mysteries are not to be answered."

"I am of the guild, Kimasa," he countered. "I seek answers, and effect solutions."

"Temi does not question Sela, Rodani. You are much more than guild. You fit no mold. That is the source of much of your disaffection in life."

"The source, a'Selaso," Rodani replied formally, "is not with my opinion of myself, but with others' opinions of me."

The emotional charge between them was enough to rouse Cara from her own pain. It sounded like an old argument, oft repeated. "People who break molds," she said slowly, "often live uncomfortable lives, a'Selaso, but they have great gifts to give to the world."

Kimasa turned and stared at Cara as if she had sprouted fins. "Do all humans feel so?"

"The wise do."

Kimasa looked at Rodani. "I begin to understand." And back to Cara. "Are you rational again?"

Cara's eyes flickered from Kimasa to Rodani, to the armoire to her right. "Yes."

"Another offense?" Kimasa wasn't pleased.

"I would assume you offended her, a'Selaso."

"I did not."

Rodani double-checked Cara's expression before replying. "You did."

"You are the size of a child to me, a'Cara. And you have the impulses of one."

"If I were a child, a'Selaso, Rodani would not be sharing my bed."

She inclined her head. "If it offends you so much, I will refrain. Why did you run from me?"

"Because," she replied, testy with pain, "no one told me anything. And my people don't get pulled from their homes to be taken who knows where, unless they're accused of something terrible." She waved one badly injured hand. "Why shouldn't I think the same thing, here?"

"The Enclave does not kill people for their choice of bedmates, a'Cara."

"That information would have been more useful a few hours ago," she replied with heat.

"And that is regretful."

Cara raised her enlarged, mutilated hands. "And *that* is an understatement."

"Kia."

"Aisu," she retorted. "If the selaso wishes to discuss this while I'm bedridden and full of pain, she has to understand that my courtesies are at low tide levels."

Rodani turned to Kimasa. "You are not seeing her at her best, a'Selaso."

"That is acceptable," she replied. "One sees things that are otherwise hidden."

"I would prefer you see her after she has healed."

"I would not." The high priestess settled back in the chair.

Cara pulled her arms off the shelf and rolled her body toward the wall. The shelf rocked over her hips. She grunted in pain. "Kia," came Rodani's voice, but this time there was no censure in it. Her left arm hung down awkwardly. There was nowhere to rest it, and nowhere to stare besides the armoire and unadorned stone wall.

"You do not understand the selaso's visit," he told her.

"You are correct."

"She is not here to your detriment. Do your best, and I will support you."

Cara rolled back upright. Rodani lifted the shelf and helped her settle in, then replaced it and the padding. She rested her arms on it and stared at her swollen hands. They not only throbbed, they tingled painfully, like someone was jabbing needles into them. Her nostrils flared with each shallow breath.

Rodani glanced into the doorway behind Cara's head and made a circular motion with his finger.

"You feared for your life?" the priestess continued.

"And Rodani's."

"You thought us so evil?"

"I didn't know what to think," Cara said, frustration bringing a sharpness to her tone. "No one told me anything."

"Nevertheless, you thought we would kill you, and Rodani."

Cara's face screwed up into a grimace. "Yes," she replied, "because someone already tried to."

Kimasa paused in the silence. Cara felt her eyes bore into her as she focused on Rodani's weapons belt, hoping to concentrate on something besides the uncomfortable aura that emanated between them.

"We are not evil." Kimasa's back was straight as a new fencepost, her hands rested decorously in her lap. Her eyes never left Cara's face.

"I didn't say you were."

"Running would not have saved Rodani."

Cara turned her head aside, face tensing against the sudden influx of raw emotions. Another tear fell from the corner of her eye.

Rodani laid a hand on her arm. "Do not fear to speak, kia."

She glanced over to where Serano stood, leaning against the wall with arms and ankles crossed. "I would speak more freely with fewer people in the room."

Rodani turned around. "Serano."

He shifted his stance. "I have been requested to learn all I can of this unfortunate incident."

Rodani's pupils narrowed in thought, then he turned to Kimasa.

"A'Serano," she said, "I concur with the preference for privacy."

All three waited for Serano's next move. If Kusik gave him the orders, he would leave. If Arimeso, he would stay.

He left without a word.

The eyes came back to her, one set violet, one set a light grey. Only Rodani was other than monochrome on his body. Fleetingly, Cara wondered what Kimasa looked like under her robes, and where one would find her channel of life. Then another pulse of pain took away her curiosity. Cara tried to flex her fingers, but they wouldn't move.

At a rustle in the doorway, Rodani looked up past her head, then down. "Are you hungry?"

Cara considered the question. "I can't eat."

"Why?"

"I can't use my hands."

"I will help you."

A wry smile crossed her face. "Thank you. But not in front of visitors."

"Please do not concern yourself with my presence, a'Cara," Kimasa offered. "I am quite used to the vagaries of existence."

"Please concern yourself with my concerns, a'Selaso."

"Kia." His tone was sharp. "Bring it in, Deremic. I, at least, am in need of food."

Deremic drew the cart into the bedroom and left it next to the bed. "There is enough for the august selaso, as well, a'tem." He bowed to Kimasa and left.

Rodani tilted his head in Kimasa's direction. She rose and filled a plate. He made one for himself and Cara, then began to spoon-feed her. Cara managed to conceal her embarrassment, but it infiltrated her conscious mind to the exclusion of all else. She refused to look at either person.

They ate in silence, thankfully. Cara had heard more than enough offenses in more than enough questions, and still, she didn't know the purpose of the selaso's visit. Hadn't the woman asked enough questions earlier? Hadn't she gotten the answers she needed? What in the deep, wide dark did she want?

Throbbing in her hands kept interrupting her thoughts, drawing her back to the ridiculous predicament she'd put herself into. Her fingers were even more swollen than before.

Rodani fed her, turn and about with his own spoonfuls. He watched her closely, but his expression lacked the stress lines it so often showed. Someone made a noise behind her, and Rodani glanced up, but no one else came in.

The skin on her hands continued to tighten.

He scraped the spoon against the bottom of the bowl, and Cara took a last bite. He put their trays on the cart and wheeled it back into the servants' quarters, then sat back down near to Cara on the bed. She wasn't sure of the purpose behind his attentiveness—worry, prevention of further insults to the selaso, or comfort. But he laid his hand on her arm, and it was enough, for now. She concentrated on the warmth of his skin instead of the sharp pains that shot from fingertips to wrists.

"Can you touch nothing, child?"

Kimasa had found her voice again and hadn't learned a thing. Cara gritted her teeth. "I have no desire to try. They hurt too much. Why are you here?"

"Kia."

"Why are you here?" she repeated, despite Rodani's chiding.

"To learn, my child."

"Learn what?"

"Whatever the goddess shows me."

"What if I don't want to be used for show?"

"The goddess sees us all."

"I have no ability to see the invisible, a'Selaso, or touch the discorporate."

"That does not negate Her presence."

"If I'm incapable of sensing Her," Cara said, "or She's incapable of making Herself known to me, then Her presence means nothing."

Kimasa's eyes opened wide. "You believe that?"

"Nothing else is reasonable to me," Cara replied. "No evidence, no belief."

"There is evidence all around you, child."

Cara sighed. Above her, Rodani's face held an expression she hadn't seen before. Sorrow? Disappointment?

Another body bustled down the servants' corridor, revealing itself as the physician. Serano followed him in, waiting at the doorway.

"You are awake," Baldar said.

"Apparently."

He stopped in the motion of reaching for her hand, glancing at Rodani.

"I believe that is an attempt at humor."

Baldar looked back at Cara, regarding her intently. "You are still in pain?"

The throbbing increased with his attention on it. "Oh, yes. It's taken hold with a vengeance."

Baldar stripped her gloves off and pushed on her fingers, provoking a yelp with each movement.

^You ever heard of bedside manner?^ she muttered in Cene'l. ^My mother could take lessons from you.^

Carefully, he palpitated the swollen digits. Every touch left a trail of pain through her hands. She squeezed her eyes shut and tried to go away. Baldar put his thumbs on each side of one of the purpling slashes and pulled. The skin parted with a rip that Cara felt down to her gut. She screamed and jerked her hand out of his grip, swearing.

"What are you doing?"

Baldar reached for her. "Opening the wounds."

She held her hands next to her chest, bewildered. "Why?"

"Because several applications are necessary." He took her arm and drew it to him, placing his thumbs against another stripe. She jerked it back, folding herself against the headboard in pain.

"Rodani," the physician said.

Rodani moved to Cara's shoulder, sat on the mattress, and held her arm.

"No, please," she said.

Baldar took her hand.

She squirmed. "No!"

He held it firmly.

And methodically, implacably, opened every excruciating red strip of mending, swollen flesh. One by one, he ripped them open, spilling blood, drawing a whimper or scream from her throat with every pull. She kicked at the covers, swore, and leaned over the side of the bed in a vain attempt to be released. Baldar didn't budge from his course of action, nor did Rodani let go. Tears ran down her cheeks and into her clothing. She fought and squealed and begged him to stop, begged Rodani to release her from her torment.

From the sidelines, Serano and Kimasa watched, silent witnesses to her torture.

When Baldar was done, he tugged her off the bed and into the facilities. The astringent didn't get any better, nor did her reaction to it. She fought, hard.

"Control, Cara," Rodani said.

Dinner rose in her throat, tasting bitter and hot. She swallowed convulsively. "I'm going to toss."

"Try not."

"Can't." She yanked her arm, but between Baldar's grip and Rodani's, it went nowhere.

"Calm," he told her. "Calm."

She kicked at the sink, missed, and connected to Baldar's shin. He paused and stared at her, pupils narrowed.

Dinner broke past the top of her throat. She retched and spattered the wall beside them, the floor, Rodani's pants, her own clothes. Baldar switched hands, spreading more liquid flame, ignoring the mayhem erupting in front of him. Rodani whispered in her ear, words that in her extremity she didn't even hear, let alone interpret.

By the time Baldar released her hand, the accommodation was uninhabitable, and Cara incoherent.

"Hamman," Rodani called, as Baldar packed away the astringent.

"Yes," she said, already holding cleaning tools.

"A'Selaso, tem'u," he said, "leave us, please."

Kimasa stepped back from the doorway, crossing her arms under the voluminous gold sleeves. "This must be discussed, Rodani."

Rodani bared his teeth. "Later." Banked rage provoked his rudeness. "Tem'u, bring me clean clothes."

Serano left. Rodani picked up Cara's limp body, carried it past the bed into the workroom, and kicked the door. It shut with a most satisfactory bang. He laid her on the floor carefully, knelt, and stared.

Streaks of blood stained the skin on her palms, between her fingers, and down onto her wrists. The astringent left angry white and purple wounds, open and raw. His gut clenched in reaction. Her cries had tormented him, helpless to stop her pain.

This was the woman he was duty bound to protect, to keep from harm. And he had failed, terribly, catastrophically.

Calm, he urged himself, as he had done to Cara earlier. *Temper will not solve this.* He flexed his hands and gently began to remove her noxious clothes.

Someone knocked on the door. "Rodani?"

He opened the door a crack and retrieved his clothes from Serano. "Get something for Cara."

Serano raised his eyebrows. "What?"

"Anything. Anything that will cover her."

"Tem'u," he protested.

"Then get one of my shirts. A soft one." Rodani shut the door in his face, and slipped out of his soiled clothes. He put the clean ones to the side, and removed the rest of Cara's, wiping her face with a clean portion of her pants. Then he dressed, and retrieved another shirt from Serano.

Her eyes were open and tracking his movements.

"Cold," she said.

He helped her sit, and slipped his shirt around her, infinitely cautious of her swollen hands. He tucked it underneath her and began to pick her up.

"I can walk."

He helped her stand, then followed her into the bedroom. Serano and Kimasa stood shoulder to shoulder in the corner, conferring. "Please," he said with some heat. "She needs rest to heal."

Serano left the room with a bow to Kimasa. The high priestess glared stonily at the room, at Cara, at Rodani. Folding her arms across her chest, she drifted out.

SIX

Cara sat on the edge of the bed as Kimasa left. Rodani started to help her into it. "No, I need the facilities." She hung her head. "And I'll need help. I'm sorry," she whispered.

"Au, kia, I would rather face ten times that pain than watch you battle it."

"I'll try to manage it myself," Cara told him.

"I will wait outside the door." Rodani moved up behind her and leaned back on the wall.

Cara used her elbow to push the door shut. Rodani's shirt wasn't too difficult to raise. Pressure from her wrists did an adequate job, and her unders had been removed earlier. It was the afterwards that gave her thoughts of rank humiliation. Bad enough to be small in a race of tall people, bad enough to be looked at as a child...or called one. But to go back to childhood helplessness was almost more than she could face.

When her bladder had emptied, she reached for one of the cloths folded next to her, but her fingers couldn't clutch it. Her fingertips didn't touch her thumb. She tried to slip the cloth between her fingers horizontally. It worked for a moment, then the cloth slipped and fluttered to the floor. Swollen, hot, and throbbing, her hands were as useless as she feared.

Tears welled up. Again. *Useless watering*, she berated herself. *Get a grip. You're not dead.*

"Rodani?"

He opened the door slowly and slipped in, crouching in front of her knees. He took a fresh cloth in hand and waited.

She spread her legs and motioned downward. Rodani slipped his hand in and patted her tender places carefully.

"Can you get in between?"

He shifted the cloth and tried again between her soft folds.

"Thank you."

Damp cloth in hand, he leaned forward and rested his temple against hers for a moment, wordless. Then he snatched the cloth from the floor and threw both in the wash bin.

It took her longer to get off than it did to get on, the seats being Selandu-height. Rodani waited with a hand out, just in case. She wiggled and dropped to her feet, staggering, wincing when the movement shook her painful hands. The shirt moved with gravity, covering what it ought. Rodani pushed the door open.

He settled her into bed, arranging her clothes, the covers, and her pillows.

"Will your leaders come seeking punishment of Arimeso or her house?" he asked her.

"No."

"Will your family?"

"No."

He shifted in his seat and rested his chin on his chest, stretching his long legs outward. "Will the see-ess-see complain to the Council in Hadaman?"

"No."

"No one will ask us to answer for your injuries?"

"Not when they find out why it happened."

Rodani lurched up and started pacing. There wasn't much room in the bedroom to pace, with the now ever-present overstuffed chair in the way. He strode from the corner of Cara's bed to Hamman's hallway and back again. A few steps only, for a Selandu. Back and forth he passed by her each way, hands now clasped behind him at the small of his back, then he stopped. His gaze pierced her with the intensity and drive that lay behind them. "Your species will care no more for what we have engendered here than mine does, yes?"

"Huh. Yes."

"Will you be in danger when you go home?"

That was a question not to be contemplated—for a parcel of reasons, chief of which was the very large pain residing in the depths of her chest. *Home* meant proximity to a prying lot of busybodies who didn't approve of her path in life, and the emptiness of an existence without Rodani.

"Kia?"

"I don't think so, not physically. But you're assuming they'll know?"

"That is a possibility that cannot be denied. Not now."

She stared back out into her workroom. "I'll pay the price."

Rodani shut his eyes for a moment. "There are tasks that need doing, kia. I will return."

"Go. I'll survive. Awake or asleep, I don't know."

SEVEN

As Kimasa walked out of the taso's office, Arimeso stared at her own palms. The idea of another radio call across the hills made her ears twitch, and her jaw clench. Complications were compounding, twisting the lives of those who lived in her house.

Kusik slipped into the doorway between her office and the private quarters they shared, crossing his arms.

"You *will* be relating this to the ambassadors," he said in a tone that bordered on insolence. "Yes?"

"I have already considered it, my mate. And," she answered in a similar tone, "you *will* refrain from giving me orders. Yes?" The last word came out in a hiss, and the glare in her eyes matched her keso's. "Baldar told me she will heal. And, *if you remember*," she left a pause for him to consider, "just last week she refused a'Mena'hem's offer to return home after Shurad's attack." Arimeso swept a hand across her desk as if she wished to sweep aside the looming complications, then fixed her gaze on its empty surface.

Kusik leaned against the door frame in the hope it would mask the tension that flowed between them. "If you wish me to make the call, I can do so."

Suspicion crept into her eyes, narrowing them. "Why would I wish to?"

Kusik tossed her question with a wave of his hand. "They do not frighten me, tisal."

Arimeso froze for a moment, then slowly rose from her chair. "Do think about what you're implying, a'keso." The low growl in her voice filled the space between them. "You can only push me so far."

***

Temi's knives, what a disaster. Serano walked through the back halls, eyes on the toes of his boots. Rodani was radiating rage. So was Kusik. Get them too close together and the manor's stone walls would melt from the heat. Kimasa was visibly agitated, a portent of which no one wished to divine. Anything that rippled the calm in the selaso's seas was a storm that threatened lives and livelihoods. Arimeso's impatience was rising geometrically. Anything that interrupted the smooth workings of her house and the output of her artisans threw the taso's inner circle into whirling dervishes, desperate to calm, to soothe, to patch and—where necessary—to punish.

Serano wanted to kick something. Anything. Anybody. His taso for inviting that be-damned human into her house. His partner for the life-threatening misjudgment of crawling into the human's bed. His keso for treachery. His high priestess for...well, maybe he could hold off on that one. And the unknown pointer-of-fingers...fuel on an already raging fire.

Arimeso prided herself on running a peaceful house, and Serano was proud to be a part. Artisans, on the whole, were not normally an argumentative, violent lot. Competitive, of course. They tended to throw paint bottles and clay at each other, not knives. But an alien in the midst made the tufts of everyone's ears stand up. Order. The taso rules. The guild protects. The Enclave counsels and guides. Selandu men approach Selandu women. Children obey. Everyone follows commands.

Simple and neat.

Serano knew he was partnered to a breaker-of-rules, a walker of his own path, regardless of the stares and mutters from those more properly constrained within society's bounds. But until now, Rodani's errors in judgment had been of the twitch-your-ears, roll-your-eyes type.

Now, now...

How many lines had the temichi crossed? Serano didn't want to count that high or total the cost. He could only hope, as Kusik did, that the taso would regain her senses and send the human home. Surely this would do it, this devastating injury? Worse, in damage, than Shurad's attempt on her life. And how much did the humans know?

Surely the goddess would send down a bolt of wisdom and set things back on track.

Serano hated change.

***

Late that eve, Iraimin left Cara's rooms, angry. Muscles tense, head a-whirl, she muttered words Sela would never want to hear from an ex-acolyte. It was bad enough Cara was relegated to the company of a cold, morose, rule-breaking guardian who kept her a virtual prisoner. But for her hands to be ruined? To have the use of her creativity stolen from her? Swollen, agonizing, useless appendages where once an artist's power resided?

Iraimin shook her head, but the images wouldn't leave. Cara, comatose, resting in bed with her hands propped up, hands that were twice their normal size. Hands striped with raw wounds, pungent with the scent of ziss.

She couldn't believe it when Misia had called her. She'd run through the halls and pushed past Deremic when he opened the door, stopping at the entrance to Cara's bedroom, transfixed by the carnage.

Rodani had eyed her with a look that shouted *Go away*. "She is asleep." And at her silence, added: "You cannot help her."

Her pupils narrowed. "We can try."

Goddess, Goddess, please don't let it be permanent, she prayed as she walked. She blew through the doors of the Enclave and sped past the empty desk.

Kimasa was conferring with her second-ranked priestesses in an inner alcove. Iraimin stopped and bowed deeply, properly, not all her training forgotten. It gave her a little leeway with the priestesses—sometimes.

"A'Selaso," she whispered.

The high priestess turned to her.

"A'Selaso, I request a healing."

Kimasa's expression didn't change, but her voice held a touch of warmth. "How are you injured?"

Iraimin bowed again. "For Cara, a'Selaso. Not for me."

"She does not believe."

"She will, a'Selaso, when she improves under your ministrations. Please."

"I will consider."

"I would help, if it would be allowed."

"You are no longer of the Enclave, Iraimin. I cannot allow it."

A third time, Iraimin bowed. "But...you will help?"

"I will consider."

Iraimin turned, knowing herself dismissed, then spun around. "You have seen her? You have seen what happened?"

"Yes. And I know why. Do you?" came the pointed question.

"No."

"Leave it in the goddess's hands, painter."

***

The next morning, Cara sat on the edge of her bed, shaking. The stinging smell of Baldar's astringent still hung in the air. At least she hadn't thrown up this time, and managed only a few tears. Breakfast was due shortly. Rodani rearranged the bedding as she pushed herself up to the headboard and laid down.

"What do we expect from Kusik now, aisu?"

Rodani settled into the chair, wordless. He didn't look at her, either. He took a deep breath and stretched his long legs.

Cara shifted her arms around her body, but no position stopped the burning. "Will he kill me? Will he keep finding ways to hurt me?"

"It does us no favors to guess, kia."

"Wouldn't Arimeso keep him within bounds?" She curled into the quilt that lay over her. "Gods, he frightens me."

"That is his nature and his inclination. He has ever been such."

"I'm glad he wasn't assigned to guard me."

"Arimeso would not have made that mistake."

"So, what do I do? Just lay here?"

"Exercise your hands." He pulled out an orange ball from a pocket.

With an anticipatory grimace, she took it and tried to squeeze. And again. "Not working." And again. "That miserable, dishonorable, ugly, spiteful..." Cara dropped the ball in her lap. Her hands kept burning, immobile as ever.

Rodani sat on the edge of her bed, put the ball back in her palm, and started working it with his hands. She hissed. "Arrogant, bombastic..." She kicked her feet under the covers. "I'm running out of words, aisu."

"I will bring you your dictionary." He kept massaging, working her fingers around the ball, then stretching them outward.

A bolt of pain shot through them. "Stop!"

"Last as long as you can."

She bit her lip. Counted to ten. Rocked in place. Counted to twenty. "Enough."

Rodani switched to her other hand.

"If I ever get that man in a vulnerable position..."

Rodani paused in his ministrations, cocking an eyebrow. "You will...?"

"I don't know. Beating him would satisfy me, but kissing him would offend him more."

His eyes went wide, his jaw lax. "Au, kia, do not." Then he started back in on her hand.

"I wouldn't do it for pleasure, aisu. I'd do it to shock him to his core."

"Do you not have enough wounds?"

She huffed in wordless agreement. "It's fun to dream of."

"I thought you did not approve of revenge?"

"I don't. That's why it would only be a dream."

An ache started up, low in her gut.

"Do not add to our dangers, please, kia. Keep it a dream."

"I will." The ache deepened. Recognition bubbled into her conscious thoughts. *Oh, no. It's too early for...* Pulling her hand from Rodani's, she sat up and felt a familiar wetness. "Oh gods." She kicked the covers off, dislodging him from her bed in the process, and got out. She had no unders on, and no way to wipe.

"There is blood on the sheet," Rodani said from behind her.

"Damn." Cara crossed her arms, another humiliation to add to all the others her stupidity had caused her. *Damn.*

Rodani bent over the sheet to inspect the spot. "Is this injury, or is it what you told me of before?"

"It's my red tide. Look, maybe I can just..." *What? Sit on the facilities until your hands heal? Right, fem.*

"What do you need?" Rodani asked calmly.

I don't think I can do this. "Um...the red bag in the wardrobe..." *Oh, gods.*

Rodani retrieved it. "We do this in the facilities, yes?"

"I'm sorry, aisu. I really am."

"For?"

"You having to deal with this."

"You deal with it."

"It's my body."

He herded her forward. "And I spend more time with your body than anyone but you. Besides, kia, I am Guild. Bodies do not offend me, nor what they produce."

Afterwards, Cara slid a knee onto her mattress, preparing to worm her way back into bed without using her still-stinging hands. Talk about bad timing. She glanced in Rodani's direction.

His eyes were wide, alert to something outside her awareness. He looked into Hamman's hallway, his hand reaching toward his weapons belt. Then he relaxed.

"Aisu?"

"You have guests."

Hamman's whispery voice came through the hall, welcoming someone. A rustle of bodies followed. Kimasa appeared in the doorway, leading three other women.

"A'tem, a'Cara," she said. Remote as always, she seemed to take charge of the room, making Cara an interloper in her own space. The high priestess waited, expectantly.

Quite out of mind-reading tricks, Cara just stood there, blinking. *Field this one, Rodani, would you please?*

"A'Selaso." He bowed. "You honor us with your presence. Would you wish refreshments?"

"No." She swept her hand around the room. "We are here to do a laying on of hands." Proud, she was. Assured of her welcome, her beneficence, her majesty.

Rodani turned to her. "Did you request this, a'Cara?"

Formality, in front of the unknown priestesses, she reminded herself. "I don't even know what *this* is."

His head swiveled back to the gold-clad priestess and her entourage. "A'Selaso?"

"We offer you the healing of the goddess, a'Cara. We have decided it is necessary."

Cara cleared her throat. She glanced at Rodani, whose face was masked of all expression. She shuffled her feet and curled her aching hands in front of her. "Have you discussed this with Baldar, a'Selaso?"

Kimasa pursed her lips and lifted her chin. "Baldar is not of the Enclave."

"Yes," Cara agreed. "He's the physician, and I'm under his care." She nodded to the only man in the room. "And Rodani is assisting."

A moment of confusion passed across Kimasa's regal features, as if it were a rare occurrence. "Sela is the keeper of all healing."

Cara slumped against the wall next to her headboard, refusing to meet Kimasa's eyes. *I am not in the mood for this.*

"Lay yourself on your bed so that we may commence."

Adrenaline flooded Cara's body at the order. What is best here, courtesy to the ridiculous, or honor to her own standards? Rodani was silent, a warning she could read but not interpret.

"A'Cara?"

"No. But thank you."

Silence.

A miasma of silence, with stone-still bodies.

"A'Cara, the goddess wishes—"

"Your goddess doesn't speak to me. No, thank you."

Kimasa's eyes went wide, pupils narrowed into slits. She drew herself up like a child preparing for a temper tantrum. "You refuse the goddess's help?"

Cara glanced at Rodani. "I mean no offense, a'Selaso." *Yeah, I do.* "But Baldar will be a more than adequate healer for my needs. Thank you for your kind offer. I'm sorry you made the trip to my rooms for no reason." Her aching hands shook in tune with her defiance, but she owed the woman nothing, nothing that she could see. Her cramping gut echoed the complaints in her head.

Kimasa pointed her helpers to the door. As they filed out, she headed for Cara. Rodani, all the empty gods bless him, put himself in her path.

"No, a'Selaso."

"She dare..."

"Kimasa, you offered spiritual healing to a person who does not share your beliefs. It is within her right to refuse."

"Everyone believes."

"She has already discussed this with you."

Kimasa took a step closer. Rodani held out both hands, a breathing wall and stop sign. "A'Selaso, Cara has thanked you for your concerned offer, but prefers Baldar's services to your own." He dropped his arms to his sides. "I also thank you."

The high priestess turned with a swish of long cloaks and stomped out of the room. How she managed to stomp in slippers, Cara couldn't figure. She scooted onto the bed and laid down. "She and Kusik are a matching pair."

"I stood up for you—"

"And I thank you very much."

"—but you may regret it."

"Are they killers?"

"No. But they are influential."

"You and Arimeso are the only people I need to please."

"Kia," he began.

She held up a swollen hand. "I know, aisu. I was rude. I tried not to be, but it seemed there was no way to refuse her superstition and not be offensive."

"Why did you not accept?"

Cara stared at her palms. The shooting pains returned with her focus on them, moving from one wound to another. "Is there any evidence that what they do works? We got into space with science, not magic. We found food and medicine, and made shelters and boats with science, not magic."

Rodani seated himself in the overstuffed chair and settled in. "There would have been no harm in accepting. You would have offered respect to her and the Enclave."

"I don't respect others controlling people with nonsense."

His jaw dropped. "And I thought you were tactless before."

Cara chuckled. "I wouldn't have said that to her. Or any priestess."

"That is well."

"But you could have told her I figured out one of her 'magic' tricks."

Rodani looked away from her, then back, rejecting the suggestion. "I will not provoke her. Not in such an overt way. Especially in light of our affinity."

"I guess I have enemies enough."

"Unfortunately for us both," he replied.

"I hope I heal."

"You will."

"I wish I had your optimism."

He smiled. "Trust in medicine? Trust in science?"

"I'll get you trained right, yet," she said, humor running through the pains. "Give me time." She wrestled with her covers ineffectually. Her hips ached from too much time in bed. "Rodani, what am I going to do all day? I can't craft. I can't dance. You're going to be bored into raining if all you do is watch me heal." She heaved herself up into a sitting position. "Do you want to sing? Practice your Cene'l? You haven't for a while."

"Honestly, kia, I would wish to rest. But I have one more question."

^Okay.^

"Did you really believe you would make it home?"

Chagrin flooded her in a wave. "I had some thought," she said slowly. *Suck it up, fem.* "That if I stayed nearby, and you were alive, that you'd come looking for me. If you didn't, or couldn't, then I'd head south."

"You do realize—"

"Yes, yes." She clenched her eyes shut. "I realize all sorts of things, now that I'm not panicking." She patted the mattress with the back of her hand. "I have some empty space over here."

"Would you not rest better alone? Given your pain," he added.

"My body might rest better alone, but my mind and heart are calling out to you."

"Which takes precedence?"

"Oh, gods, aisu, don't make me choose. Just come lay down. Please." She tried to scoot over but succeeded only in rumpling the sheet further. Rodani kicked his boots off, removed his weapons belt, and laid his long body out beside her, closing his eyes.

She reached over to him and whispered her deepest fear. "I thought you were dead. I thought they'd killed you."

He wrapped his arms around her and pulled her eye-to-eye. "No, kia," he said softly, plaintive. "I am sorry. I am sorrowed for all that has happened."

His was an expression she hadn't seen before—guilt, maybe. She rested her injured palm on his cheek.

He looked so alien, and yet so familiar. He now lived in that juncture of still-very-different and becoming-almost-normal that made her brain do flip-flops when she thought about it. It was a dichotomy her mind couldn't process. She shoved it aside and whispered. "You have done so much for me, aisu. I would do about anything for you, even if it is just to help you rest." She caressed his cheek with the back of her hand. He took her wrist in his fingers, kissed the swollen flesh, and laid her hand between their bodies, leaving his palm where it lay on her arm.

EIGHT

Arimeso sat in her accustomed place behind her desk, poring over the house accounts. As Kusik entered the room, he slowed at the sight of her bent head and slumped shoulders. She worked too hard, spent many—too many—hours in slavery to Barridan, to her people. He took what burdens from her she would allow, but it was too few, too few. And now, more conflicts crowded the air between them.

He approached the desk and brushed the back of his fingers across her cheek. A wan smile drifted across her features. "You did not even deign to look up," he said.

Her smile widened into something worthy, something Kusik saw too seldom. "I know your walk, esuva. I even know when it is you who opens the door." She slumped wearily against the chair back.

Kusik pulled out his chair and sat down next to her. The perfume of Kimasa's incense lingered in the air. "That human becomes more of a liability each passing day, tisal."

Arimeso glanced at her mate fondly. "I care not what her opinions of the goddess are. What concerns me is her hands, and her further ability to craft."

"She offended the selaso. Again."

"I knew there would be offenses when I tendered the invite." She erased two numbers on the paper in front of her and wrote the corrections.

"I would see her gone," Kusik complained.

Arimeso sighed at the oft-repeated refrain. "But you will abide."

In turn, Kusik sighed, resting his arms on his weapons belt. A double keso, he was both security first and taso first—her husband, first among the men Arimeso bound to her by loyalty through the affections of her heart and body. She ruled him, and through his allegiance, honored him with the responsibilities and status he craved. Through her, he was who he desired to be.

"And if the human wishes to leave?" he asked.

"I have heard no hint of that in the reports I receive."

"But if?"

"She is not a prisoner."

Kusik shifted his weight. His gun clunked against the hard edge of the seat back. "And Rodani?" he ventured.

Arimeso laid down her pencil and leaned back to look at him. "Why do you continue to walk down paths we have already trod?"

Kusik stared at his hands.

"Because you do not approve of my answers," she answered herself.

He still stared.

"This experiment, despite its problems, despite one lone Riverchild's violence, is a success. Every one of the human's quilts has sold, either within the house or outside. One even went to Hadaman. Her new works are eagerly awaited, despite her presence causing some consternation. She does not follow our customs or courtesies to the level most would like, but she is quick to apologize, and quick to learn. She also," Arimeso added. "chose to stay here despite Shurad's treachery."

"And Rodani?"

"I confess myself curious to see where their affinity will go. It was a most surprising development—"

Kusik pushed himself out of his chair. "And you see no danger?" He began to pace in front of her desk.

"Your disapproval of the man and his choice blind you to the possibilities."

"And your curiosity blinds you to my concerns."

Arimeso retrieved her pencil and glanced at the papers in front of her. "No."

Kusik crossed his arms, brooding. "And there it stays?"

"And there we stay."

"A'Taso," he said, bowing. His boots clicked loudly as he walked away.

Kimasa was in her quarters when he arrived. Acolytes scurried away from him like autumn leaves in a stiff breeze, declining to even bother him for an explanation as to his entrance.

"A'Selaso."

Kimasa smiled graciously, offering him an ornate chair across from her table. Odd trinkets decorated its surface, along with a goodly supply of incense and two different holders, and a fire starter.

Kusik leaned forward. His eyebrows drew downward, his pupils narrowed. "I will see her gone before the year is new."

"Your verbal courtesies are as proper as ever, a'Keso."

"She refused you."

Kimasa tossed the statement with a wave of her fingers. "I find myself in a challenge."

"Challenge, Kimasa? She offended you. Denied the very reason for the existence of the Enclave."

The high priestess took a pinch of incense, dropped it in the burner, and lit it. "She sees us both as culprits, colluders in her injuries."

"And she is as wrong as ever."

"Perhaps."

"I am in need of assistance."

The pinch of incense smoldered into ash and went out. The high priestess lit another, then folded her hands on the tabletop. "Be clear in your request, a'Keso."

Kusik clasped his hands and rubbed them together. "Help me create a situation where the human will wish to be sent home, or where Arimeso will change her mind."

"I am not in the habit of contriving, Kusik. My actions are led by the hand of Sela."

"Then ask Sela."

Kimasa's mouth thinned into a line. "Now you offend."

"No," Kusik said quickly. "I offer a wish for Sela to hear me. She will listen to you."

"She listens to all."

"Including Rodani, apparently."

"You must be patient, Kusik. If Sela is offended by the affinity, She will make Her displeasure known."

"You will not assist me?"

"I will not go against Arimeso's orders. And the goddess has a hand in this as well. We must listen for Her whispers."

Kusik stood and walked to the doorway. "Tell me what She whispers to you, Kimasa. I need to know."

He made his way to the hall of healing, heedless of the Selandu artisans who scattered as alertly as the acolytes had. Years had gone by since he noticed such triflings. He did, however, remember the first time he met Rodani. He'd found the youth wandering back hallways where only guardians were allowed, and Kusik had used his considerable voice and presence to warn the careless youngster away from the area.

And see who and what the man was now. Kusik sighed. Arimeso was admiring the clouds that hung over the treetops and ignoring the brush fire at her feet. And Rodani... Kusik's slow burn heated up again. Rodani should never have been allowed into guild training. Kusik had fought it at the time, arguing with his predecessor against proposing the boy. But his efforts had proved futile.

Kusik growled in frustration as he entered Baldar's domain, scattering a third set of Selandu—this time, healer assistants and apprentices. *Meek, frightened little people, all of them.*

"Where is the master healer?"

A young man stuttered, his eyes blinking rapidly. "In...in the second view...viewing room, a'Keso." He pointed down a hall.

"Tell him I will speak with him." Kusik crossed his arms, filling the hallway with purposeful disruption. "I will wait."

"He is with a patient, a'Keso."

Kusik took a step forward.

The apprentice fled in the direction he'd pointed, then came back a moment later. "He will see you in his office, a'Keso," he said, pointing to the end of the opposite corridor.

Kusik made himself comfortable in the cramped room. Papers and medical drawings cluttered the physician's desk. Several rows of potions and ointments rested on narrow shelves against the wall.

Baldar came in, laying notes on the corner of his desk. "A'Keso."

"What is the status on the human, Baldar?"

His gaze went off into the distance. "Healing, but slowly. More slowly than I anticipated. I am still using the astringent on her hands. I expect the scarring to be severe."

"Will she continue to craft?"

"That cannot be seen."

Kusik took a deep breath. "Your knowledge and skills are tailored toward us. Would she not be better treated by her own people?"

"I have not heard Arimeso speak of bringing a human healer here."

A cough threatened Kusik's composure. "In her own land, Baldar."

The physician's dark pupils narrowed. "Camabarin trees do not grow in warm climates."

"Yes. But she may heal more promptly surrounded by those more like her."

Baldar tilted his head, looking down from his great height. "Can you mark your trail more clearly, a'Keso? I am having difficulty following you."

Kusik moved to the far wall and turned back to face the physician. "You say she is healing slowly. You say she may not heal much at all. You do not know if she will craft again. Yes?"

"Possibly."

"Then I would ask you to counsel Arimeso to have her sent home, where she can recuperate among her own people, and not be a drain upon our taso or the house accounts."

Baldar glanced over the detritus on his desk, evidence of years of healing and advice-giving. An image of Rodani's angry face arose in his mind. By nature or training, fighters may haggle, argue, and hit. By nature or training, physicians heal.

"A'Keso, it seems appropriate for her to remain under my care as the only person she knows who has experience with the toxin. I will report further when Arimeso calls the follow-up meeting."

Kusik stiffened.

"Bleeding lacerations do not wait for long conversations," Baldar said, bowing. "I bid you a pleasant day."

***

Iraimin let go of Cara's hand and returned the orange ball to her, then sat back in the chair on the other side of the sewing table. Rodani sat on the side with a pencil and leaf of paper, scratching out designs. "They hurt still?" she said, nodding in Cara's direction.

She lifted her hand and waved it in the air. "Yes, but Baldar's damnable liquid hurts more."

"I heard that your pain was great."

"So was the nausea." She glanced at Rodani, who declined to comment.

"The swelling has gone down."

"Only a little. It's been *days,* and I can't wear my rings, I can hardly hold a spoon, and I can't button my blouses to save my sanity." She gripped the ball with what strength she had, squeezing, squeezing, as if a few more tries would bring her hands back to health. "These wounds may never heal. Every time Baldar comes in, they start screaming at me, fearing they'll be ripped open again."

"It is said you ran from an Enclave inquiry."

Good gods, if she ever lived down that mistake, it would be a bloody miracle. "I did," she said, pursing her lips in self-disapproval.

"Why?"

"Fear of the unknown." The answers came by rote, now. Between the times others had asked her the questions and the times she'd lambasted herself with the same ones, it had become a litany of shame. She waited dourly for the next question in line.

"What did you fear?"

Right on schedule there, fem. "Being in trouble. Being accused of something and unable to prove my innocence. Being punished unfairly. Being considered dishonorable when I had not been."

"What did they ask of you?"

Rodani laid the pencil down, trapping it under his fingertips. "Someone had reported me, Iraimin. Someone thought I was mistreating her or taking improper advantage of her."

"Were you?"

Cara didn't have to look at him; one glance at Iraimin's face told her the painter knew she'd made a mistake. "No," Cara said, clearly, slowly. "He wasn't."

Iraimin looked away from Rodani and focused on Cara, her expression fading from fright to mask. "That is well."

Cara pushed fabric pieces around in front of her with tingling, unresponsive fingers. She flexed them several times, willing life and movement into them despite how little they moved. Iraimin borrowed an unoccupied pencil near the sewing machine and a sheaf of paper, and began to sketch the outlines of a face.

"Kimasa was disheartened at your refusal, Cara," she said.

Cara chuckled. "She was more than disheartened. She was livid. I thought she was going to hit me."

Iraimin stopped sketching. "Hit you? Never."

"Rodani had to step in front of her to stop her."

The painter glanced at them both. "She would not."

"Cara," Rodani said, "likely that was not Kimasa's intention. Iraimin is correct on that point."

"That wasn't what it looked like. But I offer my apologies."

"I accept them on her behalf," Iraimin replied. "Why do you not believe Sela exists?"

On that note, Cara went back to squeezing the exercise balls in her hands. *Onward into the fray.* "There's no evidence for Her existence."

"There is."

"No. No one can see, hear, smell, taste, or touch Her, not reliably. Any explanation for Her actions has a simpler explanation in real life. And everyone who claims to see or know Her describes something different."

"She is multi-faceted."

"Or She's a product of everyone's imagination."

Iraimin sat back, eyes narrowed. "That is very offensive."

"Which is why I don't usually have these types of discussions. I'm sorry."

"You would find contentment in Her."

"Contented people don't strive to better themselves, or the world they live in," Cara explained.

"You always have an answer." Iraimin rolled her pencil between her hands and sighed. "I would wish the selaso to talk to you, Cara. She would explain it so that it made sense to you."

"No." Cara smiled sadly. "She might use different words, but she'd say the same things you're saying: 'Believe because I believe,' and 'Believe because your lack of belief makes me uncomfortable,' and 'Believe so that I can predict you and judge you by my standards.' I won't do that."

"But—"

Cara laid her wounded, scarred hand on Iraimin's arm. "Please take no for an answer. Among my people, it's a sign of great wisdom. You'd show yourself to be the person of honor that I know you are."

Iraimin paled at the backhanded compliment. Her eyes roamed the tabletop between them, pencil clasped in her fist, forgotten. "Will your quilt be ready for the next exhibition?"

Cara regarded her swollen fingers, contemplating the mess they represented. "Likely not."

"Then I will pray that Sela grants you quick healing." The painter stood and bowed, her face masked. "Pleasant eve a'sel'ai."

As the painter walked out, Cara picked up the largest ball and leaned back in her chair. Tangles within weaves within webs. Was she making things worse or better by answering their questions? Facts were one thing. Diplomacy was another, and Cara's diplomatic skills were erratic at best. She glanced at Rodani. "Will she ever return, aisu? Or did I just offend her permanently?"

"Likely, and likely not." Rodani regarded her with a steady gaze. "Certainly, Kimasa will send her again after she reports tonight's failure."

"She spies?" Cara asked, astonished.

He pursed his lips in thought. "I would not be so harsh as that. It would be quite a coup if the selaso were able to bring a human to the goddess."

"Did what I said offend you?"

"No." Rodani rustled in his chair and laid his arms on her worktable.

Her worry lingered, along with a vague discomfort that she had irreparably damaged her friendship with Iraimin—if friendship it was. There wasn't a good correlating term for what was common among humans. And if Rodani were right, and Kimasa was behind it all, maybe "friend" wasn't the right term to use. She frowned down at the fabric pieces that lay in disarray, waiting for agile hands to create something worthwhile.

Rodani returned to his sketching. "I feel as if this is my fault."

"Iraimin?"

"No. Your injuries." His pencil scratched over the paper, random doodles appearing.

Cara made a determined effort to pick up two pieces of fabric. Her fingers barely touched her thumbs. "It isn't, any more than it's mine." The fabric dropped from her right hand, and she tried again to pick it up.

The pencil scratched again. "If I had not approached you—"

"Then we wouldn't be sharing pleasures, would we?" Cara smiled, then grimaced in frustration as she rubbed the two pieces together, trying to line them up.

A small smile appeared on his face.

"I had a choice, too, you know," she said. "You made sure of that." The fabric fought her, refusing to align properly. She bit her lip and sighed, then tried again.

"I did, yes. Do you have regrets?" he said softly. The pencil lay quiet in his hand as he watched her attempt to ply her trade.

Cara let her arms drop on the table. One fabric piece slipped through her fingers, fluttering to the tabletop. "About you? None." She shook her head. "I only regret trying to run. It made sense at the time, but later, seemed impossibly stupid."

A real smile crossed his face. "I will not deny that."

"You're too honest to deny that." She sighed. "Temi's demons. I'm not crazy, you know. I do think. A lot." She swept one hand over the fabric piece, drawing it into her grasp. Her fingers let out protests of pain. "I just don't think well when I'm threatened." Again, she tried to place the two pieces against each other, attempting to line them up. "How did Iraimin find out about my hands?"

"She came seeking you the first night. I presume she overheard from one of the acolytes in the Enclave."

"Why would they tell her?"

"She used to be one."

"Oh. Why did she quit?"

"That is not a question that is asked, kia."

Another set of footsteps came into her bedroom, another body appeared in the doorway. Baldar. Every muscle in Cara's body clenched as he approached. Much as she tried, it was impossible to keep her expression masked. "A'Baldar."

"A'Cara."

She got up and walked toward the dour physician.

Opening the deepest, unhealed wounds was almost worse now. Cara moaned and shook, and swore to herself she'd learn some new words, even if she had to make them up. All she needed was hard consonants, after all.

The astringent still burned. When it was done, she collapsed against Rodani, thankful she hadn't vomited all over him. The poor man put up with enough already, all on a volunteer basis.

As Baldar left the room, she crawled into bed, crafting and orange balls forgotten. And every shooting pain, every burning throb, brought her out of any semblance of calm acceptance.

"Lay down with me, aisu," she said. "Please."

He did as she bade. She rolled into him, into his warmth and scent. He wrapped his arms around her, cautious of her hands. "I don't know why you're so good to me," she told him.

"I do not understand why you think I would not be."

"Maybe I never met the right man until now."

"Maybe you needed to meet a guardian." He bent down and kissed her.

"Mmm..." She nuzzled his neck.

"Surely you are not ready for joining, kia?"

"Gods, no. Besides, I'm bleeding. Remember?"

"And remember that such things do not concern us in the guild?"

She opened her eyes to see him—two inches away. "You'd do that?"

"It would be an interesting experiment."

"Messy one."

"We have cleansers."

Cara smiled, despite all the pain. "Are you trying to make me laugh?"

"I concluded it might help."

She snuggled close. As the fire in her hands dimmed, she dozed lightly. Dreams stirred her, images of Rodani—and blood. She woke to the sound of a cart—Deremic bearing dinner.

Rodani rolled out of bed and escorted the servant to her sitting room, helping him lay out the meal. Cara followed them with the forlorn hope she could feed herself.

Dinner that evening was a trial she failed at, as her hands couldn't hold the flatware. By the time they finished, she was severely disgusted with the whole process, but at least she could feed herself with her fingers—however undignified it might be.

"I want to try again at crafting, aisu," she said, leaving the table to wash her hands. "If I can't quilt, I can't stay here."

Cara called up her meager patience, breathing deeply and relaxing her muscles. But every pair of shapes she tried to align together remained crooked, time after time after time.

"Maybe a day more," Rodani said with a glance. "Maybe two. Squeeze the balls instead."

Well, bored was better than being sent home crippled. She did as he bade, content for a while to watch him as he worked over his designs.

Smiling, she put down the balls and attempted to straighten the mess on her table. Unusable thimble in its case, scissors beyond the sewing machine, pencils in the box. Pins, now pins were a problem, just as much as the fabric shapes were. Too small to pick up with her swollen fingers, too oddly shaped to roll evenly. One made its way to the edge of the table and dropped in her lap.

Rodani leaned in close. "Au, kia, pins can be dangerous. You do not wish an injury in another important place." He reached out and, with exaggerated care, plucked the offending weapon from between her legs. Boldly, she pushed two more pins into her lap. Rodani's pupils spasmed. He leaned forward, staring into her lap.

Serano clattered into the doorway. "Tem'u."

Rodani looked over his shoulder. Serano nodded toward Hamman's room, some kind of high sign, obviously.

"A moment," Rodani said, and slowly, meticulously, he plucked the two pins out of Cara's lap. He held them up triumphantly, a warm look in his gaze. "I will return."

Rodani followed Serano out the door, passing by Deremic on his way to pick up dinner's leavings. "Yes?"

Serano walked across the hall to the rooms they shared together before he spoke. He sat down at the table in the center room and rubbed his palm across the wood. "You took Cara out to the stables nearly a week ago."

"Yes."

"Did Cara say or do anything inappropriate when you were there? Something that should be kept private?"

Rodani's eyes went wide. His ears flexed against his head in agitation. "Something very small."

Serano folded his arms across his chest. "Tem'u, you cannot take this into your own hands."

Rodani rose from his chair, looming over his partner. "Who?"

Serano remained seated, unaffected by the power implicit in Rodani's tense body.

"Tem'u, you must—"

"Who?" Rodani gripped the back of his chair.

"Is there no one in the stables who would take offense? No one who would be pleased to see you punished?"

Eyes flashing, Rodani clutched the chair and threw it across the room with a massive heave of his arms. It broke into pieces, clattering in a jumble against the wall.

Serano shot up as Rodani grabbed a chair leg from the broken pile. "You cannot."

Rodani twisted the wooden leg in his hands, growling.

"Think, tem'u. Think. If you hurt him, someone will notice. What will he say? That you beat him for no cause—"

"No cause?" Rodani exclaimed.

"In the Enclave's eyes, he had a right, and you know it."

Rodani raised his arm high in a circle and brought the wooden leg down on the rest of the chair. It snapped in two with a resounding crack.

"Look what he did to her!"

"That was an unintended consequence. Yes?"

Rodani shut his eyes and willed his body to calm. The rage, the rage he pushed deep inside, hidden where he kept everything else he'd endured.

"If you touch him," Serano said, "you will face punishment of your own."

Rodani's body vibrated in rage. A vision came of Cara, sitting on the privy, her bloody hands in the sink. Another vision of her wrapped in his arms, the stink of the astringent in his nostrils, as she screamed in agony.

No. Temi's sharpest knives, *no*.

Rodani glanced down at the chair he'd destroyed. "I thank you for the information," he said levelly.

"If I must, I will blatantly deny having this conversation." Serano sat back down at the table. "I will not let you bring me into this."

Rodani tapped the chair parts with the toe of his boot. "Understood." He walked into his bedroom and flopped on his bed, the bed he hadn't slept in for four nights—courtesy of Litelon.

Courtesy of Litelon, the screams of his bedmate rang in his ears. Courtesy of that bedamned adolescent, spying in the stables, he had to watch Cara struggle to feed herself and take care of her body's needs. Thanks to an idiotic stableboy who wouldn't know what to do with his hormones if a woman walked up and laid hands on him, Rodani was contemplating murder.

Serano leaned on the door frame. "What are you thinking?"

"What kind of excuses I could lay at the taso's feet for beating him bloody."

"Do not ask me to care for you when you, in turn, are bleeding."

"I will not."

"What will you say to Cara?"

That. That was the stone wall that stopped him cold. She didn't approve of physical punishments. But to let this go unavenged? Where was the honor in that?

Rodani rubbed his eyes with his palms, then stopped. Even that Cara couldn't do without pain.

Serano left the doorway. The outer door opened, then closed again. Rodani waited a time, then followed his partner out of the room.

This would take some preparation.

NINE

The night was cold, damp with the threat of rain. Both moons had set early. Rodani took this as a sign from Temi, even while knowing it for the superstition it was. He crossed the many yards of grass that lay between the two buildings, making his way to a pinpoint of light—a torch in the front door of the stable house.

The stables emanated their nightly noises. And their odors, Rodani thought as he stood outside the back entrance. A cold wind ruffled his hair and worked its chilled fingers through the gaps in his clothing. With more patience than he felt, Rodani worked his way past the door lock and into the stables. He stepped to the side and into the noisome darkness. Straw crackled underfoot with each step. Rodani swore at himself for his impatience and wormed his way more slowly along the walls.

The gloom deepened, swallowing him into the dark.

First, Stirachi's stall door, dimly seen as a dark shape outlined in darker black.

Andalia's stall, smaller. Another, then a fourth, and Rodani pushed gently against the door. The hinge squeaked, freezing him in place for a space of heartbeats. He pushed again, meeting no resistance. Inside was the darkest of darks. No shadow, no shape, no signal to a wary temichi full of righteous indignation.

Rodani waited out the minutes. A glimmer of outline appeared at the far end of the stall. He crept toward the unmoving shape that lay sprawled out on a cot in the corner. Rodani stood over the shape, flexed his fingers, and lunged. On the cot, Litelon fought the hand over his mouth and weight on his chest, but Rodani's strength won out over the boy's shock and panic.

Rodani pulled him to his feet, pulling him against his own body, the mouth still covered.

"Walk," he hissed.

Litelon took a hesitant step. Slowly, the shackled pair made their way outside. Rodani kept them going, making their way to a lean-to many yards distant. He threw the boy up against the side. The wooden wall snapped and cracked in protest. Litelon's pale, frightened face shook under Rodani's hand.

"Be silent and you will live. Scream and you may not." Rodani lifted his hand a fraction of an inch from Litelon's trembling mouth.

"A'tem," he whispered against the skin of Rodani's hand. He raised his own hand to grasp the guardian's. Rodani batted it away and dug his fingers more deeply into Litelon's night shirt.

"You have the honor of a rutting beast," Rodani said through clenched teeth.

"A'tem, please, honorable temichi, I have done nothing to—"

Rodani yanked at his shirt and slammed him back into the wall. "Lies," he said, and slammed him harder. "Lies." Litelon squealed in pain. "What were you thinking?" Rodani balled his fist and drove it into the side of his mouth. The skin on his lower lip split and began to drip blood. "What were you trying to prove?"

Litelon gasped deeply and shivered under Rodani's fierce grip.

"Talk ki'oto," he said, then slapped the young man for his refusal. Litelon's head thumped against the wood. "Talk!"

Litelon pressed his trembling body against the weathered wall and turned away. "I did nothing, a'tem."

Fury crawled up Rodani's spine, making his pupils pulse. He drew up his knee and ground it into Litelon's groin. The boy squealed. Rodani clapped his hand over his mouth.

"Tell me why," he growled as Litelon panted with pain. "Tell me what duty you thought you were performing, what justice you thought would be served."

Litelon took a deep breath. His face fell into mask, making him look years older. "I know you," he said grimly. "I know what you are."

Rodani's fist shot upward, connecting to Litelon's jaw. "You do not know me. You know only what the mewlings of ignorants say within your hearing." The next blow went to his eye. "You thought to punish me?" Then a heavy blow to the chest plate, shaking both their bodies. "To take from me what you could not have for yourself?"

A blow to his stomach doubled him up. Litelon coughed and retched. He sucked blood from his lip and squinted through swellings. "She deserves better," he spat.

Rodani yanked his cuffs from his belt and clipped them on Litelon's wrists, then spun him around and hung him from the hook attached to the eave of the lean-to. He grabbed the nightshirt.

"Do you know what your thoughtlessness did?" With a jerk, he ripped the shirt from Litelon's back. "Do you know what your childish arrogance caused her?" He pulled his belt from his pants with a whisk, raised it, and whipped it down across Litelon's back, forming a dark stripe. Litelon yelped and bucked against his restraints.

"Deserves better?" Rodani asked. Rage filled his body with strength as he dealt another blow. "You are a child," he said as the belt fell again. "You think you have a right to a woman," the belt whistled and landed with another sharp crack, "just because you desire her."

Litelon cried out with each lash, his body shaking as he hung by his wrists. Blood ran down his back in trickles.

"Silence," Rodani hissed, and laid one more stripe. Litelon writhed against the wall. Splinters worked their way into his chest as blood drained from his back. "Stop," he begged. "By the goddess, please!"

Rodani paused. "What goddess?" he said in a low voice and brought the belt down for the last time. "You should pay," he said as he slid the belt around his waist, "as Cara paid." He walked to the corner of the shack and came back with a bucket. "But instead," he whispered as he sat it down, "a stablehand should smell like the stables." He pulled the cuffs off the hook, threw the young man down, and unlatched the cuffs from his wrists. As the boy moaned, Rodani lifted the bucket and poured the fertile contents on his head.

Litelon swore and spat, batting at the sticky matter. Then he winced, curling inward with a moan. "They will know," he said hoarsely. "They will know who did this, whether I talk or not."

Rodani put his boot on a clean spot on his arm. "Remember my words, ki'oto." He strode away quickly, silent, anger and grief still smoldering. Cara would be indignant if she discovered what he'd done. But honor was at stake, and the punishment deserved. He could have willingly killed the boy, but there was a fine line between honor and revenge, and Rodani knew where he stood.

He spent what was left of the night in his own bed, unsleeping, and got up at first light. He showered and dressed in fresh, neat clothes. For this meeting, he needed every benefit he could muster.

***

The taso's quarters were quiet, but someone was always at the communications station outside. "I would see the taso," he told the guardian, "as soon as she is receiving." Rodani settled into a chair to wait while the message was passed.

After a short while, Arimeso opened her door and ushered Rodani into her office. It was chill with moisture and smelled faintly of incense. Kusik stood behind her in the doorway to their private quarters.

"A'Taso," Rodani said with a deep bow. "I beg private speech with you."

Arimeso lifted her eyebrows as if to chide him for his request so early in the morn. But she waved Kusik off and sat down at her desk.

At her gesture, Rodani sat across from her, leaning in to whisper.

"A'Taso," he said, choosing his words with care. "When you offered me the assignment to guard a'Cara, you told me to protect her, teach her, and help her. Yes?"

"Yes." She leaned back in her chair.

"A'Taso, as I have come to know her, I have come to feel that I also have a duty to her honor."

"And you come to this thinking through her bed."

Rodani winced inwardly. As always, his taso was sharp of mind and sharper of tongue. "No. Before that, a'Taso." He clasped his hands on his knees. "When I discovered her creativity, her intelligence, her sense of fairness, and her humor."

"And you bring this up before breakfast because?"

"A'Taso," he said, a jumper hesitating at the edge of a cliff. "I assumed the duty to avenge her honor last night. And I offer myself to you, to you alone, for judgment."

"What did you do?"

"A'Taso, I come to you only because I fear the keso would not have the wisdom to see what you would see."

Arimeso's eyes narrowed. She rose from her chair. In deference, Rodani rose also, clasping his hands behind his back.

"What did you do?"

He took a breath. "I punished someone."

Arimeso walked around her desk and stood in front of Rodani. "Go on."

"A'Taso, I was able to discover who it was that reported us to the Enclave, and thereby causing the terrible damage to Cara's hands."

A feigned casualness fell over Arimeso. It didn't reassure him. "And who gave you permission to take on this punishment?"

"It is not unknown for a temichi to do as honor dictates without direct orders."

"Insubordination."

"Initiative, a'Taso."

"Who?"

Deep. Goddess, her voice dropped deep. Rodani braced himself mentally. "Litelon," he said. "That is twice his adolescent cravings have nearly gotten her killed, a'Taso. Twice."

Arimeso now stood face-to-face with him, her grey eyes narrowed, pupils mere slits. "What did you do?"

Rodani squared his shoulders and lifted his chin. "I flogged him."

In a flash, Arimeso slapped him across the face. "It is not for you to decide such things." Again, she slapped him, creating a resounding crack in the room. Rodani held still. It wasn't the strength of her arm that twisted his innards.

"Now I know why you requested private speech." She stepped back, glaring with a ferocity that had quailed many temichin.

"A'Taso—"

"You dishonor yourself and the guild."

"A'Taso," now Rodani raised his voice. "The boy acted out of jealousy. He desired Cara and could not have her, so he chose revenge upon me." Rodani eyed his taso resolutely. "Cara paid the price."

"You should have come to me first."

"And have Kusik weigh in on the judgment?" he asked, his words sharp with bitterness. "I know better."

"I should hand you over to him, instead of standing between you two. I am beginning to believe I have done that too many times, already."

Rodani closed his eyes for an instant, willing himself out of his anger. "Before you do, a'Taso, I beg you, come with me to see Cara to see what I see and hear what I hear. Come smell the stink of the astringent and listen to her cry out in pain when it is applied. Watch her struggle to dress herself, to feed herself, to craft. Last night, she could not hold two pieces of fabric together. That impinges on your honor as well, a'Taso." He leaned forward, eyes wide. "Please. Come with me."

***

Hamman bustled into Cara's bedroom. "Up, up," she said with uncharacteristic urgency, opening Cara's wardrobe.

Jolted awake, bleary-eyed, Cara climbed out of bed. "What?"

"Baldar is coming early, and Rodani is bringing the taso with him."

"Why?"

"I do not know, and it matters not. Dress." The maid held out a tunic and long skirt combo in dark colors, with dark, flat shoes. Together, they managed to get all the proper limbs in the proper places without too many foul-ups.

"Do I have time to brush my tee—" She clenched her jaw. Temporarily forgotten was her inability to look after herself. Temporarily forgotten were the pain, frustration, and guilt. Too temporarily. Hamman ran a brush through her tangled hair, yanking past knots, curling it into a bun. For a moment Cara was taken back to childhood, the brush in her mother's hands. She ran a sore palm over her clothing, but that settled nothing—not creases, not nerves. Moments later, Hamman took a last look at her and scurried out of the room.

Bewildered, Cara had barely sat down at her worktable before voices came through Hamman's hallway. Baldar walked in... Rodani... *Arimeso*. Oh, gods, gods of the deep night. It was so clear that she was an alien in someone else's lands.

They crowded her doorway, tall, watchful. Her heartbeat shot upward. Even Rodani looked alien again. She swallowed a lump that threatened to choke her.

Baldar motioned, a slow roll of his fingers. She rose and approached the trio. They backed up and let her go to the facilities. Rodani followed, sitting on the seat. He pulled Cara to him as Baldar crowded in. Arimeso stood at the door. The physician held his hand out. Cara complied, and the torture began. He pulled at every half-healed wound, eliciting two curses and three gasps by the time he was done. Most of them opened, some remained stubbornly shut. Some he left alone.

But the bottle was different.

"Hand cup," he said.

And the liquid was different. It wasn't liquid at all, but a gel. It plopped in her hand and sat there, waiting. Baldar took a piece of cloth and rubbed the gel over Cara's hands, pushing it into the wounds.

Cara gasped. "It's worse! Ahhh!" She bucked in Rodani's arms as fire worked its way across her palm. "It's worse! Why?" She fought him, fought them both, but their hold on her body and hands stopped any escape. The fire deepened, burning hot in her skin. The gel stank. It clung to her nose and stung her eyes. Both began to run. Her hold on her voice let go, and she began to whimper, then scream.

"Cara, please," Rodani said as she struggled, and held her tighter. She kicked the sink and bit her lip. Rodani wrapped his lower legs around hers and bent his head to whisper. "It will stop, kia. It will stop. Be calm. Breathe."

"Noooo!"

Rodani spoke nonsense words in her ears, her interpreting failing again. Her eyes rained hot tears, and her nose leaked. Her lip was sore where she'd bitten it.

And Baldar reached for the other hand.

When it was over, Cara lay limp—up off the floor only because Rodani wouldn't let go. She saw nothing, heard nothing, felt nothing, except pain. Nothing existed of her body but her hands. They throbbed, burned like lava, and knife-like pains shot through them. She browned out. Light and sound faded. Someone whispered strange words in the background.

The world came back in bits and pieces. Baldar was gone. She felt Rodani's chest move against her shoulders, felt the weight of his arms around hers. His voice. His scent. Gods, that scent. Her brain clung to it with the fervor of survival. Safety.

"That was unexpected, a'Taso," he said behind her. "Baldar used something different on her hands. Her reaction was almost worse than the first time."

A touch against her fingers roused Cara. She jerked her hands back with a gasp. Arimeso stood over her, inspecting the re-opened wounds. Red, swollen, angry slashes. Stink. Fire. Pulsing waves of pain. Cara shut her eyes and moaned. "Hit me, aisu."

"Kia?" he asked, incredulous.

"Knock me out. Make me go dark. I can't do this."

Rodani held her closer, running a hand over her head. "It will pass. It has eased before, and it will ease again."

"Why was it worse?"

"I was too busy trying to assist you both to ask." Rodani shifted in his seat, jostling her. "A'Taso, I had thought to let her demonstrate her current inabilities, but I fear it unnecessary. You see the result."

Arimeso crossed her arms and stared down at the pain, the injury, the disability that sat before her. "I begin to regret my reaction this morning, Rodani."

"Will you intercede with the keso?"

She took one final look, then turned toward the hallway. "Yes."

The room seemed quieter, somehow safer with the taso gone.

Rodani slid Cara off his lap and held her steady. "Can you walk?"

"Maybe." She took a hesitant step, then another. "Bed," she whispered.

"No."

Cara whirled around, which was a mistake. Her head spun, taking her balance with it. "What?"

Rodani grabbed her arm to keep her off the floor. "I would offer to take you out of the manor today. A quiet day, a rest. We both need—some distance."

"A day just with you?" Cara closed her eyes and sagged. "You could convince me. But can I breathe some smoke first?"

"Yes." Rodani set it up, then pulled out his 'com. "Six, Five. Six, Five."

"Six."

"A favor, tem'u. Go to the stables and arrange for an old grandpa with a double saddle."

"Where do you go?"

"Tell me when you have it."

"Ninety-nine."

"Hamman," came the next call. "Food please. Enough for a day."

Soon, Rodani grabbed quilt and blankets, her coat, and her sketchpad and pencils—and on second thought, her red tide bag. Just in case. He hurried her across the room and grabbed a large pack that was sitting patiently in a corner. Out the hall, down the stairs, through a back corridor and short hall, and out the garage door. In the distance, she saw the reddish hide of an adult benatac.

***

For the fourth time, Litelon scrubbed his hair in a trough on the far side of the stables. The stink was no more than a memory of a scent, but the fiery slashes on his back burned humiliation into his brain. Rage fed the fire in his gut. He gritted his teeth as trickles of water ran down his bloody skin.

What should he say? What would anyone believe? Stories of crazed temichin were fireside tales for children—but realistically, everyone would assume he'd gotten something he deserved. He'd always been happier away from his own people. Animals had held his fascination from the time he learned to dig in the dirt for grubs. A new fascination with aliens was only a difference in degree, not in kind. The absolute unfairness of the world multiplied the turmoil in his innards and his anger at Rodani. Why him? Why an unbefitting, obviously unsuitable, dark-eyed mistake? Why not a future master of animals, lover of the different, the unique?

A whisper of footfalls swept up the corridor. Litelon froze with the horror of incipient discovery. Andalia peered over the door, her eyes wide in the dim early morning light. Litelon met her eyes for a moment, then lowered his head. The vet-second pushed through his door and looked over the long gashes on his skin. She strolled around him, as if inspecting a benatac ready for purchase.

"Last night?"

"Yes."

"Why?"

Litelon ducked his chin as deeply as it would go. "A misunderstanding, a'bi."

"With whom?" she asked, completing the circle. She touched a livid stripe.

Litelon shuddered. "Please, a'bi."

She circled again to face him. "With whom?"

Litelon took a deep breath, causing him to wince in renewed pain. "A temichi."

Andalia stared at his bent head, thoughtful, then left him to his misery. Litelon stole away to his tiny stall and crawled onto the prickly mattress. The cold air soothed his stinging skin, but the nerves underneath throbbed a drumbeat of misery.

It wasn't too long before another intrusion forced itself past his morose ruminations. Domendi, overlord of beasts and stablehands, crowded his bulky frame into the stall. Litelon pushed himself upward.

"Stop."

He froze, face to the pallet beneath his hands.

"Who did this?"

Litelon took a shallow breath, the only kind he could. "A temichi, a'ke." Slowly, he lowered himself back on the mattress.

"Why?"

Because the goddess detests me, of course. "A confusion, a'Domendi. A misunderstanding."

"Over?"

Litelon bit back a rejoinder, being well too aware of the man's penchant for teaching with his fists. "A female." *Yes.* That was safest. Such competitions were legion, nothing to be in a bother about. He tried to relax.

"A temichi's female?" The incredulity in his voice bled through even the worst of Litelon's miseries.

"I have that right, a'ke."

"And pay for your audacity with two days' inability to work."

"I will make it up to you."

Domendi remained standing behind him. Litelon's heart began to race. The man was never still, never lax in the demands he made on himself and on others, never without some semblance of motion. Litelon cringed inwardly, waiting for an explosion.

"I do not appreciate someone outside of my domain incapacitating my workers. You have two options, te'oto. Tell me who flogged you and why, or rise and work. Choose now."

Litelon began to speak.

***

Kusik shot up from his chair as the stablemaster and his workhand left the room. He pulled out his 'com and punched a button. "Five."

Arimeso stood as he began to pace. "Esuva, no."

"Five," he growled into the 'com, his arm shaking in a dark rage. "Five!"

"Kusik." Arimeso took his wrist in her hand as he passed by. "No."

Incredulous, Kusik stopped in his tracks. "This is why that demon-eyed spawn talked to you this morning?" He shook the 'com in his fist. "What did he say to you?"

"Esuva, I know why you are radiating, and I am sorry." She pulled on his arm in an attempt to re-seat him, but he resisted. His pupils pulsed erratically. "I am well aware that my interference discomfits you, but it is my prerogative. You cannot punish Rodani for this."

Kusik pulled his arm out of her grasp. "You cannot forgive this! He usurped my privileges, bloodied a half-grown stablehand, evaded my punishment by coming to you, and all because he broke one of the guild's most stringent rules! And he refuses to answer me, even now."

"I will not have my word rescinded."

Furious, Kusik pulled his hands behind his back and returned to his pacing. "A'Taso, you do not realize the damage you are doing here. To me, to your guild, to your house. You are letting one dishonored guardian ignore all my rules, all society's conventions, do whatever pleases him exactly when it pleases him, and you are protecting him while he does it!"

Arimeso slumped into her chair and lit a candle on her desk as Kusik made his way from one side of the office to the other. His formality was a warning to be heard, but not always heeded. She dribbled a pinch of incense over the candle flame, then inhaled slowly.

"Kusik, you are concerned with the short term, and it is something you are very adept at. But try to view the larger picture."

Still pacing, Kusik rolled his head back and forth on his shoulders, dropped his chin to his chest, then straightened.

Arimeso continued. "We do not have a choice in sharing this world with the human species across the hills. There is still an enemy up above us—"

"You do not know for sure."

"It is a valid assumption, and you know it well, my mate. We must do what we can to protect ourselves and our people if they return." She dragged one finger through the ashes surrounding the candle. "You excel at seeing and facing enemies that are near. But if they are out of the reach of your senses, you ignore them."

"I have more important things to worry over," Kusik said, refuting her.

"Then someone else must worry about the danger overhead. I have accepted that burden for my house, and I am doing what I can to prepare for it. In a house of artisans, there is little I can do." She ran her scented fingertip under the clip at her neck and sighed. "I have managed to create two very useful assets for the future Himadi House. The ambassadors who will govern it may find a cross-species affinity to be extremely useful."

"Or extremely disgusting."

"If they do, they are as blinded by unnecessary sensibilities as you are, and the Himadi venture may fail. I have more faith in it than that."

"Faith will not calm the tempers in my staff, nor assuage the rage of the Riverchildren."

"I will not be gainsaid, esuva. This is too important for the future. Leave them to ride their own path."

"And what do I do with a fractious guild?" he asked, exasperated.

"What you always do. But you must leave Rodani out of it."

Abruptly, Kusik left the room, leaving behind his taso calling his name. He stomped past the communications station and turned into his private office. Slamming the door behind him did little to mitigate the deep frustration that worked through the blood in his body and mind. Everything that he'd warned against was beginning to happen. Everything he'd foreseen was coming into view, and the most crucial visionary was playing her own hand to the limit of her imagination.

No sense. No base. No solid footing on ever-shifting ground. Duty was his best, firmest guideline, the one that gave him the stability to walk his path. But duty was being ground to pebbles between guild and mate, between taso and temichin. His head hurt; his honor twisted.

He walked out. Artisans scattered from his path. Up the stairs, down the hallway, he banged on the door to the servants' quarters. Deremic's face appeared, closed down and apprehensive.

"Where is he?" Kusik growled.

Deremic's pupils pulsed in agitation. Hyper-focused, Kusik ignored the emotion. "Where?" he shouted.

"He...he went out, a'Keso. A little time ago."

"Alone?"

"No, a'Keso. With a'Cara."

"Where?"

"I do not know, a'Keso."

Kusik spun around and banged on Serano's door. The knock went unanswered.

Frustrated beyond words, he stomped back to the rooms he shared with Arimeso, hoping he met up with her, and hoping he did not. Obedience had been drummed into him. But he had, in turn, knocked obedience into every temichi that ever had a place in his taso's house. If he didn't do something about this situation, some other temichi would. But it was his head onto which Arimeso's wrath would fall.

TEN

A few days later, Cara sat at her worktable, bored nigh to insanity. Baldar was insistent that she work on her hand strength and dexterity. Her mother would have said the same, she was sure. Cara upended the pin box for the tenth or eleventh time, scattering pins over the tabletop. She pinched her forefinger and thumb together with exacting patience, returning the pins to the box. In a sing-song voice, she spoke to herself. "Left hand, right hand, left hand, right, one by one by one."

Box full, she dumped them again and repeated the exercise with her middle finger and thumb, then more slowly with her other fingers.

Adjacent at the table, Rodani flipped through his flashcards, making notes and hunting words through the children's storybooks. "You should be thankful you are not Selandu, kia," he said, waggling six fingers at her.

His long, graceful fingers drew her attention. She'd felt both aspects of those fingers, in the heat of passion, and in the blaze of rage. Reaching out, she drew the digits to her mouth and kissed them. Laying them back down on the table as if they were unattached to a sapient being, she patted them, then returned to the pins.

Bemused, Rodani spread his hand and regarded it thoughtfully. "I had considered requesting your assistance in the maze this afternoon, kia. But possibly I should request something else."

His pupils were narrowed in concentration, his face a courteous mask. Cara smiled. "Can't you request both?"

"You are healed enough?"

She stared at her hands much as he had just done, but the bizarre array of half-healed wounds was all she saw. "They're beginning to hurt less. But they still don't work well."

"If you are willing to assist downstairs, you should wear gloves. There is little heat in our wing."

"I should."

Rodani headed for her armoire.

"Don't, please, aisu," she said. "I should do as much for myself as I can."

He unrolled his fingers in the gesture of acceptance, and she grabbed her jacket and gloves. The air downstairs proved Rodani correct. A mist rose from Cara's breath as he opened the doors to the maze. The splattered coat fit over her, but with the added detriment of making her look like a vagrant at a paint factory.

"Challenge me, kia."

"Challenge?"

Rodani brought out the Kishata and emptied it. Cara's eyes widened in dismay.

"You want me to use that?"

"Yes."

"Rodani, I can't shoot and move. You know that."

"It matters not whether you can hit me. The test is in my reactions."

"What if I hurt you?" Her voice raised in alarm. "I couldn't stand that!"

He pointed away, toward the stationary targets. "Fire it."

She aimed at a Selandu shape and tried to pull the trigger, but her hand didn't have the strength. The trigger remained in place, barely moving. She frowned and stared at the gun in consternation.

"No more than I expected," Rodani said, taking the gun out of her impotent fist. "Besides, it is empty. Come."

He walked to the maze. Cara followed behind, morose and confused. The little bit of pride she'd taken in her ability to use a pistol faded. An image of Kusik's face replaced the blank spot on the target she'd turned away from.

"All offense and no defense is no good practice, kia," Rodani said as he stopped. He handed the pistol back to her. "Run and hide as before. But this time, turn and pretend to fire at me. If I am facing you, I will see you and react. If somehow you are not in front of me, shout or make a noise."

Cara cleared her throat, unsure and unexpectedly timid. "I'm going to feel like a fool."

"Consider that you are helping me stay alive, instead."

"And that—is scary." She turned and entered the maze.

It was awkward but fun, like playing *police and perverts* with her brothers. Shouting, "Bang!" in the face of a seven-foot alien would be laughable if she weren't so scared of what he did for a living. Ever since Shurad, she'd been forced to remember the reality that the man she loved interposed his body between hers and death. It wasn't as comforting as it was supposed to be.

At the end of the maze, she was panting. Her respect for Rodani's reflexes had deepened, and her hand hurt from the weight of the gun, her palm stinging from the constant rub of the glove on her skin. Her hand burned, reminiscent of last week's torment.

They put up the equipment and walked back to her rooms. Cara headed for Hamman's room. "Ice bag, please?"

Quick on the task, Hamman brought it to her in the study.

"You are hurt?" Rodani asked her, eyeing the bag.

"Uncomfortable," she replied, wrapping her hand around the bulk. She settled back in the corner of the couch and put her feet on the tea table.

"I should apologize."

"No. I should probably toughen the skin. And I enjoyed helping you. Anything that keeps you alive, aisu."

"Except praying to Sela."

She stole a glance, catching his grin from the corner of her eye. "No evidence."

"For Sela, or answers to your prayers?"

"Yes."

Rodani laughed, a low rumble of mirth that brought an answering smile to her face. He reached for her ice-filled hand, lifting the edges of the bag to poke at the chafed wounds, inspecting the damage his practice had induced. Finished, he scooted closer, worked one arm behind her back, and the other one around her shoulders. He pulled her to his chest and rested his cheek on the top of her head. She sighed audibly, relaxing into his warmth. Something in her gut, something she hadn't known was there, unclenched and faded as he held her. Firelight flashed patterns on her eyelids.

After a time, Rodani's fingers worked their way under the hair at the back of her neck. They traveled up, down, and around, playing over her earlobes and down toward the front of her blouse. Cara smiled and tossed the ice bag on the tea table. She pulled herself away from the heat of his body and led him into the bedroom, lying down on the mattress with a smile.

Rodani crawled over top of her and took her hands in his. "You are horizontal again."

Cara laughed out loud and raised her arms and his to the headboard behind her, bringing him down nearer her.

"And so are you."

It was a heartfelt reunion, a symphony of passion. Languid and frantic by turns, they savored their senses and each other's bodies, intimacies given and gratefully received. Completion brought peace to them both, welcome after days of Cara's pain and the fear they had faced together.

Rodani shifted his weight and reached for his shirt. Without a word, he dug out a small package from a pocket and placed it on Cara's abdomen, letting his shirt drop behind him onto the floor.

It was small, this package, wrapped in nondescript paper and tied with a ribbon. Cara picked it up gingerly and looked it over, glancing at Rodani as she did so. He lay still on his side, head propped on his hand, waiting for her reaction.

With stiff fingers, she tugged on one end of the ribbon. It fell away, tickling her skin as it landed where the package had rested. With a flip of her fingernail, the paper began to unfold.

Inside lay a pair of handsomely crafted earrings, made of silver. Three thin curving vertical bars fell from a horizontal wire on top. They were separated at the bottom by two small spheres, the bars and spheres linked through by a thin chain. Each piece moved independently.

"They're beautiful," she managed to say.

He reached up and gently pulled the spiral ones out of her ears, laying them aside. "These have brought ill luck, kia."

"You're too intelligent to be superstitious." She felt for the holes in her ears and fumbled them in. "How do they look?"

"Tell me," he whispered.

"I will. As soon as we climb out." She rolled into his arms, obviously intending no such climb for a while. "Thank you, aisu," she said, heartfelt. "You amaze me."

"And you are a suede glove on a cold winter's day. I would wear you always."

"And you say you have no poesy."

Rodani's 'com crackled to life. "Five, Six. Five, Six." He fumbled for the 'com on the bedside table. "Five."

"Where are you?"

"In Cara's rooms."

A pregnant pause erupted from the 'com, followed by a droll rejoinder. "And that is the reason you forgot the guild meeting?"

Rodani swore and rolled off the bed, tossing the 'com beside her. The voice droned on. "On the very same schedule we've had for, tell me—how many years?"

He yanked his clothes on in unseeming haste.

"Are you in trouble?"

"Yes," he said, buckling his belt. "But I will survive it." He grabbed the 'com, ran a hand over his hair, and sped out Hamman's door.

Goddess of all, and Temi's tortures, he thought. Of the suite of stupid things he'd accomplished lately, this was the most obvious. Berating himself in muttered imprecations, he clattered down the stairs and sped toward the meeting room, pausing outside to breathe.

The room quieted as he entered. Every head but Serano's turned to follow him as he took his seat.

"And what," Kusik began, "is more urgent than a meeting on the day of solstice?"

"Very little, a'Keso."

Kusik strolled around the corner of the table. "And whatever this very little was, surely is a subject important enough to discuss at the table?" He bent over Rodani's shoulder and breathed in.

A frisson of fear crept up Rodani's back and lodged itself at the nape of his neck, shivering. The truth was perilous.

"A concern over Cara's injuries, a'Keso," he said, with a nonchalance he didn't believe. "The matter will be resolved."

Kusik strolled back to his chair. "You will stay behind to discuss this matter after the meeting."

"A'Keso." The shivering at his nape spiked. Disagreement was out of the question. He resolved himself to the impending punishment and attempted to focus on his job.

"With one exception," Kusik said, "there is little new about this gathering from past ones. Outlying residents will be seeing our pet human for the first time. There may be some consternation at the sight. Most will remain at a safe distance from her, but some may venture closer. You are to be alert at all times to untoward attitudes and activities.

"In another concern, the feud between the cobblers and the designers has levered upward, with accusations flying in all directions. If you see it coming, prepare to intervene. But for the taso's sake, refrain from taking sides. The guild needs no more accusations of partisan politics, even on such a minor matter. Much as some of us may wish differently, we are peacekeepers tonight, not agitators. Does anyone have any concerns?"

Deneban inclined his head. This was his first solstice gathering as a guardian.

"Yes?"

"Do we patrol the woods?"

"Is that an offer, or a rejection of the task, ki'tem?"

A mutter of laughter rounded the table. Deneban paled in embarrassment.

"It is not an objectionable question," Kusik continued. "But with the amount of intimate activity that normally occurs, the taso prefers our older members to do the patrols. We are less likely to be surprised at what we come across." He stared pointedly at Serano. "Or who."

Rodani glanced at his partner, improperly gratified that Kusik's scrutiny fell on someone else for a time. He was tired of being the prey for his keso's predatory tactics. Serano only lifted his chin, unbowed before the implied censure.

"Drink?" Naremit asked.

"Lightly or none at all." Kusik leaned over the back of his chair. "Do not let me find you otherwise. But remember," he continued, "especially you who are new, that we are not there to monitor others' choice of activities. Only to prevent harm. How many of you were not here at the last New Year's?"

Three people raised their hands.

"Consider this a practice session for the New Year's gathering in the spring."

Rodani's attention faded as his keso droned on. A decade used to the liberties his people took on the winter solstice and spring equinox, he'd heard most of it, and watched Serano go about his games with a debonair superiority. Old news, old vexations.

Cara was his main concern. No walls, no corners, no way to watch all five directions. It would not be a comfortable evening. But denying her the celebration would be a discomfort of another kind. What would she wish to do? What could he allow? Deflecting her frustrations to avoid a scene was an ongoing puzzle whose pieces morphed at every turn.

His attention came back as Kusik called the meeting to a close. The other guild members jostled out, leaving Rodani with no one to face but his keso, and Timan—who was playing witness.

Kusik shuffled his notes. It was a delaying tactic Rodani had seen before, and wished he'd never have to see again.

Kusik began to circle Rodani. "The jacket has been postponed."

"Postponed?"

"It failed its test. The bullet passed through the fabric. There was no stopping it."

"That is a major disappointment, a'Keso."

"You will, of course, have no thoughts but for her safety tonight."

"Of course, a'Keso."

"We would all be ashamed for her to die in our care."

Rodani's pupils widened. Truth, yes, but threat as well? A blue-eyed face flitted through his mind. "Yes, a'Keso."

The circling continued, slow, vulturous. How he hated that movement. It was nothing but a form of stalking, and the intimidation worked.

"You are becoming a problem, a'tem. Or a greater problem, to be accurate." Kusik eyed him with a savage glint as he passed by. "If the scent on your body didn't betray your lie, I might have believed your excuse."

Kusik stopped out of sight. "Did you not have time to wash afterwards?" The blow came from behind, a fist above the ear that dropped him to one knee. His eyes watered, his balance wavered. "You bring the stench of an alien to the heart of our group, Rodani." Kusik grabbed his hair above the clip and yanked his head back at a sharp angle. Rodani stared at the ceiling as his fear sped upward. His nostrils expanded with each panic-filled breath.

"Do you enjoy being a rebel?" The fingers in his hair tightened, locking him in a painful grip. "Do you enjoy flouting guild rules?" That voice, a hissing tenor he despised, neared his ear.

"Do you enjoy pretending you have status? And respect?" Kusik pushed him down onto the floor, pressing his face into the stone with the fist at his neck. "Leave the punishments of others in my hands, ki'oto. I am, after all, a master of the craft. You are an amateur."

He caressed the tip of Rodani's ear in mockery of a lover's touch. Rodani fought hard against expression on his face, swallowing his pain and dread.

"If I lopped off your ears, what would she caress?" Kusik whispered. "Or does she know what this touch does to a man?" He ran his finger over the tender convolutions. "Or are you even a man?"

Rodani held his breath, trembling under the threat. *Danger,* his brain screamed. Kusik of the deadly knives. Knives that could do unmentionable damage.

Kusik planted his boot in the middle of Rodani's back, pressing downward. "The taso is partial to you for some reason. She finds you strangely appealing." He pulled his fingers out of Rodani's hair with a savage twist, knocking his head against the floor. "Do not tempt me into disobeying her. You would not appreciate the consequences."

Rodani lay still on the stone as two pairs of boots left the room. In the resounding quiet, he struggled to his feet, shaking in delayed reaction. He closed his eyes and fought for stability, for the calm center that every guardian sought. Slowly, he made his way back upstairs.

ELEVEN

Serano was in residence, as Rodani thought he might be. Their rooms held a miasma of rage, invisible waves that radiated from his partner. The pain in his scalp throbbed in counterpoint.

"Stupid, tem'u!" Serano spat. "You are a perfect example of why that rule was put into place!" He planted his body in front of Rodani, nose to nose. "Have you no sense at all? No wit to see where you are headed?"

Rodani blinked slowly and focused on the angry face in front of him. "Step back, Serano. Leave it be."

"So that you can do what? Ignore me as you ignore everyone else but your adashi?"

"Step back, or I will prove the old adage that violence flows downward."

"Do it, Rodani." Serano's eyes blazed, pulsating rhythmically—excited, ready. "Do it." His fists clenched at his side.

Rodani sighed. "I have faced enough right now, tem'u. And I have to protect Cara tonight while you roll in the leaves with whoever will have you." He turned back to the door. "I will spend my time with the one who is pleased when I enter the room."

True to his hopes, Cara smiled at him from her worktable. But the smile, in turn, was replaced by a tightening around her eyes. "You look ill-used," she said.

"I am well enough, kia."

"Are you?"

He raised an eyebrow at her, a mute scold. It was not strictly proper to poke at a lie-that-was-courtesy. She waved her hand. "To humans, my comment would mean that I care, aisu. No offense meant."

***

By the time they arrived at the gathering outside, spits were turning with meat, tables had been set up and laden with food, blankets and quilts lay on woven mats on the ground, and a huge bonfire blazed in the center of the south lawn. Selandu from outlying areas were arriving as the darkening sky turned the color of fire. Wisps of clouds floated high, signals of Sela's favor, perhaps.

Cara and Rodani sat on blankets near the bonfire, enjoying the crisp air. Serano appeared in front of her with a plate.

"Thank you," she said, taking it from him.

Wordless, Serano parked himself off to the side. He looked at no one, resolutely refusing to acknowledge either her or his partner. Cara could sense the tension between them, but knew this was not the time to bring it up. A pair of legs passed in front of them, and a body hit the blanket next to Cara. It was Iraimin, drink in one hand, and plate in another.

Serano, watching the throngs of people pass by and around them, left without a word, passing out of sight in the crowd.

"He found his mark for the night?" Iraimin teased Rodani.

"Possibly."

"His mark?" Cara asked.

"This is Sela's night," Iraimin told her, waving her hand over the bonfire and past the cooks' tables. "We celebrate the birth of longer days with joinings."

"And Serano celebrates with a woman?"

Iraimin grinned. "Always, if he can find one available." She put her plate to the side and held her drink on her knees. "Why do we not see you with a woman, Rodani?" she asked. "Are you risheigi, as I am?"

Rodani turned to face the painter, eyes wide, pupils narrowed to merest slits, then looked away, watching the crowd with a frown.

"But you are mateless, a'tem. Why is there no woman by your side?"

Rodani turned back to her. "Number one, Iraimin, your intrusions are unwelcome. Number two, I have investigated the women of this estate who interest me, and found them inappropriate, or they found me the same. Number three, guardians do not make the best partners. Number four, I have twenty-five-hour duties which interfere with personal associations, and which, incidentally, put a woman at my side quite frequently."

Cara tucked her head into her arms and tried to make herself smaller as the silence lengthened between them.

"Forgive me, a'sel'ai," Iraimin said finally. "I meant no offense."

Night had fallen around them, shadows cast only by the wavering light in front of them, larger by far than it had been earlier. Logs, cool and black or red and glowing, lay crisscrossed inside the flames.

A cluster of small shapes bounced and tussled on the west side of the bonfire. Cara watched by the light of the flickering flames as the children played. Their shrill voices pierced the night air and overrode the sounds of adult conversations around her. A trio of women watched over them, but no one interacted with them.

One of the children, a small boy, stopped and stared at her, quiet and intent, the same one who had stared at her in her window. Others paused in their games. Cara bowed her head to them. The other children giggled, but the boy bowed back, unsmiling, showing a presence about him the others lacked. She walked away from the blanket and sat down near him, then opened her palm and drew her fingers inward. The boy thought for a moment, then approached her, squatting just out of reach. Soon, the others followed. They stood ranging about her in a semicircle, studying her. One of the caretakers came up, a wary expression on her face. Behind Cara, Rodani stood.

"No," he said. "There is no harm here."

The caretaker stepped back.

Rodani walked a few feet away, Cara noted, ready for—what? She folded her hands in her lap. "What is your name, ki'oto?" she said to the boy across from her.

The boy blinked several times in quick succession, and his ears twitched. "Ikemi. What is your name?"

"My name is Cara. My guardians and servants pronounce it Cah-rah."

Ikemi glanced over her clothing, and at her face, then leaned to the side to look at her hair. "You are small like a child, but your hair is dark like an elder. Which are you?"

Observant: the boy had a quick mind. Cara smiled. "I'm an adult. Not a child, but not an elder, either."

Some of the other children sat down near Ikemi.

"Why are you so short, Cara?" a girl in the second row asked her.

"Teshani!" a woman's voice called out from the side. "You have offended!"

The girl bowed her head, cowed by the public censure. "Forgive me, a'sel. I meant no offense."

"None was taken, ki'ono," Cara reassured her. "And because you meant no offense, I'll answer your question. The easy answer is that I'm short because my parents were short, and their parents were short, and their parents. My people grow that way. Children take after their parents, so I am short like they are."

She waited for that to sink in, hoping for another question from her fledgling audience.

It came.

"Is that why your hair is brown, and curly?" another asked.

"Yes." Cara smiled at the questioner. "My father's hair is brown, and my mother's hair is curly."

"And their skin is pale? And their eyes blue?"

"Their skin is pale like mine. My mother's eyes are blue, but my father's eyes are a beautiful green. I wished to get my father's eyes, but I didn't."

Surreptitiously, Ikemi scooted forward a hand of inches.

"Did you play with toys when you were a child?" another one asked.

"Oh, yes."

"What kinds of toys?"

"Dolls, stuffed animals, games of all sorts."

"Did you bring them with you?"

Cara smiled. "No. I outgrew most of them many years ago. I seem a child of ten or so, but I'm more than twice that in age."

Ikemi stretched his hand out along the ground, toward Cara's crossed legs. She thought she recognized an entreaty, but didn't wish to commit more improprieties. She was skating on thin ice, as it was. Suddenly, he spoke.

"Are your parents alive, a'sel?" His fingers made picking motions at the mat she sat on.

"Yes."

"Tell me about them?"

In a desire to emphasize similarities rather than differences, Cara stretched the truth. "Probably something like yours. They wish for me to do well in life and gain status, and to be honorable."

Ikemi looked down at his probing hand. "My parents are dead."

Cara sat stunned at the blunder she'd committed. She groped for the right words as the silence became deafening.

"I'm very sorry, Ikemi," she said softly as she grasped his outstretched hand with her fingers. "Forgive me."

With the touch of her fingers, Ikemi crawled from his place in the arc and into her lap. It was no wonder he begged for touch. Who took care of him? Who made sure he had what he needed? She folded the quilt around him as he tucked his head under her chin and his knees to his narrow chest.

"When did they die?"

"A year ago."

"You must be a brave boy to have survived without your parents for so long."

Ikemi gripped her all the harder for her words. She wondered if she'd pleased or distressed him. Stroking his hair with her hand, she rocked him gently within the confines of her arms and the quilt wrap.

"Do you have a mate?" one girl asked.

"Yes," Cara admitted. Her eyes shifted to the bonfire.

"Does he live in your land?"

Cara looked down at her side, then back across to her audience.

"He's certainly not here."

Smiles erupted from the faces across from her.

"What color is his hair?" "What color are his eyes?" "Does his hair have curls?"

This was getting entirely too close, and Cara could no longer obscure the truth if she answered. She laughed. "Enough about this man. Ask something else."

"Why do you laugh so often, a'Cara?" asked a small girl near the front.

"Humans have very strong emotions, ki'ono, and we're not taught to hide them."

"Why?"

"We can be offended, just as Selandu can. But we try not to hurt each other because of it. So, it's not necessary to keep those emotions under as much control as Selandu do." And to make sure, she added, "Neither way is right or wrong. Just different."

"Do you miss your home?" another asked.

"Yes," she answered truthfully. "But it's a great honor to be here. I hope to stay a long time."

"Do you have a taso, Cara?" asked a boy in the back.

"No. We choose leaders for Newydd Cenedyl."

"Do you take the taso's orders?"

Cara raised her eyebrows with that one. She'd better tread carefully. "While I'm here? Absolutely. When in my home, we take the orders of our leaders."

"If your leaders commanded you to kill Selandu, would you?"

Ouch.

"Such questions, ki'oto." She thought about it. And the fact that no adult listening had objected to his question meant she'd better think hard. "If Selandu were attacking my home, I would help defend it. But I would never betray Selandu to my people, or betray my people to the Selandu. That would be very dishonorable."

She hoped she'd weaseled out of that one.

"Cara," the girl who had asked her about men chimed in. "Will there be a war?"

This one she didn't have to think about.

"I truly hope not. No good human wants a war. It would be terrible for my people, and for yours, too." Cara shifted in her seat, uncomfortable with the direction the questions were going. "Forgive me. I'm growing tired. More questions will have to wait for another time."

Obediently, the children got up and moved off under the direction of their caretakers and parents. As Rodani moved forward, Cara unwrapped Ikemi. He was asleep. Rodani knelt down in front of her and looked at the child in her lap.

"Now there are two men in my life," Cara joked softly.

"Ikemi, and the one in Newydd Cenedyl?" he said, face masked of emotion.

"What man in Newydd Cenedyl?"

With a small smile, Rodani broke eye contact. It would not do for them to be caught in public, staring at each other across such a short distance. He picked Ikemi up and took him over to where the other children were being settled on the ground for the duration of the evening.

"Won't he be cold?" Cara asked, coming up behind them as Rodani gently put Ikemi on the blanket-covered mats. "Look. His jacket is too small for him, and his legs hang out from the bottom of his pants."

"He will be well for the time he is out here, Cara."

Rodani stood up and started to move away, but Cara looked down at the small sleeping form. Without a word, she unwrapped her quilt and covered Ikemi, tucking it around him.

"You will get cold," Rodani reminded her as he waited for her.

"Then I'll sit closer to the fire."

They hadn't walked far when a tall form stepped in front of them.

Demons and gods. "A'Taso," they said in unison.

Arimeso looked down at Cara from her tall height. "You have patience, a'Cara."

She could *not* look into Arimeso's eyes. Answering children's questions may or may not be an approved activity for an alien. "Thank you, a'Taso. The children seemed interested. I hope I didn't offend anyone."

"What is your interest in the boy?"

Cara felt a chill that had nothing to do with the cold air that was beginning to penetrate her awareness. "He reminds me of a human child, a'Taso. He's an orphan and was seeking comfort."

Arimeso studied her a moment longer, then turned and left. Cara hugged her arms against the cold; only for a moment did she regret giving her quilt to Ikemi. They headed back toward the bonfire.

As they returned to sit next to Iraimin, Cara noticed a new item in front of the blaze. It was a small pot on a stand with a towel draped over the rung of the stand. As she watched, a man walked up to the pot and took a handful of a powdery substance from inside. He held it for a moment, then turned his back to the fire. Muttering something unintelligible to human ears, he tossed the handful over his shoulder into the fire. Turning quickly, he watched the powder hit the fire. It sputtered a little with blue and purple flames, then resumed its normal color. As he left, a woman stepped up to take his place. She repeated his gesture, with a plea for good health for her children. The powder shot into little sparks, then colored the nearby flames. Cara turned to Rodani in puzzlement.

"What are they doing?"

"Making entreaties to Sela."

"Why?"

"It is a custom. When one has survived a difficult situation during the year, one lights a fire and wishes for better times ahead. The reaction strength of the powder in the fire is proportional to Sela's acceptance of the wish."

Cara turned to Iraimin. "Did you wish, yet?"

"Yes."

"May I ask what you wished for?" she said.

Iraimin waved her hand in a tossing motion, dismissal of her concerns. "I wished for more recognition of my work, Cara."

"Your work deserves it," Cara agreed. She then turned to Rodani.

"Will you make a wish?"

He glanced at her, then rose from the mat and stepped to the fire. Taking a handful of the powder, he turned his back to the warmth of the flames. He stared into his palm for a moment, then said simply, "A safe and successful year." With a swift movement, he tossed the powder over his right shoulder and turned. Several sparks flared, along with the change of color. Rodani wiped his hands on the towel and returned to Cara's side.

"A respectable showing," he declared.

Iraimin smothered a disparaging smile and turned away.

Cara watched others come up to the fire and make their wishes. Only a few got more than a moment of sparks and colors for their efforts.

As more people came and went for wish-making and more couples strode by, a fey mood swept through Cara like the cold wind. "I'll do that, too." She began to stand up.

Rodani grabbed her arm and pulled her back down. "No. Where is your sense? Think."

Cara sighed heavily. "Rodani—" she began.

A gunshot blasted the peace of the night. A log in the fire split and broke, scattering flames on the ground. Rodani shot to his feet, grabbed Cara in a reckless clutch, and began to run. His legs pumped;

his feet pounded the dirt. From behind him came the sounds of chaos as he shifted her to his shoulder.

"Go!" Timan shouted, running to catch up with Rodani's frantic race for the doors.

He yanked them open with a massive pull and dashed inside. He slowed as they reached relative safety indoors, his breathing deep and harsh. Then he dropped Cara on her feet and spun her around, inspecting her clothing.

"No blood I can see, a'Biso." He picked her up again, ready to maneuver if necessary.

"The goddess grant."

Timan took the lead and stopped at every corner, swiveling around with his gun in the air. They took a back way up to the corridor that led to her rooms.

Setting her on her feet, Rodani stopped at her door, studying it in the oil light, checking for unauthorized entry. Satisfied, he unlocked the door and went inside, pistol up and lethally ready.

In a few moments, he was back.

"Clear."

He pulled her in. Cara just had time to thank Timan for his escort before the door was shut and bolted. Rodani double-checked the window coverings in every room, then turned a lantern on broad beam. "Take off your jacket."

She slipped it off and tossed it on her worktable.

Front and back, no blood. No holes in the fabrics. Rodani's shoulders slumped in relief. The pair looked at each other.

"Close," she said.

"Far too close," he amended. His eyes narrowed. "Now do you understand my *no*?"

"Yes," she admitted, chagrined.

His pocket-com beeped from its place inside his jacket. "Five."

"Are you hurt?" It was Serano's voice.

"No."

"Cara?"

"No. We might have wished, though," Rodani growled, "that you had waited until Cara was safe before making your trek into the woods."

There was a moment of silence. "Yes."

"Ninety-nine."

Rodani clicked off the 'com before Serano had a chance to continue. Prudent for once, Cara kept silent. She shivered in the cold air, retrieved a sweatshirt from the armoire, and met him in the study.

"Any idea who that was?" Cara asked. "If they'd aimed right, I would have been dead."

"I am not certain at this time, kia. But it was probably someone from a neighboring estate, or one of the crofters at the periphery of Barridan."

Cara crossed her arms and planted her feet wide. "Someone who simply wished an innocent human dead."

"Unfortunate, but yes," he replied.

"I guess I shouldn't have gone out."

"We," he corrected her.

"So, I don't need to obsess over it?"

"Not obsess, no. But your safety should never be so far from your awareness. I would appreciate you making my duty easier, not more difficult." He knelt in front of the fireplace, hands busy over the grate. In a few moments, a flame sputtered up. He stood up and turned to her.

"The weather has turned. You will be warmer on the couch than in your bed. I can sleep on the floor."

"On the floor?"

Rodani frowned. "I will not leave your quarters tonight."

"Did I say I wished you to? But if you think for a moment I'm spending the whole night with you in this room, *separate*, aisu, you'd better think again."

He eyed her cautiously. "The floor is too cold for you, yes?"

"Can you carry the mattress in here?" she asked, turning toward her bedroom. "With the couch out of the way, it'll fit in front of the fireplace."

"Kia, you are scandalous."

"Why? Who will see?"

"And if someone makes another attempt on you in the middle of the night, and your rooms fill with security staff?" Rodani retorted.

"They know already, don't they?"

Rodani refused to meet her eyes. "Only three." Turning back to the fireplace, he took the long poker and shifted the logs on the fire. The flames crackled and spat. The fire grew.

Cara's surety evaporated in the silence. "Rodani."

Poker still in hand, he glanced back at Cara.

"Are you ashamed of your affinity with me?"

Laying the poker against the fireplace, he turned back to her. "No, kia. But others think I should be. It has been a disturbing day."

And it had, in more ways than she realized. "Then let's end it more pleasantly than it began, a'oto."

Rodani tended the fire in silence.

Against his continued stillness, she headed for the bedroom. With much tugging and pulling, her damaged hands managed to shift the mattress an inch or so. Around the other side, she planted her feet against the dresser and pushed. Another inch of frame appeared. Around to the first side she went, trying again to pull.

A gentle pluck on her arm interrupted her futile efforts. "Allow me," Rodani said. A lift and a pull brought the mattress to an end-up position. He tugged it off the bed and dragged it through the workroom. It fell with a muffled thump in front of the fireplace, blowing the flames away. They returned with renewed vigor.

In a few moments, Cara reappeared, pillows and quilts in hand. Slipping off her shoes, she tossed the armful of items haphazardly onto the mattress and fell down amongst them. She turned on her back and stretched invitingly.

Rodani stood at the foot of the mattress, watching her antics. "And if I choose to sleep in the chair tonight?"

She stared up at him. "Then you'll miss out on the rest of the night's entertainment. In fact, you may have to listen to me entertain myself."

Rodani's eyes widened in astonishment. Cara laughed and rose to her knees, pulled off the sweatshirt and, with effort, unbuttoned all but a few strategic buttons.

Rodani knelt down and pushed her onto her back.

Magic surrounded them, the magic of shared needs and desires. The exhilaration for life that follows a brush with death, cold winds, flickering firelight, and the fabric of affinity set a mood that was difficult to deny. The temptations of lovers on the sly wove a braid of passion that bound their bodies and minds in a formidable embrace. They romped through their increasing repertoire of moves, heading toward licentious abandon as urges that could not be denied overtook them.

And for the first time since their intimacies began, as the world closed around them and their senses spiraled inward, she crested beneath him instead of to his side.

He thought he'd already heard the strongest of her responses.

He was mistaken.

TWELVE

Not yet were Cara's hands back to normal. More than a week later, her dexterity was still a thorn in her patience, and gripping strength was ghostly. The rotary cutter in her hand was a dangerous weapon without constant vigilance. She'd had to reduce the number of layers of cloth she could cut at once, adding extra time and effort to every quilt in an effort to keep her fingers attached.

Whispering erupted in the maids' corridor. A deep voice, and a higher one. A child's voice. Cara took her weight off her arm and clicked the rotary cutter's safety cover over the blade, leaving the ruler carefully positioned on the fabric.

Hamman's soft voice drifted through Cara's bedroom, admonishing. Boot steps cut through her words. "Now you mustn't take too much of a'Cara's time, ki'oto. She is very busy." A small form stepped into the doorway, eyes downcast to the floor. Too-short pants rode above the ankles. A thin shirt clung to his frame.

Cara stood. "Ikemi?"

The little boy dared a glance in her direction and took a few steps forward. Rodani crossed his arms and leaned against the doorframe as Cara came around the table.

"He has been asking to see you since the gathering, Cara. I thought it would not displease you."

"Of course not!" Cara held out her arms to Ikemi and walked toward him. Slowly, he came forward and stepped into her embrace. She folded her arms around him and rocked him gently.

"Are you hungry? Thirsty?"

Ikemi turned his head just enough to catch Hamman's eye. She unrolled her fingers.

"Yes," he whispered.

"Biscuits, tea, milk, please, Hamman. Whatever's appropriate." Cara let go of one arm and coaxed Ikemi into the study, and onto the couch next to her.

"How do you fare?" she asked gently.

"I am well."

"Is there anything you need?"

"No."

"If you think of anything you need, Ikemi, tell me."

"Thank you," he said softly.

"I did not allow him here to ask you for favors, Cara."

Cara glanced at her guardian, who had decided to occupy the comfy chair. "I'm sure. But he can ask for what he wishes, and I'm free to say yes or no."

Ikemi's large grey eyes studied her; his expressive face held a childlike concentration.

"Ikemi," Rodani said sharply. "Do not stare."

Immediately, he dropped his gaze.

"I'm different, Rodani," Cara said mildly. "I deserve a stare or two. You can look at me as much as you wish, Ikemi, until you get used to me."

Rodani leaned back in the chair and crossed his arms, scooting his feet under the tea table with a bump to his shin. Ikemi fingered the quilt that lay over the couch.

"Are you cold?"

"No," came another whisper. Ikemi ran his palm down the design and picked at a loose stitch.

On impulse, Cara held out her hands to him. He stared at them a moment, then crawled into her lap. She wrapped her arms over him and ran a hand up and down his back.

From the side, Rodani fixed his eyes on the pair.

"What did you do today?" Cara asked. She felt down the length of his arm and onto the wrist that hung out from the shirt sleeve. It felt cool.

"Lessons," Ikemi told her.

"Rodani." Worry diverted her attention from the answer. "Does he feel cold to you?"

He got up and reached around from behind the boy, placing his hands on the slender neck, then his arms. "Some," was the assessment.

Cara pulled the quilt off the back of the couch and draped it over the boy. He curled his head into her chest and wrapped his arms around her waist. "Don't fear to offend me, Ikemi. If you need something, ask."

Ikemi remained silent against her.

"Say: 'Yes, Cara,'" she prompted.

"Yes, Cara," he replied. Hesitation was heavy in the childlike voice.

"What lessons did you have?"

"Numbers and nature, letters and pictures."

"How old are you?"

Ikemi dropped his chin, rubbing his cheek against her chest. His arms flexed around her waist.

"How old are you?" Cara repeated quietly.

"I do not know," he whispered.

Her eyes grew wide. She checked sideways; Rodani's expression never left neutral. "He is approximately five."

"Who watches over you?"

"Midalic."

"Who is Midalic?"

Ikemi plucked at her blouse with nervous fingers.

"She is a nursery assistant," Rodani interjected into the silence.

"Does she treat you well? Does she give you what you need?"

More silence. Then, "Yes."

Cara began a slow burn. She clamped down on her temper, loath to disturb the boy's fragile peace. "Rodani, escort us to the clothes storage, please."

He took a deep breath in the face of her change in temperament. "This is not your concern, Cara."

"Take us."

He pursed his lips. "Food will arrive soon."

"Is that misdirection or denial?"

"Postponement."

Cara relaxed against the back of the couch and caressed Ikemi from atop the quilt. She drew her hand up around his neck and into the hair, dislodging his clip. It fell to the floor with a metallic rattle. Ikemi's baby fine hair spilled out onto his thin shoulders.

Rodani retrieved the clip and sat back in his chair to study it. He fiddled with the catch and the hinge, bringing them close to his eyes. "It needs repair." He rose and went into the workroom.

Cara let out a sigh and ran her fingers through Ikemi's hair, snagging on tangles. He seemed content to let her touch, making no movement or noise to disrupt the motherly attentions. They sat curled in peaceful repose, lulled by shared warmth, a crackling fire, and the distant rattle of tools.

Hamman walked in, preceded by a tray, and sat it on the tea table. It was laden with a variety of snackables tempting to a child's palate. Ikemi shifted in his cocoon enough to give it a once over. Cara let go of him. He climbed off her lap to investigate.

"Hamman."

"A'Cara?"

"Who's responsible for orphans?"

The servant's gaze flickered from Cara to Ikemi and back. "We have only the one, a'Cara. The taso assigned someone to his duty."

To his duty. That, Cara fumed, just about summed it up. "And what if the duty is inadequate?"

Hamman's pupils pulsed, then she looked downward. "That would be the nurserymaster's responsibility, a'Cara."

"Or the taso?"

She hesitated. "Yes, if necessary. All unsolved problems go to her."

"Thank you, Hamman."

Rodani came in as Hamman left. Ikemi waited patiently, hands in his lap, eyes on his new benefactor. Cara turned to him.

"Eat," she admonished gently.

His eyes grew wide. He ducked his head. "The...the woman eats first," he stammered.

Gods. She'd forgotten. Rather than tromp on one more bit of Selandu etiquette, Cara took a square of sandwich and nibbled on it, then smiled at him.

He dug in with the first bit of childish gusto yet displayed. Cara uncovered a glass of milky tea and set it by his hand, then poured two cups of spiced tea. She handed one to Rodani. He laid the repaired clip on the tea table and took the cup from Cara.

"Manners, ki'oto," Rodani chided the boy.

Ikemi dropped his sandwich and shoved his hands back in his lap, pupils round with embarrassment. He stared longingly at the tray.

"Go ahead," Cara said. "Use what manners you know. We can work on better ones."

Ikemi retrieved his sandwich in one hand, and dug into a cup for a handful of bechel nuts with the other. The sandwich made it into his mouth scarcely a second before the nuts.

"Ikemi." Rodani's voice went a few notes deeper and a level sharper.

Nuts ricocheted across the tray. Ikemi clenched his empty hands together and stared at the plate.

Cara laid her hand on his arm. "Slow down, ki'oto. No one will take the food away until you're finished."

When she let go, Ikemi reached once more for a sandwich square, and scooped a piece of shishi with his spoon.

"One item at a time, Ikemi."

"Please," Cara said to Rodani. "Next time is soon enough for instruction."

Ikemi, regarding his two acquisitions, relinquished his hold on his sandwich to deal with the fruit. Rodani leaned back in the chair and brought his teacup to his lips, crossing one ankle over the other knee. He lapsed into silence.

Ikemi continued his meal. Together, he and Cara marveled at the changing consistency of bread as it got wet and laughed over the squirting behavior of shishi. Ikemi came alive under her childlike influences. He smiled and chatted, becoming animated in the warmth of her interest. Finally, he slowed his rate of consumption, and reached for the tiny, frosted candies he had saved for last. He cleared an area and dumped the bowl onto the tray, then lined the candies up by color. Each color merited its own taste description, with a request for Cara to try it and agree.

"Cara," Rodani interrupted their discussion.

"Yes," she replied, head bent, fingernail lining up the candies that had gotten pushed out of line.

"Cara."

Belatedly, she looked up.

Rodani flicked his eyes into the workroom and got out of his chair. Cara followed him out of the room, gathering her strength for battle.

"Kia," he turned to her, "you are not the child's keeper."

"Someone needs to be. It's obvious he's being neglected."

Rodani's pupils narrowed. "That is a harsh judgment."

"But an accurate one. Look at him. Was he acting as children do in the gatherings? Or when I answered questions? Look at how he's dressed."

"He is a quiet child."

"But why is he quiet, aisu? That's the question. Take us to the re-use storage. And bring him to me for a while at least, each day."

Rodani sighed deeply and looked away in thought. "I will not gainsay you," he replied mildly. "The child needs clothes, and attention. But you would regret getting into a power struggle with Midalic, or the rest of the nursery staff. They are very territorial."

Cara planted her fists on her hips. "Aren't we all? And Ikemi just became my territory."

"Kia. Before you decide all on your own to take this situation in your hands, allow me time for reconnaissance. I will not force an issue for you that causes nothing but trouble."

Cara's eyes flashed. "Helping a neglected child is nothing but trouble?"

"Tsss. Calm yourself. My words were poorly chosen." Rodani glanced over her head and into the study. "I will help you to a point of reasonableness. Not beyond. And not to the detriment of your own duties here."

"What's reasonable?"

"I do not yet know. I simply wish to warn you against invalid assumptions and rash actions."

Cara laid her hands on his waist. Her little fingers rested on his weapons belt. "Would I heed that warning?"

Rodani curled his lips into a smile and ran a finger down her cheek. "You should continue your crafting." He walked past her and back into the study. "I must return you to your room, Ikemi," he told the boy. "A'Cara has work to do."

His face fell into distant blankness. "A'tem," he whispered. Candies, now untouched, sat forlornly on the tray.

Cara's heart clenched at the return of his former shy demeanor. She crouched at his side. "Rodani will bring you back to see me tomorrow, Ikemi. Would that please you?"

A light came back into his eyes. "Yes," he said softly.

"Take the candy with you, if you wish. Tomorrow we'll have lunch together." She took his hand and drew him up, then wrapped her arms around him in a farewell embrace. The strands of his hair fell over her hands. Rodani retrieved the boy's clip and handed it to Cara, who fixed it back at the nape of his neck.

Carefully, Ikemi gathered the precious candies in hand, then hesitated.

"Can he take the bowl?" Cara asked Rodani.

"Yes, if it is returned in due time."

She held the bowl out for him to pour in his treasure. Not one candy fell outside of it. Ikemi clasped it to his chest, as if it meant all the world to him, and took three or four glances back at Cara as Rodani led him away.

She sat back down at the worktable and stared at her fabric shelves. Was he warm at night? Did anyone tuck him in? Gods, she couldn't adopt him. Rodani was right. She had duties here. But it didn't stop her from feeling sorry for the boy.

Mindful of conflicting priorities, Cara returned to cutting her fabric—at least until Rodani came back.

"The inquiry is tomorrow."

She laid down the cutter with an audible clunk. "Already?"

"It has been two weeks." He sat down in his chair at the worktable.

"What happens?"

"Three people will sit on a panel to judge the issue. The taso and the selaso will be on it. Two guardians are arriving tonight from Tendiman. One of them will sit on the panel as well. The temaso is a man you should be cautious with, but not frightened of. He is the highest ranked of us all, aside from the guild council. He belongs to no taso; his allegiance is to the guild itself. His name is Chendal. The other guest is his partner."

Cara thought back, back to a desperate run from a mama benatac. "'By Chendal's eyes!' you said."

"Yes. It is one of a handful of compliments to the talents he was born with, and his mastery of guild skills."

"And I don't need to fear him?"

"Not unless you threaten him, kia. And you will have no reason to do so. Yes?" Rodani looked at her with a bit of iron in his will.

She chuckled. "Yes. But then what happens?"

"It is simple in form, sometimes complicated in delivery. I present your side of the issue. Kusik, or someone he designates, presents his side. Witnesses are interviewed by the judges. Then the judges send us out and make their decisions in private. We are called back to hear it."

"What if they disagree? Does it have to be unanimous?"

"No. Two of three decides the case."

"And if I lose?"

"Then Kusik goes unpunished. You are not, in turn, punished, because you are not accused of wrongdoing."

"Could I be?"

Rodani sat in thought, his fingers absently spinning a pencil. "You might. But likely if you were, someone would have said so by now."

"And if I win?"

"Arimeso, as taso over both him and you, decides his punishment."

"What would that be?"

"I hesitate to judge, kia. It could be one of many things."

Cara watched her lover with an intense focus. His head was bent over the table, his own focus on the pencil rattling under his fingers. His legs were drawn up under the chair, which was unusual when he wasn't crafting. His face held the bland expression she'd come to associate with worry, or the distance he'd kept in the beginning of her stay. Neither option was a balm to her nerves.

"Do you know what you'll say?"

He hesitated, eyes still on the pencil. "Yes. For the most."

Cara leaned forward, resting her hand on his forearm. "Aisu."

Finally, he looked over at her.

"Whatever happens tomorrow, whatever the judgment, I want you to know one thing."

"That is?"

"Nothing will change how I feel about you." She shook his arm gently. "You've always done what you could for me. No one can ask more than that."

Rodani lifted her hand and placed a careful kiss on her scarred palm.

THIRTEEN

The next morning, Rodani appeared at her bedroom door. His face was again masked of all expression, his voice low and over-controlled. "It is time, kia. Everyone is assembling."

Reluctantly, Cara dressed befitting the seriousness of the occasion. Long skirt, house shoes, high-necked blouse, understated jacket. Her hair showed Hamman's careful handiwork. The only curls out of place were the unruly short ones that refused to be reined in.

Rodani laid a hand on her shoulder and turned her to face him. "Unless you are asked a question directly, do not speak. And if asked, say less rather than more. Allow me to present your side of the truth."

Odd way of putting it. Subtleties of Selandu honor indicated truth was never black or white, but always a fuzzy boundary. On whose side, Cara wondered morosely, did the fuzz lie? Hers? Or Kusik's? Time would soon tell. She took a deep breath and a firm grip on her temper and followed Rodani downstairs into Arimeso's antechamber. He left his weapons with the guard on duty.

Timan answered the knock, then led them through Arimeso's office and into a larger room on the right. A table paralleled the far wall. Two short rows of chairs ran perpendicular from it on either side. In the middle was an open area. Along the near wall on either side of the door was another set of chairs.

Rodani and Cara walked up to the table. Facing them was the taso, as expected. But on her right was not Kusik, but Kimasa, the high priestess. On Arimeso's left was not Timan, but another man she didn't recognize. Chendal, he must be. Not yet middle-aged, and commanding in his dignity. One of the best ever, Rodani had said, the type that is born once a century. He would rule the guild one day.

Timan took a standing position behind the taso. A gold-clad priestess stood behind the selaso. And another guild member stood behind Chendal—a woman—his partner, Shisa.

"A'Taso," Rodani said in a carefully formal greeting. Cara echoed the greeting in form and formality, as Rodani had advised her to do.

"A'Selaso," he said. Then, to the guild's chosen representative. "A'Temaso." Cara repeated the greetings.

Rodani turned and took a seat in the row of chairs to his right. Cara sat next to him nearer the table, willing herself into a calm barely contained. Kusik appeared through another door and walked to the table, greeting the trio in the same manner as had Rodani and Cara. He took a seat in the opposite row. Only then did Cara notice the back wall and its seated occupants in front of it.

Good gods. There were Hamman and Deremic, and Serano. Baldar. He was the only anticipated one. Cara closed her eyes to the sight, shamed and embarrassed to have brought these people into an inquiry of such magnitude. If only she'd held onto her reason. If only she'd given the situation time to develop. Time to gain knowledge she had so desperately needed.

"This inquiry is begun," Arimeso spoke into the silence. "A charge of dishonor through abuse of power and privilege has been brought against the keso of this house, a'Kusik." She turned to her left. "Security Fifth Rodani, you have brought these charges before me. Rise and state your case."

Cara felt rather than heard Rodani's slow intake of breath. He stood and angled himself toward the head table, bringing his hands around behind him.

"A'Taso," he began. "My adashi, the human, Cara, had been brought into an Enclave inquiry with me. Being uninformed about the Enclave and its code of silence, as well as the nature of the inquiry, she feared greatly for her own life and mine. She saw escape as her only honorable option. She fled into the south woods, where, before recapture, she ran afoul of a camabarin tree. Her hands were sliced open in thirty to forty places. For almost an hour, those wounds were left untreated, and three-quarters of that hour was purposeful neglect. By the time she received treatment, her hands were swollen and inflamed. The result is clearly a long-term disability in their use. Possibly, it is permanent." He stopped for a moment to let the thought linger in the judges' minds. "I consider this neglect a cruelty, a'Taso, perpetrated on an innocent and ignorant guest in your eminent household, by a keso who does not wish her here. One who has been adamant, a'Taso, against your more enlightened judgment, that she should never have been allowed onto this estate. Therefore, my charges."

"A'Kusik," Arimeso addressed her keso. "Your answer?"

He rose. "I followed established procedures and proprieties at all times, a'Taso. Honor forbade me deviating from those procedures because an alien artisan had injured herself in committing a dishonorable act. I deny the charges."

"Be seated."

Rodani and Kusik sat back down.

"A'Selaso," Arimeso said to the regal woman to her right. "There is need of your recollection."

"A'Taso." Kimasa faced the assemblage. "Two weeks ago, a resident of this estate approached me with the possibility that Security Fifth Rodani had entered into a private affinity with his adashi, and with a concern that she had not freely chosen the affinity. By law and custom, I convened an inquiry."

"Who did you call?" Arimeso asked.

"Rodani and Serano, Hamman and Deremic, and a'Cara herself."

"And the consensus?"

"The consensus, a'Taso, was that there was no coercion, no force. And therefore, no dishonor."

"All witnesses are seated in this room," Arimeso noted. "Is there dissention to the selaso's conclusion?"

A welcome silence greeted Cara's ears.

"A'Kusik," came the next prompting. He stood again, facing his taso.

"Relate your experiences with a'Cara before, during, and after the inquiry."

Kusik glued his eyes on Arimeso. "I went into her room, a'Taso," he said without preamble, voice firm in his personal convictions, "before anyone else but Serano had returned. She was polite upon my entrance, but evinced fear at the nature of my duty. She called to her servants in preparation for the inquiry and, hearing no answer, anxiously asked upon Rodani's whereabouts. Of course, I did not answer. I directed her out into the hall.

"I saw her into the holding room and returned to the antechamber. Approximately a quarter of an hour later, the acolyte approached me in obvious distress. The human had disappeared from the holding room, and there was a chair under the window. I inspected the room and immediately called for my guardians to find her. After approximately twenty minutes, they reported finding her in the woods. She was returned to the Enclave. I immediately brought her before the selaso, who had been waiting more than half an hour."

Chendal spoke for the first time, his voice a melodious tenor, his eyes light grey. "Were you aware of the human's injuries and their nature, a'Kusik?"

"Yes, a'Temaso."

"Are you aware of the effects of camabarin toxin?"

"Yes, a'Temaso."

"Why did you not take her to the physician instead?"

There was not a flinch or flicker to Kusik's eye that Cara could see. "At the time, I was not aware of the issue of timing, a'Temaso. I followed custom."

Chendal's expression remained remote. He waved his fingers.

"I brought the human into the selaso's audience chamber," Kusik continued. "She managed a bare minimum of propriety until she stubbornly refused to answer an entirely appropriate question, I disciplined her. She became more proper but slowly less coherent as the questions continued. At the end, I took her back to her rooms by the shortest route through the house."

"How did you discipline her?" Arimeso asked.

"With a slap, a'Taso."

"On the face."

"On the hands, a'Taso."

"Would the face not be a more appropriate place for discipline?"

"I felt a somewhat more painful area would be a stronger reminder of proprieties, a'Taso. I wished to avoid further offenses to the selaso."

Across the narrow aisle, Cara closed her eyes and bent her head. His words brought the fiery pain from his slap back into her palms. Rodani tapped her thigh. She forced her body upright.

Kimasa refolded her hands on the wood-grained tabletop. "Why did you not take her directly to the physician after she left my offices, a'Kusik?"

He turned to the high priestess. "I had other duties to attend to, a'Selaso. Everyone but Rodani had been excused. She would be well attended. I left her in capable hands."

"Who was there when you returned a'Cara to her rooms?"

"Hamman."

"Be seated." Arimeso focused on the far wall. "A'Hamman."

Hamman rose and approached the table, dignified and reserved as she always was. "A'Taso."

"Relate to us what you experienced when a'Cara was brought back."

Her fingers, nestled in her lower back, tensed and flexed. Hamman was not so calm.

"She was in a frightful state, a'Taso," the servant said softly. "I came into her workroom in time to see the keso slap her. She shook and moaned. After some moments, she attempted to rise to her knees. She could not stand by herself."

Hamman's eyes went to the floor. "A'Kusik was still present, a'Taso. But I helped her to her feet and into the facilities. I ran warm water in the basin. Rodani came in. He attempted to calm her, then spoke with her. Determining the seriousness of the injuries, he asked the keso if a'Baldar had been notified. His answer was no, so Rodani called, and waited with me until he arrived. After he dressed her hands, I helped Rodani ready her for the meeting in your office, a'Taso. When they returned, I helped ease her into the bed and watched as she fell asleep under the smoke."

"And in later days?"

Hamman took a deep breath, her vision focused over the taso's head. "In extreme pain for the first three days, a'Taso. She could do nothing for herself. And the physician's treatments were a trial to us all. It was very difficult for her to control her reactions to the pain."

Cara ducked her head in shame. Stoicism was not in her makeup. Even Hamman's good will couldn't deny it.

"As the days passed," Hamman continued, "she began to heal, but not completely."

"Can she take care of her daily needs, a'Hamman?" Kimasa inquired.

"At first, she could not, a'Selaso. Any small finger motions that I can see have been impaired, as well as strength. Rodani threads her needles for her. She has trouble cutting meat."

All eyes were on the woman in the center of the room, all faces masked.

"Thank you, a'sel. Be seated."

Hamman turned and made her way back to her chair.

"Bring Iraimin into the room."

Timan opened the door and motioned. She walked in.

"A'Iraimin?"

The painter replaced the maid in the center of attention.

"When were you made aware of a'Cara's wounds?"

"The day after her injury, a'Taso," Iraimin said calmly.

"How often have you seen a'Cara at her crafting?"

A moment's silence. "Seven times, a'Taso. Five before her injuries, two after."

"As an artisan yourself, give us your considered opinion upon her current capabilities." Arimeso took a sip of tea from an ornate cup.

"Impaired, a'Taso. She fights for control of her tools. Her movements are no longer smooth and sure, but clumsy."

"Compare your skills' need for manual dexterity to a'Cara's need."

Iraimin considered the question before replying. "I am a painter, a'Selaso. As a quilter, Cara has somewhat of a greater need for dexterity than I. I need only hold a paintbrush. Mobility of the fingers is required, but more comes from the wrist and arm. And gripping power."

"Have you seen improvement, a'sel?" Chendal asked.

"Yes, a'Temaso," Iraimin replied, turning to face him.

"What percentage might one put to that improvement?"

Iraimin's eyes flickered back and forth in thought. "Fifty to sixty percent, a'Temaso."

"Again, from an artisan's viewpoint," Arimeso continued, "what is her reaction to this impairment?"

"Frustration, a'Taso," Iraimin answered without hesitation. "Her mind and eyes remember the skills, but those skills have great difficulty being brought forth through the hands." Iraimin's hands unclasped and reclasped. "One may admit deep sympathies with her plight, a'Taso."

Kusik shot out of his seat to stand at attention. "Sympathies are not in order, here, a'Taso."

Rodani rose on the heels of Kusik's words. "Sympathies for frustrations demonstrate that there is psychological damage as well as physical, a'Taso."

Cara wanted to cheer.

Neither man met the eyes of the other. Arimeso glanced at them both. "You may go, Iraimin. A'Serano," she added.

Serano took his turn at the front. Cara fervently hoped their mutual dislike would not interfere with his account.

"Begin, please, a'tem, at the point where you were commanded to search for Cara."

Serano gathered his thoughts. "I left off practice, a'Taso, and met with the other searchers outside the Enclave. We followed her footprints into the woods, and discovered she was climbing from tree to tree. At one tree there was evidence of a fall. I examined the tree and noticed immediately that it was a camabarin. From there, footprints led clearly east. We ran after her, eventually catching up with her. Timan cuffed her, and we walked her back to the manor house, and into the Enclave. Later, I visited her rooms, waiting long enough to watch Baldar apply a round of astringent. Cara was in extreme pain during that time, and the pain continued until the smoke took effect."

"Be seated."

Serano bowed and took his place next to Hamman along the back wall.

"A'Rodani."

Rodani stood for a third time that hour, tall and regal in his bearing. "A'Taso."

"Your observations, please, beginning with your release from the inquiry."

He explained what he had seen, what he had learned, what he had heard, and witnessed.

"Only in the last few days has she begun to craft again with any regularity. It is still a great source of difficulty and frustration. I help her as I can, a'Taso, but I cannot craft for her."

Arimeso shifted in her chair. "When might you estimate her regaining her former output?"

"It is difficult to judge, a'Taso. It will depend upon how much she recovers and how long it takes."

"Days? Weeks?" Arimeso probed.

"If her hands fail to recover completely, a'Taso, she may never regain her former rate."

It was not a pleasant thought, and Cara had tried to steer clear of it. Voiced by her lover, it acquired form and substance and hung over her shoulders like a storm cloud.

"Be seated."

Rodani obeyed.

"Master Healer."

The physician took his place before the table, imposing and confident.

"Relate your professional opinion, a'Baldar."

"A'Taso, there was undue delay between the time of the injury and the time I treated her."

Short and to the point. *Thank you, doctor. That might repay all the pain that bedamned astringent caused.*

"How much bearing does that have on the outcome?"

"A great deal, a'Taso."

The physician was known for his conciseness. He reminded Cara of her mother. Which was, she told herself firmly, not all bad.

"Explain."

"The longer the delay, a'Taso, the longer the recovery, and the less chance for a complete one."

"What do you estimate as Cara's chances for a full recovery?"

"An estimate of sixty to eighty percent is the best range I may reasonably give, a'Taso."

"How many cases of camabarin poisoning have you seen, a'sel?" Chendal asked.

"Six, to my memory, a'Temaso."

"And how many human?"

"One, a'Temaso," was the succinct reply.

"From one unhealed case, you can judge?"

Cara winced. The man had a point.

"I judge, a'Temaso," Baldar said in stiff poise, "from the five other cases of varying extremes and the knowledge of human healing that was passed to me from Hadaman."

"As?"

"In general, a'Temaso, they heal more slowly due in part to poorer circulation and more fragile skin. It also accounts for their inability to withstand the range of temperatures we do."

"In your opinion," Kimasa said, "there is permanent damage?"

"Certainly, long term, a'Selaso. Possibly permanent."

"Thank you, Master Healer. Be seated."

Baldar hesitated. "Forgive me, a'Taso," he said. "I have patients in need of my skills."

Arimeso dismissed him without comment. The physician bowed and left the room, closing the door firmly behind him.

"A'Cara."

Cara rose unsteadily from her place at Rodani's side, but she met Arimeso's stern look with a clear heart. Just as certain in her rightness as Kusik, she was determined to tell her truths.

"Begin from when a'Kusik entered your room," Arimeso told her.

Cara swallowed heavily and put her hands behind her back. Purposely she raised her chin and relaxed tense shoulders, the better to breathe—and put forth the image, if not the reality, of strength and surety.

"I invited him in, a'Taso. He told me to dress in proper clothing. I left my quilting and asked him why. He said I was going to the Enclave to face an inquiry. I...became somewhat anxious. When—"

"Why did you become anxious, a'Cara?" Chendal asked, his face an identical mask to the other two at the long table. They looked like three statues.

"Number one, a'Temaso," Cara began, "I know next to nothing about the Enclave. Number two, I know well that it's Rodani's job to walk me from one place to another, and if a'Kusik comes to escort me, it's something important, likely involving Rodani as well. Number three, my servants were nowhere around. That never happened before. Number four, a'Kusik seemed angry, and wouldn't tell me where Rodani was."

"He could not."

"Neither did he *inform me* that he couldn't, a'Temaso. I would have benefited greatly from that one piece of knowledge."

Chendal regarded her stolidly. Cara returned the regard. The silence deepened before Chendal waved his fingers.

"A'Kusik took me into a room with a desk and a young woman behind it. She led me to a cell, and—"

"A waiting room," Kimasa corrected her.

"—locked the cell door behind me," Cara continued, refusing the slanted semantics. "Seeing the bars on the window frightened me more." She hesitated, expecting another interruption. None came. "I crawled out the window, explored for a little time in an attempt to find Rodani, and then headed toward the woods."

"Why?" Chendal's voice echoed through her heightened state of mind.

Gods. Get it wrong and the case could be forfeited. Right here. Right now.

"I feared for my life, a'Temaso."

"Why?"

The same chilly word. The same emotionless stare. She began to sweat.

"The assumptions most logical to me, a'Temaso, were that the priestesses had taken strong exception to my affinity with Rodani, and that we were to be punished. Possibly severely."

"So, you ran from punishment." He didn't blink, didn't seem to breathe. He didn't move from the direct, deadly challenge. Therefore, neither could she. A trickle of sweat ran down from underneath the immaculate bun at her neck.

"From a severe, possibly life-threatening punishment that I felt was undeserved, a'Temaso." *I love you, aisu. Pray to your goddess, I don't foul this up.* "An honorable human doesn't run from punishment that is deserved. But we don't consider it a dishonor to run from injustice. We judge the perpetrator of the injustice to be the dishonorable one."

"And if the perpetrator feels justified?"

"Then there is a conflict of honor, a'Temaso."

"And who settles conflicts of honor?"

"Those in the society who are appointed to that role. History, however," she was quick to point out, "has shown us society's judges don't always decide honorably."

Chendal fell silent. Cara took it as a command to continue. "I went to the woods and started working my way inward, climbing from tree to tree."

"Did you assume you could not be followed in that manner?" he asked.

"I could only assume it would be the most difficult way to track, a'Temaso. But I don't underestimate Serano's skills."

There was no follow-up question.

"I jumped down into a stream at one point, again in an attempt to hide my tracks. I couldn't go far in the cold. I climbed another tree and continued. At one—"

"Where were you headed?" Chendal interrupted again.

Cara winced inwardly. Chendal's questions were entirely too accurate. Too able to pinpoint her gaping weaknesses. She tossed the question. Or maybe its answer. "Away, a'Temaso. As far away as I could get. Toward home. It was all I could do."

Chendal clasped his hands and rested them on the table. "How far did you estimate you would go before being caught? What would you eat? Where would you shelter?"

A sigh escaped her lips before she could censor it. Being made to look like a fool, either a stupid one or an arrogant one, in front of the three highest ranking people she would ever see was giving rise to weak knees and dizziness.

"A'Temaso, forgive me, please. You're asking rational questions about an irrational act. I'll answer your questions as best I may, but the answers won't make sense. I was acting primarily on instinct."

Chendal considered her statement in silence, then indicated she should continue.

"I climbed from tree to tree when I could, jumped when I could not. When I came to one tree, I jumped. It...it sliced my hands. The pain was so great, I took off running." She paused with the indelibly inscribed memory flashing through her mind. "I had some thought of finding the stream again, to soak and chill the wounds. But..." it didn't want to come out. Didn't want to be blinded by the light of reason Selandu shone on almost every subject.

"By that time, I was almost incapable of thinking. I ran. And would have continued to run until I ran out of strength if Serano hadn't caught me. Timan handcuffed me. We walked back to the manor, and I was immediately brought before the selaso. She questioned me, the keso re-injured my already-damaged hands, and eventually, I was released." She stopped and waited.

Chendal waited through her silence, then said, "Continue."

"A'Kusik led me through the central hallways, handcuffed, bloody, and dirty. He brought me to my rooms and knocked me to the floor. I had no awareness of time or place. Only pain. Hamman helped me to the sink. Rodani came in. I managed to tell him what happened. He called a'Baldar to heal me. Even the simplest things have been a continual test of my temper and strength of will."

"A'Cara."

She turned left to face the selaso.

"Why did you assume you and Rodani would be punished for your affinity?" Kimasa asked.

It took a moment to think that one through. "A human in fear of her life assumes the worst scenario, a'Selaso. It helps keep us alive."

"Another irrational, instinctual reaction?"

Ouch. "Not necessarily, a'Selaso. Irrational from your extensive base of knowledge, not from my level of ignorance. Rodani warned me on several occasions not to divulge our affinity to anyone without his prior approval. To me, that meant we might be in danger because of it. When I realized what was happening, I could only think this danger had appeared."

"So Rodani's earlier warnings caused your overreaction?"

The surprise could be read by anyone with even a side view of her face. "No, a'Selaso. It was my lack of knowledge and understanding."

"And whose fault is that?"

"I..." She stumbled. "I wouldn't..." and again. "...couldn't place such blame, a'Selaso. This is not my culture." Damn if she'd blame Rodani for her insanity.

Chendal put down the cup of tea he'd been holding. "I will see your hands."

Suddenly shy, Cara approached the table slowly, raising her palms into the master guardian's view. He took one scarred hand into his and prodded it, probing the wounds much as Baldar had done. It still provoked a reaction. Chendal looked across at her.

"Pain? Or sensitivity?"

She stared down at the offending appendage. "Both, I believe, a'Temaso. Higher sensitivity slides into pain at a certain amount of stimulation."

"Does your crafting cause you pain?"

"After a little time, yes, a'Temaso."

Chendal let go and refolded his hands.

"Be seated," the taso told her.

Grateful, she returned to the comfort of Rodani's side.

"A'Rodani," Kimasa called next. He stood.

"For how long have you been watching a'Cara craft?"

"Since her arrival, a'Selaso," he replied. "Though that has increased greatly in the past few months."

"Compare your craft's needs to hers."

"Similar, a'Selaso. We both manipulate our materials with deft finger movements. It takes precision and power in tandem. It is both a gift of the goddess and an acquired skill."

"Be seated."

There was an exchange of glances between the three. Chendal sat back in his chair.

"A'Selaso," he said. "What is your opinion on the subject of human presence on the estate?"

Kimasa turned to face him. "I consider all creatures a creation of the goddess. I was not sure how the experiment would develop, but I felt it was honorable to attempt."

Chendal turned to face the adversaries. "A'Rodani, your opinion."

Rodani stood. "I have no grand philosophies, a'Temaso. I obey my taso. But I would admit to great curiosity. And I believe it has proven a qualified success."

"And what part of your body speaks that piece of wisdom, a'tem?" Kusik spat.

"Silence," Arimeso said.

"And your opinion, a'Kusik," Chendal continued, unruffled.

Kusik drew his eyes away from Rodani and faced his guild superior. "I also obey my taso. But I felt, and still feel, this experiment is a mistake. A human in this estate is a danger to her."

"From what quarter?"

"From the Riverfolk, and those who fear the aliens," Kusik quickly replied, "as demonstrated by the shot fired at the solstice gathering."

"So you would prefer the human be sent home?"

That was too easy, even for Cara to see.

"I obey my taso," Kusik replied flatly.

Another quick conference, then Arimeso sat forward. "Witnesses are released. Accusers and accused adjourn to the waiting rooms."

Those in the back row arose and left the room, singly and in pairs. Rodani drew Cara out of her chair and over to a door to their left. Kusik disappeared through a different door behind his chair.

Their room was tiny but comfortable. Table. Soft chairs. Water and the fixings for tea. A miniscule facility. A vase with flowers, a painting. Cara ignored it all.

Rodani sat down. Immediately, she crawled into his arms. His scent comforted her, as did his warmth and the weight of his arms across her back and shoulders. There was little desire in her to speak, to think too far ahead. Chairs scraped across the floor in the outer room. Footsteps came near their door, walked away, and returned again. Cara listened to her lover's heartbeat beneath her head. His nimble fingers smoothed the wrinkles from her jacket, and his exhalations tickled the loose curls on the top of her head.

"You did well." Rodani's deep voice rumbled from his chest. Her cheek didn't leave its resting position on his jacket, but she tossed the compliment.

"I did what I could. It wasn't a comfortable confrontation."

"Yes."

"Do we have a chance?"

"Yes."

"It comes to conflicting honors, does it not, aisu? Just as I said."

"Partially."

One-word answers didn't have quite the negative connotation that it did in humans, but it came close. She dropped the subject.

There would be time later to discuss it. Hopefully plenty of time. Instead, they enjoyed the relative peace the little room afforded them. Calm before the conclusions. Both were aware that the already strained professional association between Rodani and Kusik would become even more taut after the inquiry, regardless of the outcome. Rodani avowed he could deal with it. Cara didn't question the assertion—out loud.

She'd had her share of personality problems with bosses in the past. It chilled her to think of two guardians in the same house at great odds with each other. A job, one could leave. Not so easy to turn one's back on a taso, wrenching allegiance from one to another. Arimeso had a tangle on her hands. And it was Cara's fault. Partially, she amended. She'd almost give up her best scissors to know who had squawked.

Then again, maybe it was better she didn't. Rodani still wouldn't admit to who it was, or whether he even knew. A few curt words had dissuaded her from pressing him on the subject. Just because he shared her bed and body didn't mean he shared guild secrets. Nor did she share all hers. She snuggled closer.

Gods knew what they were saying out there. Discussing her sanity, likely—or Rodani's, for his choice of bedmate. What did Chendal think of Rodani? A guardian/crafter, lover of an alien, who brought charges against his keso. Who wore his differences without shame instead of hiding them.

What did Chendal's eyes see? A strange, short alien with stranger notions of honor. A guild member tripping over the edges of dishonor. Conflicting cultures. Conflicting expectations. A confrontation that needed to stop here.

Cara ran her palms rhythmically over Rodani's jacket and down his side, but it didn't take long for tactile pleasure to turn to irritated palms, then to a pain that made her stop. Damn Kusik. Damn that anonymous complainant. Cara balled her fist in impotent frustration. Rodani stepped up his caresses in response.

Arimeso would side with her keso, she guessed. Kimasa might possibly side with Cara. Chendal—if he's traditional, Kusik gets off unpunished. If he's moderate, they might stand a chance.

A tic'idi in the corner outside might overhear the judges' discussions. But Rodani wouldn't let her crack the door and put her ear to it. She toyed with the idea of asking him to put his 'com on receive in the hopes they could eavesdrop more circumspectly. But he was too honorable. She could paint onto his face the expression that request would provoke. It made her smile into the leather of his guild jacket.

"Tea?" Cara startled at the unexpected utterance. Rodani pursed his lips in humor. "Tense?"

She grinned back. "Gods of the deep. Yes."

"Relax."

"Until this is over, aisu—only in your arms."

"Then it is well we have privacy here. Tea?"

"Thank you, no. You?"

"No."

"How long might it take?"

"Tea?"

She fixed him a grinning glare. "Judgment, ki'oto."

"I make no predictions, kia. Bored?"

"No. Anxious for it to be over."

"So you can go back and craft?" he continued.

"So I may go back with an excuse to undress you."

His eyes pulsed. "If we win or lose?"

"Either. One way we celebrate. The other way we commiserate."

"And an excuse is necessary?"

Her grin went ear to ear. "Not at all."

"Kia, your logic spins me."

"As long as I'm beneath you when you fall."

And pulsed again. "You are salacious."

Cara slipped a knee between his thighs and stretched up to face him, sliding her arms over his shoulders. "Tell me it displeases you."

He wrapped his arms around her, forcing the distance between them down to an absolute minimum. A slow, meandering nuzzle took his mouth up her neck and around her ear, down her jawline and up the chin, eventually landing on waiting lips. Heat began in Cara's abdomen and flowed downward.

"You are kindling to a fire, aisu," she whispered.

He simply held her tightly. Comfort given; comfort received.

Time passed.

"A'tem? A'sel?" came a voice from outside the door. A light tapping accompanied it.

Reluctantly, Cara slid out of Rodani's arms as he attempted to stand. "A moment," he replied, straightening the clothing that Cara had ruffled.

"Kia, listen to me. Regardless of whether events go as we wish or not, you *must* remain calm. You may say anything to me you need to when we return to your rooms. But in there," he nodded over her head, "there is only one correct response. Calm acceptance." He put his hands on her shoulders and squeezed. "Is there any doubt of my words?"

"No."

They locked eyes. Satisfied, Rodani let go. "Enter," he said.

Chendal's partner, Shisa, opened the door and stepped aside. Rodani led, Cara followed, to stand in front of their seats. Shisa went to her position behind Chendal. The others filed into their own places.

Arimeso settled into her chair, and into stern impassivity. Only her eyes flickered back and forth between her opposing security staff.

"Judgment has been made." A slight motion of her hand began it.

"A'Kusik," Kimasa began. "Our culture is based on proprieties. We hold ourselves in esteem for accomplishments that follow accustomed ways. You are justly proud of your duty to those ways. There are times to break the rules, and there are times to adhere to them. Your decisions, regardless of how they are seen at the time, are nearly always correct in the final accounting." She refolded her fingers and drew her eyes away from Kusik. "Judgment for the accused."

Cara shut her eyes. Was this punishment for her disbelief, or did she really believe Kusik did right? She took an audible breath and tried to keep any expression off her face. Rodani shifted his arm just enough to touch her, whether in comfort or warning, she couldn't tell.

Chendal's turn was next.

"I consider your claim to no knowledge of the critical timing of camabarin toxin specious, a'Kusik," he said, leaning back into his chair. "I am well aware of what is taught in the guild. No one living in this area of the country and having your status and responsibilities would have forgotten such information. I believe you used this unforgotten knowledge to punish a'Cara for a judgment you made on her honor." He let the statement rest in the air a moment before continuing.

"Putting aside the question of whether her actions were dishonorable or not," the temaso continued, "the decision to punish her in any way should have been discussed with your taso beforehand. You overstepped your boundaries and caused effects that have repercussions not only upon an artisan's livelihood, but upon your taso's business as well." His voice dropped. "Judgment for the accuser."

Whoa. One for, one against. *Calm, fem. Calm. Breathe. Thank you, a'Temaso.*

"Kusik," Arimeso began. "I know you well. I know and respect your honor. But there is enormous distance in the spectrum between your power and a'Cara's. And you have misused it. To her detriment and, as the temaso remarked, to mine." She stared at Cara. "Lost abilities cannot be regained, except where the goddess intervenes. Judgment for the accuser."

A taso had just called down reprehension on her own keso. The room was still. Cara's heart beat audibly in her ears. Her fingers tingled from her shallow, anxious breathing.

They had won. But what had they won? A feud? A pyrrhic victory? She dared a look at Kusik. His face was stone. His unblinking gaze rested on Arimeso.

"You have been found," the taso continued, "in dishonor to your guild and your taso. Your punishment is three-fold. In private censure," Arimeso glanced down the rows of empty chairs, "fifteen lashes. A formal apology to whom you wronged. And for a month, restrictions on your privileges." She waved the fingers of her left hand.

Chendal rose from his chair and walked past Kusik with a motion of his hand. Kusik followed. Timan left his place behind Arimeso and met the pair in front of Kusik.

Kusik unbuttoned his jacket and passed it to his wordless partner, who took it and stepped to the side. Chendal unbuckled his belt and drew it out from around his waist. Kusik flipped his hair around to the front and pulled the back of his shirt up under his neck. His eyes fixed upon a place somewhere above Arimeso's head.

Rodani pulled Cara left a few steps, for a better line of sight into the punishment. As the recipient of Kusik's dishonor, she was required to witness. Rodani kept his grip on her wrist. Chendal drew his arm to the side, then brought it back across in a blur of motion.

<Whap>

A long red mark appeared across Kusik's back. Cara flinched in unwilling sympathy.

<Whap>

A second line of red appeared, parallel to the first.

Don't you dare turn away.

<Whap>

A third red line crossed the first two, creating beads of blood in the diamonds where they crossed.

Kusik remained frozen in body and expression until the strikes piled up one on top of another, then his reserve gave way—a prolonged blinking of his eyes, a stiff grimace, and a perceptible shaking of his body. The sound of Chendal's belt resounded through the room. A mass of red and purple stripes decorated his bare back. Blood dribbled slowly down a score of small wounds.

Then it was over.

Kusik let go his shirt. It fell down his back, soaking up the surface blood. Spots appeared as he carefully tucked it in and reached for the jacket Timan held out to him. Chendal replaced his belt and came back to stand at his chair. Slowly, Kusik pulled on his jacket, forbearing to shrug it into place. As if an outside force had to push him, he shifted awkwardly to face Cara and Rodani.

"I ask forgiveness for my dishonorable actions, a'Cara," he said stiffly.

That was it? That was all he said? She'd rather take back the beating and make him grovel a little. It didn't seem to make up for the outrages he'd perpetrated on her body and her psyche. But Rodani squeezed her wrist. Cara bowed to the inevitable and inclined her head once, slowly.

"There will be no recriminations from this judgment," Arimeso said into Kusik's stony face, then over to Rodani, "nor will it be carried further. Here it ends." She got up and left the room.

Rodani pulled Cara toward the door. Both stared at Kusik, motionless in his censure, as they passed by. As Cara entered the anteroom behind Rodani, another pair of footsteps came in behind them.

"Rodani."

"Shisa," Rodani replied to the woman as he turned, losing a little of the formality he'd held to in the inquiry. Chendal strode up behind her.

"The guild council charged us with another duty while we are here," she said. "Hurasten said we are to spend a day or two in your adashi's company. Examine the situation first on. See how she acts and relates in private as well as in public."

Rodani regarded the pair circumspectly. "The taso permits?"

"Yes."

Rodani waived his reservations and retrieved his weapons from the duty guard. Cara worked her way to one side of him as they entered the hallway. Shisa strode to his other. Chendal took the fallback position.

"Opinions?" Shisa asked Rodani as they headed for the central stairs.

"I am content."

"And Kusik?" she prompted. "Will he abide by the taso's injunctions against revenge?"

Rodani regarded Shisa silently as they headed up the stairs. "I will remind him of her commands; Arimeso listens to me. Minor repercussions I may have to eat. He is a proud man. But Arimeso has proven again that she will rein him in."

Cara's ears perked up. "Again?"

"Tsss," he admonished. "Elsewhen."

Cara smiled away the rebuke. It would take a lot to dampen her spirits at this juncture. The decision just handed out proved there was occasional justice to be found in the universe. Maimed she was. But her fighter's heart had already taken hold of the disability and was wringing the life out of it drip by drop. If only her emotions were as amenable to persuasion.

Rodani pulled out his 'com and punched in a number. "Deremic?"

Static replied.

"Tea for four, a'sel. And have someone search out a dinner table that will fit us. A'Cara has company."

Static acknowledged.

Rodani led the way down that last corridor and into the relative safety of Cara's rooms. Chendal drifted into the center of her workroom. Shisa headed for the sewing table that held Cara's machine and an assortment of fabric pieces. She clasped her hands behind her and peered down at the jumble. Cara followed, her own hands shoved deep inside her pockets. Rodani went through the bedroom on an errand.

It left Cara alone in her rooms with two strangers. Guild strangers. High-ranking guild strangers that might give Rodani orders. Cara's survival antennae shot up. Was there more here than she saw? Turning surreptitiously, she took a sidelong glance at Chendal. He was studying the layout of her rooms, carefully. Cara's glance slid past her bedroom doors. No Rodani. She then turned back to Shisa, only to find the woman staring at her. Cara blinked against the cool appraisal and took a step back.

"Excuse me." She bowed, then turned abruptly and headed for her bedroom, the skin between her shoulder blades tickling. The servants' corridor beckoned. Cara made a beeline for the place where her safety had just walked. The corridor opened up into the living room. Rodani was already turning toward the unexpected sound. Hamman stopped in mid-sentence.

"Problem?" he asked, meeting her headlong stride with steps of his own.

"You left me alone with them, aisu," she said, shaky.

"They are no danger. They disturbed you?"

"Shisa was staring at me, and Chendal was committing my rooms to memory. Why?"

"You have forgotten what it is to be around people unused to you. Do you remember the reason for their visit? Return to your guests," he chided her gently. "I did not leave you with them thoughtlessly."

"But was I wrong to be concerned?"

Rodani regarded her. "Considering the amount of guild wisdom I have tried to pour into your head, kia, no. Forgive me. I should have spoken to you."

She smiled, availing herself of a reassuring hug before returning. Shisa was still at the sewing machine. Chendal studied the knife practice board.

"Why is this here?" he asked Cara as she reentered the room.

"Rodani and I practice on it."

Chendal eyed the board. "That explains the bipolar distribution of the entrance marks." He cocked his head. "And the range of accuracy. Where are your knives?"

Something tickled in her memory. Something old, eluding her recall, sending a shiver up her spine. "Rodani keeps them." The master guardian reached into his sleeve and pulled out a slim knife, holding it out to her.

"A'Temaso," she said diffidently, "I can't—" She held out her hands. "I can't throw yet. Not with any accuracy. I'm sorry."

"Show them your crafting, kia," Rodani suggested.

Glad of something that might settle her nerves, she maneuvered behind the sewing table and sat down at the machine. The two pieces she had dropped when Rodani had interrupted her were lying askew on the table. She picked them up and attempted to align them properly.

After a moment of frustration, they lined up. She slid the pieces across the faceplate. She lifted the presser foot and positioned the fabric, hoping the pieces would stay aligned. They did. She sent the needle into action, stitching the pieces together. She pulled them out and snipped the thread with an awkward clip of scissors. It took two tries. She unfolded the new piece and laid it aside its mates to flesh out a larger block. Taking two of the earlier pieced sets, she held them and attempted to match up the inner seams. Her fingers resisted the action. Instead, she laid them on the table in front of her and rubbed the top one across the bottom one with the backs of her fingers.

"Manipulate, kia," Rodani chided her gently as he received a loaded tea tray from Deremic. Deremic retrieved two chairs from the study for Shisa and Chendal. Rodani poured cups for their guests and for Cara, then one for himself, before taking his place in the chair on her adjacent side. Cara slid the next duo into position before taking a careful grip and sip of the hot liquid. With another bit of pressure on the foot pedal, she stitched the next seam. She pulled it out and clipped the threads, laying it back into place in the incomplete block.

Another set came together after being dropped on the floor and nearly dipped in her teacup. She leaned back against the chair and sighed.

"A'Cara," Chendal spoke into the awkward silence. His pale grey eyes looked out over high cheekbones. "A portion of your time, please."

Cara glanced at Rodani, who gave no indications. She opened her palm stiffly, not reaching the full-fingered extension the gesture was supposed to have. Chendal stood up and backed into the middle of the room.

"Stand in front of me."

Mystified but willing—since Rodani was in the room, Cara obeyed. A guardian of Chendal's rank was not refused lightly.

Chendal crossed his arms and studied her. "Remove your clip."

Again, she turned to Rodani for confirmation. His glance slid upward from her to the temaso.

"There is no offense here, a'Cara," Chendal said. "I ask your patience for a moment."

Cara took off the clip that kept her bun in place. Brown curls cascaded down her back.

"Pocket the clip."

She slipped it into her jacket. Chendal reached forward and tugged at her hair, pulling strands of it over her shoulders, a gesture only Rodani had done after their affinity had begun. Rank must have its privileges for the Selandu as well. Behind her, she heard the scrape of a chair against stone.

"Put your hands on your hips."

She held her hands stiffly against her hipbones, fingers downward.

"This way," he corrected her, resting his palms on his slim hips, fingers forward and thumb back in the typical human gesture of anger. Cara imitated him.

"Now, put on a cloak of arrogance, and look me over from my head down to my boots, and back up."

What the hell kind of game was this? Rodani hadn't interrupted it. He had to be watching. Cara checked behind her to make sure. To her surprise, he had rounded the table and was standing side by side with Shisa, keeping a close eye on the proceedings.

She turned back to Chendal. Taking a deep breath, she pulled her shoulders back and jutted her chin, staring him in the face. She let her eyes drift down his long frame and back up again. He was waiting expectantly, pupils slit in concentration on her. Cara kept her hands on her hips as he waited. Slowly, her cloak of arrogance slipped off, replaced with a more natural arrogance at the man's game playing. Chendal's stare was becoming irritating. She was tiring of the game already.

"It is evening," he said slowly, confusing her more. "The shadows lay long on the hillside. Your strange, blue-colored eyes flicker from me to the garden behind me where kiniki flowers wait to be plucked."

Cara's eyes grew wide.

"You are frustrated and angry with me," Chendal continued, enunciating every word.

Her hand flew to her mouth.

"It will be dark soon." His gaze remained locked on hers.

Stunned, she shuffled backwards, barely noticing the worktable as she bumped it. "You!" she cried, placing both scarred hands on the table behind for its steadying influence. Chendal remained focused on her. Rodani approached the pair slowly, carefully positioning him in between them.

"Kia?" he asked, tentatively. She was breathing heavily, her chest moving visibly with the effort. A Cene'l expletive flew from her mouth. Hands went back on the hips in earnest. Her gaze had not moved from Chendal's face.

"Kia," he repeated more forcefully.

But Cara saw no one but the man in front of her. Heard nothing but the words that had brought back a flood of memories. "Do you know what you did to me?" she shouted.

Chendal crossed his arms and leaned forward. "As I remember, I interrogated you," Chendal replied.

"For two hours," Cara complained.

"I used the opportunity to speak with someone not an ambassador, but who spoke Selandi."

"And you questioned me so long that it was dusk before you finished," Cara said accusingly. "You made me walk back down in the dark."

"You should have been better prepared."

She put her hands back on her hips. "I wouldn't have needed anything else if you hadn't kept me so long."

Shisa picked up Cara's largest ruler and slammed it down on the table. Her grey eyes flashed. She dropped the ruler, letting it clatter to a rest. "I would see your hands, a'Cara."

She held them out while Chendal's partner inspected them in some detail.

"Cara," Rodani said, in a hard tone she'd not heard for a while. "You were in the wrong, as well as all the other humans who cross the border. Apologize to the temaso."

Cara pursed her lips, biting back what she really wanted to say to Chendal. "I know we're not supposed to cross it. I'm sorry for that part. But also, you put me in danger when I never meant you any harm at all."

"I was doing my duty, a'Cara," Chendal told her. "I meant no offense."

She looked away toward the far wall. "A'Temaso, that is as difficult for me to believe as it is for you to believe I was acting honorably when I ran from the Enclave."

She reached for a cup of tea from the tray Rodani had brought, hands shaking with anger kept buried for years. But her damaged muscles lost their grip on the handle. The cup fell to the table, splashing tea in every direction.

She swore and raced for the facilities in search of a towel. When she returned, a trio of guild kerchiefs lay soggy on her table in an attempt to keep the liquid away from her fabric. Rodani helped her clean up with an instruction to have Hamman wash and dry the kerchiefs by this evening. She returned from the errand to find Rodani had poured her another half-cup.

"Thank you," she said contritely as she sat.

Bending forward over the table prevented her from having to look at the surrounding faces with their attendant censures. Too much frustration, embarrassment, and anger flooded her soul. She wanted a quiet room and Rodani in her arms.

"A'Cara."

Her body remained poised over her cup, elbows on her worktable. But she turned her head to face Chendal.

"Do you remember Kimasa's judgment?"

She blinked slowly as she thought. "Judgment for the accused."

One corner of his mouth turned up. "Her accompanying words."

The worktable's grain reminded her of her quilting. Curves and lines in parallel, demarcating lights and darks. "You spoke of the camabarin toxin. Kimasa spoke of...propriety, and flexibility. And when each was appropriate." Her gaze returned to him.

Chendal leaned forward in his chair and fixed grey eyes on her face. "Ten years ago, I had not nearly the wisdom Kimasa spoke of. Will you forgive me?"

Forgive me?

The words echoed in her head, almost uncomprehendingly.

Forgive me.

A master guardian bent down from his lofty height to extend an apology for his younger self. Somehow, it felt many times the strength of Kusik's apology.

Rodani shifted his hand to the space between them. It was an unnecessary warning.

"Yes," she said, eyes drifting from the teacup to Chendal's immobile face. Her eyes locked with his until forced to turn away from the power reflected in them. Cara chuckled in her own discomfort, cupping both hands around her cup and resting her elbow against Rodani's arm. "You're still winning the staring contests, a'Temaso," she said. "We must have held four or five that evening."

"You were the most obstreperous child I ever escorted back over the hills," he said.

"And I apologize for that." Cara leaned toward Rodani and ran a hand over his arm, who flicked a finger past her earring, making the metal pieces chime.

Shisa leaned forward, her eyes narrowed, mouth a straight line. "You dare? Dishonor means nothing to you that you flaunt it in front of the temaso?"

Cara sat back from Rodani, but he refused to move in the face of Shisa's rage. A frisson of fear swept over her, and her breathing went shallow. She glanced at Rodani. "Who answers that, aisu, you or me?"

Rodani sighed. "I understand your anger, Shisa, but it does no one any good to rail at us."

"Someone should!"

"And what do you believe it would accomplish?" he asked her.

"It might draw you back to sanity."

"What's insane to one person," Cara said, "is the essence of sanity to another."

Shisa swept her hand through the air, as if attempting to push away what she could not hear. "You can mouth platitudes at me all evening. It does not erase the dishonor I see before me."

"I am sorry that's all you see, a'tem," Cara replied.

"Have you no sense of shame?"

Cara sighed. "If I did, it wouldn't be you I would admit it to."

Shisa pushed herself away from the table and took a step toward her, prompting an equal action from Rodani. Face to face, electric anger flowed between them.

"Fool," Shisa spat. She turned on her heel and left the room.

Rodani bowed to Chendal. "You might follow her, a'Temaso, before she ignites a firestorm."

Chendal inclined his head. "You already have." He strode out in the wake of his irate partner.

Cara let out her breath in a rush. "I thought one of us was going to be bloody soon."

"I would not have let her," he replied.

"Oh, gods, Rodani, is it worse than I thought?" He wrapped his arms around her as she stared at the door.

Neither Shisa nor Chendal returned that night.

FOURTEEN

"Normal, aisu. We need normal back again." Yesterday's judgment and Shisa's anger still rattled around in Cara's brain.

Rodani turned his design book ninety degrees and studied it, head bent over the worktable. Noontime sun showed through the window. "What is normal?"

Cara chuckled and ran her hand across the nearly completed quilt top. Her palm still tingled painfully. She stared at it. "Before the Enclave, certainly."

He glanced at her, head still bent over his book. "Before our joinings?"

"Oh, no. Not the old normal. The new one."

He blinked at her and straightened. "Contradictions in terms, kia."

"I'm human, aisu. We eat contradictions for breakfast."

Rodani stilled and blinked again. "I must have slept less than I thought," he said. "You are not making sense to me today."

"I'm sorry," she said, smiling. "I shouldn't confuse you with my word games."

"Or I should learn to play."

Cara leaned over. "Maybe a different kind of play?"

Rodani's pupils widened, narrowed to a slit, and opened again as his mouth pursed into a grin.

She got up and spun his chair sideways, then straddled his lap and wrapped her arms around his neck. Rodani drew her close and rested his chin on the top of her head. With her sensitive fingertips, she tickled the hair at the base of his neck, then unhooked the clip that held it in place. With a flip of her fingers, his long hair parted over his shoulders and down his chest. She laid her head below his chin and played with the silvery strands. Idly, possessively, she worked knots into patterns in his hair, then unknotted them and began anew.

Rodani seemed content to hold her and let her play until she lifted her head for a kiss. He obeyed her silent request with a gentle touch of his lips. "Did you not get your fill the other night?"

"Oh, you filled me more than adequately, aisu." She ran her fingers down the long lengths of his hair and brought the tail of one up to tickle his nose. "But I feel empty again."

"I have a remedy in mind."

"And in the body, too?"

"If you will honor me."

She slid off his lap and gestured grandly. Rodani took her out-flung hand and led her to the bedroom. It was the work of mere seconds for them to doff their clothes. Belatedly, Rodani locked the door to Hamman's hallway, then crawled in beside her. He drew his hands down her body, and his knee up between her thighs. She pulled him close to kiss him, wrapping her arms around his neck. His warm breath and spicy scent enveloped her. With a rush of intensity, she opened herself to him, and in a moment, he was inside. He stroked her intimate places while his hands made forays over her breasts.

The fire between them grew from a warm glow to a raging furnace, enveloping them both. They rocked together, skin to skin, the dance of joining drawing them into the here and now, their senses pared down to scent and touch. They drove each other by turns, closer and closer to completion, until there was nothing left but friction and fire. Cara cried out with the force of her crest, again and again, drawing Rodani with her to growl and shout as his body emptied itself into her in waves of voice and liquids.

They rested, breathing hard.

A bang on the door startled them both. "Brother."

Cara clapped her hand over her mouth. Her eyes went wide as Rodani looked aside, his face pale.

"When you remember that you have guests, you may open the door."

Rodani took a deep breath. "I have not forgotten, Shisa." He disengaged from Cara's body gently. "Go craft, please," he said softly. "I will deal with her."

"Brother?" Incredulous, she continued. "If she hurts you, I won't guarantee what I'll say."

"Go, kia. I do not need to fear her."

She grabbed him in a fierce hug as he started to draw away. "Don't you realize I want to defend you?"

He smiled. "I do. But often it is not the best thing for us."

Rodani dressed quickly, buckled the weapons belt around his waist, and left Cara still lying in the bed. He found Shisa, Chendal, Hamman, and Deremic sitting at the small table in the middle of the central room. Weary of controversies and confrontations, he waited for someone to speak. It wasn't long.

"Rodani," Shisa said, "we must talk."

"Likely there is nothing you can say to me that I have not already said to myself."

Shisa climbed to her feet. "You know what you face."

"Yes."

"Of all the things we were taught—"

"Shisa."

"How dare you?"

"Think back. Far back."

"There is no excuse for this blatant disregard of guild rules."

"Arimeso disagrees. I disagree. Cara disagrees."

"And to subject us to the sounds of—"

"Next time, tell me you are here."

She stopped, a look of disgust plain on her face. "Where is your honor, my brother?"

"Where it has always been. With the people who help me survive in this world. Starting with you, and ending with Cara."

"She drags you toward the muck and the mire. She does nothing to help you survive."

"But she does, Shisa." Rodani stepped closer to his sister, slipping his hands into his pockets. "Some weeks ago, she sat in front of me and listed, point by point, every positive trait she sees in me, every gift that she believes I have. And so many of those things were the exact things for which I have been reviled and beaten. Can you see what that would mean to me?"

"I see you lowering yourself to her level."

"And I see myself rising to hers."

Shisa's eyes widened in consternation. "Rise?"

"I am a better person for being with her."

"How do you say that?"

"She has taught me things I would not otherwise have learned."

"She needs to be gone!"

"You sound like Kusik," Cara said.

Rodani glanced over his shoulder. Yes, there she was, in the doorway, against his orders. But his sister sped on.

"You do not acknowledge his dishonor?" Shisa said, taking a step toward Cara. Rodani shuffled back, just in case.

"I see it as a greater honor, a'Shisa. He is honoring himself and the gifts he believes Sela has given him. And he is honoring me and the gifts I can give him. And he is honoring the taso and her house with his talents."

"Dishonor."

Cara rolled her eyes. "Are you creative at all, a'tem? Are you creative?"

"No."

"Then how can you dare judge him when you have no conception of what you're judging?"

"I am judging him on his breaking of rules."

"Do you have any idea how hard it is to ignore one's own creativity? How it's a little death to the self every time one tries?"

Shisa swept her hand between their bodies. "That has nothing to do with him crawling into your bed!"

Slowly, a smile crossed Cara's face. "But it does. You just can't see it."

"You are impossible."

Rodani stepped up. "Shisa, stop."

She turned back to him, fierce in her determination. "What you and your adashi think matters not to anyone, anywhen, Rodani. And what Arimeso thinks does not overrule guild prohibitions. Especially one as strong as this." Shisa waved her hands over them.

Cara opened her scarred palm in entreaty. "We are a successful experiment, a'tem."

"You are telling me the taso predicted this? I refuse to believe it."

"Not predicted," Rodani countered. "But when she realized what was happening, she allowed it."

"And allowed the dishonor to spread to her. That is ill-thought."

"Or more deeply thought than you realize," Cara said to her.

Shisa's gaze slid from Rodani to Cara, and she fixed her with a glare. "You have little idea of the depth and breadth of the disaster you are creating."

"I see no disaster. I see closed-minded people who can't let us live our lives the way we wish."

"Which proves my point."

"Think, a'Shisa," Cara said. "Please. Do we simply let the two species continue bumping elbows and growling at each other until another war erupts? Or do we try harder to understand each other? To learn and tolerate each other's differences? What's best in the long run? For both of us?"

"To adhere to honor."

Cara sighed and rubbed her head. "I am sorry you can't see what we see, a'tem." She bowed. "Pleasant eve." She left the room quietly. Rodani watched her go, undecided as to whether pride or anger toward her prevailed.

"You will pay, my brother," Shisa said. "Temi will bleed you when this is done."

Chendal remained silent during the fray, declining to intercede between siblings. He had his own opinions, which would come due in time.

Rodani glanced at Chendal. "I will endure that when it comes." He left the foursome to their judgments and returned to Cara's workroom, shutting the doors behind him.

She was back at the table where he'd asked her to go after their joining. He sat, declining to pick up his tools. Despite believing everything that he'd said to Shisa, there was something perverse in his adashi, something that prevented her from obeying simple orders. She would obey them when she saw sense in them. But if she lacked understanding, she ignored them—as if they didn't exist. It was their greatest problem, and one Rodani chewed on far too often. Was it a lack of trust? A lack of honor? Or just immutable differences? She didn't belong in an argument between him and Shisa, and could have caused a mountain of trouble. But she didn't listen. Or didn't care that he meant what he said.

Rodani glanced at her. Yes, she was watching him. Waiting? Well, he would end that.

He pushed off from the table and rolled over to her, leaning in. Putting one hand on the back of her head and the other over her mouth, he hissed. "I do tire of you disobeying me, Cara. I do not know what gain you intended, but again, you ignored my instructions." Her eyes widened, and he could feel the suction of her breathing against his palm. He put his face in front of hers and moved close. "Cease."

An inch from the tip of her nose, he bared his teeth and snapped them shut with an audible click. Ever so slowly, he pulled back, taking his hands from her mouth and head. With a calm he didn't feel, he pushed his chair back into position at the table and picked up his pencil, determined to ignore any human histrionics.

But Cara shot out of her chair and wrapped her arms around his shoulders from behind, planting her mouth right below his sensitive ear. Rodani froze at the touch. "Where would you be without me? Back to your boring old life?" She nipped the skin and blew a breath on the minute tufts.

"Au," Rodani said, jerking his head away. Cara reached down and tickled him just under the shoulder, at a bundle of nerves where his carapace began. He hissed and grabbed at her, pulling her away. She laughed and pretended to slap him, tapping with her fingertips at his cheek and jaw. As he grabbed one hand, she reached toward his pants with her other. When he caught the second one, she danced backward, yanking him off balance in the chair.

Goddess, what was this? Pretending to attack him? Dancing and grinning like a rahkti? She wrenched her arms in attempt to get out of his grasp. Rather than hurt her, he let go.

Mistake, he realized belatedly as she made another reach for his pants. "Temi's tempers, kia!" He grabbed the offending hand. She pulled him forward by rolling the chair, then danced around to his side, planting a kiss on his temple and tickling him at the nape of his neck.

Rodani reached back to grab the hand under his hair. But without sight, her reflexes were faster than his. As she blew a warm breath against his nape, he made a decision.

Standing quickly, he grabbed her around the waist and tipped her upside down, eliciting a peculiar, high-pitched squeal. Held to his chest, she couldn't get away, but her arms and legs were still free. Her hands inched their way to his inner thighs, causing shivers to erupt in his spine and ears. He reached down to draw her into a horizontal position, but she fought him with surprising strength. When her leg almost knocked his teeth together, he'd had enough.

He took her to the floor and pinned her legs and shoulders, then waited. Cara's breaths were ragged, but the smile didn't waver. She tried to roll away but was caught.

Did his simple censure cause this? Did he go a step too far? Their first fight overshadowed anything they'd done in anger since then. He watched her with a focused intensity.

The look in her eyes was almost feral. Rodani's heart thumped in his chest. *Goddess, no.* A surge of hormones hit his body at the thought. She reached up to caress the sides of his neck with her hands, drawing her thumbs up over his ears. He pulled away at the abrupt stimulation, which prompted another escape attempt. Rodani trapped her hands with his, drawing her arms over her head.

Cara began to struggle in earnest. The smile fled. "Let go."

Temi help me. How do I do this?

"Let go of my hands, Rodani."

He released them slowly, intent on her expressions. Anger? Desire? What was he seeing?

From beneath him, she kissed her fingertips, then pressed them against his lips.

Goddess above, her pupils pulsed. They did. His own responded, generated by the hormones deep within him. There was no help to be sought. He was alone with this. With her.

Hands free, she tickled him again. As he rolled off, she began to crawl away. He grabbed her pants, but they were loose at her waist. She pulled herself out of them and ran for the bedroom, laughing.

Rodani dropped them on the floor, followed into her bedroom, and shut the door.

***

Kusik folded up the temaso's private report and flopped it on the desk in front of him. He loomed over Arimeso, who sat quietly in her accustomed chair. "I was correct, was I not? She is a danger to you. And as long as they are scandalously enjoined, they are both in danger!"

"And he is also good for her, esuva, or did you miss that part of the report? And what is good for her is good for my accountants."

Kusik raised his fist, but found nowhere appropriate to vent his temper. The desk was his taso's desk, his chair belonged to her, as did the office in which he stood. And Arimeso herself, his taso, his mate, his formally declared spouse. She regarded his fist with wary aplomb. He let his arm swing down in unwilling defeat. "You ignore the most important portions of the letter."

"The letter does not say what you claim it does, my keso."

Kusik slammed his chair against the sumptuous desk and headed out, then stopped abruptly, head bent and arms crossed over his chest. Trapped by her punishments, he halted at the door in a boiling temper.

"Do you know what else I am ignoring, my taso?" he asked, digging his fingers into his arms. "The fact that you chose that human's honor over mine. The fact that you humiliated me with a lashing in front of her. The fact that Rodani has acted far more dishonorably than I ever have, and you refuse to allow him to be punished." Kusik spun around. "And, the fact that you are allowing him free rein to destroy my guild. I cannot believe what you are permitting him to do, Arimeso."

The taso stood up and walked to face him, her expression a mask of cold fire. "Do remember who and what you are, Kusik."

"How can I forget?"

"Your duty is to look around corners. And you do it well. My job is to look toward the sky, toward the future. And I do that well."

"And by refusing to look at the ground, you will fall. How many of us will fall with you?"

"I have heard enough," Arimeso said in a sharp tone. "Take your argument out of this office."

Enraged and blocked, he charged into the study they shared and slammed the door, then sat and stared at the radio. He clicked it on, spun a dial, and said, "I will speak with Kimasa."

***

Darkness hid the grounds outside Rodani's window. No moons cast shadows this night. Rodani stared blankly at the empty view, his thoughts churning. Nor was it just his mind that agitated. Hormones wound their way through the pathways in his body. A light touch, so far, just strong enough to put reins on his ability to rest. But the portent of that touch chilled him to his center.

What did you think, fool? That this cycle would not arrive? That you would not face another frightfully strong set of human reactions? Face them with the same level of ignorance that you had the night you approached her?

You are guild. You are strong. You survived more in your first twenty years than most do in a lifetime. You will survive this as well.

And you will do it for her sake.

The sound of a door opening in the hall put him on alert. It wasn't a soft on-a-private-errand noise, but a hasty wrench and thump. He palmed his pistol from the bedside table and waited just inside his bedroom door.

A pounding on their door proved him correct. Rodani slipped through the living room and put his back to the wall. "Who?" A thump behind him became Serano rolling out of bed.

"A'tem," Deremic said. "A'Cara woke up in a fright, saying she saw someone in her workroom."

Rodani unlocked the door and pulled it open. "You searched?"

"Yes, a'tem."

Rodani followed the servant across the hall. Cara sat on the edge of her bed with her arms crossed over a shirt hastily donned.

"What did you see, kia? Or hear?"

"Something woke me up, aisu," she said, staring into the workroom. "I needed the facilities, so I was probably sleeping lightly. It may have been a soft sound. I don't know."

Himself shirtless, Rodani stood over her like a teacher questioning an errant student. His pistol pointed at the floor, his finger off the trigger. "And?"

Cara looked up. "You must think I'm a frightened child, dreaming of bad men."

"No one should fault you for that." Rodani waved his fingers. "Did you find anything moved? Anything missing? Did this person approach your bedroom? Was it a man or woman?"

Cara closed her eyes; the skin around them tightened.

She's thinking, concentrating, he decided, and waited.

"Probably a man," she said. "Not slender enough for a woman. I think he moved from my worktable to the door."

"Did you hear him go out?"

Her shoulders drooped as she exhaled. *Relief? Concern?* Surety escaped him this time.

"I should have, but..."

"Check your room for items that have been moved or taken, kia. Any other intentions, we would be unable to discern now."

Cara approached her worktable with small steps. *Hesitant*, he judged. *Unsure?* She studied it with evident care...but touched nothing. Next, she went into the study. Rodani followed her, watching as she roamed the area. Dining table, bookcase, tea table, couch. Suddenly she stopped, staring at her 'corder. She looked closely, then leaned over the table. Bringing her hands to her ears, she spun around to face him, eyes wide.

That look did not bode well. "Kia?"

She ran past him and looked again at the worktable, then on to the bedroom. With frantic motions that hurt her hands, she searched for something. Something she wasn't finding.

"What is missing, Cara?"

A look of pain crossed her face. "My earrings," she said. "The ones you—," she glanced at Deremic, "—you made me."

Dismay washed through him, along with another wave of the hormones that had fled when the chaos started. Was she so careless, or did a thief with a key really exist?

"Where were they?"

Cara headed back to the study. "I took them out when I danced, since they get caught in my hair. I put them on the table, right by my 'corder." She picked it up and looked beneath it, then on the floor and the couch. As she stood up, her face and shoulders tensed, and she cocked her head downward. "I wouldn't have lost them, aisu. I would not have."

"Calm, kia," he said. "Deremic will stay in your workroom for the rest of the night. We will search again in the morning."

"Do you believe me?" she asked.

"About the presence or the earrings?"

"Both."

Caution, he willed himself. *Tread carefully.* "I do not dispute you, kia. Let us see what the day brings."

Her head moved in that up-and-down motion he knew as *Yes.* Rodani signaled Deremic with a hand motion and went back to his own room in an effort to calm his overloaded system. It didn't need any more agitation from being near her.

FIFTEEN

Kusik made his way through the dark hallways, disobedient to his punishment, barefoot and silent. In the far corner of the manor, the entrance to the Enclave was similarly quiet. He passed by the front entryway, the empty acolyte's desk, and the common prayer rooms. Farther beyond, he stepped into a doorway and waited.

"What did you bring me?" said a form by the fireplace.

Kusik stepped up to her and laid a tiny pile of metal in her palm.

"Earrings," Kimasa said, studying them in the firelight.

"I believe Rodani made them for her, but I cannot be certain without arousing suspicion."

"Tell me again what it is you are seeking, a'Keso."

"A petition to the goddess for return of the human to her own people. To keep our taso safe, our house safe, our guild safe."

The earrings glittered in the firelight, sparkles in the dark.

"I will need at least two days to divine the proper ritual."

"Anything you can do, Kimasa. Anything."

"Leave it with me."

***

Morning brought no answers to Rodani. The earrings had not appeared, only more powerful waves of hormones. The urges could hardly be denied, despite Cara's concerns from the night before. Knowing her hormones were also on the rise, Rodani turned her attentions away from missing items and nighttime shadows. He whispered to her, held her, stroked her, and rode her up to the crest with all the controlled passion he could gift to her.

Sated, hormones quiescent for a time, he crawled off of her body and out of her bed. She lay before him, a gentle smile playing across her lips.

Tempted, he was so tempted to crawl back into her arms. Goddess, where did his sense of duty go? Just because she was in receptive phase didn't mean the last ten years of his life could be ignored. He would take care of her needs as often as necessary, for as long as the phase lasted. But Kusik was angry enough at him. There was no sense in poking that growling beast by being late for another guild meeting.

He bent down and nuzzled his forbidden adashi and felt only a pang of guilt. Damn all unnecessary guild rules, anyway. He shrugged his body into his clothes, and with an unadmitted sense of longing, walked out.

The halls were colder. Winter was deepening, and so was his sense of attachment. Why in all of Sela's known universe did he bond so strongly with a human woman? Just because he was a little late in finding someone of his own species didn't mean he had to go haring off into the hinterlands for a compatible bedmate. Goddess of all, what a tangle.

Hormones rushed through his body with renewed strength. Everything vibrated now, from the tips of his ears to the ends of his toes, and it didn't bypass his groin. In the intervening years, he'd forgotten how distracting that sensation became. Annoying at best, a lethal danger at worst, the desires interfered with concentration and fine motor skills—not to mention short-term memory—and they weren't going away as long as Cara needed him. Receptivity was a double-edged blade for both woman and man. At its height, everyday tasks became a chore. Even eating went by the wayside for a day or so. The raging waters of hormone-driven desires washed away rational thinking in its passage. Good thing it was self-limiting.

Voices floated out of the meeting room. Was he late? Had he poked the growling beast after all?

Only one head turned to him as he entered. Timan looked him up and down as he walked to his chair. Settling in, he rested his forearms on the table in front of him. Silence slowly worked its way out from his seat to the two ends of the table. Kusik cleared his throat.

"Why are you here?"

Without moving his head, Rodani glanced over to Kusik, then across to Serano. His partner's eyes were wide.

"A'Keso?" Rodani asked.

"After all these years, you are unable to judge the state of your own body?"

Rodani swallowed but held still. Hormones thrummed inside, nearly audible from heightened awareness. His ears twitched and his hands shook slightly. "I am well."

"Undoubtedly." Kusik tapped his papers on the tabletop. "You may leave."

"A'Keso, I am capable—"

Kusik leaned forward. "Leave."

Rodani stole a last glance from his partner and pushed himself up from the table. Except for the tread of his boots, the room was without sound. He walked out as he had walked in, voiceless, filled with trepidation. Behind him came the muttering.

"He has a bedmate?"

"Temi's pants, who?"

"Goddess help her."

"Maybe that mirrored painter who hangs around the human?"

Laughter circled the table—and came to rest next to Serano. "Did you gift him with one of your castoffs, a'tem?" Imal quipped.

Rodani wandered down to a room in the hall of metals and collapsed onto his stool. He pulled an old design book toward him, then let it fall at the edge of the worktable. Opening the book, he flipped through several pages of designs, but nothing caught his attention. Only the insistent undercurrent of buzzing, making concentration difficult at best. He stuck his fingers in the toolbox, rattling a cornucopia of shopworn instruments.

A spike in his hormones brought an answering twinge to his groin. Rodani heaved his body off the stool and went out into the hallway. He wondered if Cara was out of bed, or still lingering in the warmth they'd created together. That image turned the twinge into a muscular grip in his pelvic orifice that stopped him cold in the corridor.

Temi's torment! Panting in the halls was for adolescent males, randy with their first experience of hormonal surges. He needed to seek his own room. Or Cara's. When would she need him again? This eve? Earlier? He wasn't sure how her cycle ran, and she didn't seem to be forthcoming on the subject. Wellaway, they'd gotten past worse. They would make a path through this, too. He continued to walk.

By tomorrow, he'd have to cut fluids. Bodily waste channels had a tendency to clog up under the pressure and swelling. It went along with the drop in appetite. Only one desire fed the body at the height of the ride, and fed from it, as well. The body weakened, starved of everything but sexual drive. It was a tough ride, but one that few regretted.

Rodani came out of reverie in the garage. Blinking, he looked around. Obviously, his situational awareness was worth less than a broken practice knife, so driving was forbidden as a diversion. As, by default, were benatacs. He inclined his head toward the garage master, who stared at him from under the hood of a carriage, then tripped the switch on the wall radio.

When the line connected, he heard Hamman's voice.

"Is Cara well, or disturbed?" He waited for the answer, trying to ignore a new unsteadiness of his legs.

"She seems well, a'tem."

"Thank you." He walked back inside the manor proper, and around to the library. He circled the room once, twice, running his fingers past book titles, but nothing looked likely. He wanted to call the guild library in Tendiman, but secrecy forbade that. Serano might have the answer to his question, but no, he would not share this with a disgruntled partner. Most men their age, Serano included, would have passed through this several times already.

Kimasa. The Enclave might have such knowledge. He sought the hall of priestesses and was ushered into the selaso's presence.

She greeted him with a bit less warmth than she was wont, possibly for the difficult scenes they'd shared during Cara's injury and recovery. "I can see what your body is doing, te'oto. But how can the Enclave assist you?"

Rodani perched himself on the chair facing Kimasa. "Are there...herbs...that can mitigate these symptoms?"

Kimasa's eyebrows shot up, her pupils wide. "Why would you wish to?"

"This is the first cycle with Cara, and," he clenched his fists. "I wish to be more in control of myself." Rodani fidgeted in his seat. "There may be unknowns in this, the human way. I wish not to be caught up in or cause a problem."

"It is a gift from the goddess, Rodani. Not to be presumed upon or manipulated, but shared and enjoyed."

"You do not see my concern? What of her safety?"

Kimasa blinked once, twice. "In bed?"

"Or out of bed, a'Selaso," Rodani snapped. "I am riding blind."

"Trust in Her, te'oto. She will guide you where it is proper to go."

Face masked, Rodani bowed and left. He was beginning to see Cara's side of this issue. Platitudes and empty words did not stack well against facts, against hard evidence. Kimasa would assume she had helped him in some way. Rodani knew better. Her help required his belief. He had little left.

Cara was at her sewing machine when he returned to her rooms. "You look like you need rest, aisu," she said, and nodded toward her bedroom. "Lay down?"

"Yes," he said, after a moment's distraction, not even thinking to chide her for the minor discourtesy.

Her bed sheets felt cool to his buzzing body, which brought a modicum of welcome relief. Rodani called upon his guild training in forced relaxation and drifted off to sleep.

***

Naremit wandered into the festive room. Boredom was not a state he expected to reside in after guild graduation. Aside from chasing after that dishonorable human in the south woods, he'd had little but communications duty and meetings.

No one fought in the corner ring. No bets placed; no hard-earned coins exchanged hands.

Garidemu waved him over. A bottle sat on his table, half-empty. Judging by the look in his eyes, Garidemu sat in his chair, half-full. He hadn't been a pleasant man since the human arrived, and had only gotten worse since Shurad's death. Naremit wasn't sure whether Garidemu blamed Rodani or Cara more, but the man didn't seem to be looking for a peaceful resolution to his grief and anger.

"Cousin," Naremit said as he sat.

"A'tem," came the sloppy reply.

Naremit picked up the bottle of local spirits and eyed the level of the remainder. "It is not solely up to you to keep the brewers in business."

"I know a benatac that is hankering after your body, too."

Naremit smiled for an instant, then lost what little humor he held. "Revenge is a heavy dish, a'sel. It does not digest well."

Garidemu slammed his glass on the table. "What revenge?"

Naremit's eyebrows shot up. "You were not the one?"

"The one?"

"Someone spoke to the Enclave about Rodani and that human."

"Why?"

"That I have not figured. But she dishonored herself pretty thoroughly and got injured as well. I saw it."

"What happened?"

"She ran, instead of facing the selaso."

Garidemu's eyes went wide, his pupils pulsed in surprise. "And she was punished?"

"Likely. But the best punishment she did to herself. She ran into the woods and tried to embrace a camabarin tree."

Garidemu sputtered, spewing his drink. He grabbed a napkin and coughed into it. "That is a worse punishment than getting whipped."

"I saw her hands," Naremit said. "They looked as if she had fought a knife fight without a weapon."

"Goddess."

"Yes, Sela gave you some relief for our revenge, and for Shurad's memory."

Garidemu twirled the bottle in his fingers, deep in thought. "I would do more."

"What could you do to a woman with no honor, guarded by a temichi with no sense?"

"Au, interrupt her supplies. Raid her cache of fabric. Destroy her finished projects before they're sold."

"Start rumors she is stealing," Naremit said with a smile.

"Stealing what?"

"Thread?"

The look Garidemu gave him was dirtier by lengths for the alcohol in his body.

Naremit bent close. "We could kill her."

"How?"

Naremit sat back again and reached for the bottle, a look of concentration on his face. "It would require your assistance."

"You have only to ask," the potter said.

Naremit stood up. "A bit of research, first, a'sel."

Outside the room, walking by, was Naremit's new eye-catcher. "Toranel!" The guardian glanced at him, then slowed and waited for him to catch up. "Pleasant eve," he said.

"And to you as well," she replied.

Naremit moved in next to her, matching her pace to an exactitude. "I was just discussing the human with Garidemu."

"An unpleasant subject. Why?"

"I fear our keso is caught between the taso and what is best for the House."

"That is not unusual," she offered.

"We might help."

Toranel raised her eyebrows.

"We might rid the House of her presence," Naremit said.

Toranel stopped at the door to her quarters. "And you have just the derring-do to accomplish this?"

Naremit reached out and stroked her neck lightly, just below the ear. "Will you hear me out?"

SIXTEEN

From the moment he awakened, hormones radiated through every part of Rodani's body. Despite the fact he'd sought his own bed last night after their joining, he still felt as fevered as if she'd spent the night beside him. His pelvic orifice ached, swollen and hot, with a needed release.

Rodani tried to will himself back to sleep but felt smothered by his blankets, and the ache turned into a fierce itch. The urge to allow his male organ to be released from its confines overwhelmed him, and he began to reach downward.

No, he told himself. The proper, goddess-approved release was with his bedmate, who was almost certainly lying awake on her own sheets, waiting for him.

Bleary-eyed but forcibly awake, Rodani stumbled out of bed to the privy. Yes, that relief was more difficult today than yesterday. Less water. Less food. More Cara.

He walked past his bed, then had to backtrack. *Weapons belt, fool,* he told himself. *You have a brain. Use it.*

Across the hall, he let himself into Cara's workroom and peered into her bedroom. Asleep? Well, she would not be for long. Rodani undressed quickly and slipped in beside her, his pelvis an undeniable itch that blocked out nearly everything in its demands. As Cara's eyes opened, he reached for her and drew her against him.

He groaned and shuddered as his penis pushed its way out past swollen tissues. Cara parted her legs, and Rodani wasted no time relieving the terrible itch. It took all his force of will to focus on her as well, to see that she also received what she needed. He had enough sense to realize her state did not seem to match his own, then pleasure erupted from within him, exploding outward through his body. His fingernails dug into the sheets as he cried out, gasping. When the itch mercifully faded and he regained his sensibilities, he realized Cara had remained quiet. But as he reached for her favorite places, she stopped him. That made no sense. "Kia?" he asked, to make sure.

"I'm well enough. Half asleep," she said.

Joking? No sense. But he let it go. She would explain when she was ready, or not. Her choice.

"Rest," she told him, then kissed him and got up.

Temporarily sated, temporarily free of the demanding nerve endings, Rodani drifted off.

When he woke again, it was because of a voice. A child's voice. With shaky limbs, he sought it out. Not in the workroom, but in the study.

Ikemi sat cradled in Cara's lap with a book in his hands. Iraimin sat in the overstuffed chair near the fire.

Cara welcomed him with a smile. It eased him somewhat, this accepting nature of hers. Her honor twisted him in knots, but her gifts made his life worth living. She bent her head to listen to Ikemi's recitations.

From the corner of his vision, Rodani saw Iraimin rake him up and down with her eyes and stiffen. But she greeted him properly, at least. He slid onto the empty end of the couch and tried to relax. The buzzing inside of him had returned. Not as strong as it was. Not yet. But the ache was not far behind. And then would come the raging itch. It was that which drove him to seek relief in Cara's body, knowing she felt something similar. It derailed every rational thought, every urge except the one to satisfy the craving.

One of Temi's two-faced demons, it was: blessing and burden in one.

Cara halted her tutelage to let Ikemi off her lap. He'd begun to fidget. "You didn't greet the temichi, Ikemi," she said.

Ikemi stood still and drew his hands behind his back in all the solemnity a child of five could produce. "Bright morn, a'tem."

"Bright morn to you, ki'oto," Rodani replied gravely.

"What is wrong with your eyes?" the boy said.

No, he thought. *Not here, not now.* "Nothing." He clenched his fists to keep his hands from shaking, but there was no controlling his pupils, or his swept-back ears that twitched.

"But they—"

"Nothing," he said firmly.

Ikemi cocked his head and turned back to Cara. "Did you—"

"That is not how you end a conversation, Ikemi," Rodani said with some pique.

Ikemi's eyes widened at the censure. He hunched his shoulders as if expecting a blow.

"Ikemi," Cara said. "You incline your head and address him. Like this." She lowered her head at an angle. "A'tem." Ikemi mimicked her. She smiled. "Now face him and do it."

Ikemi complied, quiet and diffident. Rodani relaxed, mollified for the moment. Discourtesy in Cara, he could overlook or correct with a few words. Discourtesy in a child rankled him for reasons he never cared to explore.

Ikemi prattled on, pulling at Cara, demanding attention, running and rolling around. Cara tickled him, smiling at his childish laughter. The boy was another enigma that hovered around his bedmate. Was it proximity to her receptive phase that prompted this bond with him? Did she really wish for a child? He hoped not. That would require her returning home.

Ikemi squealed in glee, enraptured with some trick Cara had just performed with a string. Rodani winced as the sound invaded his body, stretching already taut nerves.

"Cara." He rubbed his jaw beneath his ears with both hands. "He can go back to his room."

She looked over at him in surprise. "Does he bother you? He hasn't been here long."

A rising wave of hormones washed through him, disrupting his path of thought. *Goddess. Let it go.* In the midst of a phase was not the right time to offend her. He stood. "No matter. I will find elsewhere to be for a while." He inclined his head in an effort to further ensure her calm. "Enjoy his visit."

Shakes and vibrations were coming back into his stride. His pelvis pulsed with extra blood flow. He couldn't drive. The thought of a benatac between his thighs made his ears twitch in imagined pain. He couldn't craft, couldn't study Cene'l, couldn't sing in front of the others. Probably shouldn't practice with weapons, either.

And as the ache in his pelvis increased, sleep was out of the question.

He wandered into the rooms he shared with Serano, then paused as he realized his partner was still in residence. He ignored the quizzical look that came his way and flopped down on his bed.

Boot steps intruded into his quest for rest. "Why are you here?"

He opened his eyes to see his partner leaning against the door frame. "Ikemi is in her rooms. With Iraimin, as well."

"Au, a couple of days you will be past it all."

"And until then, all I can do is walk, ride her, and sleep. Fitfully."

Serano stared at him, arms crossed. "You act as if you have never been through this before."

"I have."

"Been a while?"

"Go climb a tree in a thunderstorm, tem'u."

Serano's expression turned hard. "If you had not chosen dishonor, you would not be paying this coin right now."

From his supine position, Rodani waved his hand in dismissal of the complaint. Another tide of hormones washed through him. He swallowed hard and breathed carefully in an attempt to keep his penis from committing an embarrassing impropriety. With each joining and release, with each increase in his hormone levels, came an upwardly spiraling drive for it to emerge by its own will instead of his. Such a lack of control was inexcusably childish, and he would not give his partner the satisfaction of noting it. Rodani turned on his side, his back to the door and to disapproving temichin.

"When are you going to end this affinity, Rodani?"

Rodani's anger flared at his partner's judgment. "Leave me be."

"Submit yourself for guild punishment. You will survive it. Regain your honor. Come back to us."

"I have not left. You and the others have turned away."

Serano banged the door frame with his fist. "Temi's knives, Rodani. You spend all your time pretending the world is the way you think it should be and pay no attention to what is in front of your face. Grow up."

Rage broke past his hormones. Rodani came off the bed with a roar and shoved his partner nearly off his feet, forbearing by a finger's width to beat him bloody. "And you refuse to see what I see because you fear it!" He pushed Serano out and slammed the bedroom door shut. "You are a coward!"

He was of a mind that Serano would kick his door down, much as he himself had done to Cara's. He waited in ready stance, shaking, hoping the door stayed shut and intact. He wasn't capable of a prolonged fight, and Serano knew it.

The door stayed closed.

Rodani collapsed on the bed. A groan escaped him as his pelvic area began to itch. He knew better than to touch it unless Cara was by his side. He got up and staggered out.

Thank Sela's mercies. Serano was nowhere he could see.

***

Iraimin said goodbye to Ikemi at the door of the nursery and headed to the Enclave at a rapid pace. Good goddess and Temi's travesties. She could scarcely believe what she'd seen. But the evidence was clear, even if her heart was twisted in knots. No adult could mistake the symptoms. Rodani radiated the effects of hormones so clearly, she could have seen it across the room. What was strange was that she didn't see the same in Cara.

Could it be someone else he was reacting to? But why wouldn't he be with that woman? Why would he be wandering Cara's rooms as if they were his? Sela, forgive her, but jealousy erupted as she admitted to herself that she wanted to have Cara for her own.

Could they have? Could he? Iraimin puzzled that out as she fled into the confines of a prayer room. With shaking hands, she lit candles and dribbled incense over them. Kneeling, she labored to bring herself under control.

Yes, she decided, he could. She'd seen and heard more than enough to believe it of him. She, herself, had told Cara of his eccentricities. What was this but one more? She knew of the guild rule but discounted it as no more than a prohibition based on superstition—something she would never allow herself to succumb to. Willing her body to calm, she prayed to Sela.

With time came a sense of quietude, a serenity that settled over her with the caress of a summer mist. She snuffed out the candles and stood, stretching the cramps from her legs.

"You looked troubled when you came in, child."

Iraimin smiled at the voice and turned to look at the speaker. Kimasa's eyes radiated warmth, her pupils wide ovals in the dim light.

"A'Selaso," Iraimin said with reverence in her voice. She bowed her head and took a deep breath. "I just gained knowledge of something. Something I might rather have not known."

Kimasa smiled. "Then it is up to you to find out why Sela gave you that knowledge."

Iraimin shut her eyes. "May I speak to you in confidence?"

"Of course. Does it deal with the taso's safety?"

Iraimin's eyes shot open. She clasped her hands in front of her, both courtesy and constraint. "I think not. But in truth, I do not know."

"Come."

Iraimin followed the high priestess into her chambers and sat down.

"Tell me what you will," Kimasa said.

"A'Selaso, all of us who spend time with the human, Cara, know that she and Rodani were called before the Enclave recently. I gave evidence at the inquiry for Kusik as to the nature of Cara's injuries."

"I remember," Kimasa said.

"At the time, I did not know why they had been called to an inquiry. Now, I believe I know."

Kimasa smiled, secrets in the upturned lips.

"You knew?" Iraimin asked, wide-eyed.

Kimasa waved her fingers, tossing the impertinent question. "And what will you do with that knowledge?"

"Not chide them. Cara seems content."

"And you, child?"

"I confess to disappointment."

"Seek Her wisdom, ki'ono. You will be guided."

Iraimin stared at her fingers, wiggling them in her lap. "If she and Rodani are truly together, she is bonding herself ever more strongly to our species, a'Selaso."

"That may be."

"Then she may still be brought into the realm of the goddess."

"She had already enjoined with Rodani when she refused the healing touch."

"You are convening a group healing session soon, I believe."

"Why would she accept the second when she refused the first?" Kimasa asked her.

"Would it hurt to ask?"

"You might know that answer better than I, my child."

Iraimin bowed. "I will try."

SEVENTEEN

Cara's hands ached, as did her lower back and her neck. In between all of Rodani's needs for attentions the last few days, she'd spent less time on this commission than was wise. But pushing too fast through the quilting process only caused more delays. Broken needles, frayed and snapped thread, mismatched seams that had to be ripped out, everything seemed to come together wrong.

Speaking of which, she wondered again what was on her lover's mind. He wasn't himself. Yesterday was a repeat of the days before. He adjusted his clothes as if they didn't fit, rubbed his arms and legs as if they hurt, and was as temperamental as a mother in labor—except with her. He seemed to tiptoe around her, treating her with exaggerated care as if she was a glassblower's latest creation.

And all the joinings? He wasn't talking. The release he got from her each time seemed to calm him for a while. Then he was back to twitchy again.

They really should talk. Really should.

Really.

But he seemed so...disoriented. Curt with everyone else. And she didn't want to set him off. Emphatically did not. A twitchy alien guardian with a waist belt full of deadly implements didn't seem to be a creature she should poke. Not now, when he'd lost his normal patience. Not now, when she had so much to lose with an unfortunate remark.

So, she would bide her time. For a while longer.

With a snap, the thread broke. She smacked her fist on the table, then struggled to make her healing fingers rethread the needle. As she grumped and cursed at it, Rodani walked in from her bedroom. Red flags popped up from her subconscious, waving energetically. He was dressed, certainly. There was the belt. His clip held back his beautiful hair. Still, he looked disheveled. *Off.*

He walked in and plopped himself down in his chair. *That was it.* His grace was gone. The graceful body moves she loved to watch were gone.

"Kia," he said with a shaky voice, "we must talk."

No shit. "Please do, aisu."

Rodani stared at her cluttered table and fumbled for his drawing instruments. "How long will you be receptive?"

She scrunched her eyes down, puzzled. That wasn't how she expected the conversation to start. "Receptive?"

He glanced at her, expectant, pupils wide.

"Receptive, able to receive?" she probed, hesitantly.

"Yes. Yes," he said, as if she knew what he was talking about. His hands shook as he played with the pencil, and a spasm of his pupils betrayed an inner turmoil that matched his outer facade.

"Receive what?" she asked.

Rodani blinked, and his ears twitched. "Receive," he said slowly, and waited, paling into embarrassment. Waited until she shook her head. "Me."

As if that added anything to her understanding. She attempted to add one and one and ended up with zero. "How long will I be able to receive you?"

"Yes," he said quickly.

"Rodani, forgive me. I hear your words, but not their meaning."

He sat back in the chair to twiddle the pencil in his fingers, contemplating what she could only guess. "You receive me," he said slowly. "We join."

Well, that much was clear. "Yes."

He opened his hand as if to offer her something. "How much longer?"

Cara rubbed her eyes, weary with a worry she'd been denying for days. "How much longer will we join?"

"Yes."

"As long as we both wish, I assume," she said. Then a knot formed in the pit of her stomach. It didn't make sense, but nothing in this topic made sense. "Are you displeased with me?"

He stiffened, as if she'd insulted him. His eyes narrowed.

"No, kia. Are you?"

"No. Then why do you ask how long our affinity will last?"

218

His hands tightened on the pencil, prompting Cara to wonder if it would survive the conversation. "That is not what I asked."

Cara huffed in rueful humor and smiled. "Then I'm missing some important bit of information, aisu. Is there another way you can ask your question?"

Plainly, Rodani was out of his depths. His ears still twitched, and he remained pale and tongue-bound. The pencil flew through a series of finger acrobatics, then fell to the floor and rolled under his chair. He retrieved it and put his attention back on the table between them.

"A woman…" he closed his eyes, then opened them slowly. "…has cycles. A man—"

"You said Selandu women don't bleed." She regretted the discourtesy of interrupting, but didn't want to make him go through this a second time.

"They do not," he replied, a touch of impatience in his hurried speech. "They have cycles. A man responds to them. When a woman becomes receptive, her mate—or others, if she is unchosen, becomes receptive to her. When she…is no longer receptive, he returns to his previous state, until the next time."

Cara ran her fingers through her hair and scratched her scalp. *A woman has a cycle. They join. Then she stops, and he returns to normal.* She scratched again, but nothing sensible worked its way out of her head. What in all the gods' names was he trying to say? What did he think they were doing?

"Every time a man joins with a woman," she said, "it is because the woman has a cycle. When they are finished joining, the cycle…" The thought slowed and became enveloped in a fog.

"No." Rodani clenched his fists on the table and bowed his head. "Goddess, give me the words," he whispered.

Cara reached over and touched his arm. He shivered but refused to look at her.

"Why is this difficult, aisu?"

He took a deep breath. "It is rarely discussed, and then only from parent to a child when he matures."

"But my knowledge is that of a child sometimes."

He glanced at her from the corner of his eye. "I am not your mother."

She chuckled, then stopped. "Hamman is a mother."

"No. I need—" The pencil snapped in his hands. Cara jumped, and noisily let out the breath she didn't know she'd been holding.

"My duty," he finished lamely.

Cara sat back and folded her hands in her lap. "I'm listening, aisu."

Rodani stood, turning his back to her. His hands curled behind him, the fingers twisting and loosening by turns. "I am ill, kia." Before she could draw breath, he rushed on. "I am ill because you have been receptive for many days. That is unusual for the women of my people. I need to know how much longer you will be so."

Cara froze; the room became still—still as Rodani was, facing the door. No sense. No sense at all. She was falling into a well of miscommunication that was frightening in its depth. Rodani was sick, and desperately trying to ask her something. Something that would heal him?

"You're ill because of our joinings?"

"Ill because of the length of time, kia," he said, turning part way around. "Not because of the pleasure I have found with you." He cocked his head in her direction, though his attention remained on the stone floor.

"Because our affinity has lasted for weeks?"

"Not affinity, kia. Receptivity. Your cycle."

Cara leaned on the worktable; arms crossed. "Would it help if Hamman explained what a woman's cycles were?"

Rodani shivered and clasped and unclasped his hands behind his back. "A woman's cycles are her times of receptivity and non-receptivity. Times when she must join with a man, and times when she may wish not to."

A dim light began to glow in the back of Cara's mind. "And how long are these times?"

"She is receptive for four days or five, then non-receptive for twice as many weeks."

The light grew a little brighter. "For a hand of days, she's willing to join, then is not willing for two or three months?" Good gods. No wonder Serano jumped from woman to woman. It began to make sense.

"'Willing' is not the right word, kia. Hai!" Rodani spun back around to face the door. "Will not, cannot, neither is correct. She may or may not. And I am inadequate as teacher."

Cara stared at his back, black-clad, all tense and stiff across from her. "So," she said slowly, "you are ill because we have been joining every day for a week?"

"Yes." The affirmation came out in a rush of air, as if he had been waiting too long to speak it. "And I see no end to it."

"But aisu, not only have you not stopped, you're making requests of me as if I'm both meals and snacks, four or five times a day."

His silver hair pulled against the jacket as he bowed his head. "Because you are still receptive. While you are willing, my body responds. Only when you are not, will I stop responding to you."

Cara stood and crossed over to him and laid her hand on his waist.

"Rodani, I'm always receptive."

He stilled. His tall body turned toward her, slowly. "Always?"

"Always." Cara saw the comprehension widen his pupils.

"You cannot. It is not..."

"But it is."

He closed his eyes and pursed his lips and turned away from her for a third time. The rejection caught in her throat. "Rodani, what's so wrong?"

"Kia, if a man is around receptive women for too long, his body betrays him. He becomes ill from the constant desires."

"You can't control your desire?"

Rodani jerked his head around for a momentary glare. "Some, of course. We are not animals, Cara." His unsteady intake of breath allowed her time to hear the reproach. "But...Goddess...we are complicated. The rhythms of our bodies ebb and flow like the tides between the stars, and our desires follow."

Like a half-completed puzzle, some pieces fit, and some lay around in jumbles, too much to deal with at one time. A gust of wind rattled the window—and Cara's uneasy mind. "If I were a Selandu woman, you wouldn't be desiring me right now?"

Rodani wandered back to his chair and sat down, with that graceless flop of limbs. "If you were a Selandu woman, kia, you would no longer be receptive right now, and my desires would have ebbed alongside yours."

His square face, normally calm, looked drawn—as if he had spent too many nights sleepless.

"And you wouldn't be ill?"

"I would not be ill."

She returned to his side, fearing another rejection. "Why didn't you tell me?"

"I was waiting for your tide to ebb. I did not realize..." His jaw tensed. "Never before have..."

Good gods. Invisible undercurrents had been towing them out to sea, and she hadn't felt a thing. "I'm sorry, aisu."

"You did no wrong."

She ran her fingers under his hair, felt the solid muscles in his neck. They vibrated like wires in the wind, tensed in a spasm when the shutters clattered. "Nor did you. What now?"

He bent his head. "I must spend some time away from you."

Now it made sense. Too damn much sense. "For how long?"

"I am uncertain."

"And when you return?"

"I will still be uncertain." Rodani wrapped his arm around her waist. "Until I return, will you accept me one more time?"

Outwardly, she took his hand; inwardly, she hesitated. His body was shaking, and he was clearly worried. She led him to her bedroom. Just as the other times, quick was the watchword. In much less time than she wished, his body spent its burden and collapsed, trapping her beneath him.

"Aisu." Cara shoved at him. "Rodani, get off!" He rolled over slowly. Cara gasped for the breath his weight had pushed out of her, then felt the line of his arm touch hers. He was shivering. "Aisu?" Cara propped herself up on one arm. Rodani's eyes were half open, the nictating membrane nearly over the pupil. She shook him. "Rodani!"

He didn't answer. Didn't respond at all, just shivered in spasms that ran from head to toe. His skin burned under her scarred palms. His swollen pelvic orifice shone a dull red, the penis neither completely retracted nor fully extended. It pulsed with the spasms that flooded his body in waves.

Cara rolled out of bed and yanked on a robe. "Hamman! Deremic!" She flipped a corner of the sheet over Rodani's nether regions. It hid little.

Deremic trotted into the bedroom and took in the scene with a quick glance. He ran his hands over Rodani's face and neck, then peered into his eyes. "A'tem?" he said. "A'Rodani?" When no answer came, he drew his gaze down the length of Rodani's body and lifted the sheet. He stared for a moment, then dropped it and ran for the radio.

"Yes, an emergency, a'sel," Cara heard him say. Rodani growled as all the muscles in his body clenched in unison. A wet spot appeared on the sheet that covered him. Cara bent over his face. "Rodani!" His eyes roved the room restlessly, unseeing. His hands tightened into fists, then relaxed, then tightened in the continuing spasms. Deremic ran back in and stood over the bed, eyes wide.

"What's wrong with him?" Cara asked.

"I do not know."

She sat down next to Rodani on the bed and laid her head and arms across his shoulders. "Aisu. Aisu."

A clattering of footwear echoed down the hall. Deremic opened the door for the physician and his assistants. Rodani growled with another massive muscle spasm. Baldar swept the sheets off the bed and studied Rodani's unresponsive body. He ran a finger through the liquid that pooled around the penis and lifted his finger to his nose. It shone with a pink tinge. Abruptly, he pulled Cara up. "Get away!"

"Take him downstairs," he ordered his helpers. "Ice bath." As the assistants scurried to obey, Baldar grabbed Cara by her arm and marched her into the workroom.

"Talk."

"He said," Cara began, and pulled away to pace. "He said he was ill. Because of our..." Gods, Baldar had seen, he had seen. Everything. It was all so obvious. Oh gods, and the assistants, too! "Because, because he thought I was receptive, he was ill."

"What about your receptivity?" Baldar shot back.

"He said it went on too long. He was too—"

"How long?"

"A week."

"How long do your cycles last?"

Cara shook her head. "I don't have cycles. I'm always receptive."

Baldar stared at her, spun on the ball of his foot, and was out the door and down the hall in a sprint that left Cara openmouthed. She shut the door behind him and flopped down in her chair.

Rodani! She'd never seen him in such straits. Clutching his arms and shivering as he stood, wide-eyed with pulsing pupils, like he was in the midst of their lovemaking. And he'd wanted to join again. The sight of his comatose body shook her to the core. Panic made her lightheaded. Had their joining sent him over the edge? Had he known? Surely not. That meant he didn't know his own body, and that made no sense. He was too smart, too wise for that.

Shuffling, and the sound of fabric came out from her bedroom—Hamman changing the sheet. Cara picked up the dirty one, searching for a certain spot.

Blood-tinged. It hadn't been her imagination. Gently, Hamman pulled the sheet from her hands. "Shall I run the shower for you, a'Cara?" she asked.

"No." She stared at the wadded-up sheet. Her soul felt just as soiled, just as crumpled. "Will he heal?"

Hamman looked away. "I will ask the physician, a'Cara. When he has time." She left to wash away the outpourings from Rodani's body, wash away the evidence of their misguided loving. The room felt chilly in her solitude, the quiet too profound.

Gone, he was gone to where she couldn't follow, gone to a fate she was afraid to know. Would anything go right between them? Would any part of their lives flow smoothly? Smooth! She'd settle for less than mountainous, thanks. Settle for something like normal.

Cowed, bowed with the weight of worry on her shoulders, she collapsed on the couch, staring into the fire.

EIGHTEEN

Kusik entered Arimeso's office. His punishment over, he longed for his life to return to routine, to everyday worries of finances, fights, politics. His temporary policy of keeping his thoughts to himself had cooled the tempers between himself and his taso. But now, a new opportunity had presented itself.

Kusik sat beside her and leaned forward, elbows on his knees. "You do not know the latest, tisal."

She turned to him. "My ears are empty."

"Do you know the word 'hadaberi'?"

She thought for a moment. "An ancient affliction, brought on by a male taso having too many females available to him."

Kusik sat up, pleasure coursing through him. There were always possibilities. Always. "Rodani is hadaberi."

Arimeso blinked once, twice. A third time. "Impossible."

"No, tisal. He is in the clinic, comatose. I saw him."

"Who has he been with other than Cara?"

Kusik smiled, the corners of his mouth pulling down, a hint of malice for any Selandu to read. "No one."

"You are so sure?"

"No one that anyone can see. I have my own reports."

"Then?"

The smile remained. *Careful, careful,* he told himself. "She is continually receptive."

Arimeso's shoulders dropped in surprise. "Impossible. Again."

Kusik touched the tip of her ear lightly, ever so gently. "Your words do not turn falsehood to truth, tisal. She admitted it to Baldar."

"It cannot mean to her what it would mean to us. She is neither ill nor insane."

"But it means to Rodani what it would mean to any man. He will have to abandon his dishonorable attentions. If he survives."

Abruptly, Arimeso stood up, her skirts rustling. "I will see him."

Kusik rose in courtesy. "As my taso wishes," he said, waving his hand toward the door. "But he will not see you. Or cannot." He pulled out his 'com. "Six, One. Six, One."

"Six," Serano said.

"My office."

"Ninety-nine."

Serano pocketed his pistol, left the practice range, and made his way to Kusik's office at a respectable speed. The smell of gunpowder permeated his clothing, leaving behind evidence to sensitive noses of his previous whereabouts. "A'Keso," he said, as he entered the room.

Kusik crossed the distance between them, silent. Serano stiffened in courtesy, watching his keso approach from the corner of his eye.

"We have been given an opportunity," he said. "Your partner is ill."

"Ill? How? With what?"

Kusik's eyes narrowed, and the muscles in his jaw clenched. "Talk to Baldar. I have no wish to discuss it further. You," he crossed his arms, "are to take advantage of it."

"A'Keso," Serano began, then shut his mouth in the face of the rising tide of emotion in Kusik's eyes.

"You will replace him as the alien's guardian. You know her, you have spent time with her. Replace him in her bed, as well."

Replace... Serano blinked rapidly and shielded his astonishment behind a bland mask. "A'Keso..."

Kusik regarded him stonily.

"A'Keso, why? Why command me to commit the same dishonor Rodani has done?"

"To destroy her affinity to him. Divide her disloyalties. Then, under the guise of misunderstandings, you will anger her and cause her to choose to return home."

Serano let out a disbelieving breath. "So simple."

Kusik stepped nearer, his breath hot on Serano's face. "Your ways with women are legion, Serano. Use those skills you boast of so easily."

"Selandu women, a'Keso," he said. "Cara does not even look at me unless there is good reason."

"Then create that good reason."

"A'Keso, this is mixing the personal and the professional."

Kusik circled to face him. "You will use what skills I command you to, to keep the taso safe."

"I cannot command my desires, a'Keso."

He moved farther around, to Serano's other side, leaning forward. "See those things Rodani sees. Find what he has found."

"A'Keso, you do not know what you ask."

Wrinkles appeared at the side of Kusik's eyes. He sidled closer to Serano, chest to shoulder. "Are you guild?" he said in a low, accusing voice. His eyes pulsed.

Serano swallowed heavily, his hands clenched. "Yes, a'Keso."

"Convince her that you can take his place in her life. Then break her." A moment more he stared, then spun and left the room, through the back way into Arimeso's suite.

Serano collapsed into a squat, arms on his knees, staring at nothing.

Temi's knives! How? How? The paths before him showed naught but failure, rejection, and alien tempers over nothing he wanted from the start. He understood Kusik's indignation. But to add more emotions to the complexities that—woman—already held in abundance? A river about to burst its dikes was what she was. Better that Rodani deal with her.

Tem'u!

He shot up and out of the office in unseemly haste. He hadn't seen much of his partner since Kusik had sent him away from the most recent weekly meeting. He knew the signs, of course, having gone through it many times himself. Every adult did. When it was a woman's time, a man responded, then his response ebbed in tandem to her cycle's end.

The clinic's staff quietly bustled about their business of healing the sick, comforting the pained, and occasionally guiding someone across to Sela's waiting arms. Serano avoided the place as much as he could. Ill health was abhorrent to someone so aware of his own body, its needs, and its desires.

An assistant healer pointed Serano on his way. He rounded a corner and into a room, then stopped, staring at the tableau in front of him. Rodani's body had been immersed in a tub of icy water. A sling held his head above the waterline, his arms floated at his sides, limp. His dark eyes were closed, his legs weighted down to stay under the water. His pelvic orifice bulged as if caught in the instant before emergence. A healer turned to see who had entered the room. Seeing a temichi, he turned his back.

"What happened?" Serano asked.

"Hadaberi."

The word rattled around Serano's mind, stirring his memories. That only happened when a man had several women available to him. This made no sense.

"When will he wake?"

The healer put his hand on Rodani's chest, waited, then lifted it. "That is with the goddess."

For the second time in as many minutes, Serano ran the manor's hallways, heedless of the stares for the impropriety. Down the main corridor, up the stairs, to the doorway he rarely entered without his partner in front of him.

Inside, Cara sat at her worktable, head in her hands. Her fingers gripped the strands of her hair with a strength that matched the pain on her face. She looked up at his precipitous entrance. "I knew it wouldn't take you long."

"What happened?" Now, he would get an answer. Would not leave until he got an answer. Tension thrummed through his body.

"He said he was ill," she replied. "Said it was from too many joinings for too many days."

Serano sat down and leaned forward. "Why too many days?" he shot back. "Did you demand of him more than you needed? More than he could give?"

Cara let out a puff of air, and her fists hit the table. "No, Serano. And it was hardly necessary. He asked me. I didn't know what was happening. Why didn't he? Besides," she added, leaning against the chair back, "had I known he would go comatose, I would have refused him. As usual, you think the worst of me." She closed her eyes and rested her temple on the chair's side post. "Please go see about him." She looked up. "Or better, take me with you."

"I have seen him."

"He'll heal?"

Those strange blue eyes stared at him, innocent, almost. Could she have not known what such prolonged attentions could do to him?

Could Rodani have not known? Goddess, help them all. "Baldar was not in attendance, and the healer would not make a guess."

Her face twisted into that ill-formed expression he disliked. Rain began to roll down from her eyes. She covered the trickles with her hands as if ashamed of the display, then bent her head to the table, resting it on her arms. Serano watched her paroxysms with the same helpless frustration he felt in all their dealings. Kusik was mad. Madness, however, did not pull a guardian from his sworn duty.

Hesitant, Serano rested his hand on Cara's arm. It was warm, but small—like a child's. He cringed at the unbidden comparison. Under his hand, the arm shook with the force of her alien emotions, emotions more appropriately kept inside. "Rodani is in the goddess' hands, Cara."

"Oh, great," came the muffled reply. Serano caught the sarcasm, even buried as it was in the crook of her arm.

"I will speak to Kimasa on his behalf," he said, "and yours."

"I just want to see him."

"He would not wish that."

"Maybe."

"Truly, Cara. Not as he is now." Her choking sounds increased at his words. Lost as to how to comfort her, he removed his hand. "I will guard you while he is away."

"Why?"

What strange thoughts prompted that question? "Because you must be guarded."

The choking sounds continued, then a "thank you" reached his ears.

"Is there aught I could get you?" he asked.

"No."

Serano rummaged through his memories. "I would hold you—"

Cara's head shot up. Her wide eyes streamed water, and her face was red.

"—for comfort."

She turned away. "Thank you, no, a'tem."

Goddess and consort, Kusik, what have you demanded of me? Serano leaned back in his chair and let his eyes wander the room. What did they do with all their time together? Rodani spent an inappropriate amount of time here, but certainly not all they did was inappropriate. What did they do?

Cara shifted in her seat and rattled the tools on her desk, then got up and walked into her bedroom. Serano followed her, but stopped in the doorway as he realized her errand. Various types of splashing came from the facilities, then a flush, then Cara came out with a wet cloth on her face. She stopped when she saw him. Her eyes flitted between the two doorways, as if seeking an escape. Serano pulled his hands behind him and stepped back, letting Cara through to her workroom. She sat down again, picked up her quilting, put it back down again, picked up a tool, put it down, spun it while her eyes roamed the room much as his had done.

Next, she started for the study. Serano got up to follow. As he moved, she stopped and looked at him, then returned to her work chair, rubbing her scarred palms.

Strange creature, he thought, as she curled into the chair sideways. Her expressions, so terribly strong and unmasked, almost made sense. Her body's movements, her posture, they almost made him doubt her alienness despite the evidence in his sight. But the rain that began again to fall was a curiosity, a conundrum he failed to puzzle out regardless of how many times he'd seen it.

"Is there another problem, Cara?"

She wiped the rain from her eyes and took a deep breath. "Yes."

"Tell me."

"I fear to."

Serano crossed his arms, shocked and confused at the bold reply. Fear? He sat back down. "Why?"

"I thought it would be obvious."

"I am here to protect you from what you fear."

She hiccupped and dabbed her watering eyes. "I fear you. Your temper."

"Temper? I am not angry."

"I fear your hands."

"My hands."

"Yes."

Well, didn't this bode well for Kusik's orders. Their last argument was weeks ago, and she was afraid of the very hands he was supposed to touch her with. *Reassurance, yes. Reassure her.* "It is simple, Cara. I would ask you not to offend me."

She screwed up her face and turned away with a great exhale of breath. A flush of energy sped through Serano's body. He leaned forward, arms on her worktable. "Like that," he said sharply.

"And that's why I fear you!" she said, sitting up with enough force to wrench her chair. "I fear being alone with you. I fear talking to you. You don't know anything but how to take offense!" As she stood, her chair slammed back into the wall, rattling and echoing in his ears. Again, she started for the study, then stopped and began pacing the workroom.

"Rodani learned," he said.

"Rodani considered it his duty to learn." Cara glared at him over her shoulder. "And he has patience."

Patience? Serano considered the agitated woman pacing back and forth in front of him. He'd known Rodani nearly a decade, and patient was not a word he would use. Intelligent, yes. Introspective, far past normal. Stubborn? Enough to make more than one of Arimeso's people rage at him. But patient?

Serano stretched out his legs and stuffed his fists into his pockets. "Cara, I am here to guard you for as long as Rodani is not." She was going to wear a pathway across the stone floor if something didn't change soon. "And I mean you no harm."

Her heavy breaths reached him over the sound of her rasping slippers. Her face was an odd sort of mask of a type he hadn't seen. Eyes wide, mouth a flat line, but nothing moved except her chest and legs.

"Why do you pace?"

"Because I fear for Rodani. Because I fear you, and he's not here to protect me. I can't sit, and I can't run. I can't think, and I can't craft."

Holy Goddess of all. It began to filter through to him, past his confusion, past his own worry for his partner. Cara paced faster, her eyes wide, her breaths coming more rapidly. This was ill news. This was a human fuse, and it was lit. He stood up.

"Cara."

She jumped—Temi's knives. She jumped at her own name. *Help me, tem'u. What would you do? What would you say?*

"Calm, Cara." He held out his hands to her panicked stare. "Calm."

Eyes on his outstretched hands, Cara backed up to the wall, her elbow bumping the knife target Rodani had built for her. She didn't seem to notice either one.

"There must be something I may do for you," he said.

Her breathing became shallow and ragged. "Leave me alone. Please."

Serano dropped one hand, holding out the other to her in entreaty. "Rodani would not leave you in this state."

The odd mask went away; her eyes tightened as she looked aside. "He could calm me."

"Show me how."

"No."

"Why?"

"I can't trust you."

"I will not hurt you."

"I don't trust you!" She spun and slammed the back of her fist into the knife target. The heavy wooden board shuddered and fell forward, hitting the floor with a bang.

Serano took a deep breath as the sound faded in his ears. One did not engage in a battle with an unpredictable enemy, except in dire need. Kusik's orders were not yet so dire. Not yet.

He bowed. "Safe night." As he headed toward Hamman's hallway, he heard a soft, "I'm sorry."

***

Evening light had faded from the edges around the shuttered window, emphasizing the flames in the fireplace. Cara repositioned the pillow in her arms. The incense she'd burned was nearly out, leaving a pungent but less intrusive scent to the room. Empty room. Empty of Rodani. Her last sight of him rose unbidden in her mind, naked in her bed, comatose, pink-tinged fluid leaking from him. Deremic's panicked glance. Baldar's sharp questions, his stern orders to his assistant. The sight of her lover carted away on a pallet.

Surely, he was going to be okay. It was just an overdose of hormones or something, right? Baldar could handle that. She'd pestered Hamman for information, but the servant held her tongue, seemingly scandalized at the very idea of discussing it. Cara shifted on the couch, her legs cramping from disuse. Half her dinner still lay on the table, uneaten, unremembered.

A whisper of female slippers came into the doorway from her workroom. Hamman, come to check on her.

But no. Iraimin waited just inside, her hands clasped in front of her, courtesy to the mood of gloom in the room.

"Iraimin," Cara said, sweeping her hand over the other end of the couch.

The painter took a graceful seat and nodded. "I heard."

Cara glanced at her. "Heard what?"

"That your guardian is ill."

Oops. Who knew? What in all the gods' names did they know? *Damn it all, anyway.* Selandu couldn't keep secrets any better than humans did. "What were you told?"

"That he had an unusual illness."

Cara glanced back to the fire.

"That it is so unusual," Iraimin continued, "most people do not think to watch for it."

"I wish people didn't know."

"Not too many do, Cara."

"How did you find out?"

"Larisi."

Of course. Lots of thanks, Serano. "I want to go see him."

"I think you cannot."

"So I'm told."

"You worry for him?"

"Of course. Wouldn't you?"

"The Enclave can help you."

Ah, crap. "Thank you, Iraimin, no."

"You did not ask how."

"No, thank you."

Iraimin fell silent, watching the flames jump and jitter in the grate. "Would you let them show you how?" she ventured.

"Iraimin, my good painter, I mean you no offense," Cara said. "But if it's a drug, I can get it from Serano or home. If it's meditation, I can do it myself. If it's anything religious, I don't share your faith, and they can do it without me in attendance." She brought the pillow up to her chin. "No." She rubbed her scarred palm over the fabric. Rubbed her eyes and ran her fingers through her hair. "But if you would stay here for a time, and share the fire with me, I'd greatly appreciate it." She rubbed her hand on the couch. "I've missed you. You left angry twice recently, I believe."

"I was not angry, Cara." She stood up. "We should have drinks. Hamman?" she called.

"Oh, forgive me, sel'u. I lack courtesies."

"No need. Your thoughts are in the clinic." She leaned over to see through to the bedroom. "Two glasses, please. And a bottle. Whatever a'Cara drinks."

They sat in companionable silence for a time, nursing the libations that Deremic brought them. Finally, Cara stepped into the minefield. "Were you surprised? About us?"

"When I first realized it, yes."

Cara's head whipped around to look at her friend. "When was that?"

Iraimin smiled. "Some days ago, when I was here."

"How did you know?"

"Any Selandu adult would have seen it. He was reacting to you. To your receptivity."

"Gods," Cara said, taking a stiff swig of her drink. "I hope no one else saw it."

"You will have to ask him when you see him next."

"I hope I do."

"You will. The goddess would not give him to you only to take him away so quickly."

Cara swirled her drink in the glass, determined to avoid any more spiritual arguments. "Thank you for the thought."

"For you to be so bonded to him, he must bring pleasure to your life."

Cara smiled, the first in a very long day. "He does."

"I do remember telling you he walked an alternate path."

"I remember." Her smile broadened, then faded.

Cara got up and stirred the fire, adding a log with a grunt and a thump. "Rodani warned me more than once that no one should know of our affinity. Now it seems half the guild and all of the Enclave know. Not to mention the healers. It worries me as much as Rodani being sick does." She settled back into the couch and picked up the pillow, curling her arms around it. "Arimeso must know. No one's told me she does, but I can't imagine she doesn't."

"She seems to know everything."

"Yeah, and I know how."

"What do you mean?"

"A month or more ago, I found a wire in this room. Someone must have been listening to me. Us."

"What did Rodani say?"

"He didn't. He refused to mention it." *Crap.* And how much did Iraimin report back? "I shouldn't have told you that."

Iraimin glanced over to her. "I mean you no harm, Cara."

She smiled, wan and tired. "I believe you. Serano told me the same thing today. I'm not so sure I believe him."

"But he is your other guardian."

"My only guardian, now."

"His skills are respected."

Cara sighed. "Guild skills, yes. His human skills are worse than my Selandu skills."

"He has had less practice."

Cara scooted down on the couch, holding the pillow across her chest. "You're always so polite. I just want to be angry."

"At whom?"

Cara smiled at the painter. "That is a very astute question."

"Cara, we could use the Enclave in a slightly different way."

"How?"

"The selaso could divine a healing ritual for Rodani."

Cara waved her hand, tossing the idea. "I'm not allowed to see him. Maybe the selaso can."

"No, sel'u. She can do the ritual within the Enclave. The Goddess sees all. We do not have to be in Rodani's room for Her to hear us."

"If the selaso wants to do that, she can go ahead."

"But you could, also."

"It wouldn't help."

Iraimin leaned forward. "But it would. Your presence, your bond with Rodani, would enhance the effectiveness of the ritual."

"Or my disbelief would detract from the effectiveness. I could kill him, instead."

"She would not, Cara."

"How do you know that's not Her design? How do you know that's not the path She wants us to walk?"

"Because She is the goddess of good."

"And maybe what She sees as good is that he dies, and I go home, and the two species remain separate for all time."

Iraimin leaned back into the couch, her face now a proper blankness. "You mock me?"

Cara took her hand. "No, sel'u. I'm suggesting that this goddess you believe in could have any number of options, not just the ones you or I want. Either all of them are possible, or none."

"No, She has a plan."

"And if this plan is so important, why would She change it because we ask Her to?"

"You lack the understanding to see what I see."

"No, I can put myself in your place, into your beliefs, and make myself see what you see. But since I don't believe, I don't stay in your place. I come back to mine."

"I would change the way you see."

Cara smiled grimly. "I wouldn't."

NINETEEN

On a sigh and a clumsy grab at her needle, Cara continued the arduous task of rehabilitating her hands. With Rodani a second day in the clinic, she had little else to do. Practice was slow work, and frustrating. Her accustomed accuracy had gone by the wayside with the crippling effects of camabarin toxin. Slow and steady, Rodani had cautioned her, was the way to heal. Unfortunately, she was not a slow and steady human. Her activities danced and spun as quickly as her thoughts did. Not her mother's step-by-step careful plodding, necessary when one is diagnosing diseases or opening abdomens. Even during the painstaking quilting process, Cara's thoughts were ever on the next design, the next choice of fabrics, the next opportunity for private playing with Rodani.

And with that thought, a pang erupted in her heart and gut. Rodani was still sick, ill with more than just a germ, and Cara couldn't go to him. Couldn't see him. Couldn't get answers to her questions. Gods of the deep night, let Baldar's skills be equal to the illness.

Bootsteps echoed in Hamman's hallway, and Cara looked up expectantly, hoping against pessimism that it would be Rodani.

Serano entered the room. Cara's face fell into mask—as best she could manage it. "A'tem." She looked down, taking another stitch in the quilt.

Serano stepped up to her table and crossed his arms. "Are you hiding a rebuke?"

Crossed arms did, Cara decided, mean the same thing in both species. "Forgive me, please, a'tem," she replied in an attempt to unruffle his feathers. "This has been a difficult week."

"For many."

That was too true for comfort.

"You work on a rest-day to regain lost time?" he asked.

"And to exercise my hands."

"Will they heal?"

"Back to their original state?" She held the offending objects out in front of her. "I don't know." She stitched a little while longer, Serano watchful at her side. "Will Rodani heal?" she continued.

"We may assume he will."

When an errant stitch pricked her fingertip a little too deeply, Cara swore and stopped. She went into the study and sat down on the near end of the couch, sucking her bloody finger. As expected, Serano followed her in, and wandered over to the bookcase.

An unwanted shadow was what he was. Shadowing her footsteps, shadowing her crafting, shadowing her mind. She slid sideways until her head rested on the embroidered pillow. She curled her arms around the other one for what comfort it could give in Rodani's absence, and let her imagination roam. The current crisis carried too much fear.

If it weren't for Kusik, she might be healed now. The anger she felt toward the keso's treachery boiled upward into her consciousness, replacing her fear for Rodani's health. In her mind, she placed Kusik in front of Arimeso and watched with guilty pleasure as he took the punishment he so richly deserved. It still seemed too little for all she'd endured. His back would heal, her hands might not. At his worst, he could eat and use the privy. She had needed Rodani's help with every single embarrassing thing she'd had to do.

As she daydreamed, a weight settled downward on the opposite end of the couch, lifting the cushions beneath her. Cara peered sideways to see Serano put his feet on the tea table and open a book. She closed her eyes and let her mind drift.

Something tickled the back of her neck. Warm fingers reached under her hair and unhooked the clasp that held her hair clip in place, tugging it off.

Cara jumped off the couch, her hair spilling down her back.

Serano sat bemused, one arm across the back of the couch, the other holding Cara's clip. He stared at her, pupils wide and reflecting, with a thin-lipped grin that curled at the edges of his mouth.

Shaken, Cara pulled away from his gaze and looked at her clip. Silent and otherwise still, Serano turned it in his hand. With great and careful deliberation, he flipped the clip over and over in his mobile fingers. His gaze never left her face.

She crossed her arms and gripped the sleeves of her sweater with all the force her injured fingers could muster. "Why did you do that?" she asked, shaky in voice.

The corners of his mouth drew downward in a rueful expression. His fingers stilled. "Rodani has never done so?"

She hesitated. "Only..."

And couldn't continue.

Couldn't give credence to the thought that was blossoming unbidden in her mind. Serano didn't like her. Thought she was an over-emotional, uncontrolled, walking bundle of impropriety.

But his gaze never wavered. His body was as still as his eyes. The only sound in the room was the snap of the fire in its grate. Cara's skin tingled with heightened awareness that Serano was waiting.

Waiting for what? An answer to a question she couldn't believe he was asking? She would not make a fool of herself. Would *not*.

"Explain, please."

The corners of his mouth drew down again, then curled up in a tight smile. "It is a request, Cara." His fingers resumed their motion, sending the clip through rhythmic flips that made the polished silver sparkle in the light.

She had to be sure. No misunderstandings here, when the cost could be so high. "For what?"

"For attentions," he replied, as if it were the most natural thing in the world.

All the holy demons and demigods. What? Or better, why? "How does one answer?"

"Traditionally," Serano explained, holding the clip with his fingertips, "you would allow the taker to retain the clip if the proposition is accepted, or take it back if declined."

Cara stiffened, then took a step toward him, arms still crossed. His gaze remained locked on her face until she neared enough to hold out her hand. He surrendered the clip with a gentle movement and release of his fingers. The smile left his face and was replaced by patient resignation. Cara gripped her sleeve again, clip safely in hand. She wandered over to the wall next to the fireplace and leaned against it, much as she had done with Rodani that first time.

But it was Serano she was facing. Serano of the ready backhand. They regarded each other steadily, then he shifted his back against the couch to face her fully, stretching his long legs out under the tea table.

"It is not required," he said, "but, traditionally, if an explanation is requested, it is given."

"And you're requesting?"

"If you would oblige me."

Her fingers relaxed their fierce grip. She replaced the clip in her hair, not even attempting to re-do the spiral bun. That was a job for Hamman. Or Rodani.

Rodani.

This was his partner! Would she even tell him? Yes, she decided. She would. It would serve Serano right for making such a blatantly inappropriate suggestion. "You have all the Selandu women you desire," she told him. "Why me?"

"Partly because Rodani is ill," Serano said, "and cannot offer you what you need."

"Even if I desired you, I'd never make such a decision without at least discussing it with him. *First.* Besides," Cara continued after some thought, "I've earned neither your respect nor your good will. Therefore, I question your—" *intentions*, she almost said. But Serano caught the unspoken offense. His pupils narrowed.

"You believe I would do you ill?"

"I believe the chance for offense is far too high. I won't risk it."

"You still will not trust me."

She swept her fist through the air in front of her. "I can't! If I fear your temper out of bed, how much more would I fear it in bed?"

His eyes went wide. The tension in his face went away, replaced by something less recognizable. He reached for the discarded book. "Forgive me, a'Cara," he said, standing up. "I understand now." He walked out of the room, leaving behind enough emotional residue to choke her. Cara stomped over to the tea table and gave it the swift kick she wished she could aim elsewhere.

"Shit."

She'd fouled it up again. What was it that made their every meeting end up with an offense? What had prompted him to make such an outlandish request? Why would he think she would ever accept? They could hardly have a conversation without ending up angry. Cara flopped down on the couch, wishing desperately for a rewind button on her life. It wasn't fair.

Serano stood at the workroom window watching her, his book forgotten on the worktable. He backtracked to the door. "Forgive me," he began, leaning into the doorway. "I did not mean to disturb you so."

"Did you think it wouldn't?"

He pushed his hands into his jacket pockets. "There is pleasant disturbance and unpleasant disturbance. One hopes for the former."

"Sorry."

"Are you offended?"

Like I'm gonna answer that. "No. Are you?"

"No. Disappointed."

She tried not to smile at his words, though she had to turn aside from their meaning. It wouldn't do to let charm accomplish what surprise could not. With Rodani sick, she couldn't even think of such things. To offend him by dallying with his guild partner was not only disastrous in her own mind but might be a lethal mistake as well. She'd rarely contemplated the problem of having a lover who was trained to kill, with psychological buttons she wouldn't know she was pressing. Serano could eat his disappointment for dessert as far as she cared.

He pulled himself off the doorframe and came back into the room, taking his original spot in the overstuffed chair. "Would it please you, instead, to go for a ride?"

"A drive?" Cara asked. A cool breeze to ruffle her hair would be a welcome antidote to a day without Rodani. If, she remembered, she was allowed to open the damn windows.

"A ride. From the stables."

Cara froze. "A...benatac?" she stammered.

"They are the only rideable inhabitants in the stables," he deadpanned, as if a jaunt on a cantankerous 900 lb. sharp-toothed demon were an everyday occurrence. "My favorite is a sweet beast. Good natured, with a gentle gait. You would be pleased."

"I can't. My hands won't grip the reins. I'll fall."

"There are double saddles," he told her. "Even training saddles for adult and child. One of those would do well."

"And if I offend you?"

"Then I will remember who I am with, and why I am with her." Seeing her doubt, he continued. "Come. A short ride. I need some fresh herbs. This is an experience Rodani will not give you, even when he is well. Get a coat."

"Why?" Cara asked as she followed him out of the study.

He turned. "Because it is cold. Are you not susceptible to the cold?"

"I mean, why won't Rodani do this?"

Serano looked her up and down. "Outdoor shoes, also. Because Rodani holds no pleasure in the sport. He rides only when necessary."

Cara grabbed her coat and slipped on her hard-soled shoes while Serano 'commed ahead for his mount to be readied. They went down to the garage and took the carriage to the stables.

Domendi was there to meet them. "Set and ready, a'tem," he informed Serano as they entered the row of stalls. Serano headed to the correct one and greeted his favorite benatac.

"I have a guest with me today, te'ono. Demonstrate your best behavior for her. Yes?" He patted the velvet nose and fed some rushes into her mobile lips. He ran his hand down her flank and tugged on the straps of the double saddle. He turned back to Cara, who had hesitated just inside the door. "Come in. I will boost you."

Two feet taller than Serano at the head, the animal towered over the cowering Cara. The beast's flat nose and hinged nostril flaps, bewhiskered cheeks and liquid black eyes could not hide the deadliness of a mouth full of sharp teeth. She flicked her ears and stamped her padded feet in anticipation of the ride. Serano smiled broadly, his eyes bright with an anticipatory pleasure as great as the animal's. Finally, noticing Cara's reluctance, he pulled her forward.

"Tanami," he said to the benatac. "This is Cara, our guest. We will give her a smooth and safe first ride." He pulled a narrow shelf down from the wall. Chains and hinges clanked and held it in place. "Here," he said, and put his hands on her waist. With a swift jerk, he lifted her up on the perch and steadied her. Rough wood raked her healing fingers as she gripped the wall for stability. Tanami turned her massive head and snuffled Cara's clothing. Startled, Cara backed up against the wall with a thump. Serano grinned.

"She is greeting you, Cara."

"Uh...pleasant meetings, Tanami," Cara mumbled in return.

"Here," Serano continued, pulling on a stirrup that nestled against the striped flank. "Left foot here." He took her hand.

Cara stepped across and slid her foot into the stirrup, taller, for a moment, than Serano.

"Shift your weight toward me and swing your leg across," he explained. "I will keep you from falling."

It was a struggle, considering she had little gripping power for the task at hand, and the benatac chose those moments to shuffle and dance in the stall. Cara got caught with a foot in the stirrup and a knee on the saddle. Her body resisted Serano's unintentionally intimate efforts to boost her over. The more Cara fought her predicament, the more Tanami fought the jostling. Finally, Serano called a halt, and gripped the back of her jacket with his right hand, then reached for the pommel with his left as he slipped his left foot into the stirrup behind hers. A massive heave brought him up, incidentally knocking the breath out of Cara as she slid into the smaller saddle in front.

"Apologies," he said, hauling Cara up into place in front of him. "Prepared?"

"I can only assume," she replied breathlessly.

Serano reached around her and unwound the reins, giving them a flip onto the benatac's neck. The beast shuffled out of the stall with a rolling gait that forced Cara to clutch at Serano's pant legs behind her.

"Handholds," he said, moving her hands to the saddle ledge behind her thigh. "There is another in front of you."

She tried the pommel with one hand. It proved to be less awkward, so she brought her other hand around.

"Relax," Serano chided her. "Tension only helps tire you."

"So Rodani reminds me." She tried, but it was about as relaxing as standing on the prow of a boat in moderate seas. The motion didn't stop long enough for her to feel safe. A musty odor emanated from the beast's hide as they cantered down the narrow aisle past the stalls.

They left the east stable entrance and headed out into the open. Cold sunshine poured down onto their heads and thighs. The breeze ruffled their hair. Serano leaned into Cara and wrapped one arm around her torso.

"Hold tight," he said, snapping the reins. Tanami accelerated into a charge; her head thrust forward on the strong neck. Three claws on each padded foot dug into the ground for traction. Her brown tail fanned out behind them. Cara was pressed backward into Serano. Her whole body jostled and jerked with the rhythm of the benatac's stride as they made their way across the stable's expansive grounds. The wind brought color to her pallid cheeks and her heart thumped with exhilaration drawn from the thundering power beneath her.

Serano tugged on the reins, and Tanami angled left to parallel the tree-lined dirt road that ran past the training field.

"Stop?" he shouted.

"No!" she yelled into the wind.

Serano dug in his heels. Tanami switched into racing mode. They flew north along the fence, slowing only to turn west at the corner. As Serano tapped the benatac back into top speed, Cara whooped and hollered like a child racing a bicycle down Dead Man's Hill. Furiously, the benatac raced across the grassy expanse, Serano and Cara, one controlled, one clinging for dear life, riding the massive beast. Her muscles flexed and contracted under the soft hide. Serano guided the mare toward the low spot in the south fence that mirrored the north one, bending Cara almost double in anticipation, his grip tightening on her jacket.

Tanami bunched her muscles and pushed. Gravity ceased to exist. A line of white flickered past their feet. Gravity reasserted itself with a bone-jarring meeting of earth and padded feet, rears and soft-hided spine. Cara yelped when her chest hit her white-knuckled fists. Serano leaned upright as the mare sped on toward a familiar path in the south woods.

"Are you well?"

Cara sat up and wiggled, trying to assess the extent of the damage. "Yes," she decided.

"Stop?"

"No!"

The woods closed in. Serano pulled back on the reins. "Vasi!" he shouted. The mare slowed to a canter as the first of the trees passed by them. He led the benatac along the road, Cara bouncing in the saddle. The cold wind blew curls into the hair on her head and reddened her cheeks. The air was pungent with the sap of the never-die trees that surrounded them.

Serano took a side path into the woods on their right and led the benatac carefully along a leaf strewn track. His head turned from side to side, searching. After several minutes' quiet ride, he pulled them to a halt and dismounted. Ahead of them was a stand of trees that didn't look very different from any other set of trees Cara had seen north of the hills. But Serano held out his hands to her and helped her dismount. He pulled off a bag and plopped it on the ground.

"Lay out the blanket while I search."

Cara rummaged through the bag and found a blanket and a canteen of water, along with several small bags. "Is this plant the one that gives visions?"

"No."

"Is it poisonous to humans?"

"Not that I am aware."

"Then I could help."

Serano regarded her from over his shoulder. "If you wish."

He showed her what he was looking for, and they fanned out under the trees. The plant lived abundantly in the shadows of this area, and they made short work of the task. Back to the blanket, Serano tied the bags together in a chain and stuffed them into the saddlebag. He opened the canteen and took a deep drink, then passed it to Cara. She took a swig, choked, and coughed. A pungent, alcoholic aroma arose from the neck of the canteen and stung her throat. Bending over, she held it out to Serano without looking. "I thought it was water."

"You cannot sense the scent?"

She coughed again. "Not while it was all inside. Gods of the deep night, Serano, that's powerful."

He held it out. "Take a smaller sip. You may appreciate the taste."

Cara held the canteen to her nose and took a careful whiff, then a taste. "Thank you, no," she said, handing it back. She sighed, her shoulders sagging against the weight of worries suddenly remembered. "When will Rodani return?"

"I cannot know."

"I'm not asking for absolutes, a'tem. Give me your best guess, please."

Serano capped the canteen. "No."

"What aren't you telling me?"

"I simply prefer to wait and see. And in the meantime, I will do what I can to ease you."

That, Cara thought, *sounded like another euphemism. Pass.*

Serano put the canteen aside and stretched out on the blanket. His legs lay past the edge, resting on the winter-dry grass beyond. "I will help you put your fear aside."

Right. "How?"

He lifted his hand and rested it on her knee. Cara had the absurd temptation to remove it, like plucking a spider from her clothing.

"How would you put aside your fear of a human male?" he asked.

"Time," she said. "A lot of time, a lot of opportunities for tempers to arise—and then they don't."

"What would he say?"

"Words are no use here, Serano. Actions are all that matter."

"What actions might I take?"

"Why? Rodani will be back soon. You'll have no need and no opportunity."

Serano sat up and spun to face her. "That is premature, Cara."

She leaned back against his intensity, fighting an urge to flee. Did Rodani used to make her flinch every time he turned around? Those memories were gone, replaced by deep eyes and loving touches. The sharp grey eyes in front of her held only a force that repelled her, like magnets facing the wrong way. She scooted backwards.

"We do not know when he will return. No one in the clinic will offer an estimate." Serano reached out to touch the windblown hair against her cheek. "I would ask that you allow me to earn your trust, as Rodani has."

Cara stood up from the blanket, her hands tucked in the small of her back. "You have the plants you need?"

Serano glanced down at the blanket where she had been. The winter wind ruffled the tail end of his hair. Dry leaves skittered across the open expanse between them. He pulled the cap off the canteen and took a healthy swig, then rose.

Cara folded the blanket while Serano packed the saddle bag. The benatac shuffled with their renewed activities, snuffling the bag and pulling at her reins.

"I hope I can get back up there."

"Put your hands against the saddle, as high as you can reach." As she did so, he linked his fingers for a foothold. When she stepped in it, he lifted her with a powerful surge of strength, neatly flinging her all the way up. Unfortunately, her legs rested on one side, her arms and chest on the other. Serano vaulted into his seat. He grabbed the back of her pants and her arm, and lifted her into her place in the saddle, eliciting a squeak of alarm.

"There has got to be a more dignified way to get me up here."

He clucked at the mare and headed her back the way they had come. The ride back was uneventful. Unfortunately, Cara didn't know if that boded good or ill. Nor was she surprised at Serano's refusal to stop by the clinic on the way up to her rooms. But when he followed her in, she began to wonder at his insistence.

Priorities, she reminded herself.

"Hamman? Deremic?"

The manservant appeared at her call and bowed. "Please check on Rodani, a'sel. Find out if he's improved. Find out when he'll be well enough to return."

Deremic bowed again. Cara sat on the bed to await his answer. Serano followed her into the bedroom and perched himself on the opposite corner of her bed, almost as if he belonged there—or wanted to.

Cara bit down on a renewed urge to flee. The ride had gone alright. They'd managed not to flare up at each other. But comfortable? No, let alone comforting. Where was Deremic? She was about to get up and search when he returned.

"A'Cara, the temichi regains consciousness, but fades again before he can speak. Nothing else."

She shot off the bed. "But I can see him now. He'll know me."

"No," came the answer from both directions.

"But I can...I can..." *What, fem? Set him off again by your presence? Who knows what you would do to his hormone levels?* She hung her head, shamed by what she couldn't help, and what she couldn't do for the man she loved. She wanted to hide. The bed looked inviting as a refuge.

But not with Serano on it.

"Thank you, a'sel," she told Deremic. "Please check again before you retire tonight."

He bowed. "A'Cara."

She sat at her worktable, disinclined to do much of anything. Her new shadow dumped his collected plants where Rodani normally worked and started sorting.

"Will those leave a residue on the table?"

"Does it matter?" he asked.

"Might stain the fabric."

"Then no."

Cara picked up her box of pins and scattered them lightly over the worktable. One by solitary one, she began picking them back up again. One by solitary one, as she had done before, she dropped them back in the box. Only this time, there was no Rodani watching and waiting for anything to fall into her lap. Serano leaned over.

"What do you do?"

A pin bounced as it fell among its brethren.

"Exercise. *Dexterity* is the word, I believe."

"How many times have you done this?"

Another pin landed.

"Far too many times."

"If you hadn't enjoined an affinity with Rodani, you would not be injured."

Her hand stopped over the box, pin trapped between finger and thumb. "Thank you so much, Serano. If you hadn't told me that, I would never have figured it out on my own."

The pin dropped.

"You would have, I am sure."

Cara looked at him from underneath lowered brows. "That was an offense I gave you, a'tem. I'm sorry you didn't notice." She reached for another pin, switching fingers.

"Cara, I would ask you again to end this wrongful affinity."

Cara reared back to look him down and up. "And you asked me for the same thing." She picked up another pin. "Because Rodani isn't here to take care of my needs, you said." The pin plopped in the box.

Serano's face went to mask. He looked away.

"Something smells here, a'tem," she said. "Like a week-old fish."

"Does peace between our people matter to you?"

"Of course. If it didn't, I wouldn't be here."

"But you are ready to throw another war into the mix for your own pleasure."

"Exaggerations don't help your case."

He leaned in close. "Does it matter if he dies?"

Cara winced but held on. "Using crass words instead of polite ones doesn't change my reasoning. And you have absolutely no idea what I would feel if he crossed over." She leaned into his space. "Don't even try to tell me you do."

"Does your own life concern you?"

She dropped another pin in the box. "Yes. And it is mine to live as I see it. Not yours."

"What about the rest of the people here in Barridan?"

"What about them?"

"How many will cross over when it comes to violence?"

"If people get violent, Serano, then Rodani will discuss it with me, and we'll make our decision. If people get violent, it'll be because they made judgments on someone else's private life." Another pin fell. She switched fingers. "It isn't their business."

"It will be. They will make sure of it."

"Then Rodani will talk to me about it."

"Unless they kill him first."

The thought hit her gut and lodged there, taking over like a virulent virus. Cara dropped the pin she was holding and ran her fingers through her hair, gripping tightly. Losing him to revenge was worse than losing him to safety. Then a memory rocked her. She lifted her head and stared at Serano, eyes wide. "And then you'd kill me, wouldn't you?"

Serano stilled in his chair, his face again a mask of hidden emotions. His eyes flicked around the table, alighting on everything, stopping on nothing. Then he leaned back. "I will not answer that."

"Why?"

"That is my choice."

Cara stood up and began swiping Serano's plants back into the carry sack they'd come from. "Any man who could ask to join with a woman—," leaves and dirt spilled onto the floor as her hands shook, "—then kill her the next day—," she thrust the bag into his chest, "—is not a man I wish to have in my rooms."

The bag fell into Serano's lap as he watched her. She stepped back and crossed her arms. "Please leave."

Kibi in the headlights, she thought with some satisfaction, as he continued to stare. Maybe she'd gotten through to him this time. *Or not.* The bag stayed in his lap, untouched.

Cara grabbed it and stomped to the door, hearing his chair move as she opened it. She tossed the bag out into the hallway. As Serano came up behind her, she waved her hand grandly. "Pleasant eve and safe night, a'tem."

His eyes narrowed; his lips thinned into an angry line. But he left, reaching down for the carry sack as Cara shut the door.

TWENTY

Another day. Another day without Rodani, another day Hamman and Deremic told her that, no, she couldn't see him. It was too dangerous for her presence to increase his hormones again. Another day wondering just how many lies surrounded her, and how many truths she was ignoring. Serano's words haunted her.

She pulled her latest quilt into her lap and began to stitch the binding. Who was she supposed to believe? *What* was she supposed to believe? It didn't make sense that Rodani would ignore danger. Gods, he wouldn't let her leave the windows open if he wasn't there. That meant there really was danger all along, as he'd tried desperately to tell her.

Shurad was gone, courtesy of Rodani's shooting skills. Of course, that didn't mean the danger was. But she didn't trust Serano to tell the truth standing in front of Temi's shrine. Wait. Just...wait. Rodani will be back. That was the only way through this morass of ignorance.

Her fingertips began to ache with the repetitive pressure of the needle going through fabric. She rubbed them together, wishing for some kind of numbing lotion. *Dae, there's another one for your research list, okay?*

And again, it wasn't Rodani who strolled out of her bedroom from the servants' quarters.

"Pleasant day," Serano greeted her.

"Pleasant day," she said, declining to look at him.

"Where is your pleasantry?"

Her head shot up. But no, there was no anger in his face she could see. A tease? *Bad timing, a'tem.* "In the clinic, with my bedmate."

Serano lowered himself into Rodani's chair. "Your words and actions from last night caused me some concern, Cara." He rested his hands on the table and leaned forward. "Your fear of me prevents me from being the guardian you need. I offer you an apology."

Her needle jabbed the layered fabric. "For which part?"

"Any that offended you."

"Why?"

That brought a quizzical mien to his face. "Why? I have just told you."

She drew the needle out of the fabric with a sharp pull, which knotted the thread. "Why do you care?"

"It is my duty to assist you, as it was Rodani's." He wheeled closer to her, taking the thread between his fingers to tug at it.

"No." She swatted at his hand. "You'll make it worse." As she pulled at the loop of the knot with her needle, Serano bent down, comically close, to study the task.

"If my hand slips, you'll be bleeding, Serano."

"It will not be the first time in my life."

"You've been warned."

He grinned and sat back, eyes still on the motion of her hands. "What do you get from this?"

"I enjoy working with my hands, and the feel of fabric, and making useful things."

"Do you not miss mingling with others?"

"Occasionally." The knot came free with a last tug.

"Do you miss the outdoors?"

"Yes."

"We could go out on beast-back again."

"Thank you, no."

"Why?"

Cara stopped her stitching long enough to think, to look for a handy rationalization. "It's too far. And too secluded."

"That did not concern you before."

Cara sighed, heavy with impatience and distrust. With Rodani, the truth was best. With Serano? Misdirection, prevarication, game-playing. All those things she loathed.

"Thank you, no."

Serano got up and unlatched the shutters behind her head, flinging them back against the wall. He opened the window, then leaned out and took an exaggerated breath. "You might rethink your choice."

"Thank you, no."

Fingers lightly tapped the top of her head. "Is that the only phrase you have memorized? I thought your linguistic skills were higher than that."

She pulled her head out from under his hand and continued to stitch. "Sometimes repetition gets the point across better."

Now the fingers moved to her temples. She batted his hand away as if it were an irritating insect. The tickling moved to the back of her head, then to the side of her neck. But by the time she smacked at it, it had moved and all she hit was her own skin.

Serano laughed softly. "Your reflexes are ill-timed."

"Go 'way."

Now the touch went to the tip of her ear, feather-light. She jerked away and turned around. "You're wasting your time, Serano. Our ears aren't as sensitive as yours."

His smile stretched wide, showing an array of Selandu-sized teeth. He retook his seat and leaned toward her. "So, tell me what is."

"If you're so bored you have to bait me, go find Larisi instead. At least you know you'll get a *yes* out of her."

"What will it take to get a *yes* out of you?"

Cara threw the quilt on her table and lurched to her feet. "What is wrong with you, Serano? Why won't you leave me alone?"

He leaned back in the chair, fingers interlaced on his belt, the smile gone. "I am attempting to establish the same duty to you that Rodani did."

"Have I not made myself clear on the subject?"

"Going outside might improve your demeanor, Cara. I know a place very close. A place you haven't been to before. A place where you will still feel safe."

She sat back down, pulling the quilt into her lap. "I have a deadline."

"Even Arimeso knows a crafter cannot work all day, every day." He stood up and held out his hand.

Cara studied it dispassionately, this hand hanging mid-air in invitation. It wasn't Rodani's hand. His was broader, and the little finger on his left was bent slightly. *An old injury*, was all he'd said. And *don't ask* was the unspoken end to his explanation.

"Come."

Nor was the voice Rodani's. Not quite as deep. Quick-spoken, clipped as if in a hurry. The fingers waggled at her impatiently.

"Benatac?"

"Feet."

She got up and wove the needle into the fabric for safekeeping, not quite sure she was doing this. Her mind was elsewhere, watching her from a distance, like a dream. She folded the quilt methodically, side to side to side.

The dream vaporized as he took her hand. She yanked it back and tucked it under her arm, safe from further intrusions. *Sit down,* something in her mind told her. *No,* she chided herself. *He's not going to hurt me. I need to get out of here anyway.*

They walked side by side through the hallways, downstairs, and into a corridor she recognized as being the guild's. But instead of stopping at the practice room, Serano opened a door at the far end of the hall. Inside was a small, dimly lit room with nothing but a staircase in it. As it wasn't wide enough for two, Serano started up, motioning her to follow.

"I don't think I like this."

"You will. Come."

She put her foot on the first step. "And if I don't?"

He turned around and looked down at her. "Then I will apologize, and you will spend the rest of the day in your rooms as you wished." He continued up the stairs, leaving her with not much choice but to follow.

They climbed three flights. At the top was a door, shadowed, with a thin sliver of light surrounding its edges. Serano brought out his keys again and opened it. Bright light flooded the stairwell, discomfort to her squinting eyes. She stepped through the doorway and onto the roof of the house of Barridan.

On her left was an upward-sloping roof; to her right, a short guardrail protected the careless. Behind her, a water wheel, fed by the stream she'd run in weeks ago, clacked as it circled. Under her feet was a wide stone walkway that followed the edge of the building, its width approximately the height of an adult Selandu. She looked down over the fence. A wave of dizziness came over her, and she drew back to stare south toward the hills. A stiff wind blew against her face in gusts, pulling tendrils out of her hair in its bun. The crisp scent of woods and leaves invaded her nose as she breathed. She closed her eyes to the sun as it warmed her skin.

She opened her eyes to see Serano grinning at her. She waited for him to throw a stinging barb, but he only motioned her forward. Beyond him was a lounge chair, the type you could lie back in and stare out into the horizon.

"I come here at times," he said, "when I wish to get away but cannot go far." He motioned to the chair. "You may sit."

It was Selandu-long, and twice her width or more. "No, thank you."

She crouched down at the edge of the railing and stared out into the distance. *Aisu, I wish you were up here.* The emptiness threatened to engulf her. Fear prickled her skin. *You'll live. You have to.*

Serano squatted next to her. "A pleasant view. Yes?"

"Yes." She squinted at the sun as a cloud pulled away from it. "Thank you." An afterthought, but spoken, nonetheless. Her blouse fluttered in the stiff breeze, and loose hair fell across her eyes. She pulled the strands back behind her ears, knowing it was fruitless.

Serano took a finger-full and tugged at it in an attempt to tuck it into the bun. She let him try without objection, idly wondering why. His touch was dangerous. Everything about guild guardians was formidable. But Rodani, she trusted. Serano... Serano was a live and spitting wire.

Cara sat down on the stone and crossed her legs, feet under her knees. It earned a sidelong glance from him. "Yes, I know," she said. "It's scandalous to you." She leaned her arms on one of the rungs of the rail.

"That is an invitation in our culture."

"Then I revoke it."

"You are purposely impudent."

The remark came out with a surprising lack of rancor. Cara glanced over at him. "No. Purposely not caring. That's different."

As a grey cloud crossed over the sun, Cara began to realize how cold it really was. She crossed her arms and leaned forward. "I can't stay here long."

Still in a crouch, Serano shuffled around behind her, going down on his knees. He leaned against her back and brought his arms up to lie outside hers on the railing.

The warmth felt good, and he was trying to be nice, but his ulterior motives rankled to the core of her heart. She bit back on the first rejoinder that popped in her mind, and the second. And the third. Instead, she sighed and tried to enjoy the blustery day. To her right, the tops of the trees swayed in unison, a green and brown dance. Entranced, she swayed with them, the rhythm giving a measure of calm to her agitated nerves.

"How many camabarin trees are there on the estate?" she asked him.

He was quiet for a moment. "Two to the south that we know of, where you were. A few others to the west and north. A few around Tendiman."

"Any other dangerous trees nearby?"

"Contemplating running?"

She snorted softly. "No, but I haven't ruled it out, either."

"There is one out there that has roots with poison in the bark. You would be wise not to touch it."

"How would I know it?"

"The roots stick up vertically."

"Vertically? Strange."

The sun flashed bright and dim by turns as the minutes sauntered by. Birds flapped and cawed in the distance, heading for the southern hills. Cara leaned her elbows on the rail as the scent of rain intruded into her awareness.

As she crossed her arms against a cold breeze, Serano drew back and wrapped his arms around her, leaning into her neck.

"Serano, please."

"Please for what?" he whispered. In her mind came the memory of Rodani's first whispers to her, standing behind her on a cool, dark night.

Cara dropped her head on her chest, tired. Scared. Petrified that she might not hear that voice again. "Please, don't push me."

"I could learn to please you. Rodani did."

"I respect your skills. I respect your status. I honor your duty to my safety, Serano. But it's not you I want. I want him."

He squeezed her tightly and nuzzled the base of her neck, then released her before she could fight. As he stood up, he reached down for her hand. "Your skin is cold."

"I know."

"I will warm you when we get back."

She pulled herself up by the railing, ignoring Serano's outstretched palm. "The fire will do adequately, thank you."

Back in her room, she crouched in front of the fire, wanting to keep the cool wind in her memory, but needing the warmth.

"You could have lain on the chair," Serano said, casting himself onto the sofa. "It was big enough for both of us."

"Which is why I refused it."

He was silent for a moment. "Am I truly that disturbing to you?"

"At times, yes."

"And at other times?"

"Only slightly less disturbing."

Serano sighed and got back up, wending his way to the bookcase. He picked up a couple of the children's books she'd translated for Rodani, flipping through the pages.

"Cara, Rodani may not be back for a while."

She shoved at the crumbling logs with the poker. "I hold out hope."

"And in the meantime, you have needs that should be met."

Cara stood up and stretched the kinks out of her legs, brushing ashes off the fabric. "And you know much less about my supposed needs than you think you do."

"Teach me."

For an instant, she heard Rodani's voice after their first joining. Then reality reared its ugly head. "You don't have the patience."

"I am a fast learner."

"When you wish to be."

"Rodani would not be offended—" she spun around, glaring at him, "—if I satisfied you while he was away."

She stomped her way to the dinner table and sat with her back to the wall. She looked out over her workroom.

"You believe it not?"

"I didn't hear it from him. Just you."

"I could take offense at that. You deem me a liar."

She turned to him. "And you deem me stupid enough to believe you."

Serano rose, walked over to her, and lifted an errant curl from her temple. "No. I have come to believe Rodani's judgment, there. You are not stupid."

She pulled her hair out from between his fingers. "Only petulant, uncaring, talkative, offensive, and childish. Yes?"

Serano slid his palm under her hair at the nape and bent down near her ear. Cara shot out of the chair in the opposite direction and headed for her workroom. He stopped her headlong flight with his arms spread wide.

"Don't you dare, Serano." She stood, shaking. "Don't you dare."

"To offer my attentions?"

"To trap me. In my own rooms. With no weapon at hand."

He smiled. "Your temper is a formidable weapon."

"And so is yours, a'tem. Which is why I keep refusing. Now move, please."

He stepped to the side with a gracious wave of his hand.

***

For the twelfth time, Litelon pulled the Enclave's letter from his private storage. Tucked up on his cot in the stall he called home, Litelon unfolded the paper and read.

"Goddess grant you long life and prosperity ... undertaken an investigation of the charges you brought ... interviewed several people ... discussed this matter with the taso..."

Unwillingly, his eyes raced to the bottom of the page.

"We are pleased to report that there is no sign of any coercion or other misuse of power or status by the temichi Rodani in regard to his human adashi. The goddess thanks you for your concern in bringing this to our attention. May She smile upon you always."

He wanted to tear the paper to powder. Almost had several times since receiving it. Instead, he stuffed it back into the pouch it came in, and into the storage box. Rearranging his fresh clothes, he took a deep breath and headed out of the stables, toward the manor house.

Rest-eves meant the festive room was warm, noisy, and crowded. Paradoxically, it also meant privacy, if one spoke in whispers. Litelon dropped a hard-earned one-tenth coin on the bar and grasped a bottle. Only one small table remained unoccupied, a two-seater near the musicians. Litelon lowered himself into the chair and rested his arms on the table, staring blankly at the lip of the bottle.

"You drinking that, or willing it to tell your fortune?"

Litelon raised his eyes slowly, supremely uninterested in socializing. But the woman sat down, anyway.

"I am Iraimin," she said. "And I know who you are."

"Your name means nothing to me. And mine is unimportant."

Iraimin reached under his nose and pulled the bottle toward her, taking a healthy-sized drink. "I am a'Cara's companion. Now does my name mean nothing?"

Litelon sat back, eyes wide. "Why do you speak to me?"

"To give you advice."

"I need it not."

"You still pine for her."

That sat him up. He grabbed the bottle from her and slammed it on the table. "What do you know, and how?"

"I hear things, a'sel. I mean you no ill."

"Then leave me be."

"You need to look elsewhere."

Litelon's pupils pulsed at the unwelcome intrusion, while the musicians put up their instruments for a break. The room quieted. Selandu voices created an interweaving tapestry of conversations, soft and loud.

"You have no right," he said slowly, in a tone meant to block debate.

"Yes. But I have no wish to see another of Sela's children wallowing in unrequited desire. I have been there too often myself."

More people entered the room in ones and twos, meandering toward and away from the bar, sauntering past tables. Litelon bit back a score of rejoinders, a few choice vulgarities, and a most discourteous growl. "I do not need your advice."

"You will not win her."

"I can still try."

"She is spoken for."

Litelon shot to his feet, glanced around at the turned heads, and slowly reseated himself. Iraimin took another swallow of the dry wine as he rearranged his jacket.

"I know she is," he hissed between clenched teeth. "I know what they are doing."

Iraimin licked the wine off her lips and regarded him steadily. "How do you know?"

"How do you?"

"I have been around them. I have seen the signs. You?"

"I saw them." He took another swallow and choked it down, along with his rising fury. "In the stables. She touched him. Twice."

"There is no dishonor in simple touching."

"I saw her face. And his. Temi damn that guardian!" Down went the bottle with another bang. "How dare he?"

"Their choice, te'oto."

"Even I know he is proscribed from her. Everyone knows that. She is his adashi! He should not even dare." An adult-level growl escaped his throat as rage flared in his gut.

"There is no sense in us burning over what we cannot have."

Litelon gripped the bottle, his knuckles turning white. "You desire him?"

"No." Iraimin pulled the bottle out of his fist. "Cara."

Litelon's face fell into mask. His rage turned to embarrassment, and he paled at her frank admission. "If she is with him, she is not risheigi."

"She is not. That does not quell my desire. And the fact that she has accepted him does not quell yours." Iraimin leaned forward, her forearms crossed on the table. "Sela has Her own paths for us. It does us no good to rail against Her wisdom."

Litelon rubbed his face, then took another drink. The level inside was diminishing rapidly, as was his ego. His rage, however, remained at peak. "How can you bear knowing they are together?"

"Sela wills."

Litelon turned his head aside. "That chokes me every time I hear it. Too much unfairness, too much dishonesty and dishonor hide behind it." His thirst for socializing was disappearing as rapidly as the wine. He stood and inclined his head. "A'sel."

Bottle in hand, Litelon maneuvered his way through the crowd, seated and standing. The doorway beckoned with bleary edges. With a few more impatient nudges, he found himself back out in the cool hallway. His ears rang in the quiet. The knot in his gut began to unwind.

"A'sel," said a voice behind him.

Litelon spun to face this new unknown. He blinked slowly, trying to focus.

"Be at ease," the man said. Dressed in black, he stood with a confidence Litelon was beginning to despise.

"A'tem," he said.

The man smiled politely. "I am Naremit. And you seem to have more knowledge of guild dealings than a stablehand might."

Litelon narrowed his eyes. The man raised his hand, then lowered it. "I do feel I should find out how you know so much." He raised his other hand, which held a bottle, a nearly full one. "However, I should not fail to offer you something in return. My room is near."

Litelon's shoulders sagged. He rolled his fingers outward, then in.

Naremit motioned to him, then began to walk.

TWENTY-ONE

Three days, now. Three days of change-induced turmoil. Three long days since Serano's partner fell ill, and he'd been given the task of guarding a frightened human female. Three days since his superior had demanded he find a way to seduce and abandon a woman who wanted nothing to do with him.

A scourge on both of them would suit his tempers today. He rounded the corner to Kusik's security office and waited for acknowledgment.

Kusik sat at his desk inside one of the many rooms of Arimeso's central quarters. "I have not received a report from you."

"There has been nothing worth relaying, a'Keso."

"No? I have reports here from Hamman and Deremic. A ride on a benatac, two card games, three dinners, a lunch or two, a rooftop excursion, conversations, arguments, and yet, nothing from you?"

"Perhaps I should have specified no successes to report, a'Keso."

"Why?"

"Because her bond to Rodani is as strong as I suspected."

Kusik leaned back in his chair, the better to stare. "And such bonds cannot be broken? I have my doubts."

"There has to be a reason, a'Keso. And I am not enough of one to do the breaking."

"If we knew the reasons they bonded, we might counteract them."

Serano bit back a sigh, a response that could be disastrous when Kusik was agitated. Even if he knew the reasons for sure, prevarication seemed to be the safest trail.

"I am not informed enough to estimate, a'Keso."

Kusik's eyes narrowed, and his pupils did the same. "Your lack of knowledge is irritating, a'tem. Are you partnered to Rodani, or not? Do you share the guarding of this human, or not? Do you talk with him?"

"I am. I do. And we do, a'Keso. But as I lack the patience to deal with her tempers, Rodani has taken over nearly all her matters. He leaves me with little to do for or with her, and that is my preference."

"And that preference is preventing you from completing the task I have assigned to you."

"A'Keso, you cannot know—"

Kusik beat on his desk. "What I know is that she needs to be gone from Barridan, and she is not!"

"I understand your frustration, a'Keso. But one cannot force—"

"I am not discussing force, Serano. No one wishes her to take tales of attempted rape back to her leaders."

Serano bowed his head, mute and unwilling acquiescence. "I can only continue, a'Keso. And Rodani will not be ill forever."

"Which brings me to my next point." Kusik sat forward, his hands clasped on the desk in feigned harmlessness. Serano knew better. "You will return to the human and tell her that Rodani has requested removal from this assignment, and that I have graciously granted it."

Open-mouthed disbelief was not an expression any guardian wanted to show to his seniors. But Serano clamped his jaws shut far too late to hide his dismay.

"You will convince her," Kusik continued.

"That will not work, a'Keso."

"I tire of your negativity."

"Reality, a'Keso."

"Make a new reality."

Temi's knives. Am I a goddess? It took every scrap of his willpower and all his training to keep a lock on improper reactions. "I will try. And she will not believe me."

"Make her believe."

"A'Keso, her bond—"

"Make her believe!"

"She will ask—"

"Deny it. Deny her. Break her will."

Serano breathed deeply, almost desperately, trying to stay calm. This would be an explosion of massive proportions, and he was the fuse that Kusik had just lit.

"How will I keep them apart?" he asked.

"That, I will begin. You keep the subterfuge going—for as long as needed."

"I will not be able to keep him from her."

"Take the key to her rooms while he is still moribund. Hamman and Deremic will obey my instructions. You will reinforce them."

"And what will you tell Rodani?"

"Timan will go to the clinic and tell him that the human has requested a new guardian."

Serano closed his eyes, just for a moment. One did not tell a powerful leader that his plans were disastrous. That very rule was what had kept anyone from dissuading Arimeso. Now it was Kusik. Was there any sanity left in Barridan?

"The more intricate a web you weave, a'Keso, the more fragile it will be."

Kusik pursed his lips at the cliché. "You are guild. Save the elaborate words for writers. Go to your duty."

Serano left the office with a sense of doom roiling in his innards. He started for the garden outside, but stopped in mid-flight. Hiding would rain down censure upon him, and it was anathema to his core nature. Delay would improve nothing. He turned for the stairs instead, took them three at a time, and let himself into Cara's workroom. She eyed him without raising her head. He sat down at the worktable gingerly, as if something were paining his rear.

Cara looked at him more carefully. "A'tem?" Her eyes widened, and even her human pupils expanded. "Rodani?" she said, her voice strained. "What happened?"

Serano raised his hands to forestall her. "He is slowly improving, Cara. Be calm." Sage advice for his own self, he thought. But it was not to be. "There is other news."

The skin on Cara's face blanched. It did nothing to calm his anxiety. Cara made a rolling motion with both hands, splaying them outward. "Play your cards."

Serano leaned forward in the chair but kept his hands free. Facing a rahkti was less problematic. At least it was predictable. "Rodani has asked to be put on another assignment."

She looked confused for a moment, her eyebrows drawn down. Then she stood up, eyes wide. "No. Never. You're wrong."

"I am not. I am sorry, Cara."

Her fists went to her hips, a signal he'd seen before. "This is impossible, Serano. I refuse to believe it."

"Your refusal does not alter the facts," he said. "Do you believe he has no right to change his mind? He nearly crossed over that night."

"I don't believe you," she replied, waving her arms erratically. "He would talk to me directly, not pass the task to someone else." Arms now crossed, she stared at him, gaze never wavering.

Serano sat back, the better to move if needed. Here was the genesis of the impasse he'd foreseen. Here was the stubborn human. Worse, she was correct. Rodani would not have delegated this task.

"Cara, I can tell you only what I know."

"I want to talk to him."

"I am certain you do."

"Then take me to him. If he's well enough to decide *that*, he's well enough to talk to me."

"I am forbidden. He does not wish it."

Cara froze for several seconds, her eyes on him. Then that strange blue gaze drifted away, toward the study. With her shoulders slouched, she stuffed her hands in her pockets and wandered over to the study doorway, then across to the knife target. Back to the study door, and again to the target. She stood in front of the hole-scarred board, staring. Serano stretched out his legs under the worktable, much as his absent partner was wont to do, waiting for her inevitable tempers to show. Slowly, Cara turned toward her bedroom.

With a lunge, she flung the hall door open. It banged against the wall and rebounded. In a flash, she was out. Serano swore and jumped up, overturning his chair in his haste. He sped out the door, only to see her start down the stairs in a rapid and uncoordinated gait. "Cara!" he said in a hoarse whisper as he ran.

Temi fry that woman. Serano pounded down the hall and into the stairwell. "Cara!" Down he flew, his feet pattering a staccato rhythm against the stone. He jumped down onto the landing just as Cara raced out of it.

This was not going to happen. He put on a burst of speed and caught her amid the lower stair steps, wrapping an arm around her waist, and a hand over her mouth. He knew better than to forget that one.

Cara struggled with a ferocity that startled him. Arms and feet flailing, legs akimbo and fingernails gouging the skin on his hands, she shouted muffled imprecations into his palm.

It was much slower going back up the stairs than down. Her whole-body agitation drew him off balance, and nearly off his feet. The only defense was a strong offense, and Serano kept a tight grip on everything that he held.

Sela smiled on him for once. The door was wide open and welcoming. He brought her back into her workroom and kicked it shut behind him. Bitten, bothered, and more than a mite battered, he let go in an instant. She collapsed into an undignified heap at his feet.

As she shook her head, Serano stepped back, wary of reprisals. But she only sat, curled into that impossible flex of knees and elbows. "Leave me alone," she mumbled.

"I cannot."

"Go away!" she shouted, hunching into a ball.

"I can no more trust you than you can trust me, Cara. I know you just well enough to see what tricks you will try to pull. I am your guardian now."

The human rolled onto her side and let out a wail that scraped the inside of his skull. He stepped backward in shock, but there was no distance to be had from the pain that erupted before him. Another scream escaped her as Hamman and Deremic appeared in frantic disorder at the bedroom doorway. Deremic pushed his way through.

"What has happened?" he said. "What is wrong with her?"

Cara pulled at her hair, her forearms covering her face. She wailed again, wordless agony. Serano told them both what he'd told her. Hamman covered her mouth, her pupils wide ovals.

Deremic knelt by Cara's head and laid a hand on her shaking arm. "A'Cara," he said. It only drew another scream from her. The scream warbled at the end and turned into a deep retch. "A'Cara."

Serano walked away, then turned and stared at her. On the floor like a child, wordless and possibly witless. Now came the dire need for his partner, and his partner wasn't here. This was his own duty. It brought an unaccustomed shiver to his muscles. He'd seen Rodani embrace her more than a time or two, comfort for her emotional upheavals. But this, this was beyond his ability to approach. He stood silent as her cries turned to rain and choking breaths wracked her body. Helpless as he rarely was with his own species, Serano felt lost in a strange, alternate world where nothing made sense. Everything he felt was ajar—corners that didn't meet, edges that wouldn't match. And emotions that made sense only if he looked sideways and squinted into the mist.

One more mess to clean up. One more dishonor to lay on the back of his partner. Serano chivvied the servants out of the workroom. "We will have to watch her very carefully. Only Sela knows what she will do."

He stared down at his adashi, still raining all over the stone floor. With a heave, he pulled her to her feet. She sagged, body limp and without will to move. With a distasteful shudder, he carried her to the couch and laid her on it. She collapsed like a farm child's doll.

He called for a drink and lowered himself cautiously into a chair at the dinner table, keeping a wary eye out for sudden moves. Cara's bouts of raining were slowing, a welcome respite to his frazzled nerves. Deremic appeared with his drink. He took a mouthful and swallowed, heedless of the alcoholic sting in his nasal passages. His mind roamed back to the memories of early summer. Arimeso's decision. Rodani's acceptance. His own disbelief at what they were conspiring to, and what would be expected of him. Disagreements. Arguments. Painful silences.

And now it came down to this: a wet alien to guard, his partner dismissed from her duty, his own life turned upside down. Impossible orders, impossible human. Serano swore to Temi and took another swig of his drink.

Cara struggled to sit up and wrapped the couch quilt around her shoulders.

"Cara."

She stared at the fire.

"Cara, we must come to an understanding."

She refused to turn or acknowledge him. Temporarily deaf or willfully disobedient, he couldn't tell, but it ratcheted his temper a notch higher. "Cara, you cannot go to him. You are forbidden. You must stay in your rooms. Yes?"

She leaned her head into her hands, elbows on her knees. The rain renewed its course down her cheeks—prompted, he assumed, by his very reasonable orders.

"Cara."

She only wiped her face with the corners of her quilt.

Serano smacked the tabletop, anger gaining the upper hand over his fraying patience. "Cara! You cannot run. Not from me. Do you understand?"

She stared at the fire.

Serano shot out of the chair and grabbed her arm—the same one. She winced, but stayed silent, swaying on her feet as he pulled her up. A side of the quilt fell to the floor, pooling in folds on the stone. "Answer me, Cara. Acknowledge what I have said."

Her shoulders bowed inward; her eyes shut.

He shook her. But instead of fighting him, she closed down. Even in her human face, he could see she went elsewhere. No expression, no voice. Had she even heard him? Normally, she wouldn't shut her mouth. Now she wouldn't open it.

Bereft of patience and out of ideas, Serano pushed her back onto the couch and left her in a heap.

***

Kusik waited for his partner, in a better mood than he had felt in many a month. His path was clearing, events were turning his way. Taking those earrings was one of his more worthy ideas. Kimasa must have worked her magic, praise be to the goddess.

Timan entered his office and bowed respectfully.

"You have a duty," Kusik said.

"A'Keso."

"You will go to the clinic and give Rodani a new order."

"He is healed?"

"No. But he is conscious, and moving." Kusik's lips thinned into a line, witness to a barely concealed disappointment that things hadn't taken a worse turn. "This illness of his, and the actions that created it, seem to have offended our human guest. She has decided that she no longer wishes him to be her guardian."

Timan's eyes went wide. "What offense?"

"I know not, and care not. You will tell him he is reassigned to communications and courier duty while he is recovering. You will tell him that he is not to approach the human or try to talk with her by any method. Those are her wishes."

Timan looked away, his gaze roaming the room. "What does the taso say?"

"She does not yet know. It is not necessary. I wish this change taken care of before she does."

"Who takes his place?"

"Serano had already taken over her guarding when Rodani became ill. He will remain in that duty."

"This will be a painful blow."

Kusik almost smiled. But that kind of pleasure at his change of fortunes would not secure Timan's faith that he heard the truth. "It is an unavoidable consequence of their unethical actions, tem'u. His feelings are not my concern. Only his duty."

"This news would better come from you, Kusik."

"He will not hear it from me," Kusik said darkly, his fist clenching on top of his desk.

"Nor from me, likely," Timan said. "You are certain of this?"

"Completely."

Timan hesitated. "What of the Enclave's judgment?"

"Obviously in error," Kusik said with a wave of his hand. "I will be vindicated, of course."

Timan stiffened in respect. "Of course."

Kusik's eyes pulsed, then narrowed. "I do not question our good fortune, Timan."

"My apologies, a'Keso," Timan said, caution in his voice.

"You will tell him."

Timan closed his eyes, then opened them quickly. "And if he reacts badly?"

The frown reappeared. "Are you second in this guild, or no?"

Timan's face fell into mask. "A'Keso."

"I expect a report within the hour."

Timan bowed respectfully and left the room.

This, he thought as he strode toward the clinic, was enough to have even the selaso's calm nerves in disarray. Why did the wretched human change her mind? Yes, it was allowed. But by the goddess, to dismiss a man still recovering from an illness she gave him—such inconsiderate behavior implied a much lower level of morality than had been argued for her species. It would do Rodani no good, he was certain. Timan sighed wearily. This experiment of the taso's had caused pain enough already. He did not appreciate a duty that forced him to increase it exponentially.

The clinic door yawned wide. Timan circled around to the room that held their recovering security fifth. Rodani looked up at his entrance, and hastily folded a set of white papers into the palm of his hand. He started to sit upright.

"Be at ease," Timan told him. *That will change soon enough.* He sat on the chair next to the bed. "An unpleasant task has been given to me, a'tem."

"A'Biso," Rodani said, masking his expression. His voice was still shaky, as were his hands.

"Word has come." He shifted in the hardwood chair. "You are to be reassigned."

Rodani sat up, then tilted sideways, clutching the edge of the bed. "No, a'Biso," he whispered. "The taso—" He pushed upward, straightening. His arms quivered with the strain.

"Rodani, your adashi has requested it," Timan said in a rush to utter the difficult words. Rodani's pupils narrowed. "You are forbidden to seek her out. I am sorry."

He leaned back into the pillow. "I refuse to believe it until I hear it from her."

"You cannot."

"She would not."

"She has."

Rodani slapped his fist against his leg with what strength he had. "This...this is utterly wrong."

Timan paused, interrupting the verbal volley. Rodani looked pale, older than he should. "You are ill, a'tem. Possibly she was thinking of your health in her decision."

"Not like this," he spat, eyes narrowed, mouth pursing into a thin pinched line. "I will not believe."

"I am sorry."

Timan looked away—had to, to get away from the pain on Rodani's face. Distance. Calm. *Not my doing, not my pain.* Give him courtesy, the courtesy of not-aware, not-notice, which was sometimes all such a difficult duty allowed.

"You will be given a messenger assignment. It is not too taxing on a healing body, but important nonetheless." He dared a look back at the bed. "I suggest you concentrate on what is ahead of you rather than what is behind. That will serve you better."

The look returned to him was both forbidding and foreboding. It was not a comfortable expression to see on anyone's face, let alone a heart-wounded temichi with a temper threatening to spill over. Timan wondered who had possession of Rodani's weapons. He put his hand on Rodani's shaking shoulder.

"Speak to no one of this, a'tem." He stood, and retreated to the doorway, hesitating. Then he walked out.

Behind him, Rodani took a deep breath, fighting the clenching of his gut.

No! It cannot be.

His stomach began to burn.

He could not have made such a mistake. Not with her. Not in this situation. His head began to spin, and his throat spasmed. He rolled off the bed and down onto his knees. Pain tore through his stomach, and he retched, dizzy with humiliation and dishonor. What little he'd managed to eat spattered the floor between his shaking arms.

His arms.

How often he had held her. How often he had rested his body on hers, linked with her. How often she had held out her hands to him, welcoming his approach. Could he have misjudged her so badly?

Pain rebounded inside him and erupted onto the floor as multiple footsteps clattered into the room.

"A'tem!" They crowded around him, touching him. "A'tem!" His skin burned where they lay their hands. "A'tem, what happened?"

No. Not a hint. Not a word. Weak with more than sickness, he let them guide him back to bed. He lay lax as they washed him, refusing any other contact. The bare walls held ghostly images of brown curls; the memory of her scent wafted past his nostrils, teasing his raw nerves.

"You look as if Sela came calling early, a'tem," Baldar said, walking into the room. But the levity left his face under Rodani's stony regard. He walked to the bedside and laid a hand against Rodani's neck. "This morning you were healing well. What happened?"

He swallowed the bile that threatened a repeat visit. "A matter more for the selaso than for your talents, a'Baldar."

One eyebrow lifted. "Shall I request her presence?"

"No." *Goddess, no.* Kimasa would understand too well what this loss would cost him. Some secrets were better kept, even when they wouldn't keep long. He shuddered to think of whispers erupting behind his back in the next guild meeting. His face burned. Not all knew of what he and Cara had initiated, but all would know of the disgrace of his reassignment. Suddenly, an out-of-house task felt welcome.

"You are still in my charge, a'tem," Baldar reminded him. "If there is something you require, you have but to ask."

Rodani bowed his head. "Thank you."

Baldar motioned to his assistants. They left, not quite in such a hurry as they came. Baldar peeled the cover off the guardian and checked his vitals, then palpitated his pelvic area. "Are you in pain?"

"No."

"How do you feel?"

"More normal." But not so normal as usual. Guild honor forbade admitting to his disgrace.

Baldar re-covered him and stepped away from the bed. "Rest, a'tem. Put whatever isn't my bailiwick out of your mind."

Yes. Of course. Easily done. "Master Healer."

After Baldar left the room, Rodani made a shaky search for his clothing. He found it in a corner drawer. There was no sign of his weapons. He sat on the bed and dressed, willing his limbs and queasy insides into cooperation. Weaker than he would admit, he aimed for the doorway. The frame tilted rakishly, then righted itself. He put a hand on the wall.

The corridor lengthened and shrank in his vision, steadying as he made his way forward. He unlocked the back clinic door with no one the wiser. He turned left, then decided against attempting the main staircase, and spun around. Mistake. The wall thumped his shoulder, then held him upright as he waited for equilibrium to return.

Fool, he raged at himself. *Double and triple fool. You should know better.*

What in Temi's name had gone wrong? Or why did he think he was right this time?

A back staircase came into his bleary-eyed view. He placed one foot carefully on the first step and shifted his weight. The leg held. He took a second step, and a third. The top of the stairway beckoned, but his mind was at war with his body. His stomach joined the battle and threatened to topple him back down the stairs. He leaned against the wall to catch his breath.

He had to talk to her.

But it was forbidden. He remembered that, somewhere inside his foggy brain. Forbidden. But forbid did not mean cannot. It meant should not. *Should* was a word he both loathed and revered. Duty gave it strength, desire weakened it. His adashi. His duty. *Should not. Forbidden. Forbidden to contact her. Forbidden. To see? To touch?*

He dropped to his knees. They hit the steps above him; his hands went to the cold stone.

Au, Sela, goddess of all that is good and right, what did You let me do? Why did You let me do it?

Light footsteps pattered down from above him. "A'tem, a'tem, are you well?"

Honor. Guild image. *Get up, fool. You must not be weak.*

Rodani grabbed the rail and fought his way to his feet. A young artisan stood above him, looking down with dismay written into her features. "I will be well, thank you, te'ono," he managed, and took another step. Warily, the woman bypassed him. He reached the top and headed the long way toward Cara's rooms, stumbling with weakness and a burning pain where his pride should be. As Rodani reached to unlock the door, someone came out from his own rooms behind him. He turned, and a wave of dizziness overtook him.

Timan grabbed his arm, steadying him. Baldar came around to his other side.

"A'tem," the physician said, "you belong in the clinic."

"No."

"You know your orders," Timan said, taking the keys from Rodani's hand. With a swift flick, he removed the one to Cara's door and handed the rest back to him. A wave of rage and pain filled him as he watched Timan pocket the key, the key to the only unqualified passion and acceptance he'd ever held in his hands.

Never to return. Rejected. Dismissed. Demoted from protector, defender, and lover, to runner of errands. Rodani leaned over, his gut a wash of agony.

"A'tem," Baldar said. "A'tem, can you walk? We will take you back." Both men pulled on Rodani's arms.

Another body appeared in his vision.

"Tem'u," Serano said.

No! No admonitions. No false pity. No murmurs of sympathy. Leave me.

Rodani felt Baldar give way on one side, as his partner took his place. Slowly, silently, they made their way back to the clinic.

TWENTY-TWO

Three more days passed and still Serano had no patience. His partner was on his feet and soon to be off-site, out of the manor on assignment. Cara had not spoken a word to Serano since she'd run out of the room to find Rodani. Not a word. Not an acknowledgment of his existence. She ate if food was put before her. She listened to music. She read. She slept, a lot. She stared out the windows until someone closed them in front of her nose. Only to that boy, Ikemi, would she speak. Not even to Hamman or Deremic.

But his biggest worry was that she was refusing to craft. Not one stitch had she taken since he told her Rodani had been reassigned. Not one seam sewn, not one slice of fabric cut. Her tools lay as she had left them, unruly and unused. Pieces of fabric lay haphazardly over the tabletop, forlorn and seemingly forgotten.

Serano didn't want to think about what Arimeso would say if she knew. His reports to her were becoming sporadic and terse, and he feared her reactions. As well, he feared his keso. At the best of times, Kusik was impatient and punitive. At the worst, Serano fled Kusik's vicinity as if a poridi were at his heels.

One lone human was putting the skin of his back in jeopardy. One stubborn woman was making him out to be a fool and a failure in front of his superiors. Selandu women he could handle. He knew the tricks, the whispers, the promises and the moves.

But not an incomprehensible human. Goddess, give him strength. A showdown was coming, and he wasn't going down without a fight. But first, he sought out an option. He walked down the hall and knocked on a door.

An answer brought Iraimin's face to his. Surprised, she molded her expression into propriety. Serano swallowed his pride and inclined his head. "I request your assistance, a'sel."

"Yes," she said hesitantly.

"I do not know if you have heard, but Rodani has asked for reassignment. He is no longer a'Cara's guardian, and she is quite distressed. I have been unable to bridge her silences, no matter what I say or do. Would you attempt to help her?"

"She does not speak?"

"Yes. Not to me, not to her servants. Only to that orphan boy."

"What do you wish me to do?"

"Talk to her. Get her to respond to you."

A look of alarm spread across Iraimin's face. "If you wish, a'tem."

"I do."

Iraimin followed Serano back to Cara's rooms, only to halt at the sight of her companion, frozen on the end of the couch, staring at the fire.

"Cara?" she said. The alien eyes flickered in her direction, but didn't quite make it. Iraimin stole forward softly. "Cara?"

The human's face tensed into a grimace that frightened Iraimin into her own silence. Cara turned away and buried her face in the quilt at the corner of the couch.

"Cara, do you hurt?"

No answer. No other movement. Iraimin drew back and glanced at Serano, who kept a wary distance.

Slowly, gingerly, Iraimin approached the cocoon Cara had made of her covering. She reached out and touched what she thought was the human's shoulder. But there was no response in the motionless figure. "Cara?"

Still no answer.

Iraimin's face went tight with thought, then she left the room, waving her fingers for Serano to follow. He shut the study door behind him.

"I have never seen her so," the painter said. "Now I worry."

"I worry more for when the taso learns she has stopped crafting."

Iraimin's pupils widened. "So? Surely no."

"Surely yes."

Iraimin sped off with a hurried patter of slippers. "I will bring the Enclave," she said over her shoulder.

Not at all reassured, Serano lowered himself into the chair at Cara's worktable, the chair that had been Rodani's. How had all this happened? Why had it happened?

He should have petitioned the taso the moment he saw Rodani falling. No sense in what Kusik wanted at this point in the affinity.

Parting a bonded pair was like muzzling a benatac after she'd taken off someone's fingers. Serano berated himself for his cowardice. No more. No more overlooking discourtesies. No more putting up with willful offenses now that his partner was elsewhere. The thought was almost cheering.

In less time than he guessed, a gold robe and slippers swept through the human's bedroom and into the study, followed by three acolytes. Serano rose and bowed. "A'Selaso."

"A'tem," she replied. "Iraimin bared her concerns to me, and I hastened to be of assistance."

"I do not know if you will be successful."

"But, of course, Sela will be, a'tem. You have forgotten your teachings."

Serano tilted his head. "Something in regard to this human plays havoc with assumptions, a'Selaso." Morose, he led the quartet to the study, and walked in.

Cara was still huddled in the far corner of the couch. Serano scanned the motionless form with guild-trained eyes. Not a crease was different since Iraimin had left.

"Cara. Cara, the selaso is here. You must rise and greet her. Properly," he added, with some justification.

The quilt didn't move.

Serano's ears began to burn. He kept them from twitching in agitation by the barest minimum, his temper ready to explode.

"Cara!" Not only did she disrespect her guardian, she dared do the same to the head of the Enclave. Serano laid both hands on Cara's wrapped body, felt an arm, and pulled her off the couch. Wide-eyed, Cara stumbled, then fell into a heap on the floor. Before anyone else could move, she wrapped the quilt back around herself and curled into a ball.

Serano reached down again, mayhem in his eyes.

"Stop."

He halted in mid-reach. *Always obey authority figures*, his father's voice intoned in his head. *Taso, keso, selaso. Dangers, one and all.* He stepped away.

Kimasa motioned to her acolytes. The four gathered around the hidden human and laid their hands on whatever part of her they found.

"Oh, great goddess," Kimasa began, "hear our pleas. Heal this human woman of her hurts. Embrace her with Your heart, Your arms, Your wisdom. Heal her of her afflictions and bring her back to us."

The acolytes muttered along with their leader, quiet and subdued.

"Au, Sela, help us bring Your healing to this woman through our hands. Make Your power, Your strength, flow into us so that we may heal her in Your name."

The quilt remained stubbornly unmoving. Serano sat on the near end of the couch, disturbed but hopeful.

The women shifted their hands slightly, and Kimasa renewed her fervent prayer.

"We know Your strength, oh Great Goddess, mother of us all. Take this child and bring her back to us. Use Your majestic power, mighty Sela, to bring back sight to her eyes, and sound to her voice. Draw her up from the great well where she has fallen. Bring her into the light, Mother. Bring her into Your sight so that she can see and feel Your presence among us."

Cara remained motionless on the floor. Serano's hopes, never high to begin with, seeped away as Kimasa and her acolytes muttered and bowed, shifting their hands with every renewed effort.

They tried to lift her, but she went limp in their arms as she had done to him. How much of this was real? What had the loss of Rodani done to her? Was this biological? Emotional? Fakery? There was no way to know a game from real pain, pretend from real loss. He watched silently, unable to judge with any satisfaction.

Several minutes later, Kimasa rose from her crouch and turned to Serano. "The goddess wills that she will remain quiet a while longer, a'tem." The acolytes crowded behind her, respectfully. "But I deem her voice will awaken within a day. It was well that you sent Iraimin to us."

Serano stood and bowed, then ushered them out. When he returned to the study, Cara was back on the couch, body wrapped, head covered down to her eyelids. He stood over her.

"Cara." No movement. "Cara, this cannot continue. You have a duty, also."

No sound.

"The taso will not be pleased to know of this withdrawal. You have tasks. Deadlines."

No response.

Serano perched himself on the edge of the tea table in the hopes it would hold his weight. "Cara, I am sorry. You can choose to accept or reject my words and my sentiments. But you cannot reject the circumstances." He leaned his elbows on his knees, moving closer. "I am here, whether you will it or not. I am here to guard you, and to help you, to see that you have what you need for your work. The work you avowed you would do."

Nothing moved on the couch. The quilt-wrapped lump didn't even seem to breathe, though if he listened closely, he could hear it. The absolute abandon stymied him, infuriated him. The stubborn withdrawal poked and prodded at his well-endowed, oft-exercised pride. With both hands, he gripped tightly to the quilt and wrenched it off her body. She jerked and flailed, but made not one sound. He yanked her off the couch, which made her collapse on the floor. Since dragging her was a little too far beyond his honor, he carried her into the workroom, and plopped her into her chair.

When she made no move toward her tools, he picked up her cutting ruler and slapped it on the table, then waved it in front of her face, and tapped her shoulder with it.

Not only did she not take it, rain began to course down her cheeks.

"Temi's damnations!" Serano plucked the stack of cut fabric and tossed it across the room. It fluttered in coordinated colors and landed on the floor in a decorative heap. He stared at her. What once would have made her livid with temper now earned no reaction at all. The driblets of rain continued down her face and began to dot the front of her blouse. She said not a word.

Serano left the room in a fog of frustration, stomping downstairs toward the keso's quarters. An undercurrent of whispers floated through the meeting room, traversing the space between the talking heads that surrounded the table. Threads of conversation made their way to his tufted ears as he found his own chair.

From his right: "I cannot believe it."

"I certainly can."

"How could he ever—"

From his left: "She made him ill?"

"That alien would make anyone ill."

"They had to toss him in a bath of ice."

"—The 'Yes' malady."

And behind him: "Does the taso know?"

"Has he been punished?"

"Does the selaso know?"

"I heard a rumor they both were brought before the Enclave for a hearing. I would bet my best knife Kimasa knows."

Serano let the nattering waft past him and tried to relax the muscles in his neck and shoulders, tension courtesy of the human's recalcitrance. Pushing her from his mind, he realized he'd predicted this. Saw it behind his eyes as he watched his partner falling afoul of the proscription.

The wall between guardian and guarded was tall and wide and thick. More than a handful of lives had been lost because judgments and discipline disappeared in the haze of mutual desires. What Rodani had done was more than an error of personal dimensions. Repercussions were rippling through the guild staff and threatening to rattle weapons all the way to Tendiman. Likely, Serano thought, that Arimeso would thwart any effort of the guild council to call Rodani back to headquarters. Officially, no taso could overrule the council in guild matters; but a sufficiently determined one might block a summons. And Arimeso, on this trail, was quite amply determined.

"Serano, did you know?" Toranel asked.

Slowly, deliberately, Serano placed his pocketknife on the table and twirled it between his fingers. "It is not my situation to discuss."

"But you must have known."

Imal leaned over. "Why would he so dishonor the guild?"

"What did he do to her that she wished him dismissed?"

The pocketknife twirled to a stop. It still had stains on it from the last batch of herbs he'd cut.

The hush that replaced the chattering voices told Serano his partner had walked in. He pocketed his knife and let his gaze rest on the chair across from him. From out of his peripheral vision, Rodani appeared. Moving slowly, he pulled his chair out and lowered himself into it. He looked wan, and carried less weight than was usual.

The battle of honor against honor that Serano had been waging for six days vibrated in his body like a too-taut drum. Damn Kusik for his meddling interference. Damn Rodani for falling into that whirlpool of dishonor. And Temi damn their taso for setting this boulder at the edge of a fractured cliff face. He composed his expression into something milder than his thoughts.

"Pleased to see you up out of that ice bucket, tem'u."

Rodani glanced his way, then off into the distance.

Kusik rapped his knuckles on the table. "This is a short meeting. First, there are two reassignments. Rodani is being assigned to communications and couriering while he recovers from his illness. Serano will take his former duty with the human."

He looked down at his notes. "As there has been no further word from Shurad's family, I am moving this issue off the active list. I expect—"

A very improper throat-clearing erupted from the far end of the table. Serano glanced over. Naremit, of course, but Vanu and Toranel were also leaning on their arms with wide-eyed attention.

"A'tem'ai," Timan said behind them, ever the peacekeeper.

Naremit turned to face the security second. "No discussion of dishonor? Of breaking guild laws? No mention of censure?"

"Those discussions have already taken place."

"When? Does the taso know?"

"Do you think," Kusik growled from the other end of the table, "that anything of such magnitude would not be known by the taso?"

"And reassignment is all he gets? Does the selaso know?"

"Yes."

"Yes? That is the answer?"

"You continually overstep your—"

Naremit attempted to mask his face, but his eyes betrayed his emotions. "I overstep? I? I am not the one who bedded his adashi— an *alien*, for Temi's sake. And I am not so old to have forgotten the many lectures we had in training! How can anyone—"

Timan backhanded the young man, forestalling worse from Kusik. Naremit fell against his chair, his ears flicking with the unexpected censure.

Serano stole a look at Rodani. His partner's gaze was fixed on the tabletop between them, seemingly wholly unaffected by the tirade against him. The look in his eyes made Serano shiver; it was the same utter blankness that Cara had been wearing for three days.

Timan stood, an uncommon occurrence. "All who need to know of this business are aware of it. The discussion is closed." His gaze ran around the table's inhabitants before he sat down.

"Arimeso does not rule the guild," Kusik added. "But I should never need to say that she has absolute domain over this house and everyone in it. And that includes you, and me, and yes, Rodani. If you have issues with her decisions, I suggest you go speak with her."

The silence was touchable, hard to swallow, and impossible to ignore. None, save a foolhardy few, ever braved the taso's presence for a rehearing. If the taso declined to bite an arrogant denizen's ears, Kusik would do it for her...and relish the task.

And Rodani, quiet and withdrawn in his chair, was one of the few who had done exactly that...and escaped unscathed. Serano still didn't know quite how he'd managed it.

"This meeting is ended," Kusik continued, "and I will receive reports from the lowest six of you on the duty you owe to Arimeso, how far that duty extends, and what you are prepared to do to obey it."

"And his report?" Naremit pointed to Rodani.

Kusik's eyes flashed. "Naremit, cease questioning my orders, or you will feel the lash."

Naremit's eyes widened under the threat, then narrowed to a thin line as he stared at Rodani.

After the meeting broke up, Naremit was first out of the room. He banged on Garidemu's door with inappropriate fervor. The sound echoed up and down the hallway. When the potter opened it, Naremit pushed his way inside.

"I would kill him. I would kill him now." Naremit walked the floor. "I will kill him."

Garidemu stepped in front of the pacing temichi, interrupting him into a startled pause. "Details, cousin. Forbear from riddles."

Naremit's pupils narrowed into slits. "Did you know Rodani was ill?"

"I heard the rumor."

"Do you know why?"

"No."

"For the same reason they were called to the Enclave." Naremit leaned into Garidemu's face, his breath harsh in his own ears. "Because they had enjoined an affinity. And they bonded so hard she made him ill."

Garidemu stepped back in shock. "An affinity? With *that*?"

"And she dismissed him because of it. Serano guards her now."

Garidemu blinked slowly. "Isn't an affinity against guild rules?"

"Yes," he hissed. "But Arimeso forbids his punishment."

"That makes no sense."

"Sense does not matter here, a'sel." Naremit walked away, then turned back. "We have it within us to effect the necessary punishment, to do what the taso will not. Can you follow what we agreed on?"

"Yes."

"Then do so."

TWENTY-THREE

Serano shook his head in trepidation as he returned from solo practice. Rodani was off-site and not due back for another day or so, thank the goddess. One-sided arguments did nothing to puncture his partner's morose, withdrawn behavior that mirrored what he was forced to face in Cara's presence as well.

But Kusik was the danger. Prodding him, remonstrating against his failures. Every day, sometimes several times a day. And Serano was getting nowhere on a painful, empty path. The issue with Cara was getting critical. Not a word would she say. Not a bit of crafting would she do. Hamman couldn't get past her silence. Nor could Iraimin. Ikemi could still draw speech from her, but he was worthless in the matter of Serano's orders.

He climbed the stairs by twos and rounded the corner, unlocking Cara's door with a quick stick-and-flip. She wasn't in her workroom. Which means she was most certainly in front of the fire, doing nothing.

Yes, there she was. He flung his body down on the couch beside her, jostling her out of her reverie. She glanced sideways but gave no other clue that she knew he was there.

"Cara," he said, "this has to stop." He put his hand on her arm. She looked at it remotely, then returned to gazing at the flames. He squeezed his fingers gently. "I will take care of you if you let me." He shook her arm. "Let me."

No response.

"Cara, I will not harm you. You have my word as guild. That should mean something to you."

Not a flicker of recognition passed over her eyes.

Serano sighed and shuffled closer to her. He ran his fingers down the side of her neck, prompting a quick jerk of her shoulder. He pulled at a few curls that caught on her blouse, tugging them back into place. "I am aware that you are in pain. I can do something about it if you will let me. But I can do aught if you do not respond."

She blinked slowly, breathed slowly, and ever refused his gaze.

"Rodani passed through your barriers, Cara. Somehow, he managed this task, and you accepted him, forged a bond. I can do the same if you will but let me."

Motionless on the couch, she shut her eyes.

Serano drew his hand down her arm and onto her thigh, lingering there. "Tell me. Tell me what I can do, and I will do it." He rubbed upward on her thigh.

She smacked his hand away, startling him. He froze, then leaned his shoulder into the back of the couch.

"This cannot last, Cara. You know it."

When she still refused to respond, he left her to her frozen mien and headed outside, swearing with every step. A human didn't belong here, any more than Selandu belonged south of the hills. That protective line was there for a purpose. There was safety in distance, after all. The ambassadors did what was needed. Nothing more.

Late that night, Serano lay in bed. His thoughts still wandered over the same beaten ground, forging no new paths through the brambles in his head. Goddess, Goddess of all, but there was no good to be had here. He floundered on a knife's edge, and the ground was crumbling beneath him.

Not many options were left—not with the time frame imposed by his keso. Not with the knowledge that Arimeso was also losing patience with her lack of crafting. That was another disaster. One last try. One last tiptoe into the minefield. He rolled out of bed, slipped on a pair of loose pants, and walked across the hall. Quietly letting himself into Cara's workroom, he peered through the darkness into her bedroom. The door was open. He waited for a response, for an outcry, but none came. Barefoot, he slipped into the room.

Cara was asleep on her side, facing away from the door to the servants' hallway. Her quilt covered most of her, but enough of her body lay uncovered to let him know she slept as most all Selandu sleep.

He dropped his pants on the floor. Slowly, ever so gently, he put his hands on the mattress and pushed down, then drew one leg onto the bed. He stopped to see if her breathing had changed, but the pattern remained the same. He brought his other leg up and lay down, pulling the quilt over top of him. He knew without a doubt that cold skin against her warmth was not the way to accomplish this.

She shifted slightly, but didn't wake. He waited, unmoving, for his body to warm. Her own body's warmth drew him to her, provoking an unexpectedly strong reaction of his own. Possibly, just possibly, this could be something more than duty. Maybe, maybe, but—*no*. He would not fall into the same trap as his partner. He would not compound Rodani's disaster with a calamity of his own.

He reached beneath the quilt to the curve of her waist, and laid his palm on her skin. It was soft, as he imagined it to be. He lay still, waiting to see if she roused from sleep. When she did not, he caressed her side, moving upward. As he touched her arm, he stopped. Next was a place of intrigue, a place where touch reigned supreme, where she might wake. Slowly, he moved his hand forward, cupping the soft mound of skin under his palm.

Cara murmured at the touch but remained asleep. He ran his hand over her breast, drawing his fingers across her nipple. It tightened under his touch. To his surprise, his own body reacted with a clench of his pelvic muscles. He blew a warm breath on the back of her neck.

She leaned back against him, exposing more skin. Serano studied her endowments in the dim light and slid his hand over to her other breast. She opened her eyes.

And shrieked as she flung off the quilt, scrambling away from him in nothing but her own skin.

"What are you doing?" she shouted.

Serano put his hand out to quiet her. She batted it away with a resounding slap.

"Get out of my bed!"

"Cara," he began. No, this wasn't the way it was supposed to happen. He climbed out as noises erupted on the other side of the door.

She picked up the timepiece from the bedside table and threw it at him as he bent down for his pants.

He sidestepped it. "Please, Cara." It clattered and echoed on the stone.

Then she tossed a slipper from the floor. "Get out! Hamman!"

"Cara?" came a muffled query.

"Get him out of here!"

The other slipper smacked him on the head as he tried to slide a leg into the pants.

"How dare you!"

He stole a glance at her wild countenance as he fled back into her workroom. Deremic, with Hamman behind him, dashed into the room just as Serano flung himself out into the hallway. As the door began to shut behind him, he heard Cara shouting at her servants in outrage.

In a mere moment, Serano was back in his own rooms, disheveled and breathing as if he'd run the perimeter of the manor. He dropped his pants on the floor in front of the door and crawled back into his bed, wishing for a drink. Well, at least he'd gotten her to talk.

***

Morning found him sitting in Kusik's office. Timan watched from the far corner.

"Is that the best you can do?"

Serano paled and froze, mortification in every line of his tall body. "A'Keso," he said, "you cannot begin to understand what I have faced trying to accomplish this task you have given me."

"What you face is nothing compared to what the taso faces, and this house. Do not give me excuses."

"A'Keso, I tire of being humiliated. She has no desire for me."

"That does not need to matter."

"There is no way to gain her trust or her interest in the time frame you have given me."

"You will continue to try."

"I have done everything I can think of."

"What of that herb decoction you give the artisans?"

"Either it does not affect her with the same strength, or she has a stronger will, a'Keso. When she was under its influence, she refrained from any desire-related actions."

Kusik clenched his fists on the desk, spiking Serano's heart rate. "And?"

Frustration bubbled up into Serano's chest, making his fingers and ears twitch. "A'Keso, I have said all that I know to say."

"There is nothing more you can do?"

"This is a matter for months or years, a'Keso. Not days, or even weeks."

"We do not have that time!"

Kusik's pupils flashed, and his voice thundered past Serano's ears. But he held himself back. Why speak unwanted answers?

Kusik eyed him darkly. "You concede defeat?"

"Yes."

The keso pushed himself up from the chair slowly, an aura of rage emanating from his body. Serano shrank back in his chair with nowhere to go, and no way to get there. A frisson of fear crept up his spine and tingled his ear tips. His eyes widened and his breath went shallow as Kusik rounded the desk.

Serano stood in deference to his approach. But it only brought his head within reach of Kusik's fist. The blow struck him under his jaw, rocking him back on his heels.

"You are turning out to be nearly as worthless as your partner. Get out."

Serano left the room spitting out a piece of flesh from his inner cheek, and with the beginning of a headache.

Behind him, Timan pulled himself out of the corner.

"Ideas?" Kusik asked him.

Timan eyed him warily. "Let them be."

Kusik balled his fist, raising it into the air. "Not when guild honor is at stake."

"The guild's honor will survive one temichi's misplaced attentions, tem'u. The guild always survives."

Kusik slammed the door shut with an inappropriate bang. Perversely, it bounced open. "Serano has failed." The hard click of Kusik's boot heels gave vent to his frustration. "He pursues, and she refuses. He steps forward, she retreats. He claims she holds his discipline of her against him, but that is senseless."

"Yet you yourself have pronounced her that."

"Tsss." Kusik parted the air with a vertical slash. "If she is constantly receptive, no one man can satisfy her. Imagine the state of her body and mind. How can she work? How can she think?" Frustration tightened his gut as he walked out of the office. He fought it down, fought his expressions until they molded into proper Selandu configuration.

"Yet she does," Timan said. "There is more to her than we know."

"Or less."

"And the walls of Himadi House continue to rise."

Kusik stopped in mid-hallway. Two servants scurried by on unknown errands, eyes resolutely ahead. "You must mention that?" he asked, drawing out his distaste.

"Silence will not unmake it."

Kusik moved on. "Do not presume to lecture me."

"I would not."

Kusik glanced to either side at the walls as they strode toward Arimeso's quarters. The cracks between the blocks of stone seemed wider, the facings dimmer. Was it the stone? His eyes? His attitude? That damnable alien colored his days with a wash of anger, her presence a constant disruption to the orderly procession of his tasks, an irritant under the skin of his emotions.

"You still decline?"

Timan's glance slid away. "Yes, a'Keso."

"I could order you."

"I know it well, a'Keso. But I see no favor in her, and she knows nothing of me except that I forced her back to the Enclave when she was wounded in the forest, and ignored her entreaties upon Rodani's whereabouts. That will not endear her to me."

"You still see no danger?"

"From her, no."

"It is clear as a harvest sky, tem'u."

"At night."

They parted company inside the guardroom, old arguments still unsettled.

TWENTY-FOUR

Voices echoed in the hallway. Dimly, Rodani heard them. Automatically, he identified and categorized them—ally, foe, or indifferent, old guild habit. Then he ignored them. His eyes roamed the walls and doors apathetically. One who knew him well might have noticed the stoop in his shoulders, the pursed line of his lips, the shadowed look in his dark eyes, as if he had aged several years in the past few days. Or, maybe the years that had dropped from him in the previous weeks had come back to wreak revenge on his lightened step, his brightened outlook.

A few watched him as he passed, surreptitious in their glances. He eyed them coldly.

He brushed benatac fur off his pants as he walked, wishing for a hot bath. But his report came first.

The quiet chatter of a young woman floated down the broad hall steps behind him, a voice with a curious accent. Realization overtook him, and his ears fluttered in dismay.

"I will tell her, Serano. Don't doubt that I will."

"I do not."

Walk, he commanded himself. *Leave. Now.* He took a step, and another.

The footsteps reached floor level, then stopped. His hands clenched at his sides. He froze, willing himself to disappear. Would that he could. Memories coalesced into a ball in his midsection. Nausea reared his head. *No.*

"Rodani?"

He turned slowly, scarcely believing she chose to speak to him. What she saw in his face he could only guess, for she took a step back.

"Tem'u," Serano said, panic sharp in his voice. "No."

"Rodani?" she ventured more softly. Her eyes were wide, her mouth slightly open.

"No, Cara," Serano demanded, pulling her toward the other hall.

Rodani dug his nails into his palms. *Calm. You can survive this, fool. The worst is already over. Be courteous, then leave. This, you can manage.*

She lurched away from his partner, clawing at his grip, turning back to look right at him. "Rodani!"

Rodani swallowed past the nerves that threatened to cut off his air. He watched, confused, as Cara struggled against Serano's grip—as if she wanted to come closer. The thought threatened his grief-worn composure. She grabbed at Serano's hands and squirmed in his grip.

"Cara?" Rodani ventured into the tumult she was causing.

"Aisu, talk to me, please."

He blinked rapidly, not believing what he heard—his erinai. He started toward them, toward Cara, toward his partner, who was dragging her away. "Let her go."

"This is not allowed," Serano said, as he neared them. "Stop, Rodani!"

"Rodani, why—" Cara began.

Serano slapped his hand over her mouth. "I beg you leave, tem'u. Now."

Cara struggled in earnest, flailing against his strength and pulling at his hand. He shifted his weight, the better to maneuver. But when he tugged her in the other direction, she fought wildly, her shouting muffled. As Rodani closed the gap, Cara bit down on Serano's hand. He hissed and removed it, glaring at her.

"Why did you change your mind, Rodani?" she said in a rush.

Injured, Serano fumbled to recover her mouth. She captured his arm under her hands, refusing to let go. Serano pulled her farther down the hall.

Rodani stared at her as he followed them, tied to her presence with an invisible rope. Her form filled his vision, her words a jumble in his mind. He ran up and planted his body in front of Serano, but his gaze held his adashi. He had dreamed of her, ill in his clinic bed. Dreamed of her, and fought the very presence of those dreams every night since Timan had talked to him.

"Changed my mind?" he asked. Pain turned his voice into a rough parody of its normal melodious baritone. "I did not change my mind, Cara. You did."

294

Serano pulled her backwards. "Tem'u, no. Go back. Do your duty, as I must."

Cara stiffened against Serano's torso. Her weakened hands scratched at his skin. Her fingers shone white against his black shirt. Tension tightened the muscles around her eyes. "I didn't, aisu, I didn't."

"Stop, tem'u," Serano said, louder with the beginning of panic. "It is forbidden." He tugged at Cara, nearly lifting her from the floor. Rodani stood firmly in the way.

"I did not," Cara said. The heat in her voice carried to Rodani. "They said you refused to come back. That you were—"

"Stop, Cara," Serano said, shaking her.

"Too ill. Too tired. Too uncomfortable with what..." She looked away.

Heat spread through Rodani's chest; his vision narrowed and sharpened its focus. She no longer struggled. The water forming in her eyes shone in the flicker of hall torches and ambient light. He turned to his partner. Serano quailed, but gamely held his ground, locked onto Cara with a fierce grip.

"What do you know of this?"

Serano took a steadying breath. "I obey orders, tem'u. As you do. As you should be doing right now."

Rodani dug his fingers into Serano's arms and shook him. "What were you told?"

Serano blanked his face of expression. "To obey."

The world went quiet. The questions in Rodani's head stilled. He raised his fist, and with one blow, sent Serano to the floor in a heap. Cara fell on top of him, crying out. Heads in the hallway turned as he picked her up and looked her over.

"Are you hurt?" he asked, searching her face for the truths hidden in this matter.

She rolled her shoulders and shook her arms. "No." Her eyes were clear again, wide with emotions too complex for him to interpret.

"Who told you I changed my mind?"

"Everyone."

"Who is everyone?"

"Serano. Hamman. Deremic. They wouldn't let me see you! They wouldn't even let me see the taso." Water reformed in her eyes. "It's been days, Rodani. Too many days!"

Rodani froze.

Perfidy. Treason.

His body began to shake.

Conspiracy. Collusion.

He closed his eyes, at war with his own conflicting needs. *Control!* He fought for it, willing his fury to subside. It railed against his clenched muscles, against his honor, his pride. Control. The shudders lessened slowly. Someone reached out and gripped his arm. He ignored it and opened his eyes. Serano stood at his side. Cara was still in front of him, held fast in his hands, waiting. Waiting for him. Waiting for answers. How long had she been waiting for those answers? Answers that made sense. Answers she could trust. Their betrayal rocked him to the very center of his self.

Serano put his hand on her shoulder, fingers gripping. "Rodani."

"Cara," he said slowly, "I did not ask to be relieved of your duty."

Her eyes widened, and her jaw dropped. "Then..." She seemed to stop breathing. Rodani smiled grimly to see her pupils narrow, to feel her arms tense under his hands. "Kusik," she said.

"Quietly, kia. Your voice carries. Where were you going?"

"To see the taso."

"You said you were not allowed."

"Oh, I wasn't allowed when I asked," she said. A smile with no humor stretched across her mouth. "But when I refused to quilt, she called me. And I come."

"You stopped crafting? Why?"

"To call attention to me, aisu, to my questions. And I've succeeded."

Rodani let go, and began to circle around her, running interference on Serano's attempt to part them. One uncertainty was cleared, but another still hung about his ears. "Cara," he said softly. "Do you wish me to return? As your guardian?"

"Rodani!" Serano shouted, grabbing at his arm and shaking him.

But eyes blue as an autumn sky stared up at him, round pupils wide. "Only as my guardian?"

He hardly dared to breathe. "We must have truth between us, kia." The erinai felt good on his tongue, this pet name he cherished. It would feel better, he promised himself. Most certainly it would. "What are your wishes?"

"Rodani, you are forbidden," Serano shouted in his ear.

"To go back to the way it was," Cara replied.

"In all ways?"

"No, Rodani!"

"Yes, of course," she said.

If it were only so simple. "Come." He pulled on her, much as Serano was trying to do.

"Tem'u, do not do this," Serano said in a tone too close to begging.

"Where?" Cara asked.

"To the taso. Your errand has not changed. Mine has." Rodani's confusion dissipated in the light of Cara's words. Arguments formed and reformed in his mind as she trotted along beside him. The absolute normalcy of it reassured him as he prepared for another struggle. Too many struggles had occupied his life, but it was long since one this important had held him in its grips. One wrong step, one trip over a simple word, and the hostilities that had been waged behind separate lines would merge into open warfare.

Too soon, and not nearly soon enough, the door to Arimeso's quarters came into view. Rodani guided Cara through the guild guardroom, drawing stares from his fellow temichin. He knocked on the door to the taso's offices. Forgotten, Serano trailed behind.

"Kia," he turned to Cara, "we need calm, as much as we ever did in previous times. Do you understand?"

"Yes."

The grim expression on her face worried him. He shook her arm. "Calm."

A different look spread across her features. "I'm glad you're here."

Something within him released its intractable hold on his attitude and his gut. He straightened his shoulders.

"Enter," said a voice over the speaker.

Rodani opened the door and stepped inside, Cara following. Arimeso sat at her desk. Kusik rose from his chair to loom over them.

"Where is Serano?" he asked, eyes narrowing as Rodani shut the door. He walked out from behind the desk.

Well into protective mode, Rodani refused to panic. "I do not know."

"Find him," Kusik said through gritted teeth. "And return to your duties. This is forbidden!"

"A'Taso," Cara said. "I beg you to allow him to remain. He belongs in this meeting."

Arimeso watched silently as Kusik approached the pair. As he neared, Cara interposed her body between them. Gratification warred with shame in Rodani's mind.

"So, the adashi protects her former guardian, now?"

Rodani began to move her aside, but she flung out an arm to resist him. "You will have to ask her yourself, a'Keso," he said. "I have found it perilous to assume anything where a'Cara is concerned."

Kusik's gaze drifted back up to Rodani. "Leave."

Twice in as many minutes, Rodani ignored that order. "A'Taso," he said quickly, "there has been a serious misunderstanding." Better, he thought, to sound as if it were less than terrible. Treason was a word he didn't want to voice.

Kusik grabbed the front of his shirt. "You will obey me."

Cara slid between them. Rodani tried to pull her away, and Kusik pushed at her. They battled in a silent contest of wills.

"A'Taso," she pleaded, stumbling on her feet. "Please put a stop to this. Please."

Kusik tightened his fist on Rodani's shirt, knuckles digging into skin. He began to push Rodani backwards.

"Enough," Arimeso ordered. Kusik stopped but didn't let go. Rodani eyed him warily as Cara shuffled nearby, hands out in an empty attempt to assist him. If Kusik turned his temper on her...

"A'Keso," Arimeso said sharply.

Not without a parting shove did he release Rodani, but he returned to his taso's side without further incident. She leaned forward. "I expected a discussion of your project's lack of progress, a'Cara, not an altercation before my desk. Has the topic changed?"

"No, a'Taso," Cara replied. "My work slowed because I was very concerned about my guardian."

Arimeso's pupils widened. "Why were you concerned when you had requested he be replaced?"

"But I didn't, a'Taso. I did not. That was the misunderstanding."

Caution, kia, Rodani willed her. *Take great care.*

"But you did," Arimeso said.

"No, a'Taso, please, let me be clear." Cara waved her hand at nothing in the room. "Someone misunderstood. Someone misinformed you."

Rodani stilled his body, waiting for a reaction. Arimeso planned carefully, and did not take well to her plans being thwarted, even accidentally. Kusik remained a brooding, forbidding presence at her side.

"You did not request his transfer?"

"No, a'Taso," she said with a heartfelt tone Rodani recognized.

Arimeso blinked slowly, then opened her palm to Rodani. "A'tem?"

"I was told of her request while I was ill, a'Taso, and I obeyed, not seeking her out. I was told she requested my removal, and she was told that I requested reassignment," he said. "Only now did we learn of the mistake." Bitterness threatened to leak out all over his words. He kept his expression carefully neutral, carefully attentive on his taso. Upon her only, rested his return to Cara's side.

"Do you wish his reinstatement, a'Cara?" she asked.

"Yes, a'Taso, I do."

Kusik folded his arms across his chest. Rodani's protective instincts shot upward, flooding his body with danger signals.

"But Rodani has already been reassigned," Kusik said, "and Serano has already replaced him. There is no reason to change once again. A'Cara," he continued with disdain in his voice, "has no need of another guardian. Serano is just as well-suited to her security."

The hubris floored him. Rodani opened his mouth. Cara beat him by a split second.

"Please, a'Taso," she said. "Serano is not nearly as well-adapted to me. He is—he seems...arrogant and presumptuous." Surprise filled Arimeso's face. Kusik paled. "He has little respect for me or my craft, and his temper frightens me."

Kusik leaned forward and put his fists on the desktop. Rodani edged closer to Cara.

"Frightens you," Arimeso repeated, as if she were uncertain of Cara's use of Selandu words.

"Yes, a'Taso."

"Rodani?"

"I have seen her fear of him, a'Taso," he said. "It is not unearned."

"And Rodani does not frighten you?"

Cara pulled her hands behind her back. Rodani stole a glance at her. "He doesn't."

"And your opinion on your return to her guardianship, Rodani?"

"I would welcome it, a'Taso."

Arimeso opened her palm. "Then it is done."

Over. The last of Rodani's days-old anguish poured out of his body, invisible under his taso's gaze. Smoothly, he bowed, Cara following suit. Not for a moment did he glance at his guild superior. What rested on that face was nothing he wished to see.

"Rodani," Arimeso said. "You will write a report of this event, and upon this fear Cara has of Serano."

"A'Taso," was the only answer allowed.

In the anteroom, Serano waited. Some of Rodani's elation faded as he regarded his silent partner, but beside him, Cara bubbled with pent up emotion. Without a word to either, Rodani escorted her out of the anteroom, past the still suspicious temichin, down the hall, and up the central staircase to the room he hadn't seen for more than a week. Bootsteps followed him.

It wasn't until he reached the door that he remembered he no longer had the key. Serano walked up and unlocked it. Rodani held out his hand.

"We must talk, tem'u," Serano said, pocketing the key and turning toward their own door. Rodani whispered to Cara, coaxed her into her room, and shut the door behind her. Now was not an opportune time to turn his back on his volatile adashi, but neither was refusing Serano a healthy alternative. He followed his partner into their living area.

"Tem'u—" Serano said.

"You knew," Rodani replied darkly, cutting off his partner's excuses.

Serano's pupils narrowed. He took a deep breath. "Rodani, what you must know is that everything that happened between Cara and me was because of orders I was given." Serano began to pace. "Whatever Cara tells you of that time, know that I was obeying my superiors."

"What did you do?"

"More than I wished to, less than I was ordered."

Rodani crossed his arms and tucked his chin, leaning back—solid temichi against solid door. "Who gave you those orders?"

"Kusik, of course."

"Why?"

"To keep you two apart. Why else?"

"What did you do?"

"Let Cara tell you what she wishes. Then we may talk again." Serano stopped pacing.

Deeper, darker, dank, and rotten. Rodani studied his partner, studied him more closely than he had in years. How much fraud had Serano perpetrated? What did Cara endure while he was dismissed?

"How many times did you hit her?"

"None."

"I would be displeased to hear differently from her."

Serano flung out his hand. "And what if I were ordered to hit her? What if I were ordered to kill her? Then what would you threaten?"

A frisson of fear sped through Rodani, uncrossing his arms and bringing him away from the door in full ready mode. "What have you heard? What has been said? Speak, or—"

"Nothing, tem'u. I meant that I will follow orders, by the oath I took in the guild." Serano took a step toward him. "Will you?"

Rodani's face fell into mask, his heart thumped heavily under his chest plate. His pupils narrowed to the merest slits, but Serano held firm in front of him. He tore open the door and stomped out.

"Tem'u!"

Rodani crossed the hall and put his hand on the doorknob, before realizing that Serano still held the key. He took a deep breath and moved to the servants' door. A knock brought Deremic into view. The manservant let him in, not without hesitation.

"I have been reinstated," Rodani said, sweeping past him. Then he turned. "If you feel required to verify my statement, speak to the taso, not to Kusik."

Cara was curled up on the couch, a glass of shigeli in her hand, another of eisenico on the tea table, waiting. He studied her from the doorway, willing his mind to a calmness he didn't truly feel. His adashi's posture, the set of her head, the expression on her face, all showed a defensive, wary demeanor, but no overt upset. In a moment, he realized she studied him just as intently.

Barriers. Barriers erected and needing to be breached. Goddess! Once done, twice as easy, as the old saying went.

When Cara held out her hand to him, another crack appeared in the shell he had built, another piece of his dis-ease fell away. When the woman you'd bonded with made the first token gesture, it engendered a ray of hope. He took her hand and sat. Not next to her. Not so close yet. But not too distant. What had it cost her to face what she thought was his rejection? How badly had it pained her to beg him to answer?

A crooked smile crossed her face. "Shall we draw cards to see who speaks first?"

"If you wish."

"If it helps any," Cara told him, "I'm determined to be patient tonight, and hear whatever it is I need to hear. You can go first if you wish."

A jumbled matrix of issues sprang to his mind. What did she need to hear? How much? How much could she take without a breakdown? Security, politics, sex, health, fear, competition. It was a maze with no beginning and no end in sight that he wanted to face.

Cara shook his hand like she was tossing seeds in a garden. "Start somewhere. Or I will."

He took the out she gave him. "You."

Cara turned sideways to face him, crossing her legs. A good sign, he thought. She put her other hand on his and began to massage his palm with her fingers. And again, a sign. Another piece of his shell broke off. "Do you remember the last time you did that?" he whispered.

She stopped, but didn't let go. Her eyes widened as she looked up. "After that terrible fight. I bit you."

"Because I slapped you."

She returned to the massage, rubbing the skin on his fingers. "Seems ages ago."

"Yes."

She began to rock, to and fro, to and fro, bent over his hand. "I tried to come see you in the clinic, aisu. I tried every day. They wouldn't let me." She rubbed the whole of his palm with hers. "I wanted to take care of you, as you did me when my hands were damaged." Her head dropped. Rodani expected the rain to begin, but her eyes remained dry. "I was so afraid for you," she said. "I hated that."

"What is that word?"

"Mixture of fear and anger. Causes bad things in humans."

"Who angered you?"

"Everyone who wouldn't let me see you."

"And what of your days?"

"Serano hovered about, every day. For some reason, he developed a conscience or something. Wouldn't leave me alone."

"What did you do all day?"

"When you were ill, he followed me around as I crafted, read, and sang. We played Tasos and Temichin. Went out to gather herbs. Said he would keep me safe and occupied while you were away."

"You did not fight?"

"Argued. Didn't fight. Aisu," she stopped, looked away, off into the fire. He recognized this signal, too, and waited. She swallowed, and bit her lip. Another sign. "Serano did something."

He waited. "And that was?"

Cara closed her eyes, as if she feared to see his reaction.

"He tried to persuade me to join with him."

Rodani went still. It made sense. Quite clear sense. Serano's words echoed in his head. *What I did, I was ordered to do.* Rodani studied her demeanor in detail: her head, shoulders, eyes, mouth; the rocking had returned. Not fear. Shame? "Did you accept him?"

That brought her head up, with her eyes wide and mouth open. "That would dishonor you, aisu." She looked down at their hands. "I didn't."

Rodani covered her hands with his free one. "Forgive me for offending you. That was not my intention." She sagged sideways against the couch, relieved, he judged. "I merely wished to know your answer to him."

"Did you think I would?"

"I do not know your cultural mores on the issue, kia. And guild partners have been known to share."

"Oh. Well, he seemed to think there was no dishonor in asking, but I kept refusing."

"Kept refusing?"

"He tried more than once. Three or four times, actually."

"How did he react to your refusals?"

"Didn't seem to matter much to him. He just kept trying. Wouldn't take no for an answer, which to us means disrespect."

"I would ask you to withhold too harsh a judgment of him, kia. He was put in a difficult position with little knowledge and less guidance."

She raised her face to him, her eyes and mouth tense. "If I had said yes, would you be as calm?"

It drew him back for a moment. But before he could reply, she looked away. "No. Forgive me for asking, aisu. It doesn't matter, because I won't dishonor you like that."

Mercurial. A rocking boat at high tide. Her oscillating moods wearied him. But to be fair, she couldn't be less disturbed than he. Rodani lifted his free hand, but left the other one in Cara's grasp, content for it to be there as long as she wished. For all the frustration and forced ignorance she'd had to endure for several days, she was remarkably calm. And Rodani wanted her to remain that way. He took a sip of eisenico and leaned into the couch, subconsciously mirroring her.

"Tell me of your refusal to craft," he prompted into her silence.

She smiled, but it wasn't a pleasant one. "It was the only way I could think of to force my complaint." She ran her hands down his, past his wrist, and onto his forearm, then back. Long slow strokes encompassing the entire length. Her body swayed back and forth as she caressed him.

"I couldn't shout." She continued. "No one listened. Screaming was too embarrassing. I tried sneaking out, but that brought Serano's temper far too close to the surface for my comfort."

"Did he strike you?"

"No. But he wanted to. He held himself back. I could tell."

"I commend his restraint."

Cara smiled.

"So, you stopped crafting?"

"Completely. Wouldn't even sit at my worktable."

"What was said?"

"Oh, Serano badgered me, in between attempts to importune me. Hamman chided me, Deremic just watched from a distance. Watched a lot, as a matter of fact. Not sure why."

"And Arimeso finally demanded your presence?"

"Yes. I didn't want to face her. But she was my only link to you. She was the only one I thought would listen to me."

Abruptly, Cara stopped stroking his hand. It felt cold immediately, bereft of her touch. Her gaze fixed on no particular point between them, her face masked. Rodani held his breath for a heartbeat, and another, and another, waiting for whatever difficulty she needed to speak.

"Who told you I wanted you gone, aisu?"

Goddess. Of all the places he could go with her, this was the one he most wanted to avoid. Gently, he squeezed her scarred fingers. "Timan."

"Why did you believe him?"

And there was the cliff edge. *Temi help me.*

"No acceptable reason, kia, but many assumptions. I have not known Timan to be a liar. As well, I was still ill, and not thinking too rationally. Serano backed him up. Kusik, of course, seemed pleased that you had changed your mind. And, most importantly, I was forbidden to see you, to verify."

"You had access to Arimeso."

"Yes. But I am under far more strict orders than you are, kia, or ever will be. Despite how I act, despite what I have done, there are very real limits to how far I can tread off my path as a guardian. And I have stepped off of it too many times."

Her eyes went wide and began to fill with water. The reflection of the gathering rain in those eyes flickered in the firelight. The rain did not fall. Not yet. "Kia?"

"Have you...decided...we can't be together? Because you've gone too far?"

"No, kia, that was not a leap I meant you to take."

"Then can you be clearer?"

Rodani breathed away the new heat in his chest and spoke slowly. "I believed Timan only because I could not find anyone to tell me differently, and you were forbidden to me. I am more pleased than you know to find out I was wrong. But how far down this path we ride does not depend on you, or on me, or Kusik, or even the guild council in Tendiman. Only on Arimeso. I strayed past Kusik's boundaries when I began to craft with you. I have not yet walked past the taso's boundaries. If I do, I will certainly find out."

Cara remained silent, her eyes traveling, roaming the room as she thought. Her hands remained on his, her body still. "And your illness?"

"I can only say we will have to proceed cautiously."

"It could happen again?"

"Absolutely."

"What started it? Was it something that I did?"

"I have tried to return to those days, kia, to answer that question myself. And I believe that, unknowingly, yes, it was."

Such a mobile face. Her lips drew down, as well as her chin. The eyes widened and blinked rapidly, scanning the scene in fits and starts. Her whole head moved, just a little, vibrating to some inner tension.

"I'm sorry, aisu."

"No apologies, kia. You could not have known. I do not have that excuse."

"But you didn't know you would get so sick."

"I knew, in some remote way, that it had occurred in the past. I did not know that was the trail I was following."

"How do we prevent it?"

"I have some ideas. But it would take discipline to implement them."

"We're adults. We should be able to do that."

"Shoulds are not always coulds, kia. The path from one to another is often a perilous one."

Humor blossomed across Cara's face, a welcome sight in a dark room in the midst of dark conversations. "Well, considering the subject matter is bedroom activities, we might as well have fun while we solve it. Yes?" She kissed her own fingertips, then reached out and touched his lips. "I will help deal with the safety of your body, as you deal with the safety of mine." She caressed his cheek. ^I love you.^

His eyes narrowed in thought. "I know the first word, and the last one. But what does the middle one mean?"

"It can mean," Cara began, "a lot of things. Including honoring and respecting you, the wish to share my mind and heart with you, the wish to spend a lot of time together, to grow together, to share my life with you—as much as you'll allow it." She curled her hand in her lap. "It means I wish to help you have a happy and safe life—with me. Every human would give you a slightly different definition. But I offer to you something no one can take by force. It can only be earned. It means that when you're in trouble, I put your health and safety ahead of mine." She looked down and grinned ruefully. "I could go on and on. But I'll stop there."

Rodani clasped her hand lightly. He stood up, the question painfully evident in his wide, reflective eyes. Cara smiled and let him lead her into the workroom. But when he stopped, she leaned around his body for the cause of the delay.

Kusik stood in her bedroom doorway, solid, unmoving, mayhem written in his face and in the ready fists held still at his sides.

Rodani pulled Cara away and pushed her behind her worktable. As Kusik strode into the room, Rodani scooted backwards into the study. The grim dance went on for a dire handful of seconds. Rodani passed out of sight of her table, into the far corner.

When the first thump resounded on flesh, Cara froze, stifling a hoarse outcry. She tiptoed to the doorframe, too fearful not to look. When the second hit came, Rodani bent over, a grimace of pain crossing his features in the flickering light.

Cara ran into her bedroom, and out into her servants' quarters. "Hamman! Deremic!" she called. A chair scraped over the stone, and Deremic came into view at the end of the narrow corridor.

"Call the taso, please!" She ground to a halt in front of him. "Please!"

"Why?"

"Don't you hear that?"

"It is a guild matter, a'Cara. We do not interfere."

She swore, pushed him aside, and headed for the door to the hall.

"A'Cara!"

"You call her," she said, hand on the doorknob. "You call her, or I go find her. Choose."

Deremic pressed a button on the radio and spoke. When he motioned to her, she spoke. "A'Taso? A'Taso?"

"What in Sela's good graces could be a problem so soon, a'Cara?"

"Your keso," she said.

"Excuse you?"

"A'Taso," she said, her accent thickening with haste and fear. "Why would you allow Rodani to return to my duty, only for Kusik to come up and beat him? Where is the sense, a'Taso? Where is the honor in this?"

Arimeso was silent for a moment. "He is there?"

"Yes! And he's hitting Rodani! Make him stop. Please."

"Deremic," she demanded.

Shaking, Cara stepped away. Deremic listened as Arimeso spoke, acknowledged her, then turned around. He placed two fingers against Cara's lips and pulled her behind Hamman's bedroom door, then walked through her rooms.

In a long, too-long moment, Kusik stomped through the corridor. Cara heard him mutter, curse, and click off the radio. It wasn't until the door slammed that Cara let out a long, ragged breath. As Deremic walked past, she sped out the door to her study, stopping just inside the entrance. Rodani still stood at the far wall, arms wrapped around his midsection. His head lifted as she entered.

"What did you do?" he whispered.

She took a few steps toward him, uncertain of his mood. "Called Arimeso. Asked her to call off her poridi."

His eyes went wide, pupils opening into ovals. He looked at the fireplace mantle, as if seeing through the wall in the direction of Kusik's retreat. She came closer, diffident, waiting. Rodani looked down at her.

"Aisu, come lay down with me. Whether we do anything else or not," she tossed the comment into the air of uncertainty. "I just need to hold you. And be held."

Then it was her turn to hold out her hand, Rodani to take it.

As he pulled away from the wall, he spoke. "I have a response to your new word, kia. The one you explained."

Cara raised an eyebrow.

He spoke low and softly. "You are my all."

TWENTY-FIVE

Garidemu closed the book he'd been studying intently, replaced it on the shelf, and sauntered out of the library. *It would do. It would do.* He smiled, short and sharp.

Down in the garage, he badgered an apprentice for a vehicle. There weren't many that afternoon, and he meant to have his way. A little extra height, a certain expression, a little extra growl in his voice, and a touch of alcoholic vapor on his breath—it was enough. Intimidation was an art form. He owned an imaginary master's sigil in it, and Naremit was his earnest pupil.

He jammed the key in its slot and pushed the button that transferred power from the batteries. In moments, he was on his way to town.

It wasn't much to speak of, this place. But it claimed a gunsmith, a dry goods store, an apothecary, a seamstress, and one quite favorable eatery. However, it had been whispered in the festive room that a new business had opened recently. A certain small place, with small beds, and a few women who were easy with their gifts. He wouldn't be the first to visit, but he emphatically wouldn't be the last. Another smile crossed his face, self-satisfied, proud.

The apothecary shop's mud-spattered door opened with a noisy protest. Water? Soap? He shuddered and hoped that the mortars and pestles in use were far cleaner than the entrance.

The druggist greeted him.

"Dabuul," Garidemu said, imperious.

"We carry only small quantities, a'tem. It is very powerful."

"Which is why I need it." He rustled in his breast pocket and scattered a few coins on the table. "The sooner, the better."

The druggist pulled open a drawer near the back and brought out a dark bottle, hardly half the height of his palm. "Three-tenths."

Garidemu's eyes widened. "You beggar me!"

"No. It is a costly and time-consuming process to refine it."

The potter glared, but pushed the coins forward and retrieved the rest, then pocketed the vial. He turned with a dismissive nod and headed for the door.

"Vermin?" the druggist called out.

Garidemu looked back over his shoulder.

"Yes."

***

Cara swallowed a bite of steak and pointed to Rodani's dinner plate with her knife. "He's abusing you, aisu."

Rodani took a sip of eisenico. "It was not always this way."

"But it is now," she argued. "Will you just stand there and take it?"

He set his glass down with careful precision. "Few other options exist, kia, none of them honorable."

"There is no excuse for the pain he's dealing you."

"In normal circumstances—"

Cara slapped her palm on the table, bringing a sting to her still-healing wounds. "But it's abnormal circumstances that prove a person's worth, aisu. That's why you are worth one hundred of him. One thousand! I wish you could see this from my perspective."

"I do try."

"I know you do." She laid her sore palm on his hand. "And that's another part of your great worth. You stop. You listen. You think. Who else tries? Serano? Any other guardian? Kimasa?" She shook her head, "You, Iraimin, Arimeso," then joggled his hand. "And on a daily basis? You. Just you."

Rodani left his hand under hers for a moment, then pulled it free. He took a sip of his drink and stared into its depths as if it held the answers they sought.

"What happened to the rule about no one abusing another by status or power?" Cara asked. "Remember discussing that, when I was first hurt?"

Rodani sliced another piece of the slab of meat on his plate and held it before his eyes. "There are rules within rules." He put the piece in his mouth and began to chew, slowly, with deliberation.

Cara stabbed a mass of water greens and twirled them in their sauce. "In some ways, Rodani, your people are just too similar to us."

"In what way?"

"Power corrupts."

"In dishonorable hands."

"Are there any honorable hands when it comes to power?" She eyed the greens and pulled half of them off her fork.

"Arimeso seems to do well. The Guild of Scientists dwells easily under Tuka's hand."

"But if they were dangerous to their people, what could be done?"

Rodani took another sip of his drink. "Petition the Counsel of Three for their removal."

"Who would do the removing?"

Rodani pursed his lips to hide a smile, and turned his attention back to the diminishing slab of meat on his plate.

"It wouldn't be the house's own guild, would it?"

He took another mouthful of vegetable.

"Someone in Tendiman?"

Chewing seemed to take up all Rodani's attention, his gaze on his plate, unwavering.

"Chendal? He's certainly capable."

"Cease, kia."

The rebuke stung, but only a little. Refusals to theoretical questions didn't bother her as much. She attacked her dessert with gusto—a sweet pastry with yellow-tinted nuts on top.

"You said something once about having to be sponsored to guild training. Is that true?"

He considered a moment. "Yes."

"Why did Kusik sponsor you if he disapproved of you so strongly?"

"He did not. There was a different keso when I arrived. Kusik ranked beneath him."

"What was his name?"

"Tokennen."

"Did you respect him?"

Rodani glanced off into the air, and back in time. "Very much so."

"Tell me about him, aisu. What made him special?" She finished off her dessert with a swipe of her finger.

"There is little to tell. But he treated me with respect when few others did."

"What happened to him? Did he die?"

"No. He and the taso," Rodani hesitated, searching for words. "Could not sustain their affinity."

"And by the time you graduated, Kusik was keso?"

"Yes."

"If you knew Kusik disapproved of you so strongly, why did you return after earning your knives?"

Rodani laid down his utensils and leaned forward. "This was the only place where I thought I would be part of the guild staff and also be allowed to craft, as I had been trained."

Cara smiled in sympathy and laid her hand on his arm. "It mattered that much."

"Yes. And I felt a great deal of allegiance to Arimeso."

She moved to the couch, Rodani following. They stretched out back to front, Cara sitting on his lap, facing the fire.

"And that was worth what Kusik does to you?"

Rodani slipped his hands around hers, enveloping them in warmth and a tingling touch. "That came later, kia. He never respected me or my skills, but he had no direct antipathy for me. It was only when I accepted this assignment last year that he began to chastise me frequently, and only since I broke the guild rule has he fallen into physical abuse."

"So, it's my attentions and his abuse, or neither."

"Yes."

"Rotten choice," she judged. "Arimeso won't stop it?"

"Often she does not know."

"Why don't you tell her?"

"Status among the other guild members," he replied. "Pride. Tradition."

"Ugh."

Rodani smiled. "That had an ill sound to it."

"Matches an ill attitude, too."

The whisper of slippers passed through the workroom. Cara turned her head just in time to see Iraimin stop inside the doorway.

"Sel'u!" she greeted the painter, clambering off Rodani's lap with a wide grin. On impulse, she hugged Iraimin. Startled, the woman took a second to return the favor. But the hug felt genuine.

"Sit down. Sit down," Cara gestured. "Drink?"

"Anything you have available would be more than welcome." Iraimin bowed to Rodani before passing by him to take the overstuffed chair.

Cara took a glass from the dining table and poured shigeli, then handed it to her. "What brings you?"

Iraimin glanced between the two of them as Cara sat back next to Rodani. "I heard the blessed news."

"Aww, now you can't give your goddess the credit, Iraimin. I worked hard to get him back."

Iraimin smiled at the jibe. "Of course I can. And I saw the hard work you did."

"Do you think ignoring Serano and all his diatribes was easy? I wished to craft, too, but knew I'd ruin my argument if I did."

"We can agree that we disagree."

"We always do. And I can claim evidence for my argument."

"Which you always do."

Humor flowed between them as Cara leaned back against Rodani's shoulder.

Cara took a sip of her drink. "Who told you?"

"I overheard Serano in the gathering room during dinner."

Rodani waved a hand in dismissal. "My partner rarely speaks so loudly that others can eavesdrop."

"He did in this instance. More than just my head turned to listen. However, he left out any details."

"And you wish for them?" Cara asked.

"No," Rodani countered her intention.

Cara rolled her eyes and cocked her head. Iraimin's answering smile prompted Rodani to lean around and peer into Cara's face. She turned her head, kissed her own fingertips, then made a tossing gesture over her shoulder.

"How do you fare, a'tem?" Iraimin asked. "I have not seen you for many a day."

"Well enough."

"You might write a warning pamphlet about your illness."

Rodani lowered his brows. "No one else is likely to need it."

"What about Himadi House?"

"I do not venture to guess."

"And you, Cara? What do you guess? Would other women of your species follow your path?"

She stared into the fire for a moment. "Likely not. Or very few."

"Why?"

"Fear of the unknown, mostly. And social…" she waved her hand in frustration, "I need my dictionary," she muttered. "…shunning by other humans for crossing the species line."

Rodani reached for his drink. "Your people would treat you no differently than we are treated."

"Unfortunately, yes."

"How would you fare at home?" he continued.

"Anywhere from acceptable to terrible, depending on who knew and how much they knew."

"Then I have a question for you," he said. "Later."

"If it has to do with ending the affinity, Rodani, the answer is no."

"What would you do if you went home to censure and shame, Cara?" Iraimin asked.

"I'm not sure. Either isolate myself, or walk boldly through it all, waiting until someone else's shame turned their cackles and growls to another direction." She planted her heels on the tea table, causing Rodani to lower his brows at her. She grinned. "And knowing me, I would hide one day, be bold the next, and hide again the day after that."

Iraimin swirled the shigeli in her glass. "Litelon still pines for you."

Rodani stiffened on the couch. "Why does that matter?" he asked, his voice so deep it was almost a growl.

Cara chuckled and patted his thigh. "Calm, aisu. Breathe," she said, mimicking his many admonitions to her. "I can't help him, sel'u. He's on his own."

"I only told you so that you would be aware. He has not forgotten you."

"I wonder what he sees in me? He knows nothing about me."

Iraimin glanced at Rodani and back at her. "Some people prefer the new and different. Others only fear them."

Cara saluted the air with her glass. "Rodani and Kusik, the great and the terrible."

TWENTY-SIX

Kusik stomped from one end of his study to the other. The room wasn't nearly wide enough to contain all his rage at being thwarted twice in his plans. Humiliated again by the taso, his bonded mate, he was barely thankful that this censure took place in private.

Goddess of all, he thought himself immune to the sting of words. It shamed him to find Temi's defenses so weak inside of him. All because not one person enmeshed in this concern could do what was needed. Not one person put duty ahead of personal gain, or failure.

It was tempting. Temi's demons, it was tempting to dismiss both guardians at the next opportunity. With Rodani and Serano gone from his staff and from his life, the human would not be far behind.

But Arimeso stood behind the curtain, pulling strings. And he was the marionette.

Kusik clicked on the radio in the room. "I need Kimasa," he barked at an acolyte.

He resumed his pacing, caring not a whit that the selaso outranked him. Nothing he said to Arimeso changed the outcome that he foresaw. Even his partner, his biso, couldn't see the precipice they were nearing.

Kimasa stopped at the entrance to Kusik's study, then perched herself decorously on the softest chair in the room, as Kusik rose to greet her.

"What brings me to you?"

Kusik took a deep breath, the better not to growl at the head priestess. "You heard the ill news?"

"Ill news." She paused, dramatically. "No."

"Both Rodani and that human disobeyed orders, met up, and took their poor, dire woes to the taso."

"Did they?"

"And she, of course, granted their wishes to reunite."

"And you, a'Keso, what did you do?"

Kusik closed his eyes and turned his face to mask. "Swallowed it, though it choked the breath from my chest."

"And what will you do now?"

Kusik sliced his hand through the air, cutting away the unwanted inquiry. "Kimasa, what happened to the ritual you divined? Did you perform it?"

The selaso leaned back and raked him with her eyes. "Do you think I lie?" she said, her voice smooth and cool.

"No. You might have postponed it. You might have changed it. I cannot know."

"I performed it, exactly as it needed to be."

"There is no question it failed."

"Au, my keso, there is every possibility of questions. Who can know the mind of Sela? She may be waiting for the correct moment, the one moment where all your machinations come to fruition."

"And how much more damage to my staff and this house before that moment comes, Kimasa?"

"That is not mine to judge, Kusik. And you know it."

Kusik pushed himself out of his chair and began to pace again. "I tire of delays. I tire of disobedience. I tire of rules broken and punishments undelivered. I tire of the worry that my taso's house will fall and I with it; or worse, the blame will land on me."

"No, Kusik, your fears creep through your mind, sabotaging you. It will be Arimeso's name that attends the rise or fall of her house."

"And I rise or fall with my taso."

"Sela's plan will unfold as it is to be. Your worries avail you of nothing."

Kusik stopped his pacing in the middle of the room and turned to her. His eyes glowed reflectively under a lowered brow.

"Trust in Her," Kimasa said.

He turned his back and studied his corner shelves. Half a lifetime of objects decorated it, joyous and painful moments memorialized together. "Do you still have the earrings?"

"I do."

He returned to the center of the room and held his hand out for the hated objects.

Kimasa only stared at his open palm. "I foresee an opportunity to return them myself." She stood, stiff and regal. "Thank you for airing your concerns with me, a'Keso."

***

"A'Cara." Hamman slipped through her bedroom and walked into the workroom, a modest-sized box in her hands.

"What is it?"

"A package from your home." She placed it on the worktable and backed away, watching.

Cara gingerly replaced the fabric pieces back in their proper places on the floor before getting up.

The box was unremarked. Just her name, inexpertly printed, and the word Barridan. No return address. Odd, but not worrying. Cara shook it gently. It was heavy, but didn't rattle. She thought for a moment of calling for Rodani, then dismissed it with a shrug.

At her motion, Hamman cut the cords holding it together. Inside was a mug. She reached for it and studied it. Carefully crafted, with delicately carved designs on the outside, it shone a bright blue. She tipped it over. No markings showed, no name, date, or location. She sat it on the table, admiring it.

"What do you think, Hamman?"

"It looks like a piece from a master crafter, a'Cara."

"It does. I wonder if it will hold tea without staining?"

Hamman wiped a finger around the inside of the mug, then looked for residue on it.

"Anything?"

"No, a'Cara."

"Well," she said, "when you get a chance, you can fill it."

Hamman inclined her head. "A'Cara."

Cara sat back down on the floor, wishing for the umpteenth time that she had the Selandu grace. Maybe it was practice. *No, ki'ono. That is not how you rise from a low position. Why are you sitting on the floor at all? It is crude, and ill-mannered. Up. Now, this is what you do.*

She smiled in reverie as she pinned her newest quilt top to its sandwiched base. One more nearly done, one more hopefully sold.

Bootsteps echoed behind her. Recognition of the sound and pattern brought another smile to her face. She waited for the matching voice, the deep baritone that stroked her soul. First came the creak of his chair.

"Have you exercised your hands today?"

"No, aisu, though I've been using them a lot."

"Strength training is different. Did I not explain?"

"Yes. I just haven't taken the time."

"Do so."

"You could take me to the range."

"I no longer need that practice for now." Tools rattled in his toolbox.

"What do you need?"

"Ground fighting. Grappling." The sound of metal rasping against metal erupted behind her.

"Like the fight you and Serano had after I was shot?"

"Yes."

"I could try."

"No, kia." Humor filtered through his voice. "I suspect any grappling we did would end in a ride. And you are not strong enough to test me."

Behind them, Hamman returned, bearing a tea tray and the mug. She set them down on the other side of the worktable and poured, adding the sweetener Cara liked.

Rodani bent forward. "That is new."

Cara turned, looking up over the edge of the table. "I just received it."

"From whom?"

"I'm not sure," she said, refocusing on the quilt top.

Rodani rose from his chair to lean over the table. "There was no note?"

"No."

"No name?"

"No. Why?"

When no answer came back to her, Cara looked around. Rodani was turning the mug in his hands, inspecting it with a critical eye. He opened the window and tossed the tea out into the winter air.

"Is that necessary?" Cara asked, rising from the floor.

"I was trained to be suspicious, kia. I am doing my duty." He took a piece of paper and wiped the inside of the mug. He repeated the action in another area of the paper, rubbing harder. He smelled each spot, and watched them carefully. A faint tinge appeared where he had wiped. Head bent, lips pursed, he studied the paper and the mug, then seemed to make a decision.

Cara watched forlornly as he carried the mug out into the hallway, shutting the door behind him. She turned to her servant. "Another mug, please?"

Rodani didn't reappear until half the afternoon was gone. By that time, Cara's newest quilt was nearly finished. Only the binding was left.

"What did you do with the mug?"

Rodani sat down to his previous task. "Testing a few things, kia."

"Do I get it back?"

"Maybe."

"When do I get it back?"

"Patience."

Cara sighed. "I do appreciate your one-word answers."

Rodani glanced at her. "Do you?"

"That was sarcasm, aisu."

He blinked. "Ah."

From the servant's quarters, the radio spoke, muffled by distance and volume. In a moment, Hamman bustled through the bedroom with a stride that bespoke a social emergency. "A'tem, a'Cara," she whispered. "The selaso will visit. She is on her way."

Cara cursed under her breath. "Wonderful."

Rodani stood. "Tea, and a proper nibble tin if you can procure one, Hamman."

"A'tem." Hamman folded herself into an anxious bow and scuttled away.

Cara moved to the tiny dinner table, holding onto her temper by the shred of a thread.

"Calm, kia."

"Yes, you said that last time."

Rodani laid his hand on her arm. "And I will repeat it as often as you need to hear it."

"Or more often."

"Is that a request, or a rebuke?"

Cara let out her breath with a snort. "Not sure."

"Remember the last time you saw her? Your pain was dire, and your courtesy non-existent. Please do better this time."

They both rose to their feet as Kimasa entered the study. Behind her, Hamman carried a tray overburdened with teas, sugars, and dainty snacks. As she set it on the table, Rodani waved the selaso into the overstuffed chair.

Give it a try, fem. Cara took a calming breath. "How may we assist you this day, a'Selaso?"

Kimasa's pupils widened, then the corners of her mouth turned up. "I can see that you are feeling better, a'Cara. How goes your crafting?"

Cara inclined her head. "Well enough, thank you."

"You suffer no ill effects?"

"A few, a'Selaso. Those will probably never fade. But with continued practice, I hold out hope."

Kimasa turned to Rodani. "And you, te'oto. You have had your own troubles, so I hear."

"I am well, a'Selaso." He inclined his head in a slow genuflection.

"So, as the goddess has deigned to shine Her light on you in these several matters, and as I am Her emissary, I require a boon from you both."

Cara glanced at Rodani, who said nothing. "I don't know that word, a'Selaso," she said.

"A gift, a task, a'Cara, a token of note for the Enclave."

Silence fell between them. Cara began to fidget, annoyed for more reasons than she could count. As Rodani was unmoving beside her, she drew her hands behind her back and willed herself to stillness.

The silence lengthened. Kimasa watched them alertly, waiting for some sign. As Cara didn't know any, she concentrated on her breathing. *In-one-two, out-one-two. In... Do something, please, woman. Better yet, go away.*

Finally, Rodani spoke. "We await your pleasure, a'Selaso."

"And a pleasure it will be, te'oto," she said with assurance. "I have discussed this with my seconds, and we have agreed. You and Cara will make an announcement at tomorrow's dinner, proclaiming for all to hear that our mighty goddess has proven Herself again." Kimasa waved her hands majestically, like a symphonic conductor on opening night. "You will tell the house of your recent tribulations, and how She has stepped in to set every problem right, to soothe every concern, to turn you back to the paths you were on, and that She smiles upon your future."

The selaso sat back, beaming in spiritual harmony with the voices in her head. Rodani remained standing, solid as ever. Cara collapsed on the nearest chair, wondering when reality had left and fantasy had taken over. A score of disparaging replies sped through her brain, and it took all her reserve to bite back on them. *Take it, aisu. Step up.*

Rodani lowered himself onto the couch and clasped his hands in his lap. "A'Selaso, you honor us with this task, and I thank you. But it is far, far too dangerous to perform it."

"Rodani, I know you are cautious by nature. But this is a gift."

"A gift I cannot give to you, Kimasa. I am sorry."

"It has already been given to you, and you refuse to affirm it?"

"I must."

A look of bewilderment flew across her face, as if she couldn't fathom why anyone would demur. "You will."

"A'Selaso, as willing as I would be to profess these miracles, my duty to Cara's safety prevents me. I must respectfully decline."

"But you will be safe, Rodani. Safe in Her arms as you expound on Her bountiful goodness. No one would dare harm you in declaring such beneficence."

"No, a'Selaso." He glanced down and back up again. "Please forgive me. I mean you no disrespect."

Kimasa stared at Rodani with as grim a demeanor as Cara had ever seen on her. She breathed heavily, mouth pursed, and pupils narrow.

"A'Cara," Kimasa said, startling her. "Of course, you see the goddess's hand in the return of your good fortunes."

Cara stared back at the high priestess. From long ago, she heard her father's voice. *Simple is safer, Cara. Don't confuse the issue.*

"No, a'Selaso."

"But of course you do, a'Cara. It is the only explanation."

Cara laid her elbow on the table, and her cheek in her hand. "Please don't tell me what I think, a'Selaso. It's very discourteous."

Their eyes met and held across the small room, but Cara refused to lower her gaze. There was no fault here for her, no shame for this. No stupidity. It was about time for a bit of quiet pride.

Kimasa held her hand out in front of her, palm up. "You cannot even admit to the truth in front of your eyes?"

Gods. It's Iraimin all over again. Now I know where she gets it.

"Rodani fought with all his will to regain his health," Cara said. "Baldar and his assistants helped him. I fought with everything I had to be heard past the lies I was told. Rodani took a chance and listened when I named those lies as lies. Arimeso listened to us both when we brought the treachery to her ears, and she gave us back our affinity." Cara leaned forward. "Nowhere, a'Selaso, do I see evidence of a goddess."

"She guided it all! Every step of it," Kimasa said in outrage.

"Maybe She did. But there's no objective evidence for it."

"You refuse to see it."

"I can't see what's invisible, a'Selaso. And I won't claim to see something that I can't."

Kimasa stood up and lifted her chin. "You are as ignorant as you are arrogant."

Rodani rose up. "A'Selaso, she is an alien from a culture you know nothing about. You do the Enclave no kindness to demean her so."

Kimasa's eyes widened. Her pupils expanded and contracted. "So, that is your final word?"

"As her guardian, I must say it is."

With a swish of robes, she was gone.

Cara heaved a sigh as she flopped onto the couch. "Who was the arrogant one here, aisu?"

He frowned.

***

The next day, Rodani made his way into the maze of rooms in the healer's clinic. Baldar greeted him with a respectful nod on his way from one minor crisis to another. Rodani slipped into a back room cluttered with boxes, bins, vials, and assorted contraptions. On a high shelf was a cage. At its side, an empty box. Inside the cage lay a blue mug. Inside the mug was a motionless, furry ball.

He lifted the cage and sat it on the only available corner of a table. He opened the cage door and turned the mug over. Gingerly, he prodded the furred shape. It made no movement in response to his probing. He put two fingers on it, and rolled it. Stiff and cold to the touch, it lay with its eyes open.

Rodani's rage, which had only simmered overnight on a lack of information, began to boil. He put the cage back on the shelf and carried the mug out of the clinic, snug inside its box. First stop was the kitchen.

"Cassig," he called out to one of the chefs. The man inclined his head in respect for a temichi, and waited. Rodani pulled a kerchief from his pocket and lifted the mug out of its box. "Do you recognize this make?"

Cassig took it from him, studying its shape and consistency. He turned it over, and peered inside with his nose inches from the fired clay. "Yes."

"Someone here?"

"Yes." The chef continued to stare at the mug, absorbed in some intricacy of its nature.

"Do you wish me to guess?" Rodani prompted him.

Cassig looked up. "Forgive me, a'tem. It is one of Garidemu's."

Fresh rage washed through him, leaving a residue of shivers. "How do you know?"

Something in his tone alerted Cassig, his attention now drawn to the temichi he faced. "Problem, a'tem?"

"Tell me how you know, a'sel."

Cassig's attention went back to the mug. "The curve at the base, the concave bottom. That color of blue seems to be one of his favorites, as well." He pointed to the handle. "And here, the half-twist at the base of the handle. That is one of his signature details."

"I thank you, Cassig," Rodani told him as he retrieved the mug. "You have helped me today."

The chef again inclined his head, acceptance of an unexpected compliment.

Far down the hall and away from delectable odors, the aging postmaster sat in solitary activity, his work hardly begun this day. He looked up at Rodani's entrance. "A'tem," he said. "A package to send? You must tie it up."

"Not this time, a'sel. This package arrived yesterday." Rodani placed the box on the counter and spun it around. "Do you remember it?"

The elderly man looked it over, inside, and underneath. "Yes, I believe so. Quite a grand mug that was inside it, I see." As he reached for it, Rodani grabbed his wrist.

"Please, no, a'oto."

The man blanked his expression. "I meant no offense, a'tem."

"And I took none. Please do not be concerned. You are certain this is the box?"

"We had only two yesterday. The other was large and quite heavy. Metal, I believe, from out west."

Rodani inclined his head. "That would please me."

"Au, it would, honored temichi. That it would." The postmaster bowed.

Rodani's return visit to the clinic left the cage empty. Last stop, back upstairs. He let himself into the servant's entrance.

"Deremic? Hamman?"

Deremic came out of his room at the far end. "A'tem?"

"Did you retrieve this package from the postmaster yesterday?"

"No, a'tem. Hamman did."

Rodani looked around. "Does she abide?"

"In her room, a'tem. She has taken a sickness, and rests in bed."

Rodani's eyes flew wide. In a scarce moment, he was inside Hamman's bedroom, laying the box on her headboard.

"Hamman," he whispered as Deremic followed him in. Rodani shook her arm gently. "Hamman."

The maid rolled onto her back and opened her eyes. The nictating membranes were wide and yellow, and lingered near her pupils.

"Forgive me, a'sel," Rodani began. "But I must ask you a question."

"Of course, a'tem," she whispered, courteous even in illness.

"Cara received a blue mug yesterday. You brought her tea in it?"

"Yes."

"Did you touch it?"

Hamman blinked slowly, digesting the question. "I am not certain, a'tem."

"Did you look at it carefully? Admire it? Inspect it?"

"I might have. Yes, now that I think, I did touch the inside. It had such an intriguing look to the surface."

Rodani straightened, his gut roiling. "Thank you, Hamman. Rest." He grabbed the offending box, took Deremic by the arm, and pulled him out of Hamman's bedroom into Cara's.

"Call Baldar, Deremic. Now. Get a stretcher up here."

"A'tem?"

"I believe she has been poisoned."

A very atypical look of shock spread across Deremic's face. "The mug?"

"Yes."

"But a'Cara drank from it yesterday."

"Almost, a'sel. Almost."

At last, it was back to Cara's room. "Kia," he said, sitting down at the worktable. "It is possible the selaso was correct yesterday."

"What cloud did you just walk into, aisu?"

"No cloud, kia. No laugh."

Cara sat back and watched Rodani. "What?"

He sat the box and mug on her table, then pulled a small sack from his pocket and laid it next to the mug.

"What is that?"

Rodani opened the sack and rolled its contents onto the table.

Cara shot up from her chair with a shout. "What the...?" She walked around the table and bent over the small form. "It's an animal. Mammal, probably. Bears live young?"

"Yes."

"And why are you carrying it around?"

"To prove my suspicions correct, kia. This mug," he tapped it with a finger, "is poisoned."

"What?!"

Rodani stared at the little being that gave its life for his adashi. "I fed it last night from food that had sat in the mug. Then I poured water in it, and back out into its water trough. This morning, I found it," he waved his fingers over it, "thus."

Cara flopped into her chair and laid her head in her hands. "Who did it?"

"Who do you know who is a potter?"

Her jaw dropped; she looked off into the study. "Good gods of dark space." She ran her hand over her mouth and chin, contemplating another averted disaster. "I can't thank you enough, aisu. I can't."

Rodani stood up and rattled his hand in the toolbox. "I wish you to assist me, kia."

"What?" she repeated, still bemused over the close call.

"I can tell you feel shock. Your vocabulary has narrowed." He pulled out a hammer and turned the mug upside down in the box. "Here," he said, handing the hammer across to her. "Break the mug."

She got up and looked into the box. "Smash it?"

"Into pieces. Not so small that they are not recognizable, though." He held the edges of the box as Cara moved nearer. "Mind my fingers, please."

She shook her head in mock seriousness. "Nah, I can add them to the box when I'm done," she said, winking.

The mug shattered under her lightweight blows as a cacophony of movement and voices erupted from the servant's corridor. While Rodani explained this second mystery, Cara battered the mug with renewed force, swearing threats and imprecations. "How dare he?" She swung at the box's contents in rhythm to her words. "How bloody, bloated, blasted dare he?"

"And now for the overkill," Rodani said, slipping the hammer out of her hand. Gently, as if it still had life, he picked up the dead animal and placed it in the midst of the clay shards. "Then we close it up."

"Oh, perfect." She let out an audible breath. "In other circumstances, this would be supremely amusing. As it is, he makes me regret my ethics."

"He is not worth that, kia. Your ethics matter to you. He does not."

"Who will you get to deliver the box?"

Rodani tied it closed and lifted the ends of the string with an uncharacteristic flourish. "Your most humble guardian."

Cara gasped. "Let me come. Let me watch."

"I am tempted, because you deserve it. But your safety is more important. If he catches me, defending myself is trivial. Defending us both means he knows you are aware of his treachery. I will not take the chance." He picked up the box and headed for the hall. "I am only leaving it outside his door."

TWENTY-SEVEN

Naremit left the practice room in a foul temper and stomped through the main halls. His brooding demeanor scattered artisans and servants as he made his way outside. The cold wind invigorated him, but did nothing to calm his anger. To his left, the garden looked bedraggled in its winter wear. And besides, gardens were for soft hearts. And cooks. Not for guild guardians, not for those who had earned their knives and their stolen guns. That was the one consolation the Riverfolk had earned on their own, and the guild would be forever indebted to that courageous raid. No, guardians were primed for greater achievements than planting beans and harvesting greens, weaving clothing and cobbling shoes.

Naremit followed the manor walls in a quick stride, letting the paltry sunshine warm his face. Maybe a ride from the stables. Yes. That wicked libertine, Serano, was the only other guardian to make riding beastback one of his skills. Well, two could take that path. And one, sufficiently determined, could overtake the other. That would be a slap in the face for both of them, the lothario and his despicable partner, and a note of warning to the keso that he would *not* be held back in rank or status. Would not be held down by seniority, by the selaso's favor, or even the taso's. Or, he thought with grim humor, by the fact that one's sister is partner to the temaso. Naremit straightened his shoulders beneath the jacket as he paced down the wall toward the corner.

As Naremit strolled around the corner, high-pitched laughter floated out from a second-story window. He came to a standstill in the brittle grass and looked at the window over his head. "Au, goddess," he whispered. "Blessed, blessed Sela, and Temi beside her." Below the window was a very narrow ledge. At chest height was another window and ledge for the first floor. Naremit put his palm on the stone wall and ran his hands up and down the natural indentations. His thoughts began to swirl in his mind, each new one chasing after the previous.

Suddenly urgent, he raced back to the double doors, swung them open, and ran inside. With force of will, he slowed his steps, conforming to propriety, civilized. There was no value in alerting anyone that anything was different. And, after all, nothing was. Yet.

First stop was for Toranel. He pulled out his 'com. "Nine, Eleven. Nine, Eleven."

"Eleven."

"Where are you, sana?" he asked, using the erinai he'd given her.

"Com room."

"Duty?"

"No."

Within a moment, Naremit had pulled her from the communications console. "Sana, I have a plan. I would have you and Garidemu hear it together." He pattered down the hall in rapid steps. Toranel followed at his elbow.

At Garidemu's door rested a smallish box. Naremit plucked it off the floor and knocked. After more than a minute, the potter opened his door. His hands, hastily wiped, were streaked with clay and slurry.

"May we?" Naremit asked. The urgency underneath his courtesy prompted a quizzical expression on Garidemu's face. He opened the door wider and gestured.

Once in the room, Naremit held the box out to Garidemu. The potter stared at it, dismay falling over his features. "Where did you find that?"

"At your door," Naremit said, shaking the box at him.

Garidemu's hands began to vibrate as he took the box and put it on his sitting room table. He studied it a moment, then slowly opened it. When he looked inside, he shouted an oath and jumped back, eyes wide and ears flickering in agitation.

"Sel'u?"

Garidemu spun around and grabbed his carving knife off the potter's wheel, and began slashing the air. "Temi's demons," he shouted. "Cold hells and dark nights, devils and ghosts!" The ranting continued as Naremit and Toranel sidled up to the table for a careful look.

"Is that what I think it is?"

When Garidemu's lethal agitation headed their way, Toranel stepped back to the door, her hand fumbling for the latch behind her back.

"Cousin," Naremit said. "Garidemu."

It took some minutes for the potter's wrath to fade. He collapsed into a chair and stared into space.

Naremit took Toranel's hand and guided her to a beaten-down couch opposite the potter's wheel. "Rodani?"

"Who else?" Garidemu spat.

"Well, it is the second time you have attempted to poison her."

"And it would have worked either time if not for that damnable, dishonorable temichi."

"Then we rid ourselves of them both."

"How?"

Naremit glanced at Toranel and smiled. "I believe it is time for more direct action."

***

Kimasa lifted a paper from the corner of her desk and drew it toward her. On it laid a list of tasks to be accomplished. Many were crossed out, but more than a few still sat open, waiting. Soon, the Enclave's Four Hands celebration would be taking place. Not the fourth-year celebration, not the Fourth Hand celebration, but Four Hands. Forty-eight years her Enclave has existed in Barridan, and she had done her part to make it into the powerhouse it now was. As the strongest Enclave, its celebration would be marvelous. Kimasa had spent the better part of a half-year making sure of it.

As usual, Arimeso had suggested that they merge the Enclave's yearly celebration with the equinox, not too long after it. And as usual, Kimasa had placed her slippered foot directly on that suggestion. Glory to the goddess was not to be conflated with the mundane cyclings of one planet around a star far from where her species had sprung into being. Born by Sela's hand, guided by Sela's heart and mind from the moment each person was conceived to the moment she crossed over...that was what this celebration was about. And Kimasa would remind everyone in the manor of it if it took the last breath in her body.

But last on the list was an item that would not be crossed off. Sorely disappointed she was, by Rodani's refusal to grant her such a reasonable request. Stubbornness. His body's sanctity stolen by the charms of an alien, was his mind possibly stolen as well? Kimasa lit a pinch of incense, letting the fumes calm her frustration and focus her attention on listening for Sela's directions.

Just one human, she thought. If just one human could see the light, if just one human could be brought into Sela's arms to be enfolded into the faith, she would know the path she strode was the righteous one. There was room on this planet for only one deity, and it had to be the correct one—Sela, the Creator, the Giver and the Taker.

It was a scandal that Kusik wanted the human gone from this land. As if a high priestess would throw away this opportunity for a fear-sotted keso. The ritual she'd performed, ostensibly for him, had not failed. Nor had it yet worked. Sela had brought those propitious earrings to her through the hands of the guild, and she had put them to the best use she could divine.

Once one human could be brought over, a second would follow. And then a third, and then more. This nonsensical idea of different human groups believing in different gods...*gods*, mind you, not a goddess, had to be quelled, extinguished in favor of the true living Goddess. Nothing else would satisfy the Enclave.

A thought struck her, a bolt directly from Sela's hand. If Rodani and his adashi refused to witness for Sela's goodness, then she, the high priestess herself, would do it for them.

Kimasa leaned back and smiled in deep satisfaction. *Praise be to You, blessed Sela, mother of us all. Thank You for gifting me with the knowledge I needed.* An image formed in her mind. The dais, the sacred flames, her speaking the words of witness and drawing them both out of the audience to stand before the house. What a joyous sight it will be, and all glory shall be lifted up unto the goddess.

***

Cara shifted Ikemi in her lap and repositioned the book she was reading to him. Rasping bootsteps crossed her workroom and Rodani appeared in the doorway, wide and tall, a book of his own dangling from his fingertips.

"Ready?" she asked.

Rodani inclined his head.

"Ikemi," she said into the ear at her chest. "It's Rodani's turn. Can you sit quietly, and read or draw?"

"Yes, Onana."

Charmed by him calling her *Mother*, or more accurately, *Mama*, Cara smiled as she settled him next to his books on the other side of the tea table, with paper and pencil nearby. Rodani folded himself downward onto the couch. The bruise on his face from Kusik's fist was fading from purples to greens. *That better be the last time*, or she was marching down to the taso's office herself.

"You're spending a lot of time on this since you came back, aisu."

He looked up from the pages. "Does that concern you?"

"Not at all. Just curious."

Rodani's gaze slid from her to Ikemi, and back again. "I believe the more I understand of your language, kia, the more I will understand you. And your people."

She blew him a kiss.

As he began to read, she settled into her chair to watch him. His eyebrows furrowed as he arrived at difficult words, then smoothed out with the easy. He drew his fingers across the page as he read, much as she had done when learning his language, and Ikemi was doing with his own.

Ikemi tapped his pencil on the table, a child's thoughtful expression on his face. Cara snapped her fingers softly at him. He glanced up and stopped.

Rodani worked his way laboriously through several more pages. When his stumbling became more frequent, Cara called a halt. "I'll order some tea." She leaned down over Ikemi's shoulder. "What would you drink, ki'oto?"

"Water," came the reply from her side.

Cara glanced at her guardian with mocked affront. "Is there a problem with him choosing his own, my temichi?"

Rodani all but rolled his eyes at her gentle censure. He tossed her comment and went back to studying the book in his hand.

"Tea please, Onana," Ikemi said. Cara walked through her workroom.

"Hamm—" *Damn.* Her servant was still sick, thanks to that treacherous potter. "Deremic?"

The servant stuck his head around the far corner of the corridor they shared. "Tea, please. For three."

He bent his head. "A'Cara."

"A'sel," she said as an afterthought. "Is there anything I could do for Hamman? Anything to ease her, or let her know I hold out thoughts for her recovery?"

Deremic regarded her with widened eyes, then bowed formally. "I will carry your word."

"Thank you."

As Deremic headed out, Cara headed inward to the facilities. Ablutions done within the minute, she returned to the bedroom. Her eyes swept the nightstand where she'd touched Rodani's weapons belt after their second joining, then to the headboard where Hamman stored their after-joining cloths. Something was amiss. Something didn't belong.

Cara rounded the foot of the bed. *Oh, gods. Could it be?*

"Rodani," she called out, excitement in her voice.

A clamor of haste erupted from her study. Two sets of footsteps, one heavy, one light, made their way through the rooms.

"Rodani, look." She pointed to the headboard. "What do you see?"

He maneuvered his way around her and studied the small tangle of metal. Cautiously, if not quite believing what he saw, Rodani reached out and pulled it into his hand. He stared at it, then presented it to Cara—for the second time.

She plucked it from his hands with her scarred fingertips. With the help of gravity, it resolved itself into dangling silver earrings, found after many a day.

TWENTY-EIGHT

"What are you doing, aisu?"

Crouched at her hallway door, Rodani muttered something into the crack. From outside, Deremic answered in the same tone.

Cara got up from her worktable to watch. More tolerant of her questions than before, she knew if Rodani didn't answer, it wasn't time to badger him. When he pulled a new lock from the bag at his feet, Cara drew a sharp breath.

She turned back to her quilting, biting down on all the questions that erupted.

When the lock was in place and tested, the two men headed for her bedroom door and repeated the performance. When she heard the clank and clatter a third time, she followed them into Hamman's sitting room.

Her maid stood with her shoulder against the wall, arms crossed. The poisoning she had endured still shone on her features, in the drawn mouth and puffy eyes.

"Why, Hamman? Did they tell you?"

The servant looked down at Cara, directly, without rancor but without the courteous deference that was her norm. "He has concerns."

"More than the normal, I would guess?"

"He gave no details."

Cara watched them for a while longer, side by side with the woman who shadowed her days. Torn between boredom and frustration, she returned to her crafting.

Several minutes later, Rodani joined her at her table, wiping his hands on a rag. "I talked with Baldar earlier today," he said.

"Why? Are you ill again?"

"No, thank the—" His lips pursed, then turned upward at the ends. Crinkles appeared at the corners of his eyes.

Cara laughed. "It's just a saying, aisu. I don't believe in the demons and gods I swear by."

He looked away, declining the subject. "We discussed my options for preventing hadaberi, kia."

"Oh. What did he say?"

"Nothing too hopeful, I fear." Rodani leaned back in his chair. "There is a drug concocted by the guild healers in Tendiman that blunts a woman's receptivity. He thought it possible that the same drug might assist me."

"Aisu, I don't want... How do I say this politely?" She leaned forward, crossing her arms on the table. An unwelcome weight settled into her gut. "Will it ruin your desires?"

Rodani glanced into the study. "In high quantities, it does. But I would take a low dose."

"Every day? What about side effects?"

He looked at her quizzically. "Effects to my side?"

Cara shook her head. "Bad interpreting on my part, aisu," she said. "Will it have unwanted effects to other parts of your body—or mind?"

"Possibly small ones. But I will not take it every day, kia. Only when I feel myself responding to you. When I begin a generative phase, I can take a dose or two to see if it calms me or aborts the process."

"I would rather you spend one day of three away from me than take an herb that will hurt you."

"That would not be wise, kia."

"What works for a woman doesn't always work for a man," she said.

"Yes. But it is worth trying. Especially," he pushed himself up from the table, "when I am feeling a response right now."

Her face fell into worry. "Rodani, I'm sorry."

"No. Do not be." He laid a hand on the top of her head, stroking it. "I enjoyed last night, and do not wish to worry for other such times." He headed for the door and opened it. "If I can find Serano, we may go searching for the plant today."

Rodani pulled the door shut behind him, locking his adashi in the safety of her rooms. The hallway was empty. He pulled out his 'com and began walking. "Six, Five. Six, Five." As he entered the adjacent hallway, two guardians stepped out of the shadows.

"Six," Serano answered.

Rodani waited to see if the men would approach him.

"Tem'u," the 'com sputtered into the silence.

When his stalkers made no move, Rodani headed for the stairs. The men fell into step behind him.

"Rodani."

Rodani put the 'com to his mouth, taking the wide steps two at a time. "Where are you?"

"Practice room."

"Alone?"

"Yes."

"There in three." He stuffed the 'com back in his pocket. His followers made no move to stop him, or indeed bother him at all. But they stayed on his heels through the manor's hallways until he reached the guild's practice room. Unhindered, Rodani slipped through the door and closed himself in with his partner. Serano holstered his gun and cocked an eye at Rodani's furtive movements.

Rodani pulled him over to the far wall. "Would you recognize *varigestra* if you saw it, tem'u?"

"Yes. I helped concoct some of the tinctures in training."

"Can we go on search?"

"Today?"

"If it would not hamper you much, yes. Please."

Serano began exchanging the practice cartridges for the live ones. "Meet me in the garage in an hour."

Rodani inclined his head. "Thank you." He crossed the room, and waited a second in front of the door. One hand on his knife hilt, other on the handle, he opened the door. When he stepped out, a shadow appeared behind the door. Rodani pulled his knife as Naremit yanked him against the wall, hand on his throat. Rodani pressed his knife against Naremit's jacket, fear flooding his body.

Inches from Rodani's face, Naremit grimaced. His pupils pulsed in suppressed rage; his grip tightened into a fierce chokehold. Rodani pushed his knife forward, feeling the jacket give under the pressure. As his lungs began to fight for breath, he pushed harder. The leather snapped. Freed, his knife jerked forward.

Naremit yelped and jumped back, blood beginning to seep into his shirt. Knife still at ready, Rodani pulled away from the wall and started walking, glancing back with every second step. When he turned the corner, he began to run.

Instead of Cara's room, Rodani took refuge in his own, pacing the floor. Methodically, he wiped the blood slick from his knife, cleaning it far past necessity. He slowed his walk, coming to a standstill in the middle of the sitting room. *Breathe. This is nothing new to you, ki'oto. You know these games.*

He grabbed two small sacks and a heavy shoulder bag from his armoire and began to pack. When he was done, he crossed the hall to Cara's rooms.

She was still at her worktable with her current creation, a mass of fabric and batting, taking up all the space in her lap.

"Three-quarters of an hour, kia."

Her answering smile warmed Rodani from the inside out. She trotted into her room, the happiness alight in her face and in the swing in her arms and the dance of her hips. Then he checked himself. The buzzing in his body, the tiny twitches that heralded the generative state, had disappeared. He searched inward, doubting his senses. But his body remained calm, devoid of the antsy chatter of his nerves.

The fear, of course. The fear that swept through him in the guild hall had washed it away. So this trip was not as critical as he thought. Necessary, but no longer urgent. He allowed himself a smile. A few of the clouds about his ears drifted off.

At the proper time, Rodani led Cara down the back staircase to the garage. But when they drew near to the carriage, he grabbed Cara's arm, slowing their approach. A guardian stood at the hood, his back to them. As their steps faltered, the man turned and fixed them with a cool stare.

All vestiges of calm fled Rodani's body. "A'Keso."

Kusik waved his hand at the carriage's interior. "You are late."

"We're not," Cara said.

Rodani shook her arm in a gentle warning. "Where is Serano, a'Keso?"

"Elsewhere."

"He is needed on this trip."

Kusik's eyebrows drew down. His pupils narrowed. "I know what your task is. I know what you need, and why." He jabbed at the carriage door. "In," he ordered in a rough voice.

Rodani hesitated, a dangerous move. But he guided Cara inside, pushing against her as she hung back. "No," she whispered.

He bent down to her ear. "I am your safety."

The air was cold. The carriage was cold. And the trip was colder still.

Cara fidgeted in her seat, fiddled with her coat, and twisted the mended rings on her fingers. Her gut clenched, due to a pleasant diversion turned into some kind of nightmare. She stared past Rodani's jacket into the thicket of trees as Kusik drove them up into the high hills. Past the turnoff that led to the place they'd had lunch in the autumn, past the waterfall that had nearly killed her. She shivered with the memory.

Occasional flakes of snow hit the windows, melting into drops that clung to the glass in defiance of gravity. Without comment, Kusik threaded the carriage between the never-die trees that began to cluster into groups, and then turned into an impenetrable wall of forest. He stopped, shut off the engine, and climbed out. Heart thumping, Cara got out, Rodani at her heels. She stopped, frozen with dread at Kusik's proximity. Rodani put his hand on her shoulder and pushed. "Forward, kia."

The tree canopy shut out nearly all the sky. A few patches of old snow hid in the shadows of roots and underneath last year's accumulation of leaves. Kusik searched the ground, head a-swivel. When he crouched down into the wet leaves, Rodani looked over his shoulder.

"This is what you look for."

Rodani plucked it from his keso's fingers and studied it in the dim light, then held it down where Cara could see. Five red-tinged and ruffled leaves came to a sharp point at each tip. The acrid scent of rusted dirt drifted from it.

Rodani took off on an angled path, a little away. With Kusik's temper always ready to flash, distant was good. Far distant was even better, though she doubted that would come until they arrived home.

They spent nearly a half hour crouching in the leaves, brushing them aside, picking for the meager shoots, then scooting to another patch. Cara breathed on her fingers and flapped them against her thighs.

Rodani glanced at her. "Gloves, kia. They do you no good in your pockets."

"I can't pick plants with them on."

He walked closer to her. "Then clear the carpet of snow and leaves, and let me pick them for you. But for Temi's sake, put them on."

Another half hour went by. Cara salved her boredom by making random lines of damp leaves as she scraped the forest floor. Rodani's pack slowly filled. Wet snowflakes filtered through the trees, accumulating in random splotches on the ground. The trees seemed to exude a dimness, eating at the winter light. More flakes of snow fell through the heavy canopy, and cold crept into Cara's body despite the layers of clothing Hamman had insisted she wear.

"Enough," Kusik called from a distance away. With no other word, he turned toward the carriage. As they pulled back onto the path, the snowfall seemed to increase, the path slippery under her shoes.

They climbed into the carriage and retraced their way through the trees. The road had turned a mottled white. As Kusik maneuvered onto it, the carriage slipped and shuddered. They were jerked from side to side as the wheels caught and lost traction. Slowly, they made their way down the short track toward the edge of the hills. Flakes of snow cascaded in increasing numbers across the front of the carriage. In the near distance, trees faded from view and a white expanse appeared beyond them.

"Is that a snowstorm?" she whispered. Massive snowflakes splatted the windshield as they neared the turn that would take them down the mountainside. The carriage wheels slid in fits and stops. Cara moaned as Kusik fought the steering for control.

"Silence, human."

Cara leaned sideways and laid her head on the seat, fighting images of their vehicle sliding off the mountain. Her fingers clutched at the fabric of her seat, her eyes clenched tight.

"I did not know they were all such cowards," he continued. "I am surprised they made it to space."

"A'Keso," Rodani said with forced calm, "Cara had never seen this much snow until this winter. And she has never ridden in it."

With another jerk on the wheel, Kusik glanced into the back seat. "And the unknown frightens her into catatonia?"

Cara sat up in a rush of fury. "You try living in my world, a'Kusik! I'll strap you in a basket and push you into a rip tide, like my cousins did. We'll see who's more frightened at the end."

Kusik turned his head away, mute, disdainful.

The trees thinned out to show a whitewash of snow in front of them. Cara looked out, then curled back down on the seat. Kusik stopped the carriage. He and Rodani began to argue in hissing whispers and guild hand signals, ignoring her. She returned the favor while wishing she could get out and walk. Surely it would be safer.

They pulled forward, slowly. Trees passed by on either side of them, snow piling up on their branches and leaves. Kusik turned right onto a smaller road.

"This is not wise," Rodani said. His body rocked back and forth as the carriage made its way over rocks and tree roots.

"The storm will have passed by tomorrow. We wait. The human's life is not the only one at stake."

They pulled to a stop. Cara peered out of the windows. Trees surrounded three sides of the carriage. They could drive no farther. "Where are we?"

"A place to wait out the storm," Rodani replied, climbing out. He held out a hand to Cara, who followed him behind Kusik up a wide path. In his hand was a swinging lantern, dark in the dim light.

The keso halted in front of a large slab of stone, handed the lantern to Rodani, and with some effort, pushed the stone aside. Behind the stone was a vertical line of darkness. He took back the lantern and lit it before stepping inside. His boots scuffled on pebbles. Rodani pushed Cara before him, into the dank confines of a cave, into an abyss lit only by a feeble flame. Panic began to flutter through Cara's body, tingling her fingertips and constricting her chest. Behind her, Rodani let out a piercing, undulating whistle that startled her into a gasp.

"What was that for?"

"To wake anything that hasn't already heard our footsteps."

Cara retreated to the entrance, her shoulders thumping the cave wall. "I'd rather go back to the carriage."

"Too cold, kia. Here we may light a fire, cook over it, and sleep next to it."

"Sleep?"

Rodani coaxed her away from the wall with a gentle pull on her arm. "Not only must the storm end, but enough of the snow must melt for us to make our way back down to the lowlands."

"How long does it take snow to melt?"

He glanced down at her. "Even I forget how little you know of winter weather."

"Just answer my question, please."

"Hours to days to weeks."

Her panic level slid upward, making it difficult to breathe. She shuffled, hanging back against Rodani's insistent pull on her arm. Kusik was now little more than a shadow beyond her, down in the depths of the cave, highlighted by the lantern's light. Footsteps, clinks, and the rasping of clothes echoed throughout the cavern. Water, minerals, moss, and wild imaginings mingled into a noxious effluvium that twisted her innards. A great weight of enclosed space hovered around her head, and wrapped itself around her taut body. Darkness closed in on her sight, and she began to pant.

"Rodani," she whispered into the echoes, "leave me here."

Dim light from the entrance lit the edges of his face as he turned. "Why?"

"I..." she scrambled for an excuse that wouldn't seem like cowardice, "...don't see as well in the dark as you do. Please light a fire first. I can remain here by the door."

Rodani regarded her placidly. "There is little to be frightened of here, kia. Large animals cannot get in."

So much for hiding her fear.

"Come," he tugged again. "We are losing what light the lantern provides. I will guide you."

Cara allowed herself to be led for a few more paces. But Kusik's lantern was little more than a candle flame in the distance, and the maw of Stygian emptiness surrounding it threatened to engulf her. Abruptly, she sat down on her heels, bending Rodani into a curve to keep from releasing her.

"Cara, stand up," he chided her.

"No."

He pulled up on her arm. "You have told me many times that you are not a child. Do not now act as one."

Cara leaned back, letting her full weight drag against his grip. The skin on her arm twisted under his hand, making her hiss. "Let go, Rodani. Please. I'll wait here."

"As you wish." He let go. Cara fell back on her rear with a soft thump, chastened but relieved—for a moment. As Rodani moved downward toward Kusik, she scrambled back, back toward the daylight and the cold she feared less than the dark underground. Her heart beat heavily in her chest. She gasped for breath against the panic that threatened to overtake her.

Frigid air and a dim sunlight welcomed her. She rested her shoulder against the rock Kusik had moved. *Gods of the everlasting night. A cave! A dripping, mossy cavern of death.*

Noise echoed and re-echoed behind her, transforming into an acoustic nightmare that crept up and clamored in her ears. Ahead, bare trees and forest floor comprised a jumble of darks, greys, and whites. Icy wind worked its way into her coat. She stamped her feet on the ground and covered her ears with her palms.

"Cara."

Rodani appeared, wraith-like, from the depths of the gloom behind her. He put his hand on her cheek. "You are cold. Come sit by the fire. Soon it will be big enough to warm even a human." He started back down the slope to the center of the cave, then turned. "Why do you still stand in the snow?"

At least he was patient. She was going to need every bit of it, now. She sidled into the stone mouth. Rodani walked on, then stopped. He turned and crossed his arms over the bulky jacket. His eyebrows drew together.

Cara took another step, then sat on the floor. "Please forgive me, aisu."

"For what?" Behind him, Kusik started toward them.

"I don't think I can go down there."

"Why?"

"Because I fear it."

"Fear what? Kusik and I did a sweep. Nothing lives here but us."

"What I fear is not what lives, but what *is*."

"It is nothing but a cave, kia. We use it for storage."

As Kusik stepped up behind him, Cara beat her hands against her thighs. "Gods, Rodani. Have you never been frightened of anything?"

He regarded her intently for a moment. "What yet do you fear?"

She swept her hand ahead of her. "The dark. The weight of the earth above me, threatening to cave in and bury me. Can't you feel it? It's suffocating." She held out her hands, clenching them to fight the tremors that threatened to send her speeding back out into the snow.

He tucked his tall frame down beside her. "This cave has existed for thousands of years. It will not collapse while we are here."

Cara hung her head and stared at her hands. "If you could prove that, it might help."

"I can prove nothing, kia, only give you reasons."

"But Rodani, this kind of fear—we even have a special word for it in Cene'l—it can't be reasoned with."

Kusik kicked at a small stone with the tip of his boot. "And this is a surprise?" He flung out his hand. "Cave or snow. Darbati's choice."

The reference eluded her. She ignored it, assuming an insult. Rodani slipped his fingers into her hand, and pulled her to her feet. "Come." She took one sliding, hesitant step, then another. The darkness loomed in her vision. Breath caught in her throat. Her legs quivered. She fled back to the entrance, face to the frigid air, gasping.

Whispers hissed behind her back. Rodani strode up. "Forgive me, kia." He grabbed her from behind, lifted her off her feet, and started down into the depths, Kusik smirking at her from behind. Stunned for a moment, she lay against his shoulder. Then the sunlight faded, and her fears crowded around. "Let me go! Oh, gods, let me go, Rodani. Now!"

Rodani kept walking, resolute and silent. She pushed against his chest and twisted her hips, trying to free herself. His grip didn't budge. "Let me go!" When he didn't, she shut her eyes and buried her face in his jacket, clutching it as she jerked and swayed with his stride.

The ceiling hovered at her ears; the door retreated into a pinpoint of light. Her lungs refused to expand. A shriek crawled up her throat and lodged at the back of her teeth. She bit down on it and shivered in Rodani's arms.

He stopped walking and dropped into a crouch, then sat, letting her body rest in his lap. Something dried rustled beneath him. Cara's heels thumped on rock, but she kept her face pressed against his jacket. *I'm in my rooms. The den. Next to the fireplace, and it's night. The fire's warm. I feel the fire. A window nearby. Night sky and stars.*

"Kia, what are you saying? My coat has no ears."

Rodani attempted to pull her from his chest, where she clung with rigid fingers, muscles frozen.

"No!"

"Tsss." Insult from the other side of the fire.

"A'Keso, you know of guild trainees with similar reactions," Rodani reminded him.

"Yes. They are called weaklings."

A loud but muffled profanity escaped the woven fabric of Rodani's coat.

"Calm, kia. Fears can be faced."

"This is not fear," she mumbled into the cloth. "It's ^phobia^!"

"That word is unknown to me," he told her.

"Childishness," Kusik offered as a definition.

Cara pushed away from his chest in a fury, the cave momentarily forgotten.

"Why is anything different to you wrong, Kusik? Why are you always blind to any way but your own?" She leaned toward the fire. "Is there not one bone of good will in you at all?"

Kusik's pupils widened. Rodani grabbed for her as a pebble broke loose from the ceiling and clattered on the stone floor.

Cara shouted, panicky. The sound of her shout rolled and echoed. She pushed up from Rodani's lap, only to be held down by his heavy arms.

"No."

She pressed her forehead into his chest. The cave walls moved in her fear, closed in on her, tighter, squeezing her lungs. Her lower lip hurt as she bit it.

"Look at the fire, Cara," Rodani said. She shook her head, rolling it against the front of his coat. "Pretend it is the fire in your study."

"Tried that," she said into his coat. "Didn't work."

Evidently, Kusik had had enough. "Come with me, Cara."

Holy... Cara cringed, crunching herself up into a ball in Rodani's lap in a vain effort to disappear. *Oh, hell no. No way.*

She felt Rodani take a deep breath. "How can I assist you, a'Keso?" he asked.

"I will have her help me in the storeroom."

Gods dark and wild. Just that voice, that raspy voice, gave her the screaming meemies. The scars on her hands twinged in sympathy with her dread.

"I am better able, a'Keso."

"Let her go. She can walk with me."

"That is not wise."

"Let her go." Kusik's voice deepened; Cara's dread intensified.

Obedient, Rodani dropped his arms to his sides. Cara shot off his lap and headed full out for the cave door. Before she'd taken ten steps, Kusik grabbed her in a fierce grip. She fought wildly, uncoordinated, untrained.

Rodani ran up. "What good did that serve, a'Keso? To prove she is frightened, and you are not?" he spat out his words. "To prove your physical strength? To prove yourself somehow the master of her?" He yanked at Cara's struggling body. When Kusik let go, he held her tightly. "Cease," he said. "Cease."

Cara went lax in his grip, the sound of his voice a balm to her rattled soul. He retreated to the fire and pulled her into his lap.

"I do not see the worth you see in her, Rodani. I do not see it."

Rodani slipped his fingers under the coil of hair at Cara's neck and rubbed her skin, making no response to his keso's jibe. He laid his cheek on the top of her head. "Are you calmer?"

"I'm still waiting for all that rock to fall and kill us. I can feel it. It's loose and just waiting for a loud noise to start it."

"Perhaps you should turn that expert imagination to something more pleasant."

Cara drew her arms back from around Rodani's chest and started unbuttoning his coat. He let go one hand and held hers in his grip. "Kia," he chided her.

"If I could smell you, not this awful wet rock, that might help. That's using my imagination."

He let go of her hand, and she resumed unbuttoning. Reaching for his shirt, she pressed her nose against it and inhaled. Oh, gods, that beautiful essence that clung to his body. She didn't care how she looked to Kusik, didn't care what he thought. The cave walls receded as she rubbed her cheek against the cloth on his chest.

Kusik stirred the fire. "You remind me of an animal."

Damn that man, anyway. "We're all animals, a'Kusik," she replied into Rodani's shirt. "If you studied instead of just fought, you might learn some things."

"I still require your help in the storeroom. We will need to eat and prepare beds."

Rodani pushed her away from his chest. "Prepare your courage, kia. We shall both get up and walk." Rodani scooted her off his lap.

"Where?"

"The storerooms."

"Where are they?"

Rodani picked up the lantern and pointed, then took her arm, firmly.

Cara swallowed a lump in her throat big enough to choke a benatac. "I don't know if I can."

"Confidence, kia."

"Can I hold the lantern?"

He passed it to her. "Tight grip."

Kusik swept past them, pulling it out of her hand as he went by. Cara jerked in surprise, then swore. And swore again as the light faded, adding a few invectives she'd learned from her brother, Davad.

The darkness crowded in, and her courage fled under the pressure. "Gods damn this phobia." She took a step and squeaked like a frightened mouse. "I can't breathe, Rodani. There's no air!" She started gasping.

Rodani bent down. "But there is. You are breathing it. Your mind is confusing your body."

Sobs interrupted her gasps. She broke away and headed for the cave's entrance at a run. No one stopped her this time. She fell against the door to the outside, breathless in panic. The cold made her nose drip. Or was it tears? She stood, just breathing. *Gods, oxygen. Air.* You never knew how good it was to draw in a lungful of it until you couldn't.

Stupid, Cara.

No, she told herself. *Don't listen to your ama's old words. She's not here. You are. And phobias aren't stupidity.*

Cara turned her back on the door and slid one foot forward, then another. She turned around to the light outside, then stepped backwards. Feeling silly but marginally more in control, she took another, placing her shoe carefully on the pebbled stones.

You can do this. She took another step, and another, backwards down the slope. An errant stone threw her off balance. "Calm," she said out loud, Rodani's voice in her head. *Breathe.*

Slowly, Cara worked her way downward. As she moved, the ambient light dimmed, and her claustrophobia rose. About a third of the way down she sat, abruptly, breathing as if she'd run five hundred yards. Light from the doorway filtered about half of the way to her feet. It looked sickly, wan.

Now what?

Boot steps crunched toward her. "Kia?"

"Can you see me?"

"Yes." Rodani crouched next to her.

Cara drew his hand into her lap, clasping it between both her scarred palms. "Kusik spent that time complaining about me, I'm sure."

"And do you care?"

"No. I don't want to listen to him."

"I concur."

Cara laughed, the first one since they walked into the garage. It felt good. Rodani's hand in hers felt good. She put her hand against his cheek, leaned in, and kissed him. That felt good, too. No—it felt *right*. Calmed by his mere presence, Cara stood up and took another step backwards, then turned her back on the door. Suddenly, the walls closed in as before, trapping her, stealing her breath. *Nope.* She sat.

Rodani sat next to her. "Breathe. Slowly. Deeply."

She scooted a scant few inches downward, her rear perched ignominiously on bumpy rocks. "Aisu, I'd like to try something."

"That is?"

"Would you go sit by the fire?"

He raised an eyebrow, but went down to the fire without comment, leaving Cara alone in the moist dark. She stood. Taking a deep breath, she tensed her muscles and ran. Not toward sky light, but toward her own light—the one who had just disappeared into the depths.

Ignore it all. Everything but him. Oh gods. Panic flooded her brain, sending a rush of adrenaline throughout her body as she ran downward, light-headed, eyes blind of everything but the firelight.

There he was. Cara dropped to her knees and skidded the last couple of feet, knocking her forehead into his shoulder and gasping.

Rodani wrapped an arm around her. "I keep telling you to breathe. Are you breathing?"

"I don't think I can stay here," she said between gasps.

"Yes, you can."

She rocked against him and stared at the fire. "I... I don't think so..." She stood up and ran back, but slowed as the waning light reached her eyes. Forcing her feet to a stop, she stared upward, rocking in place, then began to walk backwards. As the light faded out, she turned and ran back to Rodani, crouching at his side.

"You will tire, kia."

She gasped for breath—panicked, not weary. "If I can dance for an hour, I can run back and forth for an hour." Her fingertips tingled anew, and the gasping didn't stop. "I can't catch my breath!"

"Is this a game?" Kusik said in a dour voice.

"No," she told him, curt. "This is reality. My reality." The *deal with it* remained unsaid. As the cave walls closed in, she ran back, back to the dim light.

Rodani stirred the fire and began feeding a larger branch into it.

Kusik glanced up at the cave door. "How much longer will you allow this lunacy, Rodani? You halt it, or I will."

Rodani walked back to the storeroom without answer. He brought out mats and a radio. "Have you attended to what she is doing here, a'Keso? Have you watched, or only judged?" He laid the mats around the fire, two on one side, one on the other. "On her own, with little help from me, she is systematically breaking down her fear—and attempting to overcome it. That is courage, Kusik. You do her a great disservice if you judge too quickly. I did in the beginning, never imagining what I could learn if I stopped. I consider myself fortunate."

Pattering footsteps neared, paired with heavy breathing. Cara skidded to a stop at his side. He pulled her close.

"I'm losing the light, aisu."

"You are safer down here. And warmer."

Instead of replying, Cara pushed herself away from his shoulder, grasping his jacket in her fists and pulling on it. Her harsh breathing reminded Rodani of a few of his own crises, paralyzing fear that shut down rational thought.

She did seem to be thinking, though. Her body swayed on the balls of her feet, pulling on him, rocking him sideways. Her head hung low, mouth open, eyes—he thought—were shut.

"You said she couldn't use her hands, Rodani."

Rodani's eyes narrowed as he regarded his keso across the fire. "She can grip. But she has little strength." The lack of an honorific in his reply was a rebuke, if Kusik chose to hear it. "She is still working to heal."

Cara rolled forward onto her knees and rested her forehead against Rodani's upper arm.

"Kia?"

She sat back on her heels, breathing deeply but slowly. She lifted her head. In the dim light, her strange blue eyes looked grey. The unexpected normalcy shook him deeply, jarring something new out of the place where he'd categorized it.

"Rodani." Kusik's growl interrupted his introspection.

He nudged Cara. "Kia." Gently, he pulled her fingers out of his jacket. "I must set up the radio. The taso needs to know our whereabouts." She nodded, leaning forward to put her hands on the mat as he got up. He watched her for a few moments, to see what she would do. When she made no move to run, he sat by the radio. In moments it was up and running, courtesy of one of the energy cells salvaged from their ship half a century ago, the same technology that powered the carriages.

"Barridan." He rolled one of the dials through his fingers. "Barridan, this is Rodani."

Nothing but static answered him. He picked up the set and headed toward the cave entrance, eyeing Cara as he walked by. She had scooted up to the fire and was feeding twigs into it with the fixation of a rahkti on its next meal.

"Follow him," Kusik said from behind. There was no answer. Rodani glanced over his shoulder; Cara hadn't moved.

"Go," said the rough voice.

Rodani forced his feet to keep moving, anxious and unsure of where he most needed to be. He sat down just outside the cave entrance with the radio and called again.

"Barridan."

"This is Rodani. I must speak with the taso."

"She is unavailable."

Something in the speaker's voice made Rodani's ears twitch. "Vanu?"

Nothing but silence came through the radio.

Anger flowed outward from the center of Rodani's guild pride. His hands vibrated, aching to grab the neck many miles away. "Vanu, rise up and find the taso, and tell her it will be two days or more before our keso returns to the manor."

More silence.

"Do you hear?"

Rodani sat through the ensuing silence with his temper held by a mere thread. *If you suffer fools,* he thought, *they in turn make you suffer.* The last rays of daylight became locked into the forest, blocked by dark leaves and darker trunks. Rodani's vision adjusted, and his pupils became reflective. He smiled with the memory of Cara's early curiosity. Only when she had asked to shine a hand light in his eyes did he stop her.

The radio crackled. "Rodani?"

Tension in his shoulders melted away at the voice. "A'Taso."

"Talk, a'tem."

Rodani explained the situation, keeping details to a minimum.

"I will speak with Kusik."

"A moment, a'Taso."

Rodani headed down the cave. Cara still sat at the fireside, chin tucked to her chest. Kusik had moved a little past center, the better to watch her beyond the flames.

"Arimeso is on the radio, a'Keso."

Kusik rose without comment and left the fire.

Rodani sat on his mat. "Kia?"

"Aisu."

Rodani analyzed the timbre of Cara's voice, the better to judge her emotional state. *Well enough,* he thought, and leaned toward her. "How are your fears? Have you banished them?"

Cara took a breath. He could hear the shaky quality in it and guessed at her answer.

"At least you are still by the fire," he joked, "instead of up top with Kusik."

"If he were up there, I'd be running back down."

"Yet you managed to stay here. And him within arm's reach."

"A miracle, eh?"

Rodani leaned in further, imposing himself between her chest and the fire. "Planning to play with embers all night?" Idly, he adjusted the position of a couple of stones surrounding the flames.

Cara flipped the back of her fingers against his forehead in mute response. He turned to face her, side by side. Her smile warmed him from the inside out, counterpoint to the fire at his back. When his bedmate was content, all was well in his world—despite his current difficulties. When she was not, her frowns and barbed words sent him out in a frantic attempt to cure whatever ailed her, to bring peace to her spirit.

Was this the bond? Was this what his onana had tried to explain when he was a youth? Did all the flowery words of history's poets come down to a moment of clarity? Au, he was in trouble.

Cara laid her hand on his thigh. "A kiss for your thoughts."

Rodani cocked his head. "Meaning?"

"Human idiom, aisu. If you'll tell me what you're thinking, I'll pay you with a kiss."

Rodani's pupils widened, unsure of the wisdom of discussing the topic. He needed a distraction to take her off the scent. "A kiss, kia. One of the many pleasures you have taught me." He wrapped his arm around her back and took her to the floor, cradling her head with his hand. Their lips met in a slow, rhythmic touch and retreat. He moved his mouth to her jaw and neck, a featherlight touch to her skin, a soft breath to tickle and taunt.

"How long will the old torac be up there?" she whispered.

He tried to smother a laugh, but failed miserably. "Not long enough, I fear."

Pebbles rolled downward, scattered by forceful steps.

"A'tem."

Rodani pushed upward at the rebuke in Kusik's voice. He stood with eyes downcast, fully expecting a blast of words in his face, or worse.

"Explain yourself."

Rodani hesitated. He didn't think Kusik was looking for an explanation for body contact. Neither silence nor incorrect answers assured his keso would stay his hand.

Rodani saw it coming from the corner of his eye. He froze as a blur came up and a sting erupted on his face. He waited, breathless, for another blow.

But before it came, Cara rushed them, shoving herself between the two and pushing Rodani backward. His arms shot out for balance as he stumbled. Cara turned to face Kusik, blocking him with her child-sized body. Protective instincts flashed through Rodani. He tried to step around her, but she outmaneuvered him, performing the same dance they'd done in Arimeso's office.

"Why are you doing that, Kusik?" she shouted as Rodani tried to pull her behind him. He glanced at Kusik, whose face held outraged surprise.

"A'Keso," he corrected her sharply.

"Would you do that in front of the taso?" she added.

Rodani pulled her backward as Kusik's pupils tightened. "Cara." He could only hope she heard the caution in his voice.

"And when she accepts our affinity?"

Au, that would be a "No."

"Cara." He tugged on her arm, trying to shake her out of offensive mode. This was becoming critical, a runaway festival of rage. Kusik began to move toward them.

Rodani wrapped his arms around Cara's shoulders, waiting for the decisive moment. As Kusik raised his hand, Rodani rolled, taking Cara down with him. He continued the roll back up to his feet, and shoved Cara toward the cave entrance. Moving in front of her, he faced Kusik.

"Arimeso forbids hitting her, a'Keso."

Kusik shifted around and started back to Rodani. "She forbids what is necessary and condones what is forbidden."

Rodani stayed in place with every bit of will he held inside as his enemy neared. "She forbids, a'Keso. Forbids."

"Then you will take her punishment." Kusik closed the distance, clenched his fist, and smashed it into Rodani's jaw. He spun and went to his knees. Vicious pain radiated out over his jaw, and his vision dimmed. *Cara. Protect Cara.*

An animal scream erupted nearby. He forced himself to his feet, only to see his bedmate with a glowing tree limb in her hands, face-on with Kusik. A memory flashed by—Cara and Serano, fighting.

"No!" He staggered toward her and ripped it out of her hands, then threw it on the fire.

"What does it take, Kusik?" she shouted. "What good does it do to hit him? What does that teach him?"

Kusik rounded on her, staring hard. "If he pays for your insolence, maybe you will learn."

Rodani grabbed her arm, his jaw awash in pain. "Stop." *Goddess, please, kia. You do not poke a raving beast. Can you not see?* He shook her, none too gently. "Stop speaking."

Her lips pursed into a hard line. She stared at Rodani, then at Kusik, refusing to lower her eyes in courtesy to his status. Rodani could only hope she heard him.

Kusik stared back at her, then pushed between them, circling Cara and studying her. Rodani's fear jack-knifed, overpowering even the pain in his jaw. He knew that circling. Knew what it could portend. *Goddess and consort, keep them apart. Please.* He held his breath as his keso kept circling.

Finally, Kusik stopped, walked to the other side of the fire, pulled his knife, and slashed it viciously through the air. He slammed it back in its sheath and knelt by the fire. He mumbled something about the taso and her ideas as he fiddled with the burning logs.

Rodani was just about to breathe easy, when Kusik shot up and shouted, pointing towards the storage room. "Food! Beds!"

Rodani drew Cara into the storage rooms. Dinner was dried meats and vegetables warmed in water. Beds were mats and blankets.

"The taso said the snowstorm has hit the manor," Kusik said after they were finished. "It will likely be two days before a rescue sets out, another one or two before they arrive."

Cara sighed. "Why so long?"

As Kusik only glared at her, Rodani answered. "We are very high up, the snow will be deep, and given that we will be safe here, it is too slippery to trust the benatacs' feet."

She pushed her mat as close to the fire as she dared. She sat and stared at the flames, mute. She took out her hair clip and ran her fingers through her hair. Rodani hissed at her, warning against the impropriety. She ignored him this time, and began to tie its dark strands into the interweaving knots she favored when she was bored. Neither of them had thought to bring paper or pencils.

"Why did you come here?" Kusik asked her.

Every muscle under Rodani's carapace tensed. Dread filled him with images of further fights, further punitive violence. His jaw still throbbed.

"A'Keso," he began.

"Du. I will hear her own words."

Cara shifted her legs, but her fingers didn't stop their knotwork. "Barridan or this cave, a'Keso?" Little courtesy came through her voice, though the words were there.

"Barridan."

"To craft. To live in a different society."

"Why?"

Cara's mouth thinned. "Craft or society, a'Keso?"

"Our society, ki'ono."

She heard the insult, the word and the tone. Rodani could only hope she would keep her temper for however long Kusik queried her. *Why did he start this? Why here? Why now?*

"Curiosity. A chance to use the language I spent years learning."

"Did you not know how disruptive you would be?"

"No."

"Would you still have come if you had known?"

She glanced at Rodani. "If I had known just the disruption, possibly not. If I had known Rodani, yes."

Kusik ran his hand down his blanket. "We will continue this tomorrow."

TWENTY-NINE

Come morning, Cara sat in the cave entrance, wrapped in a blanket and shivering. The grey dawn light did little but outline the trees across the path. Light grey meant snow. She'd figured that out with her fingertips. They still ached with the cold.

Her eyelids were gritty from lack of sleep. The woven mat had been unyielding. She'd nearly driven both men into tempers with her attempts to remove every single pebble underneath it before she could rest. At least the fear had lessened over the hours. Maybe it wasn't a phobia she had, just a garden-variety fear that bloomed under Kusik's glowering presence. It wasn't gone, though.

From the depths of the cave came a rustling, and patter of steps. They started and stopped, then started again, hesitated, and got louder. Cara waited, eyes forward.

A tall body folded itself downward beside her.

"Kia."

She smiled at him. "Bright morn." Then looked out. "Maybe."

"How do you fare?"

"Cold and sleepy. But too cold to sleep."

"Contradictions again."

She heard the smile in his voice. "No. Word games, aisu." She kept up her contemplation of the morning scene. Absolutely, it was art-worthy. Iraimin should be here—with nothing but canvas, brush, and black and white paints.

"I will be gone most of the day, kia."

Cara's body clenched. *That* was not a situation to contemplate. She swallowed heavily. "I can't be with you?"

"No. For the traps to be effective, I must hide my scent and tracks. We should not deplete the stores of too much of the food."

"You can't leave me here with him, Rodani." She leaned her head against his arm. "You can't."

He lifted his arm and wrapped it around her, drawing her into his warmth. "You can survive this, Cara. You need only adjust your attitude. You are easily agitated, often when there is no need. When you bristle, he reacts with his own barbs, causing you to rise to it again."

"Right," she replied in a dour tone.

"You have watched Kimasa, yes?"

"Yes."

"Pretend you are she. Put on that gold cloak and slippers and take on her mantle of calm competence. A serene countenance would do you well in many paths that you tread."

"I wasn't born with that."

He squeezed her against his chest. "Find it."

"This early in the morning, and you cannot keep your hands to yourselves?"

Cruel and cutting was that hated voice. Cara froze against Rodani, refusing to pull away unless he did. Shame was nothing she wanted to feel in his arms.

"There is hardly a better beginning to the day than enjoying Sela's gifts to the world," Rodani said.

Damn that he could be so calm, so collected against Kusik's constant agitation. Envy rose in her heart. She needed that Selandu demeanor, she really did.

"It is past time to be gone," Kusik told him.

Rodani rose, taking Cara's hand with him, and headed back inside the cave. He gathered a sack full of clanking and clattering traps, and a stoppered bottle from a shelf. Forlorn, Cara followed him back to the entrance. Kusik was out of sight. Rodani handed her a knife, and the Kishata he had tucked in a pocket. "Just in case."

Her eyes widened. "Kusik?"

"Animals," he said, drawing down his eyebrows. He lifted her up and held her tight against him. But her contentment faded as he put her down and picked his way up the slope behind her.

Don't leave. Be careful. Come back. She'd become superstitious, in a silly way, after they'd reunited. Nothing like a lesson in the changeable nature of circumstances to make her want to tap wood, cross her fingers, and be cautious with mirrors. *No more bad luck please, aisu. I love you.*

"We need firewood."

Startled, she spun around to face Kusik. He regarded her behind a mask of calculated coldness. Mindful of Rodani's suggestions, she inclined her head and walked into the woods. She skirted the edges for safety reasons. His knife hung heavy at her waist, sharp and intimidating. Just as deadly but more familiar, the pistol in her pocket flopped against her hip in counterpoint to her stride.

Several trips into the surrounding area made a respectable pile of twigs. Kusik could get the heavy ones. She started to take them inside when Kusik called to her. She laid down her own burden and met him several yards from the entrance.

"Help me with this," he said, leaning over a hefty branch that lay on the forest floor.

As Cara bent to grab the lighter end, a large, pelted animal started rustling in the undergrowth near her leg.

"Tsss," Kusik cautioned, pulling his knife. As he neared the jittery animal, it pulled away, flopping and jerking as if it were injured. But there was no blood on its fur. Instead of following its trail, Kusik backtracked from where it had come. Reaching into a brake, he pulled out a smaller, quivering version of the animal that had fled. With a further reach, he brought out another.

Cara winced. Mother and babies, obviously. *Oh, please don't—*

Methodically, Kusik slit their throats and tossed one on top of the other. He wiped his knife in the leaves and stuck it back in its sheath, then stuffed the furred babies into his carry sack. He flipped it over his shoulder and motioned her back to the branch. As she lifted the narrow end, an image of the lifeless bodies flashed across her eyes. Nature's bloody struggles were hard on any human with a soft heart.

After several minutes and a few stern looks from Kusik, they dropped their burden outside the cave entrance, on the far side of the path.

"Another," he said, nodding in the direction from where they'd come. Cara bit back a vocal sigh and followed him.

"What do you see when you look at him?" Kusik said.

"Rodani?" she asked. It was less a question than a request for verification.

Kusik threw her a look under lowered brows.

"Acceptance."

"Of what?" He stopped at another overly large branch and gave it a kick.

Kimasa's robe, she thought, crossing her arms over her chest. The Kishata bumped against her thigh. "A'Keso, this conversation should be had by itself, not when our minds are taken with other tasks."

Kusik bent over the log and tugged at it, loosening it from the ground. "Why?"

"Better, more thoughtful answers."

He motioned with his hand, a quick, jerky movement. Cara took the other end. They manhandled it back to the cave entrance. He kicked it up next to the other, then walked to the carriage. As Cara came up behind him, he opened the front door, passenger side. Cara stared at it.

"Are we going somewhere, a'Keso?"

"No." His grey eyes bore into hers, the pupils narrowing.

She backed away. "I'm content to stand, thank you."

"Why?"

"I'll be trapped."

He took his hand off the door handle. "Trapped."

"If I sit there," she pointed, "you trap me in the seat. I can't get past you unless you move."

"I offer a place out of the wind."

"Thank you. But I would rather be cold than trapped."

He shoved the door. It banged shut. He leaned against it, pupils constricting more tightly. "You are utterly uncivil."

"No, a'Keso. I'm honest, almost to a fault. But to communicate properly and learn, one has to listen. One has to think, not assume he already knows the answers to unspoken questions."

He leaned forward. A shiver ran down her spine and clenched every muscle in her body. "Are you rebuking me?" he said. "The keso?"

Cara swallowed, hard. The cold in his voice was worse than the cold creeping its way past her coat. "I..." *Kimasa's robe.* She raised her chin to look him in the eye. "I am offering you a chance to get accurate answers to questions you have yet to ask."

Kusik stared, intent on her face. "How did this occur?"

"The affinity?"

The cold intensity remained. No movement in his body, in his eyes. She wondered, fleetingly, how far she would get if she ran.

"We have...more similarities than someone might think, a'Keso."

Kusik pulled out of his intimidating lean and straightened up, shoulder to the door. "He is Selandu. Male. Guild fifth." His eyes raked her, from her flyaway hair, down past the over-large coat, the stained pants, to the scuffed shoes, and back up again.

Cara let out a breath she didn't know she was holding. "A'Keso, both Rodani and I are cut off from our own people."

"Again, you make no sense. Cut off? He walks among his own people every day. Every hour."

"Oh, yes," she said, taking a bit of his cold inside of her. "And he was demeaned, discredited, derided, or outright ignored. Every day. Every hour."

"Ridiculous. You exaggerate beyond all acceptable bounds."

Cara closed her eyes and turned her head. Where was the line of danger here? Where would patience jump to rage? *The cloak.*

"I exaggerate, yes, but only to make a point, a'Keso." She looked back up at him. So different from Rodani—in looks, in demeanor. But not in lethality. "Turn off your criticisms, your refusal to see, and just—listen. Listen without judgment."

The skin around his eyes tightened, as did his mouth. Cara stepped backward and nearly stopped breathing, waiting for an explosion. She wasn't sure where her audacity was coming from, but it was a tightrope walk.

No reaction. He just waited, frozen in place, as anger bubbled beneath his surface.

"A'Keso, Rodani is an outcast among his own people. So am I. When I came to Barridan, and he was assigned to me, we were thrown together and found ourselves partnered in exile." She gazed out over the hill where her lover had walked away. "We have a term in Cene'l: ^kindred souls^. It means we looked *at* each other, then *inside* each other, and found ourselves staring back at us."

"You are not making sense."

Cara shuffled her feet. Her gut was clenched into a block of ice, and her shoulders were as frozen as Kusik's. "We are very different on the outside, but share many traits on the inside."

"And it mattered not that you were forbidden to him."

"It didn't."

"Why?"

She turned one hand into a vertical position and parallel to her body, palm inward, leaving spaces between her fingers. "This is me." She tapped her fingers one by one. "I have traits. Craft talent, music talent, language talent, passions." Then she ran a finger through each of the spaces between her fingers. "But I have things that are missing in my life." She positioned her other hand to mirror the first and touched the new set of fingers. "This is Rodani. He has craft talent. Status. Guild knowledge and training. Intelligence. Wisdom." Then the spaces in between. "He also has things missing in his life." She interlocked her fingers. "This is what we are together."

Kusik unfroze in an instant, yanking her hands apart. "This," he said, holding her wrists in a fierce grip, "is honor."

Cara forced herself to breathe. In, out. In, out. The strength in his grip made her fingers curl inward, and her pulse beat in her hands. "One cannot live with honor only, a'Keso. It is like eating nothing but slowberries all your life." She tugged her arms against his grip. He released the pressure slowly, and she pulled them away, shaking. "It doesn't satisfy."

Kusik shoved his hands in his coat pockets. "He could have found someone else."

"Don't you think he tried?"

Kusik drew out his hand and waved it through the air. "Excuses," he said, turning away. "You both spew them like an overfed babe."

"Kusik," she said, following him toward the cave. At the improper use of his proper name, he spun around, fixing her with a deadly glare.

Robe, she thought, beginning to panic. "A'Keso." She took a deep breath. Any more of them, and she would start hyperventilating. "Can a Selandu truly, truly, *choose* who he bonds with?" She lifted her chin as she stepped closer. "Or does it just happen?"

He loomed over her. "A bond may not be a choice. Using it as an excuse to break guild rules *is*." A sneer of contempt overtook his last word, burning it into her mind.

Kusik stomped back to the entrance, drew his pack off his shoulder, and flung it on the ground. He removed the animals from the sack and tossed one at her feet.

"Skin it."

Cara stared at the lax little body that a short time ago had been full of life. Her hands began to tremble. "I can gut a fish, a'Keso, but I've never skinned an animal."

He gifted her with another look of contempt and lifted the animal by the tail. "Like this." He slit it from base to throat. "Then this." Cut off its feet and head. "Start here." He began at the top, pulling at the skin and cutting it away from the body. When she didn't move, he stared at her.

Slowly, she reached down. But instead of grabbing it, she stroked the soft fur, trying to ignore the dead eyes that looked up at her.

"Food, human!" Kusik's jaw clenched and his eyes narrowed. She picked it up. Her hand shook as she placed the knife at the base of its tail. Gorge rose in her throat and her vision fuzzed out.

Kusik bent to his task with sharp flicks of his wrist. "So, I am to simply ignore Rodani's dishonor, refuse to judge it?"

As she started to answer, a shadow moved over her head. She flinched instinctively. Teeth. Claws. A ferocious growl and the flash of a sleek body. It hit Kusik as he looked up, knocking him on his back. He crossed one arm against his throat. The other arm flew out, his knife spinning into the distance. The poridi growled and chewed on his arm, taking great strips out of the leather. Blood began to spurt. Kusik screamed in rage and fear, digging at the animal's face. He bucked his body in a frantic attempt to dislodge the beast.

Cara came out of her trance with Rodani's knife in hand. Instinct threw her into the bloody battle, the knife slashing and stabbing sideways into the poridi's throat. *Save him! Save him!*

It growled and scratched at Kusik's chest and abdomen with its claws as Cara stabbed. Kusik gouged at its eyes barehanded. It bit and chewed on his arm, blood dripping from its neck. Desperate, Cara stabbed upward into its throat. Her hand jerked as the poridi tore into Kusik's skin. She dragged the knife toward its jaw as it chewed, hoping to hit something vital. Blood spurted over her face. Slowly the poridi's fierce will faded; its eyes dimmed, its muscles shuddered. A steady stream of red flowed from its neck over Cara's hands. The fight was over.

As it toppled, Kusik's body went lax. His chest heaved; his uninjured fist clenched. Eyes closed, he shuddered and gasped. His injured arm lay motionless on his chest, a ragged mass of flesh. Gouges and scratches seeped blood through his clothes where the animal's claws had dug in.

Blood-spattered, Cara dropped her knife. *Oh, gods, what now? What now?* One crisis over, the second threatened a fit of hysteria.

Kusik was dazed, his eyelids at half-mast. Frantic, she searched among the forbidden implements in his weapons belt, her movements loose and jerky. It brought him out of his shock.

"What?" he said, voice raspy. "Du!"

"Where's your 'com?"

His bleary eyes tried to focus on her, but his head lolled to the side.

"Your 'com, a'Keso!"

Kusik's uninjured hand gestured feebly. Shaking, she drew out the precious instrument and pressed a button, then turned the knob. "Rodani! Rodani! Do you hear me?" She rocked forward and back. "Rodani, please!" *Please, aisu. Oh, gods.* No answer. She moved the knob to another number and repeated her plea.

In a moment, the 'com crackled. "Cara? What happened?"

"Kusik!" She bent over in misery. "He was attacked. A poridi."

"His status?"

"Hurt. His arm's a mess. Get here. Please. I can't move him."

"It will take me some minutes, kia. Keep him warm."

"Okay. Hurry!"

"Ninety-nine."

She closed the 'com and stood up, weaving in place. Kusik was motionless, eyes closed. So was the poridi, beyond him. Cara stumbled into the cave. "Blankets," she muttered. "Hot water. Cloths." Forgotten was her fear of the cave, of being buried alive. "Medicines. Do they have any? What would they look like? Where would they be?"

Talking kept her going, kept her focused. The adrenaline dump left her shaking, but she forged her way downward toward the fire, fighting to keep her balance.

Grabbing what she could find, she ran back up and fell to her knees at his side. Now what? What would her mother say? Do? She moved his head and listened for breathing. Yes. Kusik's eyelids fluttered and opened. She looked him over with clearer eyes. Blood, lots of it, but nothing gushing.

She dipped a cloth in the hot water and laid it across his ravaged forearm. He yelled and tried to shake the heat off his arm. She laid two blankets over his lower half and wiped his face and hands, checking for other injuries. But only scratches showed up. She checked over his chest, pulling aside his jacket and shirt. The beast's claws had lacerated his skin in several places. She started to undo his pants.

Kusik jerked and cried out. "Du!"

"A'Keso, you may be hurt there."

"Du!"

Now he was agitated, flailing his good arm and moving his legs. She re-covered him with the blanket and moved back to his arm. *What would you do, Ama? What would you do?* She studied it carefully, lifting it up off his chest. *Infection. Muscle damage. Tendons? Did they have those?* What was she actually seeing? Dripping blood and mangled flesh. Elbow was okay. Wrist wasn't too bad. Most of the damage was in mid-arm, as if the poridi didn't know any other way to get to his throat.

Cara dipped the cloth in the water. It was going to cool soon. She'd have to get more. *How do I wash a mangled arm?* What kind of first-aid training did Rodani have? *Hurry, please, aisu!*

She dabbed at it as best she could, ignoring his hisses and burning her own scarred hands in the process. Dip and pat. Dip and drip. Dip and poke. The water level got low.

She ran down for more. Brought it up. Washed the wounds as best she could. Sometimes Kusik would open his eyes, watching her, silent. She moved back to his chest and washed the lacerations. His clothes became wet. *Keep him warm*, Rodani had said. How? How, and clean him up? Which was worse? Cold or infection?

In the distance came a crashing sound, filtering down from the trees on the hill above. Closer and closer, it resolved itself into bootsteps and gasping breaths. Rodani took a flying leap off the hillside, much as the poridi had done, and landed in the middle of the path in a crouch, gun in hand. He took in the sight with wide eyes and heaving chest.

The tension that Cara had borne fell off her like a heavy mantle. *Aisu.*

He holstered his gun and knelt down at Kusik's side. "A'Keso?"

Kusik opened his eyes.

"Can you move? We must get you inside."

"Unknown," he whispered.

"Will you try?"

Kusik tried to roll to his side, once, twice, grunting with pain. Rodani moved to his other side and gently lifted him into a sit. Kusik growled and grimaced.

"Forgive me, a'Keso. I know you are in pain. Can you stand?"

Kusik shifted his weight as Rodani attempted to pull. By dint of much effort and swearing of oaths, Kusik made it to his feet. Rodani held tight, guiding him into the cave step by step. Cara followed behind with the items they'd left on the ground.

Rodani lowered Kusik to the sleeping mat and helped him take off his jacket and shirt before he lay down. When it came time for the pants, Kusik glared up at Cara with a ferocity that drove her back up the tunnel and outside.

She wiped Rodani's knife and slid it into its sheath, found Kusik's out near the trees, then plopped down in her original spot and grabbed the furry beast she'd tried to skin. With a savage temper, she cut off the tail. Each attempt with the knife caused a snap and crunch of bones. The sound worked its way down into her gut. Her hands began to shake, and her eyes to water. Roughly, she ran the knife point down the animal's underbelly and up to the throat. The skin split open. Guts protruded. Tears fell harder.

She tried to peel the fur back and slip the knife between it and the muscle. But her scarred and injured hands didn't have the finesse, and her watery eyesight made the problem worse. The cooling body became a hack job as she hiccupped through her tears. Eventually, the fur parted from the body.

With no more agility than before, she cut away the meat from the bones, laying it on a stone to her side in mutilated pieces. As the pile of meat became larger and the skeleton became clearer, Cara began to rock and sob.

Silly girl, she heard in her mother's voice. *You think you have it so bad? Grow up or you'll never make it in this world.*

Her frantic sobbing muffled the crunch of rock underfoot. Rodani crouched down beside her, waiting in silence. Eventually,

Cara managed to quiet her voice. Her mind, however, was not so amenable, and her hands shook like palsy.

"Kusik told me what you did," he said softly, slipping his bloody knife out of her hand. "I am proud of you."

Cara swallowed and wiped her nose on her sleeve like a child. "I felt like some beast had come out of me."

"We all pull strength from our animal nature in a death fight, kia," he told her. "That is no reason for shame."

A wave of fresh tears erupted, stealing her fragile equanimity, but she brought them under control a bit more quickly than before. "I never thought I could do that," she nodded at the poridi. Then she waved her hand over the furry body she'd skinned. "Or this."

Rodani picked up the fur and held it. "It is not a bad thing to learn you have unguessed strengths. You have been sorely tested and found yourself equal to the task." He turned to Cara. "Kusik owes you his life, kia. And he knows it."

"No more than I owe you."

"Yes, more," he said, laying the pelt on the ground. "I trained hard for my skills and my duty. You came here with no other duty than to craft. You defended a man you loathe with no training and no knowledge. That makes your courage all the greater."

Rodani went over and inspected the slashed poridi, dead with a snarl still on its face. He turned it on its back and inspected it. The droop of his shoulders caught Cara's attention.

"What?"

"Nothing you need concern yourself with, kia. Would you like a tooth to go with the benatac's?" He scooted around to the head and began to gouge at the massive jaw.

"Sure," she said, not sure at all. With more finesse but more trepidation, she picked up the other animal and began to strip off the fur with Kusik's knife. But her gut clenched, and gorge rose before she could finish the task. She pushed it away.

"Go inside if you wish." Rodani began a sawing motion inside its mouth. "I will clean up here."

Cara made her way into the damp darkness, down to Kusik's side. "Do you need me to get you anything?"

He stared at her from his supine position. "Where is Rodani?"

"Cleaning up our mess."

"Why are you not assisting him?"

Cara clenched her jaw on all the words she wanted to hurl at the injured keso, but only walked away. She emptied her adrenaline-filled bladder and washed her hands in the stream, bringing back more water to heat by the fire. She laid another log in the ashes and prodded the flames higher.

Finally, Rodani walked down to the fire. He dipped a rag into the water and wiped blood off his hands.

"What did you do?" she asked.

"A necessary task, kia. It is done."

Cara stared at him, then toward the entrance where the poridi recently lay. "What did you do?" she repeated more firmly.

"I would not have you more disturbed, Cara. Will you not trust me?"

Her mind linked a few facts, then flashed on an ugly deduction. "That was a female, wasn't it?"

Rodani grabbed her hand and turned toward the inner storage area. "We all need a rest."

Cara yanked her hand back. "There were babies, weren't there? Just like the ones Kusik killed."

Rodani continued toward the storage room, determined, it seemed, to keep her ignorant. She lashed out at a fist-sized rock, kicking it against the wall. It bounced and clattered, sending echoes of her rage through the cave. "How anyone could think some loving god or goddess created such a bloody world is beyond me."

Rodani returned with a jar in his hand. At the edge of the fire sat a small pot. Rodani shook a dark powder in it and stirred it with his camp spoon.

"What is that?"

"Medicine. For his wounds." He handed the spoon across to Cara. "Dribble it over every wound you see. Double-dose his arm."

"Where are you going?"

"Outside. I must call this in." He lifted the radio and made his way upslope into the sunlight.

Kusik watched her intently as she dripped the disinfectant into the gashes the poridi had left. He gritted his teeth and resisted moving his arm for her to check for missed wounds. She checked everything on his upper body that could be seen. But when she reached for the cloth Rodani had draped over his thighs, he snarled at her. Cara snatched her hand back.

"I know what a man looks like."

A growl erupted underneath his words. "Leave it."

Cara stood up and raised her hands. "Get infected."

Rodani went out to finish setting up the traps and brought back a wild bird that had stepped too close to one. The rest of the day crawled by. Rodani and Cara hacked at tree limbs, threw some on the fire, checked Kusik, cooked, and cleaned up. She didn't forget the roof of rock over her head, but something kept it at bay.

She wound up in the storage area, looking for more blankets, as rock was an unforgiving mattress. Rodani came in behind her, checking on food options. He found a loaf of hard-bread and knocked his knuckles against it. It was aptly named.

Cara spread five blankets down and tested it. She got up and folded them in half lengthwise, then sat again. Better. Barely. Rodani sat down beside her, patted the stack of blankets, and leaned close.

"It has been a half-hand of days since our last joining, kia. How do you fare?"

Her eyes grew wide. She glanced at the doorway, beyond which Kusik lay, several yards away. "I can wait."

"Three more days?"

"If necessary, aisu."

"Maybe it is not necessary." Rodani smiled and put his hand behind her head, laying her back on the blankets. He rested his other hand lightly on her mouth. "How quiet can you be?"

"What about Kusik?" she asked under his hand.

"Right now, kia, his only weapons are words." He removed his hand and touched his lips to hers. "And you are my duty," he added, smiling.

Sunk in his private misery, Kusik clamped his teeth shut as very inappropriate sounds drifted out from the storage room. From his mat, he growled in frustration, but decided the better part of healing was saving his energy instead of stomping into the room to interrupt them.

"Temi's knives," he muttered. Bad enough he had to fight his own pain and humiliation; worse that his bedamned security fifth had to break the rule within his hearing. What was wrong with that human that such activities couldn't be postponed? Why did she drain all the sense from her guardian?

Arimeso had tasked him with a duty he didn't want: to talk to that human, to listen to her, to find out how and what she thinks. To find out the why behind this illegal and seemingly unrepentant affinity. How could he do that, surrounded by unforgivable impropriety? How could he find out what she thought when he didn't even wish to know? When she provoked his ire at every turn?

More sounds came from the storage room, soft but unmistakable. Kusik grimaced, but could do naught else. Using his arm made the bleeding erupt again. The gouges in his thighs and orifice pained him with every movement. Yes, he was guild. He could move if he had to. But he knew the dangers of cold in wounds, and the lack of proper medical care. The more days he laid here, the greater the danger. He stared at the radio, wishing the weather would warm.

A mewling sound reached his ears. *Truly?* Goddess above and below. Rage flooded his body. How dare they? How dare that man, that guardian, choose lust over guild rules? Kusik began to rise, to confront, to put an end to such corruption. But the pain in his body kept him glued to the mat.

And what in all Sela's unearthly wisdom could he do about it? Arimeso refused to allow him to put a stop to it. Kimasa sat in her incense-filled office and declared that the goddess would work her magic in due time. When was that time due? When? How much more chaos would erupt in his taso's house before he could get that human away from them all? Must he kidnap her?

The thought filtered through his mind as he lay on the cold mat. He glanced at the fire. It needed tending, the logs needed shifting, and his fifth and adashi were... One more lash of anger swept through him.

Footsteps whispered across the sandy rocks in front of the storage room. Kusik bided his time.

Behind his head, Cara flopped the blankets on her mat. Rodani shifted the tree limbs in the fire. It sparked, flames reaching toward the ceiling far above their heads.

"Did you think you were silent?" he spat, as Cara bent down to check his wounds. "I can smell him on you."

"He smells wonderful." She began unwrapping the bandages on his arm.

"It is utterly wrong!"

"He feels wonderful, too, a'Keso. Outside, and inside."

Kusik wrenched his body upward, leaning on his uninjured elbow. Cara moved back in alarm. "You disgust me!"

Cara flopped the bloody cloth back across his arm. "Tend to your own wounds, a'Keso." She rose and walked away.

"Come back!" he shouted. "Return to me, now!"

She stopped, and turned to face him, scarred hands pulled around to the small of her back. She eyed him patiently. Rodani waited by the fire, watching.

"Tend to me," he ordered.

"You wish me to wash your wounds?" she asked.

"Yes," he hissed.

She smiled, walked back to him, and pulled the cloth off of his lower half.

"Demons and devils," he said, grabbing for the fabric that was just outside of his reach. Cara bent across him for the water pan in the hot coals. "Cover me! Now!"

Cara wet a cloth and began tending to each of the claw wounds that covered his pelvis and thighs. From the corner of her eye, she saw him glare daggers at Rodani, who remained on the sidelines. Some of the wounds were deep, and despite herself, she was worried about them.

Kusik sank back on the mat, muttering imprecations.

THIRTY

Arimeso stood among the rushes and tack, watching her stablehands attach a duo of benatacs to the largest wagon. Covered against the weather, it would, she hoped, bring her keso, the human, and her guardian back to the safety of the manor. It was the third day since Rodani had called her on the radio. But she would not let her worry show in front of the rescue party.

"Litelon," Domendi called out. "You and Andalia take the spare benatacs and ride ahead with Mindal. He will need to carry the medicines as fast as he can. This snow has delayed us far too long."

The unseasonably late storm had passed, but its remains still clung to the road, and the trees and bushes that followed its path.

"Make all haste, Timan," Arimeso whispered to her second.

"Yes." He held her for a moment. "I will bring him back." He climbed into the wagon. It creaked as the benatacs pulled its weight. Tracks in the snow followed its wheels.

***

Rodani's 'com crackled. "We are on the last road." Timan's voice sounded tired. "How is he?"

"Conscious," Rodani replied, glancing at Kusik. "But his arm is becoming infected."

"Be ready to pull out."

"Ninety-nine." Rodani pocketed his 'com and motioned to Cara. "Roll up the mats, kia, and wash the eating utensils. I will break down the fire."

In a matter of minutes, snow-muffled voices arose outside the cave door. Rodani shook Kusik's good arm. "A'Keso." Kusik opened a bleary eye. "Timan is here, with the others."

"Tell him he is three days overdue."

Rodani's face went to mask. "It would be better if you had that honor."

Timan strode down the cave entrance in a clatter of rocks and boots and stood over his injured partner. They observed each other with unusual intensity. There was more between the pair than everyday living brought to light.

"Tem'u," Timan said gently. "You picked an inconvenient place to be attacked." He bent down. "Good that the goddess bade Cara save you."

Kusik gave nothing but a grumble. "Relieve me of this place."

Mindal checked Kusik's wounds. He frowned over them, poured a medicinal wash over each one, then assisted with Kusik's clothing. Rodani and Cara packed quickly as there wasn't much to take, since there wasn't much that had been brought. Outside the cave entrance stood Lanata, Litelon, and three riderless benatacs snuffling in the cold air. Rodani ignored the beasts, but raked the boy with his eyes, looking for reasons to keep him at a distance. There was no reason why—

"The keso rides with me until we get down to the carriage," Timan said. "We had to leave it behind when the trail narrowed." He waved his arm. "Cara with Litelon. Rodani and Mindal, you ride alone."

Lanata and Mindal assisted Timan in getting their keso into the saddle. Kusik was weak, unsteady on his legs, and irascible.

Fuming inside, Rodani guided Cara over to Litelon, tall and thin from on top his beast. Between them, Litelon and Rodani managed to seat Cara on the double saddle. Rodani lifted up blankets. "Make sure she stays covered," he told the boy. "Her body cannot adapt to the cold as ours can."

"A'tem," he replied.

"Mind my words," Rodani said stiffly. "She will die in this temperature without adequate cover."

"Yes, a'tem."

Rodani mounted, not without a great deal of trepidation—for himself as well as Cara. He knew the boy was a better rider than he was. Cara was safer traveling with him. But it rankled. And if he admitted it to himself, he feared the icy path underneath the beast's padded feet.

The road was long and treacherous. They were all as tired and ill-tempered as Kusik when dusk fell.

"We will be at the carriage tomorrow before noon," Timan said as they gathered together in the gloom. "Lanata, take first watch. In the while, see to our food. Rodani, you and I will need to keep Kusik warm tonight. Make a bed for us near the fire while I gather wood. Litelon, see to the beasts."

Litelon and Lanata scrambled to their tasks. Rodani approached Timan, a worried look on his face. "A'Biso, Cara will not make it through such a night alone. It is too cold."

Timan bent over the injured body of his partner. "She will do well enough on the other side of the fire. Your job tonight is to help me keep the keso alive. Today was a hard ride for him."

"Yes, a'Biso. But my duty to Cara—"

Timan glanced at him, fire in his eyes. "I will not put a stablehand into a guardian's place. You will do as I say."

Rodani's fury rose into a hissing whisper. "I will not let Cara die in the cold. If I must be beside the keso, then Cara will sleep beside me."

"No."

"A'Biso, there is no good reason to say no," Rodani protested as far as he could dare. "It solves both problems."

Timan whirled to face him fully. "Obey me," he thundered, "Or you will feel the lash when we return!"

Rodani drew himself upward and clenched his jaw, the rest of his body nearly vibrating in rage. He spun around, looking for an alternative. Lanata would be best, but she would be standing on guard. Mindal would be up and down all night, tending to Kusik.

Temi's coldest hells! A painful mix of dishonor and embarrassment washed through him as he approached the benatacs, and Litelon.

"A'sel," he began, rather politely. The young man turned to him, and a wary look crossed his face.

"I am in need," Rodani continued, "of your assistance."

Litelon inclined his head and waited.

Emotions in painful conflict, Rodani took a deep breath. "I am ordered to sleep next to our keso, to help keep him warm," he said, forcing himself into a calm he didn't feel. "A'Cara cannot just sit by the fire all night, and survive. I would ask you," he looked off into the distance, then into Litelon's wide eyes, "if you would share your blankets with her tonight. Share your warmth—and nothing else—honor to honor."

Litelon's pupils pulsed. "Of course, a'tem."

Rodani leaned into him, the better to reinforce his next words. "I know the temptations you will feel, and I need you to keep them at bay. Be aware," he continued in a low voice, "that while she—and I—will appreciate you sharing your warmth, you will offend her, as well as me, if you cross any lines."

He watched as Litelon glanced over the camp's other inhabitants, probably making the same assessment as he had. "I hear, a'tem."

"See that you do."

Dinner was a cold, cheerless affair. Litelon kept his distance. Mindal hovered over Kusik and rubbed his injured arm with a pungent gel. Cara hovered by the fire, already cold and trying not to worry Rodani about it. Her nose ran, and her toes were beginning to tingle.

"Rodani," she said, "are there extra blankets?"

"No, kia. I am sorry. What we have, Timan has taken for Kusik. He is not well." He touched her arm lightly. "But I will not let you die by the fire. Nor," he removed his hand, "will Litelon."

Her expression reformed into doubt and surprise as Rodani explained. ^Okay.^

The privy was nothing more than a blanket that hid one from the others' eyes. Only her body's insistent demands made her drop her pants in the cold wind. She stumbled back to her blankets in front of the fire, curled into them, and bent toward the warmth. Was she supposed to just walk up and burrow next to the stablehand who nearly got her killed before?

The rustling of leaves caught her attention. A whispered voice. "A'Cara?"

Well, that's my answer.

"A'Cara?" Litelon crouched down behind her. "Come share my blankets, a'sel." He placed a cautious hand on her arm. "I will help warm you."

Cara sighed heavily, even knowing this was her only choice. She followed Litelon and wormed her way under his blankets, up against his warmth. He drew his arm around her, feeling for the placement of the covers. She was too cold to be embarrassed. His steady breathing and heartbeat calmed her as she waited for the shivers to cease. Eventually, she slept.

Dawn filtered its way through the trees. One shifting movement under the blankets brought others. Rodani rolled away from Kusik. His keso was still warm, thanks to—he didn't finish the thought.

"Cara," he said, walking over to where he saw Litelon's head.

She pulled the blanket away and stood up. "How is Kusik?"

"Alive. And how are you?" he answered, glancing at Litelon meaningfully. The youth lifted his chin in mute response.

"Well enough, with Litelon's help. Warmer than I would have been." She looked over her shoulder at Litelon. "Thank you."

"Pack up," Timan urged them all. "We must reach the wagon as soon as we can."

One at a time, each member of the party stepped behind the privy curtain, then folded their blankets. Litelon and Rodani assisted in getting Kusik reseated on Timan's benatac, then Cara on Litelon's. She adjusted her blankets as Rodani climbed back on his. They moved out.

"Thank you for saving my life last night, Litelon," Cara said softly.

"I was pleased to be of help, a'Cara." He held the reins lightly in his hand. "Thank you for reassuring Rodani."

She turned her head to whisper. "You did nothing wrong."

"Sometimes people of high status care only for their pride. He probably felt shame that he couldn't protect you."

"He's very protective."

Litelon was silent for a moment. "A'Cara, I would ask a few questions, but I do not wish to offend you."

"Ask. But I may not be able to answer them."

He leaned forward, over her shoulder, whispering. "Does he treat you well?"

She smiled. "Yes. Yes, he does."

"You are aware that if a problem arises, the taso and selaso can assist you?"

"Yes. I've talked to them both, Litelon. Thank you, though." She patted his leg affectionately. "I appreciate your concern."

"There are people in Barridan who take exception to you and your guardian's activities."

Cara wrenched her head around. "How much do you know?"

Litelon tossed her question with a flip of his hand. "Only a little. No one notices me. But I hear things."

"They should mind their own business."

Litelon opened his mouth to say something, then shut it. A few minutes later, he spoke. "You should be able to be safe in the manor, a'Cara. That is difficult when so many are angry."

Again, she turned in her seat. "How many?"

"The house guardians know. Half of the clinic knows, and most of the Enclave."

"You must listen to a lot of people."

"One of my talents, a'Cara."

THIRTY-ONE

"How much do you remember about the recipe?" Rodani asked his partner. Stiff on the couch in their sitting room, he wanted to both watch and turn away. The skirmish within him was turning into a pitched battle in his gut. Between Kusik's infected arm being removed, hostile and stalking guardians, and a renewed touch of generative disturbance, calm was as distant as the Himadi Hills.

Serano dropped a few more varigestra leaves into the pestle and continued to grind them. "You are radiating, tem'u. Find your calm, or you will fly into pieces."

"But it has been a decade since you've made the tea." He crossed and uncrossed his arms. "Or more."

Serano inspected the ground-up leaves with a practiced eye, then dumped the contents into a small bowl. "While you were relaxing in that cave, I radioed the healers in headquarters and received explicit, exacting instructions." He cut the roots from the stems of several plants and began dicing them. "The goddess blessed you, Rodani. This plant doesn't lose its potency after picking, or you would have had to make another trip."

A guttural "Au" was the only reply. Rodani got up and started pacing.

"Tem'u, please. Go bother your alien instead."

"Do not give me orders."

Serano leaned back from the table. "Do not give me tempers, or you can take this to one of Baldar's assistants."

Rodani stopped his back-and-forth, heeding the rebuke. What he wanted was a drink, but his duty wasn't done for the day. As a fact, his duty now blended from day into night into day again, with nary a break. But the perquisites, he reminded himself, gave worth to what might otherwise be drudgery.

Rodani headed toward the manor's vast kitchen, certain he could wrest a couple of bottles from Cassig. The man had taken a leap in status from cook to chef when he'd badgered Hadaman's head chef for human dietary restrictions. And hadn't made one mistake.

Preparations for the noontime meal battered his hearing as he entered the room. Searching for Cassig among the crowd, he spied him in the corner.

"A'sel."

Cassig turned and bowed. "A'tem, does a'Cara require something special tonight?"

"Not that I am aware, honored chef. However, if you have any treats at hand, we both could use one." He glanced down at the keys that Cassig carried at his waist. "And we are nearly out of drinks."

"Well, that is the simplest to remedy, a'tem."

Rodani followed Cassig to a locked door and into a narrow corridor with wall-to-wall wooden bottle racks. The chef pulled out a bottle from a shelf near the floor, and another near his head on the other side. He handed them to Rodani with a flourish and dipped his head.

Rodani looked them over. "No tampering?"

"We inspect them regularly, a'tem." He tapped the smaller bottle. "Especially now that we know which one a'Cara prefers."

From a shelf in the kitchen, he retrieved a nibble tin.

"Thank you, Cassig. May your pans never rust." Rodani wound his way between the milling cooks to the entrance and stepped into the hall.

A body took him to the ground.

Rodani folded into a fetal position in an effort to save the liquor. Naremit's fists pummeled his skull, and from the side, he took a savage kick to the ribs. He let go of his burdens and swore in rage, sweeping Vanu's feet out from underneath him. As Rodani struggled to stand, Naremit grappled him. They wrestled for a moment as shouting erupted from nearby. Hands grasped Naremit and pulled him up. Other hands yanked Rodani to his feet. From the corner of his eye, he could see Cassig fighting Vanu for the bottle of eisenico.

A female form stomped out of the kitchen. The cooks scattered from her path. "Cease this!" she bellowed.

Rodani rearranged his shirt and took the bottles and tin back from Cassig. "Thank you, a'sel."

"Who caused this uproar?" the woman asked. Only Rodani dared look at her.

"He was set upon, a'Menidi!" Cassig said. Outrage put a stammer in his voice. "A'Rodani came to me for those bottles," he stretched out his arm and pointed, "and he was attacked as he left. I saw it!"

Menidi marched up to Naremit and Vanu, who retreated in the face of her wrath. "How dare you attack your superior?" she shouted into their faces. "You are a disgrace to your guild. If I see either of you in the festive room before rest-day, I will drag you both into Kusik's office."

As the two men took off, the master chef turned to Rodani. "From where comes this disobedience, a'tem?" She raked him up and down. "And how do you allow it?"

Rodani glanced aside in an effort to see where they'd gone. "Someday, a'Menidi, I hope to be able to tell you." Pointedly, he bowed at her and at Cassig, then headed for the safety of his own corridor. When Hamman answered the door, he pushed through quickly, kicking the door shut.

"A'tem," she said, quietly as always.

Rodani tore the wrappings off each bottle in turn, tossing them to the floor.

"A'tem?"

Ignoring her, he grabbed two glasses from the cabinet and sloshed liquor in each. Without another word, he traipsed down the hall, through the bedroom, past the empty worktable, and into the study. Cara looked up from her translating and eyed his abrupt entrance.

"Something wrong?"

He plopped their drinks down and sat next to her on the couch, stretching his legs toward the fire.

"Rodani?"

He rubbed his hands on his thighs, staring into the flames. "Adjusting, kia. That is all." He reached for their drinks, handing the shigeli to her, then taking a hefty swallow of the eisenico. "Some days are easier than others."

"Can I help?"

He cut the air with his hand, making a sharp stroke. "I have work to do," he told her. "We were five days gone. I have two necklaces due next week, weapons practice, and exercise to attend to. Sitting with you makes me soft."

Cara grinned. "We could dance," she said, nodding to the 'corder that had sat quiescent since before the cave.

"If I could dance as you do, that would be an acceptable alternative. But I am neither ethereal nor gymnastic."

"You haven't tried."

"And there is not enough eisenico to induce me to."

She took another sip and glanced at the fireplace. "What about horizontal dancing?"

Rodani pulled his glass from his lips. "Horiz—" His eyes grew wide.

"You seem on edge." Cara pulled the glass from his hand and set it on the table. "If I can't help in any other way, I can help with that." She nudged at his arms, coaxing him until he wrapped them around her. As she paid attention to his lips, Rodani ran his hands over her back and up under her shirt. Even in winter, in a room needing a working fireplace, his hands were warm. Other parts of her body had been quite pleased in this regard. Many times. She pulled away from his face and smiled, then placed a careful fingertip on his ear and ran it down from tip to lobe and back up again, tickling at the top.

Rodani removed her hand and turned, laying her down on the cushions. He ran his many-fingered hands across her abdomen and down her thighs, then spread her legs with a gentle nudge. Sliding in close, he pushed his hand past the rumpled fabric of her shirt and cupped her breast.

Behind them, a chair moved with a clunk against the stone. In a flash, Rodani spun around, grabbing his knife. He stared into the corner. Crouched under the table was Ikemi, eyes wide, his small hand over his mouth.

"Stand, ki'oto," Rodani said, getting up. He pointed to the floor in front of his feet.

Slowly, Ikemi crawled out from under the table. His slender body shook against his effort to hold himself properly still.

"Here." Rodani pointed again. Ikemi shuffled forward.

Closing her shirt, Cara sat up on the couch and held out her arms. "Ikemi?"

"No." Rodani waved his hand in her face. "What were you doing, Ikemi?" he asked, as Cara dropped her arms into her lap. The boy blinked hard, staring into the floor as if it were shelter that would hide him. He swallowed visibly.

"Answer." Rodani's voice held a hardness Cara hadn't heard in a while. She held her breath, not liking the cold aura in the room. Ikemi shook like a leaf in the wind, and just as ready to fall.

Rodani leaned down and slapped him.

"No!" Cara shouted. Rodani hissed at her in censure. Ikemi kept to his feet, but continued to shiver and blink.

"Answer, ki'oto. What were you doing?"

"I wished to see a'Cara," he said in a small voice.

"And why were you hiding under the table?"

Ikemi clenched his eyes shut, then opened them as if by force of will, stiffening his arms at his sides. Cara read the signs—a small child trying with all the courage he had to face an adult's wrath.

When he remained silent, Rodani slapped him again, harder. Ikemi lost his balance and fell to his hands and knees.

"Tell me," Rodani said with a growling undercurrent in his voice.

No, Cara thought. *This is not going to happen. Not here. Not in front of me.* She pushed off the couch and wrapped her arms around the boy, drawing him out of Rodani's reach.

"Leave him, Cara," Rodani said, stepping forward. "This is his discipline to face, mine to deal out."

"You are not going to hit him."

Now he looked straight at her, his violet eyes flashing in the firelight. "I will treat him in the manner of our people."

Cara pulled Ikemi back farther. His body shook in her arms. "You say what you need to say. But keep your hands off him."

"You do not give me orders, Cara. He has done wrong and must face his punishment." He swung again at Ikemi's cheek, but Cara's hand struck it away before it connected. Rodani froze momentarily, then grabbed her arm and heaved her off balance. Ikemi slipped out of her arms. "Do not interfere!"

"Run, Ikemi," she whispered.

With a fierce grip on her arm, Rodani shook her. "Be silent!"

Cara reached out with her free arm and pushed at Ikemi. "Run!"

Ikemi scrambled for the study door. Rodani let go of Cara to follow, but she slammed the door shut in front of him and collapsed against it. Infuriated, he grabbed her by the shoulders and yanked her away, then opened the door and started to run.

Cara sped out on his heels. As Rodani went tearing into the hallway after the boy, Cara leapt at his legs, catching one in mid-stride. Rodani went down on one knee and spun on the floor to face her. "You dare?" His teeth snapped shut on a growl that erupted from his chest. His pupils shut down to slits.

Sprawled on the floor on his legs, Cara squeezed with all her strength. "You don't hit children!"

"Let go," he spat.

"Don't hit!" she shouted, voice echoing down the hallways.

He raised his arm for a backhand slap. Cara froze. "Really?" she said with all the ice she could muster. "Hit me because you can't hit Ikemi?" She let go of his leg and stood up. Adrenaline rattled her as badly as the boy had shaken. Her hands tingled.

Rodani got to his feet, his chest heaving, his face a cold mask. Wordless, he took her arm and pushed her back into the workroom, shutting the door between them. As he turned away, she opened it and spoke to his departing back. "If you're going out to find and hit him, you're no longer welcome in my bed."

Rodani turned slowly in that whole-body move she hadn't seen in months. It shook her down to her toes, but she held on to her resolve. "Come inside, so we can talk. Please, Rodani."

Unblinking, nearly unbreathing, Rodani glared at her. His pupils reflected the torches through the narrowest of confines, his face a mask of stone.

"Please." She held the door open for him, mute invitation. After a moment, he walked toward her, past her, past the workroom where they spent so much time, and back into the study. She'd swear a cold draft followed him. It chilled her.

Rodani refused the couch, standing stiffly by the dinner table. Cara climbed into the overstuffed chair, brought up her knees, and wrapped her arms around them. She took a deep breath.

"First and most important, Rodani, I'm sorry." She paused to watch his reaction, but there was none. Just a deep, dark withdrawal.

"My intention was not to offend you, or dishonor you. My only intention was to prevent him being hurt." Cara sighed heavily. But the knot in her gut was not to be assuaged by mere breathing. *Gods, let me get this right.* "If you had done nothing but talk to him, I would have stayed out of it. But it goes against everything I believe in to watch a child be hit."

"And you took what should have been a simple discipline and turned it into five types of dishonor." Now he turned his head, and his face held something she never wanted to see. Hard, cold. No masked expression could hide the fury that radiated outward.

"And I would create fifty times the offenses to keep one child safe from harm. Aisu," she took a chance with his erinai, hoping it would offer a touch of calm, "you are my guardian. It is your duty to keep me from harm. Yes?"

"Yes."

"You would step between me and someone who wanted to harm me. Yes?"

"Yes. And I see the path you are walking, but it does not lead where you wish it."

Cara splayed out her hands, scars plain to see on her palms. "But it does to me—"

"I was disciplining him, not harming him."

She grabbed her pant legs, tension in every muscle in her body. "You could have taught him everything he needed to know without touching him. And what did you teach him?"

"*You*," he spat back, "taught him that he could run from me when he should have remained where he was."

"And you taught him that he should forever fear you. And fear making any kind of simple mistake in front of you."

"You taught him dishonor."

"No! I told him to run from you for the same reason I ran from the Enclave. Do we need to cover that again? It's not dishonor to run from unearned punishment, or abuse."

"I do not abuse children."

"But you will treat them with excessive harshness when it's completely unnecessary?"

"That was excessive harshness?" The incredulity in his voice stopped her in mid-thought.

"Augh. Not excessive, no. That was a poor choice of word. But...unnecessary. You didn't show him anything but anger, and he didn't learn anything but fear."

"And dishonor."

Circles upon circles, and they were leading nowhere safe. The pain in her gut grew tentacles into her heart, and her brain. "Please sit down, aisu. Please." She crossed imaginary fingers, then crossed her real ones for good measure.

He sat, finally, on the far end of the couch by the door. To be as far from her as he could, or for a fast getaway? The thought hurt, knowing how often she did the very same thing—for reasons she didn't want to contemplate right now. The wall she'd created between them with her interference threatened her fragile composure.

Silence lay between them, a threat all its own. Rodani was back to staring into the distance, somewhere deep inside his own head. Cara's heart beat in her throat. Any minute now, Rodani would get up and walk out. Any minute now...

"Did you mean what you said in the hall?" he asked. Nothing moved but his mouth, like he was afraid something would shatter if he blinked. "That you would no longer share yourself with me?"

"Oh, gods." She rested her head on her knees and spoke to the fire that crackled at her left. "I want to say no. But I'm not sure."

"Do I matter so little to you?"

"Please don't think that, aisu. You mean more to me than any other man ever has." She began to rock back and forth. "Ending what we have would hurt like—like Temi stabbing me, over and over. But it was another way of protecting myself. I can't share my life with a man who resorts to violence."

"Ever?"

"No, *not* ever. When Shurad was shooting at me, I was happ— relieved that you killed him. You saved my life. But Ikemi is not a murderer, he's a child. He's no threat to either of us. He doesn't deserve that punishment."

He glanced over, just a bit more toward the fire than at her. "'Deserve' is one of those words that is species-dependent."

"More than that, aisu. It's personal to everyone who uses it."

"Then that leaves us trapped, does it not?"

"Rodani," she said, still rocking, "when you give me orders about my security, I obey them." She ducked her head. "Almost always. And I do it because I respect your honor and your knowledge, not because I agree. Not because I want to obey them. I do it because it matters more to you than to me.

"I can't command you. But I'd ask you to," she fought for a good, non-offensive word, "to adopt my way in this, because it matters more to me than it does to you." She lifted her head and willed him to look her way, but he stared at the fire resolutely. "A fair exchange. Honor for honor."

"And what would your way teach him?"

"If I get a chance, I'll show you."

Rodani looked away from the flames and stood up. Panic flooded Cara, frying what was left of her synapses as she watched her lover walk away. When the outer door clicked shut, the finality of the sound made her want to vomit. She crawled onto the couch and laid her head on the warmth his body had left behind.

A black cloud rolled over her, smothering any hint of the happiness she'd felt earlier.

And the rain dripped from her eyes.

***

An hour...a day...gods, a month later, Cara lay on the soggy patch of couch and listened to the fire snapping and tapping behind her. Tapping? She lifted her head and waited. There it came again, a faint scratching. Vermin. No. She tiptoed into her workroom and listened. Someone was on the other side of the door.

Damn sure it wasn't Rodani. She looked toward Hamman's hallway. Nothing was stirring. *Shades of Litelon's visits!* It hadn't been that long since someone had tried to kill her. *What now? What now?* Ignore it was the best bet. But wait...the sound—it came again—from the bottom half of the door. No seven-foot Selandu would ask for entrance at knee height. She crept forward.

"Who's there?"

"Onana?" a small voice said.

She reached for the doorknob, then froze. "Who's with you?"

"No one."

Cara put her mouth to the door frame. "Look around you. Do you see anyone? Hear anyone?"

She waited, then: "No, Onana." Twisting the handle slowly, she opened the door a crack, just enough to let Ikemi's slight body through, then shut and re-locked the door.

His eyes were wide, and his arms were wrapped across his narrow chest. Cara swept him up and carried him to the couch, plopping them both down next to the warmth of the fire. She grabbed the quilt off the back and wrapped it around him, pulling him close. Dirt decorated the edges of his ears and his forehead. Pieces of leaves clung to his hair.

"Are you hurt?"

"No, Onana."

"Where did you run to?"

He rubbed his face on her shirt, burrowing. "To a place where I hide."

The matter-of-fact words jarred her, shifting her emotions further off-kilter. "Do you hide often?"

"Almost every day."

"Can adults find you there?"

"They cannot get in."

"So, it's like a tunnel somewhere?" He shut his eyes and nestled more deeply; his fingers clenched at her waist. "Never mind," she said at his silence. "I won't ask. Don't tell me." She rubbed her hand up and down his back, willing him to relax. "What did you see when you came in the room earlier?"

"I saw him lay down on you, covering you up."

"What did you think when you saw that?"

Ikemi put a dirty fist to his mouth. "That he was hurting you."

"Did I act like I was hurting?" Cara asked gently. "Did I shout, or fight him?"

He considered that for a while, rubbing his hands on the edges of the quilt. "No."

"You were confused. Yes?"

"Yes."

"Ki'oto, I need your help."

Ikemi lifted his face to look at her.

"I need to talk to Rodani. And I need you to talk to him, too. Will you help me?"

Ikemi drew his knees up, squeezing his eyes tight and tucking his head into her chest. Cara fumed. This, this was the problem. And she was sure Rodani was only the latest perpetrator. She slid Ikemi off her lap and sat him on the cushion. "Stay here. I'll be back soon."

As she called for Deremic, he appeared out of the farthest room, his bedroom. He, too, looked a little off-kilter, his eyes a little too wide, his gaze unsteady. "A'sel," she said quietly. "Please go across the hall and ask a'Rodani—as politely and carefully as you can—to please come over and talk. Tell him Ikemi came back. Ask him with all the courtesy you can."

Deremic bent his head and turned to obey. Cara grabbed her brush and her smallest shirt on her way back to the study. She smiled her best, letting it crinkle around her eyes and uncover her teeth. "Let's get you out of those dirty clothes."

She helped him remove his outerwear, only to realize he had no inner wear. She slipped her shirt over him without comment, but scratched another mental mark on the tally of neglects the child was suffering. Her shirt hung on him awkwardly, but nothing else came close to fitting. When she sat down, Ikemi crawled back into her lap and tugged at the quilt. As she wrapped him, he snuggled close.

Cara removed his hair clip, careful of the tangles that twisted and caught. She brushed his hair in long gentle sweeps, enjoying the silky feel of the silver strands through her fingers. They sat in silent reverie for a hand of minutes, Ikemi relaxing with her motherly ministrations.

A whisper of slippers crossed the workroom. Ikemi's eyes went wide, pupils circles of panic. He tensed visibly in her lap. Cara's gut did likewise, invisible and volatile. Rodani stopped in the doorway, clad in loose clothing. He looked them both over before lowering himself onto the couch where he had been not too long ago.

"Thank you for returning, aisu. You honor me with your patience."

His gaze was back on the fire in the fireplace. He tilted his head in mute acceptance.

Cara pushed Ikemi into a sitting position. "I will begin, ki'oto. I will apologize to Rodani and ask his forgiveness."

She did so, formal in her demeanor, knowing Ikemi was watching. Again, Rodani tilted his head, saying nothing.

"Ikemi, do you know what your mistake was?" she asked.

"No," he whispered.

"A'Rodani, will you tell him?"

He turned to the boy. "You came into the room without greeting, and hid under the table. The only reason we knew you were there was because you made a noise. One might think you were spying."

"Ikemi, will you apologize to Rodani for your mistake?" He started shaking again, his slender limbs vibrating in Cara's hands. "Just say the words," she prompted him.

"I am sorry, a'Rodani," he whispered. It was a good thing Selandu had acute hearing. She barely heard him, even from her lap.

"Now ask him to forgive you."

"Please forgive me, a'Rodani."

Cara looked over at him, silent on the other end of the couch.

"Yes," he admitted after a pause. "And when you ran?"

She held up a hand. "That was my wrongdoing."

Now he looked straight at her—"and he should not have obeyed you,"—and down at Ikemi. "What do you say to me?"

Ikemi quailed before that look, but whispered, "Please forgive me."

"Do not *ever* run from an adult, ki'oto. No matter who tells you, you do not. Do you understand?" Evidently confused, Ikemi glanced up at Cara, which riled Rodani further. "Do you understand?"

Cara bounced the boy on her legs, moving him out of his frozen state. "Go ahead. Answer."

"Yes, a'Rodani."

Cara sighed in relief. She could only hope that his apology took the edge off Rodani's temper. The level of contained rage in his demeanor frightened even her. What would it do to a child? She rested her hand on Ikemi's back, feeling his breaths against her palm. From the corner of his eye, Rodani watched, stiff and silent. After a hand of painful minutes, he broke his silence.

"Are you done with this?"

Startled, Cara looked away from Ikemi into Rodani's face. The ice was still there, and underneath it, a raging fire. "I think so," she whispered.

Rodani left the room without another word.

A crush of emotion enveloped her as he disappeared. She clung to Ikemi as her renewed sobbing broke out.

"Onana, Onana," Ikemi said, tapping her on the face. "Are you hurt? Onana?" He struggled in her arms and pushed his way out. "Hamman!"

***

Morning sunlight shone through the shutters, throwing patterns on the floor. Rodani walked in from Cara's bedroom, still quiet, introspective, face masked. Cara let the sewing machine come to a stop and looked at him through still-puffy eyes. "Bright morn," she said carefully.

Rodani sat down in his accustomed place. "I have not had such a sleepless night in many a year, Cara."

Cara folded her hands on the table in front of her. "I'm sorry for my part in it." She breathed shallowly, waiting. For what, she couldn't know.

Rodani brooded in the silence, eyes on the tools scattered between them. His jaw clenched and unclenched. His breath came in deep gulps.

"I cannot agree to your interpretation of last night's events. What I did was not wrong, and you should not have interfered."

Cara put her hands to her mouth, elbows on the table. She couldn't bear going over it all again, so she waited. Waited to hear what had gone through his head in his sleepless hours, waited to hear what her immediate future would bring.

"And I do not appreciate the threat you gave me."

Oh, gods. Here it comes.

"But I believe I understand it."

"You do?" she asked, surprised.

He took a breath and looked down to the table's edge, rubbing his fingers along it. "You are powerless here. You have very little voice in what happens to you, for you, or because of you. When it comes to fighting for what you believe, your hands are nearly empty. You use what leverage you have." His nimble fingers picked at a splinter, breaking it into tiny pieces. "When everyone around you was lying about me, you ceased quilting so that Arimeso would hear you." His gaze rested on something in the workroom. "When you thought I was hurting Ikemi, you were willing to end our affinity. You use what weapons a defenseless person has."

Damn, that he thought so clearly while her mind was still fogged.

"Cara, I am helpless against that weapon. It is an all-or-nothing demand—that I submit to you or lose what I have found." Rodani bent his head in her direction, as if he were not quite ready to look her in the face. "It is too dire a weapon to draw upon for nothing more than a slap across a child's face."

"I was afraid of your anger, aisu, and afraid for Ikemi. I didn't know what else to say."

Rodani grasped a saw-toothed file in his fist; his arm vibrated with tension. "Never use that threat, Cara, unless you are ready to carry it out."

^Okay.^

"Reply in Selandi, please."

Cara gathered the words in her head. "I promise that I will not use that threat unless I am willing to carry it out."

Rodani thought a few more moments, then drew another long breath. "There are two people you wish me to treat in the manner of your culture," he continued. "Yes?"

"Two people."

His hand swept along the table in front of him. His eyes followed. "And if I offer that obedience to you, what do you offer in return?" His body stilled, waiting.

Cara gnawed at her knuckles. It all came down to this. All that they'd had, all that they'd won. "What do you ask?"

Rodani sat up straight. "That you cease interfering in concerns that are not yours. Do not argue when it is not your argument. Do not fight when it is not your fight." He turned to face her, pupils narrow in a fierce focus. "Learn when not to speak. Keep your mouth closed when I bid you do so."

Holy deep space. That was one of Temi's knives, right there. And she was bleeding. She took a deep breath. And another. "And if we disagree?"

"You obey nonetheless, and we discuss it after."

There was nothing for it, in his world. Not a lot else to say. This was a lesson she hadn't seen coming, not even on the far horizon. Humiliation for breakfast. Tasty. ^Okay.^

"Selandi."

Her lips pursed. "I affirm." She waited a second. "But..."

He uncurled his fingers in acceptance.

"First, I need you to remember how close you came to hitting me yesterday and think about how badly that would hurt our affinity. Second, the outrage that made me fight you over Ikemi is the same outrage that made me call Arimeso when Kusik was hitting you, and when Serano called you out for a dominance fight after I was shot at. And it was the same fury that made me fight you that first time. It all comes from the same source, the same sense of honor." She laid her forearms on the table and hunched her shoulders. "You've made it clear that my honor can't always supersede yours. I accept that. But," she clenched her hands together, "do you really want me to stay quiet while Kusik beats you?"

"Yes."

She had to look away on that one, biting her lip. "That's hard."

"Can you?"

"Yes." She paused. "I think so. But only because you're an adult, and strong enough to take it. And willing. And...oh, demons." She bent her head. "I don't want to say yes."

"But you will."

Her eyes clenched shut, then opened. "...Yes."

Now it was Rodani's turn to breathe deep. His eyes roamed the room, landing on her sewing machine, the throwing-knives target, the door to her study, a quilt on the wall. But not to her. Not to her. He pushed himself up from the table, turned sideways, and held out his hand.

Cara stared at his open palm, dumbfounded for a moment. His mood was still fey, his gaze still elsewhere. But it was either trust him now, or never trust him again. She took his hand.

He led her to her bedroom and shut the door behind them, then lifted her and held her, wordless. She let him have his way; no suggestions, no requests. He took what she gave, and gave it back in full measure. They lay in the quiet aftertime, a fragile peace between them.

THIRTY-TWO

Serano opened the manor's south door, knocked the dirt off his boots, and walked toward the rooms he shared with Rodani. Listening to his partner and their adashi rage at each other had set off dreams that kept him from proper rest last night. A ride on beast-back, however, had cleared his mind. Cold day, bright sky, a warm hide between his legs, a trail to follow, these were Sela's gifts. And he wouldn't give them up for anything—except the knives he'd earned in guild training.

Larisi would be waiting for him, of course. Her time was drawing near, and she requested his proximity at every opportunity. And he would attend to her with all the solicitude at his fingertips. This would be their first cycle together, and Serano ached for the experience with every muscle in his body. Including those that would be exercised the most. His eyes narrowed with the thought—

Arms gripped him from behind at neck and knees. He toppled forward, then fought against the attack, bucking his body to rid himself of someone's weight on his back. He felt one of his arms dragged behind him, then the other, while something dry was shoved in his mouth. As his eyes were covered by a dark wrap, he berated himself, swearing a multitude of oaths. Then his mouth was covered, the cloth pulling tightly between his lips.

A whisper of footsteps receded into the distance. Serano yanked at his wrists, but they were tied tight. He wormed around on the floor, rubbing his temple against the stone. Inch by inch, the blindfold moved up, until he could see well enough to stand and orient himself.

Goddess, get me safely hid, away from laughing eyes. He launched himself down the hall with a desperate attempt to remember his training, while trying to push the mass in his mouth forward against his teeth. Whoever his attackers were, they had soaked the rag in something noxious. It assaulted his nasal passages as he breathed, and tasted like a three-day-old fish.

Ahead of him was a piece of luck—Timan's office. *Please, dear Goddess, let him be there.* He knocked on the door with his forehead and waited.

"Enter."

Au, yes, and how will I do that? he thought. With a savage jerk, he kicked at the door and shouted a muffled curse through the gag.

"Who dares—" Timan asked, opening the door. His pupils expanded into saucers as he took in Serano's predicament. Serano pushed past him and kicked the door shut, wanting no more humiliation than he was already suffering.

Timan drew his knife and cut off the gag, the blindfold, and the ties around his wrists. He tossed the items on his desk and planted his fists on his hips. "Who in Temi's name did this?"

Serano shook his arms, ran his hands over his hair, and spat into the waste bin. "I do not know. Goddess, that tastes foul."

"Tell me."

He spewed out his words in a rapid patter, wanting the explanation—and the censure he knew was coming—finished and past him.

Timan stared at him with narrowed pupils. "Have you forgotten your training? Where was your awareness?"

And here it is. "Not where it should be, a'Biso. But this is home, and we are not at war."

"Are we not?"

Serano blanked his face of the puzzlement that erupted inside. "Are we?"

"How long has it been since you have spoken with your partner?"

That one took some rummaging through his memories. "Since he came back with Kusik," Serano answered after a moment.

"Why?"

"We do not... There has not..." Serano sighed. "There has been no reason to speak."

Timan motioned him out. "Stay near. I am requesting a guild meeting."

***

The room was full. Rodani had waited, risking lateness, the better to avoid further abuse. He took his seat. Across the table, Serano refused to meet his eyes.

Kusik stood. The loss of his left forearm stood out by its absence. There were no papers at his hand. No pencil, no notes. "A'tem'ai," he addressed them, "we have an issue that must be addressed." He looked down the table at his partner. "Or more accurately, we *are* the issue." His eyes scanned the table, the bodies—men and women—who obeyed him, who served their taso, her plans, her visions.

"Is there anyone here who does not know our priorities?" No one moved. "Is there anyone here who does not know who gives the orders in this house?"

Without shifting, Rodani glanced around. Younger faces at the far end of the table were tight, wrapped in the fierce blankness of emotion suppression.

"No one ever claimed," Kusik continued, "that being a guardian was simple. No one ever taught you that disagreements do not arise." Kusik stepped away from his chair and began to circle the table, walking slowly behind the backs of his house guild. "But there was one teaching that was never shirked; one lesson that should never be forgotten. And that is this: when you join a house, when you give your allegiance to your taso, you set your own opinions aside. When you accept her beneficence, you vow to protect her. When you vow to protect her, you also vow to protect her house, the people in it, and the choices she makes for us all.

"Even the best of tasos make decisions we would rather they not. And our august taso has done that very thing." He paced back and forth behind Timan. "Do not think that I have withheld my voice from her. Do not think that I deny your concerns on the issues that face us. But I must remind you that after we have voiced our disagreements, we continue to obey. That is our duty. It always has been. It always will be.

"A'Tem'ai, the ripples from the taso's decisions on the human are turning into storm-tossed waves, waves that are threatening to sink us. Not because of the human. But because of our reactions to her presence."

Rodani froze in his chair. *Kia.* Fear rushed through his body, making his heart pound. Never had Kusik or Timan broached the subject of his adashi in this way. He fought against the urge for his ears to twitch and took deeper breaths to hide his anxieties.

"We guardians," Kusik said, "are the rock upon which each taso and her decisions rest. And we must hold firm. Our fights are not with each other. Our enemies should not sit among us. We cannot guard each other's backs if our foundation shatters. And yet, some of you have decided that you have enemies at this table."

At the far end, Naremit began to stir in his chair. His demeanor mutated from cool disdain to hot rage.

Kusik strolled up behind Rodani's chair. "You have not only attacked those you think are guilty, but those who are not. You are heaping dishonor on top of disobedience, and it must stop. Your taso demands it. I demand it."

Toranel laid her hand on Naremit's arm, but it did nothing to curb his agitation. "What honor has the guild when rule-breakers walk unbloodied?" he shouted.

Serano spun to face them. "And who of you attack the innocent?" He slammed his fist on the table. "And why?"

"A man who supports the wicked," Vanu said, "is no longer innocent."

Serano pointed a shaking finger at the man. "And who gives you the authority to judge?"

"Judging is not the point here." Kusik rounded the corner and stood behind his own chair. "Actions are. Who you judge and what you judge are your own concerns—until you act against others because of them."

Rodani sat still amidst the volley of voices, fighting the burning in his gut. Someone had attacked his partner. This miasma of malice was widening to engulf the undeserving. Only Arimeso had the wisdom needed here, and the authority. This snarling pack of poridi would shout themselves hoarse and cease only when night drew to dawn. Only a tight grip on his temper kept him from screaming at the idiocy of the inflexible and the obstinate.

Far too many noisy minutes later, Rodani found himself immured in the haven of Cara's rooms, and Cara's presence. His midsection still burned. Leaving the room had been another Darbati's choice: go quickly and be deemed a coward or leave last and be forced to listen to the dregs of the arguments.

"A'tem," Deremic called from the doorway. Both Rodani and Cara turn to face him. "The taso calls you to her office, a'tem."

Rodani put his elbows on the worktable and his hands to his mouth. He'd only just sat down.

"Aisu?"

He was silent for a moment, then pushed himself away from the table. "There was...some talk in the meeting. This may be a continuation."

"You look worried."

He looked down at her. "And you are discourteous to mention it, kia."

Her eyes widened at his reprimand. As she bent her head in contrition, he swept his fingers along the base of her neck, under the clip. She would know that touch, he thought, know it for a reassurance.

Rather than leave through her door, he took the servants' hallway and the door nearest the stairs. But it availed him nothing. Naremit and Toranel peeled themselves off the wall and followed him into the stairwell, taunting him with whispered threats and insults. Irritated, he stopped at the landing and looked back at them, clenching his fists in a rhythm of warning. Insults to his own self he could swallow without choking. Wine bottles may be replaced. But insults to Cara reddened his vision with a wrath he rarely felt since his youth. His tormenters stood on the steps above his head, blank-eyed and waiting. Rodani pattered down the steps and made his way to the central quarters, defiant footsteps echoing behind him the entire distance.

He took a fierce grip on his temper and greeted the taso properly. Misplaced rage in this room was an error in judgment he couldn't afford.

At her motion, he sat. Kusik, to his relief, was not in attendance.

Arimeso studied him, calm and remote on the surface, but with an intensity unnatural to her normal demeanor.

"Even I see the marks on your face and hands, te'oto. This must stop."

Rodani splayed his hands in his lap. "When my keso does nothing in my defense, there is little I can do on my own."

"He has been talking to them privately."

"And that has accomplished what, my taso?"

She lowered her gaze, admittance to the truth in his question. "Less than you would wish, I am certain. Why do you not discipline your lessers?"

"I am outnumbered at every turn."

"What of your partner?"

Rodani tossed the question with a flick of his fingers. "I know his opinion of what I have done."

"You must ask him, anyway." Arimeso tapped her nail on the desk in emphasis. "You cannot allow this insubordination to continue."

"And what measure of partnership dare I claim if I must force Serano to do something he should wish to do—and will not?"

"I confess to a loss for suggestions, Rodani. I have never been a guardian."

Rodani stared at the worn tips of his boots. "Never have I been quite so far outside the bounds of my society, a'Taso." His gaze traveled up to her face. "And never has the distance been more worthy."

"What does a'Cara say?"

"She believes my injuries and agitation are Kusik's deeds."

Surprise flowed into Arimeso's face. "And you do not correct her error?"

"I do not discuss it with her at all, a'Taso," Rodani said. "If she knew the extent of the abuse directed at me, her anger would create more problems."

"Why?"

"Because she would wish to defend me, and she cannot. Her frustrated demands for justice would bedevil us both."

Arimeso laid her arms on her desk and clasped all dozen digits into a ball of tension. "I will ask again, Rodani. Do you wish me to put an end to this? You seem not to have the strength to do it yourself."

"No," he said with heavy emphasis. *Good Goddess and consort, no.*

"As you wish, child." Arimeso waved her fingers in the direction of the door.

Rodani rose and bowed his way out, then checked the communications room carefully. Imal was in residence this time, but studiously ignored Rodani's presence in favor of the task at his hand. Rodani stood in the doorway, then poked his head out and looked both ways. The hall seemed clear of people—of guardians, he corrected himself as the weaver and her apprentice passed in the cross-hall.

Rodani sped down the corridor in the fastest walk he could manage and still hold to his dignity. But as he neared the base of the staircase, he heard a door open behind him. He headed up the stairs at a frenetic pace. Rapid boot steps marched up behind him. A heavy tread: *Naremit*, he thought. What attack method would it be this time?

He sped over the landing and up the second set. As he reached the top, Toranel rushed from the side hall and crashed into him. They fell to the floor in a tangle of legs and arms.

Stung by his taso's words, Rodani was ready this time. In moments, he was on top, pinning Toranel underneath him. Rodani drew his knife and pressed it against her neck. Heavy steps neared his head.

"Stop, Naremit," he shouted, voice hoarse with effort, "or I will slit her throat!" When the footsteps refused to move away, Rodani spun them both. Now he was on the bottom, his legs curled around Toranel's knees, the knife steady at her throat. "Cease this, or I will end it now."

Naremit backed up a pace, then another. Rodani jabbed the knife tip into Toranel's skin. A dribble of blood welled out. "Get out of here. Out of my sight!"

Naremit started down the steps, then stopped. "If you kill her, I will set you aflame and watch you burn, traitor."

"And hearing!" Rodani shouted. The steps continued downward. "Now what?" he growled at his captive. "If I let you live, will you walk away? Or attack?"

Toranel's breaths were the only movement. Through the haft of his knife, Rodani felt her swallow. "I will walk."

With a sharp movement, Rodani released the woman's arm, grabbing her hair instead. He pulled the knife from her skin but kept it at eye level. "Up," he commanded. "Slowly."

Toranel rose stiffly, stumbling, caught by her hair and a ready knife. As Rodani let her hair slide through his fingers, Toranel spun sideways and launched herself at him, batting Rodani's knife away. Rodani grabbed Toranel and crouched, letting her momentum lead them. He planted a boot in her gut as he sat on his heel, and with all the rage he could muster, flipped her over his body and sent her flying into the stairwell behind him. As he spun up on his knees, the woman hit hard. She tumbled downward, limbs akimbo, and came to a rest on the landing, looking like a rag doll.

A shout of rage thundered up the stairwell. Rodani stood and leaned against the wall, watching as Naremit checked her for movement. Rodani's breaths slowed, then his heartbeat. He retrieved his knife as another set of boots pounded up the steps.

Rodani groaned. Focusing inward, he prepared for a new attack. But the boots stopped at the landing. He looked over the rail.

Serano hovered over Toranel's comatose body. He checked for a pulse, then ran up the second steps. They met at the top, hovered face-to-face. As Serano stared at the knife in his hand, Rodani slipped it into its sheath, somewhat bemused that it wasn't already there. Below, Naremit's anxious voice 'commed for the healers.

Serano grabbed his arm. Rodani allowed himself to be pulled toward their quarters. He could hear clamoring from Cara's room. Her strident voice, Deremic, Hamman. Iraimin? All talking over one another. But Serano took priority this time.

Rodani collapsed into the nearest chair. Serano paced in front of him, surreptitiously checking him out.

"Are you hurt?"

"Nothing to mention."

"How long has this been going on?"

"Since we returned from the cave."

"And no one puts a stop to it?"

Rodani turned to face the table and leaned his head in his hands. "Tem'u, I need you."

Serano stopped his pacing. "No."

It hurt, expected or not. All the way down to the depths, it hurt. "I cannot protect both her and myself at the same time. I need your help."

"And who will protect me now?"

Rodani closed his eyes against a new wave of pain. "I am sorry they have targeted you, tem'u."

"My answer remains."

"Please."

Serano put his fists on his hips and leaned forward. "I have been begging you for months to stop this insanity, Rodani. Do you listen? No."

"And I have been trying to explain to you for months that this is reason at its very highest. But will you learn? No."

"Learn?" he shouted. "Oh, I have learned. That your bedamned adashi has no logic, no patience, no restraint, very little courtesy, less modesty, and the arrogance to chide everyone else for their failings."

Rodani slapped the tabletop with his palm. "And that is why you see insanity, Serano. Because you see only through your own eyes, hear only with your own ears, and relegate everyone else's knowledge to the prattle of children."

"I tire of your insults!"

"And I tire of your dismissal of everything and everyone who is different from you."

"If that were true, I would have broken this partnership years ago, Rodani."

Rodani rubbed his temples in slow circles. "Will you leave us to their mercy, tem'u?"

"There are other guardians in this house."

"No one else I can trust to guard my back."

"Then you have a problem, do you not?"

"Tem'u," Rodani whispered.

Serano stepped up behind him and leaned over. "Leave her."

"I cannot."

"You can. Give this duty to someone else. Hand it back to Arimeso with your direst apologies. Accept your punishment and be cleansed."

Rodani bent his head. "I need her as much as she needs me."

Silence. He felt Serano pull away, felt the distance like a cold wind at his neck.

"Fool."

Steps moved off. The door opened and shut with a painful finality. Rodani laid his head down, cradled on his arms. Emotions welled up from the depths and began circulating in his brain. Fear. Failure. Humiliation. Anger. Loss. His head pounded and his eyes throbbed. Life was spinning out of control, and he was headed for a cliff's edge.

Kia.

He stumbled to the door. Aches in his body and pain in his head stole his balance. She would see. She would guess, and he would hear of it. *Goddess*, he thought, as he grabbed the door handle. *If you're there, help me. When no one else will, help me.*

If there was a reply, his headache drowned it out.

When he walked into Cara's workroom, a cold silence fell like a cloak of snow. He took a glance at the waiting bodies. "A drink, please, a'sel," he said. Deremic moved to obey.

"A'tem," Iraimin began. Rodani held up his palm, and she stopped.

"I'll tell him," Cara whispered. The painter inclined her head, took a long look at him, and left the room.

Cara waited in a silence he was reluctant to break. Rodani made his way to the couch in the study and lowered himself carefully into it.

She followed more slowly, likely digesting his mood. *Please be it so.* He needed no more confrontations. As he leaned back and stretched out, she left the room, only to return with a wet cloth and his drink. She set it down and began to wipe his face carefully. It felt cool and pleasant to his ravaged senses. He shut his eyes.

Cara broke her silence, as he knew she would. "If I ever get a chance, I will kill him, aisu. I promise you."

"Kusik is not your concern, kia. You saved his life. He will not take yours. Or mine. Not now."

"I don't trust that."

"You think I lie?"

"No. I think he's not trustworthy." Cara folded the washcloth and moved down his neck.

"Drink, please."

She reached behind and brought it around to him, undoing his shirt as he sipped. "How many new bruises do you have?"

"A few."

"Do you need an ice bag?"

"I think not."

She inspected what she could see of his chest, wiping it down with the cloth. "Don't tell me I can't kill him, Rodani."

"You wish to start a war?"

"No. I'll wait for a good reason."

"You could have let him die at the cave."

Her face fell into mask. Her eyes focused on nothing he could see. "I thought about it."

Rodani reached up and drew his fingers across her cheek. "How long?"

Her lips curled into shapes he couldn't interpret. "Not very. But oh, I thought it."

"You are not a killer, kia."

She glared at him, then took his hand and began to wipe it, long slow swaths down his fingers, the top side and then the palm. "Oh," she said. "I forgot to tell you."

"Yes?"

"Iraimin thinks she's being followed."

THIRTY-THREE

Naremit stormed out of the clinic, every nerve in his body alight with outrage. *He was going to pay, he was.* That indecent temichi with his incendiary affinity was going to pay for every bruise and scrape he had counted on Toranel's body. *How dare Rodani hurt her? How dare he defend himself against punishment for his improprieties?*

Naremit's gut knotted in revulsion, as it did every time he thought of those two together. He wouldn't even allow the vision to coalesce in his mind before he shoved it off into the darkness where it belonged. Why the taso allowed such a travesty, he couldn't fathom. It made no sense.

Then a thought curled through his mind—a thought so blasphemous that it stopped him cold on the stone.

The taso—the taso he'd sworn allegiance to, the taso in whose hands he'd placed his very honor—made no sense. Her decisions were becoming faulty. *She* was faulty.

Naremit stepped out of foot traffic and leaned against the wall to concentrate without shaking. His teachers in the guild had spoken well of Arimeso, saying she was firm without being abusive. Her houseful of artisans didn't make for a heavy duty, only a middling one.

But these recent decisions, they were so far afield of propriety that she seemed—ill, somehow.

All the more reason, he thought. He pulled out his com. "Vanu."

***

Two days later, Cara crawled out of her bed, leaving Rodani sleeping. She dressed, then padded to the study and built up the fire. Not yet did she feel any spring warmth, despite Rodani's gentle teasing. She wrapped herself in the quilt and sat down to write, filling up her journal with several days' revelations.

Breakfast passed into midmorning before Rodani showed up in the doorway.

"How do you feel, aisu?"

He let his masked expression drop. The corners of his mouth turned up. "My head has decided to stop hurting."

"It has?"

Rodani walked in and lowered himself onto the couch beside her.

"And the rest of your body?"

"Much better," he said. "Only a few bruises. Little that a bit of stretching would not ease."

"You heal quickly."

"Or the guild teaches us to ignore the least parts."

"Or both." She ran her hand down his arm. "I could massage your muscles. Warm them up and make them feel better."

Rodani's pupils pulsed. "I am not certain I am ready for a ride." He leaned his head toward hers. "But we could try."

Cara chuckled. "No, aisu." She patted the couch cushions beneath them. "Lay down, and I'll rub your back and legs."

The look of confusion and plaintive longing on his face touched a chord. A peal of laughter erupted from somewhere deep inside her. She took his hand. "Lay down."

As Rodani lowered himself, a hail of bullets splintered the shutters behind them. The cacophony echoed around them, fire on all sides. Before Cara could scream, Rodani grabbed her and dived for the edge of the bookcase against the wall, out of the way of the line of fire. They fell to the floor in a tangle of bodies, Cara on the bottom.

With a rough jerk, Rodani pulled out his pistol and spun to face the window. He fired at the broken window, Cara trapped behind him. Return fire pelted the couch and spat and ricocheted in the fireplace to their left. Rodani scrabbled in his jacket pocket for the 'com.

"Temichin! Temichin!" he called into the fragile lifeline. "Cara's rooms! Cara!" He shoved it back into an outer pocket and shouted at Cara as he fired again.

"Kishata, Cara! Back me!" He fired another shot. "And watch the door!"

Bullets answered his shouts. Cara pulled her gun from his belt and took off the safety, cocking it. All but paralyzed, she forced her mind to face what had overwhelmed even Rodani. Already, the shutters were shredded.

Cara leaned left and aimed her gun in the general direction of her workroom, then back to the deadly window. Back to the workroom. Three windows broke the safety of her small suite of rooms. Did she dare?

There. A shadow? A hint of movement? Cara stiffened in terror while another volley of shots rang out in front of her. Rodani pulled out one magazine and slammed in another. Cara leaned past him and fired into the study.

Their first assailant poked the muzzle of his gun through the broken shutters and fired low. Only the bookcase prevented him from shattering Rodani's skull. He fired back, convulsively ducking down as far as his tall frame would allow. Behind him, Cara gasped as his movement pinned her more tightly to the wall.

As she squirmed, a dark shape appeared around the doorway and raised his gun. She brought the gun up and fired as his muzzle spat in her direction.

"Fire in the workroom!" she screamed.

"Keep shooting! And keep down!"

Down any farther and she'd be crawling on the floor. She tucked her head and fired again, preventively, unseeing. Her arms trembled in fear, her hands clenched in a death grip. Rodani kept up a slow but steady stream of shots, keeping their shooter in the window from getting any good looks.

Menace number two stuck his head around the corner again. Cara took three quick shots in succession, making him jerk back. The gun reappeared without the head this time and fired through the couch into the wall above her.

Gunsmoke began to fill the room. Rodani increased his rate of fire as the laws of statistics worked against them. Cara took potshots into the workroom, hoping to keep her opponent too busy to aim.

Shots peppered the wall above them and careened off in chaotic and dangerous trajectories. Rodani fired back, then jerked and yelped in sudden pain. He twisted another inch further into the corner and returned fire.

Cara froze at his cry. Her heart hammered. Rodani's body was squeezing the breath out of her. All but deafened by shots and shock, she barely flinched when another stream of bullets came out of the workroom. They were dead. They were already dead. She went cold with the knowledge and prepared to crawl over to the base of the couch, closer to the door as more shots erupted from the outer rooms. If she were going to be killed, she wanted to take someone with her.

She fired into the workroom and tensed for her move...when a voice boomed out.

"Allies! Hold fire! Hold fire!"

Allies? Whose allies? Those outside the window? Was she being offered captivity? She didn't care. She fired off a few more, and yanked out another mag as the last pull of the trigger gave her a sharp click.

"Cara," Rodani whispered. But his next words were pre-empted by a shot from the workroom, adding another hail of splinters onto the floor.

Cara shoved the mag into her gun and cocked the trigger. In front of her, Rodani fired repeatedly through the tatters

"Who are you?" she shouted.

"Timan, damn you! Hold fire!"

Ignoring Rodani's warning hiss, she slithered over to the back of the couch, leaving room for him to scoot further into relative safety. As Rodani reloaded and Timan took fresh aim, Cara shot through the broken shutters where she thought the man was hiding. A scream of pain proved her right. Maybe he'd fall. The ledge was pitifully narrow outside her windows.

The room quieted. The ringing in Cara's ears went from a barely perceptible tinnitus to a continuous crashing of cymbals. She wanted desperately to run to Rodani to make sure he was going to live. But no one had given the all clear. It wouldn't do to make a mistake now when survival looked to be a strong possibility. She stayed put, eyes glued to the shattered shutters.

The quiet of unreality that comes in at the end of violence settled over her, and the shakes began. Cara stole a glance in Rodani's direction, watching as he flexed his arm in judgment of its capabilities. He caught her glance before returning his attention to the window.

She sighed deeply and let her head hang, but her heart raged inside her chest. Her hands wouldn't grip the gun; it dangled loosely in her fingers.

Shouts erupted from outside, orders given and acknowledged, then someone's 'com buzzed.

"Two," Timan replied.

"All clear east," came a welcome piece of information.

"Clear north," came another.

"Clear south," came on its heels.

Cara's breath quickened in anticipation. She wanted this over. Done with! Her eyes roamed over the splinters of wood and glass shards that littered the floor in front of her and, no doubt, the rest of the room. A noise behind the shutters brought her heart rate and her gun back up.

"Tsss," Rodani hissed again. "Clear south," he reminded her. "Safety."

Cara pushed the safety catch and pocketed the Kishata.

The 'com crackled with renewed static. "Clear west." Timan stepped into the study and looked around. "Ninety-nine," he replied, then flipped another switch. "All guild; all clear. All guild; all clear." He turned to someone out of view and put in an order for the physician.

Cara heaved herself up off the floor and scooted over to Rodani, who had holstered his gun and was studying his arm. The room became crowded with black-clad guardians, as nearly everyone who had answered the call came to investigate it. Ignoring Timan's continued instructions and answers, Cara bent down to get a closer look at Rodani's upper arm. It looked wickedly painful, but he reassured her it didn't go deeply into muscle, and nothing but a few stitches would be needed. Cara was dubious, but content to wait for the physician.

"You are not hurt?" he asked in turn.

"I'm not. Do you want it wrapped?" she asked quietly.

"No."

"It's still bleeding," she noted.

"By the time you wrap it, kia," he said, "Baldar will be here and be forced to unwrap it."

Cara looked around for anything else to occupy her empty hands. Anything to keep herself from thinking too deeply. Her place of safety, her sanctuary where she and Rodani could be themselves, had been violated. Was there anywhere else for them? Or would she be sent home, mateless?

She looked up at Timan, who was holding court in the middle of the study. Other guardians inspected the shutters and picked up spent shells. Rodani rose with a jerk and a hand on the wall for support. The look on his face brought cold and clammy back to her skin.

"Naremit?" he said to Timan. "Naremit?!" Pupils that had begun to constrict to a more normal width dilated again. He strode to the window, knocked some glass shards away, and stuck his head out, circling it for a 360° view with a long pause at the ground below. As Cara rose to join him, he pulled back in and turned slowly, coming face to face with Timan. His expression would melt ice in the frozen north wastelands.

Timan inclined his head slightly to the side, acknowledging, maybe, the legitimacy of Rodani's anger. Rodani began to pace the room, a killer thwarted of a neck to put his hands around. Cara eyed his unusually agitated movements with growing misgivings, wondering what new threat had set him off. She peered out the window. Three people were on the ground, two kneeling, one supine. As she watched, the third man was rolled over and handcuffed. With a start, Cara recognized the man as one who had accompanied Serano and Timan on their chase through the woods for her.

Gods of the deep night. Their attacker was guild. No wonder Rodani was going volcanic. The man's escorts brought him to his feet and led him around the manor's corner. A rope hung to her right, swaying with the movement of a climber Cara recognized as Lanata. Glass fragments sparkled on the ledge in sunlight, a rainbow glitter's violent genesis.

Cara turned back to her room in time to see Rodani's pacing interrupted by the physician. She joined them, needing reassurance for Rodani, and having an obsessive desire to do something. After a poking and prodding inspection, Baldar pronounced it little more than a flesh wound. Rodani held still and expressionless while Baldar took the requisite stitches.

Cara couldn't watch. She went to the end table and grabbed the wastebasket that had been so thoughtfully decorated by someone, crouched down and began picking up glass and wood fragments, placing them with some care in the bottom of the basket. Hands still shaking with the dump of adrenaline, Cara began to grab and toss the pieces in with an audible clink and clatter. Soon she was scrabbling around on all fours, throwing detritus with a vengeance. Cut, she sucked a breath through her teeth and licked at the upwelling of blood. A black-clad body crouched down beside her.

"Others will do that, kia," Rodani said.

She continued to toss glass and wood, heedless of the cuts they might make in her already scarred fingers.

"Kia, stop."

The tossing became violent, trash she'd already collected, jumping in response to the force behind her throws. Rodani reached out and caught her wrist. The crashing stopped.

"What do you do?"

Cara blinked rapidly, tugging on her captive arm. But Rodani refused to release her. Her thoughts skimmed and skipped over the situation and her ignorance of all that had gone on to provoke it. "Something is very wrong, aisu."

Rodani flexed his fingers on her arm and shook her gently. "The wrong is not in you."

Cara shifted her weight and flailed her unfettered fist at Rodani, who caught it. "Kusik wants me sent home, and he's willing to maim me to do it. Your sister wants me sent home, and she's willing to destroy your contentment to do it. Half the guardians here want to kill me, and probably you, too."

Rodani fought her struggles, pulling downward on her arms to keep her in a crouch. "They do not understand."

She clenched her hands, fingernails digging into the still tender scars. "And it doesn't make a stinking stable's worth of difference, does it, aisu?" She railed at him, heedless of onlookers; or possibly because of them. "We could talk until Temi comes down and taps you on the back, and nothing would change! Only Arimeso can see what we have."

Cara stopped for breath and made the mistake of staring into Rodani's eyes. Deepest black pupils were round with emotion, only a hint of violet ringing them. He stared back unblinking, distress in every line and angle of his face. She tugged against him fitfully and with waning strength.

"Do you wish to return home?" Rodani asked. He was quiet. Too quiet.

"No!" she said. "I wish to be left alone to live! With you," she added plaintively. "Human or not, I should have the right to exist."

"Kia, if most did not agree with you, your room would not now be filled with guardians, and we both would be dead."

"And you, the right to make your own decisions."

"And therein lies the problem."

Her gaze traveled to Rodani's bandaged arm. It shamed her, this carrying on like a child, and he was the one who had taken a bullet in her defense.

"Did Baldar give you pain medication?"

"It is not needed," he replied. "You are unhurt, and I will heal. However, we do have a right to our tempers."

She gave in to the calm his words always brought out in her. "Thank you, aisu," she said, heartfelt. And before she forgot: "Thank you to all who assisted us," she added, taking a good look around for the first time at all the people who were watching Rodani cope with his ill-mannered and temperamental bedmate.

And standing in the doorway, taking in every word, were Kusik and Arimeso. Cara hung her head between her hands and taught Rodani some more adult-level Cene'l. It never failed.

But maybe they needed to hear it said.

Rodani pulled her to her feet. They bowed to and greeted the taso, as did Baldar, who was leaving on another call. Cara's fear of Kusik moved into her brain, shoving aside the disaster she'd just survived. Damn her verbal indiscretions. If her humanity didn't get her killed, her mouth would. It didn't matter that the whole household knew about Kusik's hatred of her and had learned of it even before her arrival. No self-respecting Selandu would voice it in public.

But Arimeso remained silent, as did the keso. She raked the two survivors up and down with her cold stare, then ran it around the room slowly, as if digesting the destruction, or committing it to permanent storage in her memory banks. Maybe there was nothing left to say. Or maybe she was saving it up for a private censure, or a public one.

Cara shuddered. And shuddered again as Kusik fixed a stare on her face that ruffled the hackles on the back of her neck. Security first with a missing forearm. And as cold as they come. She knew there was no love lost between them, despite the fact that she'd saved his life.

Without a word, they left.

Cara went through the doorway to see the damage that had been done to her workroom. She stepped through with Rodani at her heels and stopped dead at the sight of a body on the floor. Still uncovered, the man's dead eyes stared up at the ceiling, his chest a pool of blood.

"Enemy? Or ally?" she asked Rodani.

"Enemy," he said through gritted teeth.

Cara closed her own eyes and turned away. Enough violent afterimages haunted her dreams already. She concentrated on her tools of trade, desk, frame and its quilt, and her shelves of fabric. All seemed thankfully undamaged. But the man had indeed shot his way in. Glass and wood splinters crunched under her feet.

"Exchange those slippers for outdoor shoes, kia," Rodani told her, evidently noting the same sound.

It being good advice, she did as he bade, only to come across a second body in her bedroom. Another man, lying on his stomach between the window and her bed. Another broken window, another ruined Selandu. Cara cringed.

Timan had done his work well, she thought as she exchanged shoes. Two, to his credit. Cara, and even Rodani, pinned as they were, had not managed any. She left the man and turned back toward Rodani, only to notice the holes in her bedsheets and the quilt she'd brought from home.

Bullet holes.

They'd have been dead in each other's arms.

Cara fled the room.

But there was no place to retreat. More bullet holes came to her sight, this time on the wall and the door to the hall. Her attackers had planned well. Success and failure had come down to a matter of a few minutes, minutes they'd spent debating instead of...her memory shied away from the holes in the bed behind her.

"There is no reason to stay here during clean up," Rodani said upon her return. "There is too little to see."

"And too much." The bed drew her eyes with indecent curiosity, an image of bloody death too easy to envision. Holes. There would be her chest. There, Rodani's head. There... Cara spun around and leaned into the wall.

Rodani motioned to Hamman, ordered two drinks to be delivered across the hall, then pulled Cara toward the door.

"Rodani."

He turned.

"Who fired the Kishata?" Timan asked.

"Cara."

"Your training must not have been as worthless as we thought. She got a piece of both Garidemu," he gestured to the inert form on the floor at his feet, "and Naremit."

Rodani bowed to his biso, then tugged on her arm. "We will be in my rooms if we are needed, a'Timan."

"Shouldn't you stay and see if there is anything else to be done?" Cara asked as they settled into Rodani's couch.

"Normally, yes," he replied. "But my duty is still to your safety, even when that duty seems to be shirking duty."

"Shirking? No one had better call what you just did *shirking*."

Rodani smiled wanly. "We have earned the right to rest while others clean and repair." He relaxed into the cushions and stared into the cold fireplace.

"Aisu, you should lay down," she chided the worn guardian. "Is your bedroom safe?"

"Yes. There is someone still on the roof."

"Go to bed."

"I am well enough."

"You'll rest more properly in bed."

"And it will be more difficult to attend to duties if I am pulled from a deep sleep," he said, his voice dropping into cool tones.

She took the hint.

The final tally for the day was two dead, two wounded, and one frightened nearly out of her human wits.

Twice Rodani left her, for short periods that anxiety stretched into hours. Dinner was a quiet affair, broken mostly by the clinks and chinks of tableware, glass, and plate. As night drew close, he tucked her into his bed and crawled in beside her. She stretched out against him, breathing in his scent, fervently wishing that her dreams behave.

But the first time Rodani woke her, she cried out as her muscles unlocked from the dream state to flash at her unseen attacker. The second time she woke with a pounding heart and sore muscles from the vision of dead men with glassy eyes and bloodied chests, and fingers that groped for her. For the third time that night, she sought Rodani's comfort, waking his light sleep with the weight of her arm across his chest.

She woke the next morning alone. Someone stirred in the shared living room. She rose from the bed.

Serano turned to her. "He is across the hall."

Humph. "And bright morn to you, as well."

His pupils narrowed, but he only reached for the doorknob. "Come." Cara followed him across to her rooms and stood in the doorway in abject dismay.

They'd bricked up her windows.

Rodani's voice rose from her bedroom, sharp with ire. "From what dingy storeroom did you drag that? Take it away and bring back something more suitable to the taso's guest."

The heavy thump of a mattress followed his words. Two servants carried it past her and down the hall. Rodani appeared in the doorway. Something in his expression closed down when he saw her.

"Kia." He shut the door behind her, then double-checked that it was locked.

"Rodani, how can I see outside? I need sunlight."

His eyes roamed the walls, the worktable, the floor. "Forgive me, kia. It was necessary."

"Necessary? You've turned it into a prison."

He turned toward her. "I have made you a safe haven."

A safe jail. At least before, she could feel the sun's warmth, smell the fresh air. Now even that was denied to her.

Rodani continued. "We cannot make someone live on the roof so that you can look outside, kia."

Why not? she thought. *I'm the damned taso's damned human guest.*

The door's lock rattled, and Timan stepped in. "Rodani," he said.

Rodani inclined his head and followed his second out the door. It shut behind them with a bleak finality.

THIRTY-FOUR

Rodani closed his eyes. *Calm,* he willed himself before walking into the guild meeting room. *Breathe.* The intonation hardly worked better than it did when he said it to Cara. But something in the cold, clawing anxiety that wrapped him opened up as he thought of her. Again, she'd surprised him with her courage, her defense of his safety, as well as her own. The rage that had overtaken her was his as well—the aftermath of treachery and death, the shattered illusion of safety at home.

The meeting room was a riot of voices: shouting, blending and separating, talking over one another like a child's game of slap-the-hands. Rodani hesitated in the doorway.

"Where is the right and wrong here?"

"Wrong from both sides."

"Forget wrong, where is honor?"

"How could they—?"

"How could *he*?"

"Why did she have a gun?"

"Some of those shots were hers."

"How could anyone blame Naremit? First fault is worst fault!"

"What will be Rodani's punishment?"

"Why? They were defending themselves."

"Defending their dishonor, you mean."

"Naremit should be released!"

"No, he should not!"

The rage that Rodani had so recently buried crept up his spine. Loud-mouthed, small-minded people, most of them. Only Timan seemed divorced from the cacophony. And Misheiki.

Rodani strode into the room to stand behind his accustomed chair, back against the wall. He crossed his arms and stared in unfocused attention at the milling bodies around the table. His bedmate wasn't here to defend herself, so his task was doubled. *Bedmate. Au, the term hardly seemed adequate anymore.*

Focus, fool, he chided himself as seats were taken and silence fell. Toranel rocked back and forth in her seat. A moment's sympathy was all Rodani had the inclination for. She wasn't the one with a bullet hole in her arm, or her bed shot up.

"Chair broken, Rodani?" Kusik said.

Rodani glanced at his keso, then ran a hot gaze past his fellow guardians. "No, a'Keso. I will stand." As the silence filled his ears, he felt, rather than saw, Kusik's stare.

"To what?"

"To my right to face you all and ask why no one knew, why no one spoke, why no one tried to prevent this. Violence in the guild should stop at fists." He took a breath. "I can guess Naremit's reasons. I can recite them in my sleep. But a failure to prevent is still a failure. And a necessary death is still a tragedy. I am stalked and beaten by the very people whose backs I help watch."

Imal spoke first. "You should know the problem, Rodani. You have broken one of the guild's oldest rules, and not one iota of punishment have you received. It is a slap in the face to all of us."

"Our keso has already addressed this," Rodani replied.

"Not to my satisfaction."

Kusik leaned forward. "What satisfaction do you require? Whatever does or does not go on between this guardian and his adashi, the taso is aware of it, and has chosen not to interfere. Nor does she allow me to do so."

"That is wrong," Imal said.

"So, tell me. Is disobeying a taso's direct order a greater or lesser error than breaking any other ancient rule?"

Imal remained silent.

"Perhaps you could take your dissatisfaction to the taso?"

He only looked away.

Rodani leaned forward from his place at the wall. "No one here has the right to act against me, because the taso is not offended." He swept his hand over the heads at the table. "You may think anything you wish. But it stops there. We all took vows to the guild, then took vows to the taso that bind us further."

Pavanec pounded his fist on the tabletop. His pupils were slit and glowing, his face a rictus of anger. "There has always been conflict between honor to the guild and honor to a taso. That is nothing new.

You chose your side, we choose ours. Rule-breaking with permission from her is still rule-breaking. And we have a right to be offended."

Rodani's heart rate climbed rapidly. "You have that right," he shot back. "But you do not have a right to act on it."

"You killed a guardian!" Pavanec shouted as he stood up.

"I did not, actually. And he tried to kill us!"

"Because you break guild rules and dally with an alien!"

Rodani leaned back against the wall and slipped his hands behind his hips. "And now we hear the real problem. Yes? Even Cara sees it. Fear of the unknown. And disgust of it."

"No," Serano countered. "The real problem is you, Rodani. As it has often been. You are stubborn and misguided. Always you walk your own path, regardless of rules and the authority behind them. Few of us wished for the human's presence here, but we were willing to abide while she kept her place."

Rodani's eyes widened at the open censure from his partner. "She is still in her *place*," Rodani spat.

"And you crawled down into it and sullied yourself, taking us with you. You dirty us. You offend us. You make us ashamed to uphold our honor among others."

Rodani took a deep breath, but nothing stilled the fury inside him. "No one shames you but yourself, a'tem. And it is I and my adashi who were almost killed. Not you. Not anyone else here."

"And if she were only your adashi," Serano said with rising heat, "we would not be speaking thus! I cannot believe how far you have allowed yourself to fall. Do you care for nothing but your own pleasure?"

Rodani took a step toward his chair, his arms itching to reach out. "How dare you speak to me of pleasure? That is all you seek!"

"But I seek it from my own kind."

"I cannot believe the ignorance I am hearing," Rodani replied.

"Ignorance of what?" Pavanec said in white heat. "Guild rules? Social proprieties?"

Rodani folded his arms and stared at him in a fierce focus. "I obey my taso. The people who attacked us did not."

Kusik shifted in his chair. A series of creaks erupted. "Stop."

All eyes turned to the head of the table.

"Rodani, sit down."

Rodani looked at his boots. "A'Keso, I have no wish to sit at a table where I do not know who to trust."

"Sit. Down."

Rodani swallowed heavily, unfolded his arms, and lowered himself into his chair.

Kusik inclined his head at Timan, who opened a side door. He went inside and brought out Naremit, gagged and handcuffed. Timan stood him up at the side wall as Arimeso and Chendal walked in. Kusik bowed to both and gave up his seat to his taso. Chendal took Timan's.

Toranel's rocking motion became ragged. The lips she was biting were reddened.

Timan swept the gag off of Naremit's mouth. Immediately the stable gates opened, and a flood of refuse poured out.

"Why am I here and your real traitor is there? Why?" The chains clanked as he tried to gesture. "I am not your enemy, a'Taso, a'Keso. He is!"

Arimeso folded her hands on the table, calm, as always. "A'tem, you are hereby accused of acts of perfidy against your taso and your house, in an attempt to murder a fellow guardian and an alien guest, a gesture which brought death to two of your conspirators. Confirm or deny."

"I deny it, a'Taso. I deny it with every breath that is in me. Why do you refuse to see who—"

In a flash, Timan stuffed the gag back into Naremit's mouth. He glanced over to Arimeso, waiting for a signal. She waved her fingers. Timan removed the gag.

"A'tem," she continued, "I was hoping for something more coherent from you, something that would explain your actions."

As Naremit drew breath, his face formed sharp lines of rage. Rodani looked away. Closing his eyes would be a dire offense to the taso and temaso when someone's life was at stake, let alone a guild member. So would stuffing his fingers in his ears. But his immunity to Naremit's venom had run out weeks ago. *Goddess, let this be over soon.* At least Arimeso hadn't changed her mind about their affinity. Nor had Chendal forced any confrontation, rightful though it might be to his eyes.

And where was Shisa? Was she still so offended by his proclivities that she refused this attendance? A pang erupted in his midsection. They had been so close when they were young. Why couldn't she see him? Him, not his faults, not his misfit status among their people.

And Serano. His partner sat across from him, a chasm separating them. Would he lose them both? Could Cara take both their places, sister and partner?

No. An affinity bond was not a calculation. Math had no function here. He would gain and lose as the goddess—*No*, to that as well. There was no sense on that path. There never had been.

Naremit screeched and wailed in the background. Chendal droned, Arimeso insisted. Shisa entered the room. Then, abruptly, all was silent.

"Rodani," Arimeso said. "As it was you and your adashi who were put in death's way, it will be your duty to finish this."

His face went to mask. *No, please.* He inclined his head. "A'Taso."

Toranel whimpered.

***

Cara looked around. For the most part, her rooms went back to normal: shutters replaced, new mattress on its way, patches in the stone where bullets had sent chips flying. The quilt in her frame had escaped any noticeable damage, thankfully; the second assailant had aimed for where her head and chest would've been, not her hands.

Deremic accompanied her as she checked the rest of her belongings, temporary reassurance that all was well. She rested on the couch for a while, poked the logs in the fire, watched while servants brought in the newest mattress, and Hamman remade her bed. But the moment she sat in front of the former window at her quilt frame, a prickly sensation erupted between her shoulder blades and crawled up the back of her neck into her scalp. She could not sit there, bricks or not.

Could *not.*

She slid off the chair and pulled it noisily across the stone to the corner nearest her study, then did the same with the frame. Deremic watched with bland curiosity. She sat back down with an emphatic thump and waited for another chill to erupt.

There was none.

"Problem?" Deremic said, as he studied the necklace Rodani had been sanding yesterday.

"Not now." Cara picked up the needle and began to stitch, then yelped as something stuck her. She yanked her hand back to see a dot of blood on the outside of her little finger.

Deremic came over to investigate.

"There's glass in it!" she said, pointing. Cara sat back in the chair and stared dejectedly. A magnifier and tweezers would take hours, or days. It wasn't quite to a washable state. And she had nowhere to brush it off and no brush to brush with.

"Deremic, I do need your help." She unrolled it and held it out. "As I'm not allowed a window anymore," she added with annoyance, "please take this, hold it out a window, and shake it. Shake the shards out of it and bring it back."

A bit nonplussed at the order, Deremic made the trip, after a promise she would stay meekly behind in her room. When he returned, she rolled the quilt back onto its frame.

Rodani stepped into the room. Shisa arrived behind him, solid and silent.

"Why did you move the frame, kia?" he asked, picking up the necklace.

She ran her hand lightly over the quilt top. "It was very uncomfortable sitting in front of the window," she told him. "Or what used to be one."

"It is bricked," he said with a side glance, as if to confirm what he knew well to be true.

"No bullets will go through it," Shisa added, breaking her silence for the first time.

"My foremind knows that, a'Shisa." Cara tapped her forehead. "But the primitive part of my brain refuses to listen." Cara returned to her work. "You're here because of yesterday's fight?" she ventured.

"Yes."

"And is Chendal here?"

"Yes."

"Where?"

"Downstairs," Rodani answered for her.

Cara turned her curiosity back on Shisa. "Are you and Chendal always the guardians sent to settle disputes involving guardians?"

"Yes. And we guard the ambassadors when they are in Hadaman."

"Hopefully there will be no more firefights."

"One may hope," Shisa replied.

Cara studied her, then glanced over to Rodani. "You two don't look much alike, a'Shisa."

Shisa glanced at Rodani before returning her regard to Cara. Rodani spoke up.

"She carries our father inside her. I carry our mother."

Odd way of putting it. "Whose eyes do you carry?" she asked him with a smile, knowing it was a provocation.

"I have never received an adequate answer to that question."

"Why do you ask?" Shisa asked Cara sharply. Her pupils had narrowed.

"I'd like to thank him. Or her."

Rodani looked at her. "Likely he has long been ashes, kia." He turned to his sister. "Shisa, I would ask you to excuse us for a while."

Shisa contemplated them both for a moment, then bowed to Rodani.

He stared at the necklace in his hands. "Kia, it was a difficult meeting downstairs."

Cara refocused on her bedmate, switching gears and paying attention. "What happened?"

"Most I am constrained from discussing. But I spent much of an hour listening to Naremit spew stable sweepings and threats at you. It was not pleasant."

"I'm sorry," she said, heartfelt.

"There is going to be a censure."

"Naremit?"

He pursed his lips. "Yes. And I find myself in need of your comfort." He turned dark eyes on her. "Will you accept me?"

Put that way, it was unthinkable to deny him. She held out her hand.

The doors got shut, and the locks turned. A pleasant time passed, and Rodani lay spent and shuddering on Cara's ample curves. Silver hair spilled out over his shoulders and mixed with brown curls, tickling her face. She brushed tendrils of both colors away as her own breathing slowly returned to normal.

"Aisu," she whispered, a last bit of comfort before their bodies parted. Rodani rolled over and wrapped Cara in a full-length embrace, then let go again—much too soon.

"Forgive me, kia. The call may come any moment. I must be there promptly when it does."

Cara opened her scarred palm in acceptance. Rodani took it and tugged her off the mattress. When they'd washed and dressed, he pulled her back down to a sit on the edge of the bed.

"Kia," he said, resting his elbows on his knees, "this censure will be difficult."

"Why?"

"Against that I am constrained as well. But you must remain seated, and you must remain silent. Serano and Shisa will sit with you. And I will return here as soon as I am released from the platform."

"That bad?"

"I suggest you remember what he did."

Rodani was dark, deep in serious duty, both private and professional. She wondered what they all faced. "I can't feign sudden illness?"

Rodani declined to share her attempt at humor. "It would be a nearly unforgivable dishonor for you and your species if you fail to be there...or walk out prematurely. For the sake of our affinity, do not."

"Because he's being punished for what he did to us, I have to be there?"

"Yes."

"I'll honor your word," she said, formal in the face of his urgency.

They shared one more embrace before his 'com buzzed.

"Five."

"Time, a'tem."

"Ninety-nine," Rodani paged his partner. In seconds, Serano was at her door, Shisa behind. He entered; Rodani left.

THIRTY-FIVE

Disturbed by his enigmatic warnings, Cara went into her study and knelt in the corner where she and Rodani had nearly come to an abrupt end. It brought back an echo of the terror they had faced. She heard again Rodani's yelp as he was shot. She forced herself to envision his body on the floor in front of her, skull shattered as Shurad's had been, sightless violet eyes staring at her.

A lump formed in her throat and tears welled up. Hurriedly, she rose to leave the room as Serano looked in to see what she was doing. He walked her down the familiar route to the gathering room. Shisa strode behind them. The room had several long rows of simple chairs facing the double tiered dais, and there was a red rug covering the lower tier.

Serano shifted a couple of people out of the near chairs in the first row and sat Cara in the second seat. He took the outer one, Shisa the third. Cara settled her body and attempted a settling of her stomach, to no avail. No one was on the platform yet. People took their seats around the trio, singly and in groups. Cara kept watch on the far-left door. Was Rodani there? Or Naremit?

The door to their left opened. Out walked Timan, Arimeso, and Kusik, then Rodani, with Chendal at his side. The trio took their accustomed places, Arimeso in her seat, Kusik at her right hand, Timan at her left. Rodani stood at Timan's side, Chendal at Kusik's.

The door to the right opened. Naremit walked out, flanked by the second-tier guardians, Lanata and Imal. Naremit was handcuffed and shackled. Each escort had a grip on one elbow. As he turned toward the platform, he stumbled and began to fight, eyes wide. Lanata fetched him a blow at the temple. It took both guards to wrestle him to the red covered dais.

"Naremit," Arimeso began. "You are charged with disobeying orders, perfidy, treachery, and sedition with violence—bordering on treason against my house. You have deliberately disobeyed my direct orders in the matter of my human guest, planning and carrying out a three-fold attack on her in her private rooms, nearly killing her and her guardian, Security Fifth Rodani. Instead of pursuing your duty and maintaining honor, you embarked upon a twenty-year-old vendetta, defying all orders to the contrary. You have dishonored yourself and your guild, therefore, you shall forfeit both."

Naremit renewed his struggle. Lanata and Imal tightened their hold on his arms with an arm through his elbows and Lanata's knife at the base of his skull. He panted and blinked rapidly. His feet made stepping motions on the red carpet.

"A'Kusik," Arimeso continued. "As head of my security staff, do you concur?"

"Yes," came the reply.

"A'Chendal, as chosen representative of the guild council, do you concur?"

"Yes."

"A'Chendal."

Chendal walked forward to Naremit and pulled a knife.

"By your dishonorable actions," he said, "you have forfeited your place in the Guild of Guardians." He stepped around behind Naremit and lifted his hair by the end of his clip. One quick slash, then another x-ed out a guild brand at the base of his neck. Naremit jerked with pain. Red spilled out from the cuts and down into his collar. Chendal wiped the bloody blade on his kerchief and replaced the knife, then walked back to his place at Kusik's side.

"Rodani," Arimeso intoned.

He stepped in front of the taso, turned to face her, and bowed deeply.

"It is no one's—" Naremit began to shout, until Lanata muzzled him with her hand.

"You have had your say," Arimeso spoke coldly, as Rodani stepped aside in deference to her voice. "Be silent or be gagged."

Rodani watched her, awaiting a go-ahead glance. She gave it.

In the audience, Cara's breathing became shallow; she began to feel dizzy. Even not knowing what was coming, she wished only to shut her eyes and bury her head in her arms, but Rodani's warning lay on her mind and heart. With sweating palms, she balled her fists and tucked them between her knees. At her motion, Serano pulled on her nearest wrist and grabbed her hand. Shisa did the same. There was no going anywhere now, even if she had not already promised Rodani.

He walked slowly down the platform until he was nearly face-to-face with Naremit. Rodani said something to him in a voice too low for Cara to hear the words. Naremit was visibly shaking. Imal tightened his grip on Naremit's arms.

Rodani stepped down off the covered dais and, for a moment, faced the assembled household. Horror dawned in Cara's mind as Rodani parted his jacket.

He pulled out his pistol, looked to Naremit, aimed behind his ear, and fired.

The boom echoed, short and sharp. Naremit crumpled. Blood shot out and shards of bone flew.

Imal and Lanata, splattered in red, guided the body into a jumble of lifeless limbs. A river of blood flowed into the red carpet. Rodani slid his weapon back into its holster and turned again for a bow to the taso.

A hot, acid gorge rose in Cara's throat. She bit her lip and buried her head in Serano's side.

There was no walk-by. None was needed. Serano pulled Cara to her feet as Imal and Lanata folded the red cloth over Naremit's body. Timan and Chendal met Rodani in the center of the platform, conferring in muttering voices. Cara stumbled behind Serano. He hurried her up the stairs, shutting the three of them inside her rooms to await Rodani's return.

Cara retreated to her bedroom, climbed into the new bed, and covered her head with the bullet-marred quilt. There were no tears, a measure of the depth of her shock.

It was unreal. A hallucination. It didn't happen. It couldn't have happened.

Her lover, the man who played her body like a maestro on strings, didn't shoot down another man in cold blood in front of the house. Shurad she could distance herself from. Even Naremit she didn't give a whit for, based on what he'd done. But Rodani. She couldn't distance herself from him. He resided inside her. And had just committed a cold kill.

The dark and the fabric warmth made a well, one that threatened to become a bottomless pit. She tensed with the effort to keep the visions at bay. Rodani. Face-to-face with Naremit. The push at his jacket. The pistol calmly pulled from its place of residence. The smooth aim. The...

NO!

Naremit deserved it.

Rodani had no choice.

Naremit knew the consequences.

Rodani was following orders.

Naremit tried to kill them both.

Rodani would have killed him yesterday, given the opportunity.

So would she.

NO!

Cara sat up in bed, quilt twisted around her body in disarray. Every cell in her body shouted, *Wrong!* But no one here thought so. It was sick. But Rodani wasn't sick. It was dishonorable. But Rodani was the most honorable being she knew.

She pulled the quilt off her face. Her attention latched onto the marks of yesterday's battle. The holes in the wall were patched. She and Rodani were patched. Walking wounded, one physical, one emotional. She wanted him there. Wanted him to walk off that platform and leave the killing to Kusik, who would undoubtedly enjoy the duty. Wanted to have killed Naremit herself in self-defense yesterday. Wanted her lover to be someone he couldn't be. She crawled off the bed and went in search of the only other type of comfort available here.

"Hamman!"

Hamman appeared in her doorway in a flash. Waiting there, probably. Watching, most likely.

"Shigeli, please," she requested with some heat. "Keep it available."

The servant hesitated a moment, then left.

Cara walked across the workroom with her eyes glued firmly on the floor in front of her. Shisa and Serano watched silently as she passed by, entered the study, and dropped out of sight. Their eyes met.

Serano eased into the doorway. Cara sat crouched by the wall near the fireplace, hunched as if in pain. He wanted his partner back in the room promptly, despite the anger that burned inside of him.

He wanted not to have to deal with a human in this mood. He knew her emotional insanities. And if she went unstable, he was responsible for controlling her—without harming her.

Serano could tell she was riding the edge, thanks to the week he'd tried to spend with her. He stepped inside the room but made no move to approach her. Leaning against the fireplace mantle would have to do for his duty.

Shisa sidled into the room, next to him. "Is she hurt?" she whispered.

"No," he whispered back.

"What is she doing?"

"I am uncertain. But she is in deep distress."

"Why?"

Serano looked at his partner's sister. They'd met some months after he and Rodani had been assigned to each other. He knew the bond they shared. Knew she was as deep as her brother. Knew why, too. "Rodani did not discuss it with you?"

"He had no chance. Said only to assist you in guarding her."

"That we do. The rest we leave to him."

"What is she likely to do?"

"I hesitate to imagine."

Shisa studied the still form against the wall. Strange sounds emanated from Cara's throat, as she wiped water from her eyes with the sleeves of her jacket. "Andrew and Mena'hem do not act like this."

Serano rolled his fingers open, attempting as well to swallow his tempers. "She has led us to understand her emotions are much stronger than other humans. Much closer to the surface, and therefore much more uncontrollable."

"Is she this way often?"

"Twice have I seen her in similar straits."

Shisa stared at the quilt-covered lump on the floor, perplexed. "Is Rodani still pleased with their affinity?"

"Yes," he said grimly. "She seems to give him something he needs."

Hamman stepped quietly into the doorway. Serano reached past Shisa to take the glass from Hamman's hand. He sniffed it. "She requested it?"

"Yes, a'tem."

He dismissed the servant and turned to Shisa. His eyes flickered from the glass to her to Cara and back again. Shisa made no move to aid him. He was on his own. He took a breath and walked over to the wall cautiously, setting the glass on the floor near her. Unharmed, he returned to his station at the fireplace. After a moment, Cara raised her head. With her back to the door, she sat up and took the glass, drinking as if to quench her thirst.

This was not a desirable situation. Twice Serano had seen Cara inebriated. Both times she had been inappropriately indecorous. Where was Rodani?

***

A fresh fall of tears ran over Cara's cheeks and dripped onto the knees of her pants. Sobs broke out of her throat in short, staccato hiccups. Black clad legs appeared at her side, close enough to touch. Close enough to smell, had her nose not been stuffed. Where did they come from? She'd heard no footsteps. The knees bent. Rodani's face came into view.

"Kia." The voice held no censure, no anger. Weariness, maybe. Acceptance of the inevitable. He stroked the feathers of her curling hair with his fingertips, pushing the unruly tendrils back from her scalp. She jerked away from his touch. Her head banged the wall, producing another wave of tears.

Rodani rested his arms on his thighs, hands dangling between his legs—worthless as comfort. "I knew you would be distressed. I am sorry."

Cara bent her face to her knees and turned toward the wall.

"I asked Arimeso to relieve me of the duty," he told her. "Others could have honorably done it. She refused. I explained my reasons to her, and she still refused. I had no choice."

"You killed him. In cold blood."

"Cold?"

"Cold," she shouted, turning to stare at his shoulder. His face, she couldn't yet manage. "You walked up to him, raised your gun, and shot him. He could have been confined instead."

Rodani rubbed his ear. His pupils constricted from ovals into a narrow line. "For the rest of his life?"

"Yes."

"We do not do such things."

"No. You take a life for a life. And that's wrong." *You. The man I love. You took his life with no more thought than that it would upset me.*

Rodani leaned forward, reaching out for an embrace. Before his hands more than lightly touched her, she shot out of her crouch and retreated to the edge of the fireplace, fingers clutched in the quilt. She leaned her shoulder against the stone and rested her temple on a sharp knob of rock. It felt better than her soul.

He took a cautious step in her direction. "Kia, you have told me touch comforts you." He raised his hand. "It seems obvious—"

She flinched. "Don't."

He lowered his hand slowly, as if not quite believing that his tool of last resort was no longer available to him. "Why?"

"Because when I see your hand, I see it holding your gun, pulling the trigger. And then I see Naremit die." Slowly, she collapsed onto the floor. "I'm sorry, aisu," she said into his silence. Maybe she was wrong. Maybe she was doing him a grave disservice. But she couldn't see past the images burned in her brain.

He crouched down beside her. "But what else has this hand done?" he asked quietly, holding it out for her inspection. She remained silent.

"What did it do not more than an hour ago? Tell me."

"I can't."

"Why?"

"Those thoughts are gone."

"Then bring them back."

"The bloody ones crowd them out."

Rodani's shoulders slumped. His fingers curled into a fist, which dropped down to his thigh and lay there, impotent.

"Kia, I am not just the man who crafts with you, or nuzzles at your earlobes. I am Guild."

"Obviously."

A pregnant silence filled the space between them. "I was not chosen as your guardian because of my ability to sit on the floor and discuss life with an alien."

"Don't patronize me, Rodani."

"You cannot cut me into pieces and throw away the parts you do not want." His black boots scraped the floor as he shifted his weight. "Nor can I do the same to you."

The parts you do not want. Gods. What of her did he want to throw away? This part, for sure. What else? Was she so terrible? Was she so wrong?

"Kia, look at me."

She bit her lip and turned away.

He lowered his body a few inches, and sat back against the wall, legs nearly touching her slippers. "Then I will sit here until you can."

Damn that determined, unalterable patience. Like he could wait days, unspeaking, unmoving, for her to come to her senses—the senses he thought she should have. Guilt washed through her in a hot wave. Guilt that she could only see him through human filters, through her own sense of justice and equity, not his own.

But was he right? No. He was not. An eye for an eye makes the whole world blind. Who had said that...ages ago? The idea had passed through the centuries, through the violence her own people had forever perpetrated on each other when their desire for retribution equaled the damage done.

Was she wrong? No. But could she condemn Rodani because he was? No, again. Vengeance wasn't in her.

Another body walked over. She knew the arrogance in that stride, knew the scratches on those boots.

"Pathetic."

She looked up. In front of her, Rodani stood, his expression growing hard, his pupils turning to slits. "Tem'u." Cold lingered behind the word.

Serano tapped his foot in her direction. "What value you see is beyond me."

"And that, too, is obvious."

Chendal and Shisa remained in the doorway, wordless witnesses to the emotional battle within the room. Cara stared up at the stiff tableau between the two guild partners. *Thank you, Rodani. Thank you for reminding me of the other pieces of your nature, the parts I fell in love with.*

Serano made the tossing gesture with his hand, then left the room. Rodani reclaimed his seat on the floor and glanced cautiously in her direction. His gaze rose to her face, and she didn't look away. His pupils, black within the violet, softened into ovals and then into wide circles as she regarded him without flinching. His wounded arm rested against the wall.

She crawled to him, nestled into the crook of his shoulder, sighing against his warmth. She felt his arms wrap around her, a comfort that melted into her bones. The day's images didn't disappear, but they faded into the background, lingering on the edges of her thoughts. *Gods of the deep night.* How far does "I love you" carry into this mess? How can you tell someone he's forgiven if he doesn't understand what you objected to? How can you explain that "I'm sorry" doesn't always mean "I'm wrong"?

Chendal shifted out of his stance and settled into a chair at the table. Shisa followed him. They began to talk in lowered voices, about who the hell knew what. Cara closed her eyes.

Serano came back into the doorway. "Rodani."

He glanced up, preoccupied.

Serano shifted his gaze to the hall door and back and made a hand sign.

"Later."

Serano banged the door with his fist. Cara let out a squeak, startled. "Now," he said, then made another rapid length of signals.

"Rest, kia. I will return."

Stiffly, Rodani arose from his place on the floor and followed Serano across the hall. Serano barged into their living area with an intent toward mayhem. "Where is your sanity?"

Rodani took a fresh grip on his temper and sat down. He stretched out his legs while Serano paced in front of him. "My sanity is where it has always been, tem'u. With the safety of me and mine at the fore of my honor."

"And Vanu, Naremit, and Garidemu are dead because of you. Where do you stop?"

"Those deaths were not of my doing. Their choice, Serano. *Their choice.*"

"But it was your choice that brought theirs into being. Without you breaking the—"

"No!" Rodani shouted. "My choice had only to do with my life, and Cara's. Had the others kept their ignorant zeal to themselves, it would not have happened."

"This ill-thought independence of yours has caused more trouble than any hundred guardians before you!"

Rodani blinked, confused at his change of track. "I did not know you were the new guild historian. I congratulate you. Now, where is your evidence?"

Serano knocked his chair against the table. "Evidence. Evidence. Now you sound like her."

"If you make claims against me, you should have the facts to go with them."

"Facts? Here." Serano tapped his fingers. "One, you should never have accepted this duty. Two, you should have rescinded it once you found yourself falling. Three, you should never have walked that path to her. Four, you should be back-tracking as fast as you can, right now, and you are not. You sit here arguing with me while three bodies rot!"

Rodani stared at the fireplace, tired in body and mind. Tired of the anger, the wrongful judgments, the confrontations, the offenses, the stalking, and the threats. He felt Cara's plaintive cry in his gut— the desire to be left alone to live as they saw fit. "Every one of those supposed facts of yours is naught but an opinion, Serano."

"Opinion?" Serano's eyes went wide. He gripped the back of his chair and rose on the balls of his feet. Tension flowed through his shoulders and arms as he bent over the table. "Break away from her. Now!"

A million years of protective instincts roared into Rodani's head. Defenses honed by his childhood brought him up off his seat. Serano took a single step back, fists clenched. "Hit me?" he taunted. "That will fix everything?"

Rodani slid to within biting distance of Serano's face. His partner's chest heaved with audible breaths. "You will not demand *any* such thing of me. *Ever.*"

The growl beneath Rodani's words brought an answering flicker from Serano's ears. He bared his teeth in response. "And that is your final word?"

"Yes."

Serano turned his back, wrapping his arms over his chest. "I am done with you." He stomped into his bedroom, grabbed a large bag, and began to stuff it with anything he could find. Clothes, toiletries, a few books, an assortment of items from his headboard.

Rodani watched from the living room. "Tem'u."

Serano pushed the items down into the bag and threw a couple of knives on top. Then he jerked on the strings. The bag closed up with a snap of finality.

"Tem'u," he repeated.

Serano grabbed the strap and pulled it over his shoulder. "You have none."

THIRTY-SIX

"A'Cara."

Cara looked up from her spot on the study's floor. The shock of what had happened was receding, but mortification was crowding into its place. She heaved herself up, wishing again for a measure of Selandu grace. "A'Temaso."

Chendal stepped back into her workroom. "Talk with us."

Holy fried fish in the morning. Cara passed by him and planted herself in her work chair. Chendal took Rodani's usual place, while Shisa brought a chair in from the study and stood behind it.

Eyes wide, Cara clasped her hands in front of her and began to rub her thumbs over one other, unsteadily. The scars quickly became sore. *Rodani, come back. Please.*

"You need not be so anxious, a'Cara," Chendal said.

She glanced from his face to Shisa's, which was set in a cold mask. Rodani's voice popped up from her memory. *Kimasa's robe. Deep breaths. Radiate calm.* "A'Temaso," she replied.

"How much do you realize of what has happened here?"

Cara thought for a moment. "That's an unanswerable question, a'Temaso."

Shisa leaned forward, eyes narrowed. "Why?"

"The temaso knows I'm human and can't see this with Selandu eyes. If I don't know the scope of the problem, I can't estimate my level of ignorance."

Shisa's gaze traveled back to her partner's. Chendal shifted in his chair, leaned to the side, and rested his arm on the table. "Allow me to rephrase. Tell me what you see here, a'Cara."

Cara stared down at her table, eyes unfocused. She spoke in slow cadence. "Ignorance. Suspicion. Rage. Disgust. Fear. Death. Prison."

"Is this what you wish for our people? And yours?"

"I would wager you know the answer to that question, a'Temaso."

"Answer him," Shisa ordered.

"I don't wish it."

"And yet you have brought it on us," Shisa continued.

"No, a'tem." Anger forced her words out. "It is not *me*. It is both of us or neither. Don't blame me for something we both did."

Shisa balled her fist and laid it on the table. "You were the instigator."

Cara eyed the fist. "I really do disturb you, don't I, a'Shisa?"

"Do you know what you did by taking Rodani to your bed?"

She smiled grimly. This was beginning to sound like her first meeting with the selaso. "Accepted his attentions, a'tem." The smile widened. "Pleasured him."

Shisa raised her arm, fist at the ready.

"Sit, tem'u," Chendal said. "Or I will send you off on a worthless errand while I finish this."

Shisa obeyed, reluctantly. Defiantly. It shone in her eyes, in the pupils that shut down to slits and the line of teeth behind her lips.

"A'Cara," Chendal began.

Cara dragged her gaze from her new enemy to her old.

"Have you ever guarded anyone?"

"Children."

"From death? From disaster?"

"Not in an immediate sense."

Chendal ran his hand over his mouth and chin. "A guardian's duty to his adashi, if the duty is not resentful or antagonistic, creates a bond."

Cara waited, but he remained silent. "I thought," she ventured into the quiet, "that a bond was a bad idea. Which is why others have a problem with us."

Chendal's gaze returned to her face. "No. A guardian-adashi bond is never truly appropriate, but it is expected. Trust builds it. The actual problem is the second bond."

At his words, Shisa stiffened, frozen into a statue of contained fury. Chendal continued to look at her, waiting.

"So...the second bond is joining? And it makes the first one worse?"

Shisa unfroze. "The second bond is toxic," she shouted from Cara's left. "That is why it is forbidden."

"Tem'u," from her right.

"It destroys impartiality, human." Shisa was in full rage mode, now. "The ability to make proper decisions. The distance needed to judge honor and dishonor. The strength not to commit improprieties."

"A'temichi." Chendal's voice fell into a growl, which Shisa promptly ignored.

"It reduces attention to danger," she continued in a heated tone. "It causes a loss of focus on anything but the second bond. When you took him within you, you created a double bond that is nearly unbreakable." She stood up and pointed a rigid finger at the table. "You *will* leave this place one day. With you gone, and both his bonds damaged, he will never be the guardian he once was. You have ruined him!" She swept her hand through the air, coming far too close to Cara's nose. "Ruined his livelihood, his honor, and the place he earned at his taso's side. And it will destroy what peace he still has when you are done with him."

Chendal rose to face his partner. A flurry of hand signals flashed between them. Shisa balled her fists, bowed to her partner, and walked out.

Cara shrank into her chair as she watched Rodani's sister leave the room in a deadly tempest. Shisa's rant echoed in her mind, unnerving with its possibilities. "Then why did Rodani approach me?"

"I suspect his judgment was already compromised," Chendal said as he retook his seat. "What did you do to cause that?"

"Asked him to socialize with me."

"That would not be enough."

"Taught him to make music with his voice. Taught him my language."

"Nor would that. Keep tracking."

Cara leaned her head on her hand and looked away. "Told him that it wasn't dishonorable to be different."

"The trail grows warm."

"Told him that he was a better man than all the ignorant, angry, narrow-minded people that surrounded him all his life."

"And I believe we have arrived."

Cara's head shot off her hand as she stared back into Chendal's eyes, the eyes that guardians used as an oath, testament to the deadly skills he held within him. "So, telling Rodani the truth, telling him he's not the wrong-headed, improper, unwise man that all of you think he is, ruined him?"

"Telling him that ignoring his own culture's mores is appropriate is what has caused this problem."

"I would rather tell him the truth and make him feel good about his talents, than destroy him with lies."

"But what is good for a person is not always good for his society."

"Which one he chooses is no one's decision but his, a'Temaso."

"And he will pay a price for it."

"We all pay prices for our decisions. The only difference here is the magnitude."

Chendal fell silent. The muscles around his eyes went lax as he stared at the worktable. He seemed to drift inward, no longer focused on her.

She waited out his silence for a few moments. "What happens now, a'Chendal?"

The temaso drew back from wherever he'd gone. "As long as you are here, and his problem remains localized, it is all in the taso's hands."

"And when I'm not?"

"Then he will be brought before the guild council in Tendiman, and I will be ordered to flog him—or kill him."

***

Rodani clasped his hands on the back of his neck as Serano closed the door. He curled his fingers through his hair, then crossed his arms over his chest. His heart thumped painfully under the casing, and his ears twitched erratically. "Tem'u," he whispered. But there was no answer. No sound in the room but his own breathing.

Thoughts flickered through his mind in rapid succession. *He is only angry. No, it is more. He will change his mind. No. That is denial. This will cause further repercussions with the guild staff. Now that, you fool, is the first rational thought you've had for a time.*

Rodani lowered himself onto the couch arm. Slowly, so slowly he hadn't seen it, a shifting had occurred. Everything from his old life was eroding. Sweeping vistas were being walled off. Freedoms curtailed. Companions and guild compatriots, what there were of them, were turning their backs. The scope of his life was an ever-decreasing perimeter, centered on his adashi and the tiny suite where she spent her days.

Rodani shot up off the couch arm and strode back and forth across the room. Restless.

Partnerless.

Bereft.

No guild to guard his back.

No tem'u to walk at his side.

Every guardian carried his own fears, faced them in the solitude of his own mind. But to be without a partner was madness. Serano's rejection had left a burning hole in his psyche. The desertion carved out a portion from his essence, and left it open and bleeding.

Rodani grabbed the back of the couch and brought his head to his hands, bent in pain that overflowed into the physical.

Always, he'd thought that they could mend their disagreements, heal their rifts, salvage their damaged feelings. Always, there had been a way to fix their problems. To winnow facts from ego, cooperation from competition. But this was a knife in the gut.

And it was no one's fault but his.

Rodani began to shiver. Convulsions rippled through him, shaking him from head to toe. His knees lost their strength. He crumpled, resting his shoulders and head on the back of the couch, his insides empty and on fire. He needed to spew. But nothing would get rid of the remorse that crawled through his nerves.

After a time, he pulled himself up to a drunken stand and weaved into his bedroom. He found the bag that was identical to his partn—to Serano's and tossed it on the bed. His gut roiling with loss, he shuffled from place to place. The wardrobe, the headboard, the facilities. When the bag was full, he hung it over his shoulder. "I am returning," he said into his 'com.

As he stepped into the hall, his shadows appeared.

"We heard, a'tem." Pavanec's voice dripped with contempt.

Rodani walked the angled path to Hamman's door.

"We saw your partner leave you, a'tem," Pavanec said. "Do you think now that no one will remind you of your dishonor?"

Rodani rapped sharply on the door.

"You would be mistaken." Pavanec leaned into his face. "You will pay for what you did today."

Deremic opened the door. Rodani passed through, leaving the threats behind. He requested drinks, then headed into Cara's bedroom. His steps were heavy, his heart a hollow drum in his chest. He dropped his bag next to the armoire.

He stopped when the worktable came into view. Cara and Chendal sat nose to nose. The look of horror he'd seen on her face a quarter hour ago still resided there. *Strength, a'tem. Dig deep. For her.* And where was his sister? The block of dread in his midsection grew heavier, his need to spew stronger.

"Aisu," Cara said, then stood up. "Are you well?"

Rodani made it to the table and sat without collapsing. "Yes, kia. Where is Shisa, a'Temaso?"

Chendal tossed the question. "She was angry. I bade her walk away from it."

Rodani placed his hand on the worktable with careful deliberation. *See, no shaking.* "From what, this time?"

Chendal's gaze raked him up and down. "We were discussing the nature of the double bond. Cara was not aware of it, or of its consequences." He tilted his head with an expression of mild censure. "You did not explain it?"

"I did not." *This needs shutting down, now.* "I am not convinced the stories are accurate. I will not fill her ears with vague alarms."

Cara drew her hands up to her mouth. "Shisa was anything but vague."

"And the accuracy?" he asked, close on the heels of her accusation.

Cara spread her empty hands. Chendal caught one of them.

"And that is why I did not say." Rodani leaned back and looked at Cara, attempting to quiet his burning gut. They both had tree damage, did they not? It was something else they shared, something that he hadn't told her.

"You are healed," Chendal said to her, prodding the scars on her hand.

"Mostly." The whole side of Cara's body jerked as he pushed at a too-sensitive spot.

"They are still tender, a'Temaso," Rodani said. "Please be cautious. She needs them."

"The discourtesies are circling the table even now."

Cara chuckled. Rodani was in no mood for humor.

Chendal gave Cara's hand back to her. "What did Serano have to say?"

Rodani froze, shutting down his expressions. Likely not fast enough for Chendal, but more than adequate for his mate. He flashed a hand signal.

Cara sucked in a breath to speak, then bit down on whatever she was going to say. Rodani made a mental note to praise her for remembering their agreement.

"A'tem'ai," she began, in place of whatever bit of offense she was going to rattle off. She glanced at Chendal first, then Rodani. Good. Proprieties were in focus. She looked past him. "The study is much more comfortable. If it would not offend."

Rodani checked in a visual with Chendal, who signaled agreement. As they rose, Deremic brought in drinks. Cara sat hers on the tea table and flopped into the corner of the couch like an untutored child. So much for courtesies. Rodani laid another log on the fire and prodded the coals with the poker.

"What is the name of your drink, a'Temaso?" Cara said behind him.

"Yolaro."

"Aisu," she said in a softer voice. "Would it offend the temaso too badly if I asked for a taste of his drink?"

Rodani turned around to face her and glanced at Chendal. But he was already offering his glass to her. She inclined her head and took the glass from his fingers.

"Clench tightly, kia."

She smiled up at her bedmate. *Happiness, where she might have taken offense*, he decided. A tiny bit of the burning inside him faded. He waited for her reaction as she brought the glass to her lips. Her eyebrows rose. *He knew that one: surprise*. Now she turned her smile on Chendal. "Good."

A fleeting expression passed across Chendal's face, almost too quick to see, let alone interpret. It didn't seem to be anger.

Rodani sat down on the couch next to Cara and took a sip of his drink. Cara curved her arm around his abdomen. "May I?" she whispered.

He felt his eyes widen. "Within reasonable bounds, yes." Cara sat her drink down and wrapped her arms around him as far as they would go. He repeated the gesture, tucking her into his body. As she nuzzled into his shirt, another small flame of burning loss died down. Just a little.

Chendal watched them, quietly, dispassionately. Arimeso had made her wishes clear to him, and he had chosen to respect them.

For now.

***

Toranel lay on her bed, her mind awash in misery. Her receptive time was only days past, and the exquisite sharing she'd enjoyed with Naremit would never be repeated. The ache of loss in her mind echoed in her body, trapping her in a suspension of movement. She'd begged Kusik to let her remain away from the censure. But he had refused. "Too obvious," he had said. "Your duty is to the taso and her orders," he had said.

The blast from that immoral guardian's gun had shattered her heart. She still heard the shot, still felt it as if it had been aimed at her. *Why? Why was the wrong man alive, and the right one...*

Au, Goddess, you may have him in your arms, but he belongs here. In mine. Temi's knives! It was all the fault of that ill-begotten guardian. And that ugly shrunken human—she looked as if someone had taken a mallet and pounded half the height out of her. How could anyone imagine an affinity with a rotund, fleshy child who couldn't keep her emotions constrained or her mouth shut?

Toranel pushed her face into her pillow. Her fists tore at the weave of the sheet underneath her. Her adult life had barely begun, a bedmate newly found then destroyed. Where was justice? Where was the comfort Sela promised?

She was lost. No purpose, no trust in the guild staff that remained. No mate, no will to endure endless duties of weapons maintenance, practice, door-guarding, or trail- or perimeter-walking. For a real fight, for just one real fight, she would give her life. To avenge Naremit, to avenge the guild that accepted her, trained her, and released her into the world.

And Vanu. Her partner. How could she forget him? They'd been paired for less than a year, but it was more than enough to create a bond. Guilt began to intrude its tendrils into the gloom of her sorrow. Her chest tightened with the double calamity. After all their meetings, after all the planning, she never once believed they would fail. A single guardian with an illicit bond and a careless human, intent on each other. Failure was unthinkable.

But the unthinkable could still happen.

A soft tap on her door pulled her out of her gloom. With monumental effort, she dragged herself from the bed.

Pavanec's face greeted her at the door.

"Sel'u," he said.

She turned her face from his offer of connection, but opened the door.

THIRTY-SEVEN

"Deremic," Rodani said as he walked through the servant's corridor.

"A'tem?"

"Call Cassig, please. There is a small meeting room outside the main kitchen. Advise him that I would wish to talk with him there."

Rodani unlocked the door to the hall and slowly stuck his head out. The hall seemed empty. Behind him, Deremic spoke quietly.

"Five minutes, a'tem?"

"That will do." Rodani slipped out the door, pleasantly surprised that he made it to the kitchens without incident. Cassig followed him in a few minutes later, wiping his hands on a rag.

"A'Cassig," Rodani began, noting the chef's raised eyebrow at his courtesy, "I have a concern."

"A'tem?"

"I trust your knowledge and your caution when you choose what foods to serve a'Cara. But how much trust do you put in the food that you choose?"

Cassig slid into the nearest chair, thinking. "I am not certain I understand."

"Then I will speak more plainly. And you will, of course, refrain from passing my concerns to anyone else."

"Of course, a'tem."

Rodani leaned toward the chef. "How simple would it be to poison Cara's food before or after it is made?"

Cassig sat up straight, his pupils wide. "Is she ill? Have I—"

Rodani sliced the air with his hand. "No, a'Cassig. Be calm." He glanced around the room, and at the wall that cut them off from the main kitchen—as if he could watch the many cooks and helpers beyond it as they went about their work. "It is a concern that I have."

"Why now? Why not in the beginning?"

"Additional reasons have crept up."

Cassig looked down at his hands and folded the rag carefully, once, twice, thrice. "I have heard rumors, a'tem."

"And what are your thoughts on those rumors?"

"They are not my concern, a'tem."

"But you see how others might decide to eliminate part of the problem?"

"Yes."

"Then back to my question, please. Are there precautions taken for the safety of the food before you cook it, or after?"

"No."

"Then I would ask you to take those precautions."

"How?"

"You know better than I each step our food takes from the world outside to our cook pots and dishes. Think upon it, please. When you have ideas, you may discuss them with me." Rodani stood. "Me only, a'sel."

Cassig rose from his chair and bowed. "Of course, a'tem."

Rodani took a different path back from the way he had arrived. His head swiveled from side to side as he walked. A few artisans passed him, slowing, bowing. He acknowledged each with a dip of his head. Their respect contrasted with the lack his fellow guardians were showing rekindled the anger he'd so recently banked.

***

Cara clipped loose threads from the wall quilt she'd just finished. She collected the tailings into a little pile on her worktable, musing on Rodani's recent comments about craft trash on the floor. Well, if it made him less irritable, she was willing to compromise. No sense in fighting over the small stuff when there were so many bigger issues at hand.

At times, it was all she could do not to rage, not to rip pictures from the wall and toss books from one room to the next. The bruises and cuts she found on Rodani's body were almost more than she could bear. It was probably for the best that he never took her to the dinner gatherings anymore. At least he would understand if she made a scene, even while he berated her for it. Best to avoid that altogether. And avoid being in the sight of Kusik. *Gods, for one good spit in his face.*

"Onana, why do you smile?"

"Ikemi," she said, flinging the quilt aside. The boy walked in from her bedroom door. Hamman's shadow waited behind him. "How do you fare?"

"Well, thank you," he replied. Rodani's courtesy lessons were evidently working. "But," he moved in close to whisper, "there are guardians outside your rooms."

A heavy weight dropped into Cara's stomach. "Guardians?" she asked, keeping her tone light. She guided him into the study.

"Yes. They watched me. Stared at me."

"Did they touch you?"

"No."

Cara sat on the couch and pulled Ikemi up to sit beside her. "Well, put them from your mind for now, ki'oto. I will ask a'Rodani about them later."

Ikemi wrapped his arms around his slender chest and made a valiant effort to conform his expression into a proper Selandu mask—devoid of emotions, calm and waiting.

It tore at her, this withdrawal into a shell. The human need for expression was strong, and burying it became so harmful in the long run. She wanted to shake him, bring life back to his face. A smile, a frown, a spate of childish laughter.

But she was the interloper. Ikemi had to live here, had to fit in. She took a deep breath and forced her own emotions back under wraps. "Choose a book?" she asked him.

Ikemi pulled one off the table, and they cuddled together as he opened it, smiling.

Then the smile turned to alarm as a heavy thump battered the hall door. Cara slipped off the couch. "Stay here."

Scuffles, bumps, and grunts bled through the door as she went into her workroom. The weight in her stomach came back. *Rodani!* He was there. She knew it. Outside her door, getting hit again. *Damn Kusik*, she muttered through clenched teeth. She picked up her rotary cutter, aching to draw blood.

Rodani shouted. Voices answered, voices she didn't know. Something metallic clattered on stone. Hamman scurried through Cara's bedroom and pulled her back toward the study. Cara fought the pull wildly. "He needs help!"

"Tsss," the maid said, tugging at her arm.

Cara flung her cutter on the table in helpless fury. Her man was out there, and by her own promise to him, she was forbidden to interfere.

After a lifetime of minutes, the hallway tumult stopped. The door handle moved, and Rodani lurched inside, leaning against the door as it closed behind him. He glanced around the room, then shut his eyes. His chest surged with each breath, his hair hung awry about his shoulders, and the jacket he kept in immaculate condition fell open, buttonless and ripped.

Cara tiptoed toward him. "Aisu?" she whispered. His breathing slowed to something resembling normal. "Are you hurt?" she asked.

His mouth formed a *Du*, but his eyes remained closed. Cara slipped a hand on his waist, above the weapons belt. He ignored her touch. "Ice bag? Analgesic?" *Please, aisu, let me comfort you. Let me not be utterly helpless against what's happening to you.*

"Eisenico," he said, and peeled himself off the door. Hamman ran to obey. Cara followed. *No one* was going to hand him that drink besides her. When she came back, Rodani lay sprawled in the comfy chair before the fire. Ikemi, stiff and silent, sat curled at the far end of the couch with his book untouched beside him. Cara handed Rodani the drink, her hands shaking in delayed reaction. Strangely, his were steady. She folded herself into the near seat on the couch.

"That was not Kusik," she said, her voice low.

His gaze flashed to her, then over to Ikemi. With that look, the boy curled more tightly into a ball. *Who needs comfort more?* she wondered. But this was not a scene for children. She lifted Ikemi into her arms and carried him into the study, rubbing his back. "A'Rodani is unhurt, ki'oto," she said. "And you did nothing wrong." Ikemi nuzzled her shoulder and clenched his thin arms around her neck.

"Deremic," she called, walking into the servant's corridor, then stopped.

Deremic stood at the table, his arm a smear of red. Hamman bent over it with a rag, dabbing it. "Shallow," she said. They both turned to her.

"A'Cara?" Deremic's voice was calm, despite the blood seeping into his shirtsleeve.

Cara held Ikemi more tightly with the realization of what she was seeing. "You fought?"

454

"I assisted Rodani, a'Cara."

She swallowed, hard. "I'm sorry you've been drawn into this, a'sel."

Deremic studied his own arm as Hamman slathered on an ointment. "You would defend him if you could, would you not?"

"Of course."

"Then you need no sorrow for my duty."

"...Yes. Thank you." She turned around, locked in the rooms with nowhere to go, and no one to see Ikemi safely back to his dormitory.

"But you needed something?" Deremic asked.

"Ikemi..."

"Yes, of course, a'Cara. We will see to him."

"But you should rest."

"And you should attend to Rodani."

"I will." She planted Ikemi on his feet and gave him a parting hug. "I will see you another day, ki'oto. Yes?"

His wide eyes shifted from her to Deremic to the door. Cara drew away from him with the only thoughts she could—Rodani.

He now sat on the edge of the tea table, his drink in one hand, the poker in his other. Flames licked around a new log. Cara came up behind him and rested her hands on his shoulders, then reached around with her arms and laid her temple against his. "Talk to me, aisu."

Rodani dropped the poker. It bounced against his boot and clanged on the floor. He pulled her hand away from his neck and moved to the couch, drawing her down beside him. "There is less to tell than you believe, kia."

"Start somewhere."

He sighed and took another sip. "'Somewhen' is the term, I believe." He stretched his legs and rubbed at a sore spot. "You are correct. That was not Kusik."

"Then who?"

"Some of the house guild."

"The guardians? Your own guild is attacking you?" Outrage ran through her. "More of them? Why?"

"Because they know, kia. They are aware of our affinity."

"Yes, I heard."

Rodani's eyes went wide. "How?"

"Litelon told me on the way back from the cave. When we were riding together."

"How did he know? What did he say?"

"He said he listens a lot because no one pays attention to him. He said all the guardians and half the clinic are aware, as well as the Enclave."

"I was not aware you knew."

Cara tossed the admission with a wave of her hand. "So, this is what it's come down to? The rest of the guardians break rules as retribution against rule-breakers?"

"Not all of them, kia. And this is not just about rule-breaking. This is about fear and disgust, which changes nothing."

"What can I do?

"Refrain from adding to the fight." He leaned forward to touch her arm. "Support me. Be the comfort that I come back to."

That wasn't what she wanted to hear. Wasn't all she wanted to do. This whole situation was impossible. "Is that all I can be?"

"It is the best of a small lot."

Cara huddled in a ball, her eyes focused on the flickering fire.

"You just wrapped an invisible quilt around you, kia." He peeled her hand away from her other arm, unlocking her defensive posture. "I know you wish to stop this, to solve it. But you cannot." He pulled her against him. His warmth flooded her, unlocking a battered door in her heart.

"I don't even know where to touch you, aisu. I don't know what hurts. I don't know what you need to hear." Her voice began to crack. Mentally, she kicked herself. "I'm supposed to be comforting you. But you're the one comforting me. As usual."

"No." His arms tightened around her. She felt him shiver. "This is mutual."

They rested together, head to chin. The fire crackled and spat. An early spring rain pounded against the walls, and thunder grumbled in the distance. Hamman appeared in the doorway, waiting for acknowledgment. Rodani looked over at her.

She handed him a leather envelope. "From the council."

Rodani tugged at the flap and pulled out a note. "They approved my design." He stuffed it back in and tossed the hide on the tea table, then took a sip of his drink. "And of course, they wish it already done." He rose from the couch. "I must go back out."

"Why?"

"I need to check the silver supply, choose the proper slab."

"Can't someone do it for you?"

"No. I trust this to no one else. It is my duty as a crafter."

Cara thought of her fabric stash. It made sense. But... *Oh, gods, her promise.* "Be careful."

"Always. Besides," he said, bending down to plant his lips on her forehead, "they have never marked me more than once a day since this began." He turned and walked out like nothing had happened, like he hadn't just been attacked and beaten by his fellow guardians. The anger in her gut exploded, a flashover that burned through every vein and artery. She lashed out at the tea table, sweeping the remnants of his drink onto the floor and heaving a kick at the leg. The poker lay where Rodani had dropped it. She grabbed it and swung. It rebounded against the mantle with a clang, wrenching her arms. She batted it again, over and over, swinging with all the strength that blind rage gifted to her. Chips flew.

"A'Cara, a'Cara," voices shouted. She swung again, the metal poker ruffling skin on her scarred hands. "A'Cara!"

She spun to face her servants, poker held in front of her like a sword. "Leave me alone!" Another clap of thunder, closer this time. She bared her teeth at the mantle and bashed the poker against the stone once more, then flung it in the corner with the wood pile. It bounced, rattled, and lay still. Refusing the stares that were no doubt turned her way, she leaned her forehead against the mantle, gasping for breath. For calm in the face of the unacceptable. For a measure of peace against helplessness.

True love was supposed to make you happy, wasn't it? Smooth away your problems. Bright futures, shared joys.

Yep. Nice fantasies.

An odor of liquor crept into her nostrils, past the scent of burning wood and chill air. She looked down under her arm at the brown stain on the floor. "I need some rags." She pulled her arms off the mantle.

"My duty, a'Cara," Hamman said.

Cara walked past her. "Not your duty to clean up after my tempers." She pulled some cloths from her private stash in her headboard.

"No, a'Cara, please." Hamman took them back and laid them down on the stack. She headed into the corridor. Cara retreated to the study. The fireplace mantle sported several white patches, gouged by the force of her blows. Chips of stone lay scattered on the floor. She sat on the tea table and leaned over, retrieving them one by one. When Hamman returned, Cara stopped her, taking the cloths from her hands. "My duty." She looked down. "A broom, too, a'sel. Please."

Rain continued to beat against the wall outside, coming and going in waves. Cara swept the floor, willing herself into quiescence with the knowledge that there were, after all, forces stronger than she, stronger than her enemies. Thunder rumbled through the walls and into her body.

When she was done cleaning, she righted the poker in the corner and took the rags and broom back toward the servant's quarters. She heard a pounding sound—Hamman's door to the hallway. A large weight dropped into Cara's stomach. Anything now, anything out of the ordinary, caused anxiety. But when Hamman came running into her bedroom, anxiety erupted into panic.

"A'Cara, step back, please." Hamman tugged on her arm, pulling her toward her workroom. Voices came through the narrow corridor ahead of two large bodies. No, three. Four? A scream forced its way up her throat. Cara clamped her hands on her mouth and stared as Timan and Baldar laid Rodani down on her bed. One eye was black and purple. Blood welled from cuts on his cheeks and mouth. His jacket was gone, and his weapons belt. No—it dangled from Deremic's fist. Rodani tried to curl up, but Timan held his legs down as Baldar sliced his shirt open.

Cara clutched the door frame, desperate not to collapse. Blood, bruises, and cuts covered Rodani's chest. As Baldar tugged his pants down, more bruises came into view. Below his waist, on his abdomen, and even—*Oh, gods. No.*

Baldar inspected the damage clinically. No blood, but the orifice looked red and raw.

Cara whimpered, sick in heart and mind. She rushed to his side.

"Remove her," Timan ordered, bending over Rodani's naked, beaten body. He bit back a cry of pain, and his whole body jerked in unison. Cara stuffed her fingers in her mouth and ground down on them, to block the pain she mirrored. Rodani's pain.

Someone grabbed her, pulled on her. She reached for her mate but was hustled out and into her study without a word.

***

Sometime later, Cara lifted the quilt from her head, and her head from her arms, freeing herself from her emotional cocoon. Quiet had fallen. The storm was gone. So were the screams in her mind. So were the urgent voices. She glanced around. So was Hamman gone. She shuffled to the doorway, unsteady on her feet. The workroom was empty, and the door to her bedroom was closed. She made her way across the room, step-by-step, listening—for anything that would tell her...anything...about what happened. No servants whispered. No barked orders from a physician, no rough, contempt-filled voices of guardians. Cara put her hand on the door handle. It was cold. The door opened, a crack, a finger's width, an inch.

She put her eye to the opening, then slowly pushed forward. Rodani was on his side, facing her. Eyes closed, mouth slack, his hands were on an ice bag at his crotch. Paste adhered to his many wounds. Cara folded herself into the chair to watch him. It seemed strange, now that it was her turn.

Rodani cracked an eye and focused on her. She willed herself to calm. "How are you?"

The eye closed again. "I will mend."

"You don't need to give me courteous denials, aisu. The truth will do." She leaned her head into the corner of the chair. "When you're ready."

Silence enveloped them. It beat against her eardrums, deafening her. She wanted to rage. To kill whoever did this. To slice them open and watch them bleed out at her feet. But no, it was hard enough to do that to an animal, even when it was attacking.

Rodani tried to shift in the bed, but did little except move his head and lower legs.

"Can I help you, aisu?" she said, getting up. "Can I get you anything? Cover you?"

"No, kia."

She started to sit back down, when Rodani took an audible breath. "Will you lay down with me?" She came forward. "Carefully," he added.

As she slid onto the bed, each of his bruises and cuts came into focus in the dim light. Red and purple bruises, raked and ruffled skin. Open cuts with a green paste dabbed on them. With the blood wiped clean, the real damage showed more clearly. "Is there a place I can touch you without hurting you?"

Rodani pulled one hand away from the ice bag and dragged it along the mattress. Cara took it and brought it up between them, kissing his knuckles. "This wasn't Kusik either, was it?"

"Du."

"How many?"

"Va." *Three. Against one.* Bitterness erupted within her, souring her gut and thoughts. How could anyone do that? Over love? He looked like he'd been gang—

Rodani shook the hand she held. "Do not squeeze."

Cara jerked her hand back. "Aisu," she glanced down at the ice bag. "What did they do to you? Did they...force themselves into you?"

"Du." His one good eye pierced her with a solid stare.

She put her hand back on his. "You promise me that's the truth?"

"On my duty to you, kia," he mumbled through swollen lips.

A breath shuddered its way out of her. "They kicked you?"

"Sai."

"Please tell me what I can do for you."

He closed his eye. "Stay with me while I rest."

"Can we get you the smoke that you brought me for my hand pain?"

"Du."

"Why not?"

"I do not wish to be drugged." It came out sharply, a warning to remember her promise. "The goddess wills."

"What goddess, Rodani? Where is She? How can She watch this happen to you? To us?" Cara rubbed her hand gently over his arm and through his hair. "I know you speak of her because that's what you learned as a child. But there's no one out there listening. It's up to us," she nodded toward the servant's rooms, "and the few others who matter, to stop this."

Rodani squeezed her hand. "I must rest."

She kissed him on the temple and settled down beside him.

THIRTY-EIGHT

The first day passed quietly. By the second, Rodani was up and limping. Barely. And against Baldar's orders. But just as Cara had refused the physician's curt instructions to leave the room while ministering to Rodani, Rodani himself had refused the orders to remain in bed.

"No. Try again, kia," he said from his corner of the couch. "Not all guild skills are difficult." The fire roared its warmth toward the quilt he covered himself with, the same one Cara had used. "Put your feet down more slowly."

"I'm placing them as slow as I can, Rodani. And my legs are getting achy."

The silence made her look up. Bright marks and dark bruises, the color of pain, marred Rodani's handsome Selandu face. Suddenly, Cara was ashamed of her childish complaint. She ducked her chin. "Tell me again why you suggested this?"

"I thought learning some of the silent commands would keep your mind on something worthwhile as I mended."

Cara looked down at her foot, contorted on the floor in an attempt to walk silently. Try as she might, however, Rodani's superior hearing nearly guaranteed her failure. "But why this?"

Rodani's lower lip curled downward. "As the knife-throwing, kia—something you may take home to your family that you have learned. You may find it useful."

"You don't know my family, aisu. My mother will care only that another three years have passed without me giving birth. And my father will wonder again what I'm going to do with the rest of my life."

Rodani shifted on the couch, wincing slightly. "Does no one appreciate your skills?"

Cara put her foot flat on the floor and looked at her lover beneath her brows. "Only you. No one else in my family."

Rodani's pupils spread wide. "I am family?" he asked, voice low and hesitant.

She stared right back at him. "Yes."

His ears twitched; his body shivered in response. His gaze never left her face.

Wan, weak...to see him in such a state was a gut-wrenching turnaround from the rest of her time here. Rodani was the guardian. The strong one. The tempered metal that would bend not break, the unstained honor. The steadfast wall that protected her from the blasts that came from her every direction.

To see him hunched in the corner of her couch as she had done countless times, it hurt. Hurt to the center of her heart. She wanted to pick him up and comfort him as she had done Ikemi. The improbable was merely daunting. But the impossible...

If only she could pay those guardians back. Were there times when it was okay to ignore one's dearly held ethics? Really? Or was it just weakness in her mind, a monkey-response for revenge?

"Sit," Rodani bade her. "Leave off the walking." He patted the couch beside his leg.

Now *this* was more like it, even though it would have been nice to have attentions he wasn't capable of right now. She curled down next to him and waited. Something shone through his eyes. Some depth she couldn't see.

"I have little to give you, kia, but I will give you what I can."

"You've given me more than you know, aisu."

Rodani tilted his head in a slow slide toward his shoulder, a soft rejection—one without insult.

Behind her, a set of shoes intruded on their privacy.

"Deremic," Rodani said.

The servant walked toward them and bowed.

"What did Iraimin say?"

Deremic pulled his hands behind his back, as Rodani did when facing his taso—or that hated keso of theirs.

"She said she has both heard and sensed people following her, a'tem."

"Did she say who?"

"No, a'tem. But she believes they are guardians."

"Why?"

"Because they are much too adept at not being seen."

"Have they touched her? Stopped her painting? Damaged her property?"

"Not as yet, a'tem."

Rodani pursed his lips and stared at the fire. "Does she ask aught of us?"

Now it was Deremic's turn to hesitate. "She knows of these troubles. She knows she is potential collateral damage." He stared at the toes of his shoes. "She asks if she should speak to the taso."

Rodani rubbed his forehead with a bandaged finger. "Tell her that is her choice. Arimeso will not take offense, but likely she will do little to help."

Deremic bowed and began to leave.

Cara spoke up, uncertain if it was allowed. "Serano could guard her."

"No."

The force in Rodani's voice startled her. She waited a moment to see if he continued, as Deremic left.

"Talk to me, aisu."

He leaned his head back into the corner of the couch and closed his eyes. Beneath the quilt, his hands dropped to his lap. "Why did I move my clothes to your bedroom, kia?"

"Because you didn't want a fight every time you needed to change."

His lips curled into the barest of smiles. "Wise guess. But incorrect."

"Then why?"

"Because I no longer have a guild partner."

Cara sat up straight and spoke with a catch in her voice. "You left him?"

Rodani's expression closed down into a tight ball of pain. He turned his face to the fire.

No. It couldn't be. "He didn't!"

Rodani opened his eyes to the fire but refused to meet her gaze.

Say something, aisu. Anything.

But his eyelids closed down as he shifted his sore body under the quilt.

Cara jumped up. "I'm going to find him and teach him some new words, Rodani. And everyone will hear."

"No!" Rodani's body jerked upward, hand out as the quilt edge dropped into his lap. "No. You promised."

Cara slammed her fist against the door frame. "He left you! He turned his back on you when you need him most!"

Rodani turned away. "And your words stab me again for that which I have already been wounded."

Cara swore, her heart on fire. Pain given and returned, a volley of heartache that burned in each of them. She sat against him, pulling her legs underneath her. "I will never forgive him for this."

Rodani's eyes were fever bright, mirroring the twin pains he carried. "And likely he will never forgive me for this," he said, waving his hand into the air between them.

"When did he leave?" Cara whispered.

"After the censure."

She opened her mouth and inhaled—

"Ask me no more questions, I beg you."

Chastised again, a roil of pain and guilt rushed through her, leaving a wash of shame that crawled down every nerve. Weeks and weeks had gone by as she enjoyed the fruits of their affinity, while Rodani hid the price he'd been paying. How much worse was it? What she could see was bad enough. How much regret was swirling through his body? How close was he to ending the whole mess with her? Would that even help? What could he do to get back the respect he'd lost?

Suddenly, Chendal's words came back to her. "And I will be ordered to...."

Oh, unholy space and time. An image of a striped and bloody Rodani curled on the floor, shot through her vision, warping it with nausea. She couldn't envision the other option. It refused to come to mind. "Gods of the deepest night," she whispered. She curled up to him, close as she could get without aggravating his healing wounds. "I did this."

"Kia?"

"I did this to us. To you. This is my—"

"Cease. Cease. You told Shisa it was the work of the both of us. And you were correct." He reached out with a bruised hand and swept back the tendrils of hair that had left her clip. "I had the wider vision. I knew what could happen. You did not."

She let out a heavy breath and leaned into his palm. "What now?"

"We look forward." His thumb brushed her cheek. "Always."

"Will Hadaman take us?"

The answer was a while in coming. Cara held her breath.

"I believe not, kia."

"Why? You could join the guild staff there. I could be a help to the ambassadors."

"Chendal intimated that they were content with who and what they have."

"So, if I can't help you and Kusik won't stop them, what do we have left?" She pointed to him, her palm open in entreaty. "This?"

Rodani brought both hands out from beneath the quilt. "You should continue to practice walking silently." He took her hands in his and shook them lightly. "And speaking silently."

***

Kimasa, the high priestess, sat at her desk, as satisfied as she had been in many a year. The Ceremony of Four Hands was only days away, and her heart was full of joy—Sela's joy, of course. Minor crises were being solved, plans coming to fruition. Not in their years in this colony has there ever been such an undertaking, such a spectacular celebration for the goddess who created their species and guides them all with Her wisdom.

The selaso brushed the curtains away, letting the afternoon sunlight into her private office. The rain that pounded the manor earlier had disappeared over the horizon. Deeply, she breathed Sela's air, bowing over Sela's landscape, the trees, grasses, the vast plains that ran to the north, all created and watched over by Her all-seeing eyes.

As Kimasa held still in prayer and supplication to the goddess, the abrupt sound of distress clamored behind her. A body. A body in slippers. Breathing hard and uneven. Rushing toward one of the contemplation rooms as if Temi's demons bit at her heels.

An acolyte followed, whispering. "A'sel, a'sel, be at peace. Peace. Here, allow me to assist you."

Kimasa took a calming breath before following the audible chaos. An affinity gone wrong? An inebriated crafter crossing lines?

An unwanted unborn? A wanted one who had slipped away? Kimasa straightened her already-stiff shoulders and entered the room.

Iraimin, master portraitist and ex-acolyte, lay crumpled on the prayer cushions in the far corner, her abdomen heaving with the effort to catch her breath. The newest acolyte, Cusara, knelt at her side, hands on her shoulder in an effort to calm the shaking woman. "Tell me, a'sel. Tell us. The goddess hears you. She hears us all." Cusara ran her hands lightly over Iraimin's covered arms. "Speak your pain, a'sel, and let it depart from you."

Kimasa walked around to the cushions and watched the display, one seeking comfort and one seeking to offer. Iraimin rubbed her arms with shaking hands and pressed her cheek against the cushion. The scent of painting oils wafted up from her hands.

"Holy Mother of all, bring forth Your healing powers through my hands," Cusara intoned. "Ease our sister, take away her hurts and fears. Hear us, Almighty Mother."

Kimasa leaned down and inspected Iraimin's face. Gone was the calm and contemplative aura that had permeated her essence in her office.

Marks.

Marks on her face.

Kimasa moved the acolyte to the side. "Who did this to you, my child?"

Iraimin whispered. "I do not know. I could not see his face."

"His?" the selaso prompted. Ire began to burn hotter. *Calm*, she willed herself. *The goddess heals all.*

"He was tall. I think he was a guardian. He grabbed me. Hit me. I pulled loose and ran." Iraimin curled herself into a fetal position. "But I did not turn to look. Could not. I am sorry."

"Who would do such a thing, Iraimin?" Cusara asked. "Why?"

Iraimin looked at the selaso, then over to the acolyte.

"Au," Kimasa sighed. "You have been caught up in this?"

"Sai."

"All will be better, my child," she said as she rose. "Four days hence, you shall sit at the head table with me, and witness the transforming power of She Who Guides Us All."

***

Rodani flattened Cara's hand between his injured ones, then posed it in a vertical position and pushed downward for a moment. "Stop," he said. "This is the position and gesture for the word 'stop.' You have seen me make it."

"Yes."

"The strength with which you gesture relates the strength behind the word." Rodani flattened his own hand and drew it out and down slowly, as between two antagonists. "This is meant to signal calm. To cease disagreements and arrest any anger." He brought his hand back, then slashed out and down, a quick, heavy chop. "This is also 'stop.' But it is meant to be forceful. An order, one to be obeyed without question."

"You did a slap at the end of it once."

Rodani smiled. "That was in lieu of slapping both you and Serano."

"Thank you for refraining."

The smile widened. "You are most welcome."

"So, if that's 'stop,' what is 'start'?"

The smile slid away. "'Start' or 'go' is similar to the 'as you wish' gesture. But instead of rolling your fingers out into a horizontal position, it is done vertically." He demonstrated with a quick unroll of his fist while straightening his wrist. "As with 'stop,' the urgency or force of command is denoted with speed and power."

"Is 'come here' the same as everyone uses?"

"Sai. Show me."

Cara pointed her fingers toward Rodani and curled her fingers and wrist down and back toward herself. "Same calm and urgency as the others?"

Rodani inclined his head.

"What else?"

"More than too much to teach in one day, kia. But here is one you need." He lifted his first two fingers and tapped them against his lips.

Sighing, Cara shook her head in resignation. "Is there a gesture for sarcasm?" Into his silence, she asked, "what about 'yes' and 'no'?"

"'Yes' is one or more fingers held upward. Toward the goddess, traditionally." A glint of humor shone in his eye. "'No' would normally be one or more fingers held downward. 'Temi's claws, no!' is a draw of the finger across one's neck."

"And, of course, that could also mean 'I'll kill you.'"

"Depending on context."

Cara shifted in her seat, anxious and animated with the chance to learn something new. "What about 'help'? I need? I want? Do you want? Can I? Can you?"

Rodani drew his hand downward slowly, in a stop gesture. *Calm down.*

Heedless, Cara spouted back, animated. "Nouns, aisu! Things! Chair, table, door, hall, dinner, food, pain, hurt, fire?"

Again, Rodani gestured, this time with fingers against his lips.

"But there are so many—"

He glanced toward the fire, then in a flash, reached out and clamped one hand on the back of her head, the other over her mouth. Her eyes went wide, but she held still.

"Hand signals are silent commands, kia, or answers to commands," Rodani said with some heat. "If you cannot obey a silent command, there is no sense in going further."

Cara's body wilted under his hands. He let go, waiting for the reaction he was sure would come. He glanced over her body, watching for tension in her muscles that might presage a bout of temper. But the stillness with which she sat held its own concerns.

"Why are we doing this?" she asked.

Rodani ran the words through his head, adding the extra quiet of her voice, the stillness of her body, the width of her pupils, and height of her eyelids. The sum did not reassure him. The discordant signs of childlike emotion and adult-level intelligence warped his default view of humans into something that was uniquely hers. Though he would never admit it, her stare unnerved him.

"For now, kia, it is something we may occupy ourselves with. I ask you to be content with that."

Slowly, from his cocoon in the couch, he taught her the gestures for every important item in the room, and for movement. When he gestured her into the workroom, he followed her in and continued the lesson, mixing new and old gestures as he had been taught in guild training. He did not, however, raise welts on her skin with every mistake she made. Those lessons he kept to himself.

When Deremic came into the room, Rodani called a halt. Cara obeyed the gesture, waiting quietly for the next order. When Rodani gestured *work* while pointing to her latest quilt, she rolled her eyes and sat down as he followed Deremic back into the servant's quarters.

When Deremic related the attack in the corridor and Iraimin's escape, the banked anger in his chest began to burn anew. "Come with me."

Deremic eyed Rodani's bandages and the cockeyed slant of his hips as he favored one leg. "Where?"

"The taso."

Deremic drew his expression into a mask of propriety, the only answer to Rodani's wild desire to venture into the halls still injured. "Allow me to see if she is available first, a'tem." Rodani gestured acquiescence, and followed Deremic out into the hall when the "yes" came.

They met no enemies in the halls. Deremic stayed in the communications alcove as Rodani was ushered into the taso's office.

Arimeso rose in alarm. She circled him, eyeing what could be seen and what could not. Sitting down in the heavy, carved chair that belonged to her alone, she drew her brows down. "Te'oto," she began.

Rodani bowed deeply, but with one hand out in the gesture of *No*, the other open on his knee in supplication. It was a dangerous beginning for an entreaty. He held his breath.

"How long before I lose my patience with this entire experiment, Rodani?"

The burn in his midsection turned up to high at the tone in his taso's voice. She was, indeed, losing her patience. And that meant nothing but ill for Rodani and the woman with whom he had bonded. Double-bonded.

"A'Taso, I am deeply sorry for any disorder and distraction my actions have caused you," he said from his bowed position.

Arimeso tapped her curving nail on the top of her desk. Silence rode behind it. "And you limped down here to tell me that?"

Rodani took a deeper breath. "A'Taso," he began.

"Sit down before your body sits for you, te'oto."

Rodani sat carefully in the unadorned chair facing the taso's desk, facing the taso. Facing his future. "A'Taso, I wish to take Cara out of the house for a time."

Arimeso's nail stopped tapping. She sat back and regarded him with narrowed pupils. "Where?"

"A'Taso, my parents," he swallowed, "have a cabin near the base of the hills south of here. I could take her there, and no one would know where we are."

"You assume you could take her that far away with no one the wiser?"

"Yes, a'Taso."

"You would be betting both your lives on it."

"Yes."

"You would lose," she told him. "Even if you got her there safely, you could not defend her and yourself if you were found. It would be a death trap."

Rodani drew several deep breaths, keeping his hands still in his lap. "A'Taso."

"No."

Another breath. "A'Taso, we need to get away. For a time. Just…a time, a'Taso." Temi's demons, where was his control? He clenched his jaw and kept his ears still with the last bit of will he had left. "Allow the others a chance to calm as well. It may help. It may." Demons, devils, and claws, he sounded like a child begging at his mother's knee. "A'Taso."

"No, Rodani. I understand your plea, and the logic behind it. But I cannot let the human go outside the grounds. If I let her outside my safety net, and she is killed, it will be a double calamity on my house, our names, and our species. No."

With the last of his willpower keeping his hands in his lap and his face masked, Rodani could only lower his head.

"I will speak to them again. Tomorrow evening, after dinner. This violence in my guild has to stop. Even if I have to take charge of it."

"They have taken it outside, a'Taso."

Arimeso leaned forward. "Outside?"

"The guild, a'Taso. Iraimin has been attacked."

Arimeso stood up, slowly. She seemed to rise forever, a statue carved of sacred stone. A glint shone in her eyes. A light that Rodani recognized as kin to the one in Cara's when she went feral.

"Return to your room. Or yours and Cara's, since you left yours."

Serano. She knew.

Rodani retreated as bidden, Deremic at his side.

Back in the servant's quarters, Rodani sat himself, Hamman, and Deremic at their table. He spoke quietly. Gave orders. Explanations. Suggestions. More orders. Timetable. Gave Deremic the key to his old rooms.

"Questions?"

There were none. Rodani limped back into Cara's study. He gestured for silence, and for Cara to stand. "We will continue."

He motioned for Cara to walk, coupled with the gesture for silence. Motioned for her to roll up her quilt. Several times he halted her and made stronger gestures for silence. When Hamman rolled the dinner tray in, he motioned her to sit. Motioned for her to eat. Motioned her to drink. All with the silence gesture, doubled and tripled in strength. When dinner was done and Cara got up from her chair with an audible scrape, Rodani stood up and threw a series of gestures at her, anger in the whiplike motions of his hands.

"Game?" she whispered, her expressions easy for him to read this time. Her eyes widened as he held one set of fingers up, one set down.

Let her bite on that one for a while, he thought.

He kept her at it for the rest of the evening, taking breaks when she seemed to need them, but enforcing his teachings all the while. Bedtime was no different, even if the armoire drawers refused to open silently. Five times he made her retry it before she finally refused, jabbing her finger at his face and back to the noisy drawer. With seeming infinite patience, he opened it. Not a creak was heard.

Cara threw up her hands, then grinned widely. *Let's see him silence what I do in the facilities.*

When she crawled under the covers, it was with an audible sigh of relief. Rodani put his nose up to hers and put his fingers on her lips.

She nipped them.

THIRTY-NINE

Rodani woke her, covering her mouth when she mumbled a complaint, slashing a "no" motion with his hand when she tried to question him. "Test yourself," he whispered into her ear. "See how long you can remain silent in word and movement." He rolled quietly out of bed and pulled on his clothes.

Cara attempted the same, not without a handful of furious gestures from him as reminders.

Deremic opened the door (quietly, as well) and motioned to them. They followed him out the servants' door and across the hall to Rodani's old rooms. Inside his bedroom, the window on the south wall was open to the night and the chill spring wind. Rodani bent his head to Deremic's ear. "All is ready?"

He pointed upward.

Rodani motioned Cara to stay behind as he walked noiselessly to the window and peered out into the night. Another motion brought Deremic up to him. He made a few hand gestures, to which Deremic gestured another yes.

Deremic leaned out the window slowly into the pitched darkness and grabbed something. Pulling, he climbed out of the window and disappeared down out of sight. Rodani motioned for her to come forward. He whispered.

"Climb down the rope. Deremic will assist you when you are near the ground."

Cara looked closely. A dark shape resolved itself into her servant, and another, larger, one stood nearby. "Benatac?" she mouthed.

Yes, he signed, and pointed to her foot, then patted the windowsill. He helped her up and out of the window, as Deremic held the rope from below, guiding it into her waiting hands. Slowly, she slid down, grasping the thick cord as best she could with thighs and damaged hands. Rodani kept a fierce grip on her jacket for as long as she was within his reach, then let go.

Her hold on the rope slackened, her wasted hand muscles unable to keep up with the task. She began to slip. "Help," she whispered into the dark.

"Drop," Deremic whispered back. She slid a little further, reaching the height of the first floor. Then her hands gave out. As she felt them go, she pursed her lips tightly to keep any sound escaping. She fell with a soft thump into Deremic's arms.

As soon as she did, Rodani climbed out and let himself down, hand-over-hand, behind her. They got her onto the benatac in record time. Rodani clambered up and into the back seat of the saddle. "No sound until I tell you, kia," he said right behind her ear. Then he flipped a blanket over her and onto his shoulders. The beast began to move toward the forest.

Rodani aimed it southwest, heading toward the area where Cara had run after escaping the Enclave. Nothing but the soft padding of benatac feet against the ground marred their nighttime passage. In a short while, the beast slowed down, and Cara began to hear the sound of leaves brushing against cloth. Rodani removed the blanket and laid it across the beast's haunches behind him. He placed two fingers against Cara's mouth, emphasizing their continued need for silence in the woods.

They followed the stream eastward for a half-hour, then Rodani dismounted and led the benatac forward more slowly. They came to what looked like a crooked row of vertical wooden columns, like close-set fence posts. The columns were no wider than her palm.

Rodani looped the reins around a nearby branch and pulled Cara off the saddle. He stood her on the forest floor and stepped over to what looked like fence posts but were actually tree roots. Cara started to follow him, but Rodani threw out a hand behind him to stop her. He readjusted his jacket and reached between the posts for something. Rasping sounds erupted in the air as he maneuvered two somethings she couldn't see into place between the roots. Then he pulled Cara up to the fence and motioned for her to walk forward. In front of her face, almost invisible in the midnight forest, were two thin, tall panels, tangent to the two roots, creating a short corridor. Rodani pushed her forward, guiding her in between the panels, squeezing her. She came out into a dim circle of posts around a tree trunk. She felt a tap on her shoulder.

One by one, Rodani handed her several sacks that had hung on the benatac, passing them through to her between the panels. He leaned inward to speak softly. "Put them on the ground by the tree, then sit with them. I will return in a while." He took the reins in hand. "Do *not* touch the roots," he warned her. "The rest of the tree is safe to touch. Be patient, kia," he whispered again. "There is little to harm you within this wall. I need to return the beast to Deremic. He knows where to meet me."

Cara motioned to the panels. Rodani pushed them inward until they barely rested against the posts, warning her silently to leave them alone. He handed her a knife, then disappeared into the darkness.

Cara stared at the knife in her palm, questions banging around in her head, unsought and unspoken. She sat down in the dark with her back to the tree, one arm resting on top of the nearest bag, and waited.

Time passed slowly. Did she dare sleep? She'd gotten little, earlier. But this place, this time, was not where she should let down her guard. Her eyes had already adjusted, and still, she could see nothing much but shadows. Wind rustled the new leaves around her. Grass beneath her tickled against her skin. The eerie scream of a wild hunter startled her out of a doze, her limbs jerking at the sound.

Was that a footstep?

Wood rasped against wood. She stood up in anticipation. Her guardian slipped through the panels and pulled them through afterwards, laying them flat on the ground inside.

He laid a hand on her shoulder and pushed her into a sit, then sat down beside her. "When you can see again, we will work," he whispered. He pulled her to his chest and wrapped his arms around her. "Now, we rest."

Later, light began to filter through the trees. Rodani shifted Cara away from him and stood up. He dug for one of the larger bags nearby, then began to climb the tree. Cara watched, and soon he was out of sight. After several minutes, he came back down empty-handed. He stopped on the lowest branch.

He motioned to the nearest bag, then himself. Cara brought it to him, pushing it upward, near his feet. He grabbed it and carried it up into the layers of branches that grew out from the trunk. One trip for each of the larger bags, one for two or three of the smaller.

Did he have a tree house up there?

Cara bit down on her questions, waiting stubbornly to see when he would say she could talk again. In another part of the circle of roots, she relieved her morning bladder, then waited at the base of the tree for him to come down.

This time, he jumped to the ground. Without a word, he lifted her up, so that she was lying on the branch he'd jumped from. She pulled herself up onto it. Rodani clambered up after her. Branch by branch, they climbed into the tree. The branches shrunk in size from massive, to extra-large, to large, before Rodani stopped. Above her hung a hammock.

She looked down between her feet. The ground seemed very far away.

Rodani boosted her to the next branch, then himself. He put one foot into the hammock just below the branch, then the other foot, keeping hold of the branch and balancing carefully. With one arm, he brought Cara down into the hammock, pointing to a rope that was wrapped around the branch near her shoulder. She grabbed it, then folded herself down into the hammock. Rodani curled up beside her.

"You may speak softly, now, kia," he said finally.

She knew what she wanted to say first. "Are you proud of me for staying silent so long?"

Rodani smiled. "As you are objectively not guild, I suppose I must be."

"What in the gods' dark night are we doing, Rodani?" she whispered.

"Taking a much-needed respite from the house."

"No one will find us here?"

"Very unlikely."

She looked around. "What will we do for water? And food? And facilities?"

"Much of what we brought is travel food. There is a stream nearby for water. Facilities are a minor problem, but I have rigged a waterproof basket lower down that we can use when reaching the ground is not advisable."

"They'll smell us."

"Not if we are cautious."

"Then you should rest." She patted his leg. "I know you still hurt."

He stretched into horizontal and stared at her. "I could consider that discourteous."

"But you won't." She leaned over him. "Even if you are guild, and can't admit to pain, you know it's simply that I worry for you."

She looked around. "I wish I'd had the time to take a book, or drawing materials."

"Already walked that path," he replied, eyes closing. "Green bag."

As the sun rose to mid-day, Rodani's 'com went off. "Five, One. Five, One." He grabbed it and shut off the sound of Kusik's voice, turning the volume down as well.

"Fool," he muttered.

Cara smiled. "You or him?"

He thought. "Both."

"Do you think they know we're gone?"

Rodani fiddled with his 'com, manipulating it in ways she'd never seen. "It would be better if they did not know yet. But when I do not reply, it will be obvious. We must remain cautious." He put the 'com on the branch above his head and tied it down with a string.

"It is set to receive only, now. And it will warn us if there is another 'com in the area."

"Really. It has unguessed talents, aisu." She lay down next to him, her head under his arm.

"Tomorrow will be the first test."

"Why?"

"Kimasa has scheduled a ceremony in honor of the goddess. The full house will attend. I assumed you would not care to witness it."

"Gods, no. Thank you, aisu."

"That is why we left in the night. It is possible that the timing of the last attack on me was to make sure I was visibly bruised and hurting during the congregation."

"Damn them. It pleases me that you fooled them." She twirled her fingers in a circle. "What's with those posts in the ground? And the boards we walked through?"

"They are the tree's roots. There is poison in the bark and sap of the roots."

Cara drew a breath. "Oh. Serano told me about them. When you were sick."

"What did he say?"

"Not much. Just that they were dangerous."

"He is correct."

They rested against each other. Rodani pulled an errant strand of hair away from her bun. "It would please me if you would wear your hair down while we are here, kia."

"Loose, or clipped back like yours?"

"Either. Whatever does not offend you. Whatever you prefer."

She let the bun roll out, and clipped her hair at the nape, like Rodani's. "It can get in the way."

"Yes." He pulled a long strand away from her shoulder and wrapped it around his finger. "I know you will need a ride soon."

Cara reared back, eyes wide. "After they kicked you there? Please, te'oto. Not until you heal."

"I enjoy tending to your needs," he said softly.

"When you're ready."

Rodani stared into the distance and began to smile.

"What?"

He looked down at her. "My fingers will be ready before the rest of me."

***

The day of the Four Hands Ceremony had dawned auspiciously. Everything had flowed into place as it should have, guided by the munificent hand of the goddess.

Unfortunately, it had not ended that way. Kimasa strode down the second-floor east hallway, imperious in her anger.

How dare he? How dare he humiliate her with their absence from the ceremony? The selaso pounded on the servants' door as her handmaidens gathered in a golden flutter behind her.

Hamman answered the door.

"I will speak with Rodani."

"I have not seen him today, a'Selaso," the servant said quietly.

"Where is a'Cara?"

"She is not here."

"Where are they?" Kimasa demanded.

Deremic came up behind Hamman as she answered, "We do not know."

"How can you not know? Is it not your duty to attend to her?"

"A'Selaso, please forgive us," Deremic said. "We were not told where they would be."

Kimasa leaned into their faces. "Everyone was to be there!" She stamped her golden-slippered foot. "Everyone." She enunciated each syllable, imbuing it with her fury.

"That information was not given to us."

"When will they return?"

"Nor have we been told that," he said.

Kimasa drew herself up in offended pride. "This is unconscionable!" She turned and headed for the taso's inner quarters.

Arimeso was just pulling her lounging gown together when Kimasa flew into her office. "A'Taso," she called out.

By habit, Arimeso wiped her face of expression before entering the room. She had an idea what this was about.

"A'Selaso," she said. "Please sit down. Would you care for a drink? Some tea?"

"Nothing, a'Taso. Just the ears of that missing guardian!"

"Please calm yourself, a'Selaso, if the goddess pleases."

"I can tell you what the goddess is displeased about, Arimeso. Did you see what they did?"

"Who?" she asked, though she could very well guess. Let the selaso have her say. It was better for all that she spew it out first.

"Rodani. And Cara. They were both absent from the ceremony."

"Why was it necessary that they attend?"

Kimasa's eyes widened in disbelief. "I told them days ago that I wished them to witness to the house for all of their good fortune in reuniting," she said. "Rodani refused me. Refused me! Claiming that he could not, for safety. Safety? I was incensed! How dare he think that the goddess would not protect them for witnessing? How dare—"

Arimeso held up a palm. "If he already refused you, why did you call on them today?"

"I was going to offer it for them, of course, since Rodani was reluctant for them to do so themselves." She rushed on. "I was giving them the opportunity to affirm to the whole house and its outliers that the goddess shined Her beneficence on him, and on your human guest as well. Oh, it was to be marvelous. A proclamation of the clearest, most undeniable—"

"A'Selaso, Rodani was correct."

Kimasa's face folded back into anger. "The goddess protects Her most fervent followers, a'Taso."

"And sometimes the goddess forces us to protect ourselves. I am sorry that Rodani and Cara were not at the ceremony. But it would have been better had you not mentioned them."

Kimasa stood up. "I see."

With a turn as sharp as her words, she left the office.

In the inner doorway, Kusik sighed. Arimeso waited for whatever would come out of his mouth next.

"And you will let him get away with this as well?"

"It is the selaso's fault just as much as Rodani's, tisal."

"Are we always to prioritize this muck of stable sweepings from opposite directions, esuva? If Rodani hadn't started it..." he said in one voice. "If others would let them alone..." he said in another, sarcasm dripping. "The dichotomy will never be made whole if we cannot heal this divide."

It was Arimeso's turn to sigh.

***

Up one floor and around the corner, Toranel let her co-conspirators into her room, and shut the door behind them.

FORTY

"Another day, aisu," Cara said. She marked her place in *The History of Selandu Cultures* and put it on the tree branch above. "All I need now is my quilting supplies."

A fleeting expression flowed across Rodani's face. "We will both be late on our commissions, kia."

"Will we be in trouble?"

"There will be words, a few tempers. Otherwise, likely no."

"What will we face when we go back? Will they stop beating on you?"

"I have some hope that Kusik will have reined them in."

"How forlorn is that hope?"

Rodani drew her close, refusing to answer. He rested his hand on her head, then on her breast, caressing gently. "Are you in need?"

"You aren't healed yet. I can still see bruising. I can wait."

He looked at her steadily as his thumb rubbed across her nipple. "Are you sure?"

"I'm not going to ride a bruised organ, Rodani."

His hand moved lower. "You will not."

"If you're just using your fingers, I'll be the only one receiving pleasure. That isn't fair."

"Untrue. You will simply be the only one receiving a crest."

She thought about it, about what he'd been through, about what he meant to her. "That's acceptable to you?"

"Today, yes. With no doubt." To prove his point and, by the way, removing any chance of protest, Rodani sat up and tugged her clothes off. He sat sideways in the hammock, his back curved. He tapped his chest. "Lay on me."

Naked to the breezes, Cara started to climb on top of him.

"No. Your back to me." He pointed. "Face the forest."

Somewhat mystified, she slid onto his chest and abdomen, resting her head in the curve of his shoulder. "Don't let me slide down on your bruises, aisu."

Slowly, he pulled her knees up and apart, bringing his legs up behind hers along her inner thighs, to hold her legs in place. "As far as you can stretch, kia. Stop me before I hurt you."

And he bared her private flesh to the sky and the trees.

His hands began to roam, up, down, round and round, side to side, and most importantly, over and between her nether lips.

He left them, returned to them, left them, and returned to them, both hands constantly in motion. He couldn't see her face, but he listened closely to her breathing and watched for the signs of arousal in her body and its movements.

This, he thought, *this time, this place, this activity, I must commit to memory.*

Rodani narrowed his focus and his finger movements, found her place of greatest pleasure, and began to ride it with his thumb—cautiously, ever so gently, watching...listening...

Soon, her breathing began to change. His fingers drifted downward to her channel, testing it. *Yes.* He pushed two fingers in. Farther...farther. *There.* He pressed upward rhythmically, then refocused on his thumb. With a crafter's patience and coordination, he rode her higher toward the top of her hill.

Goddess, the sounds she makes. His own pelvis pulsed with desire, but twinged in pain as well. He ignored it for the pleasure above him.

Caressing her face, her breasts, her neck, he quickened the movements of his lower hand, pushing and pulling in minute movements of pressure. Her voice went up an octave. He knew this sign, too.

He felt increased pressure on his shoulder as she arched her back. *Yes, yes.*

Ride, my ki'tana. Let me hear you.

Cara gasped, then froze and went silent. Quickly, Rodani covered her mouth with his free hand. "Kia," he whispered.

She cried out, over and over, her body bucking through the waves of pleasure he gave her. Chills started at his ears and rushed downward over his body as he pushed her through to the end. Only when she laid her hand on his, did he stop.

It almost sounded as if she were raining. But he knew better, and smiled.

Cara pulled his arms across her chest and began to caress them. After a few minutes, she shifted. "Clothes," she whispered.

Rodani let go, remembering how easily she became chilled. She slipped her clothing back on, then nestled against him. "Thank you."

Au, he thought, gratitude was most welcome, but her sounds of pleasure were second only to his own passionate desires. Daily—no, hourly, when they were in close contact, he marveled at the changes she had wrought in his life. Boredom and loneliness had transformed into a state of unbounded ardor and attachment that he wore with pride while in her presence, but left him empty and anxious when he was away from her.

He remained aware of how much he had, in turn, lost. His partner foremost, much of his freedom a near second, companionship, such as it was, with his fellow guild members. He refused to look too deeply into the balance. He had thrown his dice and played the hand that spread out in front of him without ruminating on regrets. It was a stubbornness not too different from his adashi's.

They dozed in the stippled sunshine, arms wrapped around each other, while new leaves fluttering in the breeze.

Rodani's 'com broke the silence with a soft buzzing noise.

Instantly he was alert, shifting Cara's body away from his. He motioned her to silence, then crawled across to the end of the hammock and unwound the string holding his 'com on the branch. Slowly, he spun it through a 360° flat plane.

Talk to me. Tell me where they are, he thought.

West. West of him. *Two, maybe three? Hunting*. He motioned to Cara, hand signals again. *Watch. That direction.*

She crawled unsteadily down the other half of the hammock to peer over the edge. The tree trunk blocked quite a bit of her view, but Rodani knew she would do what she was able.

He waited, unmoving in his knotted perch that hung many times his height from the ground. After several minutes, he spotted movement below. Two guardians walking east, approximately ten feet from each other. Slowly, they walked nearer to the circle of roots surrounding their tree, then under its branches, then beyond. They stopped, started, and stopped again to search the ground and environs for someone's passage.

Rodani knew what they hunted. This close to the manor, wild animals large enough to feed a crowd had lessened over the decades. They could be after only one thing.

The 'com came to life again, volume turned low. "Tracks," he heard one guardian say.

"Where?" asked another.

"What kind?" asked a third.

"Boots."

They converged several feet east from the ring of roots, nearly out of Rodani's sight.

"Temi's knives! Does your 'com read anything?"

"Many small readings. Naught of what we're looking for." Anger bled through the speaker.

"Where do they lead?"

"Stay that. Where do they come from?"

The trio fanned out.

"South," said one voice, excited.

Yes, Rodani thought. *Follow the trail, fools. You think me an amateur? Serano must not be among them.* To his surprise, he found some satisfaction in that.

He watched as they tracked out of sight, his breath becoming somewhat less constricted. He glanced up at the water bag. It held enough until tomorrow. Reaching out, he tapped Cara's extended leg. She turned to look at him.

He motioned. *Did you see anything?*

She mouthed a *Du,* then shook her head, answers in both languages. He motioned her to keep looking, but as they listened and watched, the 'com remained silent.

For now.

Rodani tapped her leg again and motioned her away from the hammock's edge. They came together in a huddle of arms and legs.

"Did I cause that?" Cara whispered.

Rodani berated himself silently. "If you did, kia, it was by consequence of my actions."

How long did they have here? Returning to the manor made Rodani's stomach burn. Though he never voiced it, and never would, he knew his own unwise actions were the root of their current dread. Had he kept his hands—and body—off of his adashi, she would now be safe in her rooms. And he...he would be free from the ever-present uproar and violence that dogged his boot heels and hovered over his ears. At this late point, it would matter to no one but them that the proximate cause of their misery was his fellow Selandu choosing to pay attention to that which was not their duty.

His thoughts veered in directions he fervently did *not* wish them to go. Deeply disturbed, he drew Cara closer and fixed his attention on the sight, scent, and feel of his bedmate in his arms.

FORTY-ONE

Kusik stomped his feet and muttered as he circled his desk and his taso's.

"They cannot be far. Serano has checked the cabin that Rodani's parents own. Timan, the cave and the waterfall. The new knives checked the south forest and the east."

He spun and stomped the other way. "The temaso tells me they are not in Hadaman, nor in Tendiman. They must be south. That is the only location where recent footprints were seen."

Arimeso leaned back in her chair to regard her keso, her mate of ten years. "You may consider waiting them out, esuva. They will run out of food and clean clothes."

"Or they will continue to run."

"You did send a notice to the surrounding towns."

"Yes, yes."

"I doubt a'Cara would leave her belongings behind. Many of her tools are not hers. They belong to her people."

"I do not predict what an uncontrollable and dishonorable human might do, tisal." He stopped pacing and faced the office door. "My guild is cloven in two. It is war."

"You must put a stop to their violence, esuva. I do not wish for Rodani's affinity ended before its time."

"Sela may not allow that wish."

"Punish the attackers."

"I have. It does not stop them."

"Then dismiss them, my keso."

"I—"

"Do not tell me you cannot. You can."

"And still no punishment from the guardian who fled his duty?"

"Rodani did not flee his duty, Kusik," Arimeso said firmly. "He took his duty with him."

***

The new day had dawned soft and was heading toward warm.

Cara sketched a few more lines in her notebook, then erased a few errant ones. Rodani watched her, remaining still as she'd asked.

Drawing had become her haven these past four days, and drawing Rodani was the best part. Strange and cold in the beginning of her stay in his land, he'd become handsome with familiarity.

And vocabulary, mustn't forget that. Her cheeks still burned with embarrassment at the new words she had pushed Rodani to give her as he lay naked in the hammock. She smiled wickedly.

In his turn, Rodani had coaxed her out of her own clothes (again!) and begun a dictionary of his own. As well, he had added to her notebook, sketches and detailed drawings. The shock of them when she had opened the pages had brought a grin to his mouth. One that rarely appeared as they whiled away the hours high above the ground.

She looked more closely at his face. At least his bruises were going away, including the ones under his clothes. Anger still burned when she remembered Baldar and his assistants bringing Rodani's battered body up to her bedroom a week ago, blood leaking from more cuts than she could stomach counting.

Suddenly, the 'com sputtered to life.

"Rodani."

His eyes went as wide as hers. They both looked toward the communicator above their heads on the tree branch.

"Rodani, I know you can hear me."

It was Timan, Kusik the hateful's guild partner. Timan of the long walk while her bound hands burned.

They waited.

"Rodani, it is enough. Meet me, *with Cara*, at the base of the rapids. One hour, a'tem."

Rodani bent his head in thought. A million questions flew through Cara's mind but, for her promise, she clamped down on them. For now. This was Rodani's call. His summons, his choice, and his responsibility to its consequences.

"Retrieve your knife. Come." He began to climb down. She followed him, holding out a hand for assistance when the distance between branches was too far for her own grasp. At the bottom, she jumped into his arms. When he set her down, he spoke.

"The rapids are near the head of the stream coming down from the hills. I will walk south, then cross over as I near them. You will cross the stream now, then head south on the other side. Walk slowly and quietly as you near us. Try to pass by us at the rapids, turn around again, and meet us as you walk north."

She thought it through. "You don't want him knowing our hiding place, either."

Rodani led her to the crossing stones he'd laid down two days ago. "Use those new skills I taught you, kia. I will see you soon." He gave her hair a gentle stroke, then headed south on the west side of the stream. He didn't take the time to walk quietly. Neither did he stomp and rage. He would meet the coming remonstrance with calm assurance.

Timan rested his rear on a rock next to the rapids.

"Where is Cara?"

"She will meet us here, a'Biso."

"When?"

"As soon as she arrives, a'Biso." Rodani stood in front of him, clear-eyed, knowing his words were tinged with insolence. But his regard for discourtesies hung fragile.

Timan's eyes narrowed. "You are taking far too much privilege upon yourself, a'tem."

"And my fellow guardians are taking far too many liberties with their rage. I tire of the damage."

"You would both do better to let Kusik administer control of the situation."

"When will that begin?"

He saw it coming and stood unmoving to face it. Timan's slap stung his face, but it was far less than what Kusik had already dealt him.

"So you believe you can do what you wish," Timan asked, "when you wish, and you will not be denied?"

"No, a'Biso. I am well aware that I can be denied at any time. But while I wait, I deal with my own safety and Cara's as best that I can manage. There has been precious little safety in the manor of late."

"And not one person in the inner circle has failed to mention your insubordination and flouting of guild rules," Timan said, anger rising.

Rodani accepted the stern rebuke with a mask of calm. "The taso looks toward the future. I have seen the wisdom of doing the same."

"And here you hide, even from me, while your crafting and hers sit unmade and behind schedule."

"I have been forced to make us both a prisoner of her rooms, a'Biso. It was becoming difficult to endure."

"Then you have lost much of your strength of will since guild training, a'tem, if three rooms and three meals a day are so difficult to tolerate."

"My intolerance comes from Cara's difficulties, not my own."

"Please tell me, Rodani, what difficulties do her rooms, meals, and warm showers present to her?"

Rodani bit down on all the hostility he wished to spew and told his nervously quivering ear tips to behave. "What she objects to is the treatment I have received at the guild's hands, a'Timan." His voice rose. "Were you there when she frantically begged Arimeso to stop Kusik from hitting me after we were reunited—with permission? Did you watch as she screamed and beat chunks of stone out of the fireplace for my injuries? Have you listened to her rage and rain out her frustrations?"

"And every complaint of yours, and hers, stems from the guild line you should never have crossed."

"Have you asked the taso's opinion of our affinity, a'Biso?"

"I need not. I am well aware of it."

Ahead of him, beyond Timan, Cara stepped out from behind a tree.

"I obey my taso, a'Biso." It was his most basic defense, oft stated, and he held to it with all the strength of his will.

With a rustle of cloth, Cara crossed her arms. Timan's eyes widened. As he spun, Rodani grabbed his wrist—the one that had already palmed a gun.

Maybe she felt the tension in the air. Possibly, she remembered at the last moment the necessity of courtesies. But Cara lowered her hands and bowed to Timan, a proper one.

Timan breathed deeply and released the grip on his gun. "Are you well, a'Cara?"

"Yes, thanks to Rodani."

Timan ran his gaze over her unbound hair for a few moments before she continued.

"Have you asked Rodani if he is well?"

Au, I know that look, Rodani thought. *Know that tone of voice, those narrowed eyes.* "Cara, it seems a'Timan is not here to attack me."

Timan motioned to the ground. "Sit."

Cara waited, motionless except for her eyes. They flit from Timan to Rodani and back.

Timan pursed his lips. "Sit," he commanded.

Cara looked only at Rodani.

Now Timan's shoulders stiffened. Quickly, Rodani pointed for her to sit. Cara walked to his side and folded herself down into a tangle of supple limbs. Rodani sat beside her, across from his second, the divide between them now incarnate.

Timan lowered himself gracefully to the ground. "A'Cara, do humans obey rules?"

"Have you never met the ambassadors, a'Timan?"

"I have not had that honor."

Cara remained silent.

"Do you not see the rule Rodani has blatantly broken?" he asked. "Do you not see the trouble it has caused?"

"Humans are rule-breakers as well as rule-followers, a'Biso. Trouble may be worthless or very much worth it."

"And as you are so often disturbed, does the chaos before you not caution you at all?"

Cara leaned forward, aggression filling her face. "Given the chance, I would take a fireplace poker to every one of their faces, a'Timan. What Rodani and I do behind closed doors is no one else's concern."

"I see you both have discussed this and come to an agreement."

Cara smiled, a wide inappropriate one, from Rodani's judgment. "I believe we agreed to that the first night we joined, a'Timan."

Much to Rodani's amusement, his second paled in embarrassment.

"Have you no shame?" Timan countered.

"Whatever I feel shame for, a'Timan, is not something I'll discuss with you."

"I am attempting to assist you both."

"By doing what?"

His biso and his bedmate stared at each other over the wall of culture and honor that divided them. Rodani began to despair of a tall enough ladder ever being built.

"You know, a'Biso, if you want to help us, guard Rodani's back for him, will you? Since his own partner decided to desert him, he could really use some help."

Rodani froze.

"Please, a'Timan," she begged.

Timan drew his gaze back to Rodani. "You will return to the manor tomorrow."

"Rest-day we will return, a'Biso."

"Day after tomorrow."

"Rest-day, please, a'Biso. I am long due a holiday. I requested one a few days past, and I am asking again, now. I see no definitive reason why I should be refused."

"No. Because you left without permission, just as you enjoined an affinity with your adashi without permission. We tire of your insolence, Rodani. It stops here."

"Be specific, please. *What* stops?"

"Your disobedience. Your illegal affinity."

"I will stop fleeing the manor when I am no longer abused by my fellow guardians. And I will stop my affinity when the taso demands it."

"You are making a choice between your guild and taso, and an alien woman."

"The choice has been forced upon me, a'Biso. It is not one I wished for."

"Come home."

"Home is where the words and hands I feel are welcoming, not wounding."

Timan's masked expression fell away. Incredulity took its place. "A'Cara," he said sharply. "Walk away."

Cara stared at Rodani with a look of fear.

"Find us a fish for dinner, kia," he replied. *Be calm. Temi's knives, obey me.*

She got up and walked down the stream.

Timan leaned forward. "What hold does she have on you, te'oto?"

"Do any of us truly know what bonds us to another, a'Timan? What holds you to the taso in second place?"

"Cease. Prying."

Now it was Rodani's turn to lean in. "Yes," he hissed.

"This affinity is destroying you!"

"In what way, a'Biso? My guild and craft skills remain. I have lost neither. Where is this destruction you see?"

Timan only stared.

"Or is it the house guild you see destroying itself?"

Now Timan's face returned to anger.

"Where does the fault truly lie?" Rodani continued.

"In all of you. And you began it."

"Did I?" Rodani adjusted his seat on the ground, as if readying for a fight. "Let us walk back up the trail, the two of us."

The speed of his words went into high gear. "What caused my affinity? Cara's needs, plus my own. Why were Cara's needs my duty? Because the taso assigned them to me. Why did the taso assign them to me? Because she needed someone to watch over Cara. Why did the taso need someone to watch over her? Because the taso brought her here. Why did the taso bring her here? For money. For the future. Why does the taso concern herself with money? Simple. Why concern herself with the future? Because she is wise. Why is she wise? Ask the goddess, a'Timan. Sela does not speak to me.

"Is that far enough back, or shall we walk farther? Shall we speak of the River War and the necessity of preventing another?"

"Cease."

"I *beg* you to, a'Biso." His rejoinder came from the heart. He only hoped his second could hear it.

With no other word, Timan got up and walked away.

Rodani dropped his head in his hands.

It was still there when Cara came back.

"I saw him leave," she said, kneeling in front of him. "Was anything settled?"

"No."

"Let's go back to the tree."

FORTY-TWO

It felt good to be back in a proper bed, despite the peace they'd left behind in the forest. Cara stretched under the covers, bumping her knee against Rodani's thigh. She patted it. "Many things to do today, aisu. Deadlines."

Rodani muttered something unintelligible.

"Clean clothes and a hot breakfast." A polite tap on the door interrupted her attempt to kiss him awake.

"A'tem, a'Cara," Hamman's agitated voice came through the gap at the edge of the door. "The selaso is here to speak with you."

"Temi's demons," Rodani whispered. And louder: "This is not an auspicious time."

"Yes, a'tem. So I told her. But she has waited days for your return and will not be gainsaid."

"Tea, please?" Cara slid out of bed and threw on a hodgepodge of clothes.

Rodani went to the facilities and came back combed. Guild black, of course, was all he would wear. He tapped on the door to let Hamman know they were dressed.

Hamman bustled in with a tray of tea, bread, and jam. "She seems in a state, a'tem. Will not sit, refused tea, refused all courtesies." Cara and Rodani followed her into the study.

"Is this about the Four Hands Ceremony?"

"I do not presume, a'Cara." It was as close to a censure as Cara had ever heard from her servant. She closed her mouth and waited.

Kimasa paraded into Cara's rooms in a swirl of gold. "A'tem," she said, stopping in front of Rodani. He stood in the guild rest position, feet apart, and open, empty hands on his thighs, courteous but cool. The priestess glanced down at Cara, then lifted her chin. "You failed to attend the ceremony, Rodani."

Rodani inclined his head sharply and held it there a few moments, acknowledging the truth of her words.

"You were aware of my order to you, that you would avow the goddess's hand in your life. That you would attest to Her beneficence in reuniting with your adashi."

"I was aware."

Kimasa waited, eyes wide, expecting something. When it wasn't forthcoming, she jumped into the silence. "It is absolutely imperative that you make this admission."

"Why?"

"Why? It will show to the whole house, the whole of Selandan, that the goddess not only guides your life, but Cara's also. She and her people must be brought under the Enclave's canopy. It is the only way to ensure peace between our peoples." She motioned to Cara, and past her. "Surely you see the necessity of this, Rodani?"

"And surely, a'Selaso, you remember that I could not do so, for security reasons?"

"The goddess is your safety." Imperious, Kimasa stomped her slippered foot. "Do not thwart Her, or She may withdraw it."

"And so, She would punish me for my duty to my adashi? What would Temi say to that, a'Selaso?"

If Kimasa was angry before, now she was livid. "Do you dare? Do you dare, a'tem? I, who spend my life divining Her nature and our duty to Her, and you—you..." Wordless was not a condition one saw in the selaso. It didn't last long. "Do you deny the truth in my words? Do you refuse the gift of Her favor?"

Rodani thought over his words. Eight months of listening to Cara's unusual pronouncements on the subject, coupled with his own dubious beliefs, left him with few sincere replies. Wisdom, however, dictated caution.

"I refuse nothing beneficial, a'Selaso," he said finally. "Neither do I make any claims to facts."

Kimasa waved away his equivocation. "The facts," she stated boldly, "require your obedience to the goddess, a'tem. You will state the goddess's benefaction to the house on the night of equinox, with Cara at your side. I have spoken." Kimasa headed for Cara's workroom.

"And I refuse." Demons would eat at his heart before Rodani would spill guild business to the house, let alone his private blunders. "I honor the assistance you have given me in the past, Kimasa. I do not forget. But if you persist in this adverse request, Cara and I will not attend the celebration."

Rodani's 'com sputtered. "Five, Two. Five, Two." Rodani opened the channel. "Five."

"Meeting. Now."

"Ninety-nine." Rodani held his hand out in an attempt to usher the furious priestess out of the room. She stared back at Cara.

"A'Selaso, Cara is under my orders just as I am under the taso's." He chivvied her forward. "Please do not distress her."

"It is my duty to bring all peoples to the goddess."

"If you wish, we will take this to the taso after my meeting. We can discuss it there."

Protest in her every movement, Kimasa let herself be persuaded to leave the rooms. They parted at the base of the main staircase.

The guild meeting room was nearly full, guardians shuffling into their chairs with a cacophony of scrapes and bangs. Two chairs remained empty. Rodani took his place across from his former partner. Serano refused to meet his eyes.

Kusik wrapped his only set of knuckles on the table. Rodani wondered idly if his keso bothered to remember who had saved his life.

Kusik waded in. "Now that Rodani has returned from his unauthorized leave, we meet again together to discuss the behaviors of this guild." Several pairs of eyes rolled at the table, and faces went further into mask. He ignored the infractions. Rodani stared at a spot just shy of Serano's right hand.

"I have been in discussions with the taso about the widening fractures in this formerly united group. She is very much concerned, as I am.

"Disagreements are to be expected. Occasional fights are overlooked. But systematic violence against fellow guardians is against the very tenets of the guild. Intimidation of the innocent is likewise unethical. The taso and I will no longer abide by it in any form, at any time. I have spoken to each of the known perpetrators singly, and now to all of you as a group. This is my last warning."

Kusik looked at each face at the table, one by one. Some refused his direct stare. Others met it with their own. "The taso has ordered," he said, precise in his diction, "that anyone who commits violence against another guild member, or continues intimidation tactics against non-guild, will be dismissed from this house and returned to headquarters for reassignment."

He waited out the shocked silence, then the expected mutters, before continuing. "I will obey the taso on this. Make no mistake in her intentions or mine, a'tem'ai. If you disobey this command, you will be packed and removed within the hour."

He leaned forward, jutting his chin. "Are my words clear? Is the seriousness of this pronouncement evident to all ears?"

Silence was the only response.

"I will hear your answers!"

A chorus of "Yes, a'Keso" broke through.

Kusik ended the meeting with a wave of his hand.

Rodani swallowed a catch in his throat and waited behind as the others filed out. "All honor to the taso," he began, as Kusik let the rage he'd kept hidden flow across his face. "If it would not offend, I have a critical question."

His keso was vibrating with repressed violence of his own. "What must you ask now?"

Timan walked up from the other end of the table to join them.

"A'Keso, if someone disobeys your command, may I defend myself? Without punishment?" A simple enough question on the surface, he thought.

But Kusik turned away to pace. After a long minute, he stopped and faced the far wall. "Yes. If it is within reasonable bounds. Now remove yourself from my sight."

"A'Keso." Rodani removed himself. With alacrity.

He walked the short distance to Arimeso's quarters and requested admittance.

"Rodani," she said.

He bowed, stiff and formal. "All honor to you, a'Taso." It was a greeting with a warning beneath it.

"Continue."

"A'Taso," his words came slowly and cautiously. "Forgive me for annoying you with such a matter, but there is an issue with the selaso."

She rolled her fingers out and back in. Nothing else on her body moved.

"A'Taso, the selaso wishes for me to make a statement to the house. A statement that admits to my affinity with Cara, and an admission that the goddess favored us in your allowing us to begin and continue that affinity."

"And where is your issue?"

Rodani blinked. Surely it was evident. The taso was no dullard. "With security, a'Taso. Our safety. Cara's safety, primarily, but mine as well."

"Half the house already knows. What do you fear?"

"It would be a provocation, a'Taso, on top of our mere presence. It is one thing to be aware of my rule-breaking. It is a far different reality to have it shoved in one's face."

Arimeso regarded him steadily. "What does a'Cara think of this admission?"

"I believe she is aware, to an extent, of the security problems in such a statement. But as well, she is explicit in her disbelief of the goddess. I conclude that any statement Kimasa approved of would be objectionable to her." He glanced down at his feet, and back up to his taso. "Kimasa has made it clear, even before our affinity, that she wishes to bring Cara—and all humans—under Sela's shelter. Cara has ever resisted." He splayed his hands. "Neither of us wish to make a statement."

"It seems to me there is virtue to be found in admitting to moral imperfections."

Rodani swallowed the rebuke. "While claiming Sela's approval of my failings?"

Arimeso pressed her fist against her forehead as a compliment to his retort. "I believe you are in a quandary, te'oto."

"A'Taso, I have fought hard to remove myself from under the cloud that followed me here. It clings to my ears still, but I would prefer not to subject myself to more."

"And yet you still approached her."

Rodani closed his eyes and sighed. "I believe I do not wish to admit to my moral imperfections, a'Taso."

Arimeso sat back in her chair. "I should refuse you, Rodani."

He looked down at the floor.

"You have no apology to give me for stealing away against my orders?"

"I will give you any apology you demand, a'Taso."

"I should let you give it to Kusik."

"A'Taso, the pressures from the other guardians are becoming unsustainable."

"And still, you do not deny her. And still, you do not repudiate your affinity to her or the violence it has caused."

Rodani could not meet her eyes. "I do not."

Arimeso let out a sigh. "I will speak to Kimasa."

Rodani bowed and made his way back to Cara's rooms. His rooms, now, as well.

Cara greeted him with arms folded, her gaze under lowered brows.

"Kia?"

She shrugged. "Trying not to interfere in what's not my business, while wondering what happened." She looked him up and down. "You don't seem to have been attacked while you were out."

Rodani took his chair at her worktable. "The taso has forbidden it."

"When did that ever help?"

He gave her a glance of reproval. "She is threatening them with dismissal if they disobey."

"Will that be enough?"

"One can hope."

She laid her hand on his arm. It was warm, and the muscles were tense. "Two can hope."

His pupils relaxed, and a small smile arose on his face.

"And Kimasa?"

"The taso agrees with me. She will speak with her."

Cara hung her head in relief and swept her hand across the fabric in front of her. "Do you ever stop to think how much worse things would be if we didn't have Arimeso's support?"

"Only every hour, kia."

She began to run a duo of fabric pieces through the machine. "I've been thinking..."

"Of?"

"I assume the festival will have dancing?"

"Yes."

"We could put my 'corder in the gathering room, and dance together. I could teach you one of my ancestor's dances."

His lips thinned. "No. I have no wish to embarrass myself, and there is not the time to learn. I have no objection to you dancing, however." He looked away. "Au, let me amend that. I would have an objection to you dancing that swaying dance. The one where you turned your back to me repeatedly."

Cara laughed in delight. "You appreciated that one?"

"Far too much."

Someone pounded on the door of the servants' sitting room. Rodani got up in an unexpected hurry and strode toward the sound. Cara followed him, but stopped in her bedroom.

"Who?" demanded Deremic. Rodani stood behind him, hand on his gun.

"Litelon," came the voice.

"What brings you?"

"I must speak to Rodani, a'sel. I have terrible news!"

Rodani stepped up. "What news?"

"I do not wish to talk in the hallway, a'tem. Please."

Rodani glanced at Deremic, who stiffened to guard position. Rodani opened the door a crack, and glanced out, then widened it. Litelon danced in place in front of him, agitated nearly beyond sense.

"Tell me quickly."

The stablehand wrung his hands and glanced both ways down the hall. "A'tem, in the stables, I heard—"

"Heard?" Rodani's voice deepened.

"A'tem, there were guardians in the stables. They did not know I was there. They were talking. I..." he breathed in heavily. "I heard them plotting to kill Cara! And you!"

Rodani yanked the young man through the door. "Details, te'oto. Now."

"Au, a'tem," he stammered. "I do not know. They are planning something. At the festival!"

"Before, during, after?"

"I am not certain, a'tem, but probably during or after. They are going to steal benatacs, and escape! Run from the house! I heard them make plans."

Rodani clenched Litelon's shoulders. "You have done well. Now, we go downstairs. You will not run. You will not gasp for breath. We will walk sedately down to the taso's quarters." He peered into Litelon's eyes. "You can do this?"

Litelon took a deep breath. "For Cara, anything."

"Deremic, stay with her." Rodani pulled his 'com and called for Kusik and Timan.

Arimeso was still at her desk, one hand on her forehead. Rodani took a second to sympathize, then drew to attention. Litelon followed.

The taso glanced up, then studied them both. "Yes?"

Before he could reply, the security first and second thundered in behind them. "What is this?" Kusik spat. "What is the emergency?" His pupils spasmed in anger that hadn't yet faded.

"Litelon, tell them what you heard," Rodani said.

Litelon repeated what he'd said upstairs. At the end of it, Arimeso sat back in her chair, her mouth a small O.

"How many?" Kusik asked in a sharp tone. "Who did you hear?"

"I cannot be certain, a'Keso. I heard at least three voices, but the only one I am sure of was a'Imal. Maybe Toranel, as well?"

"How long have you lived here?"

"A...a'Keso," he pleaded.

Kusik slashed his hand through the air. "Is there aught else you can tell us?"

Litelon closed his eyes as three guardians and a taso waited. "After they have done what they mean to do, a'Keso, they are going to steal benatacs and quit the house. They discussed what they would pack as provisions."

Kusik stomped around to his chair beside Arimeso. "That is all?"

"All that I remember at this time, a'Keso."

"Then return to your duties."

Litelon's eyes widened, and his head drooped.

Rodani leaned over. "I will make sure the stablemaster knows of your loyalty."

Litelon bowed to his superiors, then stumbled toward the door.

"Walk, te'oto," Rodani cautioned him. "Breathe. Tell no one else."

"Yes, a'tem."

Rodani watched Kusik, and saw it coming. The slap against his face was sharp and sudden and eminently earned, if one were to be truthful. As Kusik's rekindled rage seethed over him, Rodani willed his body and mind into stillness. If he were very lucky, Kusik would keep his fists to himself.

"Imal?" Arimeso asked. "Were you aware, esuva?"

"No."

Rodani saw the guilt in his eyes. It flashed, then vanished. Vindication was not an honorable emotion for a guardian, but Rodani had been threatened, slapped, and beaten too often by his keso to deny himself the pleasure.

Timan spoke, finally. "Imal has always been closed, a'Taso, though he voiced his disapproval of Rodani's rule-breaking. Once or twice."

Arimeso turned to him. "What will you do with only a stablehand's word for evidence?"

Kusik gritted his teeth. "Halt the festival."

"No. I will not punish the rest of the house for the possible treason of a few. What will they do, my keso? How will they do it? Run in and shoot indiscriminately? They would hardly survive a few seconds."

"A few seconds is all it needs."

"I cannot see them suiciding. Especially when they are making plans to run."

"We cannot see what is inside their heads."

Timan spoke up. "We could incarcerate them for the duration."

Kusik eyed him, his lips pursed in disappointment. "And the next day? And the next? When does their menace fade? Even dismissing them from the house does not end their danger." He turned back to Arimeso. "Send her home. Send Rodani to Tendiman for punishment. Eliminate the provocation, and you eliminate the threat."

"No."

Kusik stared, then bowed to her. "Then please enlighten us with your military strategy, a'Taso."

Anger flared across her face, then Arimeso glanced at Rodani, who waited in silence. "Let Rodani and Cara attend the festival.

Guard them. If the others show any sign of violence, arrest and dismiss them."

"And again, you choose the hard path. The most dangerous one."

"The one best for my house and the world, a'Keso."

Kusik spun and left the room, Timan on his heels. Rodani followed them into the communications room.

"Leave," Kusik spat at him. "Go to your duty while you still have her."

FORTY-THREE

Cara heard the door to her servants' quarters open again. She slipped out of her chair and stood at her table, waiting. As Rodani walked through her bedroom, she crossed her arms, protective reaction against...something. Something in the voices she'd heard, the abrupt departures, Rodani's downcast eyes as he returned.

She refused the questions that fought to come from her mouth. As he came into the room, he looked at her, measuring her attitude with his eyes. Silent, he took his seat at the worktable, staring at the tools that waited unused.

Cara remained standing, watching his mood as well.

"Sit, please, kia."

When she still stood, he got up, and reversed his request. "No." He looked away, then back into her face. "Dance."

She uncrossed her arms. "Dance?"

"For me." His pupils waxed full.

Anxiety crawled through her nerves at his expression. Something wild shone behind his eyes.

He turned toward her bedroom. "I will find the skirt."

Well. Cara took a deep breath, the first of many. She changed into her dancing skirt, the one with the slits up the thighs. Rodani moved the couch aside and waited at her 'corder. When she approached it, he fingered the buttons of her blouse.

"Take this off. Please," he added. He reached into the slit of the skirt and tugged at her unders. "This, too."

Cara smiled to herself, and did as he bade, then chose two songs for her dance. In nothing but halter and skirt, she danced her way through the songs. Rodani's gaze was riveted on her as he straddled the table chair. When she finished, he shot up from the chair and lifted her into his arms. One hand palmed the back of her head, the other on bare skin beneath her skirt.

"Please," he whispered.

"Why are you still in your clothes, aisu?"

Rodani carried her into their bedroom and bounced her on the bed. He stripped her of what she still wore, and kept his eyes pinned to her nakedness as he removed his own. He crawled up her legs and buried his face in her abdomen, hands on her breasts. Almost, he was tempted to put his mouth where the goddess forbade it to go. But he resisted. Instead, he let his hands roam over the many curves of her body, curves that wove through his dreams. He fondled her nether lips as he sucked on her breast. He felt her hands curl into his hair and roam over every place on him that she could reach.

When she spread her legs for him, he felt her welcome from the tips of his ears to his pelvis. He settled himself between her thighs and pressed himself against her entrance.

"Open your eyes, kia. Look at me."

Cara's startling blue eyes stared into his as he pushed inside her. *Goddess, help me.* The bonds he'd let develop from the shameful weakness in his soul wrapped themselves around him, tighter and tighter. He rocked against her, his adashi, his forbidden flame.

He drew himself out of her, placed the tip of his penis against her sweet spot, and pushed downward between her lips. She shut her eyes, riding with the pleasure he knew he was giving her. Her pupils didn't pulse as his did. But her mouth told him everything he needed to know. He watched it grow from a small circle to a grimace as he stroked her delicate parts.

He rose up and took one last, long stroke on her outside, then plunged inside again. She cried out at his intimate invasion.

Her channel had swelled. Engorged, it raised his pleasure to a peak, driving waves of passion throughout his body. He knew what it meant. What each of her body's signs meant. He shifted his hips to give her the last of what she needed, in the place she needed it. He felt a growl gather in his throat and erupt.

She fought with him, underneath him, then froze. With a guttural cry, he emptied his body into hers. Her screams of pleasure filled his ears and heart as he continued to pound against her, making sure she completed her ride.

She tapped his back, relaxing as he stopped. Supremely sated, he rested against her, skin-to-skin, his face buried in her hair. His shivers died out. As his passion floated away, satisfaction took its place, and pride. Pride. To shelter and defend her as no other guardian could. To play her difficult body like a musical instrument, drawing her pleasures forth as they crested the hill together—nothing else in his life matched it. He was lost to her, and he knew it.

And knew the cost that was coming, the price they would eventually pay.

After a short time, he lifted himself from her and sat back on his heels. Her beautiful body, still warm from their activities, rested in front of him. He caressed her legs, then picked up her skirt from the floor and pulled it into his lap. He folded it and smoothed it out over his thighs.

Cara watched his caressing hands. "I think you have things to tell me, aisu."

Rodani folded the skirt twice more, then laid it on the bed. "Not yet."

He leaned forward, reached behind her, and slid open one of the cubbies in the headboard. He withdrew a package and held it out to her. It was small, about the length of his palm. She sat up and turned it over in her hands.

"Aisu," she said hesitantly, "I didn't know there were gifts for the equinox. I don't have anything for you."

"No. This is different."

Cara untied the bow. The wrapping fell away. Inside was a hair clip. Silver, carefully wrought in curves and angles, highly polished. It looked familiar. "It's beautiful. Is there something wrong with the one I wear?"

"It is identical to mine, kia. I wish you to be my chosen mate."

Her jaw dropped, and her eyes widened into ovals. "As in...wear the same clips, and wear my hair down instead of up? As in, proclaim it for everyone to know?"

He interleaved his fingers and rested his hands in his lap. Unsure of her thoughts, he simply said, "Yes."

"Rodani, I'm honored. But you have to explain. You have to tell me what you expect. My...my people know nothing about..." She looked down at the clip. "Help me understand."

"It is..." He stopped, similarly tongue-tied, and began again. "It is similar to what we have now, kia. But formal. A promise. An agreement."

She took his hands in hers, six fingers enclosed in five. "What are we agreeing on?"

His chest expanded in a deep breath and his fingers tightened against hers. "Will you continue what you do now? Support me as I do you? Keep yourself for me? Guide me, and allow me to guide you? Teach and be taught?"

"I can do those things." She smiled. "And I've already refused both Litelon and Serano. Refusing anyone else is no problem."

"Will you obey my security restrictions?"

She sighed heavily. "Yes. As best as I am able."

"Will you respect my honor and my skills?"

Cara thought. "As fully as you respect mine, aisu."

"I hear," he said quietly. "I hear you."

She squeezed his fingers. "Will you talk to me of your anger, instead of using your hands?"

"I have, and I will continue to."

"Will you continue to compromise with me?"

Then he smiled. "That is a must, kia. For us both."

Cara ran her fingers over the clip. She pursed her mouth, bent her head and twisted her shoulders. It was a complicated action Rodani couldn't interpret. He held his breath.

"What happens if, sometime in the future, one of us decides it's a mistake?"

He tossed the question with a wave of his hand. "Then we part ways, and the record of it is wiped from the Enclave's books."

She considered, then slowly raised her hand to the back of her neck and unfastened the clasp of her clip. Her hair fell in waves down her back. Rodani took the new one from her hand and clipped it in place. He let his hands fall back into his lap.

"I don't think I can tell my mother about this," Cara said.

Rodani smiled. His chest expanded, and his breathing became easier. Temporarily. "Nor can I mine, kia."

They faced each other on the bed. Her soft regard tugged on his bonds and his protectiveness. To find himself mated, accepted, cherished—he might say, if he were to admit it to himself—felt strange. Unstable. But that had been his life for eight months. The steep learning curve he'd fought against had turned shallow, and his focus had sharpened. He would persevere.

From a different cubbyhole, he pulled out a small book and opened it to a list of names. "This is the official record. We each sign. It registers our decision with the Enclave."

Cara slipped off the bed to retrieve her pen from the armoire and handed it to him.

"The woman signs first, kia."

She signed, then Rodani followed, and placed the book on the headboard.

"What now?" she asked.

"I believe we have earned a short rest."

"No celebratory drink?"

Rodani climbed out of bed. "You are correct. Tonight may be better than tomorrow." He opened the door a crack and made the request to Hamman, then climbed back in and laid down, pulling Cara next to him.

"Why not tomorrow?"

"We will need to be even more cautious."

Cara's eyes narrowed. "Why?"

He hesitated. This was dangerous ground, and he walked on it newly mated. He'd weathered other tempests, but hoped to not cause another one so quickly. "There is a new danger."

"Your guild again? Is that the news Litelon brought you?"

"Yes."

"What will happen?"

"We do not know. There will be people at the festival who, more than ever, will oppose our affinity. We can stay in our rooms and have a private celebration, or we can go and face them. If we go, they may stay their hand. If we celebrate alone, we may still not be safe. I leave the decision to you, kia."

"Wait, wait." She put her hands on his chest. "Remember what you told Kimasa, aisu? The terrible things that would happen if we let people know?"

"That ship has already set sail."

She stilled in thought. "I could keep my hair in a bun."

"Au, kia, you can still be naïve. Hiding our mated status will not erase their rage at our affinity, and your presence on the estate." He ran his hand over her brown waves, now unbound. "You make the decision to wear it up or down."

"What about Kusik? Timan? Do they know? What are they doing?"

"They have talked. We are taking precautions."

"Should we just not go to the festival?"

Rodani looked her over, pupils wide, trying to prepare for a reaction he couldn't predict. "It may," he hesitated, "be best that we do that; avoid it."

She pouted, then her lips thinned. "That bad, huh?" One eyebrow raised.

"Yes, kia."

She looked off to the side. "I was hoping to dance for everyone."

"The way you dance, that would be a dangerous provocation. I am sorrowed for your disappointment."

Cara was silent for a short time. "What about the tree? Should we go back there again?"

Rodani waved his hand. "That is a more worthy suggestion. But we will still need to return sometime. As long as the threat remains, so does our danger."

"So, if it doesn't end here, we stay scared the rest of the three years."

Rodani swallowed a hot ball of emotion. It nearly choked him, and his hands began to shake. "It is my belief that you will not be here three years, kia. Possibly not even one."

Her eyes went wide as she sucked in a breath. They looked the same as when he had asked her to mate with him. "Months?"

Rodani could only look at her. He let his emotions flood his face.

"Weeks? Rodani?"

"I cannot know, kia. Let us enjoy what we have without looking for the end."

"But what about," she flipped her hand toward the clip in her hair, "being mated? What happens?"

Rodani rested his forehead against hers and closed his eyes against his inner misery. "Wait to ride that trail until we see it."

A tentative tapping filtered through the door. "Your drinks, a'tem," Hamman said. "I will set them on the floor."

Rodani pulled himself out of bed and back into his clothes. He retrieved the drinks and took them to the study. Cara put her dancing clothes back on and followed him. He took a large swallow of his drink and turned to her. "Kia, I must leave you for a little while. I have errands."

"You'll be safe?"

"I believe so." He drew his fingers down the side of her face. "I will return soon." He headed down the halls to the first floor and the taso's environs. He knocked on the door to Timan's private quarters.

"Who?"

"Rodani."

Timan opened the door, glanced at Rodani, and let him in. He pointed Rodani to a chair at his table. Rodani sat, pensive. Timan sat and waited for him to speak.

"A'Biso," he said at last. "I have decided not to go to the festival. Cara has reluctantly agreed."

"And what will you do instead?"

"Stay in my former rooms," Rodani told him. "The less we are walking through the house, the fewer people will be able to report on our whereabouts."

"Of what worth is that?"

"At the least, a'Biso, it keeps danger away from the rest of the household. Better, with well-placed misdirection, we may confuse them enough to stay whatever attack they had in mind."

"And if they simply postpone?"

"We will have more time to catch them, or gather enough evidence to have them sent to Tendiman for punishment."

Rodani bent his head, not only in thought, but in shame he didn't want to admit. "A'Biso, may I speak plainly?"

"...Yes," he replied slowly, as if considering a refusal of the request.

"I would wish to avoid the keso as much as possible in this critical time. Would you allow me to discuss the possibilities with you, and you carry them forward?"

"Why?"

"Because," Rodani admitted, "I doubt his resolve to plan anything worthy of the effort for our security, with me in the room. "

"Temi's demons, Rodani. Where is your courage?"

He stared back, unflinching, now. "Being used to safeguard my chosen mate, a'Biso."

Timan leaned back in his chair. "Have you talked to Serano about assisting you?"

"I will not."

"Then your bond is severed?"

"If it is, a'Biso, Serano cut it. I will not seek out someone who left me unguarded when I needed him."

Timan waved his hand in the air. "I wish you would have avoided this affinity."

"Reason says I would not have begun it had I known. My emotions say it was worth every pain."

"You will have to face the guild council."

"I am aware."

"She means so much?"

Rodani shivered with internalized panic. "I have asked her to be my mate. She agreed."

Surprise spread across Timan's face. "You may lose everything you have fought for."

The ball in Rodani's gut burned anew. "I am about to lose it anyway, am I not?"

Timan fell silent.

Rodani waited, knowing the die was cast, the cards played.

"Does she know the danger?" Timan asked.

Rodani took a deep breath. "I attempted to explain it in a circumspect way. But no, she does not know what we know."

"I will discuss it with the keso." Timan stared at Rodani for a moment, then waved him out.

Rodani bowed, then made his way back to Cara after stopping off in his old room. She was curled up on the sofa, drink in hand.

"How many have you had?" he asked wryly.

"This is only my second, aisu." She handed him his own as he sat beside her. His gaze roamed over her clothing.

"You still wear the skirt." He observed with a side eye.

"You noticed." Her voice slid down and up an octave, in tune with her smile.

"Have you something in mind? Again? Maybe I should have some of my varigestra tea."

She jumped up and went to the 'corder, choosing a new song. Loud, fast, it got her feet tapping. First, she sat on the couch and patted out the song's rhythms with her hands on the tea table, swaying to the beat. On the next song, she stood and danced in front of Rodani on the couch, swinging her hips. She waved her hands in his face and leaned forward for his second-favorite glimpse of curves. The song revived her spirits, and her antics made Rodani's pupils pulse.

She took his drink from his hand and set it aside, then caught his hands. "Stand up, my mate."

He resisted, but allowed her to pull him to his feet. She tugged on his arms, one, then the other, as she danced. He tapped his feet a few times and attempted to sway his hips. But mostly he held his arms out with Cara's hands and turned as she moved in a circle around him. His eyes shown reflective in the firelight, and a wide smile graced his lips. She laughed again and spun underneath his outstretched arms, then put her hands on his waist.

"You dance so well horizontally that you must be hiding your vertical skills, Rodani."

"Then I will pin you to the wall next time."

She stopped dancing as his comment began to make sense. "That wasn't what I meant!"

"Yes." He grinned. "I know."

***

Deremic reached for the radio in the living area he shared with Hamman. As she was celebrating early with her pregnant daughter, Deremic was working extra hours. He set the dial for the stables.

"Andalia," came the answer. "A'bi, this is Deremic, from a'Cara's rooms. Is Litelon available?"

"A moment, a'sel," she told him.

After a short wait, the journeyman spoke, "A'Deremic?"

"Litelon," the manservant began, "I have an order for you, coming from a'Timan through Rodani. You are to contact Imal, and tell him these things.

"First, it is possible that too many people will be riding away to celebrate elsewhere. Both Rodani and Hamman have requested beasts, and because of that, Imal and his group may need to double up on the benatacs. Second, you are to ask Imal where he is going, because that may matter for what beasts are made available to him.

Then you will relay this answer to me, promptly," he added with emphasis. "Do you understand?"

"Yes, a'sel."

"Do not alert him that anything is amiss. That is very important. We await your answer, and thank you."

"Of course, a'sel. Right away."

Deremic clicked off the radio and sighed. Just by living with Cara—and then Rodani, he knew both more than he wished, and not enough.

***

Timan left the taso's office, where she and Kusik were still debating the merits of the planned diversions. *Goddess grant us a quiet night,* he prayed. Occasionally, he mused, Sela came through with a miracle. He fervently hoped this would be one of those times.

Why Arimeso was still adamant about Rodani's affinity with his adashi was a puzzle he had yet to solve, one that may fly into pieces soon.

In reaching the door to the Enclave, he hesitated and closed his eyes, reaching out with his mind for the presence of the goddess. *Maybe, maybe...*

"Adonsa, is the selaso in residence?" he asked.

The acolyte rose and bowed. "A moment, please, a'Biso." She scurried away, then neared again as Kimasa exited a prayer room and entered her office.

Timan followed the acolyte's instruction to enter the selaso's quarters.

"A'Selaso," he began, "I have a welcome message to relate to you."

The high priestess's pupils widened, and a smile drifted into place. "Pleasant surprises are always welcome, a'Timan."

A little uneasy, Timan shifted in the chair. "This one must be kept secret until tomorrow at the festival, a'Selaso. Will you abide?"

She leaned forward, eyes bright with anticipation. "Whose order do you carry, a'tem?"

"The taso's, a'Selaso. You may, of course, verify with her if you feel it necessary."

"Of course not." She gestured with her open hand, eager.

Timan took a breath to settle his nerves. Lying to the high priestess was fraught with unwelcome consequences—to this world, and to the next.

"I have been informed that Rodani and Cara wish to make the proclamation tomorrow evening; the one you have repeatedly asked for."

Shock in the selaso was a rare occurrence. Unfortunately, Timan had no wish to see it. Not in this place, not at this time.

"Timan," she spoke, enraptured. "But this is wondrous! My plans have come to fruition at last!" She stood up and raised her palms to the ceiling. "Oh Great Goddess, mother to us all, we thank you for your beneficence, your bounty!" Her gold-colored robes swayed and reflected like dancing glitter in the candlelights on her desk.

Timan rose to face her exuberance. "I beg you, a'Selaso, to cloak your joy and prayers until tomorrow eve. The taso expressly wishes it."

"Of course, a'Timan. Of course."

Timan left her presence with a bow and a speed that was not quite appropriate for a guild second. *Now, to lie to the guardians.*

***

The next morning, Timan walked into the bustle of a busy festival day in the kitchens. He wandered through the throngs of people slicing and dicing, stirring, pulling spices off of shelves, and stoking fires.

He checked in with the head chef, Menidi, the hunters bringing fresh meat, the head bartender making sure there were enough bottles to fill the revelers who wanted them.

It was a task not too different from his end-of-day sojourns around Barridan, checking for problems both real and potential.

At one table, he spied his quarry. *This is utterly normal, Goddess and consort, be sure that no one notices my errand. It is of no importance, no consequence.*

Cassig turned to him as he neared. "A'Biso."

"A'sel," Timan answered. "I have a small task for you."

Cassig inclined his head in silent acceptance.

Timan attempted to lean himself closer to the chef, without seeming like he was doing so. And speaking barely loud enough to be heard above the cacophony surrounding them. "You are bringing lunch to Rodani and Cara this noon, are you not?"

"Yes, a'Biso."

"You will," Timan explained, "bring them a second meal at the same time. A dinner of whatever is available. And," he continued, "you will deliver it to Rodani's rooms."

"Two meals at once?" Cassig verified.

"Yes, and," he eyed the chef with a forceful glare, "you will not mention this fact unless you are specifically asked. If anyone queries the unusual amount of food, tell them Rodani is expecting visitors. Otherwise, you know nothing and tell nothing."

"A'Biso," Cassic replied with a bow.

FORTY-FOUR

Her room was quiet. Morning tea sat at her left hand. The sewing machine waited. Cara sketched another thumbnail design on her drawing pad.

She was married. Married!

Sort of, she amended. She doubted her own people would accept it as legal. Her new husband towered over her, tried his best to curb her excesses, and whispered words she couldn't decipher when he lay with her.

Good gods, what strange paths life could take. She tried to imagine explaining things to her mother. The picture both horrified and amused her.

"An alien, Cara. A killer! And you can't even have babies with him! What's wrong with you?"

"Yes, yes, Ama, I never do anything right, do I?"

She felt Rodani's clip at her nape, and the hair that hung down her back in waves. She thought about the warnings Rodani had told her of yesterday and wondered what the year would bring them. How many weeks or months did they have? The thought of returning to Glaniad, to her parents' house, brought a new wave of anxieties. No one waited there for her. No one really missed her. Did anyone care if she lived or died? Maybe her father; or Davad, her brother; or her youngest sister.

Why had she ended up bonding with an alien man and not a human? Life made no sense at times. The scars on her fingers and palms still ached, and not all of her hand strength had returned. The memory of bruises and cuts on Rodani's body still filled her with anger, as did Serano's ever-impatient and disrespectful treatment of her. And Kusik. Gods, Kusik. Now there was a guardian who fit humanity's perception of an assassin. She shuddered.

The lock on her door rattled, and Rodani strode through. He stopped at her table long enough to nuzzle at her ear, then reached for his designs.

"Busy this morning?" she asked.

"Yes, kia."

Cara sat back in her chair, anxiety again building in her gut. "Guild meetings?"

He eyed her, pupils narrowing. "Of which I cannot speak."

"I know." She reached for the eraser in front of her. "At least you say yes or no, now. It's an improvement."

He tilted his head and studied her. "Is that an offense?"

She smiled and shook her head.

"You will need to be ready to spend the day and night across the hall. Find quiet things to do."

Cara turned to him, eyes wide in disbelief. "We have to be quiet the whole time?"

Rodani glanced at her. Amusement fought with worry at the prospect of her complaints as the day wore on. "Quiet, not silent, kia," he corrected her.

"And we're doing this why?"

"So that certain people do not know where we are."

"Rodani," Cara said, "you're telling me just enough that I assume someone else is after me. *Again,*" she added.

Silent, Rodani collected pencils, papers, a needle and thread, a pair of pants with a torn seam, and two books that Cara had been translating into Cene'l for him to practice with. "Do you have what you need?" he asked, purposely calm.

She plopped onto the chair at her worktable. "Remember when you told Arimeso how important it was to keep me informed? So that I'll make better decisions?" She stared at his back, willing him to face her, and to speak. Not of inconsequentialities, but of hard facts. Knowledge that led to wisdom.

"You are correct, kia. And I will explain what I can when we are settled in. What I cannot do is explain what will happen. No one knows."

He walked through their bedroom and into the servants' hall. "Deremic?"

"A'tem?" was the quick answer, as the manservant met up with him.

Rodani spoke softly. "Check the halls nearby for prowlers." He tapped the pocket that held his 'com. "Tell me what you know when you know it."

"A'tem," Deremic said, and slipped out the door.

Rodani returned to Cara and eyed the carry sack that hung from her shoulder. "You are ready?"

"Yes," she replied, with pursed lips and lowered brows.

When Cassig had left lunch and dinner with them, Rodani peeled the sheet off of Serano's empty bed. He scuffed the rug that lay next to it with his toe.

"Cara, take the rug to the door, please." He carried the sheet, and with trial and error, tucked it through the crack between the door and the wall, on the top and sides. When he finished, he pointed to the rug Cara held behind him.

"Do the same with it," he said, pointing to the bottom of the door. He sat on the couch and watched her stuff the rug under the door. When she sat next to him, expectantly, he stretched his legs out toward the fire.

"Here is what I can tell you of what I know."

***

At the entrance to the gathering room, Deremic took a deep breath and shook the tension out of his shoulders. Not for the first time, he wished he'd received the same level of training that guardians received. *Sometimes,* he thought, *it might help.*

The festivities were finally under way. The room was festooned with bows and streamers, and pots of seedlings that celebrated the new life that the spring equinox brought. To his left was the taso's table. As usual, there were five seated there. Imal nearest the door, Kusik, Arimeso in the center, Timan, and Lanata. He approached the table with his palms out, and bowed to the taso.

"A'Taso," he began, "please forgive my interruption." He paused for permission to continue.

"Yes?" she prompted him.

"A'Cara has related that she feels ill this evening and has elected not to attend."

Kusik leaned forward, his lips firm in distaste. "Why does that matter?"

Arimeso glanced at her mate, then turned back to Deremic. "That is a sorrow to hear. Remind Rodani that the clinic is open today, if it is needed."

"A'Taso," Deremic replied, bowed, and left the gathering room. As he exited, he caught a glimpse of Imal, who seemed to be staring at his compatriots who sat at a nearby table.

Will this day ever end? Deremic thought as he headed back, and *how will it end? May the goddess hold us all safely in Her arms.*

He entered the rooms he shared with Hamman, walked into Cara's study, turned on the 'corder, and left. He knocked once on the door to Rodani's old rooms, then strode down the hallway as if he had somewhere important to go.

He'd offered himself as a second bodyguard to Rodani while he was sequestered with Cara. But the temichi had quietly declined, saying more people in the rooms meant more opportunities for Cara to speak, question, and agitate.

It was well that Deremic kept his thoughts to himself.

***

"What do you think will happen?" Cara whispered, as she finished her lunch.

Rodani quietly scraped the last of the gravy off his plate. "You asked me that earlier. I do not know."

"What do you think *won't* happen?" She leaned back in her chair and studied him. laying her hands on her abdomen.

"I do not know that, either, kia." His face was masked more than usual. What he was hiding was what she wanted to find out.

"So, what else *do* you know?" she asked with an airy tone.

Rodani pursed his lips and tried not to glare. "That you are asking unanswerable questions."

Thwarted, Cara rubbed her fingers together in her clasped hands, with force and concentration.

"Are you not hurting your hands?" Rodani asked, noting the action with a raised eyebrow.

She unlocked her hands and wrapped them over the opposite arms. "I hate waiting for an explosion."

"What choice do you have?"

Cara grimaced at his rejoinder, her eyes squinting in frustration. Her shoes tapped the floor erratically.

"You must learn to relax, Cara. Like imagining Kimasa's cloak, it would do you well in life."

"Relax?" she shot back. "Now? Suuure." She drew the word out like a bowstring with an arrow notched. She needed only a pointed word to let it fly.

"Breathe deeply. Relax your muscles. Concentrate on your body," he told her. "Come over to the couch, and we will practice."

As the afternoon passed into evening, Rodani's 'com went off. "Five, Two. Five, Two." He moved into the bedroom and shut the door to speak less softly.

Cara followed him in, and sat on the edge of his bed.

"Five," he answered.

"Imal left the festival a few minutes ago," Timan told him. "And Pavanec just followed. 'Ware your surroundings."

"Who is watching them?"

"Serano and Misheiki. I'm waiting for Toranel to leave the table."

"Lanata should trail her," Rodani offered.

"Yes." There was a pause. "And now she walks."

Rodani considered the situation. "And it will be difficult to stalk and not be seen."

"Being seen," Timan replied, "may change the situation."

"Ninety-nine."

Hearing the sign-off, Cara pulled herself off the bed. "Breathe," she reminded herself quietly. "Relax." She turned to Rodani. "And now, three more guardians plot against us. They couldn't have been put into the cells in the Enclave? They're free to walk?" She slapped her palms on her hips. "Knowing they're after us? Where's the sense, Rodani?"

Postponing a reply, Rodani got up to check on the dinner that had arrived earlier, with lunch. He had little appetite for food, and

Cara's pointed questions reduced it more. His stomach was beginning to burn, as it had before in times of high stress. Fear. Not of his own death. Fear of failure. Fear of dishonor. Fear of Cara dying in the mess he'd made of their lives.

Fool! he berated himself. *What was that Cene'l word Cara used? Fuck. That was it. Fucking fool*, he called himself. Almost, he wished Cara would say it out loud.

"We do not pen people like animals," he replied.

"Not even to survive?"

Rodani made one of those stiff, whole-body turns toward her. He meant it as a warning, one he hoped she'd heed. "This is *not* the time to argue our methods, Cara. Stop."

He softened his demeanor, and drew her onto the bed. He laid down beside her, facing the bedroom door. She noticed he still had his boots on. That, more than anything, waved a flag in her face. Rodani *knew* something was coming, and he wouldn't tell her.

"If we survive this, first chance I get, I'm biting your ears," she whispered into his face.

But he pressed two fingers against her mouth. "Rest."

Yeah, right. She listened and listened, her heart pounding in her chest. Her gut was a ball of anxiety, with no way to relieve it. She sighed, stretched her legs, shifted her shoulders, wiggled her feet, clenched and unclenched her fists, tried to rest, and began the cycle over again. No tender words or touches passed between them. Rodani remained still, his hands on or near her arms. His eyes were wide, his vision fixed somewhere beyond where he lay.

Minutes went by, and more. Then more. Bloody hours went by, as far as Cara's time sense told her. The only thing she heard was Rodani's breathing.

When a loud crash penetrated the bedroom walls, Rodani slapped a hand across Cara's mouth before she could shout, then spun her out of bed and into the armoire. He pushed on a panel at the back. A dark corridor appeared. He pulled her into the corridor, then shut the armoire door and the inner door, and laid something heavy across it.

Nearly blind in the dark, Cara stood behind him with her heart in her mouth, her claustrophobia rearing its ugly head. She bit down on her lip to keep silent. "Two, Five, Two, Five," he called softly to

Timan. "Cara's rooms likely breached. We are in the south passageway, heading toward you. Call the others."

Rodani picked her up one-armed and ran the hall. It angled downward. In the near-dark, he kept one hand on the wall, the other on Cara. She bounced against him. A boom echoed down the corridor. Crashes followed. As Rodani reached the first-floor turn, the armoire door they'd come through banged and thundered. He pulled his 'com a second time. "They are following us," he whispered in a harsh tone.

As they made the turn, Rodani slowed his headlong rush. He switched Cara to his other arm and ran his fingers along the wall to his right. After several paces, he stopped and put her down. Breathing rapidly, he bent to fiddle with a lock. The catch eluded him. He swore something about putrid and flaming. Fiddled again.

Distant bootsteps in the passageway pounded toward them from both directions. Closer, closer. Rodani kept at his task, then something clicked. He slammed the door open, grabbed Cara, and pushed her ahead of him into the taso's anteroom. He followed her through as a hail of bullets shattered the dark and the silence, hitting the walls of the passageway and ricocheting into the anteroom as they ran. The door to their right opened. Kusik reached for Cara and yanked her through the doorway, into the taso's rooms.

Rodani turned to fire at their attackers. He backed himself into a blind spot as Kusik fired one-handed from his doorway. The door to the outer hallway slammed open behind them. Serano and Lanata fired at the deadly passageway door, working their way inside the room behind their rapid-fire defense. They spread out.

Kusik shouted over the cacophony. "Are all three there?"

"I do not know," Rodani replied heatedly.

Misheiki appeared at the hallway door, fired several times, then bellowed in pain and spun out of sight. Lanata crawled forward. Rodani went down on one knee and leaned further into the fracas. Blood blossomed on his thigh. The burn shocked him for a second, but training took over. He continued to shoot. Flashes of gunfire bruised his retinas. The room filled with stinging smoke.

Timan surged out from behind Kusik and into the room. He shot into the dark beyond the door.

A scream burst from the passageway. The shots died down.

From an angle, Timan crept toward the door. Return fire spat. He jerked and sagged to the floor. His gun fell out of his hand as red flooded his shirt.

Rodani switched out his empty magazine and rushed, limping, from his hiding spot, shooting madly into the doorway. Kusik headed for Rodani's empty spot, but a shot took him down. Rodani plastered himself against the wall next to the door and fired blindly into the darkened passageway as his keso slid down into a sitting position, his gun limp in his hand.

Rodani waited, his ears ringing, the smoke clogging his nostrils. Quiet reigned in the corridor and in the guardian-filled room. A light shone in the darkness. Rodani raised his gun.

"One, Seven, One, Seven!"

Rodani pointed a cramped finger at Lanata, who, with Kusik injured, was now the senior guardian in the room. She pulled her 'com and answered. "Misheiki! Talk!"

"I am in the passageway, a'tem. There are two bodies. I see no survivors. Hold fire. Hold fire!"

A whispered scrape of boots issued from the passageway. Clothing rustled.

Rodani leaned into that doorway, his thigh an irritating burn that dribbled blood. "'Ware your back, Misheiki!" He flipped a switch on the 'com. "Medical, medical," he shouted. "Emergency in the taso's quarters. Multiple injuries."

Lanata gripped the pale wrist of Timan. After some seconds, she placed it back on the floor and whispered something toward the sky.

Serano hovered over Kusik, trying to staunch their keso's bleeding.

Misheiki crept through the passageway door and began to pull the bodies into the room one-handed. Blood dripped from his shoulder.

Lanata, unhurt, ran to assist Misheiki. When both bodies lay in a line on the floor, she shut and locked the fatal door.

Rodani took a stolen moment to lean against the wall and breathe. Just breathe. Then he heaved himself up into an unbalanced stance. He knew where to find the taso, and his bonded mate. Hobbling, he made his way into the next room to a tall set of double doors. It looked like an armoire. It wasn't. He rapped sharply on the door. "Sela protects, with her five handmaidens."

More than one lock clicked. A triple-thickness door opened, and Arimeso stepped out. Cara stood, wide-eyed and shaking, behind her.

"A'Taso," he said, wincing and breathing heavily.

"Kusik!?" she demanded.

"Alive, thus far, a'Taso." Rodani bowed his head. "Timan... Timan has crossed. I am desperately sorry."

Her pupils pulsed. Her mouth was no more than a slash across her face. She dashed through the doorway and rushed to Kusik's side. Baldar and his assistants clattered in from the main hallway, filling the small room.

Forgotten for the moment, Cara crept toward the anteroom.

"No." Rodani held his hand in front of her.

"Aisu..."

He spun to face her. "Do you need more dream fears? There is nothing out there you need see."

Now she saw his wound. "You're hurt! Get treated, Rodani. Go!" She pushed him toward the medical staff she could see. One came toward them.

"A'tem, let me assess you. Please," the healer said.

Cara dragged a chair over. Unwillingly grateful, Rodani eased himself down on the seat. The assistant sliced his pant leg off, then bent over the leaking bullet wound. She turned around. "Pallet! Now!"

"No need. I can walk."

"But you will not." The healer waved to her cohort. "Take him."

As they maneuvered Rodani onto the pallet, Arimeso stepped to his side. "A'Taso," he said.

Arimeso glared at Cara. "She goes back to—" Arimeso glanced around, then stomped back to the study, staring at the bodies. "Who is missing, Lanata?" she demanded, as Kusik was carried out.

"Pavanec, a'Taso."

"Where is he?"

"We do not yet know."

"Likely in the stables," Serano answered for her. "Or already on the run."

"Check with Domendi, or Litelon, to verify. Then take Cara back to her rooms."

On his back, Rodani waved his hand in the air. "No, a'Taso, I beg you. Her rooms will have been damaged. Allow her to stay with me, please."

"Serano can watch her."

"You need Serano and Lanata for your own guard, a'Taso," he protested. "You are their duty."

Arimeso waved her hand sharply as if to backslap someone. "Serano, request a summons of the temaso." She swept out of the room and followed her own mate.

Unnoticed, unwanted, Cara followed Rodani as he was carried into the clinic anteroom. Selandu in the grey garb of healers ran thither and fro, intent on the crisis. When she tried to follow Rodani into the exam rooms, she was stopped by a very intimidating female.

"Du!"

The gripping hand on her shoulder pinched. Cara tried to shake the woman off and scoot forward, but the healer took her by her arms and shoved her back into the waiting room. Cara stood, arms crossed and vibrating with excess jitters that bordered on panic. Other people were beginning to crowd into the waiting room as word spread throughout the manor.

Alone, without a guardian, she sought refuge in a far corner of the room next to a small table. She watched wide-eyed at people she didn't know, people who could want her as dead as Timan now was. She didn't mourn the guild second, but wished it had been Kusik who'd taken the heart shot instead. If he lived...gods, if he lived, a late summer sea storm would be less lethal.

Even as she tucked herself down into a smaller ball, a hand gripped her and pulled her to her feet. Serano's face was a mask, but fury ran beneath it in the corners of his eyes and mouth. He dragged her out into the hall and passed her to a waiting Deremic.

"Take her to her rooms. Or Rodani's, I care not. Keep her there, and make sure she does not leave." Serano disappeared down the hall.

As Deremic reached for her, Cara pulled her arm away with a snap. She shook her finger in her servant's face. "Deremic, if it were your chosen mate in there," she pointed back into the clinic, "wouldn't you be there waiting?"

Deremic pursed his mouth and looked down his nose at her. "Serano ordered—"

"Fry Serano! He doesn't have a mate in there, either!" She swept her arm through the air, almost sideswiping a nearby artisan. "I belong there!"

"A'Cara," he began.

"If you don't want to disobey Serano, talk to Lanata. Ask her." Cara took a step back. "She's in charge, now. See what she says!" She took another step, sliding backwards.

"I will not."

She ran. Back into the middle of milling Selandu bodies, threading her way toward the inner entrance. She heard Deremic call her name but slipped in between the healers. The place was a maze. At first, people reached for her, but she kept going, glancing into rooms. Slowing at each open doorway, peering inside, her breathing ragged, her nerves frazzled.

And there he was.

"Cara!" Deremic's voice erupted behind her, full of fury she'd never heard from him before. She slipped into Rodani's room and huddled at the far corner of his bed. Rodani's eyes went wide as the healers at his bedside turned toward the chaos.

"No visitors," one said sharply.

Deremic followed her in.

"Deremic, stop," Rodani said.

The servant stopped in his tracks, his gaze traveling from Cara to Rodani, to the healers, and back to Cara.

"Remove her," the healer demanded. "Only the goddess knows what germs she is carrying."

Deremic reached for her.

Wincing as the second healer dug into his wound, Rodani shouted. "Du! She is my mate, and my duty. She stays here."

"A'tem," the first healer replied, an objection Deremic repeated.

"Every other guardian is dead, injured, or busy. She stays." He sucked in a breath as pain shot through his leg. "Deremic, wait outside. Cara, sit on the floor and touch nothing, say nothing."

"Madness. Goddess save us." The healer continued her work, muttering to her partner.

Cara slipped down onto the floor and wrapped her arms around her shins. Snips and snaps, and the rustle of fabric filtered down from the bedside above her. To her surprise, Rodani let his arm hang over the side of the bed, down near her face. She scooted forward until his hand rested on her hair. There they stayed.

Eventually, the healers placed an umbrella over his head and lit the smoke. When Rodani's hand relaxed, she put his arm back on the bed, pulled up a chair, and laid her head down beside him, hand clasped in his.

She had no idea what time of night it was, but she was where she needed to be.

FORTY-FIVE

Morning time brought the healers bustling into the room, waking Cara. Images of her mother at work made her slip back into the shadows, rotating her head against the crick in her neck. They reviewed Rodani's status quickly. His eyes opened to half-mast.

"A'tem," the senior healer said, and handed him a glass of thick liquid. "You should drink this directly. Your body needs sustenance."

"These are noxious," he grumbled.

"Yes, a'tem, but necessary. Can you hold it?"

He gripped it carefully, then set it on his stomach. "The keso?"

"Alive, by the grace of the goddess."

Rodani closed his eyes and sighed.

"As soon as you finish your drink, you can have more sleep smoke, a'tem."

He glanced at the glass in his hand. "I cannot drink flat on my back," he said, his tongue thick and dry. "I need a reed."

The second healer searched his pockets and stuck a hollow, flexing reed into the glass. Cara slipped around the healers up to his other side and held the glass next to his jaw for him to drink.

The healer patted Rodani's foot. "Drink. I will return."

Rodani took another sip. "Is Deremic still in the hall?"

A head and shoulders appeared in the doorway. "Yes, a'tem," the servant said.

"Breakfast for you and Cara, a'sel. Find it. Then you may sleep."

"I should not leave you, a'tem."

"I accept the hazard. Go."

Disapproval swept across Deremic's face, but he disappeared, his footfalls lingering in the hallway.

"You are quiet, kia." His hand brushed her curls and touched the clip at her neck.

"If I thought you could handle my pestering, I wouldn't be." She slipped her hand in his, grasping gently. "Rest."

Before he could, Serano swept into the room, a blast of anger surrounding him. He glanced at his former partner, then rounded on Cara, a sneer on his face and pupils pulsing. "Why are you here? Have you ever obeyed an order in your life?"

"I countermanded it," Rodani said.

Serano turned back to him and swept his gaze up and down Rodani's body. "Are you pleased with yourself, a'tem?"

Rodani blinked slowly. "I am pleased to see you ambulatory."

"Are you making a joke?"

"No."

"Where is Deremic?"

"Retrieving breakfast."

Serano glared at them both. "Do you accept responsibility for her, here?"

"Always."

Serano pulled away. "Payment will come due." He left without another word.

"What did he mean?" Cara dared to ask.

"We waited last night for the explosion. We wait now for the taso's response."

"I'm sorry about Timan."

He squeezed her hand and drank.

***

Kimasa unfolded herself from the altar. She'd spent the night in prayer, but had not found the peace she was seeking. She had words to say and was determined to be heard. This time, she would be answered. She made her way through the Enclave halls and into the center of the manor. But the taso was not in her quarters. The guardian stood at attention when she swept in, but only stammered an apology that Kimasa ignored.

She found Arimeso in the clinic, standing beside Kusik, who was swathed in bandages.

"A'Taso."

She turned to face the selaso, her eyes guarded, expression flat.

"I must speak."

Arimeso's eyes lingered on her mate, who watched her through a smoke-induced haze. "Not here." She turned away and walked past Kimasa as if she were a servant-in-waiting.

"A'Taso!"

Arimeso slowed down to allow Kimasa to catch up with her. As they walked, everyone in the nearest vicinity plastered themselves against the walls. Neither woman noticed.

The taso's anteroom was bullet-battered and bloodied. A puddle of deep red showed where Kusik had sat, and a larger one showed Timan's fatal resting place. Kimasa halted in the doorway.

"Goddess above," she whispered. "A'Taso, you refused to listen to me last night, and now we see the results." Kimasa swerved around the mess, following Arimeso into her inner sanctum. "I told you. I told you that disobedience to the goddess would cost you. Cost us all."

"I need healers and guardians now, Kimasa, not censure."

"If you had not disobeyed, ignored me—"

Arimeso planted her fists on the center table. "I am the taso."

"The souls of the dead will haunt us all, Arimeso."

"Then I will talk to them directly, not through an intermediary," Arimeso replied.

Kimasa let her gaze roll over the bloodstains behind her. "How could this have come to happen, a'Taso? What chain of events wrapped itself around your guild?"

"A'Selaso," Arimeso said, weariness in her voice, "the guild carries every proper and improper impulse inherent in our species. Morals and ethics, jealousy and envy, anger and disgust. And desire. I allowed Rodani his improper affinity with Cara against Kusik's wishes. I do not regret my decision, nor does Rodani, but only its end result."

"I feared your experiment would fail when your human refused to bow to Sela and my authority."

"One cannot force another's faith."

"Rodani abetted her in that refusal."

"It was his duty."

"His duty as a guardian is also to me," Kimasa snapped. "And after his repeated refusal to aver in front of the house for 'security reasons,' this happens?"

"A'Selaso, what is your real concern here?"

"With the souls of our people, the goddess's directives, and the status of your house and my Enclave."

"Kimasa, could you have done anything to stop the violence that occurred here?"

"If they had come to me, surely the goddess would have—"

"But they did not, any more than Cara or Rodani did."

"A'Taso, I believe that a'Cara has been a negative influence on Rodani in the matter of his faith. I request that he be sequestered in the Enclave for meditation and guidance."

"He goes to guild headquarters first, Kimasa. If he returns safely, I will consider it."

"I will expect him." Kimasa turned toward the door. "When you are ready to pray for the spirit of your second, I will be waiting."

Arimeso closed her eyes and looked away.

***

Chendal yanked on the reins of the benatac between his legs. It came to a halt at the entrance of the manor, dim in the evening light. One of Arimeso's door wardens took the beast as Chendal dismounted.

The halls were unusually empty. He would check the gathering room later, and the festive room. It was always wise to listen to the rumors that floated in the aftermath of calamity. He strode past Arimeso's security desk and the lone guardian who attended it. Inside the anteroom, a washerwoman was cleaning, a small mound of bloody rags near her knees. Chendal studied the room, its layout and furniture, the bullet holes, the door to the back passageway. It wasn't the poor accuracy of some of the shots that vexed him. It was that the shots existed at all.

Arimeso appeared in the doorway to her study. "A'Temaso."

"A'Taso." He looked her over. This was not the poised, self-assured woman he had come to know. They regarded each other in silence. "Begin somewhere, Arimeso."

She turned back to her room. "Drink?"

"No, I thank you. I need my wits."

"Tea?"

"Tea is sufficient. And Kusik?"

"Alive." Arimeso poured the tea.

"Awake?"

"Yes."

"Prognosis?" Chendal continued.

Arimeso made the tossing motion. "Hopeful."

"How did this happen?"

She sighed and folded herself into her favorite chair. "How many players do you wish on your list?"

"Do not play games with me, a'Taso," Chendal said with some heat. "This is an inter-species crisis we have not seen since the River War, and you are in the center of it."

Arimeso glanced aside. "I play no games, Chendal. My honor is dented, I have lost my taso second, I may lose my mate, I will lose income from Cara's crafting and Rodani's, and every other artisan who cannot keep her mind on her work. And I must pay for several more guardians."

She leaned her elbows on the desk, drink in hand. "I am a fool. I thought I could better the world. I thought I could prove something to myself, to my house, to the naysayers and the frightened in this land. I failed."

"If you cannot start at the beginning, start in the middle."

"The middle," she mused. "Human females do not have cycles as Selandu women do. When Rodani became ill, word seeped through my guardians that Cara was the cause. Many took exception to Rodani breaking the guild rule, and some became disgusted, much as Kusik was, with the idea of joining with a human. The landslide began there."

"What did they do?"

"Stalked him, harassed him, threatened him. Beat him."

Chendal's ears began to twitch. With some effort, he banked his anger. "And Kusik?"

"Was torn between agreeing with them and trying to stave off rebellion." She swept her hands over her desk. "Eventually, rebellion won."

"You both deserve censure for failing to manage it."

"I have already heard from Hadaman. My ears still smolder."

"Why did you not call me?"

Arimeso folded her hands in front of her, clenching her fingers together. "A'Temaso, we have already called you here twice in the last four months. We thought we could control it." She looked down. "You are expensive."

Chendal shot out of his chair. "You put wealth ahead of guild lives?" he shouted.

Arimeso met his wrath on her feet. "Spoken as someone who never had to feed and house 200 people, a'Temaso!"

Chendal stomped back and forth in front of her desk. "I would never have thought you so obdurate, Arimeso."

"I am not," she spat. "I rolled against Temi's demons and lost."

Chendal reseated himself. Tempers were useless here, however provoked. "What will you do?"

"What I must."

"You can no longer protect Rodani. He will face the guild council whether you wish it or not."

"He is injured as well, a'Temaso."

"As soon as he is able to ride, we travel together."

Arimeso tossed the comment. "As you will."

"Is anyone else still alive who shares the guilt?"

"The stablehand who notified the Enclave. Pavanec."

"Where is he?"

"Gone."

"What direction?" Chendal spat.

"Ask in the stables," she said flatly.

He leaned forward, incredulous. "You have not commanded a search?"

Arimeso mirrored his movement, pupils narrowed. "Chendal, I have *two* unharmed, experienced guardians. Two of twelve! What would you have me do?"

"I will request replacements for you."

"And with neither keso nor biso, what will I do with them?"

Chendal regarded the tips of his boots, well-worn with miles and years and experiences, some of which he wished to forget. Temi's demons must have orchestrated this. "Who survives, Arimeso?"

"My keso, injured. My fourth, unharmed. Fifth, injured. Sixth, unharmed. Seventh, injured but ambulatory, and a very new twelfth."

"It was the new knives who took the most offense?"

"With the exception of Imal, my third, yes."

That will be an issue to take to the council, he thought. Chendal rose from the chair, tea in hand. "I will investigate." He bowed. "With your permission, of course, a'Taso."

FORTY-SIX

"You're moving better today than yesterday," Cara told Rodani as he limped around the clinic's small room.

"Only because the healer demanded I get out of bed." He leaned against the wall to rest his quivering leg muscle. "She said one day was enough in which to laze."

Footsteps echoed through the doorway. Cara turned, expecting to see the physician, Baldar, with permission to leave the clinic.

Instead, Serano walked in, eyeing them both grimly. "A'Cara, go with Deremic."

"Why?"

He turned away from her, toward his ex-partner. "I am not obliged to answer unnecessary questions. Do as you are told."

Cara looked over at Rodani for confirmation. Expression blanked and frozen, he inclined his head. She started out. "Bad as Kusik," she muttered.

Rodani turned to face Serano. Regardless of their severed partnership, he retained his higher rank. He lifted his chin.

Serano broke the silence first. "The taso demands your presence."

Nausea welled up inside him. A burning ran along his nerves. "Where?"

"Her study."

Rodani pulled himself away from the wall and made his way slowly from the clinic to Arimeso's quarters, his limp more noticeable the farther he traveled. He halted in the anteroom, staring at the bloody stains that hadn't been completely removed.

Arimeso looked up at his entrance. Her eyes were shadowed, her pupils narrowed into slits, the nictating membranes visible. She was on the edge of an explosion. All that was needed was a spark.

He walked into her office, bowed his head, and lowered his shaking body to kneel.

"The injured do not prostrate themselves, Rodani."

"A'Taso." Unstable in mid gesture, he rose with a body weakened from grief and pain.

"The injuries and deaths are on both our heads, a'tem."

Rodani swallowed his fear. It sat in his gut and burned. "I understand your point, a'Taso. But I will forever claim I am not responsible for the prurient interests and rabid emotions of others."

"As you have claimed since the beginning of this affinity."

"Which you allowed," he whispered.

"To my utter dismay and regret." She leaned forward. "At least you remember whose permission you needed."

"Always, a'Taso. Even Cara knows and has remarked upon it."

"And does Cara know and remark upon my options here as well?"

Options. I need options. "I have bade her patience, a'Taso. To keep her calm."

"And what tumult will she engender when she is parted from you?"

Rodani shut his eyes. A sharp pain shot through his chest, followed by a numbing dread. "A'Taso, please." He drew the word down into himself, an impotent prayer.

"Do not argue with me! My artisans are in an uproar, my guardians at war with each other, their ranks halved." Her eyes held a fire that burned him without touch. "I have lost my security second, and nearly lost my mate, not to mention the deaths of four other guardians and a crafter, and one who has disappeared."

"A'Taso, I can take Cara elsewhere," Rodani suggested.

"No one else needs her."

"We can hide, a'Taso. In the cave."

"And what kind of life will you have there? She must go home."

"She might return," he replied with waning hope.

"To where?" Arimeso shot back. "To here? No. Not for the foreseeable future. You have no other options that I am aware of."

Rodani held himself tight against the shudders that threatened to tear him apart. His chin dropped to his chest, his injured leg shook in weakness. "A day, a'Taso. A week. Let calm return. Please."

"I take no pleasure in breaking apart what you fought so hard to build and protect, Rodani. But my house is in pieces. It takes priority."

"Allow me to take her to my parents' cabin in the mountains, a'Taso."

"No. She must be seen back in her own land."

"A'Taso, I beg you."

Arimeso shot to her feet. Her glare pierced him exactly where his guilt lay. "Do not. I have decided." She walked into the anteroom, motioning Rodani to follow. "Radio. I will speak to Ambassador Mena'hem."

Rodani sat down at the transceiver and twisted the dial. He spoke into the mic, calling for an answer. After a few minutes, the line came live with a human voice.

"This is a call from the Taso Arimeso in the Barridan estates," Rodani replied. "She will speak to Ambassador Mena'hem."

"Is this an emergency, a'tem?"

"It is urgent. Please find him."

"Immediately, a'tem."

After another endless several moments, two human voices came on the line. "Ambassador Menachem," said one. "Ambassador Second Andrew," said the other.

"A'Taso," Menachem said. "How may we assist you?"

Rodani recognized the anxiety in the ambassador's voice, courtesy of his dealings with Cara.

Arimeso leaned over Rodani's shoulder. "A'Reiti, I will be plain. I am forced to send a'Cara back to you. She will be in Soldan in the late afternoon and will take the first boat south."

Ice, Rodani admonished himself. The long-ago words of Tokennen, his first keso. *Find the ice inside you to keep you still when your world is in flames.*

"May I ask what happened, a'Taso?"

"My house has finally decided against me, a'Reiti. There was a fight. She cannot stay."

Breathing came over the line, and voices conferred in the background. "Please accept our deepest apologies, a'Taso. Is there some error or fault of Cara's that has caused this?"

"No. This is nothing she could stop."

Rodani bit down on his lip and dug his fingernails into the fabric on his arms. The 'I know who could' hovered in the air, berating him, unvoiced.

"You will have someone there to retrieve her?" Arimeso asked.

Menachem's voice carried through the radio. "Of course, a'Taso. Thank you for alerting us."

Arimeso waved her hand over the cut-off switch and turned her back. Rodani mumbled thanks, then cut the link and slowly followed her back to the office. Inside the door, he stood at attention, but with his chin on his chest. "Is there no other possible—"

"Stop, Rodani. You know as well as I that if I have enemies on the inside of my house, they exist outside as well. It is done." They regarded each other over an uncrossable gap of pain. "Tell Serano to bring her to me. You will wait here while I give her my decision. You will say your goodbyes while the servants pack up her belongings."

Rodani's knees started to buckle. He held himself up by the thinnest of strings. "A'Taso—"

"Your life is in peril, Rodani. Do as I bid you."

He bowed and pulled out his 'com. Nausea and shakes flooded him.

***

Serano bobbed back into Cara's workroom, much to her utter disgust. He looked grimly pleased about something, despite the terror that had descended on them all. The damaged door to her servants' quarters had been hastily replaced, but the marks from the explosion still decorated the adjacent walls.

At least Rodani was going to mend. And the worst of the fight was over, the adrenaline rush had passed. But a fake reality had set in. She could imagine her brain sparking and spitting with chemicals that hadn't subsided, burning in new memories.

Serano neared the table, watching her carefully. After a moment, he motioned her to follow.

"Where are we going?" she asked.

Serano didn't respond with his usual glib retorts. *Still in Kusik mode*, she thought. But he motioned to her servants, who stood aside as they passed by. At the door, he took her arm and pushed her out.

Cara tried to slow him down, pulling back on her arm. "Please don't treat me like the keso did, Serano."

Serano spun her around. "Do you know how many people have died while you are here, Cara? Because of your presence here?"

"I'm very sorry, Serano. But how many were my fault? Mourn them. Do rituals for them. But don't blame their deaths on me."

"I tire of your lamentable sense of honor." Serano pushed her down the main hallway with not a care for her stumbling feet or stinging arm. Compared to what happened two days ago, it was no more than a nuisance. Cara kept her mouth shut. But the closer she got to Arimeso's quarters, the harder her pulse beat. When Serano pushed her into the office, she saw Arimeso first, stiff and distant behind her desk. When Rodani turned around, she saw his hands fly through a series of signals. Then she saw his face, and froze.

"Rodani?"

He closed his eyes and moved to stand beside her, turning to the taso. His body was visibly shivering. *Clinic*, she thought. *He's hurting. Bad.*

"A'Cara," Arimeso said.

^This doesn't look good,^ she whispered to herself. The taso wasn't pleased. The look in her eyes was nothing Cara wanted to see.

"My house is in danger. My guild is shattered." Arimeso's mouth thinned to a narrow line. She clasped her hands in a rigid lock on top of her desk. "I do not blame you, but others will."

From the periphery, Cara saw another shudder roll through Rodani's frame. A sense of dread began to permeate the room, infiltrating her body. Nausea rose in her throat.

No.

"A'Cara, there is no way to soften this blow."

No. Oh, gods, NO!

"I am sending you home."

Cara slapped her hands against her mouth and moaned. "A'Taso, please."

Rodani shivered beside her, painfully silent.

"I have no choice, a'Cara. I told your ambassadors that I found no fault in you, that this was directed at you, not because of you."

"A'Taso, no—" Her voice choked on her words as Arimeso called down doom upon all Cara had worked for, on her chosen mate, and on all they had accomplished. "Is there nowhere—"

"I have already answered those questions for Rodani, a'Cara. There is no answer that you wish to hear."

The room wavered as tears welled in her eyes and began to fall down her face. Shame, terror, and grief fell with them. She began to shake as badly as Rodani. "A'Taso…"

"Serano will take you back to Soldan." Arimeso stood up. "You have an hour for your parting."

Wordless, hand firmly around her arm, Rodani hobbled out of the office beside her and up the main staircase. Cara had to hold herself to his slower pace when she wanted to run, screaming; wanted to hide. He unlocked his old room and pushed her inside, mimicking Serano's actions of minutes ago.

Cara sagged next to him, crying audibly. He drew her into the damaged bedroom, standing her in front of him as he sat on the edge of the bed. It was an agonizing reminder of their first joining. Cara sobbed on his shoulders. His arms wrapped around her in a grip that was almost painful.

Another shiver ripped through Rodani's body, vibrating in her arms. "Kia."

"No," she wailed into his neck. "This can't happen. It can't." She hiccupped and coughed, her sleeve wet with drippings from her eyes and nose.

"Kia, listen to me."

A grief-stricken keening erupted from her throat. Rodani jogged her shoulders. She wiped her eyes and tried to focus. On him. On the man she loved. On the man she was losing—

"I saw this coming, kia," he said, flexing her arms in emphasis. His grip would have hurt had she not already been reeling.

Her nose ran, her fingers tingled, and her legs shook. "What?"

"I knew it would not be long."

She stared at him, uncomprehending. "You said it would be weeks. Or months." The sobs continued.

"I hoped it would be…and knew it might not."

She burrowed into his chest, seeking comfort, seeking something that couldn't be given. "I can't go. I can't let you go."

"We have no choice." Rodani stroked her hair, her shoulders, her back. He pulled her in closer, right up to the line of his body.

"I can't do this. I can't."

"Kia, my bonded mate, you are chaos incarnate. You will rain and thunder the entire way home." He put his hands on either side of her face. "But you are strong. I have seen it, time and again. You will abide."

"Oh, gods," she grabbed his hands, eyes wide. "Ikemi!"

"No, kia. There is nothing more you can do for him."

She shook her head, eyes streaming. "He won't understand!"

"I will ask Hamman to look in on him."

Cara hit her forehead with a hand, forcing herself out of despair, and her brain to concentrate. "We...we could go into the mountains and live along the border."

"Where guardians walk every morning and evening."

"Hadaman could use me. Somehow. Or Himadi House."

"Hadaman has the ambassadors. Himadi will not open for months."

"I know Soldan needs an interpreter. I was there."

"Not without official permission."

She sagged against him, lost and hopeless. "You've thought through all this already."

"Yes."

"And there's nothing we can do?"

"There is nothing, my obstinate adashi..." He leaned into her ear and whispered, "...at this time."

Cara widened her eyes. Rodani tapped her ear and gestured to the ceiling. He hadn't lived in this room for a month, but he was telling her it could be wired. He reached under the mattress for a piece of paper and tucked it into her halter, then bent again to whisper. "Read this when you are safely home—and alone."

Confused and desperate, she pulled her blouse forward to pull out the folded note.

"No." Rodani pulled her fingers away and kept them cradled in his hand.

She wrapped her arms around his neck. "I can't do this."

"You must. And do not fight the ride home. Serano will win against you, every time."

"Fuck Serano."

"Kia, he is looking for an excuse to hurt you. Do not give him one."

His voice was deep and resonant. His scent, that spice... The long fall of hair, soft as a baby's. His shirt under her scarred fingertips. The strength in his body, and the passion it contained. Remember. Remember all of it.

As the rain renewed its course from her reddened eyes, Rodani leaned in again. "Kia." Not a whisper this time, not a secret.

"Wha-at." A sob interrupted the word.

"You have a choice to make."

She tried to breathe through the hiccups, but all that came out was a stair-stepping shudder. "What choice?"

He pulled away from her, then leaned his forehead against hers. "Do you wish to remain mated to me? Or would it be better at home if you are not?"

"No."

Rodani's pupils widened. He pulled away, his expressions retreating behind a mask.

Quickly, she put her hands on his face and turned it back. "No, it wouldn't be better at home!" The words tumbled out, nearly incoherent. "No one will know. I won't tell. And when they wonder why I still wear a clip? So what? They already think I'm stupid. I don't care." She moved in nose-to-nose. Rodani's face regained its softer mien. "You are all I care about, aisu."

He smiled gently. "You will remember your family when you are home."

"Not like I'll remember you."

Minutes passed. Memories flipped through her mind, sharp. Their first joining. The cave. Singing together. The tree. His soft words as he bent over her at the window. His hands on her body.

They breathed together in abject silence, clinging like storm-tossed sailors.

In the middle room, the door opened. Rodani bent his head into her shoulder, hiding his eyes; shallow breaths drew in against her skin. He whispered. "We will meet again. I swear it on the clip you wear."

Footsteps came up behind her. She felt a hand grab her arm. A silent battle of wills began as she fought to keep her arms wrapped around Rodani's neck. The hand held her more tightly, squeezing it into pain. She whimpered. The grip on her arm became a vise, digging down to the bone. It pulled on her, inexorably. She felt Rodani release her, slowly, reluctantly. His hands dropped from her body and came to rest in his lap. His eyes remained on her face.

The hand pulled her backwards, away from her soul, from her life, from the only love she'd ever believed in. Gasping, eyes streaming, she reached back for the blurry visage behind her. But as the hand pulled her away, Rodani's body receded, obscured in a haze of tears, then hidden by the door.

In the hallway, Cara screamed. Then it was cut off—a creature trapped in agony, helpless to escape its fate.

Rodani rocked back and forth on the edge of the bed, doubled over. Shaking, biting back his own howl, he pulled his knife from the belt at his waist. He lifted his shirt and slashed his chest. Once, twice, an X over his heart. Blood flowed. It dripped down his skin in crimson lines and pooled at the beltline. As he let go of the shirt, the stain invaded it and began creeping upward as if in defiance of gravity.

"A'tem," came a worried query from the door. Misheiki walked in, staring at the crimson spread. The security seventh swallowed heavily, waiting for a response. Rodani gave him nothing but silence and a blank stare.

"Chendal requests your presence, a'tem. In the taso's office."

Rodani sheathed his knife and limped out.

***

Despite Rodani's warnings, Cara struggled in Serano's grip, fighting one last battle—and losing. She bent toward his hand.

Serano shook her. "If you bite me, Cara, I will send you home with bruises. Is that what you wish?"

When they reached the garage, a covered wagon was waiting, harnessed to a duo of benatacs. Litelon popped up from the other side of the beasts. "A'Cara." He bowed, slowly and formally.

Out of words, she ignored him. All that was left was raw emotion. Hot and cold by turns, numb one second, nauseated the other.

Serano pointed. "In the back."

The road was bumpy, the ride long. The men sat in front. Cara flopped down onto the floor of the wagon, sobbing. Everything was on fire—her heart, her head, her gut, her thoughts and fears and grief.

In extremis, she coughed, retched, and spat. Memories intruded. Even the happy ones were drained of joy. They only brought more pain, more rain.

Up front, the men spoke in lowered tones.

Litelon glanced behind him. "What are those convulsions, a'tem? Is she ill?"

Serano waved his hand. "Nothing but emotions. Ignore her."

"I have never seen—"

"I have. And I am pleased that this is the last time."

Litelon shifted in his seat, rearranging the reins in his hands. "Timan has really crossed? You are certain?"

"I am certain."

"Who fought?"

"Guild."

"Cara was there?"

"Yes, but she did not fight. Nor did the taso."

"But why, a'tem? Why fight a battle in the taso's very presence?"

"It did not start there. It ended there."

"Why?"

An impatient sigh filtered back from the front of the wagon. "You are beginning to sound like her, te'oto. I cannot answer every question that fills your head."

"But it was due to Rodani and Cara. Yes?"

"Yes. And since you were the one who reported them to the Enclave, you bear a piece of the guilt for what happened."

Cara froze at Serano's words. Rodani had never told her, had refused to say anything.

"I paid for that report," Litelon replied. "With blood."

"As did many other people," Serano reminded him.

The hours crawled along as slowly as the wagon wheels. Finally, the seaside hamlet of Soldan appeared on the horizon. Litelon drove directly for the docks. Serano pulled Cara out of the wagon.

"I can walk, I can walk," she snarled.

"Then walk into the boat," he spat, "and take the ghosts of the dead with you."

"You believe in your ghosts, Serano. They're not mine."

"Kusik is injured and Timan is dead because of you, along with almost a half-dozen other guardians."

She refused to look at him. "Kusik can die for all I care."

"He fought for you!" Serano snarled.

"No! He fought for Arimeso. I watched him beat up Rodani. I know what he tried to do to me. He can freeze in your hell, and I'll laugh." She gazed out over the waves. "Timan," she said more slowly, "Timan, I mourn. He helped Rodani when you turned your back on him. When you walked away, Timan walked up. I'll honor him for that."

Serano slapped her, one last time. Dazed in despair, she didn't even care.

Cara stood on the dock, her heart a solid mass of pain, her body heavy with grief. Her skin felt numb in the sea wind. Her eyes saw nothing but the salt-corroded wood at her feet.

Clouds blotted the sun, graying out the day to match her existence. Crashing waves drowned out the muted voices around her as dockworkers maneuvered bales and boxes in orderly chaos.

Serano stood beside her, finally quiet. The quiet fed her loss, fed the yawning emptiness inside that threatened her very sanity. She was held in a net of nowhere. Barridan was locked behind her. Home held no meaning. The connections of memory to emotions had been severed. Pictures of home in her mind were flat and dull. They held no homecoming, no welcome. Part of her had been gutted, the part that offered life, love, happiness, a future.

Now there was no future, and the past no more than a painting on a wall. The moment held her in a timeless ache, buffeted with every heartbeat.

The End

The Fabric of Choice
Expected in the spring of 2025

Rodani made his way through the back hallways and stairs to the rooms he had shared with Cara. He walked up to the door slowly, staring at it. How many times, how many times had he walked through that door to see Cara's welcoming smile? He'd not been in her rooms since before the final shootout.

The rooms are empty, he told himself. *She is not there. Nothing resides inside but memories. Walk away.*

Instead, he slipped his key in the door and went into the workroom. Her table was there, but no sewing machine whirred on top of it. The shelves sat to his left, but they were empty of fabric. The oil lamp remained unlit, adding to the gloom. He turned left.

Her bedroom. It drew him, almost against his will. The bed lay empty. Only a few pillows rested on top. Rodani could hear her laughter, her whispers, smell the scent of her body. He sat on the edge of the bed and ran his hand over the sheets. Slowly, he laid on his side and drew up his legs, not even deigning to remove his boots.

Kia. The erinai had become his mantra, every repeat of it a balm to his aching soul. He pulled a pillow under his arm and tucked it to his chest. He shut his eyes.

For the first time in nearly a decade, he released his emotions in full. His mind filled with the pain of his loss, his mistakes, his ignorance—willful or not. His body shook in spasms. Deep, repetitive coughs erupted from his chest. He retched. His hands clenched spasmodically as his body convulsed and his back burned.

If he could have seen himself, heard himself, he would have noticed the similarities between his own breakdown and one of Cara's. But he was sunk too deeply to see it. The biggest difference was his eyes that did not rain.

GLOSSARY

Bolded names and words are the more important or most often use ones.

Cara MacLennan	crafter, the lone human visitor in Barridan	CARE-uh
Rodani	Security Fifth; Cara's guardian and lover	row-DON-ee
ai	suffix; plural of a noun; ex: a'tem'ai; a'sel'ai	aye
'com	pocket communication device carried by all guardians, and occasionally by others	
'corder	music playing device; brought down from shipboard	
a'	prefix; honorific; formal courtesy of address	ah
a'sel	honorific form of addressing any regular Selandu person	a-SELL
a'selaso	honorific form of addressing a high priestess	ah-sell-AH-so
a'taso	honorific form of addressing a taso directly	ah-TAH-so
a'tem	honorific form of addressing a temichi directly	ah-TEM, as in "temp"
a'temaso	honorific form of addressing the head of guild guardians	ah-tem-AH-so
adashi	one who is guarded from others by a guardian	a-DASH-ee, as in "and"
affinity	love/sex relationship	

aisu	Cara's pet name for Rodani: "night eyes"	AYE-soo
Ama	Cara's name for her mother	AH-mah
Andalia	Veterinary Second (f)	an-DAL-ee-ah, as in "dally"
Andrew Lieu	Ambassador Second; pronounced Andreh' by Selandu	Lee-ooh
Arimeso Osanin	taso of Barridan	Air-ih-MAY-so oh-SAH-nin
au	interjection; onomatopoeia; open-throated exclamation	As in like: ack! Or ow! Or oh!
Baldar	physician; Master Healer	BALL-dar, as in "dart"
Barridan	estate that Arimeso rules; house full of crafters and artists	BEAR-ih-dahn
bed-mate	lover; no formal declaration; short- or long-term	
benatac	large horse-like animal; toes and sharp teeth; irascible	BEN-ah-tack
biso	Security Second	BEE-so
Cene'l	human language; based on the Welsh language intermixed with English and common words from other languages	ken-EL
Chendal	head of the Guild of Guardians; the temaso	CHEN-dahl

CSC	Cultural Studies Center where humans study the Selandu language and culture	
Dae	Cara's name for her father	day
Davad	Cara's next younger sibling; male	DAH-vahd
Deneban	Security Twelfth (m)	DEN-eh-bun
Deremic	Cara's second servant; has some training in protection	Deh-REM-ick
Dienata	Rodani's gun	dee-en-AH-tah
Domendi	Stablemaster (m)	doh-MEN-dee
du	no	dthoo short sound, don't extend the "oo"
eisenico	Rodani's drink	aye-sen-EE-ko
erinai	pet name for a lover	AIR-en-aye
Enclave	both the area in the manor where the priestesses live and work, and the name of the group of priestesses themselves	AHN-clave
festive room	recreation area; drinking, dancing, music, wrestling, betting	
Garidemu	potter; hates humans	gare-ih-DEY-moo rhymes with "dare"

gathering room	for large dinners, celebrations, punishments	
Glaniad	Welsh; it means landing or touchdown, the town Cara is from	GLAHN-yadth
Hadaman	capital city; north and somewhat east of Barridan	HAH-dah-mahn
Hamman	Cara's senior servant; middle aged	HAH-mun
Himadi Hills	low hills separating Selandan (north) and Newydd Cenedyl (south)	hih-MAH-dee
Himadi House	manor under construction on the Himadi Plateau where Selandu and humans are to live and work together	(same)
Himadi Plateau	flatlands north of the hills	(same)
Imal	Security Third (m)	IH-mul
inner circle	name for a taso's group of trustworthy advisers	
Iraimin	painter; risheigi; friend to Cara	ih-RAI-min, as in "rye"
ke	first	keh
keso	Security First	KEH-so
ki'oto; ki'ono	little man, male child; little woman, female child	kee-oto; kee-ono
kia	little one	KEE-uh

Kimasa	head of the Enclave of priestesses; the selaso	kih-MAH-sah
Kishata	gun that Rodani lets Cara use (smaller)	kish-AH-tah
Kusik	The keso, Security First; Arimeso's husband	KOO-sick
Lanata	Security Fourth (f)	lah-NAH-tah
Larisi	Serano's lover; new acolyte of the Enclave	lah-REE-zee
lie-that-is-courtesy	an obvious prevarication for courtesy's sake	
Litelon	a mid-adolescent stablehand, who has a crush on Cara	lih-TELL-on
mate; bonded mate	spouse; formal declaration of joining lives	
Menachem Mboto	Ambassador First; pronounced Mena'hem by Selandu	men-AH-(flegm) mm-BOH-toh as in "boat"
Misheiki	Security Seventh (m)	mish-AY-kee as in the letter "a"
music with the voice	singing (long forbidden by the Enclave)	
Naremit	Security Eleventh (m)	nah-REHM-it
Newydd Cenedyl	Human land south of the hills (Welsh; means "new nation")	NEY-width KAN-a-dill
ninety-nine	sign-off on a given command or exchange over 'com	

ona	mother	OH-nah
onana	familiar form of mother; mama	oh-NAH-nah
ono	woman	OH-noh
oto	man	OH-toh
Pavanec	Security Eighth (m)	PA-van-ek, as in "pal"
poridi	a nasty, clawed, 100-150 lb. canine/feline animal; fast and always dangerous	pour-EE-dee
reiti	**ambassador**	**ray-EE-tee**
risheigi	homosexual person; also: mirrored	rish-A-gee
River Samida	river where the battle was fought; also name of the battle	sah-MEAD-ah
sai	yes	sigh
sel'u	informal name for Selandu companion ("friend")	SELL-oo
Sela	goddess of the Selandu	SELL-uh
Selandu	species' name	seh-LAN-doo, as in "land"
selaso	head of the Enclave; high priestess	seh-LAH-so

Serano	Security Sixth; Rodani's guild partner	seh-RON-oh
shigeli	Cara's alcoholic drink	shih-GAY-lee
Shurad	Riverchild; writer; tried to kill Cara in *The Fabric of Honor*	SURE-add
slowberry	berry that ripens in the fall; nutritious but sour if not ripe	
Soldan	ocean-side town where boats from Newydd Cenedyl dock	SOLE-dahn
taso	head of a manor house and all its inhabitants.	TAH-so
Tasos and Temichin	card game	
te	middle; middling (age, size, etc.)	teh
te'oto; **te'ono**	young man, male youth; young woman, female youth	TEH-oto; TEH-ono
tem'u	informal name for guild partner; close companionship	TEM-oo, as in "temp"
temaso	head of the guild of guardians (only three people in guild council are higher)	teh-MAH-so
Temi	consort to the goddess; worshipped by guardians	TEM-ee, as in "temp"
temichi	Selandu name for guardian	teh-MEE-chee
temichin	plural of temichi	teh-MEE-chin

Tendiman	town holding the Guild of Guardians' training center	TEN-dih-mahn
tic'idi	finger-length insects active during the day	tick-EE-dee
Timan	the biso, Security Second; Kusik's guild partner	TEE-mun
torac	400-500 lb. bear-like wild animal; dangerous if provoked	TOR-ak, as in "tore"
Toranel	Security Ninth (f)	TOR-an-el, as in "tore"
Tuka	head of Guild of Scientists; Arimeso's nearest neighbor (a little west and north)	Too-kuh
Vanu	Security Tenth (m)	VA-new, as in "van"

AUTHOR'S BIOGRAPHY

J.A. Komorita is a born and raised Hoosier, who moved to Texas in her late twenties. Within two weeks, she met the man who would become her husband. They raised twin sons and a daughter. They live in a very crowded home with two cats, 900+ books of nearly every genre, and more art and craft supplies, completed and unfinished projects, notes, designs, and ideas than she will ever use in three lifetimes.

She would like to borrow and modify a quote from the esteemed SF author Anne McCaffrey: "My eyes are blue, my hair is grey, the rest is subject to change without notice."

www.ingramcontent.com/pod-product-compliance
Lightning Source LLC
Chambersburg PA
CBHW032059310726

48972CB00001B/31